Also by Sam Barone

Dawn of Empire

Empire Rising

Quest For Honour
(Also published outside the United States as
Conflict of Empires)

Coming soon – Summer 2012

Battle For Empire

ISBN-10: 0615511759
ISBN-13: 9780615511757

Eskkar Enterprises

Please feel free to contact the
author with suggestions and comments.
www.sambarone.com

SAM BARONE

ESKKAR & TRELLA
•THE BEGINNING•

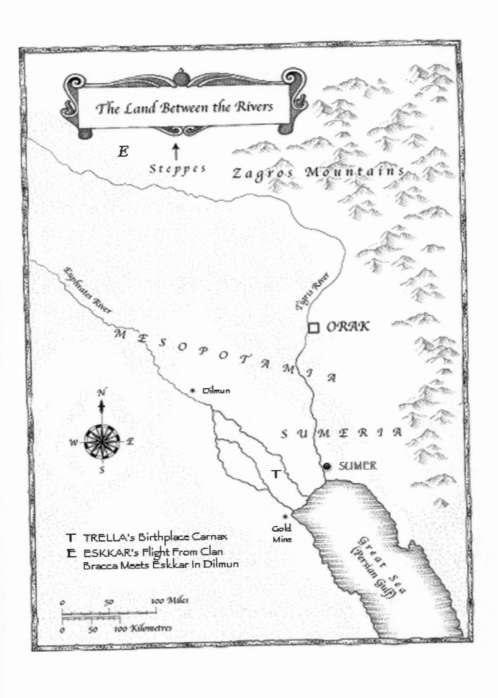

The Land Between the Rivers

E

Steppes

Zagros Mountains

Euphrates River

Tigris River

M E S O P O T A M I A

☐ ORAK

* Dilmun

N
W   E
S

S U M E R I A

T

● SUMER

Gold
Mine

Great Sea
(Persian Gulf)

T TRELLA's Birthplace Carnax
E ESKKAR's Flight From Clan
   Bracca Meets Esskar In Dilmun

0   50   100 Miles

0   50   100 Kilometres

Prologue

Somewhere west of the Zagros Mountains, 3173 BC . . .

Each day, the Great Clan of the Alur Meriki resumed its endless journey across the face of the world. Behind the relentless caravan, the ravaged countryside lay bare, crops burned, the ground picked clean, its inhabitants either dead or scattered to the winds. Ahead, the fruitful land awaited the same fate.

Indifferent to the suffering and death their passage inflicted, the Alur Meriki people, horses, and wagons traversed the earth. Serene within themselves and confident in their strength, little disturbed their progress.

Descended from ancestors who rode down from the northern steppes generations ago, the Alur Meriki warriors formed one of the fiercest and most powerful clans in the land. Each day, it sent forth bands of mounted and well-armed fighting men to scour the countryside, searching for loot, horses, slaves, anything of value. They lived and grew strong by taking from others. The Alur Meriki way of life demanded a constant supply of grain, livestock, tools, and new slaves.

The harsh existence of the Great Clan inured them to the misery of others whom fate placed at their mercy. According to their customs, only those in the Clan were worthy of survival. Outsiders and dirt-eaters, those who farmed the land for their food, deserved the death and destruction that accompanied the warriors' passage.

For the terrified villagers, herders, or farmers in their path, the approach of the Alur Meriki appeared as a punishment sent by angry gods. Prayers and pleas for deliverance rose up to the spirits, accompanied by promises of sacrifices in abundance should the supplicants be spared from the barbarian wrath.

If the dirt-eaters had sufficient warning, they buried their stores of grain, seeds, and tools, before scattering their herds and fleeing for their lives, desperate to escape the merciless horsemen.

To resist the implacable warriors meant certain death; piteous acceptance might mean the dirt-eaters' lives would be spared, at least for the present. With their fields burned and animals taken or butchered, even those who survived the Alur Meriki's passing often failed to live through the aftermath. Long after the barbarians departed, the ruined crops and slaughtered herds brought famine and disease to those who remained alive.

Despite the chaos and catastrophe the Alur Meriki inflicted on others, order ruled within the Great Clan. Everyone, starting with the lowest slave, knew his place and understood his duties. Life seldom varied from day to day, and years passed in much the same manner.

Men, women, even children labored from dawn to well into the darkness. With their clumsy wagons and straggling herds and flocks, the elongated column could only travel five to ten miles a day. Yet each morning, the Alur Meriki caravan rolled ever onward, as unstoppable as the north wind gusting down from the mountains.

The Alur Meriki had to keep moving to survive, as the countryside they passed over soon became empty of grazing, vegetation, and game animals. As a result, the Clan seldom remained in one place for more than a few days.

The constant migration imposed a hardship on its people, but the warriors had existed this way for longer than anyone could remember. Over time, the Clan grew steadily in number, and the grim horsemen extended their reach and power over the ever-widening swath of land they traversed.

At the end of the day's journey, with the sun still a hand's length above the horizon, the halting horn sounded and the great caravan creaked to a stop. Thousands of weary men, women, children, slaves, and animals looked forward to a night of rest and thanked their gods that another arduous day had ended. Up and down the straggling line of wagons and horses, preparation for the evening's work began.

The women, girls, younger boys, and slaves, who'd walked beside their family's wagons all day, now busied themselves setting up the night camp for their kith and kin, pitching tents and gathering wood or dung chips for the campfires. With long switches in their hands, young maidens not yet women shepherded the numerous flocks of sheep, cattle, goats, and pigs that accompanied them. The weary animals nosed about for their final foraging, before settling down to their own respite.

For the Alur Meriki warriors accompanying the cavalcade, most of their duties ended when the last wagon ceased its movement, and they worked swiftly to help their women unload their possessions and settle in for the night. But as soon as they could get away, the men and older boys turned their attention to their precious horses.

Horses, unlike women or lesser animals, announced to everyone a warrior's success. The number and quality of steeds a man possessed measured his status within the Clan, and strong mounts marked the most powerful warriors.

Every family safeguarded its horses with care, checking them for injuries before darkness set in, and making certain the animals had enough grazing to keep them strong. Slaves and the youngest warriors guarded the herds at night to ensure none wandered off, or, the gods forbid, were stolen by outsiders foolhardy enough to attempt such thievery.

Afterward, the men took their ease, or practiced with sword or bow until it grew too dark, or their women summoned them to their meal. A few warriors, those lucky enough to have wine, would gather together; some imbibed too much. Quarrels might erupt, and sometimes men would fight. Such drunken altercations often turned deadly when proud warriors reached for weapons to avenge even minor insults.

The most serious conflicts took place over honor. An imagined or real slight to a warrior's pride often resulted in drawn blades and flowing blood that could quickly escalate to entire families feuding, with more bloodshed.

Another source of fighting centered around women. Jealous husbands and fathers guarded their women as best they could, but an unwed girl bursting into womanhood might smile at a warrior as he passed by or touch his arm, and trouble would result.

Even so, the most frequent and discordant note in the regimented nomadic life of the Alur Meriki came not from men competing over women or honor, but from the older boys, those still not mature enough for the rite of passage into the warriors' ranks. Trained by their fathers to ride as soon as they could cling astride a horse, and to fight from the first day they could lift a wooden sword, these boys formed secret groups and gatherings, created their own honor code, and abided by their own customs.

The Alur Meriki produced strong, aggressive boys eager to be inducted into the warriors' ranks. The powerful urges of youth, encouraged by their older brothers and approving fathers, led to fights among themselves that marked the metamorphosis of boys into men. The stronger and harder a boy fought, the more battle skills he exhibited, the sooner he would reach the rank of warrior.

Once a young man attained that status, he could partake in the raids and warfare against outsiders that would enhance his reputation. Only in this way could the new warrior enjoy women and slaves, gather loot, and in time, take a wife and start his own family.

Just as brothers within a family often wrestle amongst themselves, so too did the twelve sub-clans that made up the Alur Meriki contend among themselves. Each of these smaller clans had its own leader and obeyed its own customs.

The largest of these clans fought under the standard displaying the ruler of the animal world – the black-maned lion. The Lion Clan dominated the others, and its leader, Maskim-Xul, ruled all of the Alur Meriki as the Great Chief. Quick to anger and cunning in his dictates, he demanded the total allegiance of each and every clan leader.

The smallest of the twelve clans comprising the Alur Meriki was the Hawk Clan; its standard displayed an image of the desert hawk, a powerful hunter despite its diminutive size. Jamal, an experienced and wise leader past his fortieth season, led the sixty warriors and their families who constituted the Hawk Clan. One of Jamal's sub-commanders was Hogarthak, a strong fighter who'd earned the respect of those he commanded.

The long struggle described in the Alur Meriki chronicle songs begins with these three men – Jamal, Hogarthak, and Maskim-Xul. Their actions in a single night set the wheel of fate spinning in an unexpected direction, turning mankind onto a new journey whose end is still unwritten.

Book One

Eskkar

1

=

Early spring, 3173 BC . . .

The sun hovered just above the distant horizon when Nasir strode up to Eskkar and shoved him so hard that he landed on his back.

"Don't get up unless you're willing to fight." Nasir's loud voice made the challenge straight-forward. At least ten of his companions ranged behind him, encouraging their leader and laughing at his latest victim.

Eskkar, surprised by the unexpected attack, reacted fast enough. He rolled to the side and rose to his feet, feeling anger flare through him. He never thought about staying on the ground, admitting Nasir's authority over him in front of everyone.

"Not here, you fool," Nasir said, shaking his head at his opponent. "You don't want the warriors to see you beaten, do you? Come down to the stream. We'll cross over and fight there."

Before Eskkar could reply or change his mind, Nasir had already turned his back and jogged off, moving easily across the ground. A crowd had gathered, and most of them followed, leaving Eskkar and a few of his friends behind.

"You don't have to fight him," one said. "He's nearly two seasons older than you."

Eskkar didn't care. Just into his fourteenth season, he knew what it meant to ignore a challenge. "I'll fight him," he said, the flush still hot on his face.

Nasir had pushed him down as easily as a woman, and treated him with just as much scorn. Eskkar felt his honor at stake, and he wouldn't take the insult, not in front of his friends. Without hesitation, he followed Nasir and the others through the lengthening shadows, his fists clenched in anger. Plenty of daylight remained for a good fight.

Wading across the tiny stream, Eskkar then stepped another hundred paces to where Nasir waited, hands on his hips, surrounded by his taunting friends. Eskkar hadn't sought out this fight. In fact, he'd purposely stayed away from the older boy.

Everyone knew Nasir's reputation for quarreling, and Eskkar had never even considered challenging Nasir, who would soon be accepted into the ranks of the warriors. Nevertheless, the fight had come to Eskkar, and now all he wanted was to smash the grin from Nasir's face.

Eskkar had grown both taller and stronger in the last few months. He'd wrestled many boys his own age, even some older, and had been beaten only once. But those scuffles sprang from youthful exuberance and the desire to test one's strength against another.

This time he faced the victor of at least ten fights, and Nasir's disdainful insolence made this a personal attack on Eskkar's honor, not just another boyish challenge. For the first time in his young life, Eskkar felt the battle rage burning in his blood, the all-consuming anger that banished both fear and thought.

As he walked toward his waiting opponent, Eskkar unloosened his belt, and let it and the knife fall to the ground. If he had drawn the knife, as was his right, then Nasir would have to meet the attack in kind.

Such death fights sometimes happened, but a killing fight held too many implications that even headstrong boys couldn't ignore. Both could die or be wounded, and the victor might even be killed afterward by the loser's kin. Bloody clan feuds had started for smaller insults.

Nasir unbelted his own weapon and handed it to one of his followers. By that time Eskkar had reached him, launching a clumsy blow that Nasir easily dodged – except Eskkar had already shifted his feet, grabbed Nasir's arm and jerked him forward. In the same motion, Eskkar extended his leg and sent Nasir tumbling to the earth.

A ripple of groans from Nasir's supporters sounded at the unexpected maneuver. But Eskkar's outnumbered friends drowned them out, cheering and jumping up and down at the sight of the local bully sprawling in the dirt. Other camp idlers, observing the knot of boys and men, wandered over, attracted by the noise and always eager to see an interesting fight.

Nasir's eyes brimmed with rage at the ignominy. He got up, taking his time, staring hard at his opponent, then began moving closer, feet sliding cautiously over the sand, hands extended. "You'll pay for that, boy."

Eskkar's height and longer arms had the reach on Nasir, so he moved back, letting the older boy come to him, waiting until...

Nasir dove at him, expecting to wrap his arms around Eskkar's stomach and wrestle him to the ground. But Eskkar slipped to the side and using the heel of his hand, landed a blow on Nasir's ear, again sending him rolling on the ground.

This time a wave of jeers greeted Nasir, who clearly hadn't expected his younger opponent to be so resourceful. A growing ring of pushing and shoving onlookers formed around the two boys, all the spectators excited to see the exchange of blows, and shouting encouragement and suggestions. Most were youths their own age, though a few older warriors, their faces impassive as suited their status, joined the onlookers. Even some women heading for the stream put down their jars and pots to join the ever-growing crowd watching the contest.

Everyone in the camp knew Nasir and his reputation as a bully; he'd bested many boys to achieve his position as leader of those soon-to-be warriors.

The two fighters ignored the crowd as they met head on. Eskkar's greater reach again let him land the first blow, but Nasir shook it off, dodged the second, and caught Eskkar's arms.

The two boys wrestled, straining against each other, feet churning the loose sand, hands slipping while they struggled to find an advantage, each grunting with the effort. Eskkar stood a good hand's length taller, but his adversary equaled Eskkar's weight, and his muscles were rock hard from riding and handling horses.

With a quick move, Nasir twisted to the side, relaxing just enough to unbalance Eskkar, who found himself hurtling to the ground. He tried to regain his feet, but Nasir stayed with him, their legs entangled.

A fist slammed against Eskkar's cheek, knocking his head against the earth. He struggled harder, but Nasir hung on, both boys gulping air from their exertions. Each kept trying to land a stroke, but Nasir remained on top, using his body to keep Eskkar from rolling away.

Eskkar blocked one fist, then another, but the third blow caught him square on the forehead, slamming his head back. Before he could react, Nasir thrust his body forward, his weight now fully on Eskkar's chest, his leg pinning one of Eskkar's arms.

Another fist landed, brushing aside Eskkar's hand and smashing into his mouth, and he felt the taste of blood gush between his lips. Something crashed into Eskkar's left eye, then another blow to the forehead stunned him, then another and another. Dazed, Eskkar could do no more than try to cover his face as each blow landed.

With a shout of victory, Nasir raised his fist, ready to pound his opponent senseless.

"Nasir! Stop!" The voice of command cut through all the shouting, silencing the vociferous crowd in a moment. A broad-shouldered warrior moved through the crowd, striding past the ring of shouting young men, knocking them out of his way as if they were children. "He's finished, Nasir," Ekur said. "Let him be."

Nasir, breathing hard, heard the command in his father's voice, and nodded. The victor pushed himself upright, raising his fist in the air.

His friends cheered loudly, moving to his side, stepping over the prone loser who still lay there, dazed. The crowd led Nasir away, back toward the stream, where he could rinse Eskkar's blood from his hands and face while accepting their congratulations.

Eskkar tried to get to his feet. It took two attempts before he could even sit, and his eyes refused to focus. When he lifted them, he saw his father, Hogarthak, standing over him.

"All of you, go back to the camp," Hogarthak said, ordering Eskkar's friends away. A tall man, Hogarthak reached down and pulled his son to his feet. "Come with me," he said, and strode off in the opposite direction.

Eskkar, embarrassed to learn his father had witnessed not only the fight but his defeat, stumbled after him. It took a few moments before he realized they were headed away from the camp.

"Where are we going?" His voice sounded weak and childish, adding to his distress. A hot tear ran down his cheek and Eskkar blinked hard to stop more from coming.

Hogarthak didn't answer, just lengthened his stride, forcing his son to keep pace.

The fading light dimmed even more as they passed into a stand of trees that hugged the base of a small hill. Eskkar wiped the blood from his swollen lips with the back of his hand. His mouth stung, and he could feel the split in his lower lip. Pain throbbed in his cheek, and his forehead hurt. He had trouble focusing one eye, and tripped twice in the gathering darkness, cursing his clumsy feet and still-blurry vision.

Hogarthak either didn't hear the small sounds of his son's distress or didn't care about them. Eskkar found himself following his father up the diminutive hillock, and in a few moments, the trees thinned out. The ascent grew steeper, and near the top even Hogarthak had to lean forward to finish the climb to the crest.

Breathing hard, Eskkar looked around. The campfires of the Alur Meriki burned in their hundreds, each marking a small circle of flickering orange light in the growing darkness, each fire a beacon for a warrior and his family.

Hogarthak found a boulder and sat. The rock had just enough room for two, but Eskkar knew better than to sit in his father's presence without permission.

Eskkar tried to prepare for what would come. Hogarthak would be angry. Angry at the fighting, and even more angry at the fact that his son had lost.

"Sit, Eskkar. Let me see your face."

Eskkar sat beside his father, feeling his legs tremble with weakness. He lifted his fingers to his swollen face, and winced at the contact.

Hogarthak turned toward his son. Hogarthak leaned close in the growing darkness and examined the damage, taking his time.

"You'll be lucky not to have a scar on your lip, boy," Hogarthak said as he finished his scrutiny. His hand clasped Eskkar's shoulder for a moment. "Your mother won't like that. She wants you pretty until she finds you a wife."

The idea of marriage held no interest for Eskkar, though lusty thoughts took up nearly every idle moment of his days and nights. Lately he stared ever harder at girls his own age and older, even some of their mothers. And he'd noticed that several of the wives had smiled at him in passing, though both his parents had warned him about that danger, too.

"I don't want a wife," Eskkar said, his wounded pride and injured body leaving no place for thoughts of lust at the moment. He ran a finger over his teeth, thankful that they all seemed to be intact, though one felt a little loose.

"You'll take a wife when you're told to," Hogarthak said calmly. "When your mother and I arrange it, or, if you're lucky, when Jamal finds someone for you."

As Hawk Clan leader, Jamal had some influence over nearly every aspect of his followers' lives. Only the Great Chief of the Alur Meriki, Maskim-Xul, wielded more authority, but the Great Chief never interested himself in the petty affairs involved in governing such a small clan.

"We'll talk of marriage later," Hogarthak said, dismissing the idea for the present. "Now, it is time to talk about being a warrior."

Eskkar tried to clear his head, to keep pace with his father's words. "Father, I . . ."

"Why did you fight him? He'll be a warrior in a few days, as soon as his clan rides out."

"He pushed me down . . . challenged me."

"Nasir is older than you, is stronger than you, and he carries more weight," Hogarthak went on, ignoring his son's words. "If you hadn't caught him by surprise with that first rush, he would have taken you down soon enough. Instead you hurt his pride, the last thing he wanted to happen before the warrior rites."

"But what could I do? My friends . . ."

"You could have laughed when he knocked you down, told him he was too old and too strong to challenge. He would have laughed with you, and helped you to your feet, another easy victory to add to his string."

Shocked at his father's words, Eskkar could hardly speak. "My friends would have thought me afraid to face him."

Hogarthak leaned close to his son and stared into his eyes. "When he pushed you down, did you think you could win? Tell me the truth, boy. Forget your anger for a moment."

Eskkar closed his eyes, reliving the moment when he looked up at Nasir's grinning face, trying to remember his thoughts. "No, I thought he would beat me."

"So you fought a fight you knew you couldn't win," his father said. "That's not the warrior way. A cunning warrior doesn't fight a battle he knows he can't win. Suppose twenty dirt-eaters challenged you to a battle? Would you fight them?"

The thought of running from dirt-eaters had never entered Eskkar's head. "I'm not ... I don't know."

"I would laugh at them, and ride away," Hogarthak said. "That's what I'd do. Then I'd gather a few more men, four or five would be enough, and come back. The sight of a handful of warriors coming to attack twenty dirt-eaters would break them before the first arrow landed in their midst."

The idea that his father might ride away from a challenge shocked Eskkar more than his own defeat.

"I've another question for you, boy. Suppose five years from now, when both you and Nasir are fully grown and seasoned warriors, suppose you have to fight him then? I mean a real fight, to the death. Who would win that one?"

"Why, I don't know. I suppose ..."

"Nasir would win," his father interrupted. "He'd win because he'd remember this day. He'd remember how you tricked him and threw him down while he was still smug in his strength. So he'd be on his guard, take his time, and cut you down."

Hogarthak took a deep breath, then put his arm around Eskkar's shoulder, a surprising and rare display of affection. "That's what you did, boy. You gave away your strength today. Nasir will never forget that." Hogarthak laughed, but the grim sound had no mirth in it.

"But suppose you'd conceded to his strength today. Suppose you laughed it off, and let him think he'd bested you without a fight. Now when you had to fight him to the death, who do you think would win?"

Eskkar, trying to keep up with his father's thoughts, opened his mouth, but his father didn't even give him time to speak.

"This time, Nasir would remember the easy victory, the boy acknowledging the man. He'd look at you and laugh. Then you'd kill him, gut him as easily as your mother slices a sheep's belly."

"But my honor was at stake, Father. He challenged me."

"A boy has no honor, not until he's a warrior. You keep forgetting that. Only when you're a warrior, and only when your honor demands it, only then do you fight. Never start a needless fight, Eskkar."

Hogarthak took a deep breath, then let it out. "Remember, every fight tells all those who watch something about your skills, tells them your strengths and weaknesses. A good warrior studies the fights of others, learning from what they do, and remembering how they move and what tricks they have. That's why you should fight only when you must, and then fight to the death."

His father's words churned through Eskkar's head, adding to his misery. His mouth and eye hurt more with every moment that passed. And now his pride added to his anguish, stung by ideas and insights he'd never expected from his father.

"I'll remember... I'll try to . . . I'm just sorry you had to watch me. How did you know..."

"Word was all over the camp. Nasir has a big mouth. He'll be a loud-talker as a warrior. He was boasting of what he planned to do to you." Hogarthak shook his head. "Ekur must know his son. That's why he sent word to me about the fight."

Once again Eskkar felt the shock of his father's words. A loud talker meant one who boasted of his fighting skills, and usually wound up getting himself killed because of his pride and stupidity.

"Tomorrow, walk by Nasir's tent," Hogarthak said. "And don't show surprise if you see his face all bruised. Ekur was shamed by his son tonight, and I'm sure he'll take it out on Nasir. First by how easily you threw Nasir down, and then by the fact that Nasir would have beaten you to death if Ekur hadn't stopped it. Then I would have killed Nasir."

His father's calm words unsettled Eskkar more than any outburst.

Hogarthak ignored the surprise showing on his son's face. "I would have waited a few moons, until Nasir returned from his first raid. Then I would have insulted him, and made him grovel in the dirt or take the challenge. After he was dead, I might have to kill Ekur as well. All because you were too proud to think like a warrior."

Stunned into silence by the chain of events his actions might have launched, Eskkar didn't know what to answer. He lowered his head in shame, thinking about what disaster he might have brought on his father and his family.

Hogarthak pointed to the fires burning brighter in the night. "Look, Eskkar, what do you see?"

"I see the campfires of the Hawk Clan, all the clans. I see the horse herds and ..."

"What I see, my son, are men. Just men, trying to survive in a harsh world that permits few mistakes. Some men are strong, some are weak. Some beat their women, some treat them honorably. Most of them never use their wits for anything but finding their horse or their supper. They avoid trouble, if they're lucky. Most of them do as they're told, never think about tomorrow or the next day or the next year. If you want to be a leader of warriors, then you must learn to think and see things differently from the rest. Do you think Jamal or Maskim-Xul spend their days worrying about their honor? Or about how brave everyone thinks they are? Or how many horses and slaves and women they have? Well, do you?"

Hanging his head, Eskkar thought about Jamal, about how wise he seemed, how capable. Everyone regarded him as a just leader who cared for his people. "No, Father, I suppose they don't think of such things."

"Good. At least there's hope for you, if you ever learn to use your wits instead of your muscles. Since you were old enough to stand, I've tried to teach you something each day, something that might keep you alive when you face your true enemies. Don't make me wonder if I've wasted all that effort. Learn to think more and fight less. You'll live longer, and maybe rise in honor."

He stood. "Time to get back to the campfire. Your mother will be angry at both of us for staying away so late."

Eskkar got to his feet, then felt a wave of dizziness pass over him. His father had to help him down the steep hill, holding his arm until they passed through the trees.

"You'll make a fine warrior some day, Eskkar," Hogarthak said, as they walked side by side.

"But only when you learn to think first, before you fight. A real warrior fights best when his blood runs cold, not when it boils up like stew in a pot. Pick your battles, boy, and use your wits, if the gods gave you any. If you can do that, you may even become a clan leader some day."

They crossed the stream and approached the campfires, Eskkar thinking hard about his father's words. Not every man spent as much time teaching his son the warrior skills. Many fathers preferred to spend their time with their horses, their women, or even their wine-skins. Suddenly Eskkar appreciated what his father had given him.

"Go on ahead, boy. Have your mother tend your face. Tell her I'll be along later."

For the first time in his life, Eskkar understood his father, grasped his true meaning without being told. His father was letting him go to the women alone. Without Hogarthak's presence, Eskkar's mother and sister could tend to his bruises and his wounded pride, and he wouldn't be embarrassed in front of his father.

He'd always considered his father a brave man and a skilled warrior, but it never occurred to Eskkar that his father possessed any particular wisdom. Now that Eskkar thought about it, of course Jamal would only appoint someone with insight and good judgment as his subcommander. Even the slowest-witted warrior in the clan could comprehend that.

By the time Eskkar worked this out, Hogarthak had nearly disappeared into the darkness, heading toward the horse herd. He would eat a cold meal very late tonight, or not at all, to allow his son's pride to recover.

"Father, thank you for ..."

The words trailed off into the night. If Hogarthak heard them, his shadowy silhouette gave no sign before it vanished.

Eskkar stood alone for a moment, trying to sort out these new concepts. Finally he trudged back to his campfire, where the women would tend what little remained of his wounded pride as much as his cut lip and bruised face.

2

Late fall, 3173 BC . . .

"Where's your brother, Eskkar?"

The boy didn't answer, a new habit acquired in the last few months. Ever since he'd started riding with the warriors, he paid less and less attention to his mother, another irksome rite of passage on his journey to manhood.

Laliya sighed. Approaching his fifteenth season, her son would soon take his own wife, and the oldest of her three children would be gone. And her favorite. Every time she looked at him, she smiled. Already girls approaching marrying age stared at Eskkar with open interest, and a few of the wives had taken note of his well-toned and still growing body.

Girl or woman, they all thought him handsome, and Laliya worried about that. Discord over women caused many fights within the Clan. A father determined to protect his daughter's honor, a husband concerned about an erring wife, or rival youths quarrelling over the same flirtatious girl, it often took only a word or a glance to spark a fight.

And such fights could turn deadly for young men not quite warriors. Eskkar's father, Hogarthak, had presented his son to the leader of their clan nearly three months ago. Jamal noted Eskkar's tall frame that promised to carry plenty of muscle in the coming years. He'd approved of the young man, and given Eskkar permission to carry a long knife and continue his warrior training.

That day Laliya, watching her son strut around the camp bursting with pride, felt tears welling up. Before anyone noticed, she walked away from the wagons and found a place she could be alone – and wept. Her boy-child had grown into a man, and would soon leave Hogarthak's hearth fire for one of his own. She knew she would cry when that day came, too.

Nonetheless, Laliya gazed with satisfaction on her eldest son. He had the same deep brown eyes as her father, who'd been a handsome man favored by many women, though her son promised to be much taller. Dark brown hair, as lustrous as her own not that many years ago, swirled around his face and shoulders whenever he forgot to tie it back, a task Laliya enjoyed doing for him more and more, though she still scolded him each time.

She sighed again. Perhaps it would be best to find a bride for him sooner rather than later. The responsibilities might keep him out of trouble, and at least he wouldn't be gaping at other women for a few years, until the first rush of emerging manhood and its raging passion wore off.

"Eskkar!" This time Laliya put authority into her voice. "Your brother has work to do."

"I don't know where Melkorak is, Mother," Eskkar said, putting down the sword he'd been swinging, practicing his movements against the wagon. Nicks and gouges along the top rail testified to his growing arm strength. "He may have gone to check the horses. I'll go look for him."

"Yes, anything to shirk his chores. And don't you use him to avoid yours," she commented. "Make sure you get back here …"

"I'll find him," Eskkar said, returning his father's second sword to its place inside their wagon. Only full warriors accepted at their clan leader's council fire could carry a sword in the camp.

"Is the wagon ready for tomorrow?" Despite herself, Laliya softened her voice. "Has the water barrel been filled?"

Eskkar gave his mother and sister a wave and jogged away toward the rear of the encampment. Laliya watched him move easily between the wagons and tents, dodging the women and children setting up the night camp and preparing supper for their families.

"Make sure the animals are fed," Laliya called after him. The three goats and two sheep that belonged to Hogarthak and several other families were herded together. To keep the animals fat and healthy, they needed to be tended and guarded by their owners.

The boys, and the men, too, for that matter, preferred to spend their time working with their horses and training them to ride into battle.

At Laliya's side, her daughter giggled, but kept to her task of chopping squash and onions gathered along the day's march. Zakita, a year younger than Eskkar, doted on her older brother, following him about whenever she could.

Laliya brushed the hair away from the young girl's face. "You'll cut yourself if you can't see what you're doing, Zakita," Laliya said. She looked down at her own hands, rough and scarred by countless encounters with the cooking knife over the years.

Zakita had no scars, moles, or birthmarks anywhere on her body, a blessing from the gods for which Laliya often gave thanks. Her daughter's auburn hair, wholesome face and attractive smile would ensure a good number of suitable young men offering themselves as husbands when the time came.

"I'll finish the vegetables. Take the slave and gather more firewood. We've barely enough to cook dinner, and it will be cold tonight.

Her daughter put down her knife, wiping her hands on her dress. Laliya shifted her gaze toward the slave who'd just returned from fetching water from the stream. "Go with Zakita," Laliya commanded, her voice hardening. "Make sure you come back with plenty of wood."

Tarana, the newest addition to Hogarthak's family, set the water jug down with care and obediently started after Zakita.

The two girls walked off, and Laliya returned to contemplating her life. First her son would go, then her daughter. In a few more years, she would be an old woman, worn down and relegated to caring for her grandchildren. Thankfully her husband provided well for his family, and her advanced years would be less wearisome than many of her friends and kin. In the Clan, women did most of the hard labor, work that grew no easier with the passing of the years.

She pulled the dented copper pot full of rabbit parts closer, and added the chopped vegetables, along with a double-handful of green beans and chickpeas, all gathered today along the march. At least the Great Clan's present route took them through a bountiful land, full of wild vegetables and plenty of game.

Laliya and her daughter had taken turns searching for these delicacies all during the day, hunting alongside the slow-moving caravan and competing with the other women engaged in the same activity.

A handful of dried onions would fill out the stew, and along with the two rabbits Eskkar had hunted during the afternoon, meant everyone would have some meat. Warriors needed meat to maintain their strength, but none of Hogarthak's kin had managed to kill a large game animal in the last six days.

Tonight even firewood was scarce. Zakita and the slave might have to walk a long way, picking up sticks and twigs as they went, before returning to Hogarthak's wagon.

Laliya's husband had obtained Tarana only a few days ago, after he returned from an extended raid. A valuable gift from their clan chief, Jamal, she accompanied Hogarthak's promotion, a public sign of Hogarthak's growing importance.

Now her husband stood at Jamal's side, promoted from a leader-of-twenty to third in command. Hogarthak had proven both his fighting skill and his wisdom over the last ten years; the other warriors within their clan accepted and respected him.

After her husband took his new station, Laliya had spoken with most of the women in the Hawk Clan, but heard none of the usual grumblings when an unpopular choice rose in the ranks. Hogarthak also happened to be a nephew of Jamal, not that it mattered. Nearly everyone in the Hawk Clan was kin in some degree to one another.

She felt as much pride as any of the men about Hogarthak's rise. Until Tarana's arrival, Hogarthak possessed only one slave, Sargat, whose sole duty involved caring for his master's horses. With his new station, Hogarthak would receive a share from every game animal his men hunted; the extra food would more than compensate for what Tarana would consume.

In the next few months, there would be more slaves. Laliya and her daughter would have less to do themselves, though she knew they'd still be busy managing the slaves and personally caring for the men in their family.

Zakita, midway through her thirteenth season, would soon become a woman, and Laliya and Hogarthak would have to find their daughter a suitable husband. No doubt Jamal would suggest some young warriors he favored and Zakita would be married within the year, too.

Jamal had awarded the slave girl Tarana to Hogarthak after they returned from their last foray. Hogarthak led the frightened girl back to his campfire, and pushed her toward his wife.

"A gift from Jamal, to ease your labors. Train her well."

Laliya had taken a stick and beaten the girl hard, across her back and bottom, ignoring her cries, continuing long after Tarana sobbed uncontrollably and squirmed in the dirt, begging for mercy. Laliya then told Tarana what would be her duties, and how she must obey every command instantly or face even more painful beatings.

That night Hogarthak bedded the still-crying girl, indifferent to her tears. Laliya had knelt beside them, the stick always handy at her side, watching to ensure the slave not only performed well, but understood the unspoken message.

The slave had to learn that her life now depended on her obedience to Laliya as much as the enjoyment she provided her master. The sooner Tarana accepted her role, the less she would suffer.

Laliya had to beat the girl twice more, but now Tarana seemed to understand that any failure to obey only added to her woes. She would be a slave the rest of her life.

Last night, the two of them pleasured Hogarthak, Laliya guiding the slave, telling her what to do, even showing the inexperienced girl several other ways to please her master. Afterwards, when her husband fell asleep, Laliya had mounted the girl herself, straddling her mouth until she reached the pleasure of the gods.

She took care not to awake her snoring husband, though she knew he would ignore the act even if he did wake and take notice. Many warriors frowned on such activities, forbidding their wives to do such things, but when a slave was involved, the act meant little.

Laliya, well satisfied for the first time in many days, fell asleep beside her husband, oblivious to Tarana's muffled crying.

A slave's tears meant nothing. Laliya's children ignored them as easily as they did their father's lovemaking, another familiar sight to any family that slept together in a tent scarcely large enough to hold them.

Laliya brought her thoughts back to the present. She started the cooking fire, making sure it burned steadily before putting the pot over it. In truth, she was glad of Tarana's presence.

The girl, scarcely older than Zakita, was beautiful, and possession of a well-favored slave girl would further enhance Hogarthak's standing in the clan. The addition of new slaves would improve Laliya's life as well. And Laliya now preferred her husband to seek his pleasures with slaves, rather than risk another pregnancy.

Melkorak, her second son and youngest child, came only after a long and difficult birth. Twice after that, Laliya delivered stillborn infants, both times nearly bleeding to death in the process. No, better that Tarana and other, younger women take the risks of childbearing.

Over the years, Laliya had learned different ways to satisfy her husband's needs, ways that reduced the chance of again being with child. Besides, the children of slaves remained slaves themselves, so they presented no threat to her own sons. As head wife, Laliya could even put a woman slave to death, though such a drastic action rarely happened.

Year after year, Laliya had worked hard to provide for her husband and their children. Already her once dark tresses glinted with gray, as she approached her thirtieth season. It would be good to relax a little, and enjoy the benefits Hogarthak's new position would bring.

Tonight he attended his clan chief Jamal at a full council meeting of all the clans. Afterwards Hogarthak would return to take his supper and relate to her what the leaders of the Great Council had decided. He would be hungry, and she would make sure he ate well.

A small skin of wine still held half its contents; perhaps tonight would be a good occasion to offer it to her husband, before the wine turned vinegary. She tossed more twigs on the fire and stirred the food pot, humming a simple rhyme from her childhood, and anticipating the night's modest pleasures.

The summons from the Great Chief Maskim-Xul had come soon after the caravan stopped for the day. Hogarthak had ridden at Jamal's side most of the afternoon. Since Jamal's two grown sons had already departed to check on their horses before the summons arrived, the bodyguard task fell to Hogarthak.

Now Hogarthak sat on the ground behind Jamal, another link in the outer chain that circled around the smaller, inner ring of clan chiefs. Hogarthak's role, as he sat behind Jamal, was to listen, watch, and keep his mouth shut. Each of the twelve clan chiefs of the Alur Meriki that formed the inner circle had a single bodyguard to attend him.

Hogarthak had performed this duty only three times before, but already the novelty had worn off. It wasn't as if he got to hear anything secret or special. Whatever the Council decided, even for matters of importance, the whole camp generally knew before turning in for the night. Hogarthak thought more about his wife's supper than the droning words of his leaders.

As sundown drew near, the ruler of all the Alur Meriki clans, Maskim-Xul, took his seat on a low stool at the circle's head, his sword resting across his knees. The copper medallion that indicated his authority, as large as two clenched fists, glittered on his chest.

Hogarthak knew better than to stare at the great ruler, but an occasional glance was permitted, enough to see the raw power of the man who led the twelve clans and held sway over all their lives.

Maskim-Xul had entered the prime of life, just short of his thirty-eighth season, and he'd ruled the Alur Meriki for more than fifteen years. Not only ruled them, he had increased their power and wealth beyond expectations.

Everywhere the Alur Meriki marched, they stood uncontested, the whole world helpless before them. No other clan had sufficient numbers to challenge them. Now the Alur Meriki not only terrorized the helpless dirt-eaters, but actively sought after other steppes clans. These they absorbed, either by a forced joining under threat of the sword, or by actual conquest.

In the first case, Alur Meriki numbers grew by simple addition. Warriors from the conquered clans were scattered among the Alur Meriki, where these new members swore oaths of fealty to their new leaders. If any steppes clan resisted the joining, Maskim-Xul unleashed the fury of his warriors in war, and fighting raged until the opposing force suffered total defeat and surrender.

For the losing side, that meant the distribution of their horses and women to the victors, with any surviving warriors once again dispersed throughout the Alur Meriki ranks.

With all the wealth and resources of the rich and fertile land available to them, the number of Alur Meriki warriors under Maskim-Xul's command grew steadily, as many of his fighters took second and third wives to provide even more strong sons for the Great Clan. Plentiful food, either from the hunt or taken from the dirt-eaters, insured that most babies survived, to swell the force of ever growing fighters.

And in every case, whether born into the Clan, absorbed, or conquered, each warrior swore undying allegiance to his clan chief, and every clan chief bowed before Maskim-Xul's power.

Hogarthak seldom considered such things. The Great Clan grew, as it had always grown, and would continue to grow. A warrior's duty was to obey his clan leader, and fight the clan's enemies.

Tonight's duties involved attending Jamal at the council. Once again Hogarthak's thoughts returned to his delayed supper, as he ignored the preening of clan leaders eager to impress each other.

"Then the route chosen for the next few months is settled," Maskim-Xul announced, his deep voice carrying easily around the circle. "The scouts say a small clan of warriors traverses these lands, the Mittani. They will join with us, or be destroyed."

The other clan chieftains seated on the ground nodded approval. More wealth and slaves would flow into their hands, and their warriors would have yet another chance to demonstrate their prowess. Raiding and looting dirt-eaters might be necessary, but brought no honor. The pitiful farmers or frightened villagers they encountered seldom offered any resistance, and even if they did, they had no force of warriors who dared stand before the Alur Meriki.

The news about the Mittani meant nothing to Hogarthak. Jamal's clan had just returned from an extended raid, and wouldn't likely be dispatched for another ten or twenty days. Bored with listening to Maskim-Xul and the clan chiefs, Hogarthak concealed a yawn and breathed a sigh of relief as the council meeting drew to a close. The sun had dipped below the horizon, and it would soon be dark.

But just as Hogarthak expected the council to be dismissed, Maskim-Xul's son, Seluku, seated just behind his father, rose to his feet.

"Clan Chiefs," he began, "I led the last raid against the villages to the north." Seluku's loud voice and pompous words grated on Hogarthak's ears. He'd heard the same tone many times each day for the twenty plus days that the raid lasted. "There is much about the raid the council should know."

A bull of a man, just entering his twenty-first season, Seluku wore the gold and gemstones of many conquests glinting on his fingers and arms. Taking a step into the circle of leaders, he began to describe the last raid, recounting the fighting and looting, and listing the wealth of slaves, grain, and animals they'd captured.

Hogarthak listened, his mouth falling open in astonishment, as Seluku claimed for himself and his clansmen all the credit, ignoring the accomplishments of Jamal and the Hawk Clan. While Maskim-Xul's son spoke, Hogarthak noted that Jamal began to squirm, listening to the boastings and half-truths spoken by the younger Seluku.

"We took many slaves," Seluku went on, his eyes darting around the inner circle, "but the division of what we captured was not done fairly." He glanced at his father for a moment, then turned toward Jamal and pointed toward him.

"The clan of Jamal took more than their share. Not only more, but they took the fairest women, choicest horses, and strongest slaves. This insult I did not mind, but the share of the captured goods that belonged to my father was not enough. I see now that the portion allotted to our great leader fails to show proper respect and honor."

"Seluku speaks unwisely, and reveals his inexperience," Jamal said, when he could keep silent no more. "The Hawk Clan warriors did most of the fighting. We led the way into every village. One of my warriors died in the last skirmish, while Seluku and his men, stayed to the rear or chased down stragglers attempting to escape."

Jamal rose to his feet, though custom dictated that only one speaker at a time should stand. "Since my clan rode in the forefront of each attack, custom decrees we earned the right of first choice of spoils."

Hogarthak had rarely heard Jamal speak so forcefully, even when berating members of his own clan. A wise leader, Jamal ruled his clan with justice and moderation for almost twenty years. But the Hawk Clan numbered just over sixty warriors, one of the smallest in the Alur Meriki. Despite the size of Jamal's force, many of the other clan leaders held him in respect, and his words were heeded within the council.

Seluku ignored Jamal, directing his words to the rest of the clan chiefs. "The horses left for Maskim-Xul and me were inferior, good for little but pulling an empty wagon. The slave woman chosen for my father is already dead, as is the one I chose for myself. Those taken by Jamal and his men still live, and . . ."

"If Seluku knew how to handle his horses or his women, they'd all still be alive," Jamal said, his voice cold with scorn. He remained on his feet. "And not once did Seluku offer to lead the way, to risk even the slightest danger. No, he stayed behind my warriors, where he would be safe. Then after the fighting ended, he demanded first pick of the spoils, against our ways."

Hogarthak heard the murmur of astonishment at his leader's words. Jamal had accused Seluku of cowardice again, this time openly.

His face flushed, Jamal went on arguing with Seluku, both men growing more agitated with each angry word exchanged, while Hogarthak sat there stunned. These kinds of accusations were rarely brought up to the council. A clan chief with a grievance went to another clan leader, who presented the facts to Maskim-Xul.

The Great Chief would then speak to each leader separately, to decide on the truth of the claim, before presenting his decision to the council. If it were not done this way, blood would be spilled at nearly all council gatherings over every trifle.

Hogarthak stared directly at the Great Clan Chief. He'd said nothing, just listened as his son Seluku made his charges. Maskim-Xul still sat there, but something about the man's posture had changed, something Hogarthak couldn't detect, some slight ... Maskim-Xul's feet had shifted, positioned for him to rise, and his sword, resting across his knees, had moved, too, the hilt now resting beneath his right hand.

Jamal's damning words that implied Seluku's cowardice had removed the smiles from the Council's faces. Hogarthak felt his mouth go dry. Only a fight to the death could wipe out the insult, and Seluku, a dangerous fighter, led nearly seventy men, almost half as many as his father, Maskim-Xul, commanded.

Hogarthak gaze darted around the inner ring, and saw many had their eyes down, avoiding contact with Jamal and each other. They, too, had seen the signs. Blood would flow, and it would likely be Jamal's. His prosperous clan would be broken up, its families distributed among the rest of the clan chiefs, with most going to Seluku.

Jamal's warriors would bear the insult for years; they'd suffer the worst assignments and receive the least gain from every conquest, until the humiliation faded away with the passage of time.

Hogarthak noticed movement on either side. Some of Seluku's guards gradually drew closer to the circle, and others had disappeared. No, not disappeared. A quick glance over his shoulder showed they'd shifted behind Jamal and Hogarthak. Without moving, he tensed his muscles and made himself ready to rise.

He felt the itching in his back, knowing that Seluku's men stood there, moving ever closer. Now Hogarthak understood. This was no sudden burst of ill-will by Seluku, but something planned in advance, something... he had to stop it, before Jamal ended up dead.

Though forbidden, Hogarthak rose to his feet. He reached out and touched Jamal's arm. Jamal scarcely felt the touch at first, then turned in surprise to see his subcommander standing just behind him.

"My Lord," Hogarthak said, keeping his voice calm, "perhaps there is some truth to what Seluku says. I was given a slave girl taken in the raid. Let me give her to Maskim-Xul, to distribute as he sees fit. And my share of the gold, and the horses."

But the proud leader of the Hawk Clan refused to bow to such insults. Jamal, mouth open, stared at Hogarthak, shocked that his underling would dare to speak at the council, and even more surprised to hear his subcommander urge conciliation to Seluku's demands.

Jamal shook off Hogarthak's hand. "Keep to your place. There will be no change in the division of spoils. Let Seluku give up some of his wealth to his father, if he feels our great leader has been slighted."

"Your subcommander's words show I speak the truth," Seluku said, pouncing like a lion on Hogarthak's efforts to sooth his leader's temper. "Now all the council knows that Jamal is not only a liar, but a coward."

The fatal words hung in the air but for a moment. Enraged, Jamal's hands went to his belt, left gripping the scabbard while he drew his sword with the right. "Let us see who is a coward, Seluku, or are you afraid of facing me with a sword in your hand?"

His teeth bared, Seluku drew his sword as well, but he stepped back as he did so, and his guards quickly pushed into the circle, their swords rasping from their scabbards.

Jamal, too far gone with rage and anger, moved forward, taking a cut at Seluku's head, but one of Seluku's guards moved in, his blade raised to deflect the blow. By then three men were advancing on Jamal, who suddenly realized he'd been tricked into drawing his blade first.

For a single instant Hogarthak hesitated, knowing what was at stake. Jamal must have seen his own death coming, but if Hogarthak did nothing, if he stepped back, then he might well survive. Then the brief moment of weakness passed. Hogarthak drew his own sword, whirling around so that his back pressed against that of his clan leader, to find two men with bared weapons only a step away.

I'm going to die this day, Hogarthak thought. Then he forgot everything as his battle rage came over him.

He moved half a step to the side, striking at the closest warrior and halting his advance, then shifting so quickly that he thrust home his blade into the second man's stomach, catching him by surprise with the quick shift. Ducking under the first attacker's counter stroke, he slipped to the other side and slashed viciously at the man's neck, sending a spray of blood over the council members, many of them scrambling to get out of the way.

Behind him, Jamal killed the first man to reach him, but the other two fought with skill, stopping Jamal's advance, and in a moment, driving him back. As Hogarthak turned to join his lord, one of Seluku's men struck Jamal's right arm, the blade cutting through flesh and into the bone just above the wrist, wrenching a gasp from the Hawk Clan leader as the weapon slipped from his grasp, the fingers of his sword hand no longer obeying his command.

"No!" Seluku moved back into what remained of the circle, halting his men before they could administer the death stroke. "I'll kill him myself."

He stepped toward the wounded man. Jamal, still attempting to fight, fumbled with his left hand, trying to reach the knife hanging on his belt.

Hogarthak heard the words, but two more men had pushed through the gathering crowd and advanced toward him. Jamal's cry of agony rang out as Seluku's sword thrust into his stomach. Hogarthak faked a cut at his attackers, slowing them for an instant, then ducked low and swung around, his left arm encircling his dying clan leader and holding him upright.

But in the same movement, Hogarthak's sword slipped under Jamal's bloody arm and thrust hard, the concealed stroke catching everyone by surprise, and half an arm's length of bloody bronze entered Seluku's stomach, a hand's width below the breast bone.

Then the satisfyingly shocked face of Seluku vanished, and Hogarthak felt cold metal sear through his own back once, twice, sending his body into a spasm and wrenching a cry of pain from his lips. He screamed in agony before another blow severed his head from his neck in a final flash of white hot light.

Hogarthak's head landed beside the body of Jamal. The lifeless eyes of clan chieftain and subcommander stared at each other, so close that not even a hand's breadth separated them.

No one moved or uttered a sound. Maskim-Xul, on his feet, stared in surprise and anger at his son, who'd stumbled backwards before falling heavily and clutching his stomach. Otherwise, Maskim-Xul's scheme to destroy the Hawk Clan had worked perfectly.

Despite the small size of Jamal's clan, his influence and stature within the council had steadily increased over the last few months. Maskim-Xul had watched as more and more clan chiefs sought Jamal's advice and took their direction from him. Maskim-Xul permitted no threat to his power, no matter how small or how subtle.

And so, as father and son had planned over the last two days, Seluku goaded Jamal into drawing a weapon, and the guards had moved swiftly and efficiently to bring Jamal down.

Yet Seluku, foolishly wanting to give the death stroke himself, now lay in the dirt at his father's feet, coughing blood and gasping for breath, somehow killed by Jamal's insignificant subcommander an instant before the man's own life ended.

No one dared to speak. As Maskim-Xul took in all this, Seluku whimpered in pain, his feet kicking feebly and hands clutching the bloody wound in his stomach.

Maskim-Xul, rage contorting his face, glowered down at his son. He drew his sword and struck down, driving the point deep into Seluku's heart, silencing him. No one would hear a son of his whimper in his death throes. Withdrawing the blade, Maskim-Xul grunted in satisfaction. If Seluku's death was the price Maskim-Xul had to be pay to rid himself of a potential rival, so be it. He lifted his gaze to take in the other clan leaders, staring open mouthed at the dead heaped within what remained of the council circle.

Maskim-Xul raised his voice, to make sure all could hear. "To pay for my son's death, all of Jamal's family is to be put to death. His name, and the name of his clan, is cursed from this day."

No one said anything, the rest of the chiefs stunned and frightened into silence. They'd all seen Maskim-Xul's rages before, but Seluku's death changed everything. Each clan chief had to think about his own life, knowing those closest to Jamal would feel Maskim-Xul's anger for months to come. More blood would likely flow before the Great Chief felt fully avenged.

Maskim-Xul took a step forward and kicked Hogarthak's severed head, intending to send it flying. But the bloody head rolled into Jamal's body and rebounded, tumbling back to rest against Maskim-Xul foot. Hogarthak's eyes now stared sightlessly up at Maskim-Xul, almost as if to mock him.

"And this one," Maskim-Xul roared, pointing with his bloody sword, "find his family and kill them all. Let everyone know the penalty for killing my son!"

For a moment, the clan leaders stood there, surrounded by Seluku and Maskim-Xul's tense guards, drawn swords still in their hands.

"GO!" This time Maskim-Xul's voice echoed over the shocked figures standing about him, galvanizing them into action. "Go, and kill them all!"

⸺⸺

"Mama, something's happening," Zakita said.

Laliya didn't bother to look up. She dipped her finger into the pot, tasted the stew, and decided it was ready. "Yes, child," she said soothingly.

Something was always happening in the camp, women arguing over wood for the fires, children running wild through the wagons and causing trouble, warriors getting drunk and quarreling, boys fighting, slaves getting beaten. Nearly every night brought its own excitement.

"Mama!"

The urgency in her daughter's voice made Laliya turn her head, just as five men approached, following the line of wagons stretched out haphazardly throughout the camp. The men stepped purposefully, and carried drawn swords in their hands.

A chill passed over Laliya. Where was Hogarthak? He should have returned by now. What had happened? She recognized the foremost of the warriors, a grim man named Romar.

"Is this the wagon of the traitor Hogarthak?" Romar spat the words at her.

"This is the wagon of my husband, Hogarthak," Laliya said, getting to her feet and wiping her hands on her dress, "but he is no traitor to his lord Jamal."

"The filth Jamal is dead," the man answered, glancing around, relieved to see no warriors nearby. Most of Seluku's guards had gone to Jamal's wagons, eager to take first pick from Jamal's horses and women.

The sounds of fighting at Jamal's campsite could now be heard up and down the caravan. Jamal had sons, as well as plenty of close kin who would fight to avenge their leader's death, no matter what the odds.

Romar and four others of Seluku's followers had been dispatched to find and finish off the subcommander's family. More men would be coming soon, but until they arrived, Romar and his men might find themselves outnumbered by Jamal's followers, if any came to the family's assistance.

"Summon your children," Romar ordered, "you are all to come to the council meeting."

Laliya knew the man lied, knew something dreadful had happened the moment she heard of Jamal's death. Hogarthak must be dead as well, though she couldn't quite make herself believe it.

"Zakita, go find your brother," she said, grasping the girl by the shoulder and shoving her on her way. "Tell him Clan Chief Jamal is dead and ..."

Romar reached across Laliya's body and grabbed the girl's arm. "You'll both stay here. Tell me where your sons are."

Like a striking snake, Laliya leapt at Romar, her hands outstretched and fingers clawing for his eyes. "Run, Zakita," she shouted, "find Eskkar and ..."

Caught by surprise, the warrior exploded in pain and rage, unaware that he'd already been blinded in one eye. Romar knocked Laliya down, then thrust hard through a bloody haze with his sword, driving the blade through her belly and into the ground, impaling her.

Zakita darted away, but one of Romar's men caught her by her hair, then twisted her arm up behind her back and shoved her to the ground. She screamed in fright, and he pushed her face into the dirt, then began binding her hands. The girl had to die, of course, like the rest of the family, but not right away, not until she'd provided some amusement to Seluku's men.

Laliya, clutching her blood-soaked belly, cried out, helpless to stop anything, feeling the terrible burning in her stomach as her life's blood gushed from the wound. Behind her she heard laughter, the high-pitched, vicious laughter of the slave, Tarana, as she watched her mistress bleeding to death.

"Hurry up," Eskkar said, pushing his brother along. "There won't be anything left for us to eat."

"They always save food for me," Melkorak said, though the boy quickened his pace. Nearly three years younger than his brother, Melkorak had yet to show whether he would attain Eskkar's size and frame.

In temperament, they could not be further apart. Where Eskkar tended to be slow and methodical, Melkorak seemed full of energy, unable to remain still even for a moment.

As expected, Eskkar had found his brother down by the horses, galloping one of their father's smaller mounts back and forth across the holding area, raising dust and annoying all the horse tenders who wanted to eat their evening meal in peace. Half the herd milled about, nervously eyeing the boy racing back and forth while whooping war cries in his high-pitched voice.

As usual, several families from Jamal's clan had pooled their forty or so horses together within a flimsy rope corral anchored to a mix of bushes, trees, or even rocks; they were cared for by a handful of slaves. For warriors, a good horse had far more value than any slave, and they attended their animals as dutifully as their wives and children.

As Hogarthak's stature within the clan had risen, he'd taken more horses for himself, the true mark of a successful warrior. Eskkar's father now possessed seven mounts, and kept a slave whose only duty was to tend them. Sargat had been a slave all his life, born into the clan, but even as a child he'd taken to horses, and had grown old herding them for Jamal, Hogarthak, and a few others.

Even with three or four extra slaves to help him, providing the care needed for that many horses took all of Sargat's time.

All the same, whenever the clan made camp for the night, Sargat always found time to teach the excitable boy how to feed and tend to the herd. Somehow he put up with Melkorak's noisy antics, allowing him to help train and exercise the spirited creatures.

Too mature to chase after his brother, Eskkar kept walking, and didn't notice the shouting that echoed along the wagons until he'd nearly reached his family's campsite. Then he recognized Zakita's voice, a scream that rose above everything else. He broke into a run, but by then Melkorak had reached the wagon and disappeared around the other side.

Eskkar burst into the campsite only a few paces behind his brother, just in time to see a burly warrior struggling with Melkorak.

"I've got him," the warrior shouted.

In the flickering light from the small dinner fire, Eskkar saw other warriors, swords in their hands. One held Melkorak, who squirmed and twisted in the man's arms, while another knelt over Zakita, binding her hands. Then Eskkar saw his mother laying on her back in the dirt beside the fire, blood pooling the ground around her, while a bleeding warrior stood over her, holding a red-streaked sword.

"Kill them and be done," Romar said, trying to get the blood out of his remaining eye.

"Mother!" Zakita's plea could hardly be heard over all the commotion.

"Save my family . . . someone . . ." Laliya cried. She struggled to lift her head, clutching her blood-stained stomach.

"There's another one," a fourth warrior called out, pointing his sword at Eskkar.

Eskkar's eyes widened in horror. He reacted without thinking, darting into the firelight. One of the warriors lifted his sword. Eskkar ducked beneath the blade and, still moving, drew his knife.

The man grasping Melkorak had pushed him to the ground, holding him there with one hand just long enough to drive the sword through his chest. The boy's shriek of agony masked not only the noise of Eskkar's rush, but the warning shouted by the other warrior.

Before the man could withdraw his sword from Melkorak's body, Eskkar had plunged his knife deep into the man's back with a fury that buried the blade to the hilt.

Cursing, the warrior who'd let Eskkar slip past swung the sword again, and this time Eskkar had to fling himself to the ground to avoid the cut.

"Run, Eskkar," Laliya gasped. "Save yourself . . . run. Leave the clan . . . run!"

Romar's now-gory left hand still clutched his empty eye socket, as he blinked the blood away. "Damn you to the demons." He lowered his sword and thrust it hard forward, driving the blade deep into Laliya's throat, silencing her.

Rolling to his feet, Eskkar had time only for a single glance. He saw his mother take the death blow, Zakita lay senseless, dead or dying, on the ground. Melkorak, already silent, lay pinned to the ground, the warrior's sword protruding from the boy's body.

Eskkar's knife remained embedded in the killer's back. Two men closed in on him from either side, trapping him against the wagon.

They attacked, and all Eskkar could do was fling himself down and under the wagon, rolling beneath it and out the other side, on his feet and darting back into the darkness. His head pounded and tears blurred his vision, but he had no time for anything except to run, run as hard as he could. He could hear the men shouting as they gave chase.

Laliya's dying words echoed in his mind; she told him to run, flee the clan, and he knew what that meant. Without thinking, he retraced his way back to the area where Sargat tended the horses and slept each night beside them.

The two warriors gave chase, but Eskkar, unencumbered by any weapon, fairly flew through the shadows, jumping over obstacles and pushing women, children, and even warriors aside. The men hounding him might be older and stronger, but ever since they'd attained full warrior status, they'd given up running for riding. That and the darkness helped Eskkar widen his lead over his pursuers.

Eskkar splashed across the tiny stream and reached the horses, his sudden approach startling the animals, who whinnied and pawed the earth at the abrupt movement, their ears flicking back and forth. Sargat, tending a small fire with a few other slaves, looked up in surprise at the boy's abrupt appearance, his mouth open to protest.

Gasping for breath, Eskkar reached the pile of halters and blankets, ignoring Sargat's confused questions. Without stopping, Eskkar grabbed a halter and dashed into the herd. He went straight for his father's best horse, a sturdy animal with plenty of endurance.

Eskkar had ridden the animal often enough, and before the surprised horse could protest, Eskkar slipped the halter over its head and fastened it snugly. He grasped the mane, swung himself up and put his heels to the horse's flank.

The animal resisted, tossing its head, unused to such rough handling. Eskkar kicked the horse again, but the animal lowered its head, whinnying in annoyance.

Seluku's two warriors arrived, breathing hard, swords in their hands. They shoved the slaves aside and made for Eskkar. But now the milling horses blocked their way. The beasts moved back and forth, surging against the rope, frightened by all the sudden move-ment, their natural instinct telling them to run.

The grim warriors forced their way through the herd, pushing animals aside in their haste, and just as one of them raised his sword, Eskkar reached down and smacked the nearest horse on its rump as hard as he could.

With a loud snort, the startled animal bolted. Eskkar shouted, and suddenly the entire herd surged forward, his stallion under control at last. The rope held them back for a moment, but then it snapped, and the frightened mass, sensing freedom, began to move, taking Eskkar and his mount along with them.

The small stampede quickly grew. Another herd, a hundred paces away, caught the excitement and strained against its own retaining ropes, before breaking free and galloping away into the night. The whole camp by now had erupted into chaos.

Cursing warriors not even involved in the fight between the two clans rushed after their horses, while those from Jamal's clan tried to gather together for protection. If they wished to stay alive, they dared not interfere with the Great Chief's death order, but no one knew what might happen next.

In all the confusion, the horses vanished into the darkness, taking the fleeing boy with them.

—⊶⊶—

The two men chasing Eskkar stopped, out of breath and full of rage.

"Shouldn't we ride after him?" The younger warrior looked toward his older cousin for guidance.

"On what? We'd have to catch a horse first." He looked around; the nearest herd was two or three hundred paces away.

"I'm not going to risk my life riding after some fool boy in the dark. Besides, he'll probably break his neck and save us the trouble of killing him." He rammed his sword into its sheath.

He turned away and walked back toward the tiny fire, the younger warrior following reluctantly a step behind. The hapless slaves, unaware of the quarrels of their masters, stayed on their knees, heads down and shaking in fear.

But slaves and their terrors meant nothing to warriors. "You, slaves," the older one said. "Make sure you round up all of Hogarthak and Jamal's horses, and bring them to the tent of Seluku in the morning. Every one, you hear?"

They nodded.

Still breathing hard from their long run, the two men trudged back toward Hogarthak's campsite.

"Ulor's dead," the younger one said.

"And his brother lost an eye," the older countered with a laugh. Neither Ulor nor Romar, both toadies of Seluku, were popular with the rest of the men. "And with Seluku dead, Romar One-Eye has to face Maskim-Xul and explain how a woman blinded one of his favorite warriors. Romar may yet lose his other eye before the night's over."

They both laughed at that thought.

"What about the boy who got away?"

The older and wiser warrior considered that for a moment, then shrugged. "What's one boy? Where can he go, what can he do? Besides, the family's dead ... enough blood's been spilled. Seluku was a pig anyway."

"But Maskim-Xul said ..."

"As far as I'm concerned, the boy's dead. Unless you want to spend the next two or three days galloping over the countryside chasing after him. Let those riding patrols run him down tomorrow. Besides, Romar won't say anything, not if it means admitting he let one get away. Romar already lost an eye to that she-wolf. He won't want to risk his head."

The younger warrior thought about that for a moment. "What will happen to the boy?"

"He's already good as dead," the older one answered. "Even if he gets away, the dirt-eaters will finish him off soon enough. Saves us the trouble."

"Then it's over," the young warrior said, grunting in relief.

"Yes, that's the end of it, until the next time someone offends Maskim-Xul."

"Who'll take Seluku's place, do you think?"

"Hmm, Maskim-Xul's got plenty of sons." The older warrior slowed his steps as he pondered the question. "What's that other boy's name, the one that's always hanging around the council fire, listening to everything . . . Thutmose . . . perhaps he'll take Seluku's place at Maskim-Xul's side."

"He's too young, isn't he?"

"For now," the older man agreed. Suddenly he laughed. "But cunning as a fox, they say. Different mother than the ugly whore that whelped Seluku. You know, Thutmose may be our ruler someday, thanks to Hogarthak's lucky thrust."

By now they'd reached Hogarthak's wagon. Romar sat there, his fists clenched, trying to ignore the pain. A woman with trembling lips leaned over him, bandaging his eye. Fresh blood already soaked through the strip of cloth. Another warrior stood close by, eyes watching the sullen followers of Jamal who stared back at Seluku's men from nearby wagons, hatred and fear plain on their faces.

"Did you get him?" Romar asked, his teeth clenched against the pain.

"He's dead. He stampeded the horses, and got trampled beneath them," the older man said, his words making the death official.

Romar tried to focus his remaining eye on the man. Despite the throbbing in his head, he sensed something not quite right.

"Where's the . . ." Romar let the question trail off, staring at the grizzled warrior's face. Romar didn't want, he decided, to ask any more questions. "Then Hogarthak's line is ended."

"Yes, it's finished." The older warrior said the words firmly, meeting Romar's gaze until he nodded agreement.

Whether the boy lived or died, the old warrior really didn't care. He'd seen enough of these clan fights in his time, arrogant chiefs killing each other and their followers over some assumed slight to their pride or even just simple greed.

Better to sit by his campfire with his woman, and eat his supper in peace. He knew one thing for certain: one boy more or less wasn't going to change anything, not in this world, and not in his lifetime.

—⟶⟨⟩⟵—

Eskkar clung to the horse's neck and galloped through the darkness. At first other horses running loose followed along, but they gradually turned away or stopped. Even dumb beasts knew better than to rush about in the darkness, let alone race for more than a few hundred paces. But Eskkar drove the big stallion, keeping it at a run until even the light from the hundreds of campfires disappeared behind him.

When he finally stopped, both he and the horse were breathing hard. Eskkar dismounted, his legs trembling from the close escape and the reckless ride. A single misstep, a hole in the ground, even a loose rock could have killed both horse and rider.

As soon as Eskkar had his breathing under control, he strained his ears, listening for the sound of pursuit. Behind him, he knew cursing men would be rounding up their horses, searching for those mounts still missing, and herding the jittery animals back to camp.

Naturally the men wouldn't recapture every one, despite losing a night's sleep. For the warriors, that meant half the morning wasted, tracking and chasing after horses all too happy to be running free.

Whether any searchers would be coming after him, Eskkar didn't know. He had to assume they would be on his trail, if not tonight, then as soon as the sun came up. Eskkar had gotten out of the camp, but he hadn't escaped the danger, not yet.

All he knew for certain was that he was alone. Not only alone, but a renegade. Some horrible calamity had destroyed his family; even those he could call kinsmen would turn him away, unwilling to face Maskim-Xul's wrath. Eskkar's father must be dead, or he surely would have returned to the family wagon from the council meeting.

That likely meant Jamal had died as well. Certainly the men who'd come to Hogarthak's campfire didn't belong to Jamal's clan, and the proud clan leader would never permit anyone else's warriors to come for one of his own.

Only the Great Chief of all the Alur Meriki, Eskkar realized, could order an entire family put to death. The men who murdered Eskkar's family must have come at Maskim-Xul's bidding. Otherwise there were numerous ways of punishing a wayward warrior.

Horses could be taken, a wagon, slaves, any warrior's possessions could be confiscated; a warrior could even be beaten, the worst kind of public humiliation. In the most severe case, an entire family could be banished from the Clan, forced to dwell forever away from kin and to live, or more likely, die, in disgrace among the dirt-eaters.

Instead, Eskkar had seen his mother and brother die, and none of Jamal's clan, not even their closest neighbors came to their defense. Zakita might already be dead, too. He hoped she was. Otherwise, as soon as the warriors finished raping her, they'd slit her throat, and laugh as she bled to death.

Tears of anger ran down his cheeks. He loved Zakita, always watched over his sister, but there was nothing he could do to help. Even if he turned back, Eskkar would be dead long before he reached the wagons.

For a moment, his shoulders shook with sobs, as the hot tears coursed down his cheeks. He couldn't stop himself from crying, something no warrior should ever do. But he wasn't a warrior yet, not really.

In the two raids he'd been on, Eskkar had done little more than ride behind the warriors and tend to their horses. His father hadn't finished Eskkar's training, and he'd never fought in a battle, nor killed anyone.

Yes, he had, Eskkar recalled with sudden satisfaction. The man who killed his brother Melkorak had died by Eskkar's hand. He shook the tears away as he remembered the feeling, the hard thrust into the man's back, the quick gasp of pain before the man slumped forward, already dead or dying.

Eskkar opened and closed the fingers of his right hand. Whatever his father's offense, Eskkar had at least repaid part of the debt to his spirit. Aloud, he swore to avenge his family's death, the harsh words echoing into the night.

When his tears ceased, the silence and the darkness surrounding him remained unbroken. He was alone, as alone as any boy could be. Tomorrow men would be on his trail, eager to hunt him down and kill him. Time to get moving again.

Eskkar checked the moon's position, and studied the stars shining above. The Great Clan had been moving in a north-easterly direction. Tomorrow they would do as they did each day, send riders out to patrol either side of the caravan, and to its front. But the lands to the west would be barren, stripped bare by the Alur Meriki's passage. Eskkar felt tempted to ride due west, but he hesitated.

The land wouldn't truly be empty. Though many dirt-eaters and villagers had been killed or enslaved, others would have escaped, and they would return to their land sooner or later. Should they come across a lone Alur Meriki warrior, especially a young, inexperienced, and unarmed one, they'd have no trouble killing him to revenge their own dead.

He decided to ride to the southwest, away from the Clan's raiding and scouting parties, but not too far from the lands the Alur Meriki had already ravaged. That path would take him down from the steppes, and deep into the lands of the dirt-eaters.

For Eskkar, for anyone driven out of the Clan, all this meant a new and frightening prospect. All his life, Eskkar had considered himself one of the chosen, destined to take his place among the fearless warriors who ruled the land, who could travel where they pleased, and take what they wanted.

Now, instead of growing into a proud and dreaded Alur Meriki warrior, Eskkar would become the hunted, an outcast renegade from his own people.

The enormity of what he faced washed over him, and he felt the weakness sap the strength in his arms and legs. For the first time in his life, he contemplated the likelihood of his death. Eskkar should already be dead, killed like the rest of his family.

He might not survive tomorrow, not with warriors hunting him. If not tomorrow, then the day after that. Without weapons, without food, and without friends or kinsmen, he would be fair game for anyone. Each day would bring danger he could only begin to imagine.

His mother's words, called out just before she died, returned to him. "Leave the Clan," she'd cried, her pain echoing in her voice. The worst fate any warrior could imagine, even worse than death, was to be banished from the Clan.

Yet that's what she uttered with the last of her strength. The tears came again, but this time Eskkar blinked them away and focused on his mother's last command. She wanted him to live, even if that meant a life outside the Clan. With her dying breath she'd told him what to do, how to survive.

Eskkar took a firm grip on the halter, gazed toward the southwest, and started walking, leading the horse away from the Great Clan. He would guide the animal through the night, taking care to avoid any obstacles. The horse was all he had, and had to be protected. Fortunately, the animal hadn't been ridden that day, so at least Eskkar had a fresh mount.

But tomorrow, both he and the horse would be put to the test, with a long and hard ride ahead of them. The patrols circling the line of march would cross his tracks sooner or later, and wonder why a warrior rode alone. Those tracks would tell them who they pursued. They would take up the trail, and they'd have fresh horses beneath them.

If Eskkar wanted to live, he had to put as much distance between himself and the Clan as possible. He needed food and weapons, but for now, flight was what mattered. He had to travel as far and as fast as possible.

His mother had ordered him to live, and he swore he would fight to the last, just as she had done. If the gods willed it . . . no, he would not invoke the Clan deities to whom his father and mother had offered sacrifices. The gods had turned their faces from his family, and he would survive or not without them.

Eskkar wiped the last tear from his cheek with the back of his hand. That, too, had ended. He vowed not to cry again, ever.

3

West of the Northern Euphrates River, two years later . . .

Eskkar sat on the rocks and watched the rider coming toward him, a low cloud of dust trailing behind. The man lashed the horse again and again, running the animal flat out and ignoring the danger to both rider and mount should the animal stumble over the uneven ground. Even at this distance, Eskkar could see the lather covering the horse's neck. The fool must have galloped the animal full speed since leaving the farm.

"Uraq's coming back at a run," Eskkar called down to the men encamped below, making sure his voice didn't break. In the last few months his voice had deepened, but still, when he got excited, it had a tendency to revert back to his youth. "If he keeps up that pace, he'll kill the horse."

"Anyone chasing him?" Kovar shouted the question as he scrambled up the rocks to Eskkar's position.

"No, he's alone," Eskkar answered, rising to his feet as Kovar reached the jumble of rocks. The outcropping, too small to be called a hill, provided a decent vista of the surrounding lands.

By then Kovar could see for himself. He pushed Eskkar aside as he scanned the grasslands that surrounded the campsite. Eskkar recovered his balance, though he'd nearly fallen from the rock face.

Not that Kovar would have cared if Eskkar broke his neck. He only tolerated him because the boy knew his horses.

Kovar led the band of bandits, if the motley collection of seventeen men, women, and children could be dignified by that title. Scavengers, Eskkar thought, like the jackals that roamed these arid lands, described them better.

The rider had nearly reached the camp and still showed no sign of slowing down. Eskkar frowned at the sight. In his mind, the horse had more value than its rider.

"He's risking the horse …"

Kovar glared at Eskkar, his hand tightening into a fist. "Speak when you're spoken to, barbarian." Kovar scanned the horizon once again, then turned away and began descending. "Stay here and keep watch."

Eskkar shrugged. The horse didn't belong to him. Returning to his vigil, he stared out toward the horizon, moving his eyes back and forth, side to side, searching for anything that moved, a hint of dust, birds taking flight, or some animal moving into the open. He saw nothing unusual, but kept looking. Danger lurked everywhere for Kovar's outcast band, and any group of farmers would need little excuse to hunt them down.

Even more than the rest of them, Eskkar couldn't take any chances. The bandits might be hunted, even killed, by those they'd recently robbed, but Eskkar always had to worry about the Alur Meriki, his former clan brothers, finding him. If they took him alive, he'd suffer a slow death by torture.

The dirt-eaters wouldn't treat him much better. His steppes heritage showed on his broad face. That, combined with his thick accent, confirmed his barbarian ancestry whenever he spoke.

Uraq galloped into the campsite, launching a spray of dirt and sand as he pulled the winded horse to a stop. Eskkar glanced down, though he kept his face turned toward the west. The horse stood with its legs splayed apart, head low, its sides heaving and foam bubbling from its mouth. The animal could barely stand after the hard run in the hot summer sun. Uraq's face showed his fear; something had scared the man badly.

Eskkar moved his eyes back to the landscape. If Kovar noticed Eskkar neglecting his duties, it might mean another beating, or at least another round of curses. Besides, Eskkar could hear everything and an occasional glimpse would be more than enough.

"They're all dead . . . dead." Uraq paused to catch his breath. He snatched the water skin one of the women offered, and gulped down half its contents.

"Who's dead?" Kovar pulled the water skin from Uraq's hands.

"The farmers. They're all dead. At least all the ones that I saw."

"You weren't supposed to get close, you fool," Kovar said. "Just look them over without being seen, I told you."

"I didn't see anyone, just the goats calling . . . chickens running loose. The animals hadn't been tended. So I moved closer. I found the first body near the corral. It was covered with flies, bloated."

Uraq looked around at the circle of faces that surrounded him. Except for Eskkar up above, everyone had closed in around him, eager to hear what he said, their concern starting to show.

"So you saw a dead farmer. What else did you see?"

"I rode up to the main house. It looked deserted, so I called out, but no one answered. I thought maybe they'd left, gone someplace. I tied the horse down and went inside."

"To see what you could steal for yourself," Kovar growled. "Next time you disobey my orders . . ."

"They were all dead inside. Two men, three women, and some kids. They had dried blood all over them, their faces, arms, legs, everywhere. It was the pox . . . had to be."

Eskkar felt a chill pass through him, though the sun still stood high in the afternoon sky. Beneath him, the bandits shuffled their feet, all of them edging away from Uraq. Each of them feared the disease.

The scourge of smallpox could be mild or fatal, and the healers' herbs and prayers did nothing to stop its onslaught. It ravaged your body, and you died or lived, usually with the pox scars covering your face and body for the rest of your life.

The worst kind would ravage a healthy man in a few days, leaving him too weak to move and unable to care for himself as the pustules spread over his body and bled out his insides until he died, in agony the entire time.

Growing up among the Alur Meriki, Eskkar had seen families stricken by the pox. Their neighbors and kinsmen drove them away from the Clan, leaving them to fend for themselves, at least until the disease ran its course. Only then, and only with the healers' approval, could they rejoin their kinsmen.

"Well, we can't go there now," Uraq went on, "not with . . ."

"You'll do what you're told." Kovar, a broadly built man with thick arms, tolerated no disobedience from his followers. "Now stop your yapping."

Eskkar smiled to himself. The bandits had drifted toward this desolated farm for the last two days, circling around toward the desert side to reach this place. At dawn, they would have rushed in, with the rising sun behind their backs, catching the dirt-eaters while half-asleep. Those who resisted would die. Kovar's men would take what they wanted, rape whatever women they found, and move on.

It always surprised Eskkar that afterwards some of the men, and often one or two of the women, would ask to join the bandits. His erstwhile clan, the Alur Meriki, would have killed any outsider for even daring to ask the question.

But these bandits were dirt-eaters themselves, and knew all about the curse of farming and its back breaking labor, especially this far west of the Euphrates. Yet at nearly every ravaged farm, there was always someone who looked forward to any escape from the land's slavery.

"Eskkar, you whelp! Get down here!"

Eskkar had allowed himself to get distracted. He took one last look over the empty land, and scrambled down the rocks. No doubt Kovar wanted the horse tended, since any horseflesh had value, even the weary and pathetic beasts these fools mishandled and mistreated at every occasion.

Kovar put his hand on Eskkar's shoulder. A few months ago, that would have left Kovar looking down on the youth. Now Eskkar had entered the middle of his sixteenth season, and his eyes stood level with his leader's, though the older man had plenty of weight, hard muscle really, over the still-growing boy.

"You go ahead to the farm," Kovar ordered. "See if anyone's still alive, and count the dead. Bring out anything of value."

Eskkar's mouth fell open. "But the pox! I'm not . . ."

Kovar tightened his grip on Eskkar's shoulder, and punched him hard in the chest with his other hand. The powerful blow would have sent Eskkar tumbling to the ground, except that Kovar's thick muscles kept his follower upright.

"You'll do what I say, or I'll do more than tap your chest. Tend to the horse first, then get going. We'll break camp and follow you in."

Eskkar had no choice. A barbarian outcast had no standing with even these dirt-eaters, and he needed to eat as much as he needed protection. To disobey would simply mean another beating until he complied.

Kovar ruled his band without mercy. Even the leader's two brothers, just as vicious but lacking Kovar's wits, knew better than to disregard his orders. Only a month ago Eskkar had seen one man beaten to death for daring to cross wills with Kovar.

By the time Eskkar finished caring for the horse, the four women had loaded their bowls and skins on two of the horses. Kovar, his brothers, and Uraq were the only ones who rode. Everyone else walked.

With a jerk of his head, Kovar ordered Eskkar on his way. It would be a long walk to the farm, at least four miles away, but he knew better than to ask for a horse. Eskkar might have nowhere else to go, but faced with the pox, a horse would be too great a temptation. It would be easy to just ride off. Kovar had once caught Eskkar eyeing the bandit's mount, and told him exactly what would happen if he tried to slip away.

Now Eskkar trudged his way toward the farm, the bandits following a half mile behind him. Eskkar didn't like this, but couldn't think of any way to get out of it. His skill with horses might be useful to this band of thieves, but the food he ate and his barbarian heritage made his value to them marginal. If he refused, Kovar would kill him without hesitation. Trying to run away on foot would lead to the same fate.

Nonetheless, going into the farm, if the pox had killed everyone there . . . Eskkar didn't want to die that way. The idea of festering sores breaking out over his body frightened him even more than Kovar's wrath.

Eskkar no longer believed in the gods of his clan, not after what had happened to his family, but he found himself muttering prayers for protection. Faced with the pox, only the gods could protect him.

Gloomy thoughts accompanied him on the trek to the farm. As he drew near, he crossed a field of emmer wheat, the plants turning brown and wilting from lack of water. The rock-hard irrigation channels told Eskkar no water had flowed in them for days.

That alone meant all the dirt-eaters were dead, even the women and children. No dirt-eater who could get to his feet would risk starvation that way. The crops always came first to any farmer, even before their animals. Another day or two, and the plants would die.

A small corral held a herd of scrawny goats, the seven beasts struggling to stay upright, bawling for water. Their eyes followed him as he approached. By then he'd seen the first body.

The corpse lay just past the corral and half-way to the house, an older man with straggling gray hair moving with the breeze. Dried sores covered the man's face and chest. Eskkar shivered at the sight. A flock of thin chickens appeared and eyed Eskkar warily, clucking as they tentatively moved closer.

Curse the pox and the death it brought, Eskkar thought, his eyes searching around. The herder in him couldn't let the animals die. He stepped toward the well, a simple rock-ringed hole in the ground with a rope fastened to a long stick that stretched across the opening.

Leaning over, Eskkar saw the water a few paces below, nearly concealed by the deep shadows. He jiggled the rope until he felt the bucket sink as it filled, then drew it up hand over hand. As he carried his burden toward the corral, the frantic animals began bleating even louder, until he dumped the water into a declivity within the pen.

The agitated herd bleated and struggled with each other to reach the water. By the time he returned with a second bucket, the goats had licked the hole dry. Already their raspy voices bleated for more. The third bucket he dumped beside the well, for the chickens.

The stock attended to for the moment, Eskkar moved toward the main house, a low structure made of the usual mud brick, with a grass-covered roof supported by a lattice of twisted branches. He paused at the door. The fetid odor of death wafted from the interior, moved about by the buzzing flies that circled around his head. Taking a deep breath, he ducked under the low doorway.

Inside he found the bodies, as Uraq said. Two men, three women, and two children. The stink of rotting flesh, made even more offensive by the dried pus from the pox, made him want to vomit. He clamped his hand over his mouth.

They're just dirt-eaters. No warrior would waste a moment of pity for the whole lot. Eskkar held onto the thought. Looking around the room, he saw nothing of value, not even a decent cooking pot.

Whatever clothing they owned remained on their backs, untouchable now. He saw no tools, no weapons, no stores of food. There might be valuables buried under the dirt floor, but Eskkar had no intention of probing around for anything hidden.

He stepped back outside and moved away from the doorway, taking deep breaths into his lungs until most of the stench was gone. Turning the corner, he found a second door leading to the other half of the structure.

The afternoon sun shone through this entrance, and he could see most of the interior. Smaller than the other chamber, it held nearly the same number of bodies. The remains of a young couple, with their two small children, stared up at the ceiling with what was left of their faces. This room, too, contained nothing useful.

Eskkar backed out and again cleared his lungs. He walked completely around the house, but found nothing. He looked back out over the plain, and saw Kovar and his men taking their ease on the sand about a quarter mile away, while the women set up camp. None of them even bothered looking toward the farmhouse, caring as little for Eskkar as they did for the dead farmers.

He returned to the well and drew up another bucket. This time Eskkar sniffed the water. It smelled better than what came out of

Kovar's water skins, so he lifted the bucket with both hands and took a tentative drink.

The cool liquid tasted sweet and he quenched his thirst, then dumped the rest for the chickens that now flocked boldly around his feet. At least we'll eat well tonight, he thought, already imaging the smell of roasting chicken.

Looking past the house, he saw some planks laid out on the sand, so he walked toward them. A work area, he realized, taking in the worn copper chisel and a shovel resting beside a mallet and two straw baskets utilized to carry human and animal waste for use as fertilizer. The tools would interest Kovar. He'd wrap them in a blanket and sell the lot at the next village, Eskkar thought, as he knelt down to pick them up.

Instead he put his hand to his knife. A low moan had drifted across the ground. He spun on his heel, searching for the source, but saw nothing. Eskkar felt the hair on his neck stand on end, as fear of the pox brought images of demons lying in wait, ready to slip over the sands and force the disease into his body. The chickens, he remembered, had clustered near here when he arrived. He rose up and moved toward the sound, his eyes roving over the sparse grass.

The noise came again, this time sounding like some small creature in pain. He kept moving, and nearly tripped over the blanket before he saw it. Sand and dirt and chicken droppings covered the dirty woolen cloth, blending it with the surrounding grass. A small hand, the skin burned red from the sun, protruded from beneath the edge.

The hand moved and he jumped back, drawing the copper knife from his belt. Eskkar crouched there a moment, but nothing else moved, except the chickens milling about his feet, following his footsteps and looking for food.

Leaning forward, he extended the knife and lifted one corner of the blanket, exposing a tangle of long brown hair, sprinkled with dirt and sand. A girl's eyes, unused to the sun, squinted closed, then opened again. She stared unseeingly at him, moaned again, and closed her eyes.

He shifted his body to shield her face from the sun, and, using the knife, lifted the blanket aside. Her shift had bunched up almost to her waist, and he saw the scab-scars from the pox running down her legs and inner thighs. Fighting his stomach and the urge to run, he tried to remember what he'd learned about the pox from his mother.

She'd told him you caught the pox by breathing the same air as those who already had it, or so some of the healers claimed, though no one could explain how one man might suddenly fall ill with the disease when nobody else had it. Other healers believed you could catch the pox by touching those already stricken. But Eskkar remembered her also saying that when the pox scabs started falling off, it meant the disease had run its course. If the body formed scabs, then the victim generally would live.

Carefully he examined the girls legs, looking for any sign of pustules. He moved closer. Flipping the rest of the blanket off her body, he reached down and with his finger tips lifted the dress away from her body. He slit the garment from neck to hem, then used the point to move it apart.

Her budding breasts and stomach held ten or twelve dried scabs, most smaller than those on her legs. Again he couldn't detect any open sores, though he examined the length of her body.

Eskkar exhaled, and realized he'd been holding his breath. She might live, he decided. Or she could still be infected with the pox, in which case he might already have it, from breathing the same air or touching her clothing. Well, too late now. Grimacing at his fear, he slid his hand under her neck and lifted her shoulders. Her back looked clean, with only a few loose and dried scabs. These looked darker, but that might be from lying on them.

The breeze moved her hair across her face, covering one eye. The image of his sister, Zakita, jumped into his thoughts. This girl was much the same age. He remember Zakita, lying senseless on the ground, unaware of the pain that awaited her.

Damn the gods, he thought, forgetting that he no longer believed in their existence. Eskkar let the girl down and moved away. She hadn't awakened when he lifted her. He stood and jogged back to the well.

Filling another bucket, he carried it back to her. Again he lifted her head with one hand, while he scooped water from the bucket with the other and let some dribble into her open mouth.

She swallowed once, then gagged. Her eyes opened, and she coughed up some water. This time her eyes showed her wits had returned, and she feebly raised her hand toward the bucket. He hoisted it to her lips and let her drink.

After a few moments, he pulled the bucket away, knowing too much water too soon would make her sick. The liquid sloshed over her neck and breasts as she slid back to the ground with a sigh, her eyes closing again.

At least she wouldn't die of thirst. Looking around, Eskkar found some sticks and rigged a shelter, using the blanket to shield her head and upper body from the sun. Just as he finished, he heard Kovar's booming voice.

"Eskkar! Where are you? Answer me!"

Damn the man. Eskkar ran back toward the wastelands, stopping about fifty paces from Kovar, when the bandit held up his hand. Kovar carried the only bow the group possessed in his hand, while Uraq stood beside him holding the arrow quiver.

"Don't come any closer," Kovar shouted.

Eskkar stopped immediately. The man might not be an expert with the bow, but no sense tempting fate.

"What did you find? Is it the pox?"

"Yes," Eskkar shouted back. "They're all dead. Four men and four women, and some children. All dead at least two or three days from the pox. There's one young girl still alive, but she's got the pox, too. Other than the chickens and goats, there's nothing here."

"Nothing?"

"Oh, a copper shovel and chisel, and a wooden mallet" Eskkar added. "There may be more..."

"Get a goat and bring it here, along with the tools." Kovar took an arrow, fitted it to the bow, and shot the shaft into the earth halfway between them. "Don't come any closer than the arrow. And bring a chicken, no, two chickens, too. We might as well feast tonight."

Eskkar didn't understand what Kovar meant. "Why can't I just bring the animals back to the camp?"

"No, you stay away from us. If you try and come any closer, I'll put a shaft in you. In eight or ten days, if you're healthy, you can rejoin us. If you're not, don't bother." Both men laughed at Kovar's joke, and turned away.

Feeling like a fool, Eskkar walked back toward the farm. He should have guessed Kovar wouldn't let him return. Now he was stuck here, with the pox-ridden bodies, at least until Kovar moved on.

Eskkar thought about that. The food might tempt Kovar to stay, but he wouldn't want to linger in the area more than a few days. These farmers must have neighbors who might decide to visit. Or perhaps they'd even sent for help before they died. No, Kovar couldn't stay here long. More than likely, he'd move on tomorrow or the next day, taking the goats with him.

Eskkar thought about slipping away in the night, but decided against it. If Kovar found him gone, he might enjoy tracking him down. No, better to let the man go his way, then choose the opposite direction. Eskkar found no solace in that thought; he'd be alone again, with every man's hand against him. Even the bandits' company, abuse and all, was better than none.

The dirt-eaters hated him and his kind. The fact that he'd been driven out from the clans meant nothing to them. A barbarian was a barbarian, to their way of thinking, always ready to turn on them.

He had no real choice. Eskkar could never return to his people. No other clan of steppes people would be willing to take in an outcast, especially one from the dreaded Alur Meriki, the most powerful of the clans that passed through these lands.

Eskkar put the grim thoughts aside when he found himself standing over the girl. Eyes open now, she stared up at him, face and shoulders shaded from the sun by the blanket. She'd pulled the dress back over her body, but had no more strength for anything else.

"My name is Iltani. Who are you?"

Her words came slowly, as if she hadn't spoken in some time. But by now, Eskkar understood the language of the dirt-eaters well enough.

"I'm called Eskkar. There are . . ."

"A barbarian!" Even sick and near death, fear and distrust sounded in her voice.

Though he wore the same clothes as the dirt-eaters, Eskkar's accent always revealed his origins.

"I'll not harm you," he said, as he knelt beside her. "Now tell me. How long were you sick? And the others . . ."

"My mother . . . father. Is everyone dead?"

When he told her what he'd found, her body shook with grief though no tears came. "Then I am all alone." She gazed up at him. "My father carried me out here, and put me under the blanket. He said I might live, if I were away from the others. He gave me water . . . came as often as he could, until yesterday or the day before . . . he didn't come anymore."

From the position of the body, Eskkar knew the father had died trying to reach his daughter.

The effort to speak, or the memory of her family, exhausted her. She closed her eyes and turned away, onto her side, pulling her knees to her chest and clutching them with her arms. When he was sure Iltani slept, he left her.

Near the corral he found a piece of worn rope, and used it to form a halter. Filling the bucket with water, he carried it and the rope to the corral. As the goats drank, he slipped into the pen and fitted the noose around the weakest looking animal.

Dragging the goat from the pen began a struggle that taxed his strength, as the frightened creature refused to move, terrified at leaving its companions. Fortunately the goat's weakened condition soon exhausted it, and the animal followed along, digging in its hooves every few steps and bleating for its brethren.

When he reached the arrow, Eskkar secured the goat to a bush, then jogged back to the well. Dumping another bucket of water brought back the chickens, and he snatched up the first two he could catch. Shoving one under his arm and ignoring the screeching and cackling, he wrung the other's neck, dropped it, and killed the second the same way.

By the time he reached the arrow, Uraq and two of the women waited there. Uraq held the bow in his hand, an arrow fitted to the string.

"Where are the tools?" he shouted. "Kovar wants the tools."

Cursing under his breath, Eskkar jogged back a third time, gathering the mallet, chisel, and shovel. When he returned, the women, chickens, and the goat were gone, along with the rope. Eskkar swore at himself for not keeping the rope, but knew better than to ask for it now.

"Kovar says to return in the morning, barbarian," Uraq said. "And you'd better bring something else of value."

Eskkar resisted the urge to curse at the man. Unlike Kovar, Uraq was short and thin. His boasting held no fear to Eskkar. However, the fool had the bow, and there was no sense starting something now.

Uraq hadn't asked about the girl. Kovar probably had forgotten about her. Eskkar decided to keep silent. That way she was less likely to end up dead.

Back at the farmhouse, Eskkar surveyed the area, moving in ever widening circles, searching for anything of value. When he finished, he'd collected three clay pots, another blanket, and a small copper dagger of poor workmanship, inferior even to the one at Eskkar's waist. Bundling them up, he left them near the corral for the morning. He ignored the stack of firewood behind the house. If he mentioned that, Kovar would have him lugging the wood out to the bandits' camp.

As he approached Iltani, he saw her struggling to sit up.

"No, stay down," he said, dropping to his knees beside her. "The others may see you."

"What others?" She let herself fall back, too weak to argue.

He told her about the bandits, but left out Kovar's original plans. "They're just fools and petty thieves," he ended up, "but they might do you harm if they learn you're alive."

She looked at him. "And you, what about you. Why are you with these men?"

He told her about the Alur Meriki, how something had gone wrong, and that warriors came to his father's camp to kill his family.

"I watched my brother die, and my sister taken captive. My mother screamed at me to run. I killed one of them before I fled. Took a horse and ran. They chased me for a few days, but I got away. The horse broke its leg a few months later, and I've been wandering about since."

He shrugged. "That was almost two years ago. Soon I'll have seventeen seasons."

"I have fourteen seasons," Iltani offered. "What will you do next, Eskkar?"

"I'll try and keep you safe. If Kovar comes to the farmhouse, you can hide under the blanket. If you keep silent . . . I nearly missed finding you."

"I meant about you, what you'll do next."

Her eyes showed concern, the first time anyone had looked at him with compassion since he fled the clan. "I don't know. Dirt-eaters have no use for barbarians, even those like me who've been driven out of their clans."

He smiled at her. "But now, I think I'll prepare some food. You need to eat, and I haven't tasted a chicken in at least a month."

—⚬—

Eskkar glanced up at the waning sun and decided to fix dinner first. Like the rest of Kovar's band, Eskkar never knew when he'd be eating next, and passing up an opportunity for a good meal seemed foolish. Going to the woodpile, he scooped up as much wood as he could carry, then lugged the load at least fifty paces away from the house, keeping the structure between himself and Kovar's campsite.

After stacking the wood in two piles, one to start the fire and the other to keep it going, Eskkar dug into the earth to set up a spit. The goats, scrambling around inside the pen, kept up a raucous bleating that soon grated on Eskkar's nerves. With an oath, he decided to care for them first, if for no other reason than he didn't want Kovar to send someone over to investigate the frantic cries.

Eskkar went back to the well and brought up bucket after bucket, filling the hole for the goats and letting them drink until they could hold no more. No matter what happened, they'd have enough water for another few days. A pile of dried grass stood nearby. He gathered an armful and moved it just outside the pen, so the goats could reach it. At least they wouldn't starve to death. As soon as they started stuffing clumps of grass into their hairy mouths, they stopped making that raucous noise.

Eskkar drew one last bucket, filled the cooking pot, and then set the bucket down at Iltani's side. The girl still slept, but now her face looked more peaceful. With food and water, she would recover, and for the rest of her life smallpox would hold no threat. He doubted she would consider the loss of her entire family worth the benefit.

Building the fire tried his patience, the flint sparking again and again, but the dried grasses he'd gathered refused to catch. When they did, he built it up until the thicker sticks had fully caught.

A scrawny chicken wandered by, and Eskkar snatched it up. He wrung its neck, and started plucking the bird. The simple task gave him time to think about his own situation. Kovar couldn't be trusted. The bandit would leave sooner or later, but first he'd ride closer to the farm, or send one of his followers to make one last search.

Despite what Eskkar told Iltani, they'd find her. In her condition, she wouldn't be worth raping. Kovar would put an arrow into her, just to be sure no one survived to tell any tales.

With a shock, Eskkar realized that same fate awaited him as well. Kovar wouldn't want Eskkar staying behind if he were alive, not even with the pox. Both he and Iltani had to die.

Eskkar took his growing anger out on the plucked chicken. Laying the bird out on a flat rock, he used his knife to gut the bird, then thrust a stick through it and set it over the fire. The scraps and the edible organs were tossed into the stewpot. In the morning, they would provide another meal for the two of them. Every few moments, he twisted the stick, turning the flesh so that it cooked evenly.

The thought of slipping away when it grew dark tempted Eskkar for a moment, but then he looked at Iltani, sleeping peacefully. He didn't understand why he felt responsible for her. Perhaps because of the way she'd looked at him, helpless and trusting, or perhaps because she reminded him of his sister. After failing to save Zakita, Eskkar couldn't leave Iltani to be killed.

Still, he didn't know what to do. Even if he could steal a horse, Iltani wouldn't be able to travel, not for days. And Kovar would come after him; the loss of a valuable horse couldn't be tolerated. It would mean that one of his brothers, or his loyal follower Uraq, would have to be left behind if anyone pursued him. The bandit chief cared nothing for the other men, women and children; they'd be abandoned at the first sign of trouble.

Eskkar couldn't stop thinking about Kovar and his bandits. He'd come to hate these men more every day. They killed and robbed their own kind to stay alive, and they had no honor or loyalty, even to each other. No Alur Meriki warrior would shame himself by riding with them.

He remembered his fierce kin, but that only made things worse. He knew warriors would brush these bandits aside. One or two fighters from his clan would not hesitate before attacking and killing all of them.

Even a single warrior would gallop straight at them, shooting his arrows as he came, then veer off to circle around them, running down any that tried to flee, until he'd emptied his quiver. Then the attack with sword or lance, until they were all dead or kneeling on the ground begging to be spared as a slave.

Clenching his fist, Eskkar wanted to kill them all, to put an end to the beatings and abuse he'd endured because of his ancestry. But he had no horse, no sword, no bow, only his knife. He drew the copper knife from his belt. Sharp enough, but no match for a sword. He had nothing . . .

A sword! These farmers had to have some weapons. Even dirt-eaters weren't stupid enough to try and live on the edge of the desert without something to defend themselves. He'd seen nothing in the house, which only meant he hadn't looked closely enough.

Getting to his feet, Eskkar scooped up the chicken guts and carried them away from the fire before dumping them. Iltani still slept, so he went back to the farmhouse. The sun hovered just above the horizon. Soon it would be too dark to see anything.

Just outside the doorway, Eskkar took a deep breath, then stepped back inside the first room and began searching for anything he might have missed. Any weapons would have to be inside, in case of an attack at night. They had to be still here, since no one had carried them away.

Glancing around the room, he tried to think like a dirt-eater. Where would they store a sword? Someplace handy, maybe near the entrance. He ducked back outside and took another deep breath, then moved quickly inside again. He scanned the ceiling. Just to the right of the door, he saw a gap in the mesh of branches that formed the roof. Peering in, he glimpsed the hilts of two swords slipped between the latticework.

They slid easily from the hiding place, and he saw they'd been covered with a bit of cloth to reduce the corrosion. Lungs ready to burst, Eskkar stumbled back outside and kept moving, until he'd gotten well clear of the house.

Sitting down, he examined both blades. Copper, of course. Few dirt-eaters could afford the cost of a bronze blade. These two were old and not well cared for. Neither had a good edge, but he could remedy that. The ones Kovar and his men carried weren't much better. Taking his sharpening stone from his pouch, Eskkar began working on the better of the weapons.

The rasp of the stone along the blade comforted him. The necessary but tedious work at least gave him the feeling he'd regained some control over his fate. When Eskkar achieved a sharp tip and a cutting edge, he stood and began taking a few practice cuts.

It had been months since he'd held a sword, and his muscles felt stiff. The blade seemed surprisingly light in his hand, and he realized his arms had grown more powerful. Eskkar went through the practice routine his father had taught him. Overhand stroke, thrust, slash, and retreat, varying the routine and the movement, until the blade hummed through the air.

He kept at it, enjoying the feel of his heart pounding and the sweat building on his chest. A warrior needs a sword, he decided.

Eskkar might not be a true warrior, but from now on, he would keep a sword at his side at all times. When he finally stopped, he was breathing hard and feeling hungry.

The smell of the crisping chicken made his mouth water. It was time to eat.

Taking the spit off the fire, he carried the golden brown flesh over to where Iltani lay. She awoke, looking confused for a moment. Then she sniffed the air, catching the aroma of the roasting chicken.

He held the water bucket for her to drink.

Her thirst quenched, she lifted herself up on an elbow. "How are the chickens? And the goats? Have any perished?"

He smiled. "You must be feeling better." He waved the spit in his hand. "Most are alive, apart from this one. I've fed and watered the goats, too."

Ignoring the hot flesh, Eskkar tore a leg off the spit and handed it to her. "Start with this, but eat slowly."

Iltani sat up and grasped the leg. She took her time with the first few bites, but soon finished the leg, while Eskkar started on the other one. He had to use his knife to slice the breast, and they shared that, too.

They talked while they ate. Iltani finished half the chicken herself, ripping into the flesh with strength and determination that surprised him. She said she didn't remember the last time she'd eaten. Eskkar hadn't eaten so well in some time, so between the two of them, the savory chicken was soon picked to the bone.

Iltani noticed the swords lying beside the fire. "You found the swords? You went back in the house? What do you intend to do with them?"

She asked a lot of questions for a girl, Eskkar decided. "I knew there had to be weapons somewhere. They may be needed."

Eskkar told her about Kovar and his band, and Eskkar's days with them. The words came easier the longer he talked. With Kovar's group, he hardly spoke a handful of words a day.

Her eyes widened with apprehension. "Then you think this Kovar will come?"

"Yes."

"What will you do?"

"They won't come tonight. And I think I know how to make sure they don't come in the morning." He saw the look of doubt on her face and smiled. "Now, you should get some rest."

Eskkar scooped a hole in the sand, shoved in the remains, and covered it over. He wiped his hands on his tunic, then added the last of the wood to the fire.

"I'm going to go keep watch on their camp. I'll be gone most of the night."

By now darkness had fallen, and the moon had yet to climb into the night sky. He left her there and walked back toward Kovar's camp, angling off to the side so that the dim glow from Iltani's fire didn't show his movement. The quarter mile separating the farm from Kovar's campfire took little time to cross.

As he drew closer, he dropped to his belly and crawled along, until he reached a vantage point behind a low rise about a hundred paces away. He lay down on the warm sand and began his vigil.

The sounds of laughter came from the camp. They'd pitched their three tents and rigged a rope corral for the horses. The goat and chickens provided enough meat for a real feast, and the bandits were making the most of it. The men always ate first, leaving only what was left for the women and children, but tonight there would be plenty for all.

The feasting at the camp went on and on, the fire's flames crackling and sending sparks swirling into the darkness. After they finished eating, the wine came out and Eskkar saw not one but two wine skins passed around and quickly emptied. For once, every man received a share, so Kovar must be feeling generous. With full bellies and a few mouthfuls of wine, everyone would sleep soundly tonight.

Eventually the feasting came to an end. Kovar posted one of the men as a guard. Eskkar even heard Kovar's loud voice ordering the man to keep an eye out toward the farm, before the bandit leader retired to his tent with his women.

At last the talking and laughing of the others trailed off, and the campfire began to die. Soon the sound of men snoring floated over the sand. Eskkar waited patiently, watching the moon rise and begin to creep higher in the sky. Well after the camp had fallen silent, Eskkar stood up and stretched his limbs. By now, he felt certain, all the bandits were sound asleep.

Except for the sentry. Any guard would be facing west, toward the farm, though even the women would know better than to just stare in one direction all night. Eskkar stayed in the shadows. The half-full moon didn't give much light, but as long as he took his time, he could pick out his footing. He moved silently around the perimeter of the camp, until he reached a spot that placed the sentry between him and the farm.

As he drew closer to the sleeping bandits, Eskkar wondered what would happen when the horses caught his scent. That might spook them, but they should know his smell by now; he'd been feeding and grooming them for more than three months.

He'd brought only his knife with him, but Eskkar resisted the urge to carry it in his hand. Slowing his pace even more, he began moving toward the camp, stopping every few paces. As Eskkar drew closer, he kept his eyes on the guard's back, sitting on a rock close to the horses, his head nodding occasionally.

Twice the sentry got up and moved about, no doubt trying to stay awake, and each time Eskkar sank to the ground, where he wouldn't be seen. Thankfully, the guard was as careless as Eskkar expected. He would stay awake, but only because he knew what would happen if Kovar woke up to piss and found his man asleep.

The sentry returned to his seat and in a few moments his head began to nod. Eskkar had swung wide around the horses, and the sentry heard nothing. Eskkar traversed the last twenty paces with care, making sure he made no sounds and stopping dead in his tracks whenever the guard's head shifted or jerked about.

When the horses heard something approaching, familiar scent or not, they'd react. Even so, the animals had grown accustomed to seeing men walking around the camp at night. Eskkar eased past the horses without alarming them, and he needed only a few more soft steps to reach the tents without being seen.

Loud snores came from all three tents. Eskkar knew the power of the raw date wine Kovar had stolen. By now Eskkar's eyes had grown well accustomed to the dim light, and he had no trouble spotting what he'd come for, resting on the ground just outside the opening to Kovar's tent. Unlike a sword or knife, the bow and quiver had no use inside a tent, especially with Kovar and his two women inside. Without a sound, Eskkar picked them up, and retraced his steps.

The guard remained on his rock, head slumped forward and his back to Eskkar. Taking his time and moving with care, Eskkar slipped into the shadows and away from the camp.

Back at the farm, he found Iltani awake and sitting up. He called her name as he drew near.

"Why aren't you sleeping?"

"I did. I just woke up a little while ago. I started worrying about you, and couldn't sleep any more. Is everything all right?"

"Yes," he said. "I stole their bow." He held it up proudly for her to see. "They only had the one." Sitting down, he took inventory of the feather-topped shafts. "Only fourteen arrows. I wish there were more."

"You said there are seven men. You can't mean to fight all of them?"

"They're bandits, not warriors. Without their bow, they can't kill at a distance, and they won't want to get too close because of the pox."

"But they'll come. When they find the bow gone..."

"Yes, they'll come." In truth, Eskkar didn't care one way or another. The feel of the sword in his hand this afternoon had given him confidence. For the first time in his life, he felt like a warrior, not like a runaway boy. And now the bow only strengthened that feeling.

He yawned. "Can you stay awake a little longer?" he asked, a little embarrassed. A warrior was supposed to be able to stay awake and fight for days without sleep. "I could use some sleep."

"Rest, then. I'll keep watch, and wake you if I hear anything."

Eskkar lay down a few paces away, the sword by his side, glad that she was there and grateful she would keep watch. He fell sound asleep in moments.

She woke him well after dawn's first light. Startled, he got to his feet, slapping the dirt from his tunic and looking anxiously toward the bandits' camp.

"You should have woken me at dawn." He usually stirred a few moments before sunrise.

"You needed to sleep, Eskkar," she said. "I didn't think they'd come rushing up here, not after a night of eating and drinking."

She was right, of course. The bandits might not even be awake yet.

Regardless, he'd wanted to get an early start. Eskkar picked up his sword and moved away from the farmhouse, checking the landscape and looking toward Kovar's camp. Nothing stirred, so perhaps he had time. First he strung the bow. The bowstring appeared frayed.

Checking the quiver, he found another, newer one stored between the layers of skin that made up the mouth of the case. He held it up to the light and examined every part of its length. This one looked sound, certainly stronger than the old one, so he restrung the weapon.

Carrying the bow and quiver, Eskkar crossed over to the planks that had been used as a work table. Propped on its side, it would make a decent target. Examining the arrows, he selected the worst three shafts and used them for practice. He shot twelve arrows into the board, noting where they struck, and getting the feel of the weapon.

He wished he could take some longer shots, but he didn't have time for that, and didn't want to risk losing a shaft. Eskkar unstrung the bow. He remembered his father's instructions to keep any bow unstrung as long as possible, to save the precious bowstring from unnecessary strain.

Eskkar left the weapon leaning against the farmhouse wall, then placed the older of the swords there as well. The other blade he shoved through his belt, along with his knife. Then he ducked back inside the house, emerging in a moment with the flimsy ladder the inhabitants had used to get up to the roof. It would work just as well from outside, he decided.

When he returned to Iltani, she'd gotten to her feet. She seemed a little unsteady as she moved about, but at least she could walk. Putting his arm around her waist, he led her back toward the house. She hesitated as they drew close, no doubt thinking about her family inside.

"If they come, Iltani, we'll be safer up on the roof. From there, they won't be able to rush us." He didn't like the idea of being so close to the pox, but neither would Kovar's men.

"Are you sure?"

"Yes. From up there, we can see them coming."

The roof line wasn't high – Eskkar could reach up and touch the top with his fingers. All the same, it provided a vantage point, and would take some effort to climb without the ladder. He didn't tell her what concerned him. If they were trapped up there, Kovar's men could set fire to the roof, and Eskkar and Iltani would be burned alive.

They went to the well, and Eskkar drew up a full bucket. He drank his fill, forcing himself to swallow as much as he could hold, and ordered Iltani to do the same.

Then he watered the goats once again, more to stop their bleating than because he cared about their thirst. Afterward, he refilled the bucket, and carried it back to the house, leaving it in the shade beside the wall. If they had to spend the day up there, at least they wouldn't be choking with thirst.

"Can you climb the ladder," he asked, "or will..."

"I can climb," she said, a determined edge in her voice. "But what will we do up there, in the sun, with no food?"

"We won't be up there long," he said, hoping he spoke the truth.

A distant shout made him look toward the camp. Three men walked toward the farm. Eskkar picked up the bow and fastened the quiver of arrows to his belt, then jogged toward them. He slowed as he drew close to the arrow Kovar had fired into the earth the day before. Only then did Eskkar string the bow, taking his time and making sure the bowstring fit properly inside the notches.

"You found a bow?" Surprise sounded in Kovar's voice.

The fool hadn't even noticed its loss. "Yes, right outside your tent, Kovar."

Kovar's face turned red with rage. "You barbarian filth . . . you piece of horse shit, you bring that here right now."

"Why don't you come and get it?" Eskkar heard the change in his voice and felt the battle rage coming over him. When he spoke, the first time he'd raised his voice in months, the youth disappeared forever, replaced by a young warrior.

Kovar and his men exchanged looks. Eskkar smiled, reached down, and pulled the arrow from the earth. Taking his time, he fitted it to the bow and assumed the archer's stance, feet apart, left leg half-pointed at his enemy.

"What are you going to do, barbarian? Kill all of us?"

"If I have to," Eskkar said, his voice cold with certainty. He saw Kovar's rage struggling against his habitual caution.

"The girl told me her father sent for help from the nearest village," Eskkar went on, telling the lie smoothly. "They'll be here today or tomorrow, so if I were you, I'd get moving."

"You fool, they'll turn on you. They hate barbarians even . . ."

"Even more than you do, Kovar? I'll take my chances with them."

Eskkar drew the bow, the motion making all three men move apart, ready to duck. He faked releasing the shaft, and watched Kovar fling himself to one side. Before they could react, Eskkar fired the shaft at Kovar's older brother, the one with the biggest bulk and slowest wits. Surprised at being targeted, the bandit twisted aside, but not before the shaft buried itself in his arm.

A good shot, Eskkar decided, listening to the man's howl of pain. Better a wounded man than a dead one, for now at least. "I'll kill the next one that calls me a barbarian. Now get moving before I come down there and start killing the horses."

The wounded man, already moving backward, cursed steadily as he clutched his arm, blood showing between his fingers. The arrow's bone tip had penetrated through the flesh above the elbow.

"Eskkar . . . wait." Kovar, moving backwards as well, had to raise his voice. "Bring us out the goats. Give us the animals, and we'll leave you alone."

"You can have all the goats you want," Eskkar said. "Just come and get them. If the pox doesn't get you, I will." He watched while the three men retreated.

When Eskkar felt certain they were headed back to their camp, he turned and raced back to the farm, and found himself breathing hard when he reached the house. "Time to climb onto the roof, Iltani."

He helped her up the wall, holding the ladder steady and ordering her to stay close to the corner where she could watch both doors. Eskkar handed up the full bucket to Iltani, wishing these pitiful dirt-eaters had possessed a second one. The swords went next. Finally he went back to get the blanket that had covered the girl. It would shield her from the sun.

After one last look around, to make sure he hadn't forgotten anything, Eskkar started climbing. The roof felt sturdier than he expected when he stepped off the ladder, until he remembered that the whole family would have slept up here at night to avoid the heat. Satisfied, he pulled the ladder up behind him.

"Stay down," he told the girl. "If Kovar's knows we're on the roof, he might bring fire when he comes."

Peering over the edge, Eskkar studied the landscape around the farm. Not much cover to shield Kovar's approach, and with Iltani's help, they should be able to see anyone trying to sneak up on them. If the bandits waited until night, though, the roof would be a trap. He'd have to take Iltani and try to slip away in the darkness. Hopefully Kovar wouldn't want to linger a whole day.

From the roof's vantage, Eskkar could see all the way to the campsite. The bandits were milling around, no doubt arguing with each other. Not that it mattered. In the end, they'd do whatever Kovar decided.

"Can you count, Iltani? We need to keep track of each bandit." He told her how many men and women Kovar had, what they might do. "What's most important is to not let anyone get close enough to set fire to the roof."

"I can count to ten," she said, holding up both hands.

"That's enough. There are only seven men, maybe six now that one is wounded." Thinking about the arrow shot gave him confidence. He'd killed a man the night of his escape from the Clan, but that had been from behind, as the man had struggled with Eskkar's brother, and the warrior probably never knew who killed him.

Now Eskkar had faced three enemies and wounded one of them. A feeling of power and strength flowed through him. His father had spoken of this feeling, the reason their people fought so well. They showed no fear, no matter what odds they faced, only confidence. Eskkar might not survive, but these bandits would soon learn they faced a true warrior. He swore the oath to his dead father.

"I'm hungry, Eskkar," Iltani said.

Eskkar frowned at her words. He should have thought of that himself. He took a good look at the girl. Iltani looked much better than she had yesterday. If she felt hungry again, so soon after eating a good meal last night, then she must be getting better. Sick people, he knew, rarely wanted to eat.

"Then we'll eat," he said. "You keep an eye on the bandits."

Taking the bow with him, he lowered the ladder and descended. Plenty of firewood remained, and he moved another armful to an empty space about twenty paces from the house. He collected the sticks he'd use as a spit last night, and dug them into the ground. This time the fire caught in moments, and as soon as he had it burning briskly, he went chicken hunting.

When the bird was cooked, Eskkar killed the fire, then carried the whole chicken to the roof, trying not to think about what lay just below them, or what he'd do if they fell through. Iltani waved the chicken about while it cooled.

"What do you think they will do?"

Eskkar looked toward the camp. They'd had plenty of time to break camp, but they hadn't, so they didn't plan to move on. "Kovar must think he can get the goats. Right now, five goats are worth at least one or two of his men getting killed or wounded, at least to his way of thinking."

"So he'll come." Iltani touched the chicken, and decided it had cooled enough to eat. She sat on the edge of the roof and began tearing the bird apart.

Eskkar sat beside her, accepting a chicken leg. She matched him mouthful for mouthful, neither of them saying anything until the bird had been reduced to bones and gristle. They tossed the remains onto the ground below.

He made her drink plenty of water, then went down to refill the bucket.

"Eskkar! They're coming."

Grunting, he carried the full bucket back to the roof, pulled up the ladder, then snatched up the bow and strung it. Selecting one of the straightest arrows, he fitted it to the string. Then he looked out toward the camp.

The bandits were coming on foot, all of them, including the women. Obviously Kovar would rather risk any of his band rather than one of the horses. As Eskkar watched, the bandits separated into three groups. Thankfully, Eskkar didn't see anyone carrying fire. At least he wouldn't have to worry about that danger – yet.

One of Kovar's brothers, the one Eskkar shot earlier, drove the five women straight toward the corral. The other men split into two groups of three, and moved toward each side of the farmhouse. Every man carried a crude shield of some sort, sticks and branches woven together and covered with a blanket, anything that might stop an arrow. They were going to rush the house while the women drove off the goats. Unless he cut them down.

"I'm not giving them the goats," he said. The stupid animals had pleaded with him for water. He'd fed them, and now he refused to turn them over to scum like Kovar.

Iltani stood beside him. She'd picked up the other sword, though she had to use both hands to hold it. "The women are afraid, Eskkar."

He glanced left and right. They were all going to come into range at about the same time. The men would burst into a run to reach the house, or at least try to keep Eskkar busy, and the women would rush toward the goat pen. Everything was going to happen at once, he realized, feeling his heart beginning to race in his chest.

"They're not going to get the goats," he repeated. Eskkar drew the arrow to his ear, and aimed it toward Kovar and his two men. They saw the motion and moved further apart.

Eskkar turned suddenly, and fired the arrow toward the women, giving it just enough arc to reach them. He had another arrow to the string and launched before the first one reached its target. The women shrieked as the arrow flew by, narrowly missing the one he'd targeted. The next shaft also missed, but this woman threw herself down to avoid it.

That was enough for the women. They turned and fled, and even Kovar's brother, shouting and waving his sword, couldn't get them moving toward the corral. Yet the fool tried, grabbing the first one that tried to flee, turning her round and shoving her forward. He stood still just long enough for the third arrow to strike him full in the belly.

A fourth arrow flew over the wounded bandit. "Damn the gods," Eskkar swore, angry at wasting a shot. Kovar's brother, now on his knees, tried to pluck the arrow from his body.

Eskkar had already turned, aiming for Kovar. Break him, he decided, and the rest would run. "Watch the others," he shouted. He shot five arrows at Kovar and his men before a shaft found its mark, dropping one man, and slowing their approach.

"They're here," Iltani cried.

The other three were only steps away from the house, running hard, shields raised up. Taking a moment, Eskkar deliberately targeted the last of the three, aiming low and sending the arrow into his stomach. A cry of pain accompanied the strike. This close, they didn't have much time to dodge.

The other two reached the side of the house, but they had no place to go, except inside. One man ducked in, but the other, Uraq, hesitated, remembering what lay inside. Eskkar leaned over and Uraq thrust upwards with his sword, trying to cut Eskkar's legs out from under him. The low roof didn't give Eskkar much protection, and he took a small step back. The lattice work of sticks and branches sagged under his weight, and Eskkar prayed that it wouldn't collapse.

The instant the sword withdrew, Eskkar stepped forward and shot a shaft at Uraq's exposed chest. The man tried to twist aside, but the arrow smacked into his shoulder. Uraq screamed like a butchered pig. At such close range, the arrow had penetrated deep into the muscle.

The house shook as Kovar and his brother, Nutesh, slammed into the opposite wall. A shout of terror came from inside the house, and the bandit who'd taken shelter suddenly burst out, running for his life. The sight and smell of the pox-ridden bodies had taken all the fight out of him. With two long strides across the roof, Eskkar rushed to meet the bandit leader's threat.

Screaming curses, Kovar lunged upward with his sword, sweeping the roof's edge clear. Eskkar snapped a shot at Kovar's arm, but the shaft missed. Eskkar whipped another arrow to the string, aware that only one more shaft remained in the quiver. Now there was silence. Eskkar didn't want to approach too close to the roof's edge, and Kovar and his brother hugged the wall, not wanting to give him an easy shot.

"What's the matter, barbarian? Run out of arrows?"

"I've got one left for you, Kovar." Eskkar kept his voice confident as he spoke the lie, but he felt the fear growing inside him.

They could move around the house, throw something at him. If they dared to enter the dwelling, they could thrust upward at his feet. They had him on the defensive, and he faced the two strongest fighters in the band. Only a well-placed shaft would bring down either of these men.

He made up his mind. Moving away from Kovar's side of the house, he took a quick glance down at Uraq. The man was crawling away on his hands and knees, the arrow still protruding from his shoulder and leaving a trail of blood drops in the dirt behind him. Eskkar heard Kovar and Nutesh edging along the wall, and knew the time had come.

Hoping to confuse the two men just long enough, Eskkar picked up the ladder and tossed it over the side where he guessed Kovar would be. Then, clutching the bow and two arrows tight with his left hand, he darted back to the side where Uraq had been.

Using his right hand to grasp the roof's edge, Eskkar swung down, landing a little off balance. He went to one knee for a moment, but was rising up when Kovar rushed around the corner with a roar and charged, sword held high, his makeshift shield before him.

Eskkar loosed the arrow, but Kovar drove his shield down, protecting his lower body, and the shaft struck the shield with a thud. However the motion upset Kovar's charge, and he stumbled, giving Eskkar time to leap aside and notch the last shaft.

Nutesh followed right behind his brother, sword raised high for a killing stroke. Iltani screamed, Eskkar shot, and threw himself to the ground, dropping the now useless bow and rolling once before regaining his feet, the sword coming free from his belt in the same movement.

Nutesh had gotten his shield down in time, but the shaft found a hole in the branches and the arrow passed through and into Nutesh's side. The man stumbled and fell, landing on the arrow and giving a great gasp of pain.

Eskkar darted away from both of them, watching Kovar. The bandit chief moved toward his brother, who stayed on his knees, cursing at Eskkar. Kovar's chest rose and fell, and his eyes darted around, looking for his men. He bellowed with rage, as he realized he'd have to kill Eskkar himself.

"Getting old, Kovar?" Eskkar, now confident, taunted him. He advanced toward the bandit, the sword weaving lightly in his hand. "Too much time taking ease with your women."

"You're dead, barbarian. Dead right here in the dirt." Kovar rushed forward with a mighty cut at Eskkar's head, but he slipped aside. Moving back toward Nutesh, Eskkar had time for one quick swing, striking the kneeling man a glancing blow on the shoulder, and eliciting another scream.

Then Kovar was upon him. The swords clashed once, twice, and Eskkar retreated, moving sideways, circling. He saw Kovar breathing hard. The bandit might be stronger, but his lungs gulped for air.

Eskkar attacked, not wanting to give Kovar time to recover. He struck twice, surprised at the shock that traveled up his arm from the contact. Kovar parried both cuts, and counter-thrust at Eskkar's belly.

Twisting his body, Eskkar stepped back, then charged again, the sword swinging high overhead. But at the last moment, Eskkar slipped the blade to the side, ducking low under Kovar's counter and swinging at his right leg. The bandit tried to parry, but too late, and Eskkar's sword cut into Kovar's thigh just above the knee.

Kovar bellowed like a stuck boar, and took another savage cut at Eskkar's head. But Eskkar, already down on one knee, rolled away and regained his feet in a smooth motion the injured man couldn't match. Kovar, too, had gone down to his knees, either off balance or from the wound in his leg. He had to use one hand to get back to his feet.

Eskkar saw his chance and moved in for the kill.

Kovar flung a handful of dirt into Eskkar's face.

His eyes blinded for a moment, Eskkar ducked back and shook his head. By the time he could see again, Kovar had risen to his feet and closed the distance, his sword coming down at Eskkar's head with all the strength the bandit leader could muster. Eskkar flung up his sword, the blades clashed, and the impact jolted his arm.

Then Kovar's blade flashed past Eskkar's left shoulder. Though Eskkar's sword had deflected the stroke just enough to make the bandit miss, Eskkar's weapon had shattered a hand's breadth above the hilt. He staggered back.

Kovar, shouting in triumph, raised his sword and rushed toward his younger foe.

Eskkar took a half-step back, then threw himself forward, underneath the descending blow that would have cut him in half, and plunged the jagged remains of his sword into Kovar's side.

The bandit's momentum took them both to the ground, Kovar on top and cursing, while Eskkar struggled to lift the man's heavy weight off his chest and get free. He let go of the broken weapon, and used both hands to push Kovar away, then rolled to the side. His clumsy thrust just missed, and then Eskkar was on his feet, drawing his knife and staying just out of Kovar's reach.

"Behind you!" The shout came from the roof.

Esskar whirled around to see Nutesh moving toward him, one hand clutching the arrow in his stomach, and the other holding his sword. Bleeding badly, he still had plenty of fight in him.

"Esskar!" Iltani had reversed the sword in her hand and tossed the weapon toward him. Esskar flipped the knife into his left hand, caught the descending sword cleanly by the hilt, moved toward Nutesh, feinted a stroke at his belly to make the man commit himself, then Esskar killed him with one savage blow to the neck. Hot blood gushed from the wound, some splattering on Esskar's face and arm.

Kovar, still alive in spite of his wounds, managed to get back on his feet. He shouted out in rage, screaming for his men, but none of his followers remained. Cursing, he jerked Esskar's broken sword from his body with an oath, and flung it down. Then he staggered away, weaving and clutching his side, stumbling back to his camp.

Esskar walked over to Nutesh, and ripped the arrow from his dead body. The other man, the one he'd shot from the roof, yielded another. Esskar checked to see that the shafts appeared sound and the bone tips still attached, then picked up the bow and nocked an arrow to the string, ignoring the blood that dripped off the shaft.

He jogged after Kovar, taking only moments to close up with the bandit. Badly wounded, the man would probably die from loss of blood soon enough. Esskar didn't care. Kovar, looking back over his shoulder as Esskar approached, tripped and fell. When he tried to get up this time, he couldn't. On his knees, Kovar's sword fell from his hand.

Esskar slowed to a walk, then stopped, drew the arrow back as far as it would go, then loosed it. The shaft struck hard into Kovar's chest. He fell backwards with a sharp gasp, feet twitching, but finished. When Esskar stood over him, the man could barely move.

Esskar put the last arrow into Kovar's throat, then stood there and watched Kovar's death throes. When the body went limp, Esskar tried to retrieve the arrows. The tip of the one in Kovar's chest broke off when he pulled it free, so he dropped it. However the shaft from the bandit's neck came out easily, and would be enough to finish off Uraq.

But Uraq, despite his wound, had kept moving toward the camp. By the time Eskkar got there, Uraq had crawled onto a horse and galloped off, following the trail of the bandit who'd run from the house and also ridden off.

The women took one look at Eskkar approaching and started screaming. One of Kovar's women caught another horse and rode after Uraq, but the rest scattered on foot, their children following, running back into the desert.

Eskkar stood there, looking around the camp. Tents, whatever loot the bandits had accumulated, it all belonged to him now. The one remaining horse had bolted and run off, but the animal halted a hundred paces away, eyeing Eskkar suspiciously.

He whistled at the beast, the same sound he used when feeding and grooming them. Gradually the horse's ears stopped flicking back and forth, though its wide eyes still watched him. At least it didn't move farther away from the campsite.

The smell of blood would spook the nervous animal, so Eskkar bent down and scrubbed the blood off both the bow and his only arrow with a patch of grass. He rubbed his hands in the dirt, to cover the blood scent.

Going to the small bag of grain the bandits used for feed, Eskkar scooped out a handful and walked toward the uneasy beast, extending his palm so the horse could catch the scent. It took a few moments, but the horse let him approach, extending its neck to take the grain.

Taking his time, Eskkar let the animal finish the treat before he gathered in the dangling halter rope. Then he gave the surprised horse another handful as a reward before mounting his newest possession and riding back toward the farm.

Holding onto the halter, Eskkar realized his hands were shaking, the reaction to the encounter. He'd heard whispers of such things around the clan's campfires, how even brave and victorious warriors sometimes trembled after a hard fight.

Tomorrow he would accompany Iltani to her kin, who would surely take her in. A young girl needed family to protect her, and see that she found a good husband. But there would be no place for Eskkar. No dirt-eaters struggling to survive on a farm needed or wanted a cast-out barbarian. He would have to move on. At least he now possessed a horse of his own, and a copper sword.

Then Eskkar realized something else. His first battle had ended, and he'd survived. He'd become a warrior today. And no one, he swore, would ever beat or abuse him again.

4

The western bank of the Euphrates, three years later . . .

Eskkar rode into Dimuzai, a motley collection of forty or so mud huts surrounded by twenty or twenty-five small farms. His barbarian features elicited the usual cold stares from the villagers, who paused their tasks to watch him dismount. Their suspicious looks reminded him once again of how much dirt-eaters hated and distrusted his kind.

Still, his weary horse required rest and grain, and Eskkar needed a new blanket, a fresh halter rope, and something substantial to eat. Since he had nothing to trade and no copper to buy any of these items, that meant finding some type of menial labor until he could earn enough for his wants. Or go hungry, which happened all too often the last few months.

Leading the horse, Eskkar wandered the dirty lanes that stank from too many animals and people living too close together. Accosting anyone who looked remotely prosperous, he inquired about work and ignored the occasional verbal abuse about his ancestry. Sometimes laugher followed behind him when he resumed his search. He ignored that as well.

A few of the villagers stared at him with hostility and hatred, but always mixed with fear. He received the same answer at each stop – no work, and often a suggestion to move on. Eventually he reached a large, sprawling collection of dwellings, animal pens, and corrals that butted against a pleasant-smelling field of barley.

Two guards, swords at their waists, watched him approach. Their presence told him someone of importance lived in the large and prosperous house. Eskkar had no expectation of finding work here, but he'd come this far, and it wouldn't hurt to ask.

"Greetings." He nodded politely at the men and pretended he didn't notice either their frowns or the way they kept their hands on their weapons. Dirt-eaters thought they had to look ferocious whenever they dealt with one of his kind.

"I need some grain for my horse and food for myself. Is there any work that I might do to earn what I need?"

"This is the house of Kuwari, the Village Elder," the older of the two said, not bothering to keep his tone civil. "There's no work here for a barbarian. We don't want your kind here. Better if you move on to the next village." He tapped the hilt of his sword, to make sure the barbarian understood.

Eskkar hadn't expected anything different. The village leader surely had enough servants and slaves of his own, plus the entire village to call upon, if need be. Eskkar nodded and turned away, his tired horse following docilely.

"Wait!"

The commanding voice came from the direction of the main house, and Eskkar turned to see a young man, not much older than Eskkar, walking toward them. The cleanliness of the man's garment proclaimed his status – one of Dimuzai's rulers, and one who'd never worked with his hands.

The man pushed past his guards without a glance. "I'm Kuwari, the Village Elder," he announced, his eyes appraising both Eskkar and his mount. "Do you know anything about horses, barbarian?"

"I know horses, Noble," Eskkar replied, ignoring the insult and giving Kuwari the highest appellation the dirt-eaters used, even as he wondered what the man wanted. "What do you require?"

"I've a sick mare, my best stock. She's due to foal before the next moon. Now she won't let anyone approach her, and she's not eating.

I bred her to my finest stallion, and I want to save both the mare and her colt."

The Village Elder's urgency overcame his distaste at speaking with one of the steppes people. "Let me see her then," Eskkar said.

Kuwari, trailed by his guards, led him behind the main house to a good sized corral where seven animals stared listlessly at their approach. Good horseflesh, Eskkar decided, the moment he spied them. Obviously this Kuwari knew how to breed stock. Even the Alur Meriki possessed few better, though his former people spent their lives breeding and training horses. Or stealing them.

The horses edged away as Eskkar neared the corral, all except the mare, who seemed to lack the energy even to cross the enclosure. She was a dun, reddish-brown colored, with a darker stripe down her back and some white spotting on her face.

The foal she carried showed against ribs that should have been covered with thicker flesh. The other horses looked well-fed, but even a quick look told him they needed exercise.

He studied her lines, admiring the wide shoulders and graceful sweep of her hindquarters. Built for speed, Eskkar guessed she could run like the wind. She would be the pride of any warrior's string of horses.

"What do you feed them, Noble?" Eskkar kept his eyes on the mare, whose listless eyes seemed to wander.

"The finest grain in the village, barbarian," Kuwari said, as if to display his wealth. "The rest of the horses thrive on it."

Horses needed grain, especially when ridden or worked hard. But they also needed to forage for plenty of grass, or they'd become fat, lazy, and lacking in endurance. Just like Kuwari's herd. Horses, like men, needed to work each day to stay strong and healthy. Whoever had managed these beasts had done a poor job, Eskkar decided, though now was not the time to point that out. He turned to his potential employer.

"The mare needs exercise, even now." Eskkar faced Kuwari and met his gaze for the first time – seeing a spoiled young man with a scraggly beard, soft in the chest and stomach, who appeared to be only a year or two older than Eskkar's nineteen seasons.

"She needs to change her feed, and to get out of that corral and into one of her own, where she'll feel safer. If you want, I can stay on and care for her until she delivers. Without enough exercise, the foaling will be difficult and risky. The other horses need work, too, or soon they'll be as slack and sluggish as the mare."

Kuwari frowned, no doubt hating to admit he needed an out-sider and a barbarian at that to care for his fine horse. However, his concern for the mare overcame his haughtiness.

"A copper coin every other day," he said, his mouth a thin line thinking of the expense, "with an extra three if she delivers a healthy foal, barbarian. And a safe place to sleep and all the food you need."

"A copper coin every day, Noble," Eskkar countered. Villagers loved to bargain, no matter what the circumstances. "And my name is Eskkar." He hated the word *barbarian.*

"What! That's ridiculous. That's more than my steward earns."

"You're only paying me until the foal is born, Noble," Eskkar reminded him. "But you will have to build a new corral."

They settled on two copper coins every three days, and five if the foal dropped safely. Kuwari also agreed to provide a place to sleep and meals for his new horse master. And to build a separate corral for the mare, which Eskkar reluctantly agreed to help construct. He already knew how such tasks went – with him doing most of the digging and carrying.

"Good. Then get started, barbarian . . . or whatever your name is."

The next few days passed quickly enough. It didn't take long for Eskkar to win over the dun, and soon they were traversing the countryside, Eskkar riding his own horse and leading the mare. He gradually cut down on her grain, and soon the mare munched con-tentedly on the thick grass that grew in the fields.

Kuwari called her O-po, but Eskkar thought that a foolish name for such a fine horse. He called her Arun, and after a few days she learned to come when he called her name, something she had never done for Kuwari. That became the mare's new name, and Arun soon learned to accept apples and grain from Eskkar's hand. He rubbed her down at least twice each day, taking his time, talking soothingly, as she relaxed under his touch.

By the end of the first ten days he'd weaned the other horses off the grain as well, forcing them to forage for at least half their food, and making sure they got enough exercise. He'd told Kuwari the truth. The animals needed work, plenty of it, and that kept Eskkar galloping around the grasslands outside the village most of the day, working each of the animals in turn.

To his surprise, the simple task gave him more satisfaction than he expected. Eskkar hadn't ridden horses this fine since he'd left the Alur Meriki. Dirt-eaters claimed his people were born on the back of a horse, which approached the truth more than they knew. He'd worked with his father's horses as soon as he grew tall enough to avoid being stepped on. Now spending day after day on horseback brought back pleasant memories of his youth. The hard riding strengthened his own muscles, too.

Eskkar soon learned Kuwari's background. The younger son of a wealthy trader, he ruled Dimuzai in his father's name. The father resided in another village, two days walk down the river.

He'd become rich trading in slaves and grain, shipping surplus crops up and down the Euphrates. His son had received the village of Dimuzai to rule, and to collect the tenant fees. The local farmers paid with shares of their crops and herds. Most of that wealth probably went to Kuwari's father.

Despite the passage of time, Kuwari's guards watched Eskkar like a hawk. No doubt they expected him to try and steal all the horses, and Eskkar knew it would be impossible to convince them otherwise.

So he took the horses out one by one, racing them up and down the outlying hills for a good length of time before letting them graze. The farmers bending over and sweating in the fields soon grew used to the sight, and waved at him as he rode by, chased by the occasional farmer's dog barking its head off.

Nevertheless the guards, no doubt following Kuwari's orders, kept close watch on the horses, and they took turns guarding the animals at night.

Arun, now safely ensconced in her own corral, perked up as well, and Eskkar took her out two and three times a day, leading her at a slow walk, and taking her just far enough to sharpen her appetite and maintain her tone. By now she trusted Eskkar more than her owner.

Eventually Kuwari's suspicions faded and the Village Elder appeared satisfied, though he paid the copper grudgingly every third day. After sixteen days, Eskkar's wages allowed him to buy an almost new tunic, a food pouch, and a halter for his horse.

The basics taken care of, he spent plenty of time with the village blacksmith. Eskkar's old copper long sword had seen its best days. Chipped, nicked, and weakened by corrosion, the grip had parted from the tang, and the pommel had broken off.

The smith proclaimed the blade both un-reliable and un-repairable. He offered Eskkar a good price for one of the vil-lager's short swords, which he declared he could make within a few days.

Eskkar tried to get the man to lengthen the new blade. Even a hand's length would do, he suggested, but the smith declined.

"Never made a long sword," he declared. "Wouldn't trust myself to do it right, not here. Can't get the forge hot enough to heat that much bronze evenly."

The old copper sword had served him well, but better a shorter weapon he could depend on than a longer one liable to shatter at the first hard stroke. The smith offered to lower the price in exchange for the old sword's copper content, and Eskkar agreed, grateful to get anything at all for the remains of the weapon.

When Arun showed signs that it was time to deliver her foal, Eskkar stayed awake all night with her, until the birthing started. Kuwari stood by as well, every bit as nervous as the dun, with two farmhands to help.

As Eskkar expected, the birth was awkward, and the mare fright-ened and in considerable pain. At last, well after sunrise, the most dangerous moment arrived. Eskkar helped ease the foal from its mother, always a tricky and dangerous procedure, and gently placed the newborn on the ground beside its dam.

Arun gave a long cry of relief when free of her burden. Then she licked the foal's head. Eskkar stood by Arun's side, stroking her neck and speaking softly in her ear, as they watched her spindly offspring already trying to get to its feet and nurse.

Eskkar felt as exhausted as the mare, while Kuwari beamed and strutted around, as proud as if he'd fathered the colt himself.

Kuwari's elation for his newest addition carried over to Eskkar. "I said you could stay until the foal came. But I'd like you to stay on, to keep the horses in good condition, though at one copper coin every other day."

Eskkar didn't mind either the reduced wage or the thought of staying on. Kuwari wasn't too bad for a villager, and with the horses now in better shape, Eskkar's work had lessened. The rest of Dimuzai had grown accustomed to Eskkar's presence. Their glares had diminished over the days, and now they left the tall barbarian horse master, who always carried his sword, to himself.

Of course, they accepted his copper gratefully enough at the ale house. All things considered, Eskkar agreed to remain in Dimuzai for a few more months, or as long as Kuwari wanted him.

The next two months passed by pleasantly enough, and Eskkar settled into a comfortable yet lonely existence. The villagers still treated him politely, but he made no friends, not even within Kuwari's household. But Eskkar had lived alone, more or less, for nearly five years, and he enjoyed the small luxuries of having a safe place to sleep each night, superior horses to work with, and plenty of good food and ale under his belt.

A little more than two months after Arun gave birth, the horse thieves struck.

The men rode into Dimuzai just before dawn, moving silently along the outskirts of the village before slipping into Kuwari's corral. It took them only moments to slit the night guard's throat, the fool probably asleep at his post since he never raised an alarm.

Only when the bandits opened the corral gate did the horses react to the strangers by moving about and whinnying nervously. Two of Kuwari's farmhands, accustomed to waking before daylight, came out to see about the commotion. The bandits cut them down ruthlessly, unarmed and harmless laborers too surprised to run or hide in their huts.

Eskkar, jolted awake by the cries of the horses and shouts of the farmers, grabbed his sword and rushed outside, only to find a horseman galloping straight at him. Eskkar threw himself down just in time, and he heard the sword hiss past his head. He leapt up, but another rider put his horse's shoulder into him, and Eskkar spun around before slamming into the mud hut and falling to the ground, stunned.

The rider laughed as he cantered leisurely away. The bandits had no worries about pursuit, since they'd stolen all the village's animals, or at least all those worth stealing. Only the freshly weaned colt and Eskkar's mount, long since consigned to farm work, remained.

Kuwari, clad in his undergarment, rushed outside, waving a sword. He screamed oaths at his servants and guards, ignoring the dead bodies, concerned only about his horses. Eskkar took the abuse with everyone else, though privately he thought Kuwari possessed more luck than he knew, since the raiders could probably have killed him and half his village, then looted it before leaving.

With the village awake and roused, Kuwari shouted for his guards, demanding the horses be recovered, and that those responsible for losing his herd be whipped. Eskkar, his head still ringing from his collision with the hut, tightened his grip on the sword in his hand and stared coldly at the merchant. Eskkar's duties had never included guarding the animals or sounding the alarm.

All the same, with the horses gone, Kuwari had no need for Eskkar's services. He flew into a rage when he saw Eskkar standing there.

"Get out! Get out of my village, before . . . they were your friends, weren't they? I should have you put to death! My horses . . . my horses," his voice trailed off in despair, though his face remained flushed with anger.

Eskkar had taken as much of the confusing tirade as he could. "Do you think I'd be fool enough to stay here if I had anything to do with this?" He turned his back without waiting to hear Kuwari's reply and walked off.

No one tried to stop him. Even Kuwari's five remaining guards had more wits than that. They'd seen Eskkar's daily sword practice, and knew he'd probably kill two or three of them before he went down.

Back in the hut he'd shared with three other servants, Eskkar took his time, gathering his things while deciding what to do. The village of Dimuzai nestled against the western bank of the Euphrates River. He could ride south, the direction he'd originally been traveling when he'd reached this miserable place.

Thanks to Kuwari, Eskkar had saved enough copper for a month or two. He could sleep alongside the river as he journeyed. He rolled his few belongings into his blanket, fastened each end with cords, and slung the contents over his shoulder.

"Eskkar!"

Eskkar picked up his sword and stepped cautiously to the doorway, surprised to find Kuwari standing there, accompanied only by his steward. "What do you want now, Kuwari?"

The man took a deep breath, fighting to control his emotions. "My horses, Eskkar. Can you get the horses back for me? I'll pay you well for them."

"I thought you blamed me for losing them. Get them back yourself."

"I'm . . . I know you tried . . . my steward . . ." he gestured toward his clerk, ". . . he saw them run you down."

Eskkar grunted. It wasn't much of an apology, but coming from a dirt-eater, it would have to do. He softened his voice.

"I'm sorry you lost your horses, Kuwari." Eskkar actually did feel some sympathy for the man. Kuwari loved those horses more than he loved either of his wives.

"Bring them back to me. Follow their trail. You can steal them back."

"What about your men?"

"They're no good for something like this, Eskkar, as well you know," he answered. "This needs a horseman, not a bodyguard."

"How much will you pay?"

Kuwari bit his lip, as greed struggled against his desire for his stock. "A gold coin for each horse you recover." The words came out between clenched teeth.

Eskkar said nothing, thinking the offer over. The horses might actually be worth more, but then there weren't many who could afford to buy them, let alone maintain them once recaptured. Certainly no one else in Dimuzai and the surrounding areas had enough wealth.

The more Eskkar thought about it, the more the reward seemed reasonable. With a single gold coin, he could buy himself a good horse, and have something left over. If he recaptured more than one, it might be worth the risk.

"I can't guarantee to bring back all of them," Eskkar said slowly.

Kuwari's face flushed again, but he ground his teeth together until he had control of his emotions. "Just the mare, then," he said, a hint of desperation creeping into his voice. "She's worth more than the rest."

"I'll do my best, Kuwari."

As soon as he gathered what he needed, Eskkar rode out of Dimuzai, Kuwari's useless words of advice still ringing in his ears. A pouch filled with bread and cheese fastened to his belt and a bulging water skin hung behind his back. He rode his old mount, pressed into service once again. His new bronze sword hung at his waist.

Eskkar took his time. The bandits had left a plain-enough trail, but they would probably have at least one scout hanging back, watching for any sign of pursuit. From the tracks, Eskkar guessed about six or seven men had taken part in the well-executed raid, and from what little he'd seen, they looked both competent and dangerous. Better, he decided, to let them get well ahead.

Two days later, Eskkar began to close on the bandits. Then the shock came, when he realized they'd joined up with another band of riders, probably doubling their number. He slowed his pace, avoiding hilltops so as not to be silhouetted against the sky. He scanned the horizon often.

Three more days passed, with Eskkar dodging their scouts by day, and covering as much ground as he dared by night.

The chase became even more of a challenge, as the thieves started covering their tracks as much as possible, riding through the occasional stream, keeping to the rocks, and avoiding the easy paths as they wandered slowly north. Once he'd lost their trail, and had to waste half a morning riding in circles until he picked up traces of their passage again.

Even so, Eskkar always found some indication of their trek, and so far, they appeared unaware of his shadowing them. By now he'd been on their trail for nearly seven days, and knew he had to make his move soon.

The next day he saw no scouts at all, not even a trace of one. Pushing his tired animal to its limit, Eskkar began to close the gap between himself and the bandits. That night, in true Alur Meriki fashion, he left his horse behind and sneaked up on foot to spy on their camp. He observed their movements and studied their precautions as they guarded the horses and themselves.

In the morning, he remained in concealment and watched them ride off. They looked relaxed, almost at ease, certain no one pursued them. Eskkar admitted to himself he'd done well. They'd likely have spotted any band of men following their trail, but they wouldn't expect a single man to make any attempt on their herd.

At midmorning, he collected his horse and resumed stalking their trail. Once again he pushed his horse to a rapid pace, trying to get as much out of the beast as he could. Fortunately, the bandits decided to camp early, and Eskkar saw the smoke from their fire.

He dismounted nearly a mile behind them. After tying his weary mount securely, he emptied his pouch of everything but what he would need – the three halter ropes and the small sack of grain. Eskkar regretted leaving the sword behind, but if it came to that, he would probably be dead anyway. Carrying nothing but his knife and the pouch, he jogged ahead, following the tracks in the fading light.

When Eskkar caught up with them, he understood why they'd stopped well before sundown. A small spring fed a grove of trees, and a wide patch of grass provided lush grazing for the horses. He noticed with satisfaction a small, rocky hill about two hundred paces away. It would provide a good elevation to study the camp.

He crawled through the rocks, keeping below the skyline and trying not to disturb any birds or animals settling in for the night, until he reached the hillock and could peer down between two boulders at their camp.

Two men guarded a herd of more than twenty horses penned within a night corral – a single strand of rope wound around some scattered trees and bushes to enclose a space on the tree fringe.

Another handful of men wandered about, gathering wood for the fire, and in the distance he could make out two men riding away, bows across their saddles, looking for game. Fortunately they rode northward. If they'd hunted back the way they came, they might have crossed Eskkar's tracks. If they came across his horse, tethered nearly a mile back, they'd be hunting him, not dinner. Since he had no bow, he'd be defenseless if they caught up with him.

Thankfully hunters rarely wanted to traverse land they'd already passed over. He'd seen the bandits do the same thing yesterday, though he arrived too late to see the huntsmen depart.

By now they'd probably forgotten all about the village they'd raided nearly ten days ago. At least Eskkar hoped they had. He didn't know how much longer he could keep shadowing them. Sooner or later, some sharp-eyed rider would surely discover him.

Eskkar settled in on the hard ground, and took another count. All of Kuwari's horses were there, and he saw the mare standing next to her stallion. Thirteen men and twenty-three horses. And not just plow horses or pack carriers. These animals represented some of the finest horseflesh in the land.

Even ignorant farmers or villagers could occasionally breed a fine animal, and wealthy traders always paid well for such stock, and without asking too many questions. Sold or traded in the right villages, a good horse could fetch plenty, at least five or six times as much as an able-bodied slave. The animals grazing below him would be worth a hefty sack of gold to the bandit leader.

If Eskkar had five or six men with him, he would have gambled on slipping in and cutting out the whole herd, risking a fight for the chance to steal all the horses and leave the thieves on foot.

The bandits seemed as relaxed as such men who lived by their swords could be. Eskkar lay there, waiting, going over his plan as the sun slipped beneath the horizon and the campfire grew brighter and brighter. He studied the camp below him, locating the rocks and trees that would help cover his approach.

Eskkar knew he would only get one chance. And he had no doubts about what men like these would do to a barbarian outcast caught attempting to steal their horses.

The mare would be his main target. Eskkar knew she was fast enough, although carrying his bulk, she could likely be run down by a relay of two or three of the prime horseflesh below. That meant he would need at least one more horse.

With two fine mounts, Eskkar could change from one to the other, and outrun any pursuers. And two horses might not be worth a long chase to the bandits, another good reason not to try for any more. It wasn't much of a plan, but he couldn't think of anything else.

Ignoring the laughter and loud talk drifting up the hillside, Eskkar went over his preparations, then settled in, trying to relax and snatch as much rest as he could. The night before, the bandits had relieved the guards midway through the darkness. He had to hope they followed the same procedure tonight.

With danger looming, Eskkar couldn't manage any sleep. He was risking his neck over a couple of horses, facing hard men who knew how to ride and how to fight. Time and again he thought about slipping away, abandoning Kuwari's horses and his promise of gold. But he always came back to one thought – these men had swung a sword at him and tried to run him down.

Eskkar might wind up dead, but the affront to his honor rankled. He remembered the rider's laugh as he knocked Eskkar down and rode off. Besides, the horses had been under his care, and he wanted them back for his own sake, not Kuwari's.

In a way, these men had challenged him. And that, he decided, couldn't go unanswered, and outweighed the risk. His mind made up, Eskkar finally dozed off, knife under his hand.

When he woke, the moon had climbed half-way across the star-blackened sky. Gathering his pouch and making sure his knife slid smoothly from its sheath, Eskkar slipped down the hillside. He worked his way toward the camp, moving with caution and angling his approach to keep the high ground at his back so that he would always have the greater darkness behind him.

A hundred paces from the horses, he dropped down to his belly and crawled, searching the ground with his hands for twigs or anything else that might give him away. Moving with care, Eskkar reached the position he wanted, near two trees that loomed only ten or fifteen paces from the rope corral.

He'd hardly reached his objective when the wind shifted and the horses reacted to his scent. A few of the animals snorted, looking around nervously, wondering about the strange odor wafting their way.

But five of the horses did nothing, merely lifted their heads for a moment before resuming their rest. They recognized the scent of the man who'd fed and cared for them. The mare, however, moved slowly away from the trees and toward Eskkar, stopping only when the corral rope tightened across her chest.

The rest of the horses took their cue from the unperturbed mare. They settled back down, a few snorting and bobbing their heads, but already growing accustomed to the strange man-smell in the night air.

The guards never noticed. Plenty of animals hunted in the darkness, and skittish horses reacted to any unusual scent or sound. Regardless, the sentries walked the occasional circle around the corral, passing within a few steps of Eskkar's concealment, but suspecting nothing.

The moon continued its passage, as Eskkar remained flat on the ground. At last the moon reached its zenith, and the tired guards walked away to awaken their replacements. As soon as they moved, Eskkar arose, keeping the herd between himself and the departing guards, and trusting in the darkness to conceal him if they should glance back.

He kept his movements slow, and needed only a few silent steps to reach the rope and slip beneath it. Taking one of the halters from the pouch, he stroked Arun's shoulder. The mare nuzzled his face, and Eskkar reached into his pouch and gave her a handful of Kuwari's finest grain.

As soon as Arun finished licking the last flecks from his hand, Eskkar slipped the halter over her head. Before she could react, he dug into his pouch and offered her a second handful. That disappeared as well, and then Arun's rough tongue rasped against his arm and her head nudged him, demanding more.

Another of Kuwari's animals wandered over, perhaps catching the scent of the grain. The stallion who'd ruled the herd back in Dimuzai also remembered eating from Eskkar's hand. He had time to feed him a single handful before the fresh guards, yawning, arrived at their post.

By now Eskkar was merely a deeper shadow crouching in the midst of the horses. The guards talked to each other in soft voices, still half-asleep, and Eskkar slipped the second halter over the stallion's head, following quickly with the last scoop of grain from the pouch.

Gathering both halters in one hand, he remained crouched as he moved back toward the corral rope, the two horses following docilely. The sharp knife cut through the rope in one effort. Eskkar swung onto the stallion's back, keeping a firm hold of the mare's halter, and let out a blood-curdling barbarian war cry, as he put his heels to the stallion.

Instantly the whole herd stirred. Heads jerked up, frightened by the sudden outburst of sound. Their natural instinct led them to follow the two horses fleeing the now open corral.

Eskkar bellowed out his war cry again and again, not only to spur the horses onward, but to convince the bandits that a steppes raiding party surrounded them. By the time he paused to take a breath, the shouts and curses of the guards had already faded in the distance.

Now he only had to worry about the horse tripping over some obstacle in the dark and breaking its leg and possibly Eskkar's neck. As soon as he could, he slowed the pace, letting the stallion pick its way through the dim moonlight. The other horses had already trailed off, drifting away to the left and right as their fright subsided. The cursing bandits would spend the rest of the night and first part of the morning rounding them up. Hopefully, it might take even longer.

He slowed Kuwari's animals to a stop when he reached the place where he'd left his own mount. For a moment, Eskkar felt tempted to leave the faithful plow-horse behind, but the bandits would surely track him this far, and they might recognize the beast from the corral in Dimuzai.

Dismounting, he untied the old mount and made sure he had a good grip on the halter rope. He took a moment to listen for any sounds of pursuit, but he heard nothing, no hoof beats, no shouts in the distance, only the silence of the night.

Grunting in satisfaction, he led the three horses on foot through the darkness as fast as he dared. Eskkar kept up the pace through the rest of the night. Three times he stumbled and fell, but he never let his grip on the halter ropes slacken.

As soon as it was light enough to see the ground, Eskkar mounted the stallion. His legs ached from the unaccustomed walking, but he felt certain he had a head start of at least half a day. With luck, he'd reach Dimuzai in less than five or six days of hard riding.

The gods had certainly favored him tonight, Eskkar decided. He'd half-expected to wind up dead, or captured and tortured. Instead, Kuwari would regain his two best horses, and Eskkar would earn two gold coins for recovering them.

Thoughts of keeping the stallion for himself kept tempting him, but each time Eskkar decided against it. The animal was too valuable and too well known. Besides, every horse thief worthy of the name would be after the beast, and a lone, outcast barbarian would be certain to lose it sooner or later.

Men had been killed for their horses before, and for horses a lot less valuable than the stallion. Better to use Kuwari's gold to buy a decent animal, one not as alluring to every brigand between and beyond the two rivers.

Eskkar turned his thoughts to Dimuzai's blacksmith. The man admitted he couldn't craft a quality long sword, but there were larger villages, and in one of them Eskkar would find a master smith who knew his trade. A sturdy bronze sword would serve Eskkar for many years, and might even keep him alive. By returning the stallion and the mare, Eskkar would have the gold to pay for it.

He imagined himself holding a gleaming bronze sword high overhead, astride a powerful war horse. Once again he thought about the stallion, but he'd learned enough about the ways of the dirt-eaters. Greed ruled them, but Eskkar refused to become like them. Better to be content with the reward he earned. At least his honor remained satisfied, though he doubted the villagers would even notice.

No, the time had come to move on, to leave Dimuzai behind, and resume his wanderings. He sighed at life's injustices, and quickened his pace.

5

Eighty miles west of the Euphrates, one year later . . .

"What can I serve you, stranger?"

The innkeeper put the question politely enough, but the man's eyes betrayed his curiosity. Once again Eskkar wondered at how easily they recognized his heritage, even before he opened his mouth. Just into his twentieth season, his face, his height, even the long sword hanging over his shoulder, pronounced him an outcast warrior from the steppes.

"A cup of ale and something to eat, innkeeper," Eskkar answered, keeping his voice low and lowering his head in a polite bow. It never hurt to be respectful to villagers. Barbarians, as they called his kind, made them nervous, even afraid, and frightened people might cause trouble.

"One cup of ale, and a loaf of fresh bread, for one copper," the innkeeper said, showing no inclination to move aside and allow access to his tables.

Eskkar winced at the price. A copper coin should have paid for a whole meal, including the ale and bread. In slow times, some inns would even throw in a quick romp with one of the serving girls.

"We've been short of ale for almost a month," the man offered by way of explanation. "It was a good batch, and it went fast."

"Make sure it's a full cup, then," Eskkar growled, annoyed at himself for being so weak. But he hadn't had any ale in the last ten days, and the smell of the strong barley brew lingering in the air had weakened his resolve from the moment he stepped into the alehouse. "And some grain for my horse."

"Grain we have in plenty," the man said, smiling for the first time and waving Eskkar to a table. The innkeeper called out to a young boy squatting against the wall. "Take care of the barb . . . stranger's horse."

Ale wasn't the only reason Eskkar had chosen the inn, rather than try to satisfy his hunger at the market. Twice in the recent past he'd been accused of intimidating, even threatening those selling food or spirits at the street stalls. Better to eat at an inn, where haggling with the innkeeper was expected.

This gloomy establishment, illuminated only by the light streaming through the open door, stank of ale and worse. The innkeeper hadn't bathed in days, and like most dirt-eaters, had the bad habit of standing too close when conversing. Eskkar had learned not to back away, just as he'd learned not to show his distaste at the stink of too many people and animals living together.

His former kindred lived free, in the open air, with only the honest smell of horses and cooking fires to contend with. But those days had vanished, like smoke rising from a campfire, leaving Eskkar without family, friends, or clan, condemned to spend his life wandering, always alone among suspicious strangers.

Looking around, he saw only five tables. Without thinking Eskkar chose the smallest, a rickety one in the farthest corner where he could watch the door. He sat, leaning against the rough mud-brick wall, and let himself relax, for once glad to be off the back of a horse. Even the hard bench felt good after four long days of riding.

Three men with dirty hands and mud-spattered tunics occupied another table, and they'd stared at him with open mouths. No doubt they'd never seen anyone from the steppes before. When he frowned at their rude behavior, their eyes returned to their cups, and he dismissed them as farmers spending most of the day's profit before returning home to answer to angry wives.

The ale arrived, overflowing the cup's brim, and Eskkar noted with satisfaction that the cup was large and deep. The man carried it properly, without putting his thumb in the liquid. Servers of ale and wine had many tricks, like handing a man a seemingly full cup, with the innkeeper's fat thumb inside the liquid. Or they offered small cups, or even large ones carved shallow that held little. Until he'd learned better, he'd been tricked enough times by such swindles.

"The bread's not arrived yet," the innkeeper said. "My woman should be back any moment, if she doesn't spend too much time gossiping at the well." He remained at the table, obviously waiting for payment.

Untying his pouch, Eskkar handed the man a well-worn copper coin, reducing his fortune by half at the exchange.

The ale surprised him with its smooth taste, not the usual half-fermented, foul-tasting swill foisted on ignorant field workers. Without thinking, he downed half the cup, and let his head fall back against the wall. He'd hoped to find a few days work in Nippur, as they called this mud heap, but one look at the crowd of idlers squatting in the village center told him he wouldn't find anything here.

He'd ridden in at midday, and his hunger had led him to this establishment. If he left soon, Eskkar could still get in a half-day's travel before he camped for the night. He didn't plan to waste his last coin for a chance to sleep on the dirty and no doubt bug-infested floor.

Shadows blocked the entrance for a moment, and four men entered. Eskkar studied them carefully, but without staring. About his own age, all in their early twenties, these were no farmers. Three carried long knives at their belts, real weapons, not a farmer's simple cutting tool. The other wore a short sword at his waist. Clean-looking tunics meant they did no hard labor, so they must be sons of prosperous farmers or traders.

They sat at the largest table in the center of the room and shouted for the innkeeper, demanding wine. Quenching one's thirst with wine meant plenty of coins, as even the cheapest local wine would cost twice as much as ale. Their loud voices announced that this wouldn't be the first wine they'd consumed today, nor likely the last.

The bread failed to arrive, and the ale in Eskkar's cup soon disappeared. He hadn't eaten anything since the day before, and the strong spirits awakened the growing emptiness in his stomach. He thought about the single coin left in his pouch, and decided to spend it now. Nodding to the innkeeper, he ordered another cup of ale, and a second loaf of bread. He would take that one with him for tomorrow on the trail.

By now the four men had started their second cups of wine. They drew close around the table, leaning inward, and whispered among themselves. One or another glanced toward Eskkar after nearly every comment. Each remark brought forth loud laughter, and the disdain in their looks became more apparent.

They quieted down when the innkeeper arrived to refill their cups. But by the time Eskkar's second ale arrived, they'd resumed their comments.

"Where's the bread?" Eskkar asked, his voice hard. He wanted to be off, but he'd paid for the bread, and didn't plan to leave without it.

"She should have been back . . . I'll send the boy for her now." His eyes drifted toward the other table. "Perhaps you could . . ."

"I'll wait in the corral," Eskkar said, not needing the man's hint. Even though he disliked drinking so fast, Eskkar drained half his cup before rising. The longer he stayed here, the more likely trouble would ensue. Even if he didn't start it, all the patrons would turn against him – a barbarian and, almost as bad, a stranger. Strangers always made for easy targets; they had no local kin or family to avenge them.

Carrying his ale, Eskkar headed for the door. As he passed the table, a foot shot out, tripping him. Stumbling, the ale cup slipped from his grasp, the contents spilling onto the dirt floor, and Eskkar nearly went down. The four men burst out laughing.

Regaining his feet and his balance, he stared at the men. One dropped his eyes, but the others matched his glare.

"What's the matter, barbarian? Can't hold your ale?"

Another round of laughter erupted at the speaker's wit. Eskkar moved closer to the table. The men enjoyed the joke they shared at Eskkar's expense.

"Someone owes me for the ale," he said, feeling the flush of anger in his face. He knew he should walk away, ignore the insult and avoid any trouble.

"Why should we pay for your clumsiness? Maybe you should get out, before you find yourself on the floor."

"I'll leave, when you pay me for the ale."

The man wearing the sword stood up, the smile disappearing from his face. His companions matched his movement, until all four of them faced Eskkar.

"I want no fighting here," the innkeeper said loudly, moving toward them. "I'll get you another cup of ale, stranger." He reached Eskkar's side. "I'll bring it out to you. We don't want any trouble."

Eskkar ignored the innkeeper for a moment, watching the cocky men whose smiles grew broader. But the owner of the alehouse spoke the truth. Eskkar didn't need a fight with these troublemakers. "I'll wait outside," he said.

The innkeeper stepped between Eskkar and the men, and Eskkar took a step backward before turning and approaching the door, ignoring the laughter that broke out behind him. But as Eskkar and the innkeeper reached the opening, one of the men scooped up a stool and hurled it at Eskkar's head.

Eskkar saw the movement, but couldn't quite get out of the way. The clumsy missile scraped along Eskkar's upraised arm and glanced off his head. Two more stools flew at him, before the men reached for their knives and rushed him.

The innkeeper, struck by one of the flying stools, stumbled in their way, and they shoved him aside, knocking him hard to the floor. Even so, his body slowed their advance. Eskkar had no time to draw the sword on his back, but his knife flashed into his hand, and he stepped into the first of his attackers, catching him by surprise and smashing the knife hilt into the man's face, breaking his nose and stunning him.

Eskkar shoved the man into his advancing companions. Their leader, the man with the sword, stepped aside and lunged at Eskkar, expecting to run him through with the thrust. But Eskkar twisted sideways and the blade ran past his stomach. The attack brought the sword-wielder within reach, and, without thought, Eskkar plunged his knife into the man's breast.

With a gasp of pain, the man fell to his knees, a shocked look on his face as he dropped the sword. The sight stopped the other two in their attack. Eskkar jerked the knife free, shifted it into his left hand, and drew the sword from its sheath, a difficult maneuver he'd practiced countless times. The sight of the long blade ended the fight. The two men facing him backed away, holding their knives before them.

For a moment Eskkar wanted to go after them, kill them all. He could do it easy enough. Instead he turned with a curse and slipped out the door. Outside, the bright sunlight made the madness inside already seem distant.

At the corral, the boy had finished feeding Eskkar's horse, a rangy stallion with a dark mane. He scooped up the halter from the rail and slipped it over the animal's head, pulling it close in a single motion. Something moved behind him, and he turned in time to see the knife flash by his head. One of the men had thrown the blade at him, then ducked back inside the inn.

The innkeeper came out, holding his bleeding head with one hand and pulling the door closed behind him. "You'd better go, stranger, and quickly. The man you stabbed is the Village Elder's son. His men, he has plenty of them, they'll come for you."

"They started the fight," Eskkar said, "and they . . ."

"Doesn't matter, barbarian. The one you killed, he's Maldar's second son." When the innkeeper saw his words meant nothing, he went on. "Maldar's not only our Village Elder, he's the head of the largest family. He owns most of the farms around the village. They'll come after you."

Of course it had to be the Village Elder's whelp. "Damn the luck," Eskkar growled, the anger in his voice making the innkeeper take a step backwards. Eskkar swung up onto his horse. A woman rushed to the innkeeper's side, a look of fear and confusion on her face. She clutched a large basket full of bread to her breast.

Eskkar reached down and plucked two loaves from the basket. "I've already paid for these," he said, before turning to the innkeeper.

"Make sure you tell everyone I didn't steal it." Eskkar kicked the horse into motion.

Before he passed the outskirts of the village, he heard shouting behind him. By now everyone would be blaming him for starting the fight, including the helpful innkeeper, who'd want to avoid any more trouble with his neighbors and patrons. Even so, they might not chase after him. That would depend on the Elder, how much he cared for that particular son, and how much time and gold he would spend to avenge his death.

Nevertheless, Eskkar needed to put plenty of distance between him and this stinking collection of mud huts. In a few days word would spread throughout the countryside, about a murdering barbarian running loose, killing honest men and raping women and children in their beds.

Once again, every man's hand would be against him, and it might be months before the danger faded away. Some day, if he lived long enough, he might learn to blend in with these dirt-eaters. Assuming they didn't kill him first.

Slipping one loaf of bread inside his tunic, Eskkar ate the other as he rode. He varied his pace, moving from a trot to a canter and occasionally to a gallop when the land looked flat enough. The afternoon sun still shed plenty of warmth, and he didn't want to overheat the horse.

One thing Eskkar knew well was how to get the most from his mount. Since he'd run from his birth clan, he'd ridden long distances nearly everyday. So now he kept his eyes on the ground ahead of him, always seeking the easiest path, the one safest for the beast.

It wouldn't take much of an accident for pursuers to catch up with him. The horse might stumble and break its leg, go lame, or, even worse, throw Eskkar from its back because something spooked it. Without the horse, his stalkers would run their quarry down, and he'd find himself facing ten or fifteen well-armed men.

Putting these grim thoughts behind him, Eskkar pressed on. By the time the sun began to slide below the horizon, he'd covered nearly twenty miles, a great distance to most dirt-eaters, who seldom traveled more than a day's walk from their birthplace. A steep hill challenged the tiring horse, but Eskkar wanted a vantage point while the light still held.

When they finally scrambled to the summit, he swung down from the horse and patted its neck. "Good boy," he said, letting the horse take comfort from his voice and touch. Dismounting, he stretched his stiff muscles and gazed back along his trail.

His eyes searched the horizon, moving back and forth, looking for anything moving, though in truth he didn't expect . . . but there it was, a small cloud of dust hanging low in the sky, about three miles back.

"Damn the gods," he muttered, as he watched. The cloud shifted almost imperceptibly, but it moved, and he knew it would take at least fifteen, maybe twenty horses to raise that much dust.

That sent a chill of fear through him. He hadn't expected the Village Elder, whatever his name was, to be able to assemble so many men and horses, certainly not in such little time. In fact . . . no, Eskkar decided. There weren't twenty men; probably half that number, each riding one horse and leading another. That's the only way they could have followed him so quickly.

Swearing again at his bad luck, he led the horse down the far side of the hill, angry at the time and effort wasted climbing it, but knowing he'd needed to see what was behind him. When Eskkar reached level ground, he mounted and began riding, pushing the animal as hard as he dared, until it grew dark. He rested briefly, then began walking, leading the reluctant animal through the darkness.

Eskkar determined to cover as much ground as he could. It wasn't likely his trackers would keep moving after dark, but they'd surprised him once with their rapid pursuit, and he couldn't take the chance again. Traveling at night meant taking extra risks, leading the skittish horse through the darkness, squinting into the blackness, trying to see holes in the ground or loose rocks that might cause the beast to stumble.

When Eskkar finally stopped, his legs trembled with weakness. The horse sank carefully to the earth to rest its own limbs. Glancing up at the crescent moon, Eskkar saw that almost half the night had passed.

He fed the horse the last of the grain he'd carried in his pack, grain that should have augmented the beast's grazing for another three days. When the horse finished licking the last of the precious grain, Eskkar refastened the horse blanket, making sure it fit snugly. Last he tied the halter rope around his wrist. If he had to wake suddenly, he didn't want to be groping for an excited mount.

Man and beast slept fitfully the rest of the night, waking often. Eskkar rose before dawn, shivering a little from the chilly air and wishing he'd used the blanket. After taking a few moments to piss, he began leading the horse once more, ignoring the stiffness in his legs, knowing they'd loosen up after a few miles.

Even after the sun's rosy first light illuminated the land, Eskkar didn't mount. Instead he broke into a jog, forcing the animal to trot beside him. Only when Eskkar's legs gave out did he mount the horse and begin riding. In the distance, he caught sight of his destination, a series of low hills rising in the west, fronting an even higher line of crests behind them.

The formations appeared closer than they were; he guessed about a day and half ride away, at a normal pace. Eskkar needed to reach them by nightfall, or those chasing him would catch him for sure.

Though he'd never visited these lands before, Eskkar had spoken with others who had, and he'd committed all they said to memory. They described the landmarks well enough for him to keep his bearings, even if the countryside itself was mostly empty, except for the scattered grasses half as tall as a man.

If he could get into those hills and out the other side, he'd be safe. No matter what the Village Elder demanded or how much gold he offered, few men would persevere against so much distance and obstacles searching for one man.

Eskkar looked behind him. The dust cloud still hung in the air, even closer than it had been the night before. They were closing the gap, running him down. He wondered who led them; surely no fat Village Elder would have pressed onward through the night.

"Damn all gods for sending such bad luck," he yelled, startling the horse. "Not you, boy, not you," he said, speaking in a soothing tone and patting his mount's neck. No sense making the animal any more skittish. Picking up the pace, he glanced again at the dust cloud. Less than two miles behind him, he decided, and surely with extra horses. That distance would close gradually, as the spare mounts proved their worth.

When a patch of hard ground appeared, Eskkar shifted his direction, hoping to throw his pursuers off. For a time, he'd thought they'd lost his trail, but those shadowing him found it and resumed the hunt.

Still, they didn't have him yet, and the hills drew ever closer, though slower than he liked. Every time he could, Eskkar dismounted and ran beside the horse, trying to husband the animal's strength as much as possible. By noon, his feet burned, and his battered sandals were falling to pieces. Soon he'd be barefoot.

Ignoring his bruised feet and the stabbing pain that burned in his side, he kept running until he couldn't take another step, until every breath cut into his lungs. Only then did he pull himself back astride the horse and ride, glancing behind him and seeing the dust cloud grow ever larger. Cursing under his breath, Eskkar ate the last of his bread and finished what was left in his water skin. Again and again he wondered about the man who led them, what kind of hunter of men could drive villagers on with such urgency and persistence. Even relaying their horses, Eskkar had set a killing pace.

He could feel the horse tiring. Whenever he could Eskkar flung himself down from the horse's back and ran alongside for as long as he could. He had to spare the horse as much as possible. Right now, his mount was the only thing keeping him alive.

The sun dragged slowly across the sky, seeming to take forever before it started its descent into the west. When he looked back at his pursuers, he could almost make them out now, horses and men kicking the long plume of dust into the air.

At last Eskkar reached the start of the hills. A swift-moving stream flowed along at their base, following the same line as the hills. If Eskkar read the land right, the source of the water would be somewhere deeper within the hills.

He didn't bother to look behind him now. Pausing only long enough to scoop some water into his mouth while the horse slurped noisily, Eskkar followed the small river, crossing back and forth often, depending on where the land looked easier to ride.

Once again, he twisted his head and glanced back, damning the weakness that made him look behind. Eskkar could count them now, only about a mile behind him; nine men and eighteen horses, and he knew they were closing the gap faster with nearly every stride, probably covering three paces for every two of his.

The river turned sharply, and he could see it curving up into the hills. Eskkar pushed the horse hard, using every trick he knew to keep the animal moving as fast as it could. The sun neared the horizon, and soon it would be dark, and he'd be safe. Even his hunters had to rest, at least for a time. Eskkar just needed to last that long.

Gradually the riverbank grew higher, the water cutting its way deeper into the rocky soil. Eskkar took only a moment to decide. His stalkers had closed the gap between them faster than he expected. The river would have to save him, one way or another. He slowed the horse, patted its neck encouragingly, and turned its head toward the stream.

"Come on, boy. We can lose them yet. They won't find us in the river," he said, talking as much to himself as to the horse, to distract the animal from its nervousness.

Eskkar let the horse pick its own path down the steep side of the riverbank. Once started, the animal kept going, responding to its rider's gentle urgings, and knowing that it couldn't turn back. Fortunately the water here, little more than a stream, remained shallow, and the cautious horse could see its footing.

With a splash and a loud snort, horse and rider entered the water. Resting only long enough for the thirsty and tired animal to drink, Eskkar guided the animal to mid-stream, then turned its head upstream, toward the heart of the hills.

He didn't have much time. The men pursuing him weren't far behind, and he intended to use the river to slow them down. Eskkar just needed to reach the higher hills rising ever closer in the west, not more than another mile or so away.

The stream, thank the gods, led straight to them, and might actually be the easiest and shortest way to get through the ever-higher obstacles dotting the landscape on either side, and that, he hoped, would hinder and slow those tracking him.

What would happen after he reached the steeper crests rising before him, he didn't know. Nor did he know anything more about these hills; he'd planned to skirt them on his way south. But at this moment, all he cared about were the men closing in behind him.

Once he vanished deeper into the hills, they might give up the chase. After all, he was only one man, his exhausted mind reasoned, and they had already invested almost two days of hard riding chasing after him.

Again Eskkar swore at the spiteful gods for the bad luck they continued to rain down upon his head. He regretted ever stopping at the miserable inn where ignorant dirt-eaters passed the time drinking and looking for trouble. Not that the past mattered now. What did matter was that any band of men that size would carry at least three or four bows. If they closed within bowshot, Eskkar would be finished.

Splashing along, the scattered rocks on either side turned into low hills as the stream wended its way deeper into the clefts. The ever rising hills also blocked the setting sun, which would bring dusk earlier. He'd follow the stream as long as he could, until it got too dark to see. Before then Eskkar had to find someplace safe to leave the water, before the horse turned its leg on some slippery rock. Anxiously, he searched both sides of the river. The few places that looked accessible would leave plenty of evidence of his departure, and he wasn't ready to abandon his plan so easily.

He slowed the pace as the setting sun colored the rocks a reddish gold. The tiring horse felt the danger as well, moving more cautiously and snorting every few steps. To Eskkar's dismay, the riverbanks began to rise up, and within a few hundred paces, nearly vertical banks stretched well above his head on either side.

Eskkar decided to get out of the river, now, before he found himself trapped in deeper water and had to reverse his course. His eyes scanned the banks looking for any way to climb out, not caring now if he left a trail.

The sun had vanished, hidden behind the hills, and soon darkness would be complete. The horse decided the same thing, and halted with a nervous whinny that announced its refusal to proceed. Swearing at the recalcitrant horse, Eskkar swung down, took the halter, and led the way. Freed from its human burden, the horse reluctantly followed behind, though Eskkar had to drag on the rope more than once, fighting both the animal and the swift current.

The cold water swirled and gurgled around his numbing feet, slowing his progress, as his eyes kept searching for a way out of the river. Nightfall would be on him in a few more moments, and still the river's banks continued to rise higher and higher. To add to his woes, the river began to narrow, and its depth increased. Already the water chilled his bare legs above the knees, as it impeded every step forward.

The horse neighed loudly and dug in its heels. The sudden movement made Eskkar lose his footing, and he fell, soaking himself in the cold water before he could regain his feet. He'd kept a tight grip on the halter, or the horse would have bolted back the way it came. Swearing at the stubborn beast, he jerked hard on the rope.

Then Eskkar noticed the animal staring at the riverbank, its ears flattening and flashing its teeth. Something had spooked the horse besides exhaustion and the cold water. Looking around in the little light that remained, he saw nothing but a slightly wider pool to his right, where the horse kept its gaze, its eyes wide as it snorted the air. It must have caught the scent of something, some wild beast, perhaps a wolf or mountain lion.

Eskkar stared at the eddy pool. Only a few paces away, it looked like a normal part of the river. Tightening his grip on the rope, Eskkar moved closer, dragging the animal behind him by brute strength.

As he approached the riverbank, what seemed like a solid rock wall opened slightly to reveal a narrow gap. This led to a slender ledge of rock that projected down from the cliff above. Behind the gap, the pool widened even more. But all Eskkar noticed was the sloping path that wound its way up the face of the rock.

That was what had frightened the horse, he decided. Wild animals would use this natural ladder to reach the river's waters.

They could scamper up and down its slope without too much difficulty, then hang off the rocks to drink.

Eskkar looked back at the opposite bank, wondering if anyone there could see the gap in the rocks that formed this side of the riverbank. Three large boulders leaned against one another, blocking anyone from looking directly at the entrance. And a few paces further upstream, the eddy pool would be even more invisible.

Another shiver passed over him, and he knew the horse's legs must be nearly numb by now. Despite its fear, the horse followed along as he stepped closer to the bank, man and beast willing to face whatever danger lurked to get out of the river.

To Eskkar's relief, the water grew shallower after two paces, and he saw a slab of nearly flat stone where thirsty animals could reach the precious liquid. But could the weary horse clamber up onto the shelf, he wondered.

Eskkar pulled himself onto the ledge, grunting with relief as his feet left the cold water. The horse protested at first, when he tugged on the halter, but it, too, wanted out of the chilled stream. At Eskkar's urgings, the animal tried to climb up. Twice it slipped back, its eyes wide with fright, Eskkar hanging onto the halter rope with all his strength, hoping it wouldn't break.

Despite Eskkar's encouragement, the horse couldn't make it out of the water. Swearing at every god he could think of, Eskkar jumped back into the pool. He moved along the base of the ledge, searching for the best footing.

One place seemed a little shallower, and he guided the horse there. Then he stood at the horse's side. "Get out of the water, you fool of a beast," he muttered, shaking the halter rope and pushing on the animal's hindquarters.

The horse tried, but foundered again. Eskkar smacked it hard on the rump, and this time the tired animal responded with a leap that lifted its forelegs onto the ledge, while its hind legs churned the water. Eskkar put his shoulder under the beast's hindquarters and pushed with all his strength, hoping the frightened animal wouldn't kick his skull to pieces.

Suddenly the horse found some footing; it scrambled onto some projection, and, muscles straining, pulled itself up and out of the water, hooves scraping against the wet rock. The horse snorted in excitement, and dragged itself up the slope, disappearing beyond a curve.

The horse's sudden movement jerked the halter rope from his hand, and, off balance, Eskkar fell back into the eddy pool. By the time he got his head above water, the horse had vanished, gone up the slope and out of sight. "You'd better run. I'll kill you myself, you stupid son of a donkey."

Eskkar dragged himself out of the cold water, nearly exhausted from the effort. Breathing hard, he made sure he still had his sword and knife. Then he followed the horse up the ledge, slipping more than once as he went.

The moment he reached the curve, he found firmer footing. The horse remained out of sight, though he could hear it clattering away. Breaking into a run, Eskkar chased after his stallion, using the first faint rays of the moon to guide him.

He needed that horse. Only two months ago, he'd paid hard coin for him. The trader had refused to bargain, insisting on his full price and knowing what a fine animal like that would mean to any horse-man, let alone a barbarian outcast.

The path wound back and forth between the high rocks, twisting steadily away from the river and ever higher into the hills. Eskkar, nearing exhaustion, didn't know where it led, but at least none of his pursuers would find him, not unless they stumbled upon the eddy pool.

Sounds of the horse's hooves among the rocks ceased, but he heard snorting somewhere up ahead. Moving as fast as he dared, Eskkar rounded a good-sized boulder and glimpsed the animal, a darker shadow standing next to a high cliff wall. Night had fallen, even darker in these rocks, and he had to squint into the gloom to make out the horse's bulk.

At least it had stopped running, probably because the path ended where it stood. Gratefully, Eskkar called softly and slowed his approach. He didn't want the animal bolting off again. Moving carefully around its flank, he reached out for the halter. Then he saw a hand holding it.

Before he could even think to draw his sword, something smashed into the back of Eskkar's head. He'd been leaning forward, and the blow knocked him off his feet. Eskkar landed hard among the rocks, striking his head, the last thing he remembered before he passed out.

6

The smoke from the fire woke him, wafting into his face, pushed by some stirring of air. Coughing, Eskkar tried to sit up, but couldn't move, and he banged his aching head yet again against something hard. Eskkar struggled until he realized his hands and feet were tied. He forced himself upright, his back rubbing against rough stone. Resin-rich fumes tickled his throat, more than such a small fire should produce.

"Well, he's awake at last. Thought we were going to have to dump his body in the river before he woke."

Someone laughed. Eskkar blinked until his eyes focused and he peered through the smoky haze drifting in his direction. The fire produced more smoke than light, but he made out three figures seated around it. Three women. One laughed again, and his addled wits finally made the connection.

He looked around and realized that he and his captors were inside a cave, which accounted for the smoke floating everywhere. His dry throat wanted to cough again, but Eskkar swallowed hard, trying to stifle it. He coughed anyway, a brief racking that left his throat raw before it stopped.

"What happened?" Eskkar felt like a fool the moment the words left his lips. Someone had knocked him senseless.

Another woman laughed, this time a more pleasant sound. Although she found something enjoyable in his discomfort.

"He doesn't remember, or . . ."

"Or says he doesn't," the first woman said, finishing the thought. Now her voice sounded rough and hard, and her stocky figure showed the effects of years of hard work, matching the gray sprinkled in her hair. "Maybe we should tell him." She emphasized her words by tapping the ground between them with a sword. Looking down, Eskkar noticed the blade. It was his own.

Observing his glance, she lifted the weapon, holding it steady as she turned it to and fro in the firelight. "Good bronze," she commented. "I didn't know barbarians could make weapons this fine." The muscles in her arm had no trouble holding the heavy blade, and he decided she not only knew how to handle a weapon, but had the strength to do so.

Eskkar looked around, but saw no more than the three women. The way their voices echoed off the walls told him this was no shallow hole in a cliff, but a real cave, one that might go back quite a ways into the hillside. A natural refuge this large might shelter a sizeable number of people. The men would be returning soon; they wouldn't leave a prisoner to be guarded by women for long.

"A village smith made it for me," Eskkar said, remembering her question.

"And you killed him for it?" The third woman posed the question, her voice softer than the others, though he heard the hatred underlying her words.

Whatever he said, they weren't likely to believe him. "I paid the blacksmith ten silver coins, and worked for him besides, for more than a month, until the blade was finished." No one said anything. "Why did you attack me? I was only trying to get through the hills."

"In the dark? In the river?" The first woman lowered the sword and rested it on the earth between her feet. "Your horse's legs were chilled to the bone. The poor beast shivered while we rubbed it down. Nice horse you *had*. You both must have been in the water a long time, I'd guess."

Eskkar nodded, ignoring the comment about the horse. Whether he lived or died, it wasn't likely he'd get the horse back.

"We did enter the river before sundown," he said, shifting his position a bit and using the movement to test the ropes that held him. The bindings had some give, but he'd need plenty of time to loosen or break them.

"Don't try to free yourself." The second woman's venom remained in her voice. Younger than the woman holding his sword, this one looked to have about twenty-five seasons. "If you try to escape, we'll slit your throat."

She held up his knife. It had lain concealed against her leg. Her ragged garment left her arms bare, and he noticed the wiry muscles as she gripped the knife.

"So, barbarian," said the older woman, the one holding his sword and who appeared to be the leader. "Why were you in the river? I'll not ask again."

There didn't seem much point in lying. Besides, deceit could get him killed as soon as the truth. "My name is Eskkar. Men were after me," he said. "Since midday yesterday. They were closing fast, so I went into the river and rode upstream, up into the hills, to cover my tracks." He lifted his shoulders and let them drop. "Then I couldn't get out."

"And you came right to our secret place," she said, tapping the sword again, this time a little harder. "Who told you about us?"

"No one." A noise made him look up. Another woman appeared from the direction of what he guessed to be the cave's opening. Still no men. "The horse found the pool," Eskkar went on. "Some scent spooked him, and when I looked, I saw the ledge and thought we could get out of the water from there. That's all."

The women exchanged glances. Eskkar regretted that he'd stumbled into their secret lair, probably a hiding place for bandits or outcasts. Not that it made any difference. He saw the grim looks on the women's faces and they exchanged glances.

"You think I planned to come to that ledge, with a horse, after dark? I barely got the horse out of the water." No one spoke. He looked at each of them. "Anyone else ever bring a horse out of the river that way before?"

"It doesn't matter why you came, or how you got here, barbarian," the second woman said, ignoring his question. "You would have died back in the boulders, from my club, except you hit the rocks and knocked yourself out. I would have finished you off, but Eristi wanted to talk to you first."

Eristi must be the older woman, the one in charge, Eskkar guessed. A handful of women had captured him, trussed him up like a chicken.

Well, that explained the absence of the men. They must be off hunting or raiding somewhere, most likely a band of thieves. No one would live in these rocks by choice, not unless they had good reason to hide. Surely they wouldn't kill him before their men returned.

"Did you or your men folk see who was chasing me?"

They exchanged glances again, but said nothing. With a chill up the length of his spine, Eskkar knew what the look meant.

Women wouldn't dare kill a prisoner without their men's approval, but these women would, which meant there were no men here. He was running out of time. Again Eskkar tested the ropes binding his wrists, and knew he couldn't free his hands without struggling. They would finish him long before he could break free.

"I saw eight or ten men in the moonlight, skirting the hills across the river." The words came from the fourth woman, the one who just entered the cave. She sat down close to the fire, ignored the smoke, and warmed her hands. She appeared younger, little more than a girl, with long brown hair braided down her back. "They were searching for someone, looking for a trail out of the river. They finally made camp half mile past the eddy pool. I saw their fire. They'll search in the morning, but find nothing. By then the waters will have washed away any trace of his passage."

"So many men, and searching in the darkness," the third woman said, a hint of surprise in her voice. "You must have stolen more than just a horse and a sword. Where did you come from?"

She was the only one that didn't seem ready to take his blood, so Eskkar answered politely. "A little village to the east. Nippur, I think it is called."

"Really? And what did you do there, to make them chase you for two days?"

So she knew how distant the village was. Eskkar tried to think, not sure what to tell them. He licked his dry lips while he wondered what to answer, then regretted showing such a sign of weakness.

The third woman stood, and knelt beside him. Younger than the first two, not past her twentieth season, she had no weapon, only an oval-shaped rock in her right hand. She grabbed him by the hair with her left, pushing his head against the cave wall and holding it there.

"You'd better answer, barbarian, and don't try to lie. Tell me what you did in Nippur, or I'll smash your skull." She lifted the stone above her shoulder to give her words emphasis, but she never raised her voice, and her very calmness sent a shiver of fear through him.

"There was a fight at the inn," he said, the words rushing out. "Men . . . four men attacked me, and I had to kill one to get away." She must know people in Nippur, maybe even have kin there. For all Eskkar knew, he might have killed her brother. Fear gripped at his stomach, and he had to force himself not to struggle.

"And his name," the voice remained low.

"I don't know his name," Eskkar said, his voice rising. He couldn't keep the hint of panic from showing through. She tightened her grip on his hair and raised the rock even higher.

"The innkeeper . . . said he was the Village Elder's son. His second son . . . Maldar . . . no, Maldar's second son." The words ran together. He couldn't take his eyes from the rock about to split his head.

The rock slipped from her grasp, and she rocked back on her heels, letting go of his hair. "Kassites is dead?"

The name meant nothing to Eskkar, and he couldn't tell from her face whether or not the dead man's name brought pain or joy.

"Kassites is dead?" she said again.

"If that's the name of the man I killed." This time Eskkar detected the hint of relief in her voice. This Kassites, or whatever he was called, had been no friend of hers. Then he saw tears in her eyes, which only added to his confusion.

She took a deep breath, and brushed the tears away with the back of her hand. "You've done me a service, stranger," she said, releasing his hair. "I ran from Kassites. I was given to him as a slave, after he raped and killed my sister. He was . . . cruel to his women." She lifted her eyes to Eskkar's. "My name is Anahita. Your name is . . ."

"Eskkar," he repeated, still not sure what this revelation meant to his chances of surviving another hundred heartbeats.

Anahita shifted to face the others, her leg brushing against Eskkar's. "I owe this man a blood debt for my sister. We cannot kill him."

"Blood debt indeed!" the first woman said. "We are women, not puffed-up men prancing in front of each other and boasting of their conquests. We swore to kill any man who came upon us." She softened her tone. "He didn't kill Kassites to avenge you and your sister."

"Eristi, he came here running from those trying to kill him," Anahita said. "Just as I did."

Eskkar glanced at Eristi, the oldest of the four women. Probably approaching her thirty-fifth season, she'd spoken with the voice of command. She was the one he had to convince.

"I mean you no harm, Eristi," Eskkar offered. "Let me go, and I'll be gone at first light. I only want to cross these hills and head west."

"And that is the one direction we cannot let you go," Eristi said. "The rest of us came from there. Even now, men from the west are coming for us."

Eskkar stared at her, while his mind assembled the pieces of the puzzle together. These women must be runaway slaves, who had fled from their masters and taken refuge in these hills.

Naturally their owners wanted their property back. You couldn't let even a few insignificant slaves run away; if you did, they'd all run. So slaves had to be tracked down and brought back for punishment, as a lesson to any others, who might one day be tempted to flee their masters themselves.

In Eskkar's clan, the penalty for a slave attempting to escape was death by slow torture, in front of the other slaves. The dirt-eaters, he'd come to learn, preferred keeping their property alive.

They would beat runaways, sometimes even maim or mark them, but not usually kill them, not unless . . .

He broke the silence with another question. "How do you know men are coming?"

"They came six days ago," Anahita said. "There were five of them, but we drove them off, throwing stones from the rocks above. They didn't know the passages through the cliffs, and it's not easy to climb up the rock face. They had to carry two men away when they left."

"How far from here is their village," he said, still thinking the situation through.

"About two days ride," Anahita answered.

Two days to return to the village, three or four days to gather men, weapons, and whatever else they needed, and two days to return to this place. Eskkar knew enough about villagers and how they prepared to fight.

"They could be here tomorrow," he said. "No later than the day after."

"Why are you so certain?" Eristi asked, leaning forward slightly, curious in spite of herself.

"Well, you drove them off with rocks. So they'll be back with bowmen, at least three or four men who can shoot. An archer can stand back further than you can throw a stone, and shoot you down from the cliffs. The rest, probably another eight or ten men, will bring ropes, ladders, horses, and enough food to hunt you down if you run away and try to hide in the rocks. Or slip across the stream to the east. That's what you should have done. Right after the attack, you should have gone to the east, to Nippur, or another village."

Then he remembered. Anahita came from there, and she couldn't return.

"I ask again, how do you know such things?" Eristi's voice had hardened.

"Twice villagers paid me to help chase down runaway slaves," Eskkar said, wondering how they'd react to that statement. "They needed someone who could track and work with the horses."

"I told you he should die," the second woman said. She lifted the knife. "He's as bad as any that owned us, hunting down helpless slaves for a few coins."

"You'll not kill him, Shama," Anahita said firmly. "If we kill those seeking refuge, we're no better than our masters."

"I can take Anahita away from here," Eskkar broke in, speaking rapidly before they began to argue. "On the horse. You say they don't know her. If we encounter them, I'll say she's my woman."

"Or we can kill you, and take the horse ourselves."

"Do you know how to ride?" He waited, eyes moving from one to another, but Shama said nothing. "They'll track you down . . . follow any tracks leaving this place. They'll run you to earth in a day, assuming the horse doesn't throw you off before then."

"No, Shama," Anahita said. "I won't leave you and the others. Not after what you've done for me." She faced Eskkar. "Can you take all of us?"

"The four of you? We'd leave a trail a child could follow. They'd catch up with us in half a day."

"I still say he has to die," Eristi said. "The moment we let him loose, he will turn on us. If the men come, Anahita can hide in the rocks, deeper in the hills. They're not looking for her. The rest of us will fight."

"Then you'll all die, or be recaptured," Eskkar said, his eyes moving from one to the other.

Shama answered his words by standing and lifting the knife in her hand. Eristi joined her, and Eskkar knew the moment had come. They'd push Anahita aside, kill him, and comfort her later.

"Wait," he said. "I've another choice to offer you."

Eristi stopped, but Shama took a step closer.

"I can help you fight them off. I know how to fight. At least we'll have a chance to drive them away."

"What can one man do," Eristi said, "against ten, or even more?"

"They're villagers, not warriors," Eskkar answered. "They won't be expecting a fight. Besides, you only need to kill a few to scare the rest away. They're here to hunt women, not fight a battle."

"You ran from the villagers," Shama said. "Why should we think you can help us?"

"Four men attacked me," Eskkar said, the anger rising in his voice. "I killed one and knocked another senseless. The others ran. I wasn't going to wait for them to come back with more men."

"How can we trust you?" Eristi said, before Shama could answer. "You might abandon us, or even try to kill us."

Eskkar opened his mouth, then closed it. There was no way to guarantee his words. Now that he thought the thing through, they spoke the truth, he'd be a fool to stay. He'd promise them anything. The moment they cut him loose, he'd be gone. As soon as Eskkar found the horse, he'd get out of these damned hills, leave them to their fate, kill them if they tried to stop him. They meant nothing to him.

Anahita turned her back to the women, and shifted to Eskkar's side, practically touching his chest. She put her hands on his shoulders and moved closer to his face.

"Your word . . . Eskkar . . . your honor as a warrior, sworn upon your sword. May you die unburied, food for the carrion-eaters, if you betray us. May you wander the underworld for all time if you break your pledge. Swear it, as a warrior."

Despite his fear, Eskkar felt the blood rush from his face at her request. For a warrior to swear on his sword was a serious oath, second only to the oath given to a clan brother. And to invoke the worst fate possible for a warrior, to lie unburied, defeated, his body food for the worms and maggots, while his soul wandered alone for all time, proved Anahita knew something about steppes warriors.

Eskkar might not believe in the gods, or offer them sacrifice, but only a fool would tempt fate by swearing and breaking such an oath.

Eristi stepped forward, the sword in her hand, but she held it vertically now, and she pressed the hilt against Eskkar's chest, the upright blade pressed against his cheek. "Swear on your sword, barbarian! Swear to defend us against those who come. Swear to protect us, or you die here, right now, and we'll cut you apart and dump your body in the river, piece by piece!"

The cold metal against him seemed alive, as if ready to draw the life force from his body.

"Swear, Eskkar," Anahita said, squeezing her hands on his shoulders. "Swear, and we'll let you live."

The sword felt like a heavy weight on his chest, and he struggled to breathe, both their faces practically touching his. He'd never given his oath to anyone, let alone for something like this, something that demanded his eternal damnation should he break his word.

"I . . . swear," he said, mumbling the words.

"Louder," Anahita demanded. "Let the gods above and below hear your promise."

"I swear it!" The words echoed ominously throughout the cavern, as if the gods themselves had answered his oath. He shivered at the thought of the gods hearing his words. "I swear to defend you against those who come."

Eristi stepped back, letting the sword drop to her side. "Untie him," she said.

Anahita cupped his face in her hands, then kissed him on the lips. "That was for killing Kassites and avenging my sister. Remember, your word as a warrior binds you, Eskkar. Make sure you remain worthy, or you'll suffer for the rest of your days, and again in the hereafter."

When they untied the ropes, Eskkar felt as weak and shaky as a newborn lamb. His heart beat rapidly in his chest.

Anahita took his hands and massaged them in her own. "The gods sent you to avenge my sister's death. Now, you must save us from the slave masters. When you do, the gods will favor you the rest of your days. They have spoken, and I hear their voices."

He looked at her blankly, still unable to speak, wondering about her words.

"My mother had the Goddess's gift . . . to see the future. She passed part of that gift on to me. The Goddess Ishtar first sent you to kill Kassites, then ordained that you would come here, to find me, to complete your task by saving us. I know this to be true."

Ishtar, Queen of the Gods of the dirt-eaters, ruled the heavens while Marduk ruled the earth. Ishtar was also the god most favored by women, because she ruled both men and gods by playing on their lusts.

Eskkar shook his head. "No gods sent me, Anahita. Only chance brought me . . ."

"You think chance put you in Kassites's path?" She touched a finger to his lips to silence him. "Don't blaspheme Ishtar's choice. Don't try to oppose the will of the Goddess. You might break her spell, and all will be ruined."

He nodded, swallowing hard and trying not to shake. Now he not only had men pursuing him, other men coming for him, but also the wrath of the Queen of the gods hanging over his head.

Eristi dropped his sword on the ground. "You need this, I suppose . . . Eskkar. Give him the knife, Shama."

"What if he doesn't keep his oath?"

"Then the knife won't save you," Eristi said. "Give it to him."

Muttering something under her breath, Shama tossed the knife onto his lap. "We're all fools to trust him."

"Perhaps we are," Anahita said, "but I trust the Goddess, and she sent him to us." She turned back to Eskkar. "Are you hungry?"

He nodded. "More thirsty. Is there any water?"

Eristi handed him a small clay pitcher, its lip broken. Eskkar washed the dryness from his throat, and handed it back to her with thanks.

They gave him something to eat. The women didn't have much, only a few wilted vegetables that grew wild in thin patches of soil scattered throughout the rocks. It didn't satisfy his hunger, but they had nothing better, and they shared what little they had with him.

Eskkar wondered how they'd lived in such conditions. They might get an occasional fish from the river, but for anything else, they'd have to venture out of the cliffs to gather what they could from whatever grew nearby. Obviously none of them knew how to hunt or trap the small animals that dwelt within the rocks.

The fire burned low, and finally went out, filling the cave with even more smoke. By the light of the last glowing coals, Anahita came to his side.

"Rest, Eskkar," Anahita said, spreading a thin blanket over them both. "You'll need all your strength tomorrow." She settled down beside him, turned onto her side, and closed her eyes.

He lay there, still awake, until the three women had fallen asleep around him. The events of the day and night raced through his thoughts. All this was too much for him. He'd never been so close to death before, not like this. In battle, fighting or running, he'd always been able to do something – attack, flee, anything.

During today's chase, he'd felt no fear even as his pursuers closed in behind him. But to sit here, helpless, while women came within a heartbeat of killing him, he never encountered that kind of threat in his life, and never felt such fear possess him, sapping his strength, leaving him weak and shaking.

Sleep, when it finally came, was fitful and filled with strange dreams. He tossed about, waking again and again as the demons of the night, evil and horrible, reached cold hands toward his throat. Finally his restless movements woke Anahita, who took his hand and held it.

Her touch soothed him. Eskkar turned his head against her shoulder and finally fell back asleep. This time he slept until morning, perhaps helped by the touch of Anahita's hand. For the rest of the night, no dreams or apparitions appeared to terrify his thoughts, as his weary body and over-excited mind succumbed to the stress of a long and challenging day.

7

When Eskkar woke, he found the women gone and the cavern empty. Not much light filtered into the cave, but the chamber had cleared of smoke, and he could see without having to squint. The cavern, only partially illuminated by the rising sun, looked even larger than it had last night, though the smoke-blackened walls swallowed up much of the morning sun's rays.

Sitting up, Eskkar found his sword and knife lying beside him. He slung the long sword over his shoulder, the weapon's presence making him feel safe for the first time in days.

Following the light, Eskkar came out onto a narrow ledge, and realized he was well up among the rocks. The women must have labored to drag his unconscious body to the cave, and he wondered why they had bothered, especially if they planned to kill him. He shook his head to drive away the evil thought, and the motion reminded him that his skull still hurt from last night's blows.

A glance at the sun told him quite some time had passed since dawn. It seemed logical to retrace the path down from the cave, but Eskkar went the other way, following the ledge higher and higher until it disappeared, and he had to scramble on his hands and knees up rocks worn smooth and slippery by uncounted years of blowing wind and baking sun.

Breathing hard, he finally reached the top of the hill. A vast vista opened up before him under the blue sky and bright white billowing clouds scattered overhead, the view making the climb worth the struggle.

Taking his time, Eskkar scanned the horizon, getting a feel for the land, committing landmarks to memory in case he needed to find his way. The hills, he now realized, formed a long, jagged spine that extended down from even higher elevations to the north. These foothills stretched far out to the southeast, another day's ride or more for any of his pursuers who wished to go around the ridge.

To the east, Eskkar could see the part of the river and the barren lands he'd passed through the last two days. Today that land looked empty, without a trace of those who'd stalked him from Nippur. Hopefully the men chasing him had given up, presuming him drowned in the river.

To the west, the land changed somewhat, from grassland to a more rugged terrain, with small patches of green scattered among the rocks and sand. Eskkar saw none of the usual dirt-eater farms or canals, no sign of crops growing, no herds of sheep or goats in pastures. The countryside might not be a desert, but there wasn't much water, and dirt-eaters avoided living on dry, parched land.

Which was why, he supposed, runaway slaves made for this haven in the cliffs. Too desolate and dreary to see many travelers, it yielded just enough food to keep a handful of desperate people alive for a few days, though not well fed. The women must have decided to remain, a grim enough prospect, at least until their masters forgot about them.

Thinking about food brought a frown to his face. Women, who ate less than men and needed less meat to stay alive, might subsist on a scattering of roots and vegetables. If Eskkar wanted to keep his strength, he'd need to hunt, to find some meat.

Looking at the highlands behind him, he decided there must be wild goats and sheep running about, and, of course, their hereditary enemy, the mountain lion. Gazing skyward, he saw only a solitary hawk circling above with wings extended, rising and falling as it rode the wind, patiently searching for its next meal.

He squinted against the sun, following the graceful bird's flight. It was a desert hawk, the small hunter that had been the emblem of his father's clan.

"Bring luck to me today, desert hawk," he said, mouthing the words he'd heard from his father as far back as he could remember.

Eskkar dropped his gaze and thought about the other creatures inhabiting the cliffs. Without a bow, the women had no way to hunt any of these animals, which was why they were slowly starving. An occasional fish and some undersized vegetables wouldn't keep even women alive for too long.

"ESKKAR!"

He looked down. Anahita stood a hundred paces below, waving at him, and Eskkar realized how high he'd climbed. He went down, taking his time. A slip and a fall, even if it resulted in nothing worse than a sprained ankle, might be enough to finish him today. Anahita waited for him until he stood before the cave's entrance once again.

"What did you see?"

"Nothing," Eskkar said, "no sign of anyone approaching."

"Dalza is keeping watch to the west."

"Dalza?"

"The youngest of us," Anahita answered. "Dalza just passed into her fifteenth season. She says little, and keeps to herself. Sometimes I think her wits are addled. But she works hard, and does whatever is needed."

"Where's my horse?"

"Shama penned it in a small gully. It's safe there. Do you need to see it?"

"No, not now. Perhaps later." Eskkar brought his mind back to the problem. "You said you drove men off before," he said. "Can you show me how? And where?"

She took him down the ledge, then across the top of a rock shelf. Anahita's bare feet moved easily over the rough and tilted surfaces, while Eskkar had to step carefully and make sure of his footing on the unfamiliar rocky terrain.

"Everything is uneven up here, but you'll get used to moving about." She waited patiently for him every few paces.

Still watching his footing, Eskkar wasn't so sure, and hoped he wouldn't have to experience a few falls while he acquired the skill. At last they reached the edge of the rock wall, or what he thought was the edge until he stood there. About ten or twelve paces below, another wide shelf, almost like a step, stretched beneath him. Only below that expanse could he make out the bottom of the rock face, where sand and dirt met the base of the cliffs.

"There are three ways to climb up to the lower shelf," she explained, indicating the level space below. "The men only found one of them." She pointed and he followed her finger as she traced a narrow cleft between the rocks that went back and forth upon itself until it reached the sandy floor.

"We stood down there," Anahita said, pointing a spot on the lower step, "and pelted them with rocks. They couldn't climb up through our stones. Shama had a sling, and she hit several of them."

"They had no bows?"

"No, just swords and knives. One carried a spear. They tried to throw our stones back at us, but it's a lot easier to throw them down than up." She laughed at the memory.

"And they gave up, just like that?"

"Not at first. They looked for another place to climb up, but the ways are not easy to discover. From down there, all the rocks look the same, and almost every way a person goes, you end up facing a cliff. We kept throwing stones at them whenever they got too close to finding a way up."

Eskkar thought about that. Four women had driven off five men, probably injuring one or two with the first barrage of stones. After that, the rest of the men hadn't pressed too hard. A few women slaves weren't worth getting your skull smashed, or even your arm broken.

If they returned . . . when they came back, they'd be prepared. Shields, bows, ropes, ladders, and most of all, enough men to overwhelm any resistance.

He didn't respect much about dirt-eaters in general, but he'd seen how well they could organize things, prepare for situations, anticipate upcoming problems, and how to resolve them. They might not

be good fighters, but they worked together, and even a pack of cowardly dogs could take down a mountain lion.

"You still think they will come?" Anahita broke into his thoughts.

"Yes, they'll come. They'd never live it down . . . driven off by
a few women." He glanced up at the sun. "Let's start getting ready
for them."

They left Dalza to keep watch. Eskkar followed Anahita as she
descended all the way down to the base of the cliff wall. He wanted
to see how the cliffs would look to any approaching men. She'd told
the truth; everything appeared the same from the wasteland at the
floor of the cliffs, a jumble of rocks that all looked alike. Without
Anahita leading the way, Eskkar knew he might not even find his
way back up to the cave.

Instead he and Anahita walked along the length of the rocks,
going at least a quarter of a mile in each direction. Eristi and Shama
followed them along the shelf above, appearing and disappearing
behind the rocks, and pointing out the places where the villagers
had tried to climb up, or where you could, with some effort, make it
to the first level.

Eskkar studied the rocks, trying to put himself in the attackers'
place, visualizing the way they would storm the heights.

The cliffs provided a nearly ideal defensive position. With ten
or twelve well-armed men, Eskkar guessed he could hold off fifty
or sixty attackers. But he didn't have any fighters, not even a bow.
All he had were four women. And the horse, he reminded himself.
Thinking about the horse gave him an idea.

"Anahita, do you have any ropes? Good ropes, strong enough to
hold my weight?"

"We have one rope, Eskkar. It's thick, and it should hold your
bulk. One of the men left it behind when they fled."

"Good. Maybe we can lay a trap for them, at least a few, maybe
enough to get what we need."

"What do we need?"

"One of their bows. We need a bow and some arrows. Come.
Let's go back to Eristi."

He followed Anahita, and they climbed back up the narrow, twisting passageway to the first shelf, and rejoined the others. Sitting on a rock, Eskkar explained his plan, and told the women what he intended to do.

To his surprise, no one questioned him. The dread they'd all been under for the last few days forced them to put aside any arguments or doubts. Any plan would be better than just waiting for the slave hunters.

When he finished, Shama climbed back up the cliffs, got Eskkar's horse, and led it down to the valley floor, using the passageway that the villagers had attempted to climb. The sparse grass wasn't great fodder, but the animal needed to graze, and there was nothing for it to eat up in the rocks.

The villagers might see the horse's tracks, but it wouldn't matter, since they already knew about that place. The other three women, and Eskkar, began gathering rocks. The small pile the women had accumulated near what Eskkar called the main entry, the place the villagers had tried to scale, wouldn't last more than a few moments. The passage, a twisting gully that reached back into the rocks, sloped gradually until it reached the first shelf.

Eskkar wanted enough stones to keep up a steady stream of missiles. He even practiced hurling a few stones down the cliff, making sure he knew how far he could throw a good-sized rock.

After awhile, Eskkar left the collecting of more stones to the women. Instead, he pushed larger rocks and small boulders into position, the effort making him sweat in the warm sun. The heavier rocks would crush a man's chest, and hopefully splinter any shield a man might carry.

He wanted to be able to roll them down onto anyone trying to climb up. Eristi helped him from time to time; she could shift rocks almost as large as the ones Eskkar selected, though both of them grunted from the heavy work.

By the end of the afternoon, they'd moved hundreds of stones into eight or ten piles close to those paths. Many were too large to throw, but the women could push them over the side of the cliff's walls. At last Eskkar felt satisfied with the supply of missiles.

He spent the last part of the day before sundown working with the horse and the rope. Taking his time, Eskkar examined every strand of the rough hemp, looking for any sign of weakness, searching for any worn spots or frayed places that might snap under his weight.

When he felt satisfied the rope would take the strain, he looped one end into a simple harness to fit around the horse's shoulders. Eskkar and Anahita used the horse to lower Shama down into the cleft he'd selected, then to lift her back up again. They did it three times, to make sure the horse became accustomed to the harness and to the unusual labor.

Dinner included a single rabbit Shama had taken with her sling while grazing the horse. The skinny rabbit didn't have much meat on its bones, but Eskkar noticed they gave him most of it. His stomach still rumbled from hunger. Besides a few bites of rabbit, all he'd eaten in the last two days were the loaves of bread, and the handful of vegetables last night. The women had seen him sweating all day in the sun, and knew he needed his strength.

Afterwards, Eskkar went over the plans he'd worked out during the day, asking each of them if they thought they could do what was needed. That took some time. By then everyone, tired from the long day's labor, was ready for sleep. All the same, Eskkar insisted they post a guard during the night.

"What if they come at night, when they know you're sleeping? A single torch would give them all the light they need." The women had never even considered the idea that someone might try climbing up in the dark.

Anahita took the first watch. Eskkar had planned to take the last quarter of the night before dawn, but when Eristi prodded him awake, he found Anahita pressed against his side, and the first rays of the sun shinning into the cave.

"You needed your sleep," was all Eristi said.

Shama had already gone down to the river. She returned not long after, with two fat fish she snared. They used the last of their wood to cook them. Eskkar didn't care very much for fish. As a boy, a fish bone had lodged in his throat, and his father had to pound it out of Eskkar before he choked to death.

His people might catch a fish or two when they camped by a river, but they preferred meat. This morning, however, he ate a good-sized piece, skewered on a stick and crisped in the fire; afterwards he picked the sharp bones from his teeth and spat them into the ashes.

The sun had climbed almost directly overhead when Dalza's cry echoed over the cliffs. "Riders! I see riders coming," she shouted, her voice filled with excitement.

Everyone scrambled to the high point to watch the low cloud of dust from the west that moved steadily toward them.

Eskkar waited until he got the count: thirteen men and six horses, including two used as pack animals. Four of the men carried bows jutting up over their shoulders; the rest bore ropes or whatever other implements they'd deemed useful for rooting slaves out of the rocks. They would all be armed with a sword, and most would carry knives as well. Since most of the men were on foot, their approach would take some time.

A large number of men, Eskkar decided as he frowned at the count, to chase down a few runaway slaves. He'd expected seven or eight villagers. Nevertheless, he didn't have time to dwell on that now, but he'd think about it later. Assuming he lived past the rest of the day.

Seeing them approach, Eskkar knew the first part of his plan had already failed. He'd hoped they would arrive late in the afternoon. Given the choice, villagers preferred to sit around a fire and eat at the end of a long day. It would have offered Eskkar the opportunity to sneak down into their midst after dark and hopefully steal one or two of their bows.

With that hope dashed, Eskkar still had to get one of their weapons. With a bow, he could gamble on holding them off. Without it, the odds would be slim. Now he had to hope they took the bait he'd offered them.

As they drew closer, Eskkar again considered the consequences of breaking his oath to the women. Like all warriors from the steppes, he attached no dishonor to running away from a battle against superior numbers. Steppes horsemen preferred to fight only when certain they could win; otherwise, they tended to avoid conflict, hoping to fight another day with the odds in their favor. Even now, Eskkar knew he could slip back toward the river and escape.

The thought tempted him, but although he'd renounced the gods after his family's slaughter, he didn't want to risk offending them. Assuming they actually existed, his mind argued. No one really knew, but many mysterious forces inhabited the world, and most of them needed to be placated one way or another.

Thinking about the gods gave him a headache. The villagers had their own confusing gods, seemingly in countless numbers, to whom the fearful dirt-eaters attributed everything, good or ill, that ever happened to them.

A clumsy villager would trip over his own feet, then blame an ill-natured deity. The few war gods worshipped by the Alur Meriki rewarded only strength and courage. How a man died mattered to the gods of warfare, but little else.

Cursing at his mental wanderings, Eskkar climbed down from the lookout and went to the first line of cliffs. The women waited there, looking nervous, but resolved.

"They'll be coming at us as soon as they reach the base of the cliffs," he said, squatting down in front of the four women. "You're all still sure you want to fight? Once we start down that path, there will be no way to turn back. If any of us are caught . . ."

"We know what we have to do, Eskkar," Eristi said. "For us, there is no turning back. We must fight."

Each one knew what fate awaited if they were recaptured. They would first be beaten into submission, then raped repeatedly. When returned to their masters, the real torture would start.

"Then let's hope they fall into our trap," Eskkar said. "It's the only way to surprise them. Shama, you and Dalza guard the main passageway. Remember to wait until they're well inside before you begin. Keep them at bay. We'll come to help you as soon as we can."

Shama nodded, twisting the sling she held in her hands.

"Most of all," he went on, "keep silent, no sudden movements, and don't let the villagers see or hear you. No matter what they do or say, stay out of sight until I give the word. Even if they shoot some arrows into the rocks. Can you do that?"

Each one nodded. Eskkar saw determination in their eyes, controlling their fear. For now, he thought. It might be different when the
villagers begin their attack. On the other hand, if he could capture a
bow, they might all survive the first assault.

He looked at Eristi. "You'll lead the horse when the time comes.
Anahita, you'll have to give me the signal."

They split up and went to their places. Eskkar found a cleft
between boulders already covered by the afternoon shade. Peering
through the tiny opening, he watched the villagers as they came
forward. They moved even slower now as they drew closer, scanning the cliffs for any sign of the women.

Eskkar grunted in satisfaction at their cautious advance; they
made no sound or called out any challenge. No doubt the slave
hunters hoped to surprise the slaves. If the men could get up to the
first level unchallenged, more than half their work would be done.

Eskkar wanted them to think the cliffs were either unguarded
or abandoned. The silent cliffs should reassure the villagers, make
them think they faced no resistance. The dirt-eaters continued along,
heading toward the main entry, but before they reached it, they
would pass the place where Anahita had left the trail.

For a moment Eskkar cursed his luck when he thought the dirt-
eaters' untrained eyes had missed her tracks. But at the last moment,
the leader raised his hand and the column halted, a mere hundred
paces from the cliff face.

Almost directly below him, Eskkar watched their leader study
the false trail. A single row of footprints led directly into a narrow
cleft, scarcely visible in the cliff face. While the leader examined the
tracks, Eskkar took stock of his enemy.

The man had broad shoulders, with a thick black beard, and
looked both hard and competent. Even so, he had the look of a dirt-
eater about him, someone better suited to fighting in a village or
farm than in the high desert or from the back of a horse.

Their leader made up his mind, no doubt reasoning that the
tracks must lead somewhere, and that there could be another, possibly unguarded, path up to the first level of the escarpment. Eskkar
couldn't hear the man's quiet words, but everyone on horseback

except the leader dismounted and handed off their horses to a single man, who fastened all the halter ropes together.

The four men bearing bows strung them and fitted shafts to the strings. One of the villagers produced a wooden shield, not much larger than a barrel head, which he carried before him as he led the way along Anahita's tracks, followed by two bowmen and another man armed only with a sword.

Eskkar swallowed, licked his suddenly dry lips, and waited. If the leader divided his force, if he and the others moved on toward the main entry, Eskkar and the two women with him would have to abandon his plan, and move to help Shama and Dalza.

But if their leader waited, thinking he'd discovered an unwatched entrance up the cliffs ... then the man swung down from his horse. He kept his gaze on the rocks as his men moved forward unchallenged.

"They're coming," Eskkar said, nodding to Eristi and Anahita. Crawling backwards from his spy hole, he shifted over, found the rope and quickly lowered himself down into the passageway. His grip slipped once, the rough strands burning his hand, and he slid a few feet down the rope before he could stop. All the same, he reached the bottom in one piece and without making much of a sound.

He stood at the very end of a narrow opening that went nowhere, but behind a corner that couldn't be seen from anyone coming down the passage. Anahita's footprints came straight down and turned into the blind corner where Eskkar now stood.

Eskkar silently drew his sword from its sheath on his back, and waited. Now his life depended on Anahita. If anything went wrong, he'd be trapped here. He looked up, and caught a glimpse of her head, a glint of brown hair almost hidden in the rocks.

The sound of a sandal scraping against the rock told him the men drew close. Eskkar leaned against the cliff, and mouthed a prayer to the battle gods, asking for their favor. Another sandal crunched on some loose sand, and Eskkar took a deep breath. They'd almost reached the end of the passage.

Anahita screamed, a high-pitched shriek that echoed throughout the cliffs. Instantly Eskkar turned the corner. The shield bearer stood there, only a long pace away. He'd instinctively raised his shield over his head and looked upwards at Anahita's cry. Eskkar drove his sword beneath the man's uplifted shield, and the sword pierced his chest before he could react. The only sound he made was a gasp of pain as he died.

Without pausing, Eskkar moved forward, using his shoulder to shove the man still impaled on his sword onto the man behind him. That man, a bowman, had also turned to his right and raised his bow skyward. Now the archer tried to bring his weapon to bear on Eskkar, but before the bowman could aim, the still-twitching body of the first man crashed into him.

The arrow flew harmlessly over Eskkar's head. By then Eskkar had cleared his blade from the first man's body, and thrust it hard, the sword striking low into the second man's belly.

The third man, another archer, would have killed Eskkar, but as he drew back his shaft, a stone struck him on the shoulder. The arrow flashed past Eskkar's face and rattled on the rocks, as the man cursed his pain and the stone that deflected his shaft. Eskkar raised his sword, but the bowman had already turned and fled, pelted by more rocks from Eristi and Anahita.

Eskkar knew he had but a few moments. He flicked the loose blood from the blade and sheathed the still-bloody sword. Moving quickly, he scooped up the bow and quiver from the dead archer, and collected the sword of the first man he'd killed. Then Eskkar retreated back behind the boulder where he'd waited.

Once out of sight, he dropped the captured weapons, grabbed the dangling rope, and pulled the loop over his head and under his arms. Then Eskkar bent down and gathered up the precious bow and arrow quiver, and the extra sword.

"Bring me up, Eristi."

For a few heartbeats nothing happened. Then overhead, the horse's hooves clattered against the ground, but the rope stayed limp. Eskkar heard a stone glance off the passageway walls, answered by the twang of a bowstring. Men were returning. In another moment, they'd trap him here like a rat in a cage.

Swearing under his breath, Eskkar was about to abandon the weapons when the rope tightened painfully across his chest. He clutched it with one hand, holding everything else with the other, as he ascended the rock wall, scraping and bumping his shoulders and knees against the rough surface as he went, using his feet as best he could to keep him from bumping against the cliff.

The horse, attached to the other end of the rope, gathered speed, and Eskkar was dragged over the top and ten paces beyond before Eristi stopped the animal. Swearing again at the skin scraped raw by the rocks, he yanked the rope off his body and snatched up the bow and quiver.

Staying out of sight, he raced to the main entry. The leader of the attackers had the same idea. The moment he heard the sounds of conflict, he must have ordered half his men to the main passage. But Eskkar had the shorter way to go, and he reached it in time to strap the quiver to his waist, and nock an arrow to the bowstring.

When the first man, crouching under the shield he held high over his head, came in sight, Eskkar nodded to the women. Dalza began pushing melon sized stones over the edge, and Shama's sling hurled stones at whatever she could see from across the opposite side of the cleft.

Eskkar moved into the open, and shot an arrow into the man's body, just above his hip, all Eskkar could see uncovered by the shield. The wounded man stumbled, jerking the shield down and moving back, crying out in pain. The rest of the men stopped advancing. Cursing and shouting at each other in their rage and disappointment, they retreated out of the rocks, to regroup a hundred paces away.

Breathing hard, Eskkar smiled at the sight. Two men dead, one badly wounded. The hip-shot man would fight no more today. Even if he lived, he'd be no threat. And a stone from Shama's sling had struck another man in the face; he, too, wouldn't be in any hurry to return to the cliffs.

The first villager attack had been driven off.

Keeping low, Eskkar moved as close to the edge of the cliff as he dared, and watched as the men ran back to their horses, ignoring the wounded man who stumbled after them as best he could.

Eskkar could have taken a shot, but knew it would be better to let the man live. Alive, he'd need food, water, and care. More than that, he would be a constant reminder in their midst of what could happen to the rest of them if they returned to the rocks. A dead man was just that, dead, and easily forgotten.

Anahita and Eristi slid up on either side of Eskkar.

"Are they turning back?" Eristi said. "Have they had enough?"

Eskkar didn't answer. He kept his eyes on their leader. They'd clustered together, next to their horses, and he could hear their raised voices as they shouted at each other, though he couldn't make out what they argued about. Two or three looked ready to forego the whole venture. But the black-bearded leader didn't seem willing to abandon the attack.

Eskkar frowned at what that meant, and he remembered his earlier thought. These villagers had lost at least three men. Even if they rushed the cliffs and managed to fight their way up, they were likely to lose another two or three. No slaves, let alone women, were worth that many lives.

That prompted another thought. These villagers didn't even know about Anahita's presence, since she'd come from the east. Dalza scarcely spoke; she might be young and useful as a pleasure slave, but she didn't seem worth sending even one pursuer after her. And neither Eristi nor Shama looked worth fighting over, both well past their best childbearing years besides.

To pay this many men, and outfit them for what they'd need, took plenty of silver, far more than what three runaway women slaves were worth.

"Tell me, Eristi," he asked, "what did you do to your master? Why does he want you back so badly?"

"I told you, we ran away. We . . ."

"Don't lie to me," Eskkar said, shifting to face her. "These men would already be halfway back to their village if you'd only run away."

Eristi opened her mouth, then closed it, but she stared straight into his eyes. "What does it matter, Eskkar? You gave us your word, remember that."

It did matter, Eskkar knew, but now wasn't the time to argue with her. With a grunt, he turned back to watch the men. They'd stopped their arguing, and gathered around their leader, no doubt mulling over the best way to get onto the cliffs.

"Eristi!" The high-pitched shout came from Dalza, perched on one of the higher crags, where she could watch all the passages.

Eskkar twisted his head to look toward her. She raised her arm and pointed toward the south.

"Someone's coming!"

8

Sliding away from the cliff's edge, Eskkar moved across the rocks to a place where he could see whatever had alarmed Dalza. Crouching in the shadow of a boulder, he could make out a lone rider coming toward them. Eskkar stared at the approaching horseman. The man came from the southwest, not the direction from which the villagers besieging them had originated. As the man drew closer, Eskkar felt a moment of unease pass over him.

The stranger rode a large, powerful horse that stepped lightly despite the size and bulk of its load. Horse and rider made a smooth pair, the man relaxed and moving easily with his mount's motions. Eskkar soon focused on the man himself, especially the sword hilt protruding up over his shoulder.

Villagers didn't carry their short swords that way; they belted them at their waist. Only warriors, men trained to fight on horseback against other men armed with long sword or lance, carried their swords in that fashion.

A chilling insight passed over him. This was probably the man who'd led the band pursuing him from Nippur. Only a horseman, a former clansman like Eskkar himself, could have arranged such a swift pursuit, tracked their quarry, and nearly captured him. They would have taken him that night, he realized, if not for the fortunate encounter with the river pool and sudden onset of darkness.

Once Eskkar made his escape, the others had no doubt turned back, unwilling to continue the chase. This warrior had persevered, alone, circling around the long rocky spine to the south before heading back this way, to pick up Eskkar's trail once again. Sooner or later, the tracker would have caught up with him.

By now the slave hunters had also seen the rider's approach. Interrupted in their discussion, they fell silent and separated a little, fingering their weapons and forming a rough line that faced the stranger's path toward them. The horseman from the south never changed his gait, continuing to ride at a deceptively leisure pace that covered plenty of ground without tiring the horse, straight toward the band of men.

"Who is that, Eskkar?" Anahita asked. She'd followed him to see who approached.

"I'm not sure," he answered, but already the last shreds of doubt were fading from his mind. The man was a warrior, a warrior from the steppes, the same as Eskkar. Not quite the same, he realized.

This man was a powerful, seasoned veteran, in the prime of life, who'd clearly seen many battles, and not only with dirt-eaters. Even the way he approached the armed villagers showed his fearlessness; the men facing him sensed it, too, their nervousness apparent in the way they clutched at their weapons.

The warrior stopped a hundred paces from them, out of easy bowshot. When he spoke, his booming voice carried all the way to the cliffs, and Eskkar had no trouble hearing the man's words.

"My name is Cardal," he said. "I come from the village of Nippur, sent by their Elder, the Noble Maldar, to hunt down a murderer, a barbarian from the steppes. Have you seen any tracks made by a horseman?"

The leader of the villagers didn't answer right away, turning and speaking for a moment with the man beside him. Then he told his men to lower their bows, and stepped forward.

"My name is Shulgi," he called out, walking toward the horseman. "We come from the village of Senkereh," he pointed behind him toward the west, "hunting runaway slaves."

The stranger dismounted, and led his horse toward Shulgi, who matched his advance, moving away from his men. The two met and began speaking, but now their voices couldn't be heard. Eskkar swore at this latest misfortune.

"So this man hunts you, it seems," Eristi said, unable to keep the sarcasm out of her voice as she and Dalza arrived at Eskkar's vantage point. "Who else did you kill, I wonder?"

Eskkar ignored the question, still watching the two men as they exchanged greetings and, no doubt, information.

"What's one more man, Eskkar?" Anahita asked. "One more man cannot . . ."

"That man is . . . a warrior from the steppes," Eskkar interrupted. He'd almost said a real warrior, but he'd managed to choke off the cowardly word. "He's like . . . a battle-hardened veteran, someone who's seen a hundred fights and survived them."

Eskkar swore again. "He's probably more dangerous than all the rest. If he joins with them . . ."

"Can you not defeat him?" Anahita voice betrayed her doubts.

"I don't want to find out," Eskkar said. From this distance, Cardal looked as tall as Eskkar, and he carried more bulk on his frame. With his greater experience, he'd be a dangerous opponent.

The two men kept talking, with Shulgi occasionally gesturing toward the cliff. The conversation went on for some time, until even Eskkar began to grow impatient. When it ended, Eskkar's heart sank, and he swore again at his bad luck. The two men walked side-by-side back to the rest of Shulgi's men. Clearly, Cardal had decided to join the slavers' fight.

"Damn the gods." Eskkar didn't like it when his luck changed so swiftly, always a bad omen. If the stranger had arrived tomorrow, he would have likely found the villagers gone. Now all Eskkar had was the bow and – he counted the shafts remaining in the quiver – nine arrows.

"We'll have to change the plan. Eristi, you take Anahita with you, and defend the main passage. Dalza, you look like you can run the fastest. You take the farthest passage. You'll have to fight alone for a few moments. Just shove some rocks over the side and throw a few stones to slow them down. Can you do it?"

The girl nodded, her fingers clenched tight on a stone held in her hand.

"Good. Remember, you only need to delay them a few moments. Then get back here as quick as you can." He looked at Shama. "I'll need you and your sling here. Eristi, you and Anahita will hold the smaller passage. Slow them down as long as you can."

"What are you going to do?"

"It won't take them long to see that there are three likely ways up the cliffs. They'll probably split up into three groups. With Cardal there to help Shulgi drive his men, all three groups will push ahead. If they storm the three passages at the same time, they know we won't be able to stop them all."

Eskkar faced the women. "You need to slow them down. You won't be able hold them back, but you have to delay them. They only have three bows, so they'll probably have one archer in each group. Be careful you don't get shot. Meanwhile, I'll try and kill a few more, maybe enough to get some of the villagers to turn back."

He said the words calmly enough, and hoped his doubts didn't show on his face.

"The moment you can't hold them," he added, "use the boulders for cover and run to the second position."

That refuge, atop the second shelf, covered the main access from the first level. If the villagers ever reached the second level, they'd be on equal footing with the women, not looking up at them. The defenders only advantage, higher ground, would vanish.

Eskkar moved to the edge of the rock face and scrutinized his attackers. As he'd foreseen, they divided into three groups. Cardal took charge of three men. The remaining six split into two groups. Each party had a bowman, also as Eskkar expected.

Cardal took his force toward the main passage, the one to Eskkar's left, which was the easiest to traverse, but it also doubled back on itself, and would take more time, even with Cardal pushing the pace. The brunt of the attack, led by Shulgi, was going to fall on Dalza, and she wasn't going to delay them for long.

"Eskkar, shouldn't I go help Dalza," Shama said, obviously coming to the same conclusion. "She's not . . ."

"You'll help more here with your sling," he interrupted. "I need you to distract the men coming up this passage." He explained exactly what he wanted her to do. When he finished, he looked back toward the desert. The enemy was on the way, separating as they moved and walking purposefully toward the cliffs.

Eskkar went down into the central entrance, the bow in his hand. They'd slow their advance when they entered, expecting another ambush, and this time they'd be watching their front as much as the rocks above them.

The passage he entered was steep and narrow. Shadows covered almost all of it, but the bright sunlight overhead made the contrast down here even greater. Looking up, he saw Shama waving her hand. She pointed to where the intruders were, then disappeared. Eskkar waited, breathing hard, though he'd done nothing to exert himself yet. He recognized the tiny pinpricks of fear, and tried to block them.

One fight at a time, he said to himself, remembering his father's words. Don't count your enemy, boy, just kill the man in front of you. Eskkar hoped there would be enough time to get back to help the others.

He fitted an arrow to the string, and slipped a second shaft under the fingers of his left hand, the notch straight up so he could nock it quickly to the bowstring. Eskkar heard something scrape against the rocks, and knew the men were only a few paces away.

With a crash, rocks bounced down the passageway, glancing off the sides, as Shama pushed as many of the melon-sized rocks over the edge as she could. Without looking to see what happened below, she launched more than twenty stones, sending a small avalanche on the three approaching villagers that should make for an excellent diversion.

The moment he heard the first rocks sliding down, Eskkar rounded the boulder. The man in front, shield raised to fend off the rocks, saw the movement and jerked his shield back down.

It didn't matter. Eskkar fired his shaft, not at the man closest to him, but at the bowman bringing up the rear. The distance wasn't

much, but the shaft veered badly, either poorly aimed or mis-feath-
ered, striking the third man in the arm, even though he stood only
ten or twelve paces away.

Eskkar didn't hesitate. He strung the second shaft and … the
first villager was upon him, sword swinging at his head. Eskkar
flung himself to one side, and the sword struck the rock wall with a
clang and a spray of stone fragments. Eskkar kicked the man as he
passed, then turned and fired the arrow toward the second man.

But that villager swung his shield down, deflecting the shaft as
he rushed forward. Eskkar dropped the bow and barely had time to
snatch his sword from his shoulder before the man reached him.

The second villager swung his sword, then pushed forward with
the shield. Eskkar took a step back, then lunged forward. He used
his bulk against the shield, moving in closer and smashing it with
his right shoulder, knowing he had an enemy behind him.

The unexpected countermove drove the man back momentarily.
Whirling around, Eskkar found that the first man hadn't moved.
Instead, he began to drop slowly to the ground, stunned, a gush of
blood covering his face.

Eskkar caught a flash of movement overhead as Shama ran past,
her work done. The man he'd driven back regained his balance and
returned to the attack.

This time Eskkar had his footing, and he swung hard, the blow
crashing against the raised shield, then jumped back as the villager's counterstrike hissed past him. Eskkar's blade was already
moving, and he caught the man on the arm, Eskkar's sword crunching through flesh, spraying blood.

The wounded man cried out as he dropped his sword, lowering
the shield at the same time. With a flick of his wrist, Eskkar drove
the sword into the man's throat.

The wounded archer had fled, taking his bow with him. Eskkar
raced back, ignoring the dying man choking on his own blood. He
didn't even pause to run his sword through the chest of the man
Shama's stone had stunned. Eskkar scooped up the bow he'd dropped
and started climbing as fast as he could.

At the top, he heard men shouting and women screaming. Anahita and Eristi were rushing toward him on his left, and Dalza raced like a mountain goat across the shelf to his right. An instant later Eskkar saw men burst up out of both passages. One of the bowman fired at the two women, but the shaft missed the running targets.

Eristi and Anahita still had to cross an area that curved around the base of a boulder, and the bowman would have an easy shot. Eskkar stepped out from the shadow of the cliff, drew back a shaft, and let fly at Cardal.

Just as Eskkar loosed the missile, Cardal saw him, and flung himself to the ground. The arrow missed, and the big man was back on his feet almost without losing a step. He charged straight at Eskkar, carrying his round warrior's shield before him and shouting a war cry.

Behind Cardal, the remaining bowman turned to shoot at Eskkar, now standing exposed against the rock wall. Before the villager could draw his shaft, Eskkar loosed an arrow toward the enemy archer, who flung himself to the side. By then, the three women had scampered past Eskkar and up the passage leading to the second level.

Moving into the shadows, Eskkar launched another shaft at Cardal, now less than forty paces away. But the wily fighter, much closer now, began shifting his direction, weaving from side to side as he advanced behind his shield.

Eskkar fired a third arrow that missed everyone, then turned and ran up the ledge that led to the second level, wondering if he would get an arrow in his back before he reached the top. But he made it, and ducked behind a large boulder that formed one side of the passageway to the lower level.

Stones were flying down the opening, and even Cardal hesitated a moment as missiles whizzed past his head.

Shama had caught her breath and regained her sling. With a quick whirl, she snapped a stone straight down the passage. One of the villagers failed to dodge it, and cried out as the projectile struck him in the thigh.

Regaining his feet, Eskkar drew the bow, but a quick glance showed him no targets, at least for the moment. The villagers were shouting, an excited babble of voices, and Eskkar grunted to himself in satisfaction.

Warriors would have continued their rush up the passage, taken their wounds and overpowered the defenders before they could regroup. But villagers didn't fight that way. They needed time to think after every setback or advance, and get themselves prepared for the next effort.

He took a deep breath. "Men of Senkereh!" Eskkar called out. "You've lost two more of your brethren." One had only been wounded, but Eskkar wanted them to realize that nearly half their original force lay dead or injured. "Are a few slave women worth your deaths?"

"Give us the gold, and you can keep your slaves, barbarian." The deep voice filled with hatred must belong to Shulgi, the leader of the villagers.

Eskkar glanced at Eristi, standing there with a stone in each hand. She shook her head.

"There's no gold here," Eskkar shouted. "Would anyone with gold stay in this filthy place?"

"We have no gold, Shulgi" Eristi called out, answering the man below. "Whatever your master told you, it's not here."

No one answered, and the voices below took to whispering.

Damn these men to all the demons, Eskkar swore. They should have given up. Villagers usually didn't have the stomach for this kind of fighting and dying. But gold changed everything. Men would willingly risk their lives for the precious metal. With a good amount of gold at stake, they wouldn't back down.

And now that Shulgi and his villagers had Cardal there giving them backbone, they would give it one more push. And that, Eskkar thought, would bring them up here. He and the women had prepared no other place to fight from. They could retreat into the cave, but once inside there, they'd be trapped, with no food or water.

Or they could go beyond the cave, then down the path to the river. If they did that, the villagers and Cardal would simply go back and get their horses, and pursue them. With only one horse, they'd be run down in a less than half a day, caught out in the open.

A shout from below cut short his thoughts. A villager cried out, and Eskkar heard the noise as a man slid against the rocks. Curses erupted, echoing off the walls.

"Not too easy to climb these cliffs," Eskkar shouted. They must have boosted one man up on their shoulders, and hoped he could reach the top. That meant they were huddled somewhere, probably right beneath …

"Eristi," he whispered, "can you stand over there," Eskkar pointed toward the massive outcropping that likely sheltered the men below, "and throw stones straight up? Would they fall on that place below? Can you drop them straight down, without seeing where they go?"

Eristi took only a moment to comprehend what he wanted. "I can try. Dalza, come help me."

In a moment the two women moved across the top of the rock, their bare feet making no sound, pausing only long enough to gather a handful of good-sized rocks. While they prepared, Eskkar fitted another shaft to the bow, and made sure his sword slid easily in its sheath. He had four arrows left, but if his foes got past this passage-way and rushed him, the bow wouldn't be much use.

Eristi had readied herself, holding one rock with both hands, with Dalza kneeling at her feet, five stones in front of her. With a grunt, Eristi launched the stone into the air. It only went an arm's length up before it began to descend, and Eskkar heard it rattle against the cliff face.

Still, it would be going almost straight down, falling about ten paces, right about where the men might be standing. Before the first stone had time to land, Eristi had taken a second from Dalza's upraised hand and tossed that one as well.

In moments, all six stones had crashed down, and Eskkar heard a cry of pain and shouts of anger as the men suddenly had to dodge the heavy missiles falling from more than twenty feet above.

As soon as the first stone landed, Eskkar moved out into the open, standing exposed, hoping for Cardal or someone to attempt the passage. A man's shoulder came into view, trying to avoid the falling rocks. Eskkar had time to aim and release the shaft smoothly, and heard it smack hard into the man's upper arm.

The man let out a scream of pain. A hand reached out and dragged him back out of Eskkar's sight. It wasn't a killing shot, but another villager would probably be finished fighting for the day.

The women scrambled away to gather more stones. Eskkar didn't hear anyone else cry out, so they most likely hadn't managed to hit any more attackers. Still, the villagers would resume their assault at any moment, rather than stay where they were and dodge random stones.

Eskkar stepped back, covering the passage once again, but keeping mostly out of sight. Using his hands, he motioned to Eristi and Dalza to come back to the top of the corridor. He glanced at Anahita. She looked frightened, but nevertheless gripped a rock in each hand. Shama waited just behind Eskkar, her sling dangling at the ready.

"They'll be coming now." He kept his voice low. "Aim for their legs."

Without waiting for any reaction, Eskkar took a deep breath and burst across the top of the passageway. For two long strides he was in full sight of anyone aiming an arrow from below, and then he leaped, scrambling up the rock face, climbing higher and moving to the rear of the giant boulder forming the other side of the opening.

He heard the whirr-whirr of Shama's sling, and the hiss of an arrow that went past his head. Then he reached the perch he wanted, standing alone atop the boulder that overlooked the ledge. Two more steps let him position himself in the shelter of a huge slab of rock, a place where he could sweep the entire passage. Now the attackers would face danger from two directions.

With a shout, the villagers swarmed into the cleft, driven from behind by Shulgi and Cardal. The first two held their shields high for protection, the two remaining archers right behind. One of the shield bearers slipped halfway up the slope, either from the difficulty of the climb or struck by a flung stone.

The other pressed on, through a burst of rocks flung by the women. The first shield bearer had nearly reached the top when Eskkar put an arrow in his back.

Shulgi shouted a warning to his two bowmen, but before they could turn into the angled passage, find their footing, and launch an arrow, Eskkar shot one of the bowmen in the chest.

Eskkar bellowed his battle cry at the kill. Two men down with two shafts! A stone from Shama's sling brought down the other archer, and as that man slipped and fell, he knocked Cardal off his feet, sending both men sliding back down the slope.

Eskkar launched another arrow, this time at the scrambling Shulgi. The man jumped aside, but the shaft dug into his upper arm. He, too, lost his balance and tumbled backwards, out of Eskkar's sight.

Eskkar had only one arrow left, but he doubted anyone else would venture into the passage. They'd turn back now . . . a man appeared in the opening, his open mouth gaping up at Eskkar.

Without thinking, Eskkar took the shot, the arrow feathering itself in the man's chest. Only then did Eskkar realize the man was already dead or wounded, held upright by Cardal.

The instant the shaft landed, Cardal dropped the twice-dead man and rushed up the slope, a shield held before him. Either he knew Eskkar had shot his last shaft, or he counted on moving fast enough to avoid any more arrows.

Unlike the clumsy villagers, he scrambled up the steep gully with the speed and agility of a mountain lion, deflecting with his shield all the stones the women hurled at him. Before Eskkar had started moving, Cardal reached the top.

Scarcely slowed by the ascent, Cardal crashed into Eristi and kept moving, knocking Shama down before he turned. By then a long sword was in his hand. Anahita threw a stone at his head, but he dodged aside. She stooped to gather another stone, but Cardal reached out, grabbed her by the hair, and slammed her against the rock face.

By the time Eskkar could run back across the passage, Cardal had discarded his shield and stood with his back against the rock wall. His left arm encircled Anahita's body and the edge of his long knife pressed against her throat. The blade kept her pinned against his chest, using her as a shield, while his right hand swept his long sword from side to side.

Eskkar stopped, then turned to look down to the lower level. Shulgi, blood streaming from his head and arm, was being helped away by two of his men, the three of them heading back toward the desert floor.

"Your men are leaving you," Eskkar said.

"Useless dirt-eaters." Cardal paused to take a breath. "I only needed them to get me up here. Now you'll fight me, and after you're dead, I can take your head back to Nippur."

"I think I'll go collect some more arrows, then kill you." Eskkar moved slowly up the passage toward Cardal. "Dalza, are you there?"

"Yes, Eskkar," she answered from somewhere behind him, the fright plain in her voice.

"So your name is Eskkar. A warrior's name. Did you steal that, too?"

"Watch the men leaving," Eskkar called out to Dalza, ignoring Cardal's insult. "There should be at least four of them. Follow them to the main passage and watch from there. Let me know if any try to return."

Shama had regained her feet, and reloaded her sling. "I can hit his head."

Shama's words sounded weak, and Eskkar knew she hadn't recovered from Cardal's collision. A quick glance showed Eristi still lay where she'd fallen, knocked senseless.

"Raise that sling and I'll kill her and you, too," Cardal said calmly. He pulled the knife tighter against Anahita's throat. "Stop moving, girl, or I'll slit your throat." A thin trickle of blood ran down her neck, and Anahita, still half stunned, stopped trying to get loose.

"She's nothing to me," Eskkar said, trying to figure out what to do.

"Don't lie to me. You wouldn't have stayed and fought so many if they meant nothing."

"I gave them my word," Eskkar said, "to protect them from the villagers, not from you. But if you kill her, we'll kill you."

"Ah, a real warrior," Cardal said, his scorn sounding in his words. "Then give me your word, as a warrior, to fight me, man to man, and I'll let her go. If you're not afraid to face me. Are you afraid, *warrior*? Or just a coward who ran away from his clan?"

Eskkar felt the anger inside him, struggling with the challenge. Part of him wanted to battle Cardal sword to sword, but part of him wanted to get more arrows and finish him off. Eskkar knew he didn't have time for that. As soon as Eskkar moved, Anahita would die, and Shama a moment later. Even if she launched a stone, it probably wasn't going to stop a charging man Cardal's size. Unless she got lucky and hit him square between the eyes.

Cardal would be on Eskkar almost as quickly. By the time he found a usable arrow . . . he remembered how quickly Cardal had charged up the passage. And despite his greater bulk, he'd proved faster on his feet in these cliffs than Eskkar.

"I'll fight you, Cardal," he heard himself say, almost without volition.

"Good. Send them away, back into the rocks. "

"Go back to the cave, Shama" Eskkar said.

"Tell her to leave the sling, or I cut this one's throat," Cardal said. "I wouldn't want her sneaking around behind my back."

"I won't go," Shama said. "If he hurts Anahita, I'll kill him."

"Take Eristi back up the cliff. Leave the sling. It's me he wants, not you or Anahita."

Eristi moaned and pushed herself to a sitting position.

"Now, Shama, before he kills Anahita."

She flung the sling to the ground, and reached down to help Eristi to her feet. Shama slipped her arm around Eristi's waist and started walking. Shama moved past Cardal as if he didn't exist.

The moment the two women passed him, Cardal began moving to his left, still holding tightly to Anahita, who twitched helplessly under his thick arm, her eyes wide with fear.

Walking backward, sliding his feet across the rock so as not to slip and fall, Cardal dragged Anahita away from the gully to an open area, one out of sight of the cave and the trail above. As he passed Shama's sling, he kicked it over the edge of the cliff.

Eskkar followed him, the useless bow still in his hand. Cardal kept retreating, moving farther back, until he had another rock wall behind him.

"Come closer, Warrior Eskkar," Cardal said, the sneer back in his voice. "You've always wanted to prove yourself a warrior, haven't you? Now's your chance. Kill me, and you'll earn your name."

Eskkar reached over his shoulder and drew his sword. "Let her go now, or I will go back and get some arrows."

Anahita, too frightened to even speak, looked at him. Suddenly Cardal removed the knife from her throat. Before she could do more than gasp a breath of air, he struck her on the back of the head with the pommel of his sword. Stunned, she sagged to her knees, then fell on her side.

"There, just a little tap to keep her quiet," Cardal said. He slipped the knife back into its sheath, one handed, in a single smooth motion, without taking his eyes from Eskkar.

"Are you afraid to come to me, Eskkar?" He flexed the sword, twirling it in his hand. "Warrior to warrior? What clan are you from?"

Eskkar tossed the useless bow aside. "I was born into the Alur Meriki," Eskkar said, taking a cautious step toward his opponent.

"Those filth," Cardal said, spitting on the ground to show his disgust. "Cowards, all of them. I've killed plenty of those scum. They conquered my clan, the Mittani, by sheer force of numbers. They killed my parents and my woman. Those of us who survived, we all had to vow our allegiance to the mighty Alur Meriki."

When the Alur Meriki absorbed another clan, everyone had to swear fealty to their new clan.

"So you broke your oath," Eskkar said, testing his footing, readying himself for the coming attack.

"When I was on my knee, swearing allegiance to Maskim-Xul and his clan of women posing as men, I concealed a pebble in my hand."

"The gods don't approve of that," Eskkar said, digesting the information. An oath sworn while holding a stone meant nothing; that's why all such swearing was done open-handed.

"There are no gods, as I'm sure you've learned by now," Cardal said, "not for men like us." He took another step toward Eskkar. "I had to wait three months before I could kill my new leader of twenty and escape."

Cardal laughed at the memory. "The coward begged for mercy before he died, and lived just long enough to watch me ride off with his best horses. What drove you from the clan, Eskkar?"

"My father offended . . ."

The attack came with a rush, and Eskkar realized he'd been tricked into talking instead of readying himself. He jumped back a step and met the overhand stroke. The blades crashed together, and Eskkar felt the shock travel up his arm, raw power strong enough to beat down any defense in time.

Cardal never stopped his attack. With his blade locked against Eskkar's, Cardal's momentum and the brute strength of his arm knocked Eskkar backward and off balance. Eskkar knew better than to try and regain his footing. Instead he threw himself down onto the hard rock, but moving into his attacker, tangling himself into Cardal's legs.

Eskkar's jaw took the impact of Cardal's knee in the process. But Cardal stumbled as well, lurching forward onto one knee as he tried to regain his balance. Eskkar used the moment to roll away, rising to his feet and striking at Cardal.

However the man was fast, incredibly fast, and he'd already recovered his footing and poise. Cardal met Eskkar's stroke head on, and again the hammering bronze blades sent echoes throughout the rocks. Three more strokes and counter strokes followed, before Eskkar broke away, leaping to his right and rear at the same time, determined to stay as far away as possible from the man's sword arm.

Cardal gave him no time to rest. His next attack, smoothly delivered, didn't try to knock Eskkar down. Instead the blade slashed at Eskkar's head, but shifted toward his shoulder at the last instant.

Eskkar parried the blow, and counterthrust as hard as he could, trying to drive his blade right through the man's body. Cardal blocked that thrust and another, taking a half-step back to give him time to launch a counter attack of his own.

Using all the strength in his arm, Eskkar barely managed to deflect the thrust. He dodged away, again to his right and rear. Never had he fought an opponent as strong as Cardal. Eskkar knew he couldn't block many more thrusts like that, not unless he had time to swing his blade hard enough to deflect the man's rock-hard arm.

Eskkar shook the sweat from his eyes as he raised the suddenly heavy sword into the attack position. His heart pounded in his ears, as he gulped air into his chest. For the first time in his life, Eskkar felt the fear rising in his stomach.

"You're not bad for Alur Meriki filth," Cardal said.

This time Eskkar didn't wait to be caught off-guard. He launched his own attack, feinting toward the man's head, then ducking low and attempting to cut Cardal's knees out from under him. Cardal turned sideways for a moment, then lunged in, trying to drive his sword into Eskkar's neck before he could regain his balance.

It took every muscle in Eskkar's sword arm to block the thrust, but he deflected the weapon, then cut viciously at Cardal's head. Clank. Clank. Clank. The long blades met in the tiny space between the men, and once again Eskkar leapt back and to the right, always moving away from his opponent's sword arm.

"You're getting tired, Eskkar." Cardal grinned, ignoring the sweat that covered his brow. "I see the fear in your eyes and feel the weakness in your arm. You've been living with fat villagers and soft women too long."

Eskkar said nothing, taking another deep breath, ignoring the trembling in his right arm.

Suddenly he knew he couldn't win this fight, not by strength or skill. There had to be another way. Something else . . . perhaps . . . Eskkar attacked again, using every last bit of his strength, trying to break through the wall of bronze Cardal wove like a shield around him. Clank. Clank. Clank.

Grunting, Eskkar leapt away, starting toward his right as he'd done each time before. But this time, he gambled. His movement to the right was the briefest of feints. With a shift of his body, Eskkar flung himself back to his left, moving directly under Cardal's sword, the sword that appeared ready to split him in half.

But Cardal, too, had anticipated Eskkar's backward move, and Cardal's stroke was aimed not at where Eskkar had been, but where he expected Eskkar's body to be. As a result, he'd turned sideways, leaving a tiny part of himself exposed, if only for an instant.

Crashing down on one knee, Eskkar thrust up with his sword, the tip penetrating beneath Cardal's right armpit at least a hand's length. Eskkar stayed down, rolling away, as Cardal's sword crashed onto the rock where Eskkar's head had just been, spraying rock chips into the air.

Eskkar pushed himself to his feet, as Cardal moved toward him. Eskkar braced himself for Cardal's attack, but then the man's sword slipped from his hand. Blood poured down Cardal's right side, already drenching his tunic.

Cardal bent down for the sword, but his right arm was dead and his hand refused to grasp the weapon. He drew his knife with his left hand and rushed at Eskkar. As Eskkar struck down with his sword, Cardal launched himself headfirst through the air, like a human spear. Eskkar's stroke deflected the knife, but Cardal's shoulder slammed into him, knocking Eskkar backward and pinning him against the rocky ground.

Eskkar dropped his useless sword, and caught Cardal's left hand with his right before the man could plunge his weapon into Eskkar's chest. Despite his wound, Cardal was strong, unbelievably strong, and Eskkar had to use both hands to hold the knife at bay, its tip trembling a finger's length above his chest. Using all his strength, Eskkar started to push the knife back, when Cardal's knee smashed into his groin.

Eskkar cried out, but despite the agony didn't let go of Cardal's wrist. Instead he rolled his body, pushing Cardal onto his side. At the same time, Eskkar brought up his foot, forcing it under his opponent's hip. Then, shoving with all his weight and every muscle he possessed, Eskkar flung Cardal aside.

Gulping air into his burning lungs, Eskkar fumbled for his sword, never taking his eyes off Cardal, who still had the knife in his hand. But the warrior wasn't trying to get up; instead, he pushed himself back against the rock face. He, too, had to catch his breath for a moment.

"Well, Eskkar," he said, "you're not . . . as stupid . . . as you look."

Eskkar had to take another breath before he could answer. "You talk too much, Cardal." He wanted to say more, but didn't know what.

The man looked up at Eskkar, his eyes blinking, moving back and forth. Blood still spilled from his wound, staining the rocks a bright red, and Eskkar knew the man was bleeding to death.

"Maldar offered me . . . ten gold coins for your head." He coughed, a deep, racking cough that spit blood all over the front of his tunic. When he recovered, his eyes looked up at the sky and then rapidly down at the ground. Cardal raised his voice to a near-shout. "Though he may get your head yet, I . . ."

Eskkar heard the faint *whirr* behind him, nearly concealed by Cardal's loud words. Eskkar jumped aside.

The rock hummed past his head, so close Eskkar felt the wind as it passed. Shama stood there, facing him from the top of the same boulder where Eskkar had stood before. As he stared at her, she fitted another stone into the mouth of her sling.

"Shama," Eskkar said, slow to comprehend the attack. Only moments ago they had fought together. "What are you doing?"

"You need to die, Eskkar," she spat, "just like all the rest. We need no men to rule us." She spun the sling over her head, kept it spinning, keeping him waiting, off-balance, never knowing when . . .

The stone flew at him, and he leaped away. This one grazed his arm as it passed.

Eskkar couldn't stay here, only fifteen paces away, and with a rock wall as his back. Shama would knock him senseless sooner or later. He'd have to charge straight at her, which meant crossing the gap between them and then trying to climb up the boulder right in the face of her sling.

Again Shama whirled the sling overhead, readying for another attack. Before she could loose the stone, arms wrapped around her, dragged her backwards, and then flung her to the side, toward the boulder's edge. With a scream of rage, Shama landed on the slope of the rock, going down on her knees and still clutching the sling.

But the slope was steep there. When Shama tried to crawl back up, she lost her grip and slid farther off the top of the boulder, her hands scraping for purchase on the smooth surface. With a scream, she slipped over the boulder's edge.

The scream was cut short by a dull crunch echoing up from the passageway ten paces below.

Eskkar stared at Dalza, who stood there, breathing hard and looking at him, a smile peeking through the wild tangle of her hair. Her braids had come undone, and she looked different, almost a stranger.

Another cough made Eskkar twist around, sword upraised.

Cardal shook his head in disgust. "You have a fool's luck . . . Warrior." Blood now covered most of his right side and spread slowly over the hard rock.

Eskkar moved closer, gripping the sword at the ready.

"I'm finished." Cardal coughed again. When he stopped, he dropped the knife from his hand and pushed it away. "When I saw her moving in behind you, I guessed she wanted you dead as well."

Another spasm of coughing passed over the man, and it took a few moments before he could speak.

"You'll bury me . . . deep in the earth, not leave me in these rocks for the carrion birds." He stared up at Eskkar's face. "You owe me that much."

"I'll bury you, Cardal," he answered. Eskkar accepted that the debt must be paid, the debt for Eskkar's true passage into the ranks of the warriors.

"There's gold wrapped in . . . the horse blanket," Cardal whispered, his voice weakening. "Take it . . . and my horse. Bury me with my sword."

Eskkar nodded. He knew the burial ritual.

Cardal sighed, and closed his eyes for a moment. When he opened them, all he could manage was a whisper, and Eskkar had to lean close to hear Cardal's final words. "Always watch your back, Warrior . . . even in victory. Remember that."

The eyes closed again and his breathing slowed, became more labored, and then stopped. Cardal's head sagged onto his chest. A brave warrior had died, but died with honor. For a moment, staring at the body, Eskkar wondered where and how his own life would end. Probably not with as much honor as Cardal's.

He turned to find Dalza behind him. Shama's sling dangled from her hand. "She's dead. Landed on her head, and broke her neck. The villagers rode off, they're gone." Dalza gestured at Cardal. "You defeated him."

Eskkar shook his head. "No, I tricked him. Otherwise he was too good for . . ."

"If he was so good, then he shouldn't have been tricked," she said.

Her quick words surprised him. She hadn't spoken that much to anyone since he'd reached the cave.

Dalza smiled impishly at him through the mass of brown hair, as if all the day's killings and Shama's death had never happened. "What do we do now, Eskkar?"

Eskkar lifted his eyes to the sun. The fighting, which had seemed endless, had taken only part of the afternoon. He looked around, wondering, in fact, what to do. A few paces away, Anahita stirred, moaning as she recovered her senses. There was no sign of Eristi. He looked down at Dalza.

"How is Eristi?"

"I'm not sure. She's probably still unconscious, wherever Shama had left her."

"Help Anahita first, then find Eristi," he told Dalza. "I need to find Cardal's horse."

He started to walk past her, but Dalza reached out and caught his arm. "If you leave, take me with you," she said, looking straight into his eyes. "I don't care what the others decide. I don't want to stay here."

This time not only her words surprised him, but the thoughts behind them. She'd said little more than yes or no to anyone since he'd arrived, and scarcely met his eyes. He'd thought her half-witted, or slow at best.

Now her words revealed something harder beneath the surface. She had attacked Shama with both skill and bravery, slipping up behind her and then hurling the older and stronger woman over the edge.

"I'm not leaving, not yet."

He scooped up the bow from where he'd dropped it, and went down the gully to the first level. Eskkar moved along the shelf until he could see the patch of ground on the desert floor where the villagers had camped. Men, wounded, horses, they were all gone.

Damn his luck, Eskkar swore. He'd hoped the villagers, in their flight, might leave one or two of their horses behind. But not even panic-stricken villagers were stupid enough to leave a valuable horse behind.

Movement caught his eye. Three hundred paces to Eskkar's left, a single horse remained, walking about un-tethered. Cardal's horse. Eskkar scanned the desert, but the battle's survivors had already crossed over the horizon in their haste to get away from the deadly cliffs. Only the corpses remained.

As he descended, Eskkar gathered up all the loose arrows he spotted, checking each one and only retaining those that looked sound. Arrows tended to shatter when they struck stone, or the barb broke loose, requiring precious time and tools to repair.

Still and all, when he reached the desert floor, Eskkar had five good arrows in the quiver at his hip, and he carried the bow in his hand.

Despite their rush to get away, the villagers hadn't left behind anything useful, and for a moment he wondered why they hadn't chased after Cardal's horse. Either they couldn't catch the animal, or . . . then he realized they didn't know Cardal had died. They might have feared he would come after them to get his horse back.

And rightly so, Eskkar decided. Sooner or later, the warrior would certainly have tracked down and killed anyone who took his mount.

The horse, a large, gray-colored stallion with jagged white markings spread over its back between the neck and flanks, had a dark mane, tail, and legs. It regarded Eskkar suspiciously as he approached, then snorted when it caught the scent of Cardal's blood on Eskkar's torn and filthy tunic. Nostrils flaring, it trotted off, moving away about fifty paces, while Eskkar stood still, knowing the animal would bolt if he tried to run after it.

The horse wandered a few more steps before it finally stopped, lowered its head, and tested a clump of grass. Eskkar remained immobile, talking softly the whole time so the stallion could get used to his voice. Then he began walking toward it. The horse lifted his head with another snort, and trotted off again.

The stubborn beast and Eskkar repeated this ritual five more times, moving further away from the cliffs, before the animal let Eskkar get close enough to reach out and catch hold of the halter. Taking his time, he stroked the horse's back, using soft and gentle movements and speaking to it in the language of the steppes. Eskkar's voice might be different, but the words were the same ones Cardal would have used, the secret sounds all clansmen used to control their mounts.

At last the horse's ears ceased their twitching, and the animal relaxed under Eskkar's touch. He fingered the blanket tied loosely around the horse's neck, thinking about the gold concealed within, but didn't bother to open it. At last Eskkar took up the slack in the halter rope and walked the animal back toward the cliff.

Its hooves clattering, Eskkar led the animal to the upper level of the rocks, where he found the three women waiting for him in the shade from the cliff.

Eristi remained on the ground, a bloodstained cloth on her head and a dazed look in her eyes. Anahita pushed herself to her feet, though she started swaying, and Dalza took her arm as they faced him.

"Are they gone?" Anahita's throat still showed traces of blood from Cardal's knife.

"Yes," he said. "They left only the horse."

"Then its over, thank the gods."

"For now," Eskkar agreed. "But others may return in their stead. They'll believe the rumors of bags of stolen gold, and more will come hunting it." Gold drew dirt-eaters like flies to a rotting corpse.

"There is no gold," Eristi said, not bothering to lift her eyes.

"They said you had gold. They must have some reason to think so."

"There is no gold," Eristi repeated.

He shrugged. Eristi could keep whatever gold she'd stolen. He had no interest in it, especially if it brought a horde of villagers on Eskkar's trail. Whatever gold lay hidden in Cardal's blanket would be more than enough for him.

"They'll come anyway, perhaps not soon, but they'll come. You know what happened to Shama?"

"Dalza told us," Eristi said. "Shama's hatred clouded her mind."

Eskkar nodded. "She fought well." He resisted the temptation to speak ill of the dead. "Why did Shama want to kill me? I never did anything . . ."

Eristi sighed. "Shama distrusted all men. She had suffered much abuse."

"Are you leaving us?" Anahita, still weak and unsteady, leaned on Dalza for support.

"My oath to you is fulfilled, and I still have my own enemies to worry about. In the morning, I'm riding south. I plan to put plenty of distance between me and both these cursed villages. But if any of you wish to go with me, I'll take you."

"I will go with you," Dalza said.

No one else said anything, which suited Eskkar well enough. "I have to bury Cardal before nightfall." He took up the horse's halter again and led the animal across the rocky shelf over to Cardal's body, talking to calm the stallion. "Dalza, can you hold the halter for me?"

With Dalza's help, Eskkar finally got Cardal's weight balanced across the horse's back, grunting with the effort required to lift the heavy body. Eskkar tied the dead man securely, talking soothingly to the stallion the whole time.

Satisfied the body wouldn't fall off, Eskkar led the horse back down toward the desert. Dalza accompanied him, carrying Cardal's sword and knife. Eskkar took his time negotiating the rocky surfaces, leading the skittish horse down through the twists and inclines, and making sure the body didn't slip off. When they reached the flat ground, even the horse snorted its relief.

Eskkar retraced his steps out among the grassy dunes, back to the place where the stallion had finally allowed itself to be captured, guessing that the gods might approve of this spot as a burial ground.

Without his asking, Dalza knelt beside him and helped dig the grave, using a stick to shift the loose surface sand, then digging into the harder packed earth below. It took time, since Eskkar wanted a deep enough hole, and Cardal had plenty of bulk.

Finally they rolled the body into the grave. Eskkar closed the dead man's eyes and straightened out his limbs. A proper burial required washing the dead, but that was woman's work, and couldn't be done here, with no source of water.

Eskkar used his knife to cut a square of cloth from Cardal's tunic, large enough to cover the dead man's face. That would keep the earth from soiling the warrior's eyes and mouth. Then Eskkar laid Cardal's sword on his chest, hilt just under his chin, and folded the man's arms over his weapon.

For a moment Eskkar considered taking the sword, a fine weapon much better than Eskkar's own. Even if he didn't use it himself – Cardal's weapon was heavier and a bit longer than Eskkar's, and he preferred the lighter blade – it would fetch a good price at any market.

In the end, though, Eskkar decided not to chance the gods' anger. Cardal had given him more than enough when he named Eskkar a warrior. From now on, all the duties of a warrior would be his. Foremost of those, of course, was honor.

After they'd filled the grave, Eskkar struggled with some large rocks, rolling and heaving them until a line of boulders lay atop the burial place. Dalza blocked the open spaces with smaller stones, and they finished by pushing a mound of sand over everything, nearly obscuring the rocks.

When they stood up, dirty and covered with sand, Eskkar felt satisfied the grave was well protected from the desert animals that would soon come hunting.

"Thank you, Dalza," Eskkar said. He hadn't ordered or asked her to help, and she'd worked hard beside him.

She shrugged. "I saw that burying him meant something to you. Just remember to take me with you when you leave."

They returned to the cliffs, the horse now used to their presence and following behind them. Eskkar settled the stallion in the tiny cul-de-sac that already served to hold his own mount. By then the sun's edge had touched the distant horizon.

"I'm going to the river to wash off the blood," he told the women. He followed the twisting trail back up past the cave and down to the ledge he'd crawled from only two days ago.

This time he jumped right in, submerging himself in the cold water. Eskkar stripped off his tunic and undergarment, and washed the blood and sweat from them, before tossing them back up on the ledge.

Despite the chill, he remained in the water and scrubbed himself thoroughly, feeling really clean for the first time in days. Just as he was about to pull himself out, he looked up to see Dalza standing on the edge, two blankets from the cave draped over her arm. She dropped them against the rock wall.

"Stay there," she said, then pulled her dress over her head and tossed it down beside the blankets.

Mouth open, he stared up at her. He'd thought her young, perhaps not even past the puberty rites, but the body that displayed itself above him belonged to a young woman. Pointed breasts with pink nipples jutted out over a firm stomach, guiding his gaze past the curve of her hip to a thick patch of curly hair beneath.

For a moment she stood there, letting him look at her, then Dalza smiled and jumped in beside him.

She squealed at the cold water, then ducked beneath the surface. When Dalza came up, hair flying, she moved toward him and placed her hands on his shoulders. She smiled up at him, then pressed the length of her body against his. He felt hard nipples rubbing against him as she gave a sigh of contentment.

"Anahita isn't coming," she said.

He stared at her, wondering how she'd guessed his thoughts. Eskkar had thought . . . hoped . . . that Anahita would seek him out. He'd fought for her, saved her life more than once.

"I saw the way you looked at her," Dalza said, shivering a little from the cold. "It will take time before Anahita gets over her grief at Shama's death."

"Shama . . . were they kin?"

Dalza laughed, the cheerful sound echoing against the rocks. "No, not kin. But they were . . . close." She shook her head as if mystified at his blank look, then pushed away, splashing about as she washed herself.

"Help me up," she said when she finished, her body already shivering from the cold water.

Still in a daze, Eskkar swept her into his arms, holding onto her for a moment as he enjoyed the feel of her body, before lifting her completely out of the water and onto the ledge. By the time he'd pulled himself out, she was already drying herself with the blanket, rubbing the rough fabric over her body.

But in a moment she began drying him vigorously with the cloth, wiping the water from his chest and back. Finally she leaned forward and pressed the blanket over her wet hair, using it to squeeze the river's moisture from the long strands.

Eskkar stood there, fascinated at her movements and unable to take his eyes off her body.

When Dalza finished, her hands brushed lightly over his now fully erect penis, lingering long enough to turn him rock hard, despite the chill. She stopped only to spread the other blanket on the ground, then pulled him down beside her, gathering the wet one over their bodies. Once under the blanket, a delicious warmth flowed through Eskkar's body, as Dalza squirmed and wiggled herself as close to him as possible.

"Now you must take your reward, warrior," she said, smiling provocatively at him as she nestled in his arms, still shivering from the cold, but holding fast to his manhood. She moaned when he cupped her breast, arching her back and closing her eyes with pleasure.

"And I promise you," she opened her mouth wide and kissed him, a long, lingering kiss that made him feel weak all over, "I promise you will forget all about Anahita."

9

The next morning, Eskkar and the three women walked the two horses out of the cliffs and headed south. In addition to Dalza, Anahita and Eristi had accepted his offer to travel south. As they passed Cardal's grave, Eskkar halted and looked back toward the rock walls gleaming in the sun.

This place, the events of the last few days, had changed him. He'd lived for years among the dirt-eaters, and survived. But no matter what respect, or more likely, fear they showed toward him, the nagging voice in his head had always reminded him that he wasn't a true warrior, that he'd never passed through the rites of manhood. Hence Eskkar had missed the highest goal for any young man – to be accepted by his clansmen and kinsmen as one of their own.

That feeling had vanished with Cardal's last breath, and the man's burial had completed Eskkar's duty as a warrior. If he died tomorrow, Eskkar could face his father in the spirit world with honor, and hold his head high among the ghosts of the warriors.

Somehow, he knew that was important, that his father would have wanted nothing more from his first born son, not even the vengeance Eskkar had sworn against his former clan.

A pair of jackals moved cautiously toward the cliffs, the blood smell on the wind leading them on. Vultures and the smaller carrion birds still circled the air, while others no doubt continued pecking and tearing at the unburied slave hunters' corpses. Today, without the annoying interruptions from those still living, the birds and small scavengers would have the dead bodies all to themselves, a desert feast.

"You must be glad to be leaving this place." Anahita sat uneasily on Eskkar's horse, watching Eskkar gaze at the cliffs.

"Yes," he replied, pushing aside all thoughts of the spirit world. He shifted his eyes away from the past and looked to the south.

"First you and the others tried to kill me, then Cardal nearly did, and Shama's stone almost took my head off." He shook his head. "I only hope never to see these hills again."

"The Goddess Ishtar brought you here, remember that," Anahita said.

Eskkar grunted but said nothing, though he wished he had the courage to tell her what he thought of her goddess. Instead he started walking south, leading his horse by the halter. His eyes wandered toward Dalza, who led the other horse while Eristi clung precariously to its mane.

The four of them made a strange procession. For each of the next three days, they managed only ten or twelve miles between dawn and dusk. The rugged countryside hindered their progress, and Eskkar spent most of his time showing the women how to ride or helping them get back on when they fell off.

The slow pace made Eskkar nervous. He glanced back over his shoulder at every delay, half-expecting to see riders on his trail, and longing to put the two horses to an occasional canter.

Neither Eristi nor Anahita had ever been astride even a plow horse. Finding themselves on the back of a big stallion made their eyes go wide with fear.

Naturally the horses sensed their riders' trepidations and took as much advantage as they could. They resisted commands, or suddenly broke into a trot or gallop, a pace that left the women clutching the horses' necks, while they shrieked with fright.

As for Dalza, it didn't surprise Eskkar that she knew something about riding. After three long nights of lovemaking, nothing about the woman – he no longer thought of her as a girl, despite her years – would ever surprise him again.

Dalza came to him every night. After eating whatever food they'd managed to find during the day's ride, he and Dalza would take their blankets and move twenty or thirty paces away from the campfire, leaving Eristi and Anahita to watch the horses.

Since that first time at the river, Eskkar burned with fire for Dalza's body. During the day, he found himself looking at her again and again, unable to keep his eyes from her, imagining the feel of her body and the way she hungered for his manhood. He no longer cared that she satisfied her own needs as well. Their lovemaking went on long into the night, until they fell asleep, exhausted, in each other's arms.

Eskkar had never experienced a woman like Dalza, never been with a woman who enjoyed the love act so much, who wanted to prolong it as long as possible, and repeat it as often as she could coax his response. She soon knew every part of his body, and how to excite him no matter how tired or spent. And in her passion, she had no qualms about telling him what she wanted him to do, to increase her pleasure.

Each morning at dawn, they returned to the campfire as if they'd never left, and continued their journey. As the days passed, Anahita and Eristi lost their fear of the horses, and the little cavalcade picked up the pace. The women learned to move their bodies as they rode, and so help the horse carry them. All of them took turns walking, but each day, they spent more time riding.

Eristi, who knew something about the land, spoke often with Eskkar and they worked out a route that bypassed the first five or six villages, the ones closest to Senkereh. A group of women, let alone one led by a barbarian horseman, would have attracted everyone's interest and stay fresh in their memory.

For their own reasons, neither Eskkar nor Eristi wanted any such notice taken, so they sought out the ways less frequented, where they would encounter fewer fellow travelers. Should anyone later come seeking information about them, the less people who knew of Eskkar's passing, the better.

All the same, riding alone through the mostly desolate lands brought another danger. The horses and the women would be a tempting prize if they encountered any bandits or robbers. To prepare for that, Eskkar taught Dalza how to use the bow, and both Eristi and Anahita took turns practicing with the sling. They might not count for much in a fight, but as he'd learned in the cliffs, even a small effort could swing the tide of battle.

For once Eskkar's luck held. The occasional traveler or farmer they encountered, after the first glance, paid them little heed; even the most ignorant dirt-eater knew no barbarian rode out to loot and plunder accompanied by three women.

When they did meet other wayfarers, Eskkar let Eristi do all the talking. She reluctantly doled out a few copper coins, taken from a pouch she wore beneath her dress, to buy all the food they needed. Eskkar ate enough for two men, as much to keep his strength up for the night's lovemaking as to make up for all the meals lost in the last ten or twelve days.

Nine days after leaving the cliffs, they saw the smoke from the village of Keolas in the distance. They'd traveled in safety almost a hundred and fifty miles from their starting point. Even Eristi breathed a sigh of relief at the sight. No one in these parts would recognize any of them.

Nestled against the western bank of the Euphrates River, Keolas was larger than most of the usual farming villages. Eskkar guessed that about five or six hundred dirt-eaters lived there, making it the largest village he'd ever seen.

The river made the difference, he decided. The expanded water supply for the growing fields, coupled with easy trade routes for the tiny boats moving up and down the river, allowed Keolas to grow larger than any mere farming community. A ragged and peeling fence as tall as Eskkar encircled almost half of the huts, providing protection within for both man and beast.

As he and the women soon learned, three Elders ruled Keolas, and they'd established a company of guards to patrol the village, watching for petty thieves and protecting the local merchants, at least those who paid for the service. Naturally, as Eristi explained the process to Eskkar, the Elders made sure that all their own houses and properties received the most protection.

Those guards gave Eskkar a hard glare as he rode up to Keolas's entrance, and he was forced to tell the story he and the women had concocted. With Eristi's assistance, Eskkar explained that these were his women, and that he was a peaceful man searching only for a place to stay for a few days, before moving on.

The guard looked unimpressed, until Eristi offered him a copper coin for his "help." It took a second coin before he grudgingly waved them in, warning Eskkar to cause no trouble.

Once inside, Eskkar received the usual stares. People gaped at his tall figure, the long sword jutting over his shoulder, even the big horses bred for carrying a warrior across the steppes. Not withstanding, Keolas had many strangers, all of them busy with their private business, and after a few days, his strangeness wore off, and even Eskkar caused no further undue attention.

Eristi found a decent inn and managed to rent a room big enough for the four of them at a reasonable rate. The first order of business was getting rid of Cardal's horse. The big stallion was too noticeable, and too tempting a target for horse thieves.

Eskkar and Eristi took the animal to the market, and while Eskkar found a place to stand and show the horse, Eristi walked the stalls, calling out that a magnificent stallion was for sale, and encouraging those who might be tempted to buy. A merchant wandered over to examine the horse, then another. Each offered a few silver coins, far short of the animal's worth, and Eskkar simply shook his head.

He knew better than to try to haggle with them. Merchants had years of experience in just that very occupation, and trying to bargain with them would be a waste of time. In his experience, the more Eskkar tried to bargain, the lower the price would drift. Fortunately, Cardal's horse spoke more eloquently than any words Eskkar could have uttered.

Soon another man joined the first two, and then a fourth, and finally one wearing the colors of one of the nobles arrived. Eristi had finished combing the market, and she took over the negotiations, leaving Eskkar little to do except to keep the big horse soothed. By now a good-sized crowd had gathered, everyone shouting out comments or advice, or heckling the bidders.

To Eskkar's surprise, it wasn't the noble's steward who finally met Eristi's price, but one of the merchants. He offered one gold coin and ten silver ones, and even Eskkar felt that to be a fair payment.

The exchange was made. Eskkar had to swear on Marduk's image that the horse wasn't stolen, and then he had to pay two silver coins to the noble who "permitted" the market to operate. By the time they left the crowded marketplace, Eskkar's nerves turned edgy, and he already felt the urge to climb on his own horse and ride back to the open countryside.

Dalza's promising smile changed his mind. She took his hand for a moment when he and Eristi returned from the auction. The four of them ate a good meal that night, tearing apart two chickens, plenty of fresh bread, warm vegetables soaked in oil, and everything washed down with decent ale. A plate of plump dates gave them something to nibble on afterwards, as they relaxed for the first time in almost fifteen days.

Stretching out his second cup of ale, Eskkar leaned back against the wall. A full belly topped with plenty of good ale made him relax as much as he ever did. "Well, Eristi, the horse is gone. Now what have you planned?"

She frowned at him, and it took a moment before he remembered her instructions regarding her new name. In front of others, Eristi had become "Shubure," and Anahita's new name was "Inanna." They might have traveled far from their troubles, but it behooved them not to take any chances.

No one knew Eskkar's name, so he hadn't bothered taking a new one. Dalza claimed she had no need to change her name, which made Eskkar suspect that she'd already taken a new name before reaching the cliffs.

"Tomorrow we'll begin looking for an inn or shop to buy, something that Anahita and I can manage," Eristi said. "Keolas is a growing village, and many new huts have been built, so I'm sure we'll find something. Once we find what we need, we'll settle in. If you can stay with us for a month or so, Eskkar, that would be helpful."

He nodded. They'd gone over this before. If the gold from the sale of the horse didn't cover all Eristi's expenditures, it would be supplemented by whatever gold she'd brought from the cliffs. The villagers wouldn't notice that.

"Still, the horse was Eskkar's prize," Dalza said. "And I think he should have a bigger share of its profits."

"We all fought together, and half the price is enough for me," Eskkar said, sipping at his ale. A true warrior wouldn't waste his time arguing over a bigger share of the coins from the sale of a slain warrior's horse. He had already agreed to wait a few days for that share. Besides, no one knew about the gold coins sewn into the blanket.

Eristi wanted to use the local coins to establish her venture in Keolas, rather than gold no doubt stolen from the village up north. Merchants, it seemed, had an uncanny knowledge about what gold came from which merchant.

"Well, Eristi," Dalza went on, "then perhaps you and Anahita won't mind if Eskkar and I get a separate room."

Eskkar hadn't thought that far ahead, but now he realized that four of them sleeping in one chamber would be a little crowded. Not that he cared about taking Dalza with the others watching, or at least listening, but with so much gold and silver in their possession, the extra copper for another chamber seemed reasonable.

No one said anything, and Eskkar nodded approval.

"Then I'll arrange it," Dalza said, rising from the table with a smile and wiping her fingers on her dress.

Eskkar's eyes followed her as she walked away, aware that others in the tavern were doing the same thing. He frowned at the sight. Dalza might be lissome enough, but Anahita was more attractive, yet drew less notice. Dalza, however, seemed to enjoy the attention. He found it hard to remember her as the always silent girl from the cliffs.

"Be careful with her, Eskkar," Eristi said, noticing the frown. "Dalza will attract men like bees to honey, and trouble is bound to . . ."

"I'll take care, then," he said, rising to his feet with a laugh, already thinking ahead to the private room and the coming night's pleasures. Eskkar slung his blanket over his shoulder. "Tomorrow we'll find you a good inn or tavern to buy."

Flashing eyes or not, he didn't expect anyone to approach Dalza. Few men would be willing to challenge someone of Eskkar's size and bulk over a mere woman, no matter how flirtatious she might appear.

Across the room, Dalza handed the innkeeper a coin, concluding the arrangement, and waited for Eskkar to follow.

Eristi and Anahita rose with him. Women alone in an inn at night meant only one thing, and while the two women might have liked to stay and linger over their own ales, neither wanted to stay without Eskkar's presence.

By then, Eskkar had forgotten them. Dalza led the way to the rear of the inn, entering a small, windowless room through a flimsy door, the tiny chamber barely large enough for the narrow bed it contained.

Faint light came dimly through the chinks in the wood and reed ceiling that let in a few rays of moonlight. A crooked stick across the door provided the only security. Eskkar guessed a child could have pushed down the whole barrier. Better than nothing, he decided, after fastening the door, and dumping his blanket on the floor, he unbuckled his sword belt.

He drew the blade from its sheath and set it on the floor next to the bed. Eskkar heard the whisper of Dalza's dress as she drew it over her head. A moment later, she was in his arms, her naked body hot against his chest. She helped him undress, and they eased themselves onto the lumpy bed, first making sure it could hold their weight without a collapse.

"Tomorrow you'll buy me a new dress," Dalza said, running her hands across his chest and stomach. "And a necklace. I think . . . she bent down to kiss him, letting her breasts with their hard nipples tease him, back and forth, as she held his mouth to hers, ". . . I think you owe me at least that much, warrior." She reached down and grasped his manhood, by now stiff and ready.

"The best dress in town," Eskkar promised her, his voice hoarse with passion. He put his arms around her waist, and urged her to climb atop him. They moaned in unison as they joined.

"Then I'll make sure I please you tonight," she said, leaning down and biting his ear, "though you feel so big inside me I may not be able to walk in the morning."

"I'll carry you about the market, Dalza," he said, cupping her breasts in his hands, enjoying the feel of her warm flesh, "if I'm not too sore to walk myself."

"Eskkar. Eskkar! Wake up!"

He forced his eyes open. There wasn't much light in the chamber, but he saw the morning sky through the chinks in the roof. Eristi stood there, just inside the doorway. He pushed himself to a sitting position. "Where's Dalza?" His voice sounded rough, a croak even to his own ears.

After their first bout of lovemaking, Dalza had returned to the inn's common room for more ale. They'd drunk that quickly enough, then she'd pleasured him a second time, using her mouth to drive him to a near frenzy. Finally she mounted him yet again, and rode him long into the night, teasing him, then slowing her movements, until he thrust so hard into her that he thought he would burst from the effort.

After that, they fell asleep, Dalza burying her face and hair in his chest. Eskkar had slept soundly, long past the dawn, and hadn't awakened even when Dalza got up.

"I haven't seen her," Eristi said. "I heard you snoring, and thought I'd better wake you. It's already well past dawn."

Eskkar stood up, though the sudden movement made his head hurt. Too much ale, he thought. He pulled his tunic over his body, fumbling with the garment.

"You should wash, Eskkar. We'll be walking about in the hot sun all day, and . . ."

"Yes, I will," he muttered. He reached for the sword and buckled it around his waist. Then he noticed his dagger was missing. "My knife . . . where is Dalza?"

He peered under the bed, even dragging the wobbly frame away from the wall. Eristi helped search, but the knife was gone. He lifted the blanket roll containing his belongs, though he couldn't imagine how the knife might have gotten inside. But the blanket felt different . . .

The strings holding the ends together remained fastened, but looser than Eskkar ever tied them. Moving quicker now, he unrolled the blanket, ignoring the few articles it contained, his fingers moving awkwardly along the hem, feeling . . . the gold coins were gone!

Someone had slit the hem and taken Cardal's ten gold coins.

"What the matter, Eskkar? Is something . . ."

"Cardal had ten gold coins sewn in the blanket," Eskkar said. "They were there last night. I checked them just after dinner, just before . . ."

He stood, awake now. The room felt close and constrained. He pushed past Eristi and walked through the alehouse and out into the sun. Eskkar squinted against the sunlight, but the fresh air help push the cobwebs from his mind.

"We have to find Dalza," he said. "She must have taken them. We'll search the village together."

"Eskkar, walk with me," Eristi said. She took his arm and guided him down the lane. "If Dalza took your knife and your gold, then she's probably long gone by now."

"I'll find her," he said. "She can't have gone far."

Eristi tightened her grip. "It's better if I look for her. You'll attract too much attention. I'll find her. The village isn't that large."

"But where would she go . . . why would she leave?"

"She may have left the village, Eskkar," Eristi said, still holding fast to his arm.

"If she's left the village, I'll track her down. Cardal gave me that gold as he lay dying. If she left Keolas, I'll get the horse and ..."

"And what will you do when you find her? Take back your gold and ask her to return to you? She'll have found someone else to protect her by now. No one will give up so much gold without a fight."

"I want my gold back. She took it all. We planned . . . I planned . . ."

"Eskkar, keep your voice down," Eristi said, moving directly in front of him and holding both his hands. "Listen to me, before you jeopardize all of us."

He stared at her face. Something in her voice warned him to listen to her.

"Dalza may already be gone from Keolas," she said, "probably is gone. The morning boats left just after dawn. She could be miles away by now, either north or south. This is something she must have planned in advance."

Eskkar had forgotten about the river. Eristi was right. Dalza wouldn't leave Keolas on foot, or even on horseback. She'd know he'd track her down in a few days. But the river! A few miles south of the village, the Euphrates split in two, and then one branch split yet again.

Yesterday, Dalza had strolled through the village, or so she claimed, while he and Eristi dealt with selling the horse. In that time, she could have arranged passage on her choice of vessels.

It finally sank in that Dalza and the gold were gone. She had stolen it from him while he'd lay there sleeping off the effects of last night's ale and lovemaking.

Eristi watched the emotions play over Eskkar's face, as he realized Dalza's betrayal.

"She was never the woman for you, Eskkar." Eristi softened her tone, but continuing to hold fast to his arm. "Dalza is the kind of woman who needs a rich merchant or trader, someone who can lavish jewels and clothes on her each day, not a wandering outcast from the steppes. She's gone, and perhaps, for you, that's for the best."

"But the gold! I can't let her get away with my gold."

"She'll claim it was her gold, given to her by her dead husband. It will be your word against hers. Who do you think the people will believe?"

Eskkar ground his teeth in rage. He wanted to shout out his anger, but Eristi's hands tightened again.

"Wait here," Eristi commanded, shaking her head angrily. "I'll see what I can learn. You stay in the inn, and in the name of the gods, don't drink any more ale. You've been fool enough for one day."

She let go of his hands and strode off. Eskkar watched her disappear up the lane. His stomach felt cold and empty. He didn't understand how Dalza could do this to him, how she could leave him after what they'd shared over the last fifteen days, after such pleasures they'd experienced.

And she'd taken his gold. Ten gold coins, more than he'd ever owned before, had been stolen. Eristi was right, he was a fool. Even worse, Eskkar didn't know what he missed more, the gold or Dalza.

10

Eighteen months later . . .

Eskkar let the weary horse pick its way through the muddy puddles of a village, the result of what he hoped was the end of the spring rains. Hunger drove both man and beast. Eskkar's food had run out two days ago, and both needed something, anything, to put into their bellies.

At least the animal had dined occasionally during the last six days on the sparse grass encountered during their journey. Nonetheless, Eskkar had pushed the animal hard, and now the poor beast needed some grain in addition to grass to restore its strength.

Arriving in this nameless place a little after dawn, he wandered from hut to hut, looking for any work that would earn him something to eat. The village smith had finally offered Eskkar a loaf of bread, if he'd carry six loads of round river rock from the nearby stream to the smith's establishment.

Hesitating, Eskkar had looked in dismay at the stream, flowing nearly a quarter mile away. The rocky ground looked too dangerous to use the horse, which meant he'd have to lug the stones on his own back. Much as he needed something to eat, Eskkar knew a job like that was worth more than a handful of bread.

Even the smith knew enough to sweeten the offer. "And I'll feed your horse, too, barbarian. All he can eat. I've got plenty of grain. Looks like he's been ridden hard. And my boy can brush him down."

The smith apparently felt more sympathy for the overworked horse than its starving owner. Eskkar's hunger settled the matter, and he found himself nodding acceptance.

"Good," the smith said, clearly pleased with his side of the arrangement. "Get to work, then. Use the back harness over there. The ground's too rocky for a horse. You can leave your gear in the corral."

Eskkar's "gear" consisted of a dirty blanket and a patched water skin that he'd just refilled from the well. He kept the long sword on his back. That, and the knife at his waist, were the only weapons he owned, and Eskkar had learned the hard way not to leave them lying around. He labored a month to pay for the new knife, to replace the one Dalza had stolen.

It would be all too easy for the smith to arrange for a friend to steal them, then plead ignorance. It had happened before.

That meant Eskkar would also be lugging the heavy bronze sword around while he worked, but there was no other way. With a grunt, he led the horse into the corral, picked up the bulky wood and rope harness, slipped it over his shoulders, and started for the river.

"Round stones," the smith called after him, "round, and good sized ones, about this big." He held his cupped hands together.

Muttering a curse under his breath at all dirt-eaters, Eskkar trudged his way down to the river. Once there, he drank his fill before moving into the stream, the clean water refreshing him and temporarily filling his complaining stomach.

It didn't take long to collect the first load, about twelve stones. Any more and the fraying ropes holding the basket together would snap. Not that Eskkar could have lifted and walked with any more.

By the time he returned to the corral, he was covered in sweat and breathing hard. The smith watched without offering to help, as Eskkar swung the basket off his back, stumbling to the ground on one knee as he did so.

"Good, yes, good," the smith said as he examined the stones, talking as much to himself as to his laborer. "These are the right size. They'll do." He gave Eskkar a hearty grin. "Only five more loads to go."

"Feed the horse," Eskkar said, pushing himself to his feet and slipping the basket's ropes back on his shoulders. "And maybe you could wash him down, too."

"I'll care for him proper, don't you worry."

And he would, Eskkar thought to himself, since the establishment's owner had a stable boy for that kind of work, and the smith himself wouldn't have to lift a finger.

When Eskkar returned with the second basket, the boy had bathed the horse and wiped it down, and now the rangy brown stallion stood there happily eating a mix of grains poured onto a flat rock used for feeding.

Satisfied that his horse would be well-fed, Eskkar kept working, collecting the heavy rocks and staggering back with each load, a process that took longer and longer with each trip.

Noon approached when he dumped the final basket of rocks onto the pile. Seen this way, the collection of stones didn't seem very impressive, but the smith appeared content.

"The bread," was all Eskkar said, feeling lightheaded and almost too tired to talk. He went to the well and washed his hands and face. Though he'd washed most of the sweat and dust from his body at the river, the cool water felt good on his skin.

When he returned, the smith's wife, a short, thick armed woman who no doubt helped her man with the heavy labor, brought the bread out to him.

"Thank you," Eskkar said, remembering to be polite. His appearance and size sometimes frightened ignorant villagers, always fearful of his kind, and he'd learned to speak softly around them. The aroma of freshly made bread reached his nose and made his stomach ache in anticipation.

Eskkar caught the frown on the smith's face as the man eyed the fat, round bread, and guessed the man expected his wife to bring out a smaller loaf, perhaps even one left over from yesterday. Obviously the woman had seen Eskkar laboring, felt sorry for him, and given him the largest loaf to come out of her baking oven.

Bowing to the woman, Eskkar gave her a wink, then turned to the smith. "Thank you for caring for the horse. Can I leave him here while I eat?"

Ordinarily Eskkar would have eaten as he rode, but the horse needed as much rest as it could get. Eskkar still felt a little dizzy. Heavy work on an empty stomach, with the strong sun burning down overhead, could drain any man's strength.

He carried the bread ten paces away, moving into what in a larger village would be called the marketplace. In this mud hole, it signified a few low huts facing into a common area. Eskkar sat down at the nearest hut and leaned back against the wall, ignoring the smell of piss and worse that lingered on the side of the house and the dirt beneath it.

Even the late afternoon sun had failed to burn off the foul odors, no doubt reinforced several times each day by lazy villagers. Normally, he'd have selected another place to eat his bread, but right now he felt too tired and hungry to worry about the scent of last night's urine.

Besides, all villages stank of something, if not from too many people and animals emptying their bodies, then from the smell of too many people living too close together.

At least from here Eskkar could keep an eye on the small corral across the square that contained his horse. Not that he thought it likely this insignificant collection of mud huts boasted a man daring enough to steal a barbarian's horse. Despite only being half way into his twenty-first season, Eskkar had learned much about the customs of villagers, and what he'd encountered taught him to be cautious.

Best to eat his bread alone and be on his way. Soon what passed here for an alehouse would be filled with farmers drinking after a long day's labor, and too much ale tended to start trouble, especially for a friendless and outcast barbarian.

Besides, rumors about his latest altercation might reach even this desolate place in a few days. Before any stories concerning a tall barbarian accused of stealing a horse arrived, Eskkar intended to be long gone and far away, and for that, he needed that self same horse. Trying to flee on foot from his recent and unfortunate encounter with villagers didn't appeal to Eskkar.

Biting into the brown bread, Eskkar examined both the market square and the smith's corral, though the sun's rays angled down into his eyes. There were a few shaded places scattered about, but all held villagers, both men and women, taking their rest or offering their wares for sale out of the sun's still-bright glare.

If he wanted to move out of the sunlight, he'd have to make room for himself, and that wouldn't be worth the unfriendly looks he'd receive, nor the whispers and laughter that would be directed against him.

Barbarians, tame ones, at any rate, always provided a good source of fun for villagers. Though they took care not to laugh too loud. Eskkar had learned how to stare back at them, and the long horse sword he carried usually sufficed to keep most disparaging comments out of earshot. He continued munching on the bread, trying not to wolf it down.

A shadow blocked the sun from his eyes, and Eskkar glanced up to see a man standing a few paces away. He didn't say anything, just stood there. The man looked harmless, and Eskkar went back to eating; he'd received plenty of stares from ignorant villagers before. By now half the loaf had disappeared, and Eskkar still felt hungry. He intended to save a fist-sized chunk for tomorrow's morning meal, but the rest of the loaf would soon be gone.

"You look hungry for some meat," the man said. "A man your size needs meat."

The foolish statement didn't deserve a reply, but Eskkar looked up again. This time he paid more attention to the speaker, an old man approaching fifty seasons, dressed in a dusty linen tunic that reached past his knees.

A wide leather belt supported three separate pouches as well as a long knife, and the man's feet were set in sturdy sandals laced high around his calves. A shock of gray hair growing in every direction topped a weather-beaten face browned and lined by years of living in the open. He leaned easily on a long staff taller than his head.

Before Eskkar could think of what to say, he became aware of the smell, a stench, really, that emanated from the man. The odor, thick and unpleasant, hung in the air. Eskkar must have wrinkled his nose.

"It's the sheep," the man said. "I'm a shepherd, and that's my flock you're smelling. I can't smell them myself."

More than just smelling. The stink overpowered the urine and even the clean smell of the fresh bread in Eskkar's hands. Suddenly his hunger vanished.

"Could you take your flock elsewhere, shepherd, so I can finish my bread?"

This time the man laughed, a cheerful sound that turned a few heads in their direction as it echoed around the square. "You'll get used to it."

Not likely, Eskkar thought, not unless I stop breathing.

"You haven't thanked me for providing you with shade to finish your meal."

"You can take your shadow with you when you leave," Eskkar said.

"My name is Balthasar," the man said, ignoring the suggestion. "I want to offer you work, in exchange for fresh meat. Mutton. All you can eat."

Despite the odor, Eskkar's mouth watered at the prospect of meat. He hadn't eaten anything substantial for at least eight or nine days. But Eskkar would let himself starve to death before he herded sheep.

"I'm not a shepherd . . . Balthasar," he said. "And I'm not looking for work. I'll be leaving this dung heap as soon as I finish eating."

"Which way are you traveling?"

Eskkar frowned at his questioner, who didn't seem able to take a hint. "Not that it's any of your business, but I'm heading east."

"Mmmm," Balthasar intoned, running the sound through his nose. "Strange to hear that, since I saw you ride in from the east. Perhaps you've lost your way."

The idea that a steppes warrior would lose his way was too foolish to discuss. "Perhaps," Eskkar agreed, more annoyed that the man had noticed his arrival earlier.

"I, on the other hand, am traveling to the west, into the hill country. Not many go that way, it's mostly empty land. If you care to accompany me, I'll make sure you are well fed."

"I told you I'm not a sheep herder."

"The steppes people call that woman's work, don't they? I hear they use slaves to tend their herds," Balthasar paused. "Oh, I understand. They're not your people any more, since you've left them."

Eskkar took another mouthful of bread, and forced it down, ignoring both the insult and the smell, which seemed to grow stronger the longer the man stood there. When Eskkar finally got the mouthful down, he took another bite, a smaller one this time. At least the man hadn't called him a barbarian or an outcast.

"At any rate," Balthasar went on, "I don't need your services as a shepherd. I need someone to guard me and my flock as we pass through the hill country. The western lands are crossed by many bandits, and even farmers and herders who live there might be tempted by my flock."

"I'm heading east," Eskkar repeated stubbornly, though he knew Balthasar saw the lie.

"The journey will take about eight or ten days," the shepherd continued, again ignoring Eskkar's reaction. "When I reach my destination, my brother can pay you some copper as well, say, a coin for every day of the journey?"

That put another perspective on the offer. Eskkar needed copper. In every village the dull copper coins made exchanges of services easier. A copper coin could buy food and a place to sleep for a day, or even two.

While most people bartered goods and labor for what they lacked, a wandering former clansman didn't usually have the time or inclination to trade work for food or other necessities. Copper came in handy, especially for a man traveling in haste and frequently looking over his shoulder.

Still, Eskkar had learned one painful lesson over the years in his dealings with villagers: never take their first offer.

"Two copper coins per day," he said, expecting the haggling to begin.

Balthasar didn't hesitate. "Agreed. Two copper coins per day."

The quick agreement aroused Eskkar's suspicious nature. Eskkar couldn't claim to read villagers' faces, but even he could see Balthasar worried about something more than the vague possibility of bandits. "You haven't told me why you really need protection."

The shepherd licked his lips, and for the first time thought for a moment before he spoke. "As I say, there are bandits in the hill country, and ..."

Eskkar waited, watching the old man.

"There are some people in . . . where I came from . . . people who think part of my flock belongs to them. They may try to take them back . . . back to my village."

"And if they try?"

"That's where you come in. They're not likely to challenge someone of your size and strength. I watched you carry those rocks. You're strong, stronger than most men. And that's a warrior's weapon you carry. I suspect you'd make a formidable enemy."

Eskkar didn't know what the word "formidable" meant, but he understood the man's message. "Maybe I'll slit your throat myself, and take your copper coins."

"If I had hard copper to offer, I'd be able to hire two or three villagers right here. I had used my last coin to pay some village boys to watch my flock while I came into the village. They're grazing downstream. But I don't have any more copper, and that's why none here will come with me."

Eskkar thought it over. He liked to take his time making decisions, especially in situations he hadn't encountered before. Glancing around, he saw no one taking any interest in their conversation.

"I'm riding out to the south as soon as I finish eating," Eskkar said, contradicting what he told the shepherd before. "I have some business that way to attend to."

He didn't bother to explain that his "business" consisted of leaving a broad trail to the south, in case anyone came searching for him. "So if you're heading west in the morning, I might catch up with you before noon. And there won't be any need for you to mention to anyone that I'll be joining you."

"Yes, of course," Balthasar said, nodding his understanding. "A man has to travel his own path in life with as much care as he can manage. I'll sleep with my flock tonight, and start out at dawn. Good fortune to you, then."

The shepherd turned on his heel and walked away, taking his shadow with him, and once again Eskkar squinted into the sun. He waited a moment, until most of the sheep smell drifted away, and returned to eating his bread.

Balthasar, meanwhile, went to the well, and drew up a bucket of water. To Eskkar's amusement, even the villagers standing nearby moved away, rudely holding their noses, driven off by the sheep smell. Two or three made boorish comments about sheep and their herders, and the resulting laughter made everyone forget about the barbarian eating his bread.

Eskkar grunted in satisfaction. Balthasar hadn't immediately rushed off to his flock, signaling to everyone that he'd secured a companion for his journey. So the villagers, if anyone asked later, would report that Eskkar had gone off on his own, taken the trail south, and the shepherd and his flock had moved westward the next morning. Not even these gullible dirt-eaters would believe a barbarian would take work herding sheep.

Guarding stock, he reminded himself, not herding sheep. Muttering to himself at how low he'd fallen, Eskkar returned to eating his bread. But the sheep smell still lingered in the air, and after one more bite, Eskkar pushed himself to his feet and headed toward the corral. He'd finish the bread when the stink disappeared. The horse would have to wait a little longer before it rested.

—⚏—

The late morning sun in his eyes, Eskkar sat on his horse and watched in dismay at the flock of sheep heading toward him. He'd heard their approach long before they came into sight.

A constant sound, the "ba-a-a, ba-a-a, ba-a-a," repeated by many different voices, already grated on his ears with its endless repetition. The monotonous bleating never ceased, and new voices picked it up whenever others went quiet.

Flock didn't even begin to indicate the size of the herd. Eskkar guessed at least two hundred sheep plodded along, taking their time and nibbling at every bit of grass in their path, biting everything down to the root.

So many sheep would strip the ground bare as they passed over it, leaving nothing for a horse to forage. The wooly band streamed toward him, their sharp little hoofs cutting into the sandy soil and kicking up dust that the breeze carried ahead, and stung his nostrils.

Eskkar's horse didn't care for either the dust or the smell. He snorted again and again, and pawed the earth impatiently.

"Get used to them," Eskkar said, rubbing the horse's neck as he spoke. "It's only for ten days, maybe less." The horse seemed to take as little comfort from Eskkar's words as he did.

Remembering the flocks of sheep from his clan days, Eskkar had expected thirty or forty animals. Not a herd this size, and one far too large to be controlled by one man. He saw Balthasar walking behind his sheep, following their wake and ignoring the dust they raised as he strode along, his staff moving in a purposeful rhythm as he used it to steady his footsteps. No doubt after all these years Balthasar no longer noticed either the dust or the smell, nor the weight of the large pack strapped to his shoulders.

The staff, Eskkar soon saw, had another purpose. The shepherd had helpers after all, the four-legged kind. Two big dogs, one brown and the other mostly black, ranged along either side of the herd, glancing back occasionally at their master and taking their guidance from his commands and the way he pointed his staff.

Whenever a particularly brave wooly-one drifted away from the herd in search of sweeter morsels of grass, one of the dogs would lope around the adventurous animal and begin barking. The noise usually sufficed to send the animal scurrying back to the safety of its comrades.

If the sheep refused to heed the warning, the dog would nip at its heels or shoulder, and that always convinced the animal to return to its original course. There it would blend it with the other gray and dirty white creatures until another one, indistinguishable to Eskkar's eyes, wandered away from the bleating mass and repeated the process.

When the herd drew closer, Eskkar walked the horse farther out of their way. He knew the timid animals would grow nervous at the sight of a horse and rider in their path. They might even bolt and run. Without any sharp teeth or claws, their only defense in the face of danger was to run, blindly following whatever path their leader selected.

To Eskkar's surprise, the leader of the herd wasn't a sheep, but a goat, a buck that stood much taller than his followers. As the first of the animals passed alongside, Eskkar's horse reacted, snorting and pawing the ground at the intensity of the odor. The sheep, all sizes and ages, bleated and turned their fear-filled eyes to horse and rider as they passed.

Up close, the acrid scent was even more overpowering, and before the herd had passed, Eskkar wondered if he'd be able to stand it for ten more days. Once again he cursed the foul luck that had reduced a warrior to guarding sheep.

"I'm glad to see you so early . . . you never told me your name?"

Eskkar turned the horse to walk alongside the shepherd, wishing he'd never encountered Balthasar or his flock. "My name is Eskkar."

"A strong name," Balthasar commented, as he plodded along. "What does it mean?"

"Nothing, it's just a name," Eskkar answered. He didn't intend to start a long discussion of how Alur Meriki warriors selected names for their sons, and what those names meant. Besides, Eskkar knew that names had power even for the demons above and below, and it gained him nothing to reveal too much of himself.

"Your herd, I've never seen one so large," Eskkar said, changing the subject. "Don't you need a few more shepherds to mind it?"

"At least one more. But I've no one else. My sons are dead, and what other friends I had need to care for their own flocks. Still, the dogs know their business, and the buck is a good leader. The journey will be hard, but I think we can stand it for the next seven days or so. If you can ride ahead and pick out the easiest path with the best grazing, that will help make the trip shorter."

Ranging ahead, away from the ceaseless bleating already appealed to Eskkar. The sheep never seemed to stop their bleating and mehing, an irritating background noise that somehow increased the sharp smell cutting into his lungs.

Balthasar told Eskkar about his destination, mentioning landmarks and trails, and giving directions that would have confounded any villager. But Eskkar had ridden up and down a hundred unknown lands in the last seven years, and he had no difficulty understanding the guideposts the old man described. "Then I'll ride ahead, Balthasar, and scout the land."

The shepherd raised his staff, pointing it and shouting a command. In a moment, the brown dog slipped in close to the goat leader, and nudged him a little more in the direction of Balthasar's staff.

"Good, yes, that would be good," Balthasar said, when the herd was back on track. "But it might also be wise if, every so often, you rode to the rear, to make sure no one is following us."

So Balthasar had worries of his own, Eskkar decided. Forward or rear, any place but here breathing the dust. "Then first I'll lag behind, and make sure no one is tracking us."

He turned the horse around and rode away from the sheep track, veering to the side, unwilling to ride over the ground the sheep had traveled. That reduced the odor and the horse whinnied its gratitude.

A low hill he passed about a mile back would offer a good vantage point, so Eskkar headed there. Anyone coming from the village would naturally follow the sheep's trail, a broad pathway that even the most dull-witted, half-blind farmer couldn't miss. If anyone intended to follow Balthasar's flock, they'd have no trouble.

From the top of the hill, Eskkar could see a good two, maybe three miles. He dismounted, tied the horse securely, and found a comfortable rock to lean against. He sat there for much of the afternoon, enjoying his rest, until the afternoon sun began to descend. After taking one last look around, he untied his horse and rode down the hill.

Putting the horse to a canter, he started back along the trail. He soon had the herd in sight. Eskkar didn't stop, just swung wide around the sheep and moved on ahead. This time he searched the land for any danger they might encounter, but except for a few scattered farms off to the distant north, he saw nothing.

By tomorrow, Eskkar guessed most of the farms would be out of sight, and the land would turn brown and rocky. That would slow down the sheep, he knew, as they would need more time to forage.

He cantered the horse back to the flock and managed to time his arrival perfectly. Balthasar commanded the dogs to halt the herd as Eskkar rode up.

"Nothing behind or ahead of us," Eskkar said, as he dismounted and fastened the horse's halter to a bush.

"Then I'll settle the herd for the night, and get ready for supper," Balthasar said, slipping his pack from his shoulders. "If you could help gather some firewood . . ."

Eskkar didn't need any reminders of camp duties. Everyone worked at some task, so that all could rest as long as possible. He wandered off, searching for anything that would burn. There wasn't any thick wood lying about, but he found enough dried twigs and small bushes to make a decent fire. They'd need a good one, if they intended to cook a whole sheep. So he gathered three armloads, enough to keep a small fire going well into the night.

Preparing the fire took more time. Eskkar built a rock ring around the kindling, then used his knife to fashion a handful of sticks that would be used to hold the chunks of mutton in the flames.

Meanwhile, Balthasar had circled the herd a few times, checking on some of the ewes that had given birth in the last few days, and inspecting the older animals to see which looked the weakest. The process required some time, but Balthasar made sure all the animals felt his presence and took comfort in his protection.

Only when the herd had settled in for the night, did he select an animal for the evening meal. Balthasar carried the protesting sheep off to the rear for butchering, away from the herd, where its cries and blood scent wouldn't reach the rest of its brethren.

Meanwhile Eskkar tied up his horse, using a long length of rope that would give the animal a little grazing room. Then he took the flint from his pouch and got the fire going, an event that tonight required only a few tries before the sparks caught.

It took longer than Eskkar expected before the shepherd returned, carrying the nearly unrecognizable and bloody remains in both hands. He had skinned and gutted the animal. Now he laid the carcass across a good-sized boulder, and used his knife to start slicing off meat. Balthasar put the first portion onto a stick and shoved it into the fire. Soon the smell of burning flesh floated up in the air, to counter the blood smell.

"You can't slaughter one in front of the herd, you know," Balthasar explained, once the meat began cooking. He continued skewering bits of raw meat and adding them to the flames. "It would make the others distrustful."

"Where's the fleece?" Eskkar didn't think Balthasar would leave that behind.

"Back where I butchered him, buried in sand to absorb the blood. In the morning I'll dig the hide up and place it in my pack for a few days, until it dries out and loses its scent. They're very trusting animals. And loyal. They follow their leader wherever he goes. Not like men."

Eskkar thought sheep to be even dumber than cattle. Still, he realized Balthasar, after spending so much time alone with his flock, needed to talk.

"In the clans where I grew up," Eskkar said, as he added more wood to the fire, "a leader had the same loyalty from his men. Once the warriors accepted one of their own as clan leader, they followed wherever he led."

Balthasar kept pushing meat into and out of the fire, letting those chunks crisped to a golden brown cool on the rocks before eating, while he considered Eskkar's words. "Perhaps that is why your warriors fight so well, because they have some say in choosing who leads them."

Eskkar had never thought of it in that light. Not that the average clansman had much say in his clan leader's decisions, but no man could lead if he lost the trust and respect of most of his men, no matter how many swords he commanded.

And compared to what Eskkar had seen in the villages, where petty and greedy farmers based their authority on the number of obedient and brawny sons they fathered, or hired men with weapons to enforce their will by threat, it was a decided improvement.

"Unlike villagers," Eskkar said, "warriors have weapons, which give them a say in their lives. Even clan leaders try to avoid offending someone who might put a blade in their bellies. But for villagers, how many have any choice about how they live? Or even where they might go to settle disputes or seek justice?"

"True enough," Balthasar agreed. "And it's even worse on a lonely farm, where a father rules his family as if they were all slaves."

Eskkar grunted. No sense talking about the ways of the world, ways unchanged as far back as anyone could remember. Instead he kept his eyes on the cooking meat, his mouth watering in anticipation. But he refused to take a portion from the fire; courtesy gave first choice to the host.

Balthasar must have noticed. He selected a succulent and oozing chunk of meat from the fire and handed it to his guest. "This looks done enough to eat."

Eskkar bit into the first mouthful, burning his tongue in the process. The mutton, clearly from an older animal, needed chewing, and he gave it his full attention, eating steadily and barely pausing long enough to let the next slice of meat cool off.

They ate in silence, each man hungry after a long day's labor. Balthasar kept his knife working, slicing up mutton and adding fresh meat to the flames.

When Eskkar's stomach could hold no more, he leaned back from the smoky fire and grunted again, this time in satisfaction, his belly full for the first time in many days. Even the sheep smell had disappeared. Either the crisping meat had driven it away, or Eskkar had grown accustomed to the odor.

Although Balthasar had eaten much less than Eskkar, nearly half the butchered animal had disappeared. Balthasar fed the dogs next. One at a time, he called them in from their duty for a well-earned supper. Each dog ate in a rush, crouching over its food and keeping a wary eye on Eskkar the whole time, as if expecting the stranger to challenge them for the meat.

Eskkar added the last of the wood, building up the flames again, as Balthasar skewered the rest of the mutton and placed it into the fire.

"Nothing will go to waste," Balthasar said. "Without cooking, the flesh would spoil soon enough, and now the four of us will have a good morning meal tomorrow."

The heavy meal already had Eskkar's eyes nodding. He stared at the fire, until it began to burn low. With a quick good night, he rolled up in his blanket and closed his eyes, feet toward the dying embers, his unsheathed sword beside him.

At least tonight Eskkar could sleep with little worry. The dogs would keep a better watch than either their master or his guest.

11

When he awoke just before dawn, Eskkar found to his surprise that he'd slept straight through the night. In fact, he couldn't remember the last time he slept so soundly. When he tried to sit up, he found the brown dog curled against his leg, filling the space between its master and Eskkar. Man and dog stared at each other with suspicion, neither one sure what their new relationship portended.

Across the burned out embers of the fire, Balthasar pushed himself upright, a yawn cracking his face. It took the older man a few moments before he worked the stiffness out of his body, and could stand erect. In silence, the two men gathered their things and readied themselves for the day's march.

Afterwards, they stood side-by-side, each chewing the remainder of last night's mutton, already dry and hard. They watched the rested sheep climb noisily to their feet, eager to start their search for fresh grass.

When both men finished their morning meal, the last of the scraps went to the dogs, who wolfed down the food as if they hadn't eaten in days.

"I'll scout out the trail ahead of us," Eskkar said, fastening his blanket on the horse and strapping the sword over his shoulder. "Then I'll come back and make sure no one is following."

"Good. Pile up some stones to mark the trail. Use three stones in a line to point the way."

Eskkar swung astride his mount and cantered off. He circled wide around the sheep, who stared at him, ready to bolt, yesterday's familiarity with horse and rider already forgotten.

At least his stomach didn't ache with hunger. Eskkar knew he likely wouldn't eat again until dusk, but that didn't matter this morning. Riding to the west, he scouted out the trail they would traverse, dismounting and marking the route wherever he thought it necessary.

By the time he returned and met up with the herd, half the morning had passed. He paused only long enough to tell Balthasar about the empty land up ahead, then cantered at an easy pace to the east.

After five miles of backtracking, Eskkar found another hillock, and stretched out on a wide sward of grass. Scanning back along their trail, he saw nothing but grassland dotted with small trees and clumps of hard rock jutting from the earth. Eskkar turned over on his back, flung his arm across his face to block out the sun, and closed his eyes. He'd learned long ago to snatch sleep whenever he could.

When he woke, the sun had moved a good distance across the sky. Getting to his feet, he stretched and looked toward the east. At first he saw nothing, but then, at the very edge of the horizon, he saw a thin plume of dust, scarcely noticeable at this distance.

Wide awake now, Eskkar waited another hundred heartbeats, until his eyes could resolve the movement. By then the distant cloud had turned into five separate dots, all following along the sheep's tracks. As the tiny dots grew larger, merging and shifting, they changed again, and Eskkar's keen eyes confirmed what his instinct had already guessed – a small band of horsemen riding toward him.

The men rode with purpose and at a quick pace, so he doubted they happened to be travelers going the same direction as Balthasar. Though the riders were still more than two miles away, Eskkar noted they rode as villagers do, not with the easy posture of the steppes people.

Eskkar slipped down the hillside, mounted his horse, and galloped back toward the herd, keeping well away and to the side of the broad wake left by Balthasar's sheep. If the riders didn't spread out, hopefully they wouldn't see his tracks, and villagers' eyes, used to looking only at the ground right beneath them, might not see him at all.

By the time he rejoined Balthasar, still plodding along behind his flock, the horse had worked up a good lather.

The shepherd looked up at Eskkar's rapid approach. "Is something wrong?"

"Five men are following us, Balthasar," Eskkar said, dropping down from the horse, and walking beside the older man while the winded horse got some rest. "They'll catch up with us before mid afternoon, maybe a little earlier."

Balthasar didn't speak for a moment, but Eskkar saw the old man's hand tighten on the staff.

"I hoped they wouldn't come," Balthasar said. "Yesterday, when you saw nothing, I began to believe my flock and I were safe. Another day or two, and we'd be beyond their reach."

"What do they want?"

"The sheep, of course. A herd such as this is very valuable. Sulmano, the one who leads them, claims at least half my flock as his own. His claim is a false one."

The validity of the claim meant nothing to Eskkar, though he doubted a man like Balthasar had stolen them. "I didn't see any bows, and they ride like villagers. If there are only five of them . . ."

"They'll have swords and slings," Balthasar said. He reached into one of the pouches hanging from his belt and drew out every shepherd's favorite means of protection, a sling.

Eskkar extended his hand, and Balthasar handed him the weapon. Made from two long strips of plaited flax stitched to a piece of leather that formed the cradle, the weapon could throw a stone hard enough to kill. Depending on arm strength and size of the stone, the projectile could be cast farther than an arrow.

Eskkar had used one as a boy, before he earned the right to carry a knife within the clan, and he'd managed to bring down a few rabbits and other small game with his sling. Still, he'd never been very proficient with it, not like some of his friends, who'd grown skillful enough to hit moving rabbits with ease.

Eskkar's last and only other experience with a sling had been when Shama had nearly split his skull with one of her stones. Nonetheless, a man on a moving horse made for a difficult target, and a stone wasn't likely to bring down a horse.

He handed the sling back to Balthasar, wondering if the old man could use it as well as Shama had. "You'd better gather extra stones, just in case." Eskkar hesitated for a moment. "Unless you're willing to give up half your sheep?"

"Half would no longer satisfy them. After coming this far, and all alone out here, they'll want the whole herd." He shook his head. "No. The sheep are mine, and I'll see them all safely to my kinsmen." He turned to face his companion. "You're not afraid to face five men?'

Eskkar grunted at the foolish question. Of course he was apprehensive, not that it mattered. Even so, he couldn't remember any fights where he wasn't outnumbered. "You've got a sling, and I assume you can use it. And you've got the dogs. Will they obey your command to attack?"

"They've chased thieves away before."

"Good. Then you better get the sheep moving faster. I need time to prepare."

Eskkar walked his horse away to the side of the flock. The beast and he had been together less than twelve days, with most of that time on the run, and he hadn't had much time to work with the animal.

So now he put the horse through its paces, making sure it would jump forward at a touch of his heels, and that it would wheel and turn on command. Eskkar shouted his war cry at each maneuver, until the animal became familiar with the sound.

Warriors always shouted when they charged and fought, and the battle sounds struck fear into dirt-eaters and their mounts. When Eskkar finally stopped, the horse was as ready as he could make it on such short notice.

By the time he rejoined Balthasar, the flock had covered another two miles. The shepherd had found a good place to halt the herd, where rocks and bushes formed a rough half circle. He guided the sheep within, and left the brown dog to watch them. He walked back to Eskkar's side, the black dog trailing beside him.

The horse securely tied to a bush, Eskkar looked to his sword. He made sure it drew easily from its sheath, then tested the edge for sharpness, giving it a few strokes with the sharpening stone. He did the same with his knife.

Meanwhile, Balthasar began slinging stones, whipping the thongs in a circle, then throwing the sling forward at a nearby rock. Eskkar nodded in satisfaction when Balthasar struck the target three times in a row.

Not long afterwards, five riders crested a rise. They pulled up, clearly surprised to see their quarry less than half a mile ahead, and waiting for them. After a quick discussion, they came on again, riding slowly toward the herd.

Eskkar waited until they were about three hundred paces away before he climbed to his feet, swung onto his horse's back, and positioned himself about ten paces to Balthasar's right. Pulling the long sword from its sheath, Eskkar held it over his head for a moment, letting the sun glint against the bronze. Any warrior would recognize the challenge, and even the most ignorant villager would understand what he faced.

As the five approached, Eskkar studied them. The oldest, nearly as old as Balthasar, wore a tunic made from the finest linen and carried a short sword at his waist. A carefully trimmed beard adorned his face, and he rode a well-bred horse with strong lines.

Another man half his age carried only a long knife on his belt, but Eskkar saw a sling dangling from his hand. The third man, young and burly, wore the roughest garb. He, too, had a sling, but only a short knife hanging from a rough leather strip. Eskkar guessed him to be a shepherd, brought along to herd the sheep back.

The other two men carried both swords and knives. They sat their horses better, and their tunics and belts marked them as men who spent time on horseback. One had a jagged scar on his cheek.

Hired guards, Eskkar decided. Still, they weren't warriors, and their horses looked inferior to those the other three rode. Nor had they drawn their swords, though each had his hand close to the hilt.

By then, the five had approached within twenty paces. "That's close enough," Eskkar said, putting some force into his voice. His sword lay across the horse's neck. "Best not to come any closer. You might frighten the sheep."

The riders halted their horses about fifteen paces away, in line abreast. The two guards faced Eskkar across the open space, while the oldest, Eskkar assumed him to be the leader, anchored the other end of the line, facing Balthasar.

"Well, Balthasar," the older man said, ignoring Eskkar, "you've led us quite a chase." He started to dismount.

"Stay on your horse," Eskkar said. "I'll kill the first man that dismounts."

"There's no need to make threats," the man said, but he settled back on his mount. "We've only come for what belongs to us. We'll take half the sheep, and no more, Balthasar."

"The flock is mine, Sulmano," Balthasar said, leaning on his staff, the sling dangling in his right hand. "Half were my brother's, and half are mine."

"Your brother had a wife," Sulmano countered. "Her family deserves her husband's wealth."

"If she lived, perhaps," Balthasar said. "But she died with my brother, and the sheep were given to me."

Eskkar only half-listened to the old story of a family's disputed goods. In Eskkar's clan, such squabbles would be resolved by the clan leader. But farmers and herders, living far out in the country-side, didn't have anyone in authority to decide such things. Quarrels over inheritances often followed a father's death in the household, sometimes tearing the whole family apart and pitting brother against brother.

Instead, Eskkar kept his attention focused on his opponents, studying both the horses and the men, looking for weak points. The man without a sword resembled Sulmano too much to be anything other than his son. He looked frightened, though he kept fingering the sling he held ready in his hand.

Even so, Eskkar doubted the man had much practice using it from horseback, and Balthasar's stone should arrive first.

If it didn't, Eskkar would have to duck that first cast stone. He would be on the five of them in a few heartbeats, faster than they expected. Eskkar knew how fast he could cover the distance between them, if the horse responded properly. No time to worry about that now.

While Balthasar and Sulmano continued to exchange pointless arguments, Eskkar returned his gaze to the two hired guards. Both appeared fit and capable, and neither looked likely to cut and run.

Eskkar decided the discussion had gone on long enough. Sulmano showed no sign of leaving, and he hadn't traveled for days over rough country to turn back after a few words. Which meant he wanted a fight, and the longer they wasted time talking, the weaker Eskkar and Balthasar would appear.

"Enough!" Eskkar let his words sound out over their voices. "Leave now, or I'll cut you down. You'll be first, Sulmano."

The man turned to Eskkar, as if seeing him for the first time. "You look like a dangerous man, but remember there are five of us. But there's no reason for you to involve yourself in this matter. Tell me what Balthasar promised you for payment, and I'll double it. All you have to do to earn it is ride away. No need to die here over a few sheep."

Eskkar kept his eyes on Sulmano and his men, thinking about the man's offer. After all, what did he owe Balthasar, besides a belly full of mutton? But he had eaten with the man, shared his food and fire, and in Eskkar's mind, that counted for something.

"You need not stay, Eskkar," Balthasar said. "I was wrong to involve you in this fight. The quarrel is between me and Sulmano."

Eskkar made up his mind. "You'll pay me now, Sulmano? Twenty copper coins?" He tightened the halter the slightest bit and let the animal feel the increased pressure from his knees.

A brief smile crossed Sulmano's face. "Oh, yes, I have just that much with me. I thought ..."

Eskkar kicked the horse hard, screaming his war cry at the same moment. The horse, expecting the command, flung itself forward, driven as much by Eskkar's shout as his heels. Sulmano's two fighters, already starting to relax at Eskkar's apparent acquiescence to the bribe, were caught by surprise. The battle cry startled their horses, and the two fighters fumbled for their weapons, as Eskkar headed straight for them, not Sulmano.

By then Eskkar's horse had dashed across the gap and his sword was coming down. He aimed for the man's head, but his opponent managed to get his sword up. But nothing could stop that first cut, swung with all the force of Eskkar's powerful arm behind it. His blade brushed the shorter sword aside and struck the man at the base of the neck, the bronze edge biting deep.

Without stopping, Eskkar wheeled the horse at the second man, as he let loose another war cry. The two animals crashed together, shoulder to shoulder.

Eskkar's legs remained locked tight on his horse's ribs, but Sulmano's fighter lost his grip on his mount. He managed to block Eskkar's first cut, but couldn't control his horse. It jumped back a step, the sudden motion causing its rider to lose his balance, unable to hold his seat. Leaning over, Eskkar thrust down at the man's side as he tumbled off the horse. The thrust stuck the rider's hip, not enough to kill the man, but ... a stone flew past Eskkar's head.

A hard touch of his left heel, coupled with a command, and Eskkar turned his horse to face the slinger. Another war cry drove the horse forward, this time heading for the shepherd, who'd just cast the stone at Eskkar's head. The fool should have dismounted, where he could use the sling properly.

Now the inexperienced rider couldn't handle his horse which wanted nothing to do with all the blood and noise. With Eskkar still screaming his war cry as he approached, the man tried to turn his horse and run.

His horse caught up with the fleeing man in three long bounds, and Eskkar's blade, accompanied by a savage yell, slashed across the man's back. The shepherd's untrained mount swerved away, neighing in fright and kicking its heels, the motion tossing its wounded rider to the ground.

Yanking hard on his halter, Eskkar wheeled the horse around again. He saw Sulmano's son stagger to his feet, bloody knife in hand, kicking the dog's body away from his feet. Eskkar caught a glimpse of Sulmano and Balthasar fighting, the old shepherd using his staff to keep Sulmano and his sword at bay.

Sulmano could scarcely control his horse, and as Eskkar watched, Balthasar smote the frightened beast across the face. The animal reared up, kicking its hooves and neighing in pain and nearly throwing its rider.

Eskkar arrived with a rush and shout. He swung down at Sulmano's son, but the man threw himself to the ground, Eskkar's blade missing his back by a hand's length. Eskkar never halted his charge. In any horse battle, you never stopped to finish off a dismounted opponent, not while any others remained mounted. With a soft tug on the halter, Eskkar's obedient horse changed course again, this time heading toward Sulmano.

His son screamed a warning but Sulmano never heard it, still intent on hacking Balthasar. Eskkar leaned outward, grabbing a handful of mane with his left hand, the one that held the halter. With his right arm fully extended, he shoved the blade all the way through Sulmano's back, the point protruding for a moment beyond the man's breastbone.

Sulmano's eyes turned to look at Eskkar, a surprised expression on his face. Then Eskkar galloped past the man, gripping the sword with all his might, until the blade ripped itself from Sulmano's body, the motion yanking the dead man off the horse at the same time.

When Eskkar wheeled the horse around, the fight had ended. Sulmano's son had dropped his knife, as he crawled the few paces to his father's side, crying out something Eskkar couldn't understand. The injured shepherd, already exhausted from fear and his wound, crawled along the ground fifty paces away.

The surviving bodyguard still moved, staggering along as he, too, tried to get away from the carnage. Eskkar caught a glimpse of the man's face, as he looked fearfully back toward Eskkar.

Balthasar, breathing hard, walked over to Sulmano's body and said something to the son, who sagged onto his knees and began to weep, his arms around his father's shoulders.

"Good warrior, good warrior," Eskkar said to his horse, rubbing its neck. The animal tossed its head high, and neighed, as if it had enjoyed the excitement. Eskkar hadn't bothered to give his mount a name, but now Warrior seemed to fit.

Warrior, Eskkar thought to himself, a fine name for a good horse, one who had earned its name in battle. Gradually Warrior's ears ceased their twitching, as Eskkar's voice calmed the beast.

He kept speaking as he guided the horse back toward Balthasar, keeping a little upwind of the scent of blood. The animal had done everything Eskkar commanded, and once again he remembered why the horse fighters of the steppes inflicted so much damage on their enemies. A strong, well-trained horse, Eskkar knew, could make all the difference in a fight.

The other mounts had scattered, except for the one struck by Balthasar's staff, which stood a few paces away, its legs splayed apart, still half dazed. "Tie up that horse," Eskkar shouted. "I'll catch the rest."

It took some time to round up the scattered animals, all of them still excited from the smell of blood and the screams of men. When Eskkar returned, he had a string of four horses tied halter to halter, all trailing him. Securing his newly-named Warrior and the other horses to a bush, Eskkar went over to the first man he'd attacked, already dead from blood loss.

Eskkar wiped his sword on the dead man's tunic. A thick gold ring on the body's finger caught Eskkar's eye, and he worked it free. He collected the man's weapons and pouch before rejoining Balthasar. A large sack carried by the wounded shepherd now hung across Eskkar's horse. Its contents, already examined, contained enough food to feed its previous owners for another day or so.

Sulmano's son's tears had ceased, but now he sat on the ground, still holding his father's body. His face showed the horror of the fight. Most villagers, Eskkar knew, never saw fighting like this, the killing done with speed and ruthlessness. Or at least lived to tell about it.

"You'll need to bury your father, Oba," Balthasar said, nodding thankfully to Eskkar. "This should not have happened over a few sheep, when your father has so many."

Oba, or whatever he called himself, looked up at Eskkar standing there. "You didn't have to kill him, you ..."

"He was going to kill Balthasar," Eskkar interrupted, not in the mood to listen to a beaten man's complaints about the battlefield. "I've seen that look before. One way or another, he wanted blood to flow. Your father brought this on himself. Learn from his death. Not every claim is worth fighting over. Thank the gods that Balthasar gives you your life. It's more than I would do."

Sulmano's son opened his mouth, but closed it without speaking, suddenly realizing he was, indeed, at their mercy.

"It's best if you take your horses and go, Oba," Balthasar said. "Two of your men are wounded and need your help"

"The horses are mine, Balthasar," Eskkar objected. "The dead and defeated don't need horses. Let Oba and the others walk back home."

Balthasar straightened up, but leaned wearily on his staff with both hands. "I would not make you give up your prize, but do you really want these horses?"

Shrugging, Eskkar pondered Balthasar's words. In battle, horses belonged to the victor, and these would fetch a good price at the next village. Still, perhaps the old man spoke the truth.

If Eskkar rode into a village leading a sting of five horses for sale, someone would almost certainly accuse him of stealing them. At the very least, he'd attract everyone's attention, and there would be more rumors added to those already following him across the land.

Not to mention he'd had enough trouble with proving ownership lately; he still had Warrior to account for.

He sighed. Balthasar was right. Better to let the horses go. At least Oba wouldn't be able to accuse him of stealing *them*.

"Take your horses and your wounded and go, Oba," Eskkar said, breaking the silence. "And remember to speak the truth when you return to your home, that the five of you attacked two, and that, because of Balthasar, we let you live and gave you back your animals."

While Eskkar watched, Balthasar helped Oba put his father's body across a horse. It didn't take long to tie it down, and Oba began his journey home. Riding his horse with his head bowed, he led the other animals toward his companions.

In the distance, Eskkar saw the two wounded men. The shepherd had reached the bodyguard, and both of them knelt on the ground, watching warily to see what would happen next.

Eskkar imagined their relief when they saw Oba and the horses heading toward them.

"Is it over, Eskkar?" Balthasar said, turning away from the departing rider.

"Do I think they'll come back and try to slit our throats in the night? No, Oba's heart isn't in it. The shepherd doesn't have much of a wound, but he's no fighter anyway. The bodyguard is injured too badly to fight again, if he even survives. I think they'll want to get back to the village where they can find a healer. All the same, the sooner we get out of here, the better."

Balthasar's eyes closed for a moment. "Then my sheep are safe, thank the gods for that." He looked around at the bodies, this time his eyes fixing on the dog. "I need to bury my dog."

Something in the old man's voice made Eskkar look up. He saw tears in Balthasar's eyes. Not that such emotion meant anything. Every man reacted differently after a fight. Some laughed, some cried. More than a few twitched or trembled until the battle frenzy cleared from their minds.

And Eskkar had forgotten about their own casualty. The black dog was dead, its blood staining crimson the sandy ground beneath its body.

"Bury it? Why not . . . can't you just leave it?" In his whole life, Eskkar had never seen anyone bury a dog.

"Oba killed it," Balthasar said. "I flung a stone at him, and sent the dog at him. But Oba killed the poor animal before I could get there to help."

Eskkar realized the dog had meant more to Balthasar than merely an animal to herd the sheep. Then Eskkar remembered that every-one in the old man's family had died. The dogs and the sheep were all he had left. At least Balthasar had survived, and with something to look forward to.

"I'll bury him for you," Eskkar said, surprised at the words that came unbidden from his mouth. "You tend to the sheep. Get them moving again." But the dead bodyguard would remain where he'd fallen, to feed the carrion birds. Eskkar had no intention of burying him.

They *should* get moving again, Eskkar knew. The sheep bleated ceaselessly, probably from the scent of blood. The brown dog barked almost continuously, dashing back and forth, working hard to keep the flock from bolting.

Looking around at the grim scene, Eskkar, too, felt the spirits of the dead closing in on him. "I don't like the feel of this place. The sooner we've left it behind, the better."

Balthasar slipped to his knees and stroked the dead dog's head. "This one kept me warm many a cold night in the hills, alone with my flock. Nearly ten seasons we've been together, since I took him from his mother."

"I'll treat him with care," Eskkar said, lowering his voice. "He fought at our side, and deserves a warrior's rest."

"I should do it myself, but . . . the sheep . . . if you would."

Eskkar nodded, and Balthasar pulled himself slowly to his feet. He trod back toward the herd, looking his years for the first time since Eskkar had crossed his path.

After he finished, Eskkar caught up with the flock and its shepherd. "I buried the dog deep, and covered the grave with rocks. He'll lie easy there, until he reaches the spirit world. The others are heading back, all three of them. Oba's taking his father's body home. Or maybe they'll bury Sulmano back at the nearest village."

"Oba will want his village priest to speak over his father's grave. The body will show how he died, and the two wounded will prove Oba's innocence of patricide."

"So all that Sulmano owned will now belong to his son," Eskkar mused. "A fortunate business for Oba, to get his inheritance while so young. It should keep his thoughts from turning to revenge."

"Yes, I suppose so," Balthasar said. "Perhaps the son will prove wiser than the father."

Eskkar grunted at that. In his experience, wealthy villagers' sons tended to be stupider than their fathers. But Oba had survived one foolish adventure, so maybe he would take a lesson from his father's death.

They pushed the herd along until it become too dark to see, then made camp. The extra distance wore out the sheep enough so that they dropped gratefully to the ground, most too tired to protest the long day's march or search for forage.

Even the tireless Balthasar looked as exhausted as any of his flock, another common reaction after a death fight, Eskkar knew. For those not used to the intensity of battle, the aftermath caught many by surprise.

Once again, Eskkar began searching for firewood.

"I'll pick another sheep for slaughter," Balthasar said, his voice showing his weariness. "You must be hungry." He started to rise, but Eskkar stopped him.

"Don't bother," Eskkar said, pointing to the dirty sack hanging from Warrior's neck. "The shepherd carried supplies for the group. We'll have plenty to eat tonight." He untied the bundle and dumped the contents. Loaves of bread, dates, figs, and even some cheese fell onto the ground between them. "See, plenty of food for the next few days, at least."

"But I promised you mutton every night."

Eskkar laughed. "I ate enough meat last night to last another day or two. Leave the sheep be. Besides, I'm too tired to spend half the night picking up firewood."

Actually, Eskkar could have eaten more meat. When he thought about it, he realized he felt something more than just being too tired to gather wood. Somehow it seemed wrong to butcher another sheep so soon after killing two men to save them. All the same, he knew he wouldn't ever admit such a sentiment to Balthasar.

"Yes, a change from mutton will be good," Balthasar said, slumping down gratefully once again.

They stayed close to the herd, letting the dog keep watch over sheep and men. This time Eskkar handled their dinner. He ripped a loaf of bread in half, then pushed in the center to create a hollow. His knife cut out a hunk of cheese to toss inside, and he added some figs and dates before passing it over to his companion.

They ate in silence, chewing the hard bread, each man staring into the snapping fire.

"Have you killed many men, Eskkar?"

He took his time answering. Eskkar understood the shepherd needed to talk, to empty his mind of the battle dead. "Perhaps ten or twelve, maybe less. I've been in two big fights since I left my clan. Three, after counting today."

"You are so young to have killed so many."

"I've twenty-one seasons now, almost twenty-two. Some warriors my age have killed two or three times as many."

"And these deaths, they don't trouble you? You don't think about the men you killed?"

"Balthasar, I've never killed anyone who didn't have a weapon in his hand, or who wouldn't have killed me if they had a chance. My father taught me honor. I've never murdered anyone for their gold or their horse or their woman. Or their sheep, for that matter. I won't lose any sleep over a greedy man like Sulmano."

"Your father must have been a good man," Balthasar said. "He raised you well."

"I'm sure he died honorably," Eskkar said, remembering the night he'd fled the Alur Meriki. He still didn't know what happened to his father, or why Maskim-Xul's guards came for Eskkar's family. Long ago he'd resigned himself to the fact that he might never know exactly what happened.

"Until today, I never killed anyone," Balthasar said, poking a stick into the fire. "It wasn't . . . how I thought it would be."

"I killed them, not you," Eskkar pointed out. "They would have killed both of us. You know Sulmano wouldn't have been satisfied with half the herd. Out here, with no one to question him, he'd have taken them all."

"Yet, I asked you to fight them. They died because of me."

"Men die, Balthasar. That's the way it's always been, and always will be. The strong prey on the weak. The weak grow strong, or they die. That's why men form clans, to gather strength in numbers, and to protect their wives and children while they hunt or toil. That's why farmers form villages, to protect themselves and their farms."

"You know a good deal about the ways of men, for someone so young."

"I've traveled far and seen much, Balthasar. I've known hatred and distrust, faced scorn and abuse. You learn quickly, if you want to survive."

That reminded Eskkar of something he'd wanted to ask. "Your clan, are you sure your brother and his kin will welcome you after so many years?"

"I believe so, though men do change. Sometimes they grow tired of living the same life. They become greedy, fearful of others. My brother Hermander was a good man when I left him, with a good wife. I think it unlikely he's changed much. I plan on giving him most of the herd, Eskkar. I'll keep ten or fifteen for myself, to take care of my own needs, but an old man without any family requires little."

Balthasar sighed. "As for me, I'll ask nothing more than to tend my brother's sheep, and live out the rest of my days in peace. Though you are wise to wonder about such things."

Eskkar thought of wisdom as something that came with old age. "I doubt if I'll live long enough to gain wisdom. But I'm glad for you," Eskkar said. "Most men want to live their lives in peace."

"Even you?"

"Even me." Eskkar laughed. "Though trouble seems to follow my steps at every turn. Perhaps one day my luck will change."

"Why did you fight Sulmano? You could have taken his coins and ridden away. Weren't you afraid of dying for a few coins of copper?"

Eskkar thought about that for a moment, wondering how he could explain something he didn't quite understand himself.

"I'm not sure, Balthasar. But I am an outcast from my people. I don't even think of them as my people any more. All I have left of my life and my family is what my father gave me. He taught me about honor, and about doing a man's duty. As long as I have those things, then I still have something of my family, my father, even my clan. Perhaps one day, if I die with honor, I will see them again."

He laughed again. "Isn't that what the greedy priests of Ishtar and Marduk promise? That we will rejoin our kin after we die, and enjoy endless wine and honey? And willing women!"

This time Balthasar laughed with him. He reached out and stirred the fire. "I've often wondered about such things. Sleeping out under the stars at night, you start to question everything you've been told, everything you've been promised. Look up at the stars, Eskkar. What do you see?"

Eskkar lifted his eyes. The few clouds high in the sky reminded him of wisps of smoke. Hundreds of stars, thousands even, shone and glimmered overhead. "Stars. I see the North Star that never changes, and the group that guide the way south. That way is the west, from that bright . . ."

"I see a mystery, Eskkar. A mystery sent by the gods. So many points of light. I've looked up at them, watched them for nearly forty years. They move and shift over the days and months, but every year they return to their starting place. They mark the seasons, perhaps even a man's fate. I believe they're signs sent to us by the gods, to lead us home someday."

Leaning back, Eskkar gazed upwards, taking in the starry night, seeing it differently for the first time in his life. "You speak like a priest. All the same, there may be something greater than a man, greater even than the gods. Perhaps I will learn their mystery, some day."

"I think you will, Eskkar of the steppes. I think your destiny is up there, written in the stars. When your day comes, make sure you face your destiny with all your strength."

"Now you sound like my father," Eskkar said. "That's something he would have told me."

"The father teaches the son all he knows, all he learned, so that each generation advances in knowledge and wisdom. You will be wise someday, Eskkar."

"If that day is to ever come, Balthasar, then I need to get some sleep tonight, or I'll be too tired to face even you and your sheep in the morning."

Balthasar laughed again, but this time the sound went on, and came from deep within. Eskkar knew the man's crisis had passed, that thoughts of the dead would not trouble him that night or those to come.

They bade each other good night, and Eskkar rolled himself in Warrior's blanket, staring up at the stars, but thinking of Balthasar's words. In a way, they sounded like a blessing, the kind of blessing a father bestows on a son. Perhaps Eskkar's father's spirit lived on and watched over his son, and perhaps that spirit approved of what Eskkar had done today.

Eskkar knew he'd fought well, planned his attack, prepared the horse, gotten Balthasar ready, and even studied the ground. This time, Eskkar had let the talking distract his enemies, instead of the other way around.

Everyone knew the spirits of the dead walked the earth when they felt the need. Some could take possession of people's bodies for a time, or speak through them. Eskkar wondered if Balthasar's words came from Eskkar's father as much as from the old shepherd.

For tonight, at least, Eskkar would let himself believe that his father would be proud of his son. One who fought against many, and who stood by his companion. Any father would look with pride on that.

Eskkar took one last gaze at the stars. Maybe, he thought, maybe someday, I will know my destiny.

Then he closed his eyes and put thoughts of the future and the stars out of his head. Eskkar had one last thought before falling asleep – that he hoped the brown dog would remember to bark if someone, especially someone with a knife in his hand, crept up to kill them while they slept.

12

The next three days passed with little conversation, as Balthasar drove the herd straight toward the place where the sun dipped below the horizon each evening. Gradually the land changed its shape. The ground grew hilly and the grass more sparse. Each morning, as soon as the sun rose, Eskkar rode out, first to the west to scout the day's trail, then circling around to the east, to make sure no one pursued them.

Meanwhile, Balthasar and the brown dog had their hands full with the sheep. Afraid the old man would collapse from exhaustion, Eskkar swallowed more of his pride and lent a hand with herding the flock.

At first he tried to help guide them from Warrior's back, but the horse, brave enough against armed riders, still wanted no part of the wooly creatures. His snorting excited the sheep, and his sudden movements and looming size tended to scatter the animals when he drew near.

Sheep, as Eskkar discovered, didn't react to a horse's approach in the same manner as cattle. So, mouthing prayers to the gods that no one in his clan, including the spirits of the dead, ever saw him stooping so low, Eskkar started herding sheep, on foot. He even picked up a long stick to use as a staff.

Eskkar spent a good amount of time knotting together every piece of rope he and Balthasar had, including those taken from

Sulmano's men. When Eskkar finished, he'd formed a long tether that allowed the horse to walk twenty paces behind.

At that distance, Warrior trailed placidly behind its master, content to follow the sheep as long as no one rode him. With the horse under control, Eskkar could take a station beside the herd, letting Balthasar work the rear while the dog trotted around the other side.

The dog did the most work, though the poor creature clearly missed its companion. It kept whining, especially in the morning and evening, eyes searching everywhere for the black dog, hoping it would return. It even put aside its fear of the stranger and approached Eskkar, its big eyes imploring him to help find its friend.

He found himself patting the dog whenever it came near, speaking soothing words that the poor animal would never understand, but which seemed to give comfort. Gradually the brown dog recognized Eskkar's efforts, and before long accepted him almost as an equal in the shepherding duties. Soon the dog responded to Eskkar's commands almost as easily as it did to Balthasar's.

To his surprise, Eskkar found himself enjoying the mindless task, watching the sheep bumping into each other as they argued over every blade of grass. By now he could identify individuals, ones that exhibited certain traits, usually the ones most troublesome. He found himself attaching names to them.

As the sun began to settle, Eskkar rested his tired legs by riding to the nearest high ground, to make sure no one followed. That gave him a chance to work with Warrior, and he put the horse through different maneuvers, shouting his war cry and waving his sword over the animal's head. The horse had come to trust its new owner, and, as they learned more about each other, they both became more proficient. After each practice, Eskkar allowed the animal extra time to graze on a choice patch of grass.

Eskkar knew luck had favored him in the encounter with Sulmano's men. The horse had responded well, but there might be another fight tomorrow, and Eskkar resolved never again to let slip a chance to work and train his horse. He practiced his own fighting skills each day, but his prowess could be rendered useless by a stubborn or untrained mount.

On the fifth morning after the fight, Eskkar rode off to search out the route for the day's trek. Identifying the best grazing had proved invaluable to Balthasar and the herd's overall passage. They wasted little time following false trails or searching for suitable grass. Estimating their progress, Balthasar expected they would reach his brother's pastures within another few days.

As Eskkar scouted westward, he saw occasional signs of smoke to the north, signifying other herdsmen or small farm holds. At least he guessed that's what they were; the land had grown too stony and dry for a real farm, and the hills would have made cultivating and planting even harder. However, what made for a bad farm appeared ideal for herds of sheep and goats, as long as water could be found within a day's journey.

About to turn Warrior around to rejoin Balthasar and his flock, Eskkar heard a faint shout echoing out over the land. His eyes searched the landscape, until he saw movement on one of the hill tops. A figure stood there, waving its arms and jumping up and down, clearly trying to attract Eskkar's attention.

He scanned the land around him, but saw nothing else. Fully alert, Eskkar rode toward the figure, taking his time. He felt curious enough to see what caused the excitement, but took care lest any bandits try to ambush him. It wouldn't be the first time riders had been lured into a trap, and he made sure his sword slid easily within its scabbard.

When he drew closer, Eskkar turned Warrior aside. Instead of riding directly toward the shouting, he galloped up another hill, one that offered a higher vantage point and gave a good view of the man before him.

Not a man, he realized, now that he could see better, but a boy, maybe twelve or thirteen seasons. Another figure, that of an adult, lay behind him on the ground. A flock of sheep, maybe forty or fifty animals, filled a small canyon, held within its confines by a single strand of rope.

Two shepherds, Esskar decided, and one of them injured. Making one last check that the sword remained loose, he trotted the horse downhill and made straight for the boy. By now the unintelligible shouts had turned into calls for help, and the excited figure kept waving him closer.

The boy's voice went silent as Esskar approached. Mouths agape, man and boy stared at him as he rode up. He saw the fear on their faces, and guessed they'd never seen a warrior before. The injured man, a stick fastened around his leg as a splint, fumbled for his knife, clutching it in his hand.

"What do you want," he called out, his voice hoarse with pain.

Esskar stopped the horse ten paces away. "Nothing. Your boy was the one calling for help."

"You don't belong here. Just leave us."

Esskar shrugged. The fool could barely get the words out without gasping from the pain, but didn't want help. "Fine with me. Mind if I ask you a question before I go?" The man said nothing, which Esskar decided to interpret as a yes. "I'm looking for a shepherd named Hermander. Do you know him?"

"Why do you ask?"

"I've business with him." Esskar waited, but no further information was forthcoming. "Then I'll leave you to your work." Turning the horse, he started to leave.

"Wait . . . wait. I know Hermander. What business . . . have you with him?"

Better, Esskar thought. At least the man had some sense. He brought the horse back around to face them. "I'm escorting his brother and a flock of sheep to Hermander's land. But it's been many years since his brother lived in this country, and we want to know the best trail to reach him."

The man ran his tongue over his lips, still clutching his knife. Esskar saw fever burning in the man's eyes and on his face.

"Hermander lives about twenty miles that way," he said, waving his knife hand toward the west. "You reach a stream about five miles from here, follow it until it forks, then stay to the left."

"My thanks to you, then," Eskkar said. He clucked to the horse and moved the halter.

"Wait! You can't leave my father!" The boy's high-pitched voice stopped Eskkar once again.

"Your father says he doesn't need any help."

"We need your horse. My father needs to ride home. He can't walk and . . ."

"Keep silent, son," the father interrupted.

"No, you need the horse or you'll die." The boy pulled a sling from his belt and fumbled a stone into the pouch. "Give us your horse, or I'll kill you."

A thousand curses on these people and their slings, Eskkar thought. If he never saw another one of the cursed weapons it would be too soon.

He held up his hand, and the boy, about to whirl the sling over his head, stopped. "Put the sling away, boy, and maybe I'll help you. But if you throw that stone, I'll kill the both of you."

"Put down the sling," the father ordered, shouting the words with the last of his strength.

The boy hesitated, near tears, but lowered the sling.

Eskkar slid from the horse and tied Warrior to a bush. "How were you going to get your father on the horse, boy? Or keep him there? Do you even know how to ride a horse? Warrior isn't easy to ride."

Of course neither of them would know how to ride. If they had owned a horse, it would be out here with them.

Walking over to the boy, Eskkar took the sling from his hand, tossed the stone away, looped the leather thongs into a ball, and handed it back to its owner. "Put that away," he ordered.

Kneeling beside the father, Eskkar examined the man's injured leg. "When did this happen?"

"Yesterday," the man said, returning his knife to its sheepskin sheath, "just before sundown. Slipped in the rocks chasing after one of the herd."

The leg felt hot to Eskkar's touch, and he could feel the shattered bone beneath the skin. "You have the burning. The leg needs to be set properly, or it will heal badly. It may already be too late. Where is your family?"

Sweat covered the man's face, and he'd flinched at Eskkar's touch. "We took the herd out two days ago. My farm is about six or seven miles away, to the north."

Too far to ride for help, especially over hilly ground. By the time Eskkar got there, explained the situation, and returned with the man's kin, the shepherd would be beyond saving.

The injured man understood the silence. "Can you help me?"

"I'm no healer, but the man I'm with, Balthasar, will know more about such injuries. Between us, we might be able to set the leg straight . . . give it a chance to heal."

Standing, Eskkar turned toward the boy. "What's your name?"

"Maldar, Lord. My father's name is Vromar."

Eskkar smiled at that. No one had ever called him "lord" before. Nor would anyone else likely use that title. "Your father needs to drink lots of water, Maldar. Get as much water as you can carry and bring it here. Can you do that?"

Maldar nodded, his eyes wide.

"Good. I'm going to fetch Balthasar." Eskkar glanced up at the sun, nearly at its highest in the sky. "We'll be back as quick as we can. Don't let your father move about, either. The more he tries to move the leg, the worse it will get. Understand?"

Untying Warrior's halter, Eskkar jumped onto his horse and cantered down the hill. As soon as he reached level ground, he put the horse to a full gallop.

Before the sun had descended to mid afternoon, Eskkar and Balthasar strode up the hill to where the injured man lay. Maldar had spread his tunic over a branch from a bush and held it over his father's head, to provide a patch of shade for his face.

Vromar looked up anxiously as the two men arrived. Eskkar carried two stout sticks, each as thick as a man's wrist and as straight as he could find. He also carried the long tether he used to walk Warrior.

"I am Balthasar, brother of Hermander." The shepherd squatted on the ground beside the injured man.

"My name is Vromar," the man gasped, his lips trembling with the effort to hold back the pain. "This is my son, Maldar."

Even in his short absence, Eskkar could see both the pain and fever had gotten worse.

"Maldar, my flock is below," Balthasar said, turning to the boy. "I want to you go there and watch the herd. Help the dog guard them, but don't get too close to him. He's wary of strangers."

Maldar looked at his father, but didn't move.

Vromar knew what was coming. "Go, my son. Keep a good watch over Balthasar's sheep until he's finished here."

The boy had more tears in his eyes. Eskkar took him by the shoulder and started him moving. "Down the hill with you, boy. And don't come back, no matter how much your father cries out. We need to set the leg properly and it's going to hurt."

He pushed the lad on his way and returned to the others. Balthasar had already undone the crude splint Vromar had applied, and readied the two sticks Eskkar had carried. Balthasar pulled the boy's tunic off the shade sticks, and using his knife, cut it into two long strips. That would have to do for a bandage.

"You'll have to hold him steady. He can't be moving about."

Eskkar scooped up a thick twig from the ground. "Bite on this, Vromar, and try not to move." He took the knife from the man's belt, and tossed it aside, out of reach. When the pain came, Vromar might try to injure them or even himself. "If you struggle, I'll have to knock you out."

"Do what you have to," Vromar said, before biting hard on the stick and closing his eyes.

Eskkar knelt beside him, using his knee to hold the man fast, immobilizing Vromar as much as possible by sheer body weight.

Balthasar had readied himself. He put his own weight on the man's hip, took the injured leg in both hands, and pulled it straight with a quick jerk. The first scream rose up into the air, and Vromar's body arched up, the sudden movement nearly tossing Eskkar's bulk aside. Swearing, Eskkar pressed down harder on the man's shoulders.

Balthasar began working on the leg. The shrieks came without ceasing, loud despite the clenched stick between Vromar's lips.

Twice Eskkar nearly lost his grip as Vromar thrashed around, the man's agonies giving him extra strength. Suddenly Vromar fainted, his body going limp. Eskkar plucked the stick from the man's mouth. "Hurry, before he comes to."

Balthasar methodically continued his ministrations, straightening the broken bone, and fitting the jagged ends together as best he could. Each movement made the man, despite being unconscious, twitch from pain, but he didn't awaken and Balthasar didn't stop until satisfied with his work.

Working faster now, Balthasar washed the leg clean and bandaged it, wrapping the swollen limb tightly using both strips of tunic, until a thick layer of cloth protected the break. He finished by applying the splints and fastening them as tight as he could.

When Balthasar finished, he leaned back on his heels and wiped the sweat from his brow. "That's all I can do here. You need to get him to his family, where he can be tended properly."

Eskkar sat down, facing Balthasar across the unconscious man's body. "I can take him on the horse, but it won't be easy. His leg will have to be held. If it hangs down, every step Warrior takes will be agony for him. If the ride doesn't kill him, it may make the injury worse. It might be better if I take the boy to his family, and they can return here to care for Vromar."

"How would they get back, Eskkar? If they had horses, someone would have come looking for them. They'd still need a way to carry him. Besides, by the time anyone can walk here, Vromar will be dead or dying. He needs herbs to break the fever and ease his pain, as well as someone to care for him."

"If I take him on the horse . . ."

"Then his fate rests with the gods," Balthasar said. "At least we'll have done all we can for him."

Getting to his feet, Eskkar walked to the edge of the hill. Below he saw Vromar's son sitting on a rock, his face in his hands and staring at the sheep. "Boy, come on up here."

Maldar broke into a run, racing up the hill to reach his father's side. The boy stared at his father, afraid for a moment, until he saw Vromar's chest still rose and fell.

"Maldar," Eskkar said, remembering the boy's name, "you and I are going to take your father home. You're going to lead the way, and I'll be carrying your father on the horse." He turned to Balthasar. "Can you hold the herd here for a day or so?"

"Yes, there's enough pasture nearby for both flocks for a few days. After that, I'll have to move them. You take him to his family. The dog and I will be fine. The sheep could use the rest."

Eskkar glanced up at the sun. "If we don't get lost, I should reach his farm by sundown. It'll be too dark to return tonight, but I should be back here no later than mid morning."

He drank his fill from the water the boy had prepared and they poured more into the barely conscious Vromar. "Let's get him ready. I've never done this before, but I've heard of warriors doing it."

Eskkar explained what he wanted to do. He didn't bother to mention that he'd also heard of men dying this way as well.

Climbing astride Warrior, Eskkar moved close to a nearby rock. Balthasar lifted Vromar, and carried him next to the horse, staggering a little under the man's weight. Using the rock to step up, Balthasar handed the injured man to Eskkar, who held him sideways across the horse's withers. While Eskkar held the man steady, Balthasar looped the rope around the two men, binding Vromar to Eskkar's chest.

Eskkar slipped his left arm under Vromar's injured leg. He now held Vromar almost as a father would hold a child in his arms. The rope passed under Eskkar's right arm, leaving it free to guide the horse. As long as Eskkar could stay mounted, Vromar wouldn't fall off.

"Let's go, boy," Eskkar said, already feeling the strain in his left arm. But he had to take some of the shock off the leg, or Vromar would experience agony with every step the horse took until the pain killed him. "Maldar, you can run ahead, and pick the shortest path. I'll try and follow you over the easiest ground."

The journey began, the boy jogging ahead, and Eskkar riding slowly behind. Before they'd gone a mile, Eskkar's left arm, the one holding Vromar's legs, trembled from the strain. Twice Vromar woke briefly, each time to moan with his pain, before falling back into unconsciousness.

Eskkar refused to rest until he covered at least two miles. Even then, all he could do was halt and let the blood flow back into his left arm, while Warrior and the boy rested. Eskkar didn't dare dismount; he didn't think he could get Vromar positioned properly by himself.

Another two miles passed. This time Eskkar had to rest longer, before he could continue. The boy appeared in the best shape of all. The pace wasn't too fast for him to keep ahead of them, and he could take an occasional short-cut when the terrain permitted.

The sun began to descend. By now, Eskkar had to stop after every mile, and Warrior started tossing his head in protest of carrying the extra weight. The horse worried Eskkar more than anything. If Warrior got too tired, or began to act up, he might toss them both from his back, probably injuring Eskkar and killing Vromar in the process.

So Eskkar spoke soothingly to the horse, though his mouth went dry from all the talking, and it didn't take long to empty the water skin. He lost count of how many times he stopped. The sun seemed to hang forever in the sky, refusing to move.

Under his breath, Eskkar cursed first the stupid boy who didn't know for sure how far from home they were, then the hilly ground that lengthened the journey, and finally the ever-increasing weight of his burden.

At last the boy, jogging ahead, gave a cry, and pointed with his arm. "That's our land. Our farm's just behind that hill. We're nearly there." Whatever he recognized, it renewed Maldar's strength, and he ran up the slope, shouting as he reached the hilltop.

The hill ahead looked no different from the last ten or so Eskkar had climbed, but he urged Warrior up the hill to where the boy waited, jumping back and forth. At the crest, Eskkar heard the now-familiar sound of sheep bleating in the distance. He looked below to see a small farm holding, four mud huts spaced around a mud-brick well, a real wood corral, and two separate fields planted with what looked like wheat and barley, along with small patches of vegetables. Even a few cattle wandered about.

"Thank Marduk at last," Eskkar muttered to himself, though he doubted the earth god of the dirt-eaters had done much to help him. "We're almost there, Warrior. No more hills to climb."

Eskkar let the tired horse pick its way, and hoped it didn't stumble or break its leg so close to the end of their journey. Maldar, tired by the long trek, walked at Eskkar's knee, holding his father's limp hand. Just before they reached the base of the hill, dogs began to bark, a sharp warning indicating an approaching stranger.

Someone gave a shout, and five or six men came pouring out of the huts, some carrying knives, others brandishing the usual slings. The dogs moved toward Eskkar, barking non-stop and growling as they came.

"Run ahead and tell them what happened, Maldar," Eskkar ordered, "before some fool kills your father. And call off the dogs, before they frighten Warrior."

He slowed the horse, letting the boy go ahead. Maldar stumbled toward his family, calling out for help for his father and yelling at the dogs, kicking at the closest, driving them away from Eskkar's path.

In moments, Vromar's kin surrounded Eskkar, eager hands reaching up to support Vromar's weight. A sturdy young man cut the rope securing the injured man, and Eskkar took what felt like the first deep breath since he'd started out, at least five miles back.

His kin carried Vromar into one of the houses. Eskkar, his left arm numb, slid from Warrior's back and slipped to his knees. A woman started crying, her wails rising up. Another woman joined the first, but they both became silent when they entered the house.

Someone brought a bucket of water to Eskkar, but he could scarcely lift it to his lips. When he did, he drank and drank, wasting half the contents that spilled over his chest. "The horse," he said, wiping his mouth on the back of his hand, "the horse needs water. And grain, too," he added.

Two men helped him to his feet and guided Eskkar to the side of the nearest house where he could sit in the shade, his head lolling back against the wall's rough surface. Another bucket of water arrived, carried by a woman. She held a ladle in her hand. She filled it, then lifted it to his lips.

He tried to take it from her, but his arm muscles still trembled too much to clutch the ladle without shaking, so he let her hold it.

"That's enough for now," she said. "Too much might make you sick."

"Thank you," he said, wiping his lips with the back of his hand.

"They're seeing to your horse, stranger," she said, her voice deeper than he expected. "He'll be cared for and well fed. What's your name? Can you tell me what happened?"

By now, two other women and three boys stood around him, staring with wide eyes at the barbarian. He told her, told all of them, the whole story. When he finished, he took the ladle from the bucket and drank again.

The water and the shade brought relief, and he was starting to feel better. Eskkar flexed his left arm, testing the stiffness; the numbness had already gone, but he knew his shoulder would be sore for the next few days.

Closing his eyes, he once again leaned his head against the wall. When he opened his eyes, he found the women and boys gone, replaced by two men well past their prime. They stood facing him, and the oldest, wearing a clean tunic that proclaimed he did no work in the fields, appeared to be the family elder. Eskkar guessed him to have over sixty seasons. Despite the long white hair and lined face, he noticed the strong resemblance to Vromar.

"Thank you for caring for my grandson," the Elder said, his strong voice showing no hint of his age. "My name is Araham, and this is my cousin, Turcor."

Eskkar nodded politely. "Your thanks should go to Balthasar. He set your grandson's leg. All I did was carry him here." He told them about the sheep and Balthasar's quest for his brother, but didn't think it wise to mention the fight.

"I see," Araham said, "but you still deserve our thanks. I will thank Balthasar another time. Now I can only hope Vromar lives."

"The ride was hard on him," Eskkar said. "He was unconscious for most of it."

"The women have him now. They'll do their best for him." Araham sighed. "Vromar was to take my place as Elder when I die." Shaking his head, he put thoughts of death away for a moment. "I know this Hermander you seek. He is a good man and a good neighbor. His brother's return will be a welcome one, I'm sure. For now, you must stay the night with us. It's too dark to return to your friend."

Eskkar glanced up at the sky. The sun had disappeared beneath the horizon. The ride had taken longer than expected. "All I need is a place to lay my blanket, somewhere close to the horse."

"My women have prepared a place for you in my house. When you're rested, they'll bring food for you. Now we must return to Vromar's side." The two of them turned away, and Eskkar closed his eyes again. When he opened them the first woman had returned. She knelt beside him, holding a cup in her hand.

"I thought you might want some barley ale," she said, offering the full cup with care. "My name is Chaiya."

Using both hands, to ensure he didn't spill any, Eskkar took the cup from her and drank. Despite his thirst, he noticed the ale's fine taste. He seldom could afford good quality ale whenever he frequented an ale house. Araham must have commanded they give him the best of their stock.

"Thank you, Chaiya." He set the cup on the ground, still half full. Her eyes gave the impression of a woman, and her husky voice intrigued him, but her figure looked more like a girl's. Eskkar studied her with some care.

If she minded his gaze, she didn't try to avoid his eyes. "You are a steppes warrior?"

"Not any more," he answered, giving his usual answer to that inquiry. "Not for many years."

"Five years ago, your kind raided this land. Many farmers and shepherds died at the horsemen's hands."

"The clans have raided this land for hundreds of years," he said, speaking without emotion. He picked up the cup, took another sip, and felt his strength returning. "Your people must know that."

She nodded. "Yes, and the steppes warriors will return again, some day. But that is in the past, or in the future. Not today."

"Not today," he agreed.

Chaiya gazed at him, studying his features without embarrassment. "Rest now. I'll bring food in a little while."

She left him, and for the first time since he arrived, Eskkar sat alone. The others, too concerned about Vromar's condition, had little time to think about the stranger in their midst.

After awhile, the women put their worries for Vromar aside as they returned to their chores, though they kept their voices subdued. No matter what might happen to Vromar, life had to continue.

Smoke from the cooking fires streamed crookedly into the sky. A tawny-colored dog, braver or stupider than the others, wandered over and sat on its haunches a few paces away, to stare at the newcomer.

Three young girls passed by, giggling and whispering among themselves as they cast glances at Eskkar. He followed their progress as they headed toward the sheep pen, their movements graceful, almost suggestive, and he knew they enjoyed his gaze. They checked on the animals one more time before darkness fell.

Two older boys arrived, announcing to Eskkar that they'd come to care for Warrior. They led the big horse over to the well, and began washing him, their eyes also turning to stare at the stranger every few moments. He observed them as they poured buckets of water over the horse, then rubbed him down.

At first Warrior snorted nervously at the strange hands on his coat, but as they continued, he relaxed under their touch. They let him drink his fill, before feeding him a bucket of grain.

A choked off cry came from the house, and Eskkar turned to see Maldar, his shoulders slumped, walk out of the house. The boy hesitated for a moment, then headed toward Eskkar. Maldar sank to the ground, his arms wrapped around his knees.

"How is your father?"

"He's awake. He told me to thank you for what you did. My mother says . . . they say he may not live."

"Vromar is strong, and he has many to care for him," Eskkar said. "You must be as brave as he is, to give him honor."

"I'll try, but . . . I'll try."

Fresh tears glinted in the boy's eyes, so Eskkar looked away, not wanting to embarrass him. "If you want to stay here with me for awhile, I'd be glad of your company."

"No, I must go back, to be at my father's side. He also asked that you give his thanks to Balthasar when you see him," Maldar said, rising to his feet. He wiped the moisture from his eyes and returned to the house.

Death, Eskkar knew, came to everyone, sooner or later. He wondered, and not for the first time, how his own life would end. He'd probably be killed by some drunken fool quarreling over his ale. However it happened, Eskkar knew he would die alone. At least Vromar had his family to comfort him.

Chaiya came out of one of the houses, carrying a large platter of steaming mutton. "Start with this," she said, setting it beside him and picking up the now empty cup. "I'll bring more ale."

Using his knife, Eskkar cut the meat into smaller strips. He'd nearly finished the mutton when Chaiya returned. In addition to the ale, she carried another platter. This one held cheese, bread, dates, as well as chickpeas and lentils. She placed that on the ground next to him, then handed him the ale cup.

"This is good ale," he said, swallowing a mouthful. He noticed her ragged garment, much coarser than the ones the other women wore, and wondered if she were a slave. Not many in such deserted places owned slaves, but if they did, more than likely they would be women.

"The ale is Vromar's own," she said. "His barley crop was good this year." Chaiya squatted on the ground across from Eskkar, obviously in no hurry to leave.

"Do you think he'll live?"

"It's too soon to tell."

Something in her tone told him she really didn't care one way or another. He finished the mutton, and half the contents of the second plate. His stomach full at last, Eskkar felt himself relax. Once again he leaned back against the wall.

"Are you leaving in the morning?"

"Yes, as soon as it's light. My friend Balthasar is waiting for me."

"I want you to take me with you."

The abrupt request caught him by surprise. She must be a slave, he decided, one that wanted to run away.

"Your master might not like that."

She laughed, and rocked back on her heels. "I am not a slave, and no one will care if I'm gone. They'll be thankful they have one less mouth to feed, especially mine."

He looked at her for a moment, then drained the last mouthful of ale. In the gathering darkness, neither could see the other's face clearly. "I want no trouble with Balthasar's neighbors. You should . . ."

"Oh, I'll speak with Araham. He will tell you he approves."

She leaned closer to him, studying his face. "If you will have me, I will serve you well, for as long as you want me. All I ask is that you take me away from this place. If you grow tired of me, you can leave me in the first village we come to. Or sell me in the slave market."

Her request didn't surprise him. He'd seen this sort of thing before. The life of a dirt-eater was hard, filled with back-breaking labor from dawn to dusk, season after season. Many of their young men and women, seeing such a stark future before them, longed to run away from their farms and herds, where parents and older brothers ruled their lives as completely as any slave master. Some did, choosing the unknown dangers rather than stay in the life of near bondage.

"Why do you want to leave? Would you really prefer being a slave somewhere else?"

"My husband married me ten years ago, when I reached my thirteenth season. He brought me here, to live with his family. But I was barren, and gave him no children. He died four years ago. Afterwards, according to the customs, his brother took me for a second wife."

Chaiya sighed. "But still I failed to produce a child. When a year passed, he declared the marriage ended and turned me out of his house. Since then, I've lived alone, sleeping on the ground away from the others. The women here shun me, afraid my barrenness will spread to them. Now the men worry they will father no heirs if they lie with me."

"What about your kin? Won't they take you back?"

"My parents are dead, and my kin would treat me the same way as Araham's people," Chaiya said, keeping her voice calm, almost as if she were discussing the evening meal. "A barren woman is of no use to anyone."

For a woman to have no children was a terrible burden, Eskkar knew, as bad as any curse from the gods. A woman's whole purpose in life was to bear sons for her husband, to continue his line. Without children, anything else she did was of little consequence.

"If Araham approves, I'll take you as far as the next village, someplace where you can find something . . ." He didn't know what to say, not sure what a woman alone could find.

"Araham will think it a blessing from the gods, to be rid of me and at the same time make his women happy." She gathered the two trenchers and laid the empty ale cup on top of them. "A place has been prepared for you inside Araham's house, when you are ready to sleep."

"Thank the Elder for his offer, Chaiya, but tell him I'd rather sleep under the stars. I don't like being closed in."

In truth, he didn't like sleeping in any farmer's hut, crowded with strangers, chickens, and any other farm animal likely to wander inside at night seeking warmth. Not to mention the creatures that crawled, attracted by the stink of too many people and too much food.

"As you wish. I'll tell Araham your choice."

As soon as the moon rose, Eskkar prepared himself to sleep. As Chaiya predicted, Araham returned and informed Eskkar she could leave at any time. Eskkar noticed the Elder didn't offer his blessing on her journey.

To bed down for the night, Eskkar found an empty patch of grass about thirty paces from where the boys had secured Warrior. The horse, crunching noisily away at his second helping of grain, seemed more than content with his new surroundings. And the horse would recognize his master's scent, and would feel safer, knowing Eskkar slept nearby.

Chaiya had given him two clean blankets, a real luxury, and he spread one on the ground, and covered himself with the other.

Unsheathing his sword, he lay it beside the blanket, with the knife on the other side.

With a long sigh, he relaxed under the soft wool. The stars shone overhead, and he stared at them for a few moments. Since his talk with Balthasar, he looked at them differently, no longer so certain they had no meaning other than helping travelers find their way.

A noise brought his eyes from the heavens, and he saw a shadow approaching. His hand reached for the sword, fingers finding the hilt.

"It's Chaiya, Master," she called out softly, too softly for anyone else to hear.

When she reached his blankets, she dropped to her knees, almost kneeling on the sword's bare blade. "I thought . . . since you are to be my new master, you might want a woman to keep you warm tonight. Unless you are worried about my barrenness."

Until now, Esskar hadn't fully considered what taking her with him meant. The thought of a having a woman, barren or not, sent a wave of anticipation through him. Besides, the ignorant beliefs of the dirt-eaters meant nothing to him.

"I'm not likely to live long enough to father children, Chaiya," he said. "And I'll take you with me whether you share my bed or not. So you don't need . . ."

She leaned closer to him and placed her finger to his lips, to silence his words. "For years, I've prayed to the gods every night for someone to come and take me away, take me anywhere. For me, no life could be worse than staying here with these people. Now the gods have sent you to me, and I want to please you."

"Then stay with me, Chaiya." He took her hand in his. "Unless you mind sleeping with a barbarian."

She squeezed his hand for a moment, then rose up on her knees. Chaiya gathered her dress, and lifted it over her head. Then she shook out her hair, rumpled by removing the garment.

The moon gave almost no light, but he could see the shadow of her body, and the faint gleam of her breasts. He reached out his hand, and felt the smoothness of her thigh, warm to his touch.

She slid her hand beneath the blanket and found his manhood.

His fatigue forgotten, Eskkar felt himself harden at her touch. He lifted his hand to her breast, cool and soft. He squeezed it lightly, and heard her gasp in response.

She edged closer, pushed the blanket off his body, and leaned over him, letting her breasts brush his lips, while her hand kept holding him tight.

In the darkness, Eskkar thought about her words. No one had ever suggested he might be a gift from the gods. He reached out with his other hand and guided her over his body, holding her for a moment just above him, before letting her ease herself down upon him.

Chaiya moaned softly and gripped his shoulders as he entered her. Hands on her waist, he held her tight, guiding her down as he slid deeper inside. She trembled, her body betraying her pleasure, and she cried out when she had the whole length of him within. Only then did she straighten up.

"You feel good, Master." Her voice sounded deeper, almost hoarse, and she began to rock against him.

"You are very wet," he said, as the first wave of pleasure went through him.

"Does that displease you?"

"It pleases me very much, Chaiya." Taking her breasts in his hands, he pushed up against her. She moaned again, losing her rhythm for a moment before she resumed her rocking.

Eskkar lay back, looking up at her body, her breasts swaying over him. He let her control the pace, felt her grow still more moist as she increased her movements, faster and faster, her body now pounding on his as she rubbed herself against him, her breathing growing more rapid and her hands digging into his arms.

With a sudden frenzy, she cried out, her whole body trembling, and Eskkar knew she'd reached the pleasure of the gods. After that, he had no strength to hold back, and he, too, gasped in delight as he felt his seed burst inside her.

She never ceased moving, not stopping until he could no longer stand the pleasure and lifted her away from his body. Chaiya collapsed beside him, still breathing hard. She bent over and kissed him, a long lingering kiss that only ended when they needed to breathe.

Even then she wasn't finished. Her hair fell across his hips as she took him gently in her mouth, licking him clean, and making him twitch at every touch of her tongue.

Finally he pulled her away, and she curled up against his shoulder. A jerk of the blanket covered them both, and he held her tight, almost as tight as she held him. They relaxed together, their heartbeats slowing gradually, until she fell asleep still in the crook of his arm, and he felt himself drifting off.

But then Chaiya spoke. At first he thought she'd wakened, but the way she slurred her words told him she still slept.

"You took so long to send him to me."

He needed a moment to understand her words. Then he realized that, half-dreaming, she spoke not to him, but to whatever gods she worshipped or prayed to.

He kissed her forehead and with a satisfied murmur she quieted into a deep sleep.

Eskkar turned his eyes to the stars overhead, thinking about Balthasar and wisdom, and now Chaiya and her foolish thought that Eskkar came from the gods. It must be the sheep, he decided.

Ever since he'd become involved with the pointy-hoofed creatures and their hard-headed shepherds, Eskkar's simple ideas about his life and future had become confused. He'd plodded along from place to place, trying to stay alive, without giving much thought to what the coming months and years might bring.

In truth, a warrior should have some sense of his future. Eskkar had grown to manhood in the lands of the dirt-eaters, but stood no closer to their acceptance than the day he left the Alur Meriki.

The stars remained silent, offering no words of either wisdom or encouragement. But if Balthasar spoke the truth, they might have an answer for him someday.

Where would his life end, he wondered? More important, how would it end – in honor or in ignominy? Nevertheless, despite the weighty thoughts, he fell asleep, as content in his own way as Chaiya.

The sun had just cleared the horizon, the sky a bright blue streaked with pure white morning clouds above his head. Warrior, pawing the ground, stood ready, and Eskkar waited only for the Elder to deliver his message.

"Vromar's fever has broken," Araham said, a hint of satisfaction on his weary face. "It seems the gods have answered our prayers. He may live."

"I'm glad for you and your kin," Eskkar answered. Almost everyone from the household turned out to see his departure, regular duties put aside. He felt uncomfortable, unused to such attention. Warrior, already full with another bucket of grain in his belly, tossed his head impatiently.

"Though he will walk with a limp for the rest of his days," Araham said, somehow implying that the gods hadn't quite answered his prayers as well as they should.

More than a limp, Eskkar guessed. Even if Vromar's leg healed, it would remained crooked, and as long as he lived, there would be pain with every step he took. The dirt-eaters, who tended to blame every misfortune on some god's ill-will, might even believe that Vromar brought this onto himself for some misdeed or other.

"His sons will help him," Eskkar said, smiling at Maldar who stood closest to him.

"Go with the blessing of the gods, Eskkar," Araham said, the words repeated raggedly by the others.

At last the farewells ended. Eskkar swung himself onto Warrior's back, the smooth movement drawing a murmur of admiration from the gathering.

"May I walk with you to end of the valley?" Maldar asked.

Eskkar nodded, and glanced at Chaiya. She waited a few paces away, a large sack slung over her shoulders, somehow not quite a part of the family even on this day.

He turned the horse and began walking, Maldar on his left and Chaiya on his right. They followed the easy path which, according to Maldar, led around the base of the hill and past the barley field.

"Thank you for saving my father's life," Maldar said, as soon as they left the others out of earshot. "I only wish I had something to give you in my father's name."

"Perhaps there is a way you can repay the debt," Eskkar said, a little surprised at the generous thought from one so young. "Maybe you can do something for Balthasar one day, to ease his labors when he grows older."

"I will do that," Maldar said, "I promise it."

Suddenly Eskkar pulled back on the halter, stopping Warrior. Chaiya and Maldar looked up at him in surprise, unsure of what caused him to halt. Eskkar's gaze remained fixed, his eyes focused on the edge of the barley field.

"Maldar, I think there is something you and your family can do for me right now, if you would."

"Anything, Eskkar. I'm sure Araham will give you anything you need."

Eskkar explained what he wanted. Chaiya laughed, and Maldar raced back to the house. It took him only a few moments there to find a sack, and he returned at a run, stopping at the edge of the field before trotting back to Eskkar's side.

"Here," he said, handing up the sack. "The best two in the litter."

Noon had already passed when Eskkar led Warrior down the last hill. The brown dog barked its warning, and Balthasar, sitting on the ground, looked up, no doubt surprised to see Eskkar walking and a woman astride the horse.

"You're late," Balthasar said, glancing at the sun. "You said you would be back by midmorning."

Eskkar dropped the halter and reached up to take the sack Chaiya held with both hands. "Here, Balthasar, I've a present for you. From Maldar and his kin."

Balthasar nearly dropped the sack when Eskkar shoved it into his hands. A puppy's head burst through the opening, followed almost immediately by another. Both began barking, a high-pitched yipping that made the sheep stop their grazing and stare nervously in their direction.

Brown dog, his tail low and legs stiffening as he approached, growled back at these unknown and potentially dangerous creatures, and the puppies yapped even louder, fearless in spite of the strange dog's presence.

The old shepherd sank to the ground, releasing the two pups, who immediately began running around, barking excitedly, and glad to be free from the sack.

Chaiya swung her legs over Warrior's side, and Eskkar took her in his arms and lowered her to the ground. "And this, in case you're interested, is Chaiya. She's coming with us."

Speechless, Balthasar stared at the two of them. Meanwhile, one puppy had climbed into his lap and started licking his face, while the other tugged at his fingers.

"After all," Eskkar said, "you lost the black dog, so you need another. Why not two? Maldar claimed they come from good sheep-herding stock, so they should be useful."

Chaiya took Eskkar's hand, and they both watched Balthasar, who smiled back at them.

"Thank you, Eskkar. Once again you have me in your debt," Balthasar said, unable to say anything more.

Enough of all this thanking, Eskkar said to himself. All these people thanking him, again and again, it didn't seem right, not for a warrior. Something else to think about tonight, when he looked up at the stars. He put his arm around Chaiya's shoulders. At least he wouldn't be sleeping alone for the next few days.

13

One year later . . .

Eskkar rode into the nearly deserted village of Didra, ignoring the bitter stares cast at him. The remaining villagers scurried aside, their angry faces reflecting a mix of hatred for the rider and envy for the horse. Most ignored him altogether.

Didra, nestled at the foot of the eastern mountains, had never held more than a few hundred people. Almost all its inhabitants had fled, taking whatever they could with them, everyone desperate to escape the Alur Meriki horsemen heading their way.

Almost all the people Eskkar saw would likely be dead or enslaved by sundown. They'd waited too long before attempting to escape, praying to their feeble gods that the barbarians would pass them by.

He knew they wouldn't get very far, not compared to horsemen who could travel enormous distances with ease. Villagers who'd fled the village when the first rumor came might escape, but not these poor fools.

As for the old, the young, and the infirm left behind, their only hope lay in hiding or throwing themselves in the dust and pleading for their lives from the Alur Meriki warriors. Since the barbarians held mercy in low esteem, most could expect little more than a quick death.

At the Village Elder's house, Eskkar glanced at the mid-morning sun as he dismounted, keeping a tight grip on his horse's halter. He didn't intend to leave the horse's side for any reason.

Gallred, Didra's leading merchant and Village Elder had, of course, prepared well for his own escape. Six fresh horses, all of them fine mounts, stood inside Gallred's tiny courtyard, guarded by two men with drawn swords. Given a half day head start, those horses would take the merchant and his family swiftly out of harm's range.

Along with his wife and two grown sons, Gallred had almost completed their own preparations. Two days ago the first tales reached Didra about Alur Meriki raiding parties overrunning the countryside to the northwest.

The merchant, forced to wait until his sons returned from a trading venture to the south, had dispatched Eskkar to gather information on the approaching warriors, offering hard coins to compensate for the dangerous mission.

Gallred, a sword belted around his waist, finished fastening a sack around his horse's neck before turning to face Eskkar. "Well, I'd given up on you. I thought you were dead or had run like all the rest."

"Soon enough for that," Eskkar replied, leading his horse over to the trough to let it drink, not bothering to ask permission.

"You don't have much time, Gallred. Depending on how many farms the Alur Meriki stop to loot, they'll be here by midday, maybe less. I saw at least two large bands moving this way, and at least one group of slave gatherers trailing behind."

The warriors, always in need of fresh slaves to replace those worked to death, would be rounding up any able bodied men and women they could capture. The oldest and youngest warriors usually took possession of newly captured slaves, allowing the main raiding parties to keep moving.

"Damn the gods," Gallred said. "I hoped … seven years ago they passed us by."

"This isn't even their main force, Gallred, just a large raiding party come from the north."

"How many, do you think?"

"It's a big force, maybe two, three hundred," Eskkar said. "More than enough to blanket this land."

Eskkar unfastened his water skin from the horse's neck and carried it to the merchant's well. Gallred not only walked beside him, but the merchant drew up a bucket for Eskkar, who rinsed the skin out with the first bucket, and filled it to capacity with a second.

"Didra's luck has run out," Eskkar said. "You're right in the middle of their line of march. By this time tomorrow, your village will be burned to the ground, along with your crops. They'll slaughter any herd animals they can't lead away."

Gallred shook his head in disgust at the news. "Which way, Eskkar? That's what I need to know."

"You'll need to ride hard to the southeast," Eskkar said, swilling directly from the bucket before dumping the remainder of its contents over his face and neck.

He told Gallred not only what he had seen and heard with his own eyes, but what he gleaned from others he encountered. The detailed information, Eskkar knew, might just save Gallred and his family. As Eskkar finished relating what he'd discovered, the merchant's face grew even grimmer.

"Damn the gods," Gallred repeated. "We'll have to hug the mountain until we can reach the pass to the east. At least three days ride. You're sure we'll be safe if we go that way?"

"I think they'll turn south before then. But with so many raiding parties, you never know where they might ride."

"You can come with us," Gallred offered. "I can always use another guard."

Eskkar shook his head. "No, I have to go north. I think I can slip past their advance scouts. Besides, they'll be less interested in one horseman than fat villages or farms. Or large parties of horsemen like yourselves."

True enough, as far as it went, but not the real reason he wanted to ride alone. Years before, Eskkar had ridden with other villagers trying to flee a barbarian incursion. On the second night, he'd been attacked by a mob and nearly killed. Frightened and panicky villagers made little distinction between an outcast barbarian and those chasing them.

While Eskkar fought the villagers off, one, smarter than the rest, stole his horse, disappearing into the darkness as the other attackers screamed in rage and frustration. Left on foot with the rest of the refugees, Eskkar had nearly gotten caught by the warriors. Since then, in times of chaos, Eskkar trusted no one but himself.

"Well, good luck to you, then," Gallred said. He pulled his pouch from beneath his tunic, and counted out twelve silver coins, two more than the amount agreed upon when he sent Eskkar out scouting.

Taking the coins, Eskkar nodded to the merchant. The horse had quenched its thirst, and Eskkar mounted. "Ride fast, Gallred. And take as little with you as possible."

The merchant laughed as he gazed around him. "We're already down to nothing but food and weapons. Which reminds me." He lifted a sack from the ground and tossed it to Eskkar.

"Here's some extra food I decided not to bring. Maybe you can use it. Better you than the barbarians. Come back when things quiet down. I'll probably need all the guards I can find." He turned to his family and followers. "Mount up. We're leaving now."

Eskkar and the six members of Gallred's group rode out of the village at a gallop, ignoring the curses and even a few stones tossed at them by angry people forced to move aside as the horses thundered by.

Less than a mile outside of the village, Eskkar turned aside with a final wave, and headed north, toward the mountains. Right away, the number of travelers he encountered began to diminish. Not many would be going this way, heading so close to the approaching raiders.

He kept his eyes moving, scanning the horizon for any sign of war parties. Eskkar had taken the risky job Gallred offered because, as usual, Eskkar needed the coins.

More than that, Gallred had befriended him years ago, taking him in and giving him work when no others would. Their paths had crossed again last year. Gallred not only remembered Eskkar, but respected the honest service Eskkar had done for him.

When Gallred asked him to gather information about the barbarians, Eskkar had ridden to the west. There he found the Alur Meriki war parties advancing far faster than he expected, scouring the countryside as they rode. To save his own skin, he probably should have abandoned Gallred's task.

Instead, Eskkar had continued on, stubbornly gathering as much information as he could about the barbarians' movements. Once he set his mind to a task, Eskkar liked to finish it properly.

And now the time to worry about that decision had passed. Eskkar expected the Alur Meriki warriors would drift more to the south, where the farms were bigger and the land more populous, yielding greater opportunities for pillaging.

Nevertheless, the barbarians knew some dirt-eaters would flee toward the northern hills, and the warriors might send a small force to ride just beneath the mountains, sweeping up those they found and driving the rest of the farmers and villagers back into the path of the main horde. Eskkar had to avoid that band of horsemen, if indeed they existed.

Now time had nearly run out, and Eskkar needed some luck to help him escape. He chose the most direct path toward the hills, seeking the safety of the foothills, guiding the horse with care whenever the ground grew rough. He'd possessed the horse, whom Eskkar had named "Boy" for lack of anything better, for almost a year.

Standing nearly as high as his previous horse Warrior, Boy lacked some of Warrior's endurance. To save Boy's strength as much as possible, Eskkar dismounted often to run alongside the animal, holding tightly to the halter at all times.

Without Eskkar's weight, Boy was less likely to stumble and break a leg on the steeper climbs. The horse had enjoyed little rest for the last four days, and Eskkar knew the beast needed not only a good breathing spell but plenty of food as well. Fortunately, some of Gallred's grain still remained, and when they stopped for the night, the horse would eat at least one more good meal.

As they traveled farther north, the landscape changed rapidly. A wind blew steadily off the slopes, pushing against horse and rider.

The hills grew higher and more frequent, forcing Boy to labor as he climbed up and scrambled down ever steeper slopes. Meanwhile Eskkar prayed to the gods the tiring animal wouldn't be injured.

By the end of the day, both man and beast had pushed themselves as much as they could. The place Eskkar chose to camp nestled high in the foothills. From his vantage point, he could see almost five miles into the western plains. As the sun began to set, Eskkar spotted several dust clouds glinting in the fading light, but couldn't tell their direction with any certainty, though the nearest seemed to be past Didra.

Eskkar thanked Gallred for his gift of the food sack as soon as he opened it. Four small loaves of bread, dates, nuts, even a tiny pot of honey, more than enough food for three or four days, and well worth the extra weight to carry. Ripping into a loaf of bread, he finished that off, along with the honey, a rare treat for him, and one he decided he better eat first, before the pot got smashed from all that riding.

The horse licked up the last of Gallred's grain, and filled its belly by cropping all the grass it could find near the campsite. Well fed and exhausted, Eskkar fell asleep, his sword by his side.

He woke just before sunrise, and Eskkar watched anxiously as a spectacular dawn flooded rosy light between the northern peaks and into the dark blue of the sky. Chilled from the cool night air, Eskkar took some time to work the stiffness from his limbs.

Taking another loaf of bread from the sack, he ate, using the time to scan the land below him. Movement caught his eye, and a handful of bread remained suspended at his mouth for a moment. A line of horsemen traveled along the base of the hills, moving slowly, but coming toward him and following roughly the same path he'd taken the day before.

"Damn all the gods," he said, "they shouldn't be here, not to chase down one man." Eskkar forced himself to chew the last few mouthfuls of the suddenly dry bread, all he could swallow in his anger.

Scanning the landscape again, he saw no other war parties or villagers trying to escape. He could now count twelve riders, about two miles away over rough ground. That wouldn't give him much of a lead, if they were indeed on his trail.

He shoved the remainder of the food back in the sack, then tied it closed before fastening it on the horse. Eskkar drank his fill from the water skin, forcing himself to take a few extra swallows. Better to drink it now, than have to carry it during a chase. Untying the horse, he led the animal to a small depression in the rocks, and emptied a good portion of the water skin's contents for Boy to drink.

When the animal had licked the rocks dry, Eskkar shook the water skin. Nearly empty, it held enough for a few mouthfuls for man and beast later today. By tonight, both of them would be thirsty, unless they encountered a stream.

Holding firmly to the halter, he walked beside his mount as he guided it down the slope and toward the next elevation, not rushing his pace. The horse, like its master, needed to stretch its muscles before any hard riding, and today promised to be a long and strenuous one.

Keeping his eyes on the trail ahead, he thought about the men pursuing him. With most of the farmers and villagers fleeing to the south, these warriors must have some other purpose that brought them toward the mountains.

His tracks might have supplied them with one more reason to climb into the foothills. Whether they originally sought after him or not, now that they had his trail, they would make every effort to ride him down.

If Eskkar kept climbing straight into the mountains, going ever higher and higher into the rough terrain, the warriors might abandon the chase. One man, even one with a horse, shouldn't be worth the risk of taking twelve or so animals into these rocks. The horsemen certainly wouldn't expect him to be carrying anything valuable. Even if he had some precious store of gold or gemstones, he would have stashed them under some rock by now.

For the first part of the ride, Eskkar refused to look back to see if they were still pursuing, or worse, gaining on him. When he did halt, he'd climbed nearly another five hundred paces and reached a small plateau that extended like a dagger's blade into the next line of hills.

It took only moments to locate his pursuers, now plainly following his tracks and moving at about the same pace as their quarry. They'd dismounted as well, a bad sign that showed their determination. They wouldn't be walking if they didn't intend to continue the chase no matter how long it lasted.

Either they were definitely following him, which he still found hard to believe, or for some unknown motive they headed in the same direction. Now they'd enjoy the hunt, certain that their fresher horses were sure to catch up with him sooner or later, until he turned at bay, like an exhausted mountain lion.

The warriors would bring him down with arrows, maybe aiming at his legs to take him alive. Eskkar shivered at the thought. Torture, humiliation, and a slow death would be his if they managed that. He swore to himself that they wouldn't take him alive. He would fall on his sword first.

"Well, they haven't got us yet, Boy," he said, though he wished for the tenth time he still had Warrior. Nevertheless, Eskkar knew he could depend on the beast, even if Boy lacked some of Warrior's strength and endurance.

He mounted and galloped across the small plateau and onto a switchback that provided access to the next level of hills. Eskkar didn't notice any tracks, but this could be a known trail into the mountains.

For a while, his path perversely took him toward the men approaching him, though at a higher elevation. Looking down, Eskkar could see them quite clearly, and knew they could see him. They'd gained on him, and would be at the plateau sooner than he expected.

Eskkar forced himself to ignore their rapid progress. Worrying too much about what they did would only slow him down. He had to go as fast as he could, and hope the gods smiled on him. He had eluded horsemen before, and he'd do it again.

When the trail grew steeper, Eskkar swung off the horse and began jogging, giving the tiring animal a rest. The sun moved a hand's breadth across the sky, the trail turning back on itself several times as it rose ever higher. Sometimes he could catch a glimpse of his trackers, other times the rocks shielded them from view. Looking westward toward the plains, Eskkar guessed he'd climbed a good mile above the valley floor.

By the time he reached the next plateau, Eskkar could barely take another step and his lungs burned with every breath. He pulled himself onto the horse with a grunt, and rode as fast as he dared, the beast scrambling over loose rocks that scattered behind them.

For almost half a mile, he moved downhill, and the horse made good speed, though Eskkar's heart jumped every time the animal slipped on the loose stones littering the ground. A sprain or injured knee, and they would both be dead. Meanwhile, a child could follow his tracks. Eskkar cursed, struggling to control his anger and frustration.

He hated being hunted, pursued like a game animal for sport. All his life he'd run from one enemy or another, without ever having a place of safety, a place to call his home. Someday he'd find that place, he vowed. Eskkar pushed the strength-sapping thoughts from his mind and concentrated on staying alive.

The next line of hills would have to ensure his escape. If he couldn't lose his pursuers in these twisting canyons, the horsemen would get him sooner or later. He dismounted as the hills began, and started walking, his legs immediately protesting the upward climb.

Within a hundred paces, the trail split. One path looked steeper than the other, so he chose the easier way. With luck, the warriors would expect him to take the harder branch. Even so, he took some precious time to make sure he hadn't left any sign of which path he'd taken.

Now he moved slower, taking care not to disturb any rocks that might show his trackers that he passed this way. Another split appeared, and again he chose the easier way. By now, the looping turns around gigantic boulders had confused his sense of direction. At times he couldn't see the peaks he used for landmarks. Soon he would be completely lost. Still, his eyes moved constantly, always searching for the easiest ground that covered the shortest distance.

At least he wasn't leaving any sign of his passage, and a good tracker would have to get down on his hands and knees to notice the occasional faint hoof marks scraped on the rocky shelf. The path narrowed, with towering boulders rearing precariously over his head. Just four paces wide at first, it closed in even tighter in places, barely wide enough for the horse to pass. Suddenly the passage straightened out, with only a gradual curve to his left.

Quickening his pace, Eskkar moved as fast as he dared, but still took care not to leave any sign. The slight leftward curve soon blocked the trail behind him. After so many twists and turns, Eskkar had no idea which way he was going; he might be heading right back toward his pursuers. The long, curving stretch continued, and he hurried along. By now he'd covered three or four hundred paces, and he could only hope this path led somewhere safe.

Eskkar circled around another of the endless rocks and stopped short. About fifty paces ahead, the trail ended against a sheer rock wall, with no possible way for either horse or rider to climb over it. Groaning at his bad luck, Eskkar realized he would have to retrace his steps, and hope he could reach the last split before his pursuers arrived.

"Damn . . . damn . . . damn every god and demon that haunts me," he shouted, giving vent to his rage. Eskkar tied the horse to a stunted bush growing at the base of the rocks, and climbed the side of the nearest cliff.

He needed to get an idea of where he was, though he hated the thought of wasting more precious time. Twice Eskkar slipped and nearly fell, but he reached the top, breathing hard. The sun's position gave him some direction, and the added height helped him search the rocks and cliffs for the warriors.

Eskkar spotted them soon enough. They'd already reached the first fork in the trail. They stopped for only a moment, before deciding what to do. They divided their forces, with six riders coming along the trail he'd taken not long before.

His only chance was to retrace his steps back to the second fork, the one that had led him to this blank wall, and this time take the other branch. Yet Eskkar knew that even if he got back there before his pursuers reached it, they'd be only moments behind him.

If they reached the branch first, if all six chose the same dead end that he'd taken, he would meet them face to face. Eskkar might possibly fight his way past one or two of them, but with that many. . . they would riddle him with arrows.

"Damn these cursed rocks," he muttered. He climbed down, reached for the halter, and started to untie it.

"Hello."

Eskkar's heart jumped and pounded in his chest. He whirled around, looking for the voice. He saw no one, and his heart raced even faster at the thought that the rocks had spoken to him. Fear made him reach for the sword slung across his back.

"Up here," the voice said.

Lifting his eyes, he saw a head, a young girl's head, peering at him from a ledge about twenty feet above. Her voice had echoed off the rocks, which amplified it into something spectral.

"Did I scare you?"

He had to swallow before he could answer. "By the gods, yes, you scared me out of my hide." Eskkar started to add a few curses, then closed his mouth. He stepped back to get a better look at her.

The girl rested on her elbows, holding her head in her hands as she leaned out over the ledge. She looked to have eight or nine seasons, from what little he could see of her. Taking a deep breath, Eskkar got a grip on his anger. She'd appeared from somewhere, and maybe she knew of another way out of this accursed place.

"What's your name, little one?"

"Keja," she said. "What's yours?"

"Eskkar. Can you help me, Keja?" The girl's brown eyes looked far too large for her head, what little he could see of it behind an untidy tangle of black hair. "Alur Meriki warriors are following me, Keja, and they'll be here soon. I need to find a way out of these rocks."

"Aren't you a barbarian, too?"

Gritting his teeth, he forced another smile to his face.

"I was one once, long ago, but now I'm not. That's why they're chasing me. Is there a way out of here?"

Every moment counted now, and he couldn't waste much more time talking to a child. On the other hand, she might know a place to hide, even if he had to abandon the horse.

Keja stared down at him for moment, then looked out over the rocks. "I see them," she said. "Why are they chasing you?"

"I don't know, Keja. But there's no time to waste. They'll be here soon."

"You won't hurt me or my grandma?"

"No, I swear it," Eskkar answered. He glanced back down the trail, expecting to see horsemen riding toward him at any moment. His horse snorted as the shadow of a hawk swept across the ground.

"Will you let me ride the horse?" Keja asked.

It took all of Eskkar's willpower to keep his temper in check, but somehow he managed. "Yes, I will, but I'll probably have to ride with you."

She gazed at him for a long moment before making up her mind. "At the end of the path," she said, pointing to the sheer rock wall up ahead. "There's a little trail that leads here," she said, waving her arm behind her.

Eskkar turned and stared at the end of the passage. It looked solid, and he couldn't see any way past it. Still, it wouldn't take long to make sure. Looping the halter around a rock, he ran down the trail until he reached the massive boulder that blocked the way.

The small opening couldn't be seen until he actually touched the rock face. But it was there, on his left, a low cleft between the rock face and the adjacent cliff.

"We brought a donkey through here," Keja said, her voice offering encouragement.

Again her words startled him, and he jerked his head to see her standing just above. He looked back at the opening. His horse was a lot bigger than a donkey, but Eskkar decided to give it a try. "Stay here," he ordered, "and don't let the warriors see you."

Running back to the horse, he untied the halter and led Boy at a slow pace toward the hidden crevice. Pushing the horse's rump, he first turned Boy sideways on the trail, so that he faced the gap between the rocks. Taking a firm grip on the halter, Eskkar ducked under Boy's neck and entered the crevice, tugging on the halter.

The horse refused to follow, rolling his eyes and looking nervously at the narrow sides. Eskkar pulled harder, and the horse took a hesitant step toward it, then another.

"Come on, Boy, you stubborn brute," he said, taking care to keep his voice low and reassuring. "If a fool of a donkey can do it, you can, too."

Walking backwards, Eskkar kept speaking to the animal, showing him the way, and always keeping pressure on the rope. A few more steps and Boy was inside, still looking askance at the narrow and steep path before it.

Eskkar kept pulling on the halter, half dragging the animal forward, until the path widened a bit. At last the horse, no longer fearing the confining rocks, lengthened its stride, taking the strain off the halter rope.

"My thanks to the horse gods, Boy," Eskkar muttered. He led the horse deeper into the rocks, about a hundred paces, before he stopped. Patting the horse's neck in gratitude, Eskkar tied the halter around a jagged splinter of stone protruding from the rock wall.

Now he had to make sure no one could follow his path.

"Stay here, Keja," he ordered. She had followed along behind the horse. "Don't make any noise or show yourself. The warriors will be looking for us both. I'll be back in a moment."

Then he turned and retraced his steps. On the way, he passed a low bush struggling to survive in the rocks. He twisted off a branch and took it with him. When he slipped back through the crevice, he saw nothing on the trail yet, but the horsemen could be only moments away.

Running as fast as he could, he reached the point where he'd first heard Keja's voice. Dropping to his knees, he used the branch to sweep the ground with care, trying to erase all signs of the horse's passage down the last thirty paces. If the warriors had tracked him, Eskkar wanted them to think he'd come this far, then turned around.

Several times he stopped his sweeping to scoop handfuls of dirt and loose stones, which he scattered across the ground. He spotted a black hoof mark on the trail. Using his knife, he cut off a strip of his tunic, ripping the material savagely in his haste.

Spitting on the mark, Eskkar rubbed the telling sign away with the cloth. He repeated that process twice before reaching the cleft and climbing back to his feet.

Examining the rock face, Eskkar saw a tuft of horsehair clinging to the opening, and he plucked that loose as well, shoving it into his tunic before he slipped gratefully into the crevice, breathing a sigh of relief at being out of sight.

Taking care to move without a sound, he walked back to where Keja waited, the young girl reaching up to rub the horse's shoulder, while Boy twitched his ears nervously at this strange little creature determined to keep petting him.

"Let's go further into the rocks," he said, scooping up the child and setting her on the horse. "But you must not make a sound, or they will hear us. Can you do that?"

She nodded, and he told her to cling to the horse's mane. He guided the horse slowly, trying to make as little noise as possible as he followed a narrow path that led only the gods knew where.

Eskkar had bought some time, but he wasn't out of danger. Besides, he might have slipped away from one group of pursuers only to stumble into another. Still, the farther he traveled away from the crevice, the more he relaxed. This trail seemed to lead directly into the mountains, climbing steadily as it went.

A fork in the passage, and Eskkar stopped, unsure of which path to take. One way continued the slight upward ascent, the other slanted down. He turned to the child. "Which way? Remember, we don't want to run into any warriors."

Keja pointed to the left, the track that led downward. "That's the way to our camp."

Eskkar stared dubiously at the narrow, twisting trail. "And the other, where does that lead?"

"It goes into the mountains, but you can't take the horse that way. It's too steep."

Going lower into the valley seemed like a bad choice. His instincts warned him that, sooner or later, he would hit the mountain floor, and might be trapped. Nonetheless, he must rely on the child, or he could easily waste the rest of the day's light exploring and still not be better off.

Eskkar didn't want to encounter any Alur Meriki warriors, though he doubted they knew any more about these hills than he did. Better to find this girl's kin and camp, and fight it out there, if he had to, hopefully with Keja's relatives helping. It wasn't much of a choice, but it was all he had.

Unclenching his teeth, he smiled at Keja. "Well, then, that's the way we'll go."

Guiding the horse at a walk, Eskkar started down the trail. Within a hundred paces, he again lost all sense of direction from the constant turning and twisting. The mountains loomed ever higher on either side, and he started to feel the weight of the rocks towering over him.

Born and raised on the plains, the jumble of massive stones rising up on either side made him nervous. A fall on the slippery rocks might set off an avalanche, burying him and the horse under a wall of stone for all time.

Keja appeared unconcerned, excited over the chance to ride a horse, apparently something she'd never done before. She kept wanting to talk, and he kept telling her to be silent. He had no doubt her high-pitched voice would carry farther than the plopping sound of Boy's hooves.

Eskkar had enough to do trying to guide the horse and watch for enemies at the same time. By now they'd traveled over a quarter of a mile from where Boy squeezed through the rocks. In that distance he felt as if he'd descended at least five hundred feet, well below the plateau behind him.

The trail wove around another of the endless and huge boulders, this one many times the height of a man, and suddenly Eskkar found himself staring in amazement at a tiny valley. Not really a valley, more like a circular glen, about two hundred paces from one side to the other, and surrounded on all sides by towering cliffs. He stopped short, the horse snorting in surprise as its shoulder bumped into Eskkar's back.

About a hundred paces below, a small hut nestled in the still-green grass. In the countryside surrounding the village of Didra, the grass had already turned brown under the summer sun. A tiny rivulet of water trickled alongside the mud-brick house. On the ground flanking the length of the stream, vegetables and even some wheat grew. A donkey wandered around in distress, braying from time to time. The hills and rocks had masked even that sound.

Eskkar ignored the surroundings, his eyes drawn to the knot of men fighting below. One body lay on the ground, its chest splattered with blood visible even from here. Three men struggled with another man . . . no, a woman. As he watched, she broke free from the two men trying to subdue her.

"That's Grandma," Keja said, her voice rising as she saw the struggle. "Help her. Help her!" She leaned forward on Boy's neck, her heels kicking the horse's sides.

The girl would be screaming in a moment, and everyone within half a mile would hear her shrill voice. Eskkar swept her from the horse, cutting short her protests. He shoved the halter into her hands. "Stay here with the horse, and be quiet. I'll go help your grandmother."

He had no time for anything else, just turned and ran. A winding path led to the valley floor, switching back on itself at least once that he could see. Eskkar hoped Keja would stay quiet a few more moments; the attackers might not hear his approach, at least until he reached the canyon floor.

Slipping once, he nearly fell, but he kept moving forward, cursing whenever a loose rock threatened to send him tumbling headfirst.

Halfway down, he lifted his eyes from the slope to look at the spectacle below. The men had recaptured the woman, two of them trying to hold her still. With a shock, Eskkar realized that these men weren't Alur Meriki warriors, but villagers, bandits most likely.

All the same, three men would be more than enough to restrain one woman, and he wondered why they hadn't killed her or just knocked her senseless, to put an end to her struggles.

Despite his haste, the descent took longer than he anticipated. Near the valley floor, the trail reversed itself once again, before finally straightening out and ending in the tall grass.

Eskkar took the last few paces at a dead run, and when his sandals reached the thick grass, he stumbled and fell. The turf and his left hand absorbed most of the shock, and he leapt to his feet with scarcely a pause, his hand feeling for the knife at his belt to make sure he hadn't lost it.

Running hard, he found himself about seventy paces away from the hut. Two of the men held the woman upright, while the other faced her, punching her in the stomach and shouting in her face. They still hadn't seen him, and he moved a little to one side, to keep the hut between him and them.

He'd closed to within thirty paces before one of them heard his approach and called out to his companions. Eskkar pulled the sword from its scabbard and shouted his war cry, the sound echoing against the valley walls.

The men reacted fast. One of them threw the woman to the ground, and all three drew their swords as they faced him. Eskkar never stopped moving. He charged straight at the nearest man, raised his sword, then darted away and struck at the next closest.

That bandit parried the blow, though he staggered back under its force. Eskkar whirled around and lunged at the first man, who shoved Eskkar's blade aside just in time to save his stomach.

Then all three of them closed on Eskkar, circling him, each trying to hold his attention long enough for one of the others to put a sword in Eskkar's back. His longer blade held them at bay, and Eskkar kept shifting his ground, attacking, retreating, feinting at one before shifting to strike at another.

However, these bandits knew their sword-craft, and only one needed to catch Eskkar off guard for a single moment, just enough time to strike a solid stroke. Again and again they attacked, and each time, shifting and lunging, Eskkar could barely defend himself, with never a chance for a killing blow that wouldn't leave him vulnerable.

Breathing hard from the long run, he fought to catch his breath. Eskkar realized he'd backed himself toward the wall of the hut. If he got too close, he be pinned against it, facing three blades. Even if he killed one of them, the other two would finish him.

With a piercing shriek of hatred, the old woman appeared, her dress in tatters and a knife in her hand. She struck one of the men in the back, a vicious blow that took him by surprise and dropped him to his knees with a cry of pain.

Eskkar flung himself toward the nearest man, this time extending himself in a savage lunge that stretched Eskkar down on one knee. His sword slipped under the man's guard and pierced his stomach, sending another scream rising up into the air.

Jerking his weapon from the dying man's body, Eskkar flung himself aside, dodging the overhand stroke that the remaining bandit launched at Eskkar's head. Back on his feet, Eskkar used his blade to parry two more furious strokes that once again drove Eskkar back toward the hut.

Gasping for breath, he felt the weight of his sword dragging down his arm. The bandit, fury on his face and sensing victory, attacked Eskkar, swinging his sword with such a rage that Eskkar couldn't parry the stroke fast enough.

The blade slid along his left arm, a burning cut that brought the two men face to face. Eskkar tried to hammer his enemy in the face with the hilt of his sword, but the man grabbed Eskkar's wrist and pushed it back. Eskkar managed to clutch the man's sword arm, and for a moment, they struggled, each trying to tear loose from the other's grip.

The bandit, almost as tall, had plenty of muscle, and Eskkar, near exhaustion from the long run and hard fight, felt his grip slipping on the man's wrist. With a last effort, the man wrenched his right arm free from Eskkar's grasp. But before the bandit could strike, the old woman darted behind him, another shriek of fury and hatred erupting from her throat as she plunged her knife into the man's side.

The man's eyes went wide, and his grip relaxed for a moment. With a grunt of effort, Eskkar rammed the pommel of his sword into the bandit's face before he could recover. Not that it mattered. The old woman, still in a frenzy, delivered another thrust and another, each one wrenching a gasp from the man as he died, still struggling between the two of them.

Eskkar staggered, as his opponent fell to the ground. The woman turned her eyes toward Eskkar. Her knife pointed straight at him, and he saw the same blind rage in her eyes. She meant to kill him, too.

Using both hands, Eskkar backed away and raised his sword as she paused just long enough to take a breath. Her wild eyes showed no comprehension. He'd have to knock her unconscious somehow.

"Grandma, don't hurt him!" Keja's words echoed against the walls. She'd disobeyed Eskkar's instruction and reached the valley floor, half-leading and half-dragging the horse behind her. "He's my friend, don't hurt him."

The horse whinnied, adding its own excitement to the girl's. Her shouts broke through the old woman's frenzy, and she took a step away from Eskkar as she looked at the girl.

Eskkar didn't move, but he lowered the sword. Keja dropped the halter and ran the last twenty paces to her grandmother, wrapping her arms around her waist, getting between the two of them. Slowly the woman lowered the knife and took another step backward, one arm wrapping protectively around the child.

Eskkar let the sword's tip drop to the ground and stepped back as well, his shoulder bumping into the wall of the hut. He sagged against it, grateful for its support as he leaned over and tried to catch his breath.

The battle rage dimmed in the woman's eyes. She dropped the knife, sagged to her knees and hugged Keja to her, holding her tight and swaying back and forth. Both of them started crying, the young girl from her fears and the woman from the aftermath of the fight.

As Eskkar glanced around, he realized she'd killed three of the four bandits whose bodies lay scattered on the grass. He'd seen women kill before, but never anything to equal her wrath, never three grown men.

Wiping the blood off his sword on a bandit's tunic, he slid the blade into its scabbard. His horse, dragging the halter along the ground, had reached the tiny stream and drank its fill, ignoring the bodies and blood scent. Eskkar scanned the cliffs around him, but saw no sign of anyone. He let himself relax for a moment.

Keja stopped crying, but kept her arms around the old woman. "He's my friend, Grandma Shabata. I told him to save you and he did."

"Thank you, Warrior," the old woman said, stroking the child's head.

Her voice, soft and gentle, made her sound younger than she appeared, and Eskkar took the time to study her. Long black tresses mixed with gray obscured her face and shoulders. Through wild strands sprinkled with blood, he could make out wide brown eyes that still held a hint of the battle craze.

More blood streaked her face and chest, some of it her own. Her patched dress had split down the front during the struggle, half-exposing a lean body. Her hands shook, fingers soaked with blood that continued to bleed. She must have cut herself when she struck with the knife, a common enough occurrence with a slippery blade or when someone didn't know enough to grip the knife with all their strength.

"Let me see your hands," he said. "We need to wash those cuts and bind them up."

She looked at him without comprehension, then lifted her bloody hands. "I . . . don't feel very . . ."

Eskkar stepped forward and caught her as she fainted. The berserker rage had exhausted her spirit, and loss of blood had weakened her body.

"Grandma, are you all right?" Keja cried out. "Don't die, Grandma. Save her!"

The last words were directed at him. "She's just fainted, girl," Eskkar said.

He carried the woman close to the stream and gently lowered her to the ground. The woman's dress, torn and bloodstained, would never be fit to wear again. With his knife, he sliced the garment off, ignoring Keja's protests. Pushing the torn and ragged remains away from her shoulders, he examined her body for wounds, but except for her right hand, found only scrapes and bruises.

"Keja," he said, "do you have a bowl or bucket, something that can hold water?" The girl stood beside him, shifting from foot to foot in her anxiety. "We need to wash the blood away."

She darted off, and Eskkar gathered the bloody dress and held it in the stream. The water's chill surprised him, but he kept rubbing the garment against a stone until most of the blood floated away. Then he cut off a large piece of cloth. Returning to the woman, he pushed her hair to either side of her face and started wiping away the dirt and gore with the wet rag.

Swollen and cut lips showed where a bandit's fist had landed, and she moaned a little at the contact, but didn't wake. A large welt under her left eye had nearly closed it, but no blood oozed.

He went back to the stream and rinsed out the rag. Keja returned, toting a wooden bucket by its rope handle, using both hands. The girl, eyes wide with fright, looked ready to cry again, and he decided to keep her busy.

"Fill it," he ordered. He returned to the woman and resumed washing the blood off her shoulders and chest. Keja came back, struggling to carry the full bucket. She set it down next to Eskkar, a good portion sloshing out as she did so.

"Is Grandma all right? She won't die, will she?"

"She's going to be fine, Keja. Right now we need a blanket. Bring me one. And then I want you to go back up to the rim," he pointed to where they'd entered this hidden valley, "and keep watch. We need to know if anyone else comes this way. If you see someone, run back here quick. Can you do that?"

"Yes," she said, her head bobbing up and down. "You'll take good care of her?"

"I will. Now off you go." Keja darted across the grass toward the trail. "Don't forget the blanket," Eskkar called out after her.

She changed direction and dashed into the hut, skipping over one of the dead bodies as if it were of no consequence. In a moment Keja returned, handing him a ragged blanket before rushing off toward the trail.

Returning to his ministrations, he continued washing the woman's body clean. She had, after all, saved his life. Now that he could see her clearly, he realized she wasn't as old as he thought. Eskkar estimated she had thirty-five or forty seasons, enough years to have ten or twelve grandchildren.

He didn't see any stretch marks on her stomach, but he knew some women never got them. Or they might have faded over the years.

Another rinse of the rag and he started on her legs. Brushing a clump of grass off her right thigh, he found a jagged cut still oozing blood. Scooping water from the bucket, Eskkar poured handful after handful over the gash on her thigh, until he'd washed it clean.

A different part of the dress became a bandage, and he bound her leg as best he could, before turning attention to her knees. Scraped raw and covered with dirt, they also oozed a few drops of blood through the dirt and grass clinging to them.

He rinsed her knees and wrapped bandages around them as well. Finished at last, he covered her with the blanket, tucking it under her chin. Taking the bucket, he stepped away before upending the bloody liquid onto the grass.

Eskkar took a moment to look around, checking the cliffs to see if anyone might be there, either watching or preparing to descend. He saw only Keja, perched on a rock, watching the trail from the rim.

Unfastening his belt, he let it drop to the ground and pulled his tunic over his head. Stepping into the stream, he ignored the chill that numbed his feet within moments. The shallow water reached just above his ankles, so he knelt and splashed water over his body.

His left arm stung, reminding him of the cut he took from the bandit. When he washed the blood away, Eskkar saw the wound wasn't serious. His attacker hadn't bothered to keep the edge of his blade sharp.

By the time Eskkar finished, the cold had seeped into his body. The water must come from the snow capped mountains high to the east, a small trickle that somehow had found its way down to this place.

The ground felt warm beneath his feet, after the chilled water. Eskkar used his tunic to dry himself, then forced the damp garment onto his body, ignoring the shivers on his skin. With another strip of the woman's garment, he bound up the cut on his arm.

Belting his dagger around his waist, Eskkar drew his sword from its sheath. Spots of blood still stained the blade, so he cleansed the bronze in the stream, then rubbed it hard with the last remaining scrap of the woman's dress, to dry the weapon. He slid the blade back in the scabbard and slung it over his shoulder.

When he turned his attention to the woman, she'd regained consciousness, both hands clutching the blanket at her neck, her eyes following his every movement.

He sat on the grass beside her. "Are you in pain?"

"No. Yes. Everything hurts."

Her words sounded slurred, but he decided that was from the bruised mouth, not because her head remained woozy. He smiled at her. "You fought like a lioness. No wonder you're exhausted. And I think you saved my life as well. I thank you for that."

"I had to kill them. They would have tortured me . . . tortured Keja, to get what they searched for."

Eskkar looked at her with renewed interest. "Ah, I wondered why they didn't just knock you over the head or kill you. They wanted you alive. I thought they wanted to have their way with you."

She clenched her teeth at the thought. "That would have come later, before they killed me."

"And what great treasure do you have here," Eskkar said, waving his hand at the hut and hills surrounding them, "that brought these men?"

"They were ignorant thieves. I've nothing worth taking."

"They fought hard for so little then."

A breeze found its way down to the valley floor and made her shiver. She clutched the blanket tighter. "There's a small village just to the north, at the base of the foothills. I grew up there, until they drove me away years ago. They thought I was a witch who'd cast spells on them."

She shook her head at the memory. "They told these foolish bandits that I had a bag of gold hidden in this glen, knowing they would come here looking for it. The villagers would have said anything to get the bandits to leave them alone. That's what these men wanted. They would have tortured and killed us both, and for nothing."

Eskkar didn't bother to ask if she had any gold. No one possessing a golden hoard would be living alone in the mountains. "Are you a witch?"

"Are you afraid of witches?"

"I don't know. I never met one before. Though if you are one, you should have cast a better spell against your attackers. Even so, you did kill three of them, so maybe you are a witch."

He glanced up at the rim for a moment. "At least you're safe from bandits, for now."

"How can you be sure? There could be more of them."

"The Alur Meriki are raiding lands to the east. Everyone is running from them. Many of those driven from their farms and villages fled toward the mountains, and now the barbarians are sweeping them up, killing or taking them as slaves. At least ten or fifteen of their horsemen followed my trail into the mountains, so I don't think too many more thieves and bandits will be coming this way. But if the Alur Meriki find me . . . if they find us, we'll all be dead."

She sat up, her eyes widening in fear. "How did you get here? Did you leave a trail? They'll follow you here."

"Keja showed me the way in," Eskkar said, "and I covered my trail as best I could. The ones chasing me would have been here by now, if they'd discovered the way to this place. Unless there are other entrances to this valley."

"There are, two others. But there is only one way to bring a horse down here."

She pointed toward the crest where Keja still sat, watching the trail behind them. "I found this valley nine years ago, a few months after the villagers drove me away. Almost no one knows of this place, or the passage that leads to it. Those men," she gestured at the bodies, "must have followed me when I left the hills to gather firewood. The soil here isn't deep enough to support any real trees, nothing much taller than a bush."

That explained the donkey, Eskkar realized. She'd need some way to carry wood or anything else back here.

"But your granddaughter," Eskkar said, "where are her parents?"

"She's not really my kin," she said. "I found her wandering at the base of the mountains a few years ago, her family murdered in some feud. Whoever killed them left her to die. She was too young to understand, so I told her I was her grandmother."

"What is your name?"

"I'm called Shabata. And you are …?"

"I'm called Eskkar."

"What kind of name is that? Are you really a warrior from the steppes?"

"Not for many years, Shabata," he said. "They killed my family and drove me away. Now I wander the lands of my hereditary enemies, trying to stay alive." His eyes scanned the cliffs above him once again. Keja, still perched high above them, stared at the two of them and waved. "You must show me the other entrances. I need to make sure no one else finds this place."

Shabata got slowly to her feet, the blanket slipping from her grasp as she did so. She swayed for a moment, and Eskkar thought she might fall. But she shook her head. He picked up the blanket and handed it to her. "Your dress was ruined," he explained. "I used what was left of it to wash and bandage you."

"It's all I had," she said, wrapping the blanket around her as she stared at the bodies. "Now I'll have to make a new one from the garments of the dead."

Eskkar stepped over to examine the corpses. The tunic of the one he stabbed through the chest looked the most intact. He stripped the body efficiently, leaving it naked on the blood-soaked grass. Shabata took the dead man's tunic, and washed it out in the stream, then put the still soaking garment on.

"This will do for now," she said, shivering as the wet cloth clung to her body. "Come. I'll show you where I first came into this valley. We should climb up there anyway, to see if anyone is coming." She led the way past the hut, moving over the rocky ground with ease, until she reached the rock wall.

"This is one way up, and over there is the other."

These two entrances faced the opposite end of the oval-shaped valley from where Eskkar had entered. Both trails reached the valley floor only about twenty paces apart, but they diverged sharply as they ascended the cliffs. Eskkar gazed upward, and didn't like what he saw. The valley wall here looked much steeper than the one he'd used to enter.

Shabata understood his hesitation. "Come. It's not as difficult as it looks. We'll start with the easier one."

She moved up the narrow trail, leaving him no choice but to follow, not exactly climbing, but not walking either. To his dismay, the thought of clinging to the rocks using only his own strength sent tremors of fear through his stomach. As he ascended, the trail grew narrower. Ascending didn't seem like the right way to describe progress up the arduous path; the effort felt more like climbing into the rock itself. Eskkar's bulk worked against him, as he followed Shabata up the steep and slippery cliff face.

"Are you sure this is the easier trail?" Twice he lost his footing and nearly fell, and once had to cling to the rocks like a lizard before he could continue up. He looked down, but that made him light headed, and after that, he kept his eyes focused on the rocks above him.

"They're both about the same, but this one is a little easier."

By the time he reached the top, sweat covered his face, and his hands felt raw from gripping the rough stones. In all his years, Eskkar had seldom climbed anything more lofty than a rolling hill, preferably one a horse could scramble up.

Shabata waited for him at the top, sitting there patiently until he finished the final stretch and rolled out onto the flat surface of a gigantic boulder.

"You're not used to climbing," she said.

"I'm a horseman, not a cliff dweller. I think I'll stay on the ground from now on." Eskkar looked at the tiny valley about a hundred and fifty feet below. From up here, it seemed a long way to the floor, and his stomach felt queasy as he considered the fact that he would have to make the descent.

"It gets easier the more often you do it, Eskkar," Shabata said. "Just remember to take your time and make sure your feet are well planted before you move."

"You should have told me that before I started."

She nodded. "You're right. But I've been living in these rocks for almost ten years, and the trail seems easy after all that time. Keja can climb even faster."

Eskkar remembered how the girl had appeared and disappeared on the cliffs above him. These people had lived in the cliffs for most of their lives, and they'd learned to use what the land gave them.

Glancing about, he found himself staring at a jumble of rocks and cliffs that rose and fell in no particular order. He saw no sign of a trail, no path, nothing that looked like a way out of the mountains. Only jumbles of stones piled atop one another, with a few hardy bushes clinging to the crevices. But she said there was at least one more entrance, though he couldn't see it from where they stood.

"What else is up here? Are there other hidden places?"

"Yes, there are a few secret places in these hills. If you follow that line of cliffs," she pointed to the west, "you will eventually reach the plateau. It's a steep climb, especially toward the end. I found this route months after I'd discovered the valley. No one has ever come in this way, that I know of. Those men," she gestured toward the bodies below, "used the second path."

He nodded at that. If the thieves had come in through the same trail Eskkar had used, he would have seen some trace of their passage. "And what lies in that direction?" He pointed toward the steeper elevations.

"Ah, that goes to the east, deeper into the mountains. The rocks are treacherous, but with care, you can climb even higher. That way is easier from the other trail. We'd have to go back down, and then up again."

"Not today. I've had enough of climbing," Eskkar said. If he got back down to the valley floor in one piece, he'd thank the gods for a month. "Lets get started down. I'll follow you."

"No, you should go first. If you slip and fall, you might take me with you."

He stared at her for a moment, suddenly aware that she could probably kill him with a simple push on the descent. Still, he couldn't deny her logic. He was the one more likely to loose his footing and plunge to his death.

Perhaps she had brought him up here for that purpose. A stone hammered on his hand, or flung at his head, and he'd loose his grip and start sliding. The more he thought about it, the less he liked the whole situation.

Shabata let him work it out himself. "Go slowly," she said. "Make sure of your feet and hands before every step. If you get scared, remain still, and I'll try to help you."

Eskkar gritted his teeth, embarrassed that his fear showed itself. Still, he'd never done anything like this before, and, of course, the first time would always be the hardest.

He took one deep breath, and started the descent. Eskkar moved with exaggerated care going down, making sure he had something to hold onto, a firm spot to place his feet.

Once he nearly lost his footing, but he caught himself and regained his balance; he took another deep breath to calm himself, and continued down. To his surprise, the descent went quicker and easier than he expected.

With both feet on the valley floor once again, Eskkar let out a sigh of relief. "I think one climb like that is enough for the day," he said. "I'll go up to Keja, and see if there's anything to be seen from there." At least he could walk up that trail.

She nodded. "I'll strip the bodies. You'll have to help me bury them. We can't leave them to rot on the ground."

"As soon as I get back."

His legs felt the strain by the time he joined Keja. As he approached, she jumped off her perch on the rock like a mountain goat. "I didn't see anyone. I'll go down and help Grandma."

"No, not yet, Keja. If you want to help your grandma, go back to where you first found me. See if any other men are there. But don't let yourself be seen, not by anyone. Move slowly, and listen for any sounds. Stay there until it's almost dark, but make sure you can see your way back here. And if you do see or hear something, come back as fast as you can run. Can you do that?"

Keja looked a little dubious about the idea. "You'll take care of Grandma until I get back?"

"Shabata's fine, Keja. You saw how we went up the other cliff. Besides, we have to bury the bodies, and you won't be able to help with that. You can protect your grandmother more by watching the trail. And tomorrow," he added, "you can ride the horse around the valley."

She smiled when he mentioned riding the horse. "Can I really? What's his name?"

"He doesn't have a true name yet," Eskkar explained. "I call him Boy, for now. When we've fought together in battle, then he'll earn a name."

"I like Boy," she said. "I'll go. You stay with Grandma," she ordered.

"I will. And remember to go slow and take care not to be seen on the way."

Eskkar watched her until she disappeared behind a jumble of boulders, then started back down the trail, taking his time and using the journey to think. If the Alur Meriki had missed the cleft in the rocks, they might never find this place. The bandits had come on foot by a different path, working their way through the cliffs.

As for the pursuing warriors, they wouldn't like leaving their horses behind. And if the other entrance proved as remote and inaccessible as the one he'd just climbed, he should be safe here for four or five days. By then the Alur Meriki would have moved on, and he could ride out of the hills and return to Gallred's village.

No doubt the merchant would come home sooner or later, and he would need protection, after the chaos caused by the barbarians' passage. Or he might have other tasks for Eskkar. For now, he would just stay here and wait out the Alur Meriki raid on the countryside.

Shabata had stripped the bodies of clothing, weapons, and valuables by the time he reached the hut. "The ground is deepest over there," she said, pointing to the farthest corner of the valley. "But we'll still have to pile rocks on top of the grave. We don't want the vultures circling overhead."

Eskkar had forgotten about the carrion birds. If they began hovering over the glen, any searchers would surely notice.

The grim thought renewed his strength. He grabbed the nearest corpse by the wrists and dragged it over the ground, grunting at the effort. Shabata did the same with the smallest body, but had only moved it halfway when Eskkar joined her. "You start digging," he said. "I'll move the bodies."

She went to the hut and returned with two digging sticks, probably the same ones she used to plant her garden. After he finished moving the dead bandits, Eskkar picked up the other stick and got to work on the grave, forcing the hard earth aside.

They dug in silence, the back-breaking labor providing little time for talk. The deeper the hole grew, the more effort was required. Shabata's wiry arms moved the digging stick through the stubborn earth almost as deep as Eskkar's.

His muscles protesting, Eskkar finally dropped the stick and climbed out of the hole. "I need to rest."

She stopped and sat facing him across the grave. "We don't have much time before dark. Sundown comes early in these mountains."

He glanced at the sun. "We'll get them in the ground, at least."

"Don't be so sure, Eskkar. The earth gets harder and is filled with stones the deeper you dig."

With a grunt, he stood and went back to digging. It didn't take long to realize Shabata spoke the truth. The grave's depth reached just below Eskkar's waist when he gave up any attempt to dig deeper. "We'll have to widen the opening."

"Yes, we'll lay them side by side. At least we'll have plenty of stones to cover them."

By the time it grew too dark to work, they had crammed the bodies into the grave and covered them with an arm's length of dirt, tamping down the earth as much as possible. Even Shabata looked exhausted, the whites of her eyes gleaming as she leaned on her stick. Eskkar remembered that she'd fought as strenuously as he had.

"Enough," he said. "We'll cover the site with stones tomorrow."

He dropped the digging stick and walked unsteadily back to the stream. Eskkar's hands felt swollen, his palms tender from working the stick. His back hurt from all the bending and lifting. He knelt in the water, washing the dirt from his hands, face, and legs.

When he felt clean again, he let his hands soak in the cold water for a few moments. Only then did he satisfy his thirst.

"We need to eat," Shabata said, performing her own ablutions a few steps away. "And I have to feed Keja. I'll start a fire."

"No fire. It's too dangerous. There's food on the horse, enough for all of us tonight and tomorrow."

The horse whinnied, and Eskkar looked up, surprised to see Keja appearing out of the darkness. Either she hadn't made a sound coming down the trail and through the grass, or Eskkar's senses were dulled with fatigue. Whatever the reason, he knew he needed a night's rest.

If more bandits or the Alur Meriki could move about these cliffs and rocks at night without breaking their necks or announcing their approach, then they were welcome to take him. He pulled himself to his feet, and went to his horse.

Stripping off the halter, he took the food pouch from around Boy's neck, then rubbed the horse's shoulder for a moment. Eskkar decided he didn't have to tie up the animal. The beast wasn't likely to climb the cliff on his own, not with plenty of grass and water here.

The three of them sat against the outside of the hut and wolfed the food down, nearly emptying the sack. By then, Eskkar couldn't keep his eyes open, and Shabata didn't look much better. Neither had any energy for conversation, so they entered the hut. Eskkar had to bend almost in half to duck under the doorway.

The hut, a single windowless chamber not much larger than a tent, scarcely held the three of them. Not that it mattered. Shabata showed him where to sleep, then she lay beside him, keeping her body between Eskkar's and Keja.

Eskkar unsheathed his weapons before cradling his head on his arm and turning on his side. If Shabata decided to kill him during the night, he thought, as sleep dragged his mind into emptiness, she wouldn't need much effort.

14

Eskkar woke to find the hut empty. Rubbing the sleep from his eyes, he belted on his knife and gathered his sword before he ducked under the doorway, surprised to see the sky bright with the fullness of morning. Usually he woke with the dawn, but here the mountains played tricks with the sun's rays until they climbed high enough to shine over the hilltops.

Slinging the sword over his shoulder, he found Shabata sitting a few steps from the stream, working on another garment, her hair once again flying wildly about her head. Eskkar went to the stream and washed his face in the cold water. His back and leg muscles felt stiff, no doubt from all the digging and climbing.

"There's still some food left. Keja and I already ate." Shabata handed him the food sack.

"You should have wakened me at first light," he said, easing down beside her. Rummaging through the sack, he found only a single loaf of bread and a handful of dates.

She had a long wooden needle in her hand, and her fingers moved rapidly as she stitched the cloth together. She'd washed all the bandits' garments. Now their clothing would provide material for another dress.

Shabata saw his interest. "I'll have enough to make a real dress for me, and something new for Keja. She's nearly outgrown her own."

"Where is she?" He looked up at the valley's rim, but didn't see the child.

"Keeping watch on the trail, where she found you. It's really the only path that can take a horse. If they don't find the crevice . . ."

"The bandits could have found that way."

She shook her head. "It's a much longer journey from the village. Aside from you, no one else has come through the cliffs in years. Not many know of the passage. As long as we don't venture out, we should be safe enough."

Eskkar didn't feel quite so certain, but said nothing. He finished the last of the dates and half the bread. "Let's get the grave covered," he suggested.

No vultures or hawks circled overhead, but carrion birds possessed a keen sense of smell, especially for anything dead or dying. He and Shabata hadn't buried the bodies deep enough. A body rotting in shallow ground for a few days would draw carrion hunters overhead.

"I'm almost done." Shabata held up a shapeless tunic for him to view. It looked like nothing more than a patchwork of rags. She smiled at the look on his face. "It's more than good enough for me."

Glancing at his own garment, torn and worn in spots, he realized he didn't look much better, so he returned the smile.

"I'll sew up the holes in your tunic later," she offered, following his eyes.

The horse whinnied, and Eskkar rose to his feet. But Boy was merely greeting his new friend, the donkey. Yesterday the little beast had looked askance at the much larger horse, but sometime during the night, they had become friends, and now grazed together at the far end of the valley.

Eskkar hoped he didn't have to stay long. With both animals grazing, the limited grass would be gone in three or four days.

Midday passed before Eskkar and Shabata finished the grave. Stones now covered the wide gravesite, and reached nearly as high as Shabata's waist. That much weight of stone would keep the earth pressed tight against the bodies, and no odor would escape to attract any carrion-eaters flying overhead.

He and Shabata washed the dirt from their hands and sat against the wall of the hut, resting in the shade.

"I'd like to stay here with you for a few days, until the Alur Meriki move on. Once they're far enough away, I'll ride back to the plain. Until then, I need a place to feed and water the horse."

"We'll need more food," she said, her tone showing her reluctance to have him stay.

"I'll hunt for it, and lay out some snares up in the rocks. I can feed myself, Shabata."

"I'll tell you honestly, Eskkar. I'll be glad when you leave. I don't like having a man around."

He nodded. "No more than I like staying here, sitting in this hole like a rabbit hiding from a fox. But I'll not bother you while . . ."

"Grandma!" The cry echoed from the cliff tops, but Keja had already started her descent, slipping and sliding and threatening to fall headlong at every step.

Shabata was on her feet and running before Eskkar even had his feet under him. By the time he caught up with her, Keja had arrived and jumped into her arms.

"Grandma, men are coming! Lots of men, on horses!"

A chill passed through Eskkar. Only the Alur Meriki warriors possessed so many horses in these times. "How far away . . ."

But Shabata had started running, leading Keja by the hand. Without thinking, he followed her, running hard to catch up. At the hut, she snatched up Eskkar's food sack, then darted into the hut for a moment. He ducked in after her, grabbing his water skin. He saw the bandits' weapons and couldn't bear to give them up.

Taking the finest quality short sword and shoving it into his belt, he then snatched the other two weapons and shoved them high up into the thatch roof. Even if they burned the hut down, they might miss the blades. Before he'd finished, Shabata had filled his food sack with her own vegetables, which she shoved into Eskkar's arms as she darted outside. "Follow me," she said.

In moments, they reached the base of the cliff, at the foot of the path to the top. Not, Eskkar noted in dismay, the climb he'd done yesterday. Already Shabata had started up, Keja leading the way.

Again Eskkar cursed his luck. He'd have to leave the horse. "Damn every demon that brought them," he swore, as he knotted the food sack closed and fastened it to his belt. He followed after them, trying to watch the places where Shabata set her hands and feet. At least yesterday's ascent had given him some practice.

Gritting his teeth, Eskkar climbed steadily, though the two women moved far swifter. He carried the food and his water skin, along with his sword and the one from the dead bandit. Almost at once Eskkar regretted lugging the extra blade with him, though he stubbornly refused to abandon such a fine weapon.

The additional weight slowed him down, and made it harder for him to keep his balance as he climbed. Despite his efforts, the two women opened the space between him and them, and he cursed his bad luck again as he forced himself upwards.

Halfway up, his arms ached from the strain. He glanced toward the top, and saw Keja scurry over the edge, with Shabata right behind her. Eskkar, midway up the cliff face, had reached the most difficult part of the ascent and didn't dare move any faster. One slip now, and falling from this height, he'd be dead for sure.

"Hurry! They're almost here!"

Eskkar ignored Shabata's words. He couldn't climb any faster, and he'd . . .

An arrow clattered off the cliff an arm's length from his shoulder, before falling away. Twisting his head, he saw a man standing across the valley. Others were moving to his side, all of them with bows in their hands. Another arrow struck the cliff face above him. The spent shaft bounced off his arm as it fell toward the ground below.

Ignoring the tiredness in his arms, he forced himself up, breathing hard and searching for footholds. He could feel the skin scraping from his fingers against the grainy rocks.

"Hurry! Move faster."

He wanted to curse at her, but couldn't waste his breath. The top loomed closer, but the Alur Meriki archers were finding the range now, though the distance approached the limits of their shorter horse bows. Two more arrows impacted on the cliff, one close enough to brush his side, and he felt the burn of it against his tunic.

Shabata must have realized he wasn't going to make it. She leapt to her feet, and screamed a curse at the bowmen across the valley. "Filthy vermin! Cowards! Thieves and murderers!"

Standing there exposed, she jumped up and down, moving back and forth across the top of the cliff, as she called abuse down on the warriors. An arrow flew toward her and she ducked behind a boulder, but she'd managed to distract those aiming at Eskkar for a moment.

The cliff face at last began to tilt inwards, and the footholds grew pronounced. With a final burst of strength, Eskkar clambered up the last few paces, rolling himself over the top as arrows rattled against the rocks. He had time enough for one gasping breath before Shabata, on her hands and knees, reached his elbow, grabbed his arm, and dragged him all the way into cover. One last arrow plinked against the stones beside him and he crawled behind her, dragging his sack, at last hidden from his enemies and safe behind a large boulder.

"Come. We must go." She grasped his hand and started dragging him farther into the rocks.

"No," he said, still trying to catch his breath. "I can hold them here. They won't be able to climb up with a sword in their faces."

"Look," she said, and pointed toward the heart of the mountain. It took a moment before his eyes picked out a second group of warriors, on foot and almost a quarter mile away, but moving toward them, scrambling over rocks and sliding down inclines. They must have discovered the path the thieves used to enter the valley, probably followed their trail. He glimpsed only five or six, but one with a bow would have been enough.

When he turned back to Shabata, she'd already started moving, and this time he wormed his way after her without a word. Deeper into the cliffs she went, slipping through clefts formed by massive boulders and moving faster through the rocky terrain than he could. She reached a fork in the trail and waited for him.

"You go first," she said, pointing to the left, where the path led downward. "Watch where you step, and leave no trace of your passage. They must not be certain which direction we take."

Eskkar knew better than to argue or question. In battle, one man had to lead, and every warrior had to trust in the one who commanded him, though he'd never imagined he'd be taking such life-or-death orders from a woman.

He put all his thoughts into watching his feet, placing them with care and trying not to scrape his sandals against the rocky ground. Shabata walked behind him, her eyes tracking back and forth over their path.

The descent grew steeper as they moved. Eskkar glanced up and saw massive rocks leaning precariously over his head. "We shouldn't be going down . . . we'll be trapped."

"Keep quiet," she ordered. "Voices carry over the rocks, and we mustn't be heard."

Swearing under his breath, he kept going. Twice he had to ask her which way to go when the trail branched again and again. They finally reached what he guessed must be the bottom of the cliffs. The terrain leveled somewhat, and he increased his speed, thanking the gods that they'd soon be moving upward again.

"Stop," Shabata commanded. "This is the place." She grabbed his arm and pulled him back a step. "Down here, under this rock."

One side of the cliff face had a long projection, almost like a bench, that formed a tiny hollow beneath it. He'd stepped right past it without noticing. "Go where? There's nothing . . ."

"Hurry, Eskkar. Get inside!"

The words issued from the rock at his feet, and for a moment his heart raced, thinking the stones were speaking to him. Then he recognized Keja's voice.

"Crawl in! Crawl in!"

Now a little girl was ordering him about. Shaking his head, Eskkar dropped to his hands and knees. Underneath the overhang, he saw a deeper shadow that indicated some sort of opening into the rock. Instinctively, he glanced around for snakes. Instead, Keja's face appeared.

"Will you hurry!" Shabata's voice bespoke the urgency of her request. "They're only moments behind us."

"I'm coming." Eskkar unslung the sword from his back. He passed it through the opening first, then the food sack, water skin, and extra sword. Lowering himself to the ground, he crawled head-first into the opening.

"Watch your feet, you clumsy ox! Don't leave any marks on the ground."

The rock brushed his back and his hair caught on a sharp edge, but he eased his head and shoulders into the blackness. He managed to squeeze through the narrow gap, but it took precious time, shifting his body from one side to the other, trying to get his bulk into the cave without leaving any trace of his passage.

The instant his feet passed inside, Shabata snaked her way in behind him, her smaller stature giving her more leeway. Eskkar glanced around. The blackness wasn't complete. Beside the light coming through the entrance hole, a tiny opening high above his head showed that he'd entered a cavern, with the roof about the height of three men. Keja knelt beside him, pushing his things out of the way.

"Help me, Eskkar," the girl said. "We have to move these rocks."

By then, Shabata had twisted around, sticking her head back under the overhang to rearrange a few stones upended by their entrance. Satisfied that no sign of their passage showed, she wormed back into the cave and shoved a large stone toward the opening.

Eskkar grabbed one end, and together they lifted the small boulder and shoved it against the entrance. Shabata positioned it so that it blocked about half the opening. Meanwhile Keja struggled with the weight of another stone. Eskkar realized that both stones would conceal the hole. He took it from Keja's hands and shoved the block of stone into place.

"Careful!" Shabata kept her voice at a whisper, but even that echoed off the walls surrounding them. "We must not leave any sign that we've moved the rocks. Set it in the opening with care."

He positioned the stone, about the same size as the first, and levered it by each end until the opening was nearly blocked. Shabata stopped him before he closed it completely. Lying on her side, she reached through the still uncovered slit and carefully scooped up the loose stones and rock chips that might betray them.

Eskkar waited, his patience wearing thin, as she brushed away the last traces of their activity.

"Close it up."

With both hands, he lifted the rock and set it into place, noticing for the first time that the stones fitted neatly together. Sagging back on his knees, he decided that it would take a keen tracker to see where they'd disappeared.

Keja returned with a tree limb about as long as Eskkar's arm and nearly as thick. Meanwhile, Shabata moved a third slab of rock into position behind the two that already hid the opening. The three stones almost touched, and the last stone's rear edge rested against a rock outcropping within the cavern.

Taking the limb from Keja, Shabata pushed the thick wooden stake between the first two stones and the third, then hammered it into place with a round rock. With each blow, Eskkar saw the pressure between the rocks tighten, and he realized that anyone trying to push the stones inward would find them immobile, and think them part of the rock wall and as solid as the cliff itself.

After three more blows, the stake was rigid, and Shabata set the hammer stone aside and stood. "Let's hope they didn't hear that. Come with us."

She led the way, moving deeper into the cave. Eskkar gathered his things and followed. It didn't take long before the light seeping into the cavern from above started to fade, but before it disappeared, Shabata stopped and bent down. In a moment, he heard the familiar scratch, scratch, scratch of flint on stone, and after at least thirty or so attempts, he saw the first spark flash.

She kept working steadily at the tedious process until one spark caught in a handful of dried moss. Another handful of moss and twigs kept the tiny flame going. Before it could burn itself out, she touched a candle to it, and the wick managed to catch the flame before the last piece of tinder vanished in a final puff of smoke.

For the first time, Eskkar realized that this cave, the barrier stones to seal the entrance, the stake, even the tinder, flint, and candle – a rare enough luxury even in the dirt-eaters' villages – all had been prepared in advance. Shabata had created this hiding place, and the means to secure it, for just such an emergency. He stared at the yellowed candle; he'd never seen one so thick, nearly as big around as his wrist.

As soon as the wick burned steadily, Shabata got to her feet and moved deeper into the cavern, with Keja walking almost at her side.

Once again Eskkar brought up the rear. Shabata stepped with care, her hand shielding the candle to make sure it didn't blow itself out as she walked. No breezes reached this place, and Eskkar saw that as long as she moved slowly, the candle would continue to burn.

By now he hesitated to question anything she did. But if she tripped and fell, they'd be in the dark, unable to see anything. "What happens if the candle goes out? Where are we going?"

"If it goes out, I'll relight it," she answered. "And we don't have much farther to go."

All the same, Eskkar felt the darkness closing in on him. His people lived on the plains and steppes, avoiding the hill country where deep caverns abounded. Demons lived in caves such as this, and the lower down the trio descended, the more likely they would encounter some evil spirit or dark dweller.

Snakes, too, preferred darkness, not to mention scorpions and spiders and the gods knew what other evil creatures. Eskkar's skin crawled at these thoughts and he found it hard to breathe.

Around him, the cavern walls appeared to move and shift in the flickering light, and he tried not to think about the weight of rock towering above him. The patter of water dripping from the vault overhead added a spectral sound that grated on his already stretched nerves. He moved closer behind Shabata and her guiding candle, trying to watch his feet and, above all, trying not to stumble.

Meanwhile, the tiny flame sent the shadows moving in odd and unnatural rhythms, and his fear began to grow. He'd never been in a cave like this, with no large opening to permit air and light to enter. By now he could see nothing, only Shabata's shape in front of him. The very air seemed to resist his lungs.

"Where are we going?" His words echoed off the walls, an unnatural sound that didn't conceal the fear in his voice.

"Not much farther," Shabata repeated, too intent on picking her way to give him any reassurance.

Regardless, she raised the candle higher, but it revealed nothing but blackness ahead. Something moved along the walls, a darker shadow passed over his head, and a puff of air moved against his cheek.

"Demons!" Eskkar dropped a hand to his knife. "There's something in here . . ."

"Bats," Shabata said. "Stop worrying. We're almost through."

"There's the opening," Keja said, her voice shrill with excitement.

Eskkar peered into the darkness but saw nothing. A few more steps, and he perceived a grayness that grew lighter and lighter as they approached. He caught a whiff of fresh air, and the tiny breeze set the candle flickering. Instinctively, he took a deep breath, already relieved at the prospect of getting out of the cavern.

They reached two large rocks that rose as high as his waist, and swung themselves over. Suddenly he saw daylight reflected off the upper stones, penetrating the bowels of the mountain. The path they trod widened, and fifty paces ahead, Eskkar glimpsed a pool of warm sunlight glowing off the rocks.

A few more steps, and the three of them reached the light streaming in from a large opening, taller than a man, that lay ahead. Shabata blew out the candle, and Eskkar couldn't contain the sigh of relief that escaped from his lips.

"Snake!" Keja shrieked the word as she stopped short. Shabata halted as well, and Eskkar bumped into her.

A snake in the light of day held little terror for Eskkar. He pulled the bandit's short sword from his belt and moved forward. The disturbed viper, he recognized the thick body and broad triangular head, hissed and writhed, coiling itself for a strike, and angry at the interlopers who'd invaded its home.

Eskkar bent down and scooped up a handful of loose stones and grit. Tossing them at the snake, the viper jumped and hissed. He slammed the sword down as quick as he could, but the reptile darted back, and the blade missed the creature's head by a finger's width.

Before Eskkar could strike again, the black body, as long as his arm, wriggled off to the side, disappearing back into the blackness.

Sword at the ready, Eskkar led the way, until they cleared the opening. To his surprise, they were in another hollow between cliffs that towered over them.

This place, though, was much smaller than Shabata's valley, barely fifty paces across. The rock slabs that surrounded them leaned at odd angles, their sheer surfaces polished by rain and wind. To his eyes, they looked impossible to climb, but Eskkar had gained new respect for Shabata's abilities.

"Is this where you're taking us?"

"No, this is a place we'd best avoid." She tucked the candle under her left arm, and used her right hand to make the gesture dirt-eaters used to ward off evil spirits. "Come. We have one more cavern to cross, but we won't need the candle."

Keja, recovered from her encounter with the snake, led the way again, and now Eskkar noticed a small cut-back on the opposite wall from where they'd entered.

Bringing up the rear, Eskkar followed the women through the twists and turns of yet another narrow path that delved into the cliffs, winding its way around and over a rubble of stones and boulders. For the rest of their passage, the cliff walls cut off nearly all the sunlight, but they never needed to relight the candle.

When they stepped out into the sunlight for a second time, Eskkar knew they'd arrived at their destination, another secret opening within the mountain. Only slightly larger than the one they'd just left, this one boasted a tiny waterfall. The rivulet of water that cascaded down the rocks was hardly bigger than Eskkar's hand, but the stream flowed steadily, and had carved out a pool at the foot of the cliff.

Steep rock walls encircled the glen on three sides, but rubble from the upper cliffs had built a steep ramp that led upward on the side containing the waterfall.

With a sigh of relief, Eskkar dropped his burdens and scooped a handful of water. One taste told him that the water flowed pure and cold, and he drank his fill.

"Now what do we do?" he asked, turning to Shabata who finished drinking at the same time.

"We wait. I doubt they'll keep searching for us for more than a day or two. Even if they find the place where we entered the cave, I don't think they'll be able to force their way past the rocks sealing the entrance."

Eskkar considered how a single wooden stake, cunningly levered against three stones, formed a barrier that would be almost impossible to dislodge. "They could smash the stones, hammer them apart until they shattered."

"Yes, if they find the opening, and if they have a bronze chisel and other tools."

Warriors wouldn't likely be carrying anything like that, Eskkar knew. Getting them would require a return to the plains and a close search through any number of dirt-eaters' huts. Even then, they weren't likely to find a bronze or even a copper chisel.

Eskkar had only seen a handful of the bronze tools in his life, precious implements hoarded and guarded by craftsmen. Such instruments would be well hidden at the first rumor of the Alur Meriki's approach.

"What about this place? Could they get in here from above?" He didn't think he could climb the twenty-foot ledge, but Shabata and Keja might manage it.

"Possibly. They'd need ropes to climb the cliffs behind us, and they'd have to cross some steep drops. It's more than I would attempt, not even for some rumors of gold."

"So we're safe here?"

"For now. There's never been a sign anyone's visited this place except me."

"Let's hope so," Eskkar said. "We should go back and make sure they haven't discovered where we disappeared. Or we could stay in the first cavern."

She shook her head. "That place belongs to the spirits." She sighed. "Later I'll go back and listen, to see if they've found the cave's opening. I know the way better than you."

"Even so, the warriors could be watching the trails, waiting for you to emerge and return to your dwelling."

Shabata laughed. "That's why I brought you with us, just in case." She laughed again, this time at the look on his face. "You'll be the first one out, Eskkar. We'll stay behind, until you tell us the way is clear."

"How long do you think we'll need to wait?"

She shook her head. "No one has ever forced us out of the valley before. Besides, there is nothing there for so many men to eat. They'll be gone soon enough."

This time Eskkar shook his head. "They've got water and plenty of food in your valley. They could easily leave a few men behind for longer than that. Or ride out to the plains for more men and supplies. I'd say we should remain here at least three days, until they give up the search and are certain we won't be coming back."

"There's nothing to eat in the hut."

"The burro would feed them all for a few days. After that, they could eat my horse or one of their own."

"My poor little burro." She shook her head. "I hadn't thought of that. But they'll move on soon enough. We're not important enough for them to keep searching."

"That's what I thought, but they followed me into the mountains."

"In that case, we'd better stretch what little food we have. We may be starving ourselves in a few days."

"Better hungry than dead," Eskkar said.

The Alur Meriki might waste the day searching for them, but as consolation, the warriors would be eating roast donkey tonight and sleeping in Shabata's hut. He remembered his manners. "And thank you, Shabata, for distracting the bowmen. I think I owe you my life for that."

"As you saved mine," she answered. "Besides, Keja wouldn't want you left behind."

Now he needed a child's whim to stay alive. "Let's hope no one finds us here, then."

Eskkar thought of his horse, abandoned in Shabata's glen. The barbarians would certainly take Boy with them. Damn the Alur Meriki. He'd have to buy and train another horse.

—

Eskkar spread out his weapons and kept watch over the entrance, keeping an eye out for snakes as well as intruders, but the trio spent the rest of the day undisturbed. With nothing to do but stare at the waterfall, he spent some time practicing with his sword, working through the routines he'd learned as a boy and enhanced as he'd grown into manhood, moving and shifting his feet and his stance, attacking and retreating, thrusting and slashing.

Lunges followed overhand strokes, and Eskkar practiced his footwork as well, moving sideways and backwards, sliding his feet along the ground so as not to trip or stumble over some unevenness in the ground. The whirling sword never ceased moving, as it weaved and sliced through the air.

Occasionally he paused in his movements to test his arm. He extended the sword straight out, his right arm rigid, until the weight of the weapon made first his arm, then his whole body tremble.

When Eskkar could no longer maintain the extension, he lowered the blade for a moment, and resumed his movements. A weak arm that could not hold the sword firm could be easily pushed aside, with fatal results.

Keja and Shabata watched with fascination, never before having seen such a sight. Sweat covered his body when he finished, and Eskkar washed himself beneath the waterfall.

By then sundown had arrived, the high cliff walls sealing out the sun early and forcing the three of them to huddle together for warmth. They had no blankets, something Shabata had neglected to provide, or perhaps she didn't have an extra one to store in her hiding hole.

They spent a restless night, saying little and jumping at every sound. In the morning he woke to find Shabata under one arm and

Keja curled up like a puppy against his other side. Nothing like a common foe to bring people together.

Yawning, they ate the last few mouthfuls of Gallred's stale bread for breakfast, washed down with cold water from the pool. Afterwards, Eskkar went through his practice routines again, as much to get warm as to increase his skills.

Satisfied with his exertions, Eskkar remembered yesterday's passage through the mountain.

"Shabata, shouldn't we go back to the entrance to the cave? Perhaps there is some sign that the Alur Meriki discovered it. And the little glen we passed through, is there anything there we should be watching?"

She shrugged. "Not really. But it is a sacred place."

"Sacred?" He wondered what nameless god would have chosen this place for some rite or ritual.

She heard the tone of disbelief. "Come. I'll show you. You're right, we should go back and check the entrance anyhow." She gathered her candle, tinder, and flint, and after telling Keja to stay by the pool, led the way into the rocks.

Eskkar looked up. Noon approached, and there would be plenty of light, but he still didn't like entering the cavern. However, knowing how far ahead his destination lay made the return trip easier. It didn't take long before they again emerged into the small glen.

Shabata halted in the center. "See anything unusual?"

He looked around. There didn't seem to be anything out of the ordinary, just rocks and cliffs. "What's that mark on the wall?"

"Go and see." She made no move to join him.

With a grunt, Eskkar strode toward what he guessed to be the north wall. Shadows already covered part of the rock face, but he decided that in the morning sun, it would be well lit. He approached within a few paces and stopped short.

What he'd thought to be a mark on the stone appeared to be something else. It looked almost like a shallow depression etched into the rock, a small one, to be sure, only slightly larger than one of the round loaves of bread village women baked each morning. And the rock surrounding the insert appeared different from the other cliff walls he'd seen in the mountains.

"Marduk protect me," Eskkar muttered, the dirt-eaters' prayer coming to his lips without thinking. Someone had etched a symbol on the surface of the inset, an outline of a right hand, with fingers and thumb spread wide, the distinct lines cut carefully into the rock.

Eskkar stepped closer, and held up his own hand, comparing it to the shape showing on the rock. Not many men had larger hands, but he saw the outline would encompass his palm easily. As his fingertips touched the smooth surface, he felt a slickness more like a gemstone than a rock slab.

He wondered if the builder had carved an opening in the solid rock wall, then somehow filled the opening with a thick slab of crystal, though he'd never heard of such a thing. Eskkar decided not to touch the symbol and drew back his hand.

"Put your hand inside the lines," Shabata said.

He glanced over his shoulder. She'd remained in the center of the clearing, standing there, watching him. The fact that she kept her distance unnerved him. Eskkar hesitated, hand half-raised, but he couldn't walk away and admit his fear in front of a woman, especially one who might be a witch.

"It won't bite you." Even so, she made no effort to move closer.

Licking his lips, he reached out and placed his hand inside the hand shape.

For a moment, it seemed as if the surface changed. Something gripped his hand, a stickiness that held his palm flat against the crystal, almost like the thick tar villagers used to seal their barrels.

His heart jumped, terrified the rock wall had opened up and seized him. Eskkar jerked his hand back, yet for the briefest instant, he couldn't pull away from the stone. Then the stickiness vanished and his hand came free.

He blinked his eyes. A reddish glow colored the stone just before his hand came loose, as if a bright candle shone through the rock wall. In a heartbeat, the red glow faded out, vanished, returning the rock wall to its normal gray.

"Damn the gods," Eskkar said, jumping back. Instinctively, he reached for his sword. "What demon lives in this?"

The rock face looked unchanged, not a hint of color in the inset. Eskkar looked at his palm, but saw nothing and felt nothing out of the ordinary. He wiped his sweating palm against his tunic without thinking, and gazed again at the outline, his heart racing. But the symbol looked exactly as it had when he'd first seen it.

"Touch it again." Shabata moved to his side.

"Not for ten gold coins," he said, the words rushing out. "It turned red . . . I mean, it looked . . . what is it?"

"I don't know," she said. She stepped forward and placed her hand in the outline. Nothing happened, no flash of color, and she held it there a moment before she withdrew.

"You try it again." She saw him hesitate. "Don't be afraid. It won't hurt you."

He clenched his lips at the insult, but said nothing. Taking his time, he extended one finger and touched the outline. The etching felt like rock, no sticky feeling, no change in color. He found himself holding his breath, and he let it out with a grunt. Taking a deep breath, Eskkar again placed his hand within the outline.

Nothing. He pushed hard against the surface. Nothing. The texture felt somewhat different, but he couldn't be certain; his mind might be playing tricks on him. Not a trace of stickiness. He must have imagined the sensation. Now that he thought about it, he'd probably imagined the flash of color, too. Rocks, after all, couldn't glow, not unless heated for long periods by fire.

"I thought . . . I thought I saw it glow."

"It did," Shabata confirmed. "I saw it, too, a reddish color."

So his eyes hadn't betrayed him. Or maybe they'd both been tricked by some unknown demon.

Eskkar stepped away, putting at least three long strides between the symbol and himself. Again he wiped his hand on his tunic, rubbing hard. Shabata moved beside him, turning her back to the rock face without concern.

"How long has this been here? I mean, when did you find it?"

"It's been here a long time," she said, "longer than I've lived here. Maybe the gods marked the symbol when they created the mountains. Or maybe men, wiser than we are, carved it long ago, an altar where they made offerings to some nameless god."

Shabata waved her hand toward the mountain crests. "If you look at the surrounding cliffs, you can see that the symbol once stood in the open. I think maybe a landslide, or even a great earth shaker might have covered up the base of an altar, leaving only the symbol exposed as it is now."

Whatever it was, or had been, Eskkar had seen enough. His personal agreement with the gods consisted of asking them for nothing, and expecting nothing in return. Anything else made him uneasy. "Let's get out of here. We still need to check the entrance to the cave."

They headed back toward the first passage. Eskkar couldn't resist a last glance back at the symbol, but it appeared unchanged, and by now he half-believed he'd imagined the whole thing. They reached the opening, and Shabata set the candle down and started working the flint.

"Grandma! Grandma! Help!" The voice was faint, but it echoed over the rocks.

Shabata dropped the flint and darted back the way they'd come. She taken five or six strides before Eskkar started moving. They dashed past the symbol, but Eskkar couldn't catch up with her as she weaved her way among the rocks and entered the passage beyond.

"Grandmaaaaa!"

Knife already in her hand, Shabata disappeared into the dimly lit passage that led to the clearing where they'd spent the night. Eskkar, moving as fast as he dared, found himself only a step or two behind her. He slipped the long sword from over his shoulder. Scrambling over the rocks, they burst into the clearing and found it empty.

"Grandma, help me."

Eskkar lifted his eyes toward the cry. The tiny glen wasn't empty. High up on the ledge to the right of the waterfall, he saw Keja darting from boulder to boulder, pursued by two warriors.

"Keja!" Shabata's voice echoed against the cliffs.

Eskkar pushed past her. Keja kept leaping from place to place, dodging the men's attempts to capture her, but as Eskkar ran toward the base of the ledge, one of the warriors grabbed hold of her arm and yanked her toward him. The second man caught her other arm at almost the same time. She screamed and struggled, trying to break loose, but to no avail.

Eskkar had almost reached the waterfall when Keja saw him. "ESKKAR!"

The scream, or perhaps the name, made the men looked downward. Before Eskkar could climb up the ledge, Keja sank her teeth into the arm of the first man, then twisted and jerked her body so hard that both she and the one she'd bitten lost their footing.

Her feet slid out from her, and her weight made the second warrior, already struggling to keep his precarious perch on the slanting surface, stumble as well. He, too, fell on the slippery rocks and in the next heartbeat, all three were tumbling down the slope.

Eskkar had time to take a long stride, shifting his position so that Keja, arriving first, slid right into his arms. Without pausing, he tossed the girl to Shabata.

By then the two men had landed, crashing to the hard ground on either side of him. One of the warriors had come down head first, and Eskkar heard a crunching sound. The second man landed flat on his back, and Eskkar heard a gasp as the air rushed from his lungs.

Sword at the ready, Eskkar checked the first man. One look told him the man's neck was broken. No head could turn at such an angle. Already a thin stream of bright red blood flowed from beneath the chin, staining the ground. Eskkar turned his attention to the second warrior, moving the sword's tip to the man's neck. This one appeared young, scarcely old enough to ride with the fighters. Dazed eyes stared upward, past the blade's tip.

Brown eyes, nearly concealed by a tangle of dark hair, gazed at Eskkar, while the youth sought to regain the breath knocked from his lungs by the fall. The boy looked familiar, and it took Eskkar a moment before he understood why – his prisoner resembled Melkorak, Eskkar's brother. Or at least the youth Melkorak would have become if he'd lived.

The young warrior's hand moved toward the knife at his waist, but Eskkar pushed the tip of the sword against the boy's throat. The hand drew back, formed a fist, and slapped at the hard ground in frustration.

"What are you waiting for," Shabata said. She still had Keja in her arms. "Kill him. Others may have heard our voices."

"There's time for that," Eskkar said, glancing at the cliffs above. "Take Keja and get back in the passageway. More warriors might be up on the rim, and you could find yourself with an arrow in your back. Take everything with you."

He looked down at the slight figure beneath his sword. The boy appeared to have only twelve or thirteen seasons. A single tear leaked from the corner of his eye. "What's your name, boy?"

A defiant look replaced the frustration on his face. "Kill me and be done with it." The eyes rolled toward his companion, lying a few steps away. "You killed my brother."

"Your brother broke his neck falling down the slope, though that probably saved me the trouble," Eskkar said. "Not a very heroic way to die for a warrior. I asked you for your name?"

"My brother would have cut you to pieces."

Eskkar shrugged. He didn't intend to waste time arguing over that. "Last time. What's your name, or haven't you earned one yet?" A push of the sword at the warrior's neck emphasized the question.

"Garak, of the Wolf Clan."

The young man's eyes again returned to his brother's corpse, and Eskkar saw shock and disbelief settle in, as the fact of his brother's death took hold. Eskkar reached down and took the boy's knife from his belt. Since he carried no sword, this must be his first time riding with his clan's warriors. Eskkar placed his foot on the Garak's chest, then sheathed his sword. He kept the boy's knife in his hand.

"My name is Eskkar, but I no longer have a clan. Now, tell me how old you are."

Garak stared up at his captor. "Thirteen seasons. Nearly fourteen."

Eskkar shook his head. The boy probably lied. His slender frame looked almost too short and thin to ride with grown men. Eskkar had stood far taller and with more muscle at the same age.

"Get up."

Without waiting for the boy to comply, Eskkar reached down, grabbed him by the shoulder and lifted him to his feet. Garak could do nothing to resist. Eskkar had more than twice his bulk. Tightening his grip on Garak's shoulder, he pushed him toward the passageway. In moments they passed out of sight from the ledge above.

Shabata waited for him, with Keja at her side. The girl appeared recovered from her fright, at least enough to stare at their captive with interest. "Why haven't you killed him?" Shabata fingered the knife at her waist.

"I want to ask him some questions," Eskkar said. He dragged the boy toward a space hemmed in by two boulders, and pushed him to the ground. "Get down on your belly and don't move, or I'll kill you."

With Garak helpless at their feet, Eskkar turned to Shabata. "The other one had a bow. Get his weapons, and shove the body somewhere where it can't be seen from above."

"Do you know what you're doing? Others will come looking for them . . ."

"Hurry then, before they do," Eskkar said. "And bring his sandals, too."

"Watch Keja, then," she said, running back out to the body.

While he waited for her return, Eskkar used the time to think. Something was amiss, and he swore at himself for not figuring this out before. Warriors didn't react this way. They wouldn't spend days or even a morning chasing after one lone rider, not when they had an entire countryside to loot.

But these Alur Meriki had sent a whole troop of riders after him. Not only that, but they split their force again and again, searching for him with a tenaciousness that made no sense. Eskkar had done nothing to arouse such fervor. They'd delved into every crevice and crack in the mountain searching for their quarry. He'd never heard of such single mindedness, such dogged pursuit. If he were going to get away, he needed to know why they hunted him.

Shabata scurried back into the passage, breathing hard, her arms laden down with the warrior's sword, knife, bow, quiver, and sandals. She dumped the lot on the ground beside Eskkar.

"I dragged the body under some rocks, covered up the blood stain, and splashed water all over the ground. If they stay up on the rim, they may not notice."

"Let's hope so," Eskkar said. "But likely the water will bring them down."

In these rocks, water would be scarce, and the warriors would take every opportunity to refill their water skins. Once at the base of the waterfall, they would certainly explore and discover the cave's opening.

"Watch him," he said, handing her Garak's knife. Kneeling down, Eskkar used his own blade to cut the binding straps away from the dead man's sandals. He knelt beside the boy, bound his hands behind his back with one lacing, and used the other to tie his feet.

Eskkar kept the bindings loose; he only wanted to ensure the boy didn't make a dash for freedom. Boys that age could move quickly, and Eskkar didn't want to find himself chasing some agile youth over the rocks. Satisfied Garak wasn't going anywhere, Eskkar flipped him onto his back and propped him up against the rock wall.

"Now, Garak of the Wolf Clan, let's talk. Tell me why Alur Meriki warriors are chasing me?"

Garak's mouth opened, but he closed it without speaking. Instead he stared hard at his captor. Eskkar gave him a few moments.

"I asked you a question, boy. If you don't answer, I'll give you to Shabata and her knife. You and your brother were about to rape and kill her granddaughter. She'll start by cutting your balls off. You'll scream like a woman, and I'll leave your remains for the rest of your clan to find."

The boy's eyes went to Shabata, his knife in her hand dangling at her side. The stony expression on her face would have frightened a much stronger man than Garak. Neither of them doubted she would hesitate to use the blade without compunction, either to slit Garak's throat or worse.

Nevertheless, the boy said nothing, his wide eyes glancing from one to the other.

"Enough," Eskkar said. "Cut them off, Shabata, then we'll see what he has to say."

Shabata moved forward and dropped to her knees. With one hand she jerked up the boy's tunic, then ripped down his undergarment. She reached toward his groin with the knife.

"Stop!" The boy's high-pitched cry echoed inside the cavern. "You're not Dacarra?"

Shabata looked up at Eskkar.

"Wait for a moment," he said. Shabata leaned back on her heels, but rested the blade of her knife on Garak's thigh. He couldn't withhold a gasp of relief.

"Who's Dacarra?" Eskkar recognized the Alur Meriki name, but more than ten years had passed since he'd left the clan, so the name itself meant nothing to him.

"Dacarra of the Fox Clan. I saw him once, months ago. He has only four fingers on his left hand." Garak's eyes went to Eskkar's hands.

Eskkar wiggled his fingers showing all ten. "I told you my name was Eskkar. Did you think I would lie to a boy not old enough yet to wipe his ass without asking permission? Why are you chasing him?"

Garak licked his lips. "Dacarra . . . ran away . . . he killed the son of our clan leader."

"Warriors kill each other all the time," Eskkar said. "What makes this Dacarra so important?"

"He murdered Ragnar, stabbed him in the back. Our clan leader ordered us to hunt him down and bring him back for torture . . . or return with his head. He swore the Shan Kar that Dacarra would die."

To swear the Shan Kar meant that the man could never rest, never stop, until he killed Dacarra. A blood feud, this one with a clan leader's son murdered, explained much. "What made you think I was Dacarra?"

"We knew he was heading for these mountains. We cut across your trail. You rode like a clansman . . . everyone thought you were him."

Shaking his head, Eskkar rocked back on his heels and once again contemplated his bad luck. He'd stumbled across the path of this Dacarra and brought the wrath of the Wolf Clan down on his shoulders.

Bad enough that they would kill him merely for being an outcast. Now he found himself hunted by warriors driven by a blood feud. Even worse, he knew they would never quit, never let up, not until they found their quarry, or knew for certain he'd escaped beyond their reach. At least that explained the tenacious search.

"You're sure Dacarra came here, into these cliffs. You had his trail, knew his horse's tracks?

Garak shook his head. "I'm not sure. No one said anything about tracks."

Eskkar understood the confusion. A boy this young did what he was told without asking questions. Garak probably had done little more than care for the horses. Grown warriors wouldn't waste their breath explaining their decisions or tactics to someone riding on his first raid.

"What does any of this matter?" Shabata asked, tapping her knife on Garak's leg. "He came to kill us. When he and his brother don't return, more will come looking for them. We need to move deeper into the mountains. Get away from here, before they find us. Let's kill him and be done with it."

Eskkar hesitated, his hand fingering his knife. The boy saw the gesture and despite his efforts to act bravely, his eyes widened in fear. Eskkar had killed men before, but never a helpless boy no older than Eskkar when he had fled for his life. Killing Garak wouldn't stop the hunt in any case.

"Perhaps it would be better if I left you and Keja behind," Eskkar said slowly, "and went off on my own."

"Don't be a fool, Eskkar. You wouldn't last a day on your own in these cliffs."

"You can't let him leave us, Grandma," Keja implored. "He caught me on the ledge. I'd have landed on the rocks if not for him."

He smiled at the girl. By now she'd recovered from her fright and her fall. "I don't want to leave you, Keja. But it might be the safest thing for you and Shabata. I can draw them away from you."

"And when they find you and realize you're not the one they seek, they'll be back. How will that help us?"

Eskkar leaned against one of the boulders. Leaving the women behind probably wouldn't protect them. The warriors would soon learn that two of their own had disappeared, and would know the area the missing brothers had been sent to search.

The Alur Meriki would redouble their efforts in this part of the mountain, and they would find this hideout. The waterfall made the site too enticing. They would certainly search the area around it, and probably find the entrances to the caverns.

Shabata's thoughts must have been going down the same path. "We could retreat back to the first cave. They can't search in there without torches."

"If they think we're in there, they'll guard both entrances while they send for more warriors. In another day, they'll be back with torches, hammers, ropes, anything they might need. Besides, we can't just sit there in the dark."

"How bad do they want this Dacarra?"

Eskkar shook his head. "Their leader can't stop the search now. They've come too close to catching him, and now they've lost a warrior and a boy. To return without him would be a mark of dishonor. They're just as likely to send for more men to comb these cliffs until they find us."

Eskkar moved his eyes to the prisoner. Garak sat there, the whites of his eyes gleaming in the shadows. His initial bravado had vanished, and now he resembled more boy than warrior, one who realized that his death drew closer, less than a step away.

"Suppose we let him go?" Shabata's voice sounded desperate. "He would tell them the one they search for isn't here."

"No. Even if they believed him, they would still return to search the area, to make sure we aren't hiding Dacarra. Then they'd slit our throats for making them waste all that time."

"Then kill him and we'll hide the bodies," Shabata said. "It will be dark soon, and we can slip away from here. There are other places to hide, deeper in the mountain."

"You can move through these cliffs at night?" The thought of traveling across these heights after dark had never occurred to

Eskkar. One misstep might lead to a long fall and a body broken against the rocks.

"Well, yes, as long as the moon is up," Shabata said, as if stating the obvious, "and if you don't try to move too fast. It's dangerous, but anything is better than staying here. I won't risk Keja being taken by barbarians. You know what they'll do to her."

"You say there are other places to hide? Where are these . . ." He turned to Garak, an idea taking thought. "How long ago did you lose Dacarra's trail? And where?"

Garak's eyes moved from Shabata to Eskkar, but the boy said nothing.

In one quick motion, Eskkar moved to Garak's side. He grabbed the boy by his hair and shoved his head hard against the rock. The other hand held the knife's edge hard against Garak's throat. The boy gasped in surprise and pain.

"You answer my questions, boy, or I'll kill you right now. And don't even think about lying to me. If I decide you're not telling the truth, I'll gut you like a pig and drag your body into the cliffs where it will never be found. You'll lie here, dishonored and unburied, with the demons of the night feasting on your spirit forever. Now, where did you lose Dacarra's trail?"

The boy's fright showed plain on his face, and Eskkar didn't know if Garak were more afraid of dying than of being left to rot in some cavern, his tortured soul condemned to wander the darkness for all time.

"Two days ago . . . two days," the words gushed from his mouth. "We'd come down from the north, riding along the mountains."

"Keep talking," Eskkar commanded, maintaining pressure on the knife.

"We lost his trail just before sundown," Garak went on, "and in the morning, we couldn't find it. The warriors split up, searching for his tracks. One of the bands saw you riding toward the mountain, and we followed your trail."

Eskkar grunted. "Your leader is a fool. Dacarra must have back-tracked his trail during the night, while you continued south yesterday. Didn't anyone realize I'd come from the south? Your leader reads tracks worse than a dirt-eater." He pushed the boy's head against the rock, this time more in frustration than anger. "Damn my bad luck."

But complaining about this latest ill-fortune wasn't going to help matters. Eskkar eased the pressure of the knife against Garak's throat.

"If Dacarra backtracked," Eskkar said, thinking out loud, "he would have stayed close to the mountain, where he couldn't be spotted easily. He wouldn't take a chance of descending back to the valley floor, not with Alur Meriki hordes coming at him. But he might have found a way into some nearby cliff. These fools are searching in the wrong place."

He turned to Shabata. "Is there another place nearby, probably to the north, where a man could hide for a few days from his pursuers? A place where he could bring a horse?"

Eskkar felt certain that Dacarra, like any steppes warrior, wouldn't want to abandon his horse if he could possibly avoid it. Besides, if Dacarra had, his pursuers would likely have found the animal wandering loose.

"It would have to be northwest of here," Shabata said. "There are a few clefts in the rocks where a man and a horse could hide, places not easy to find."

"The Alur Meriki seemed to have no trouble finding all these secret places," Eskkar said, unable to keep the annoyance out of his voice. Still, they had plenty of men, and with enough men, you can search everywhere.

"Can you get us there, to these hidden places? At night, I mean. Tonight."

"You want to go where this Dacarra is, go where they're looking for him?"

"Yes. We need to find him first, before the warriors find us. Or before he slips away, which is more likely with this band of fools. Then we kill Dacarra. Once he's dead, the Alur Meriki will be glad to leave these cliffs behind."

"What about the boy? Can we kill him now?"

"Not yet . . ." Mention of the boy gave Eskkar an idea. He thought for a moment, working out the steps in his mind. "No, we need him.

He's the one who's going to kill Dacarra, then take his head to the warriors. It's the only way they will end the hunt."

Eskkar loosed his grip on Garak, and the boy's head came forward while he gulped air into his lungs. "Listen carefully to what I say, Garak. Your life and your honor depends on it. Do you want to avenge your brother?"

"You killed him. You were . . ."

"Dacarra killed your brother, not me. He was the man you were chasing when your brother slipped and fell. If he escapes, your brother will have died for nothing. And Dacarra will get away, unless you do what I say. You're the only one who can catch him now. I'm going to give you one chance for vengeance. If you don't take it, you'll die here by your own knife, and Dacarra will have killed another Wolf Clan warrior."

He waited a moment, to let his words sink in. "We're the only ones who know where he is, and the only ones who can find him before he slips away. Your brother will die un-avenged."

"Instead," Eskkar went on, "you're going to help us hunt Dacarra down, find him, and kill him. Afterwards, you will take his head to your clan. You'll become a warrior for such a deed. All we ask in return is that you get your kin out of these mountains and leave us in peace. But until Dacarra is taken, you'll obey my every order, or I'll kill you so slow you'll wish you died here at Shabata's hand. Choose now."

Garak squirmed against the rock, looking from Eskkar to Shabata. But he saw no mercy in their faces. "I . . . I will help you."

"Swear on your honor as a warrior, in the name of your clan, with death and dishonor should you fail in your oath."

Eskkar took Garak's former blade from Shabata, and held the flat of the knife against the boy's heart. "Swear it on your own weapon, Garak of the Wolf Clan. Give your true oath, or have no honor for the rest of your days."

The boy, caught between instant death or giving his word, had little choice. Garak got the words out haltingly, and Eskkar had to prompt him with the proper way to rend such a vow. At last the words were spoken, and Eskkar leaned back in satisfaction.

"Can you trust him," Shabata said, "how do you know he won't betray us?"

"If he breaks his warrior's oath, he would be dishonored before all his kin. He would be an outcast from his own kind, almost as bad as Dacarra. No man would befriend him, no woman would marry him. He would live and die alone."

"Is that what happened to you, Eskkar?"

"I was driven from the clan for my father's deeds. But my honor as a warrior still holds. Garak will keep his word, but to make sure, we'll both watch him very closely."

Eskkar untied the cords that bound Garak's hands behind his back, and retied them in front, lashing the leather strips tight enough to make sure Garak couldn't slip loose. Then he cut the thong that bound his feet.

"Watch him, Shabata. But don't kill him." He turned to Garak. "Stay here and don't move."

Working quickly, Eskkar gathered up the weapons. The dead warrior's sword and knife were of no use to him, and he tossed them deep into the rubble of rocks. He inspected the bow, and found it none the worse for its tumble down the ledge. The quiver held fifteen arrows, as well as an extra bowstring. Fastening the quiver at his waist, he carried the bow back to where Shabata waited.

"Get everything we might need, the candle, the water skin, the tinder, anything else you've got hidden away. We've got some daylight left, and I want to be well on the way before it gets dark. We'll have to climb the slope and leave the way Garak and his brother came."

"We can't go now," Shabata said. "they're out there looking for us."

"We don't dare stay here. They could trap us any moment, and then we'd never get a chance at Dacarra."

Shabata had no answer for that. Instead she shook her head and muttered something under her breath as she started moving. It didn't take long to gather their few possessions. Keja helped, moving back up the slope and searching for any sign of the warriors. When they had everything, they started up.

Garak protested he couldn't climb with his hands tied, but Eskkar picked him up and tossed him onto the first part of the slope. "Don't argue with me, Garak."

He used the boy's name now, since he had sworn a warrior's oath. "I'll untie you when we find Dacarra. Until then, make sure you move with care. If you try anything foolish, like shouting or running away, I'll put an arrow in your back."

As soon as they reached the top of the slope, Keja and Shabata took the lead, followed by Garak, with Eskkar bringing up the rear, bow in hand.

Eskkar grunted in satisfaction at the way Shabata moved. She stayed in the shadow of every boulder she could find, crouching low whenever she had to cross open spaces. He followed her example, and made sure Garak did, too.

For one long stretch that took them close to the crest of a hill, she made them crawl more than a hundred paces, a laborious process that left Eskkar's knees scraped raw. Garak stopped complaining, no doubt considering such behavior to be un-warrior-like. Despite his given word, Eskkar stayed a few paces behind the boy whenever the rocks closed in and offered the boy a chance to escape.

They kept moving northwest, though they went around and between so many boulders Eskkar would have lost all sense of direction if he couldn't see the sun overhead.

Only once did they catch sight of distant warriors moving along the top of a cliff. The four of them huddled behind a crag until the Alur Meriki disappeared, then they resumed their slow journey.

The sun began its swift descent behind the hilltops. The air grew cooler and Eskkar knew the night would be cold, especially without a blanket to cover them.

Before the last of the sun's rays disappeared, they rested. Shabata and Eskkar studied the towering cliffs and jutting rock walls that surrounded them.

"Over there, that outcropping that looks like a boar's head," Shabata said, pointing to the northwest. "That's where we want to go. Behind that is a little dell hidden in the rocks, with a tiny pool of water. Our quarry might be there, or somewhere nearby."

With difficulty, Eskkar located the promontory she indicated, though to his eyes it looked nothing like a boar's head, or anything else. "It's a long way off," he said, "at least a mile, maybe a mile and a half."

"Farther than you think," Shabata said. "We won't be able to travel in a straight line. In the dark, we'll be lucky to get there by dawn. And that's if one of us doesn't break a leg in these rocks."

Eskkar shrugged. Worrying about what might happen did no good. "Just get us there."

"Do you really think this plan will work, that they'll leave us alone if we kill this murderer? Even Garak here," she indicated the boy sitting a few paces away, "doesn't look like he believes it."

"He'll believe it when he holds Dacarra's head in his lap," Eskkar said, placing his hand on her arm. "It will work. You'll just have to trust me."

Despite his words, Eskkar knew how much was working against them. All the same, there might be a chance for success. He counted on Garak working things out for himself.

The opportunity for a boy to become a warrior overnight didn't come along often. The normal process of attaining warrior's rank took years of proving oneself to his companions. But if a young man could demonstrate his prowess in battle against a respected foe, and not some miserable dirt-eater, all that could change.

If they killed Dacarra, and Garak returned to his clan with the murderer's head, Garak would become not only a full fledged warrior overnight, but an honored and respected one.

Not to mention that the boy would not want to reveal how his brother died or that Garak had given his true oath to an Alur Meriki outcast. If that came to light, Garak would be dishonored even if he stood before his clansmen holding Dacarra's head.

Garak probably hadn't figured out all the ramifications of his actions, and there was no need to go over them if they couldn't find Dacarra. In that case, Eskkar would kill the boy, and hope he, Keja and Shabata could elude their pursuers.

"Enough rest," Eskkar said, putting all such thoughts out of his head. "It's dark enough now. Let's get going."

With Shabata again leading the way, the motley procession crept over and between the rocks. The sun slipped below the horizon, and the long gray shadows spread over the hilltops. They could see little, and their movement slowed to a crawl.

The darkness deepened as they moved; the moon hadn't yet risen, and without its light, they had nothing but shadows to guide them. Again and again, Shabata lost her way and had to retrace her steps, trying first one path, then another. They all fell several times, slipping, stumbling, and tripping over unseen rocks and jagged edges.

Eskkar struggled more than the others. He carried all the weapons, as well as his water skin, and he had to keep a close watch on their prisoner. While Garak had given no indication he would betray his oath, Eskkar knew that thoughts of slipping away in the darkness would be in the boy's mind.

A moment's distraction, and he could vanish, disappear into the night where he could hide unseen until morning. Or Garak might try something even bolder. He might snatch up a stone and try to strike Eskkar over the head. If he were rendered unconscious, or even stunned for a moment, the young warrior could seize Eskkar's knife or sword.

There was no doubt in Eskkar's mind that the boy, despite his age and inexperience, knew how to use the weapons.

Determined not to let either event happen, Eskkar stayed close behind, his hand often on the boy's back, helping Garak up when he tripped, and checking occasionally to see that the ropes binding his hands remained snug. When the moon rose, their progress became somewhat easier. At least Eskkar didn't have to worry about Shabata and Keja falling off the side of a cliff.

They rested often, but the strain of groping their way through the darkness increased. Strange noises disturbed the silence, as they dislodged stones, sending them skittering down the slopes. Rocks shifted or cracked as the night grew colder. Once they heard the slithering of a snake gliding away, followed by an angry hiss from the blackness.

Garak, too, halted at every odd noise. Like Eskkar, he knew that demons prowled the earth at night, hunting for foolish or unwary men to carry back to their subterranean dens, to feast upon their flesh and souls.

Once the sun went down, warriors and dirt-eaters alike huddled around their camp fires or stayed in their huts, knowing that evil creatures waited to entrap those unwise enough to wander the land during the darkness when demons ruled the earth. If anything, Garak feared the dark more than Eskkar, who over the years had traveled by night many times.

As they picked their way through the dark and treacherous cliffs, Eskkar realized that nothing in his years of fighting and wandering had prepared him for such a prolonged and dangerous journey. Worry accompanied every step, and the danger from a fall seemed no less frightening than the approach of demons ready to take them to the fiery pits below the earth.

Nevertheless, the moon glided through the night sky, reached its peak, and began to descend. When it disappeared behind the northern mountains, Shabata halted. "I can't go on any further," she said. "I'm exhausted, and my feet are numb."

Eskkar felt the same, though he knew his guide had the more dangerous role. He'd been about to suggest they stop, but better that the idea came from her. No warrior would ever admit that a woman could outpace him.

The four of them found a hollow between two boulders, and wedged themselves in, trying to keep warm. No one slept at first, not even Keja. Without the distraction of moving, the small but ominous sounds of the mountains closed in on them.

They huddled together, as much for reassurance as to share body heat. Despite his best intention to remain awake, Eskkar's eyes grew heavy and he could feel himself falling asleep. He struggled to resist, but when he heard Garak's regular breathing, Eskkar let his eyes close for a moment. Dawn would be on them soon enough, bringing forth another day that might see him dead before nightfall.

Still, the new day would bring what it would. Eskkar could only hope his bad luck would change. He took one last look around, then tried to find a more comfortable position against one of the boulders. Weariness had already taken control of the others, and soon Eskkar joined them in a fitful sleep.

15

As the first rays of the dawn illuminated the peaks to the east, Shabata's hand on Eskkar's shoulder awoke him with a lurch. "Are you awake?" she whispered.

A quick glance showed him that Garak still slept. "Yes."

"I need to see where we are," she said. "Watch Keja for me."

Eskkar nodded, not that he thought either of them needed to worry about the girl. Garak might try to kill Eskkar, but Keja offered no threat to anyone. The young warrior remained between them, his mouth still open, eyes closed, and his breathing heavy. Keja slept, her head on Garak's shoulder and her arm across his chest.

Eskkar shifted his body, and every muscle twinged in protest. Scratches and cuts covered his hands, feet, and knees, the result of countless encounters with rough surfaces and hard objects over the last two days. Shabata's hands looked even worse.

Eskkar climbed to his feet, taking care not to wake the two sleepers. He stretched his back and arched his arms over his head, trying to loosen cramped muscles that protested each movement. Despite his embarrassment at falling asleep, the brief period of rest felt good. A drink from the water skin helped, and he'd begun to feel better when Shabata returned.

Shabata checked to see that Keja remained asleep, then moved beside Eskkar. "We're nearly there," she said, keeping her voice low.

"The hiding place is only a five or six hundred paces away, and we can stay concealed almost all the distance."

"We should get going," Eskkar said. Despite Shabata's words, it still took too much time to clamber through these rocks. "Soon others may be up and moving about, and we don't want to be seen now."

"What if the one we seek isn't there?"

"Then we keep looking. He has to be here somewhere." Eskkar gathered up the bow, and used one end to poke Garak in the ribs. Startled, the boy woke with a gasp. His movement wrenched Keja awake as well.

"Keep silent, Garak," Eskkar admonished. "Do you want the whole mountain to hear you?" He handed him the water skin. "Three swallows, no more."

Garak drank, then passed the water skin to Keja, who gulped more than three mouthfuls before handing the skin to Shabata. When she finished, the skin lay empty.

"We'd better find water where we're going." Eskkar paused for a moment, to look at Garak's hands. They appeared swollen, the bindings no doubt too tight. Eskkar took out his knife and cut them loose. "Now you're one of us, Garak. Make sure you remember your oath."

"Are you two ready?" Shabata's voice hissed like an angry snake.

They moved off, always keeping low and trying to stay behind some rock or ledge, anything that offered concealment from the searching eyes of the Alur Meriki. At least now they could see their footing, and they moved like ghosts themselves, without a sound and leaving no trace of their passage behind them.

Shabata halted so suddenly that everyone bumped into the one before them. "Sssh! I heard something!"

The four of them stood motionless, every ear straining to catch the slightest sound. Keja moved first, wanting to go forward, but Eskkar touched her shoulder. "Wait, child," he whispered. "Let your grandmother listen."

Eskkar trusted Shabata's hearing in these mountains more than his own. If she thought she heard something odd, he'd follow her lead. More moments passed and the sunlight grew brighter. Then he heard it, a noise he recognized at once, as did Garak. They looked at each other in understanding.

"A horse," Eskkar said, keeping his voice low, "and not too far away. You two stay here and try not to make a sound."

He gripped Garak's arm and pushed him forward. "Come with me. Watch where you step, and don't make any noise."

Together they crept through the rocks. Eskkar saw that Garak understood the need for stealth, and the two of them moved with care toward the source of the sound. Gradually an opening between two massive boulders revealed itself, and they reached a ledge that overlooked the depths below. Flat on their stomachs, they peered down.

A long slanting slope nestled between two sheer cliffs, a narrow strip of ground filled with boulders and rubble that, over the years, must have tumbled or washed down from the heights above.

From Eskkar's vantage point, the slope rose to his right, merging into the base of a towering rock wall. To his left, the incline led to the west, toward the lower levels of the cliffs.

The only opening into this hidden place must lie that way, though he couldn't see an entrance. A big war horse grazed placidly, seeking tufts of grass that grew in scattered clumps. As they watched, the animal moved from place to place, occasionally rattling a loose stone that the hollow amplified.

Another movement caught Eskkar's eye, and he leaned farther out over the edge. Almost directly beneath, he saw a warrior kneeling beside a shallow cascade of water that flowed down the center of the slope. He had his back to Eskkar's position, but his sword and a bow rested on the ground only a few paces away. Eskkar saw that the bow was unstrung, which meant the sword would be the first weapon reached for.

Eskkar put his mouth to Garak's ear and spoke so softly that he couldn't have been heard two paces away. "Is he one of yours?"

Garak lifted his head, trying to see better, but Eskkar pushed him down. "Keep your head down and move slowly. The horse mustn't catch our scent or hear us."

Garak wriggled forward and, his face flat on the rock, peered over the ledge and into the cleft. He stared for a long moment, then slithered back, away from the edge. "It's Dacarra."

The whispered words could scarcely be heard, but Eskkar perceived the rush of emotion in the boy's voice. Whatever Eskkar had done to force Garak here, the sight of his clan's enemy drove everything else away but the thirst for revenge. The man ultimately responsible for the death of his brother stood beneath them. At that moment, Eskkar believed the boy would do whatever he could to kill Dacarra.

"There's no way down from here," Eskkar whispered. "We've got to get below, then move to the entrance. If we're lucky, we'll sneak up on him and take him unaware."

"He's a mighty warrior. Can't you launch an arrow from here?"

Eskkar moved back toward the rim and risked another look. The horsemen's short bows were meant to fire from horseback. The usual range for such shooting was a hundred paces or less. Beyond that, the chance of hitting anything decreased greatly.

The floor of the canyon was about seventy or eighty paces below, with Dacarra almost directly beneath him. Eskkar would have to stand on the very edge of rim, and lean well over to take the shot, an awkward position for such a long attempt.

"I don't think so. The horse will almost certainly give some warning. And if I miss the shot, all Dacarra has to do is step back toward the canyon wall. He'll vanish before I get a second shaft on the string. Unless you think you can make the shot?"

Garak shook his head. "How are we going to defeat him?"

"We find the opening and block his escape," Eskkar said. "I'll give you the bow and one arrow. You'll get one chance to bring him down, so don't miss."

"Why only one arrow? Give me the quiver."

"No, I don't want you thinking you can put a shaft in me after you kill Dacarra."

"I gave you my oath," Garak said.

"And I'm holding you to it," Eskkar said, placing his hand on the boy's shoulder. "But men have broken their sworn word before.

Come, let's go, before he decides today is a good day to ride out of these damned mountains."

They slipped deeper into the rocks, and found Shabata waiting for them, her arms wrapped protectively around Keja. "Is he there?"

"Yes." Eskkar explained what they planned to do.

"I'll lead you to the entrance," she said, pausing only long enough to tell Keja to stay behind and act as their lookout, in case any Alur Meriki warriors approached from behind.

Eskkar didn't think that likely, but it gave Keja something to do, and would keep her out of danger, and perhaps save her from seeing more killing.

Shabata led the way, working her way between the boulders. Eskkar motioned Garak to follow her steps. Because of the need for silence, it took longer than Eskkar expected to descend their side of the cliff, move around its massive base, and mount the slope that led to Dacarra's hideout. By now the sun had climbed well above the peaks surrounding them.

When Shabata reached the opening, Eskkar saw nothing but more rocks and boulders. On horseback, he would have ridden right past this narrow cleft and never discovered it. Only when they reached the sloping ledge he'd seen from above did Eskkar feel certain he'd entered the right place.

Shabata halted suddenly. "We're almost there," she whispered. "The horse will likely hear us if we get any closer."

The loose gravel and sand washed down from the hills made it difficult to move silently.

However Shabata's presence gave Eskkar another idea. He handed her the quiver, then passed the bow to Garak. "He gets one arrow to kill Dacarra, no more." Eskkar kept his voice at a whisper. "Don't let him take the quiver from you. Understand?"

She nodded, fingering the knife at her belt.

"Garak and I will rush Dacarra. You follow us in. Keep your knife ready. If he gets to his horse and attempts to ride out, I'll try and hamstring the horse."

They had no idea where the horse might be by now, as it wandered around the dell searching for grass. It might be close to Dacarra or not when they went in. No matter what happened, Eskkar didn't want the warrior getting away.

"If he comes after you, Shabata, run back the way we came. He won't catch you in these rocks." Eskkar hoped that she didn't have to find out the truth of that statement. If Dacarra came for her, it would mean that both Eskkar and Garak were dead.

"One arrow isn't enough," Garak protested, though he, too, kept his voice low.

"It's all you get, all a strong warrior needs. Now get moving."

He took the boy's arm and the two of them passed around the boulder and into the cleft. Eskkar felt his heart racing. Garak was probably right, one arrow wasn't enough to bring down Dacarra, but Eskkar refused to take any additional chances.

He remembered Shama and her sling, turning on him after the fight had ended. This time he didn't intend to fight one opponent while worrying about another behind his back, ready to kill the victor.

They eased their way up the slope, covering about fifty paces without making a sound. But just before the opening widened into Dacarra's hideout, the rubble-filled ramp grew steeper. From somewhere up ahead, the horse snorted once, then again. Either the beast heard their approach or picked up their scent.

The time for stealth had passed. Eskkar burst into a run, leaving Garak to follow. The horse whinnied in alarm, the clarion sound echoing off the rocks. Eskkar raced his way up the steep slope.

Despite his size, Eskkar could move quickly when the need arose, and he'd never run any harder in his life. Rounding another of the endless boulders, he saw Dacarra, twenty paces away, his sword already slung over his back.

Eskkar kept moving. He hadn't drawn his sword, and when he slipped and stumbled to his knees he was glad he'd left the blade in its scabbard.

Eskkar saw the bow in Dacarra's left hand, his right fitting the bowstring to the upper limb. A quick glance told him he didn't have time to string the bow. Dacarra dropped the weapon and jerked his sword from its scabbard, the long blade glinting in the sunlight as he raised it to the attack position.

Eskkar had scaled the slope, but the mad dash had winded him. Dacarra wasted not a moment, and he had the advantage of the higher ground. He took two long strides, his sword whirling down as he attacked.

Eskkar had just enough time to whip the sword from his shoulder and parry Dacarra's stroke, a powerful blow that echoed off the cliff walls and sent the shock of contact up Eskkar's arm.

Eskkar stumbled back, and nearly lost his footing. He saw Dacarra's eyes take in the boy and Shabata, surprised at the sight of a woman, and probably wondering why no more warriors joined them.

As soon as Dacarra realized only three faced him, he continued his attack against Eskkar, taking a long stride down the treacherous ground, scattering pebbles and dust as he charged.

But the brief delay enabled Eskkar to regain his balance and his footing. He blocked another overhand cut. Dacarra never slowed. Without trying to strike again, he flung himself under the upraised blades and shoved his shoulder into Eskkar's chest.

A smaller man would have gone down from the blow, tumbling backwards down the slope, and even Eskkar staggered back, sliding down on one knee. He barely managed to avoid the follow-up thrust that should have skewered him. Instead, Eskkar flung himself to the side. Dacarra twisted his body around, keeping his balance, and driven by desperation, kept up the attack.

Enraged at nearly being knocked off his feet for the second time, Eskkar gathered his wits and struck back, moving to the attack for the first time. Both men stood on uneven ground that hindered their sword play.

The blades clashed again. For a handful of strokes, they stood toe-to-toe, both men hacking at each with all their strength. Dacarra stood as tall as Eskkar, and powerful muscles bulged across his chest and arms. When Eskkar saw he couldn't take down the warrior without a long fight, Eskkar broke away.

"Garak," he shouted, "take the shot."

Both swordsmen risked a quick glance at the archer. The youth, scrambling and sliding over the loose stones, tried to get his footing and searched for a clean shot.

Dacarra must have realized he faced only a young and unsure boy with no more than a single arrow. Again he shifted ground, keeping Eskkar between himself and the bowman.

"Who are you, warrior?" Dacarra spat the words, as he followed after his opponent. "You're no Wolf Clan dog."

"Hawk Clan," Eskkar said, and launched another attack. He started an overhand blow, then shifted it into a thrust at Dacarra's belly. The man twisted aside, and countered with a ferocious thrust of his own. Eskkar nearly lost his balance blocking the stroke, and had to leap back and to the side. Dacarra moved constantly, as much to keep Eskkar off guard than to avoid the arrow. Garak had already missed one opportunity at Dacarra's back.

"The Hawk Clan is no more," Dacarra answered, shifting his position yet again, always trying to keep Eskkar between himself and the archer. "They're all dead or disgraced."

"The Hawk Clan still lives." Eskkar chest heaved as he gulped air into his body. But he had the strength for those few words, and now he moved forward, gripping his sword with both hands and holding it high above his shoulder, "and still fights."

"Not for long. You'll die like the rest of your dishonored brothers." Dacarra's attack came with a rush and a war cry. He intended to finish off his opponent, and then deal with the young archer, taking an arrow wound if necessary.

Eskkar had no more time for words. Dacarra's swordplay was skillful, and the warrior, driven by desperation, had the strength of two, plus years of experience in wielding a sword. But Eskkar had fought many battles as well, and he had the advantage of needing only to hold off his attacker until Garak loosed his shaft. Putting all his years of training into play, Eskkar first slowed the man's attack, then halted it with a savage counterthrust of his own.

The bowstring twanged, but Dacarra had already whirled away, and the shaft flew past his shoulder, narrowly missing Eskkar. Damn the gods! The boy had wasted his arrow.

"You fight well for an outcast," Dacarra said, "but now it's time to die."

Again Dacarra launched his attack, swinging his sword high, then cutting low for Eskkar's knees. Eskkar shrank aside, shifting clumsily to avoid the sweeping blade. That gave Dacarra the higher ground, and he pressed home the attack, stroke after stroke, striking with every muscle in his body, driving Eskkar backward down the slope as he tried to fight and keep his footing at the same time.

The rocky ground made retreating dangerous. A loose stone and Eskkar would go down, never to rise again. He chanced a leap back, to gather time for a counterattack, but Dacarra stayed with him.

Their swords clashed, the sound ringing in the isolated canyon. Eskkar felt the man's strength increasing, and knew the battle couldn't last much longer. If he didn't defeat Dacarra soon, the man's powerful thews would overcome Eskkar's efforts.

A stone flew past Eskkar's head, brushing his ear, to strike Dacarra in the chest. The blow did little to hurt the big man, but it distracted him for a moment. Eskkar thrust forward, aiming for Dacarra's groin, forcing the man's sword down to defend against the stroke. This time Eskkar followed the thrust with his own body, throwing his shoulder into Dacarra before his opponent could bring his sword to bear.

Dacarra's bulk took the blow with scarcely a step back, and Eskkar felt as if he'd slammed into the rock wall enclosing them. He grasped his opponent's sword wrist, even as Dacarra seized his.

Both men struggled, grunting with effort, each trying to ram the hilt of their weapons into the other's face, their feet scrambling for purchase on the sloping ground.

Eskkar felt his wrist being crushed, and despite his effort, Dacarra pushed him down the slope, a halting half-step at a time. Dacarra's knee flashed up, seeking Eskkar's groin, and only a quick twist to the side avoided the painful jab. Any moment, Eskkar would be driven to his knees, and then Dacarra would strike the death blow.

A second stone struck Dacarra in the face, the impact wrenching a gasp of pain from his lips and weakening him for an instant. Eskkar ducked down, then strained uphill with his thighs. He shoved Dacarra back and tore his sword hand free from the man's grip. Before Eskkar could strike, a shaft struck Dacarra full in the chest, the arrow biting deep into the man's body.

Leaping back, Eskkar struck down with his blade, a powerful stroke aimed at knocking Dacarra's blade aside. It did more than that. The sword fell from the man's grasp, as the bite of the arrow weakened Dacarra's muscles.

Another arrow struck, this one right beside the first shaft, only closer to the heart. With a choking curse of rage, Dacarra stumbled to his knees. For a heartbeat his hand groped for the sword, then his eyes rolled up into his head, and he fell forward, sliding headfirst three or four paces down the slope.

Eskkar, gasping for breath, whirled to find Garak stringing a third shaft to his bow. Suddenly Eskkar understood why the boy had waited so long. He'd worked his way to Dacarra's weapons and gathered a handful of arrows to replace the one Eskkar had given him. Now the shaft, nocked on the string, pointed straight at Eskkar.

Garak stood about ten paces away. Even if he shot and missed, he'd have time to dart away, and Eskkar, weakened by the hard fight, wouldn't be able to catch him. From the rocks, he could rain arrows at Eskkar until one of them struck him down.

"Lower your bow, Warrior," Shabata said, picking her way across the slope toward Garak as she replaced her knife in the sheath at her waist. "You've fought bravely today. Do not ruin your new-found honor by breaking your oath. It took all three of us to defeat him."

A few more steps and she stood in front of Garak, blocking the shot.

Recovering his wits, Eskkar readied himself for a charge, feeling much the same as Dacarra must have felt only moments before.

Garak hesitated, then slowly lowered the bow. Shabata reached out and took the weapon from his hand and walked toward Dacarra's belongings, leaving the two men facing each other.

Eskkar bowed his head slightly, acknowledging Garak for the first time as a warrior equal. "You fought well, Garak of the Wolf Clan."

Eskkar glanced at the nicks on his blade from Dacarra's hammer strokes, then returned the weapon to its scabbard. "Your kin will be proud that you were the warrior who avenged their loss and satisfied your clan's honor."

As the import of what he'd just done began to sink in, Garak's shoulders relaxed. "I'm not sure . . . what will I say?"

"Come," Eskkar said, still breathing hard. "I need a drink of water." They walked side by side to the tiny stream, where they knelt and splashed the chilled water over their faces.

"Dacarra was a mighty warrior," Garak said. "You fought well against him, but I think he would have killed you."

"Perhaps." Eskkar laughed as he splashed water over his face and neck. "I wasn't dead yet, Garak. But Shabata's stone and your arrows were most welcome." They drank side by side, the water soothing Eskkar's throat.

"My arm shook when I drew the first shaft, and I missed."

"The first time is never easy, Garak. But you honored your brother and your clan, and that is what matters."

"What do we do now?"

"First, you take his sword and cut off his head," Eskkar said. "Then you take his horse and his sword and ride out to find the rest of your clan. Once they see that Dacarra is dead, I'm sure they'll be glad enough to leave these mountains."

"And you and your woman? What will you do?"

"She is not my woman. She and the girl live here in the cliffs. No doubt she will remain. I'll stay with her a few days, until the Alur Meriki move on. Then I'll ride to the west, through the lands you've already crossed."

"The dirt-eaters will not welcome you," Garak said. "They'll hunt you."

"They've hunted me before," Eskkar said, "and I'm still alive."

"I've never heard of the Hawk Clan. They must have been a brave clan before their dishonor."

The boy was too young to remember the night the Hawk Clan died, and after that day, few would mention either the clan's name or its fate.

"My father and his kin were brave enough. Whatever they did, I'm sure they kept their honor." Eskkar took a breath as he remembered his parents. "Best not to mention such things when you rejoin your people. Others might wonder why you sought knowledge of them."

"What do I tell them about Dacarra?"

"Tell them the truth, or at least most of it. That you found yourself alone in the mountains after your brother fell to his death. You came across Dacarra's trail and tracked him to this place. Then tell the truth. That you walked up the slope and put two arrows in his chest as he charged you."

"He wasn't attacking me," Garak said.

"Don't fool yourself," Eskkar said, laughing again. "As soon as I went down, Dacarra would have been in your face. I don't think one arrow would have brought him down. Perhaps we both owe Shabata thanks for her stones."

Once again, death had tried to claim Eskkar, but once again he had managed to slip from its grasp.

"You could have given me more than one arrow. It did take two shafts to bring him down."

"Well, now that you're a true warrior, you'll only need one next time. And I think you'll find that next time you draw your bow against an enemy, your arm won't shake, either."

Garak smiled, and Eskkar felt a moment of sadness. The boy would be returning to his kin and clan, to his family and friends. They would honor him for his victory, and after a few months, all the boy would remember of the struggle was shooting the arrows that brought Dacarra down.

The only good Eskkar would gain from Dacarra's slaying was the chance to live his lonely existence for a few more days or months, until death finally claimed him.

Shaking away such gloomy thoughts, Eskkar reached out and clasped Garak's forearm, as one warrior greets another. "Time for you to return to your clan, Warrior. I'm sure they're searching for you by now."

—◦◦◦—

Six days later, Eskkar walked out of the mountains, leaving Shabata and Keja in the safety of their little valley. He'd longed to keep Dacarra's horse, a fine mount, but of course Garak needed something to ride. Eskkar already missed Boy, and hoped that his new owner would treat him well.

It took almost three days before Eskkar's long strides carried him back to the village of Didra and the house of Gallred. The Alur Meriki had burned the place, but the walls still stood, and a new roof of slender branches covered with mud was already in place.

Gallred, too, had returned, and he stood with his mouth gaping as Eskkar entered the courtyard. A plank table held tools that the workers were using to rebuild the structure.

"I'm surprised to see you alive, Eskkar. We saw a war party riding north, toward the mountains. We heard the barbarians were raiding all over the mountain. How did you avoid being taken?"

"I hid out in the rocks," Eskkar replied, not wanting to go into a long story. Instead he dumped the contents of his sack on the merchant's table. Half of the loot came from the bandits that attacked Shabata, but the best pieces had once belonged to Dacarra.

Eskkar and Garak had split the warrior's valuables. Now four rings of gold and three golden arm bands lay spread across the table, including a silver ring, and two silver arm bands, and the short sword Eskkar had managed to hang onto. Even a few decent gemstones lay scattered before the merchant's gaze.

"I didn't think hiding in the rocks could be so profitable." Gallred stared at Eskkar for a moment, until he realized no further explanation would be forthcoming.

"I see you avoided trouble, Gallred."

"We rode hard to the south," Gallred said. "If they found our trail, they didn't bother to pursue. Though I never expected to see you again.

"Well, they found my trail, and got much closer than I wanted," Eskkar replied. "But I slipped away, and they gave up the chase."

"I can use your help, Eskkar," the Village Elder said, waving his hand around. "Half my men disappeared, and I need all the guards I can find."

Eskkar shook his head. "Can't stay, not this time. But I need a horse, and some other supplies."

"Let me see what I can do. Now, have some ale. We'll drink to being alive."

"My throat's dry as dust," Eskkar said, appreciative of the offer, "and I'll drink to that."

After spending two days enjoying Gallred's hospitality, Eskkar retraced his trail into the mountains, following the same path he'd taken in his flight from Didra. This time he traveled at a leisurely pace through the empty land, leading a donkey burdened down with supplies. He saw no recent tracks or signs of anyone else passing his way, but he took care to search the horizon every few moments.

Many dirt-eaters had died in the Alur Meriki's passing, and those who survived now lived on the edge of starvation, willing to risk death as much for the food in Eskkar's pouch as for the horse he rode.

Eskkar's loot had been more than enough to outfit himself with the horse and everything else he needed, and to buy the donkey. He had purchased his new mount, a scrawny mare well past her prime, from Gallred. The horse gave Eskkar no satisfaction, but the Alur Meriki had swept the land clean of horses.

Good animals were unavailable at any price, and only a few inferior animals remained. Eskkar had pleaded with Gallred, but the merchant refused to part with any of his few remaining fine horses, even for double their worth.

"I might need them again, Eskkar. Come back in a few months, when the land has settled down. I'll have built up a good stable by then, and will sell you a decent mount at a fair price."

Eskkar wasted half a day searching for a better horse, but soon gave up. He paid Gallred almost twice what the beast would have been worth only a month ago. The donkey that plodded behind Eskkar's mare cost nearly as much as the horse. The Alur Meriki had taken most draft animals, and killed many of the rest. Even a young and clumsy donkey now fetched a high price.

"You drive a hard bargain," Eskkar said, after finishing his transactions and transferring most of his recently acquired wealth to Gallred. After all the purchases, Eskkar had only a small handful of silver coins to return to his pouch.

"Look around you, Eskkar. The land is empty, the people dead or in hiding. There will be no harvest this season. Everything will cost two and three times as much as it should for at least another year. I made no profit on what I've sold you." Gallred grinned. "Well, hardly any."

Eskkar grunted, but knew the merchant spoke the truth. Not that Eskkar intended to remain in this barren and dangerous countryside for long.

With his supplies loaded onto the horse and the donkey, he said his farewell to Gallred and headed north toward the mountains. Traveling slowly, the journey lasted four days before Eskkar ascended the same trail into the cliffs where he'd first met Keja. He guided the skittish horse and reluctant donkey along the side of the precipice.

Someone called his name, and he lifted his eyes to see a figure jumping up and down, outlined against the sky. Keja guarded the trail, watching for Eskkar's return. By the time he reached the hidden turn, Shabata and Keja waited for him.

"What took you so long, Eskkar?" Keja kept dancing about in her excitement. "I thought you'd be back days ago." The donkey caught her attention and she rubbed its neck. The animal bayed happily at her touch.

"It's good to see you, Shabata," Eskkar said.

"I didn't expect you so soon." She had an unfamiliar smile on her face.

"Or even if I'd come back at all," he said, swinging Keja up into his arms and letting her sit astride the horse for a moment. "But I'd eaten most of your food, and I promised you a new donkey."

He handed Keja down to Shabata, then slid off the mare. Together they led the animals through the narrow cleft, pushing and shoving them along, until they passed through the opening. From there they wended their way to Shabata's hidden glen, guiding both animals down the slope.

Eskkar saw that Shabata had kept busy. The hut, knocked down by the Alur Meriki in their anger, had been rebuilt, with a new roof added since Eskkar's departure. The bones of the old donkey had been buried, and all signs of the temporary camp the barbarians established had disappeared.

Eskkar eased himself down against the wall of the hut, grateful for the chance to stretch his legs. The slow pace necessitated by the donkey had wearied him more than expected.

"Have you seen any other strangers in these mountains?"

"No one," Shabata answered. "Each morning and just before dusk I climb the hills and search the approaches. But we've seen no one since Garak and his clan rode out."

"The land to the west is empty, picked clean, by their passing. The villages and nearby farms have been destroyed."

"Then perhaps I'll have a few years of peace, before ignorant villagers begin telling tales of sacks of gold hidden by a witch in the mountains."

Eskkar nodded. "You're probably safe for now. But I don't think you'll have that much time." He looked at Keja. "You're growing up, girl."

And she was. Already she looked taller, not the child who once pleaded with him to ride his horse. The recent danger had added gravity to her demeanor.

He turned toward Shabata. "Another year or so, and she'll be a woman."

"Yes, I suppose I'll have to face that soon enough," Shabata said with a sigh. "But not today."

"Not today," Eskkar agreed. He stood. "Come! Let me show you what I've brought."

He stripped the donkey and the horse of their packs. Keja began opening everything, crying out in excitement at the wonderful assortment. Eskkar had brought pots of honey, hard cheese, bags of figs, apples, and dates, even two small sacks of grain. Two loaves of bread, already stale but still edible.

"No wine or ale," he said. "There's not a drop left in the countryside."

"And I've a gift for Keja," Eskkar went on. From the bottom of one pouch, he pulled out a sling. "I'm sure you'll find plenty of round stones nearby to cast. At least you'll have something to hunt with."

The girl took the leather thongs with reverence, and he realized it was the first gift she'd ever received, probably the first thing she ever owned.

After they ate, they sat around a small fire. Eskkar had gathered the wood on his journey, enough to cook more than one meal.

"And what are your plans, Eskkar?"

"I'm riding south, far south. There are lands there that I've never seen, lands that haven't been devastated by the Alur Meriki."

"You could stay with us," Keja said wistfully.

"I'd like that. Especially after all you've done for me. But there's not enough food in these hills for the three of us. Besides, an outcast barbarian won't be too popular around here when the farmers return."

Keja's lip quivered. He saw the sadness in her eyes. "But I'll stay a few days, to rest the horse, before I go."

"Stay as long as you like," Shabata said. "You are welcome here. These hills will hide you as well as they keep their own secrets."

He wondered at her strange words for a moment, until he remember the glowing symbol. Not much of a secret, he decided.

"I've also told Gallred, the Village Elder in Didra, about you. He's a good man, or at least as good as any greedy merchant. If you need to leave this place, he's promised to take you into his service. And not out of the goodness of his heart. I've already given him two silver coins in your names. You may want to seek him out as Keja grows older."

"I don't want to get older." Keja put down her sling and slid next to Eskkar. She snuggled up against his side and wrapped her arms around him.

An unexpected emotion passed through Eskkar. No one had held him like that in a long time. Before he could react, Shabata moved to

Eskkar's other side. She put her arms around his shoulder, much the same way his mother had enfolded him.

For a moment, sadness filled his heart, as the loss of his family and kin passed through him. Then he remembered his mother's words, uttered with her final breath, telling him to save himself. To live, and perhaps to one day find happiness and a family of his own. Then the warmth of Keja and Shabata banished the dark thoughts.

"At least you'll stay with us for a while," Shabata said firmly.

"Yes, a few days," Eskkar said. "If I stay any longer, I might get too accustomed to living beneath all these grim rocks."

Eskkar wrapped his arms around them both, holding them close. And this time he couldn't keep the broad smile from his face.

16

Two years later . . .

Eskkar trudged up another rolling hill, one of an endless number the playful gods had placed in his path to confound him. After two days of walking, his legs ached from the unaccustomed slow progress over the uneven ground, his steps made more difficult by the gear he carried distributed over various parts of his body.

The sword, of course, still hung down his back, but a second, shorter weapon dangled from his waist, where it slapped against his left thigh at every opportunity. Both blades grew heavier with each step. In addition to the swords, his long copper knife seemed to have increased in weight as well, and the big water skin felt no lighter, no matter how much he drank.

Two blankets, one for the horse he no longer possessed and another for himself, formed an awkward bedroll that hung over his left shoulder. His sagging belt supported a pouch full of the small necessities every traveler required, such as the flint chip needed to start a fire, a sharpening stone for his sword, and half a loaf of stale bread.

The pouch, however, contained no other food and no coins, not a single copper, which Eskkar convinced himself helped keep the weight down. Everything else, including his cooking pot, he'd abandoned over the course of the last two days. What remained of his worldly possessions, such as they were, now burdened his body. Mounted on a good horse, those same articles had seemed but a trifle.

Cursing his usual bad luck and the fate that made the horse go lame in the middle of nowhere, Eskkar plodded slowly upwards. Not that the animal had been much of a prize, but he'd paid the last of his coins to buy it, the third mount he'd possessed in the last two years.

The new horse had gone lame three days later, unable to put any weight on its right foreleg, not even able to hobble more than a few steps.

One look at the swollen knee told Eskkar that it would take at least ten days before the horse could carry any weight. Just as likely, it would never recover. In a fit of anger, he cursed his fate, the crafty trader who sold him the unsound beast, and even the pitiful horse, before packing up his things and starting to walk, leaving the poor brute behind to forage as best it could. At least the grass was plentiful, and sooner or later some farmer would give it a home.

The hill grew steeper near the top, but Eskkar gritted his teeth and kept climbing, taking care not to trip and fall. He'd done that twice since yesterday. This time, leaning forward, he crested the hill without mishap and stopped to catch his breath and survey the land beneath him.

A good-sized stream lay only a few hundred paces ahead, the clear water flowing sluggishly along its crooked path. Lining the water's edge, he saw a tangled border of green bushes on both banks, with scattered sycamore, willow, and even an occasional date palm providing shade that nearly covered the width of the stream.

Thick vegetation gave the river a cool appearance that made Eskkar wipe the sweat from his brow. At least he wouldn't die of thirst.

According to the ignorant dirt-eater who'd given Eskkar directions, he should have reached this stream yesterday. Instead, the water that marked the trail to Dilmun had turned out to be a good twenty miles of hard traveling further west. At least now Eskkar had his bearings once again. He didn't even need to cross over, just follow the flowing water to reach his destination.

With a sigh of relief, he started down the hill, which sloped a bit more gently toward the stream. All the same, after surviving twenty-four seasons, he'd learned caution. A fall, especially one that resulted in a broken leg or even a sprained ankle, would be serious, and Eskkar had no intention of hobbling around helpless or dying of starvation.

He reached the outer fringe of greenery growing beside the brook, and followed along the bank until he found an opening that gave easy access to the water. Old tracks marked this place as a ford, but the more Eskkar examined them, the more he relaxed. No one had crossed here in several days.

He dumped his possessions and dropped to his knees at the water's edge. First he quenched his thirst, then scooped handful after handful of the cool water over his face and neck. With most of the travel dust removed, he leaned over for another drink, but then stopped, his attention attracted to movement on the opposite bank.

A pair of horsemen . . . no, one man riding and leading a second horse, approached the stream from the other side. The rider apparently planned to cross the stream. Eskkar rose to his feet and made sure the sword over his shoulder moved easily within its scabbard.

The stranger looked up in surprise, saw the gesture, and halted at the edge of the water where his horses could lower their heads and drink.

For a moment, the two men stared at each other, separated by less than twenty paces of gurgling water. By now Eskkar noted that the man carried no sword, only a knife on his belt. More interestingly, he carried nothing else, no water skin or food pouch, and the second horse carried no possessions, not even a blanket.

The rider, a small man with the darker complexion that accompanied those from the southern parts of Sumeria, a good hundred miles farther south, looked fit enough. He wore a tunic with colorful stitching that might have once belonged to rich merchant, but now a torn sleeve and numerous stains left the garment barely wearable.

Despite the lack of weapons, Eskkar guessed the man was a fighter. He didn't move or act like most dirt-eaters, and his gaze met Eskkar's without fear.

"How's the water?" The voice, a deep, resonant bass, seemed out of place coming from the man's smaller stature.

"Good enough," Eskkar answered.

"Then I'll try it," he said, swinging smoothly down from the horse, patting it on the neck before splashing into the stream to cup his hands and quench his own thirst. "I have to cross here anyway."

He drank again, then stepped back onto the bank and mounted the horse, which took a stride into the water and continued drinking.

Eskkar shrugged at the words, but said nothing.

"I'm on my way to Dilmun. Is that where you're headed?"

"Perhaps." Eskkar didn't intend to discuss his plans with an unknown rider.

"I'll cross over now," the stranger said. "You won't be thinking about using that sword on me, will you?"

Eskkar smiled at the man's caution. "Not as long as you cross straight over and keep going."

But to make plain his peaceful intentions, Eskkar moved aside, stopping only to pick up the second sword he'd tossed on the ground beside the rest of his things.

The stranger gathered the halter from the second horse and touched his heels to his own, keeping, as Eskkar noticed, the extra mount between the two of them.

Without taking his gaze off Eskkar, the rider splashed through the stream, the horses stepping slowly as they waded with care through the knee-high water. When they reached Eskkar's side, the stranger kept the horses moving, guiding them through the shrubs and trees, heading for higher ground.

Eskkar watched them go. For a moment, he'd been tempted to ask for a ride, since both men obviously were heading to the same village. But his barbarian caution prevailed, and he didn't want to have to watch his back during a long ride to Dilmun.

Instead he concentrated on the horseflesh as it moved away. The rider's mount looked strong and well-fed. The other animal appeared well past its prime, dull of eye and drab of coat.

As Eskkar watched, the stranger halted about thirty paces away and turned his horses around. He rode back, stopping twelve or so paces away from where Eskkar still stood. "I see you have an extra sword. Is it bronze?"

So the man had a quick eye as well. Eskkar didn't bother answering the foolish question. Only a dolt or some ignorant farmer would lug an extra sword of copper around on foot.

"Perhaps you'd be willing to sell it."

"I plan to, in Dilmun," Eskkar said.

"Dilmun is a full day's ride from here."

Damn these villagers and their constant urge to state the obvious. "So you say."

"Perhaps we could make a trade. I need a good sword, and you look like you could use a horse."

Eskkar's eyes flickered back to the horses for a moment. "The sword's a good one, well made from the finest bronze. It will fetch ten silver coins in Dilmun, more than enough to buy a good horse."

The man ran his hand over his face, then swung down off his mount. He paused for a moment to link the two halters, fashioning a quick hitch knot that showed he knew his way around horseflesh.

Eskkar used the time to study the man's face. A dark beard grew sparsely over his cheeks and chin. A crooked nose gave evidence of more than a few encounters with fists or other solid objects, and a jagged scar stretched its way down half the man's cheek. A dirty headband kept the hair away from his dark eyes that now met Eskkar's gaze.

"My name is Bracca. What's yours?"

"Of no concern to you," Eskkar said. By dismounting, the man had shown he had plenty of nerve or an unusual amount of stupidity.

Nonetheless, the stranger remained beside his horse. If Eskkar suddenly decided to rush toward him, one good hard slap on the animal's rump would launch it forward and give the man plenty of time to draw his knife.

"You don't like to talk much, do you?" Bracca said, a wide smile exposing a mouth still full of white teeth that contrasted with the dark skin and facial hair. "No matter. Let me see the sword."

Eskkar obligingly drew the short blade from its scabbard, and held it up.

"Doesn't look like it's worth ten silver," Bracca said.

"It's not."

"I thought you said you wanted ten."

"It's worth twelve, but I'll probably have to settle for ten," Eskkar said.

That was true enough. Over the years, he rarely got the better of any bargaining with villagers. Or people with quick tongues like this Bracca. Eskkar had learned to pick his price in advance and stick to it, walking away from the deal if necessary.

"The horse is worth ten silver, barbarian," Bracca said, again smiling. "And he's right here, ready to save you a long walk to Dilmun."

Sheathing the short sword, Eskkar looped it over his belt, making sure he attached the scabbard securely. "You're right. The horse is worth the sword. Your horse, not the nag."

Bracca's eyes widened in surprise, then he burst out laughing, his white teeth flashing. "Not my horse. He's worth three of your swords. And he's not for sale."

"Better be on your way, then . . . Bracca."

"Let me see the sword."

"You've seen it."

"I mean, hold it out, let me get a feel for it."

"I know what you mean," Eskkar said, his innate caution warning him to take care. The man showed too much interest in the weapon and not a trace of worry about Eskkar's size and bulk. Surely there would be swords for sale in Dilmun.

Or maybe Bracca thought he would need the sword on the journey. Any man riding the countryside with two horses and no sword made for a tempting target, and the thought made Eskkar wonder if he should kill Bracca and take the animals.

But the horses might be known in Dilmun. Eskkar didn't want more trouble than he usually encountered when arriving in an unfamiliar village.

With his barbarian heritage stamped on his face, villagers needed little encouragement to make trouble. "If you want to look closer, walk over here."

Bracca hesitated, clearly unhappy about the prospect of leaving his horses and venturing within Eskkar's reach.

Eskkar waited. If the man came forward, he must be truly desperate.

It took only a moment. Bracca smiled again, this time showing even more teeth, and let the halter rope hang down. He took a step forward.

Taking his time, Eskkar reached up and drew his own sword from over his shoulder.

Bracca stopped, his hand on his knife. "Why the sword, barbarian?"

"You didn't think I was going to hand you a sword, did you, without my own in hand? Suppose you decided to try and use it on me?"

"Why would I do that . . . what is your name? I hate talking to someone without a name."

With his left hand, Eskkar drew the short sword from its scabbard, then flipped the weapon in his hand, switching his grip from the hilt to the blade just below the guard. He extended his left arm, letting Bracca see both the blade and the hilt. At the same time, he lifted his long sword in his other hand, pointing it straight at Bracca.

"You're not a very trusting man, are you . . . why won't you tell me your name? Do you think I'll cast a spell on you, or put a demon on your trail?"

"My name is Eskkar." Anything to stop the questioning. "Now, do you want the sword or not?"

Bracca edged closer, but stopped about three paces away. He peered at the short sword, tilting his head as if trying to make up his mind. "No, not for my horse."

"Then I'll offer you a different deal," Eskkar said. "I'll ride with you into Dilmun on your nag. Then after I sell the sword, I'll give you a silver coin."

"Give it to me now."

"I don't have even a copper," Eskkar said, for the first time giving Bracca the benefit of his own smile.

Bracca considered that for a moment. "No, I need a sword now, and one coin won't buy me a good bronze blade. The sword for the horse is what I'm offering."

"Why turn down a chance to earn a piece of silver, Bracca?"

Without taking his eyes off the man, Eskkar slid the short sword into its scabbard, then lowered his own weapon, letting the tip rest on the ground between them.

"It appears we both have the same problem, a lack of coins," Eskkar said. "But one silver coin, plus what you can sell the nag for, might buy you an old copper weapon. Or you can sell your own horse, and buy a decent sword in Dilmun. Either way, looks like you're going to lose your horse."

"Then at least two silver coins for the ride in . . . Eskkar."

"I'm in no hurry," Eskkar said. "I'll walk."

"No horseman enjoys walking," Bracca said. "And you don't look as if you have any extra food in your pouch. Not to mention that you'll look foolish trying to sell your barbarian skills in Dilmun if you don't even have a horse. Even Jorak won't pay anything to a barbarian without a horse."

"Who's Jorak?" Eskkar cursed himself as soon as the words left his lips. He should have waited, let Bracca keep talking.

"Ah, you don't know the name? You do know about Dilmun, don't you?"

"I've heard talk," Eskkar said.

Bracca threw back his head and laughed. "You're a bad liar, barbarian."

He shook his head, this time at the expression on Eskkar's face. "Everyone in these parts knows all about the fighting at Dilmun. Jorak is the Village Elder there, calls himself the Noble One. Insists that everyone bow when they greet him. He's hiring every man who can hold a sword to help him wage his war with Tuttul."

"Tuttul?"

A loud sigh escaped Bracca lips, as if astonished at the scope of Eskkar's ignorance.

"Jorak of Dilmun is waging a blood war against the village of Tuttul," Bracca explained. "That's another two days ride further south of Dilmun. Jorak has been feuding with the ruler of Tuttul for years, but a few months ago, Jorak's son got himself killed raiding the farms around Tuttul. Jorak has decided to avenge his son's death by wiping the village from the earth."

Another blood feud. The worst kind of fighting, Eskkar knew. Even in his clan days with the Alur Meriki, such feuds could wreak disaster on families. Endless killings and retaliation, until one family or another ceased to exist – unless the clan leader intervened and put an end to the fighting.

"Jorak is paying two, maybe three copper coins a day for experienced fighting men, and promising more when Tuttul is destroyed. He's already got fifty or sixty men ready to fight for him."

"And that's why you're going to Dilmun?"

"Of course. Did you think I was going there to shovel pig shit on some farm? And what are you planning to do in Dilmun? Just sell the sword, and move on? To Tuttul, perhaps?"

Eskkar opened his mouth, then closed it. Bracca was right. Eskkar might sell the sword easily enough, and for a good price, if fighters were gathering there.

But a village full of eager warriors wasn't going to let a well-armed and mounted fighter just ride away. They'd take his sword and his horse, if nothing else, but just as likely kill him, on the off chance that he might end up fighting for the other village.

Regardless, Eskkar couldn't go back the way he'd come. It would take him close to three days to reach the nearest village, and he'd find no welcome there, only trouble. Eskkar hadn't killed anyone, but he had broken a man's jaw, and the injured man apparently had plenty of kin.

Here along the fringe of the desert, Dilmun was one of the last settlements before the wastelands closed in. With no food, no horse, and no copper, Eskkar needed to go to Dilmun.

Bracca waited a few moments, letting Eskkar digest the information.

"Take the old horse for the sword, barbarian. Then we can both ride in. If we sell our services together, we can ask for more copper than we'd get alone. I know how to use a sword, and I've fought in these kinds of quarrels before. Besides, we can protect each other, if things get ugly."

The man's words made sense, but whenever Eskkar trusted anyone, he'd always come to regret it sooner or later. He'd journeyed this far in life mostly alone, and he didn't intend to change now.

"No. I'll trade you the sword for your horse. It's either that, or one silver coin for the ride in. Take your pick, or be on your way."

"Your head is thicker than bronze, barbarian. There won't be any horses for sale in Dilmun, not now. You'll be stuck in the village and end up fighting for Jorak anyway, just to stay alive. Either that, or find your throat slit the first night for whatever you get for the sword."

Eskkar didn't like his options, but he wasn't going to give up a valuable sword for a horse worth not even one silver coin.

Bracca waited, but when Eskkar remained silent, Bracca lifted both hands up to his shoulders, then let them drop in frustration. He took three long strides back to his horses, and led them away from the stream before he mounted and cantered away.

Watching the man depart, Eskkar wondered if he'd made the right choice. If he walked until nightfall and started again at dawn, he might get to Dilmun by noon tomorrow.

"Damn all villagers and dirt-eaters," he said, angry at his seemingly inexhaustible bad luck.

He quenched his thirst from the river, then rinsed the water skin, but didn't fill it. The stream ran all the way to Dilmun, and there was no sense carrying water with a stream nearby.

Gathering up his things, Eskkar followed along the tracks left by Bracca. By the time he'd climbed the first hill, sweat again covered his brow, and he wondered if he'd made a mistake not offering two silver coins for the ride, though paying such a large amount for so small a service would have rankled Eskkar for months.

Even so, he still didn't understand why Bracca hadn't accepted his offer. Another stubborn and ignorant Sumerian dirt-eater, Eskkar decided.

Keeping the river on his right, he selected the easiest ground for walking, which happened to mirror Bracca's trail. One mile passed, then another, until Eskkar crested one more of the apparently endless rolling hills and regarded the next part of the trail.

A quarter of a mile ahead, he saw Bracca and his horses. The man lay under the shade of a poplar tree, taking his ease, the two animals grazing nearby.

Eskkar straightened up and tried to stride with purpose, as if the long walk meant nothing to him. A gentle slope led down to level ground, and Eskkar covered the remaining three hundred paces to where Bracca rested.

This time the man didn't bother to get up as Eskkar approached. Instead, he propped himself up on one arm, watching Eskkar's slow progress.

"It took you long enough to catch up. Good thing I didn't ride any farther. You'd probably have gotten lost."

Despite himself, Eskkar smiled. "You know, Bracca, you're really tempting me to kill you and take both horses." Once again, he dumped his possessions on the ground and moved under the shade of the same tree that sheltered the Sumerian.

"If you wanted to kill me and steal my horses, you would have tried back at the stream. I'd have killed you, of course, if you attempted anything so foolish."

Easing himself down to the ground, Eskkar leaned back against a rock, a few paces from where Bracca still reclined. "You and your little knife? I'd have gutted you before you could fumble it out of your sheath."

"I've killed better men than you with it, men who didn't annoy me half as much. But all in the past, that, and not worth wasting words over. Two silver coins, and you can ride into Dilmun. We'll be there by nightfall, if you've got half the wits of a dead dog. I'll even buy you a mug of ale."

"One silver coin," Eskkar said, "and I'll buy you the ale. Don't forget, we're two miles closer now."

"You ARE duller in the head than a dead dog, friend Eskkar," Bracca said. "And you drive a hard bargain, but I might accept it, with one condition."

Eskkar frowned at the thought of any more complications. "What condition?"

"You lend me the sword just before we ride in, and you sell it to me for nine silver coins. That's the same as the ten you'd get in the market, less the coin you'll owe me. I'll even throw in the nag, and promise to pay you for the sword within two days."

"Why do you need to borrow the sword, friend Bracca?" Eskkar could guess the reason, but he had to ask.

"There are some men in the village who owe me a few silver coins, and they may not be eager to pay what they owe. We had something of a disagreement when we parted. So I'd prefer not to argue with them without a good sword handy. Once I get the silver, I'll pay you, and you can trade the nag and the coins for a better mount. If there's anything better to be had in Dilmun."

Eskkar thought about Bracca's offer for a moment. He'd be taking a chance, lending the sword, even if he waited until they reached the outskirts of Dilmun.

"Suppose those in your debt kill you and take the sword from your dead body, friend Bracca? Then I'd be out my silver and the sword."

"They're not going to kill me, trust me on that. They'll pay as soon as they see me and the sword."

Eskkar took his time thinking. Bracca had been clever enough to let him walk a few more miles, before offering his deal. Still, Eskkar's feet hurt, and the thought of tramping all the way to Dilmun seemed even less appetizing than before.

"Well, Bracca, I might consider your offer, but I've one condition as well. You lend me your horse, not the nag, for the ride to Dilmun. That way, if by some chance you do get yourself killed, at least I've got a decent horse, and the villagers will remember who rode him in."

Before Bracca could object, Eskkar held up his hand. "As you said, if I have to join up with this Jorak, it wouldn't look right for a horseman from the steppes to ride in on an old plow horse, while you're strutting around on such a fine beast. When you pay me the silver, we can exchange horses."

"I don't think that's such a good arrangement," Bracca said. "Suppose we . . ."

"Look, if I have to ride the nag, I'll slow us both down, and we won't get to Dilmun by nightfall. The plow horse can carry your puny weight easier than mine. Besides, if we have to camp out overnight, one of us will end up killing the other."

Bracca rubbed his lips with the back of his hand while he considered the offer.

"Enough! I thought the steppes people were supposed to be slow-witted fools who don't know how to barter. Instead, you're taking my good horse, and making me pay you for the privilege. It seems you're getting the better of the bargain."

"You know what the merchants say – someone complains after every trade."

"You talk like a merchant yourself," Bracca said, softening the insult with a grin. "I only hope you know how to fight half as well as you barter."

"Let's get started, then," Eskkar said, rising to his feet, already invigorated at the prospect of riding a fine horse.

It took only moments to get his gear onto the big horse. "And friend Bracca, you won't mind riding in front, just in case you decide to change your mind about our agreement. Not that I don't trust you, but we barbarians get nervous when strangers draw too close. And you look like the kind of man who might know how to throw a knife."

"If I ever decide to throw it, you'll be the first one I aim at, I swear it on the gods, my good friend Eskkar."

Eskkar smiled at the coarse joke, and waited until Bracca had kicked the nag into motion and moved a few paces ahead before relaxing his own halter and moving forward.

Bracca had already started complaining, about the horse and the price for the sword. Eskkar guessed that by the time they reached Dilmun, his ears would be numb, and Bracca's voice would be grating on his nerves. Nonetheless, the man appeared unlike any other that Eskkar had met in his wanderings. The chance meeting seemed like a stroke of luck, but whether for good or ill, only time would tell.

17

The horses picked their way through the gathering darkness, following the well-trodden path that led to Dilmun's gate. As Eskkar expected, the journey had taken longer than Bracca's optimistic prediction, the plow horse slowing their progress even carrying the smaller man's weight.

Approaching Dilmun's entrance, Eskkar and Bracca found a crowd of men, women, and children, all milling around. Everyone seemed to be shouting. At least that's how it appeared to Eskkar's ears.

His horse felt the same, its ears flickering forward and back at the unaccustomed sounds. A torch, shoved between planks of the stockade, added its crackling and snapping to the din as it cast its light against the deepening dusk.

The flames revealed two armed guards blocking passage into the village. One of the men held up his hand, and Eskkar and Bracca halted their horses and dismounted.

"Are you here to fight or trade? No traders allowed in until morning."

"Do we look like traders? Do you see any sacks of goods? We're here to fight," Bracca said in a loud voice, "if the pay is right."

The older of the guards studied the two riders for a few moments, disdain evident on his features even in the flickering torch light.

"Another boasting Sumerian, all of them thieves, and this one travel-ing with an barbarian outcast, even lower scum than a Sumerian."

He spat on the ground to emphasize his words, then lifted his eyes to Eskkar. "We've already got a barbarian here, but I suppose one more shiftless bandit won't matter." Without turning his head, he called over his shoulder. "Strob, take these two miserable excuses for fighters to Icarnar."

A youngster of maybe ten or eleven seasons appeared out from the shadow of the gate.

"Follow the boy, and don't try to wander off," the guard said. "If we have to come and find you, you'll regret it." He spat on the ground again, this time to show that the conversation had ended.

"We thank you for welcoming us to your village," Bracca said, bowing his head in mock politeness.

The boy started off, and Bracca trailed after their escort, leaving Eskkar no choice but to follow along behind.

Inside Dilmun, the people were even more crowded in the lanes than the rabble outside the gate, and the familiar village odors stung Eskkar's nose and eyes even more than usual.

Whatever work the villagers did during the day had ended with the setting sun, and everyone seemed determined to crowd the streets while chattering to each other, the loudest voices showing the effects of ale flowing aplenty. Eskkar wondered if the entire village was drunk.

Within a few paces, Eskkar lost sight of the boy, so he followed behind Bracca's horse, keeping a tight grip on his halter. Their journey lasted only moments. They turned once, and then the lane widened out into an open space with corrals on two sides. Bracca stopped abruptly, and Eskkar moved alongside him.

"The boy said to wait here," Bracca explained.

Eskkar glanced around. Opposite the corrals, across the open space, he saw twenty or thirty blankets spread on the ground, most with men sitting or lying on them. A few fires already burned against the coming night. Here the pungent horse smell overpowered even the village stink.

"Someone should muck out these corrals," Eskkar said. "The horses will be sick in a few days, penned in with all those droppings."

"We'll have ours out first thing in the morning," Bracca said, wrinkling his nose.

"And if I have to sleep on the ground, I'll do it outside the walls," Eskkar said, "and not with this lot."

"That's for fools too poor or too cheap to stay at an inn," Bracca said. "Follow my lead. I know an inn where we can spend the night in comfort. After I collect my coins, I'll lend you a few coppers."

For once Eskkar didn't complain about the cost. The smell from too many horses crowded together closed in on him. Out of habit, he took a quick count. "About thirty horses. Never seen that many in a village before."

"Jorak will have at least twice that many men ready to fight on foot, I expect. Horses may be good for raiding, but it's not easy to capture an armed village from horseback."

"If this Jorak has a hundred fighters, he should have no trouble finishing off one miserable village."

"Don't be so sure. I've heard that Tuttul has plenty of men as well. Both villages have been recruiting fighters for months."

Eskkar tried to calculate how much gold Jorak had already spent on hiring men willing to fight, but soon gave up. More than the other village would be worth in loot, he decided. The ruler of Tuttul must be as big a dolt as Jorak, both of them spending their fortunes trying to kill each other.

"No wonder the Alur Meriki and the other steppes clans rule the land," Eskkar said. "Instead of banding together to fight off the steppes warriors, these fools wage war on each other."

"Well, their quarrel is to our good, as long as we earn some coins in the process. So try not to insult our future allies."

Eskkar shrugged. "It's not my concern how dirt-eaters kill each other, as long as we don't find ourselves included among the dead."

"Here comes our new employer," Bracca said. "Better let me do the talking."

"You've done nothing but talk since we started for Dilmun. Why would I stop you now?"

Three men approached, one of them waving off the boy, who jogged back toward the gate without a look at his former charges. Eskkar had no trouble picking out the leader. A thick mustache and beard flecked with gray nearly covered the man's face, leaving only a few exposed spots showing old scars from the pox.

A sword hung easily from one side of the man's wide belt, while a leather pouch dangled from the other side. The two men accompanying him looked like bodyguards, trailing after their master.

"I'm Icarnar," the bearded man said, "in charge of Jorak's fighters." He looked over his newest potential recruits and their horses, taking his time and letting his glance linger longest on Eskkar. "Another barbarian. I've already got one, but I can always use more help with the horses. Even your nag,"

Icarnar nodded toward Bracca's mount. "I'm paying three coppers a day, along with a loaf of bread and feed for the horses. Everything else you pay for yourself. After we take Tuttul, you'll get a share of the loot."

"How much of a share?" Bracca asked.

"I decide the share, depending on how well you fight. Don't worry, it'll be enough. Plenty of you are going to get killed in the fighting, so there should be lots of copper to go around."

"The two of us should be worth more than six coppers a day," Bracca countered. "My good friend and I have years of . . ."

"Shut your mouth, Sumerian," Icarnar said. "I've heard it all before, and it's always the worst from Sumerians claiming to be mighty warriors. It's three-a-day, same as everyone else, or you can ride out now. And I mean right now."

"You drive a hard bargain, Icarnar."

"Make up your mind . . . what's your name?"

"Bracca. And this is Eskkar," he said, nodding to his companion. "We'll take your coins, but we need something in advance. My friend and I have been traveling for days without any ale."

Icarnar threw back his head, his booming laugh filling the market. "Not a copper between the two of you, I'll wager. You'll get your pay tomorrow, just before sundown, like everyone else. And you'll have earned it by then, too, I promise. Now get out . . ."

"One copper, in advance, for each of us, or I'm riding out," Eskkar said. "If I have to go hungry, I'll do it out on the road, not in this filth."

"Oh, so you can talk, barbarian. I was beginning to wonder. You'll leave only if and when I say so." He unhooked his hand from his belt, and rested it on the hilt of his sword.

"You touch that sword," Eskkar said, taking a pace forward, close enough to reach out and touch Icarnar's chest, "and I'll kill you and your men before I ride out." He kept his voice low so that the bodyguards, lounging a few paces away, couldn't hear.

For a moment the two men eyed each other, the fading light making it hard to read each other's features.

"Even if you kill me, you'd never get out of the village alive."

Eskkar kept his gaze on Icarnar's face, but said nothing.

"Oh, damn the gods, at least you're willing to fight, even if you are a fool. Just make sure you're as brave when we reach Tuttul."

Icarnar hitched his belt around so he could reach the pouch. It took a moment to unfasten the double knot, then he fished out two coins and dropped them on the ground. "That's in advance, so don't expect three coins tomorrow. Be back here just after dawn. If you're late, you lose one copper. Now get out of my sight before I decide to see how good you really are."

Eskkar nodded politely, and stepped back. "Our thanks, Icarnar." Yet Eskkar didn't take his eyes away from the man, and he had no intention of bending over to pick up the coins. He'd seen that trick before.

Bracca squatted down and scooped the two coppers from the dirt. "We'll be here, Master Icarnar."

Icarnar shook his head, then stalked off, his guards glancing behind them as they followed their commander.

Bracca juggled the coins in his palm. "Well, let's find that inn, friend Eskkar. I'm getting hungry."

Despite Bracca's impatience, Eskkar made sure the horses were fed and that the boys caring for the animals knew who they belonged to. That accomplished, he let Bracca lead him away from the corrals and back into the twisting lanes.

"You did well with Icarnar," Bracca said. "I'd about given up. Not that it matters. Once I find my friends, we'll have plenty of coins and a comfortable place to spend the night."

"Good. I could use something to eat and drink, and someplace where I can sleep until dawn without getting my throat cut. Where are we going?"

Bracca halted in front of a large hut. An ale cup scratched on the wall alongside the entrance marked the place as a tavern. "We're here. Now remember, let me . . ."

"Let you do the talking, I know," Eskkar said, eyeing a pair of drunks sprawled against the wall, sleeping off the effects of too much cheap spirits. The lane stank of urine and ale, and already Eskkar wished he were back on a horse and out of this place.

With so many additional men crowding Dilmun to capacity, the stink would grow worse with each day that passed. Soon men would be dying from the usual diseases that always accompanied overcrowded conditions.

"Stay behind me," Bracca said. He pushed open the flimsy door and stepped inside. Eskkar had to duck his head under the low threshold, to follow his companion.

A fire in a corner hearth shed some light over a large room filled with ten or twelve tables jammed so close together that Eskkar wondered how anyone could walk between them.

In the opposite corner, a lamp smoked, its light flickering over a rough plank table where the owner dispensed his establishment's wine and ale, and whatever else he might convince his drunken patrons to purchase.

The smell of smoke, sweat, and ale hung in the air. Eskkar guessed at least thirty people were drinking the cheap brew, all of them talking at the same time and practically shouting to be heard over everyone else's conversations.

Eskkar stood there, trying to adapt to the noise and the rank odor, while Bracca glided smoothly between the tables, heading toward the darkest corner of the inn. Eskkar considered turning around and going back outside, but Bracca still had both of Icarnar's coins, so Eskkar pushed his way through the inn's patrons after his companion.

Bracca reached a corner table, its surface nearly concealed by five men huddled around it, their heads almost touching. "Well, Gursu, I think you have some gold that . . ."

Eskkar, still watching his footing and a good three or four steps behind Bracca, lifted his eyes as the table was upended, knocking Bracca back and to the side. A thrown knife, intended for Bracca, brushed past Eskkar's arm. Swords and curses filled the air, all five men reacting in unison.

He saw Bracca kill one man, putting Eskkar's spare blade to good use, but then Eskkar had no thought for anything but his own survival, as two of the men rushed him. Eskkar didn't have time to draw his sword, although the long blade would be almost useless inside the low structure. Instead, he took a half-step back, drawing his knife and bumping into another table in the same motion.

Eskkar's first attacker, screaming something incomprehensible, raised his sword to strike, but Eskkar had already started forward, turning sideways and extending his knife arm. The sharp blade plunged into the man's chest before the sword could descend. By then Eskkar had closed in and grappled with the man. Before the dying man could fall, Eskkar shoved the body into the second attacker.

As Eskkar wrenched his knife free, a stool struck him across the knife arm, and he almost dropped the weapon. Without thinking, Eskkar caught the stool with his left hand. The second attacker, twisting free of his friend's body, lunged with his sword, determined to skewer Eskkar.

Holding the stool as a shield to block his opponent's sword, Eskkar rammed the plank seat as hard as he could at the man's head. Wood chips sprayed into Eskkar's face as his opponent's sword bit into the wood, but the rickety stool held together long enough to blunt the onslaught. Eskkar reached out with his knife, extending his arm, and his blade bit deep into the man's shoulder.

Wounded and off balance, the attacker howled in pain and stumbled backward, crashing onto another table before sliding to the floor. Whirling around, Eskkar saw Bracca fighting for his life against two men, the crash of bronze on bronze barely sounding over the uproar of the tavern's patrons, shouting and cursing as they scrambled to get out of the way, out of the fight, and out of the inn.

Shifting the knife to his left hand, Eskkar lowered his right shoulder and jerked the sword from its scabbard. Bracca, defending himself against his enemies, had retreated and somehow managed to get his back against the wall. Eskkar took a step forward and lunged, extending the sword across a table and into the nearest man's back. With a cry of pain, the man staggered and dropped his sword.

The other man took his eyes off Bracca for an instant, just enough time for the Sumerian to knock his opponent's blade aside and plunge the sword into his chest.

The lamp, knocked over in the melee, went out, leaving the cooking fire the only source of light. Pulling his sword from his victim's back, Eskkar shifted to face the man he'd wounded, but he'd vanished into the gloom, joining the last of the patrons, all struggling to get through the door and out into the lane.

Pivoting on his heel, Eskkar surveyed the disordered room, chairs and tables scattered and overturned. Everyone but the innkeeper had fled.

"What have you done to my inn, you ignorant barbarian!"

Eskkar turned again, to see the innkeeper, a sword in one hand and a cudgel in the other, still standing behind his table. Damn all the devils below, thought Eskkar. He searched for Bracca, but couldn't see him.

For a moment Eskkar thought the wily Sumerian had slipped out, leaving Eskkar alone to face the angry villagers.

"Hold your tongue a moment, Innkeeper," Bracca's cheerful voice seemed to come out of the earth. "We'll pay for any damages. Just stay where you are."

Eskkar realized Bracca was crawling around on the floor. For a moment Eskkar thought his companion had been wounded, but then realized Bracca was searching the body of one of the men he'd killed.

"Put away that sword," the innkeeper shouted, smacking his cudgel on the table. This time Eskkar realized the words were directed at him. With a muttered curse, Eskkar lowered the sword, then bent down to wipe the blade on the dead man's tunic.

While Eskkar knelt over, it took only a few gropes to find the man's purse, and he ripped it free of the belt, feeling a satisfying weight inside the supple leather. The second corpse lay only a few steps away, and Eskkar managed to cut that one's purse as well, before straightening up.

The innkeeper peered at Eskkar through the semi-darkness, but made no move to leave his place behind the table. If he saw Eskkar gather the two purses, he kept his mouth shut.

Bracca, wiping his sword clean of blood in the same fashion Eskkar had done, rose to his feet and moved toward the innkeeper who still held his sword truculently in his hand.

"No need for any weapons, Innkeeper," Bracca said, sheathing his blade. "You and I have business to discuss. And my friend and I need a room for the night, some food, and maybe one or two of your girls," he paused to gaze around the room, "if they decide to come back."

A quick glance showed Eskkar that the tavern was indeed empty. Returning his sword to its scabbard, he crossed the room, to stand by Bracca's side, as the establishment's owner slowly lowered his weapons.

"Here," Bracca said, spilling some silver coins from his newly acquired purse on the table, "one to cover the damage, one to get rid of the bodies, and one for a room for my friend and I for the night. Don't forget, we'll need plenty of food and drink, and the girls. That should be more than enough, I think."

The tavern's owner stared at the silver for a moment, then turned and hung his sword on two pegs driven into the mud brick behind him. The cudgel stayed close by his right hand, as he examined the coins. He then swept them off the table. They disappeared into his own pouch.

"And one more," Bracca said, rapping a fourth coin on the table, "to make sure you remember that it was they who started the fight, and that they died because they refused to pay me the few coins they owed."

The man looked around the room, still empty. "One more," he demanded, his voice gruff and hard. "I'll have to give the watch something, to convince them as well."

Eskkar stared in amazement as Bracca nodded in understanding.

"Then make sure the girls are good ones," Bracca said, pushing a fifth coin across the table. "I could buy your whole place for this much silver."

"You and your friend don't look like innkeepers to me," the owner said, smiling for the first time and revealing a mouthful of crooked yellow teeth, "and my expenses have been high since the war with Tuttul started."

"Yes, I'm sure," Bracca said. "Now, how about that food and ale? My friend and I have been traveling all day, and we've worked up quite a thirst."

"Of course." The innkeeper reached under the table and came up with two greasy wooden mugs. Ale splashed from a clay pitcher, filling both cups to the brim. "Find a table, while I chase down the serving girls and find someone to get rid of the bodies."

Some time later, Eskkar and Bracca sat at the same table in the same corner as the men they'd killed, sipping their third mug of ale and relaxing after a hearty dinner. The bodies had been dragged away, the dirt floor raked to cover up the blood, and about half of the customers had returned.

The rest must have decided to purchase their ale elsewhere, someplace where knives and stools weren't hurled through the air. The braver ones who returned took their cue from the innkeeper who whistled cheerfully through the gap in his teeth, his profits already assured, probably for the next four or five days.

Eskkar yawned contentedly. "And what would have happened if your friend hadn't been carrying the silver?"

"Gursu was a hoarder, not a spender," Bracca said with a laugh. "I was sure he still had all our . . . profits."

Bracca had given Eskkar a full ten silver coins as payment for the sword, then offered to sell his war horse to Eskkar for a mere eight coins.

Eskkar had agreed, and now had something in his pouch, as well as a fine horse. Though he seemed certain that Gursu's purse must have contained quite a bit more to make Bracca feel so generous.

The Sumerian took a sip of his ale, then belched in satisfaction. "All the same, I owe you some thanks for that sword thrust, right across the table. How did you get the blade out of your scabbard?"

"Good thing for you I didn't have time to think about it," Eskkar said. "If I had, I might have made a better deal with . . . Gursu. He didn't seem quite so talkative."

"Yes, he didn't want to talk about anything. He reached for his sword as soon as he recognized me."

"And you could have warned me you were expecting trouble. Instead you brought me along to back up your play."

In truth, Eskkar still couldn't believe how quickly the fight had started. One moment Bracca started talking, and then, without the slightest hint of trouble, blood was flowing. In all his fights, Eskkar had never been caught so flat-footed before.

"Well, I thought there might be some loud words, but not anything like that, I swear it."

Bracca took another healthy gulp from his cup. "But no matter now. We've got most of Gursu's and his men's coins, and we've made a new friend in the innkeeper. And we won't have any problems with the rest of the men in Dilmun, not after word gets around about what happened."

"What about Icarnar? He might not be too happy when he hears we killed four of his recruits."

"Look around you, Eskkar. Most of these 'recruits' look like villagers or raw farmers to me. Maybe they found their swords while digging in the fields. I doubt Icarnar will mind that we got rid of some useless stomachs. In fact, he may take us more seriously now. Maybe we can get more copper out of him."

Bracca laughed contentedly. "And now I'm even happier that I didn't have to kill you at the river. For a moment I was tempted. You looked so slow. For a few heartbeats back there, I really thought you were going to hand me the sword."

"Actually, I was thinking about killing you and taking the horses. I could have tossed you the blade and skewered you before you picked it up."

"Well, good thing neither of us did anything foolish. You've been paid in full for your sword, so that should make you happy."

The innkeeper came over, the satisfied smile still on his face. No doubt he had taken care of the watch with a copper coin or two, and earned even more profit on tonight's killings. "The girls are finished serving, so you can be their first customers tonight. Or keep them all night, if you like. You've got the only room with a door."

"Our thanks to you, then," Bracca said, draining his cup and rising to his feet. "I plan to show my friend here how we make women go wild with passion in Sumeria. He's a bit clumsy, but he's eager to learn some new techniques. If his face doesn't frighten away the girls and he doesn't fall asleep first, that is."

Despite himself, Eskkar smiled. "I know that hanging out with you is going to lead to more trouble, but if you don't mind, can we get through the night without having our throats slit. I really need some sleep."

"Time enough to sleep when you're dead, friend Eskkar. Now is the time to enjoy life. Worry about tomorrow in the morning."

Two of the innkeeper's girls had finally returned, and now stood beside the innkeeper, their eyes showing some apprehension despite their smiles, as they awaited their obviously violent and dangerous customers. Bracca, still moving effortlessly, crossed the room and put an arm around each one, giving each a squeeze on their backsides that made them both squeal.

"My friend Eskkar has never had a woman," Bracca announced in a loud voice as Eskkar joined them. "Who wants to give him his first lesson?" Half the patrons laughed at the joke, and one or two offered some pointed suggestions.

Eskkar gritted his teeth and sighed. It was going to be a long night. But perhaps Bracca was right. There would be plenty of time for sleeping tomorrow.

18

Eskkar's head throbbed and his stomach churned, unpleasant after-effects from last night's drinking. His manhood felt sore as well, from too much wenching. Bracca and he had shared the two girls, and Eskkar took the plumper one twice. The whores, no doubt even more excited at the thought of the extra copper Bracca promised them, exerted all their energy and skill into making their customers happy.

Waking this morning, Eskkar found himself alone, surrounded by the malodor of sweat, sex, and stale ale, the air so thick he could scarcely breathe. As soon as he could stand, Eskkar checked his pouch, his fingers fumbling as he recounted the gains from last night.

One of the recently acquired silver coins had vanished from his pouch, and Eskkar couldn't remember giving it to either of the girls. He wasted a few moments complaining to the innkeeper, who shrugged unconcernedly.

The girls were nowhere to be seen, and would either deny the theft or swear loudly a drunken Eskkar had paid them something additional for their services.

Shrewdly, they had taken only one coin. If the girls got too greedy, they might have ended up as dead as Bracca's former companions, and no one in the village would have lifted a finger over a tavern girl's demise. Still, they enjoyed a very profitable night, earning their regular pay while taking coins from their besotted customers.

The innkeeper offered a cup of water mixed with a splash of ale, and Eskkar gulped it down without pausing. He stepped out into the lane, glanced up at the sun, and swore. The time for assembly in the marketplace had already passed.

Thinking about his lost silver coin only made Eskkar's head ache more, and the bright morning sun beating down on Dilmun's marketplace made him squint, adding to his woes. Word of the bloody fight at the inn would have swept the village. He doubted anyone would call him a barbarian today, or spit on the ground as he walked by. Taking some satisfaction in that, he strode down the narrow lane, until he reached the assembly area.

Just ahead, he heard Bracca's voice complaining about something, so Eskkar pushed his way through the mass of men eyeing him with both curiosity and new respect for his swordsmanship. He scowled at all of them until he reached the front rank, then turned his eyes toward his companion.

Icarnar, hands on his hips, must have just arrived as well, as Bracca launched into a long and eloquent justification of why he and his good friend had arrived in the marketplace well after dawn.

From ten paces away, Eskkar stood there and listened to the Sumerian, who continued his fanciful explanation to Icarnar why they had to kill a few of his recruits at the inn. Long before Bracca reached the end of his tale, Icarnar interrupted by threatening to have Bracca and Eskkar stripped naked and driven out of the village.

Somehow, Bracca calmed Icarnar down. They spoke for a long time, with Bracca either cajoling or arguing, both men's voices occasionally dropping to a whisper. The other recruits obviously enjoyed the performance, as indicated by the murmurs of approval that rippled through the assembly. No one, it seemed, held much favorable sentiment for Icarnar.

Eskkar's scowl remained on his face, as much from Bracca's annoying antics as from last night's ale. The Sumerian had been pounding away on his grunting whore when Eskkar passed out, and yet the man showed no effects from the night's activities. Obviously Bracca had acquired a strong tolerance for ale, and could drink prodigious quantities without it slowing down either his wits or his tongue.

Damn the man. For a moment, Eskkar wondered if Bracca had taken the silver. Not likely. If Bracca wanted his silver back, he would have taken Eskkar's whole purse and slit his throat to seal the transaction.

Curse all these filthy villagers to the demons' pits. Eskkar condemned Bracca to the deepest pit of all, though somewhat envious of the man's smooth words. No Alur Meriki warrior could talk like a silver-tongued merchant after a night of carousing. Eskkar should know better than to drink himself senseless, a bad habit that left a man slow, defenseless, and easy to rob or kill.

While the dirt-eaters in this part of the land might be suspicious of Bracca because of his Sumerian heritage, they wouldn't likely kill him because of it. A barbarian outcast, however, might be murdered at the slightest excuse, or even without one. Pushing the dreary thoughts from his mind, Eskkar tried to focus on Bracca's words.

"Then it's settled, Icarnar," Bracca said, offering his forearm.

"This time." Icarnar ignored Bracca's friendly gesture. Instead he poked the Sumerian hard in the chest. "But if you kill even one of my men, or start one more fight, by the gods I'll have you both strung up and cut to bits."

"Of course, Master," Bracca said, bowing his head a trifle. "There will be no more problems. I'll keep a close watch on my man, and make sure he doesn't cause any further trouble."

Eskkar clenched his teeth at this impudence and considered running his sword through Bracca's back. The thought made Eskkar's hand twitch with anticipation.

"See that you do," Dilmun's war master warned, looking past Bracca to direct a glare at Eskkar. "Now get out of here and get to work. I want to see some results by noon."

Icarnar whirled away with a final oath, followed by his ever-present bodyguards, who had stood behind him during the exchange and now hurried to keep up with their commander.

Bracca strolled over, showing his teeth in a broad smile. "Did you hear all that, barbarian, or are your wits still addled from a few cups of ale?"

"I heard it," Eskkar answered, though in his misery he hadn't really been paying close attention. "Most of it. What have you got us into?"

"I've been placed in charge of Icarnar's horsemen, to prepare them to ride and fight against the treacherous village of Tuttul." Bracca clapped his hand on his hilt and thrust out his chest as he spoke, his voice carrying over the men crowded together.

"As my second in command, you will carry out my orders. Right now, Icarnar ordered me to get the damn horses out of his master's village, before the damned stink of dung and horse piss angers our exalted Elder Jorak even more than usual. Then Icarnar wants us to get the damned men and the horses in shape and ready to fight. He says there are several good places for a training camp a few miles downriver."

Eskkar realized his mouth was hanging open, and closed it. Somehow Bracca had talked Icarnar into making him a leader of horsemen.

Bracca grinned at Eskkar's confusion. "So, Eskkar, I'm ordering you to take charge of this rabble and get them out of here as soon as you can."

He glanced at the men standing near the corral and lowered his voice, so that only Eskkar could hear. "Apparently our little encounter last night proved that we're willing and able to fight. So, within three days, we're to start the offensive."

Eskkar jaw dropped in surprise. "In three days! Are you mad, or . . ."

"Keep your voice down," Bracca said. "I know it's not enough time. But I told him you are the best horse fighter within a hundred miles, and if anyone could do it, you could."

Bracca gave Eskkar a broad wink, "Besides, I've convinced Icarnar to increase our pay. And it's not like we have to do any actual fighting in three days. As long as we're ready to start riding around and terrorizing a few helpless farmers to impress Jorak. That should give us another ten or fifteen days to get the men in shape. So, are you with me, or do I need to look for another horse master?"

Eskkar felt his temper rising, but clamped his lips shut. Bracca was right. They signed up to fight, and the sooner Eskkar came to grips with that, the better for both of them. Besides, he had no other option, nor anywhere else to go. One fight was as good as another. He didn't expect to die in his sleep anyway.

"I'll do it, damn you," Eskkar said. "How much more did you wheedle out of Icarnar?"

"A silver coin a day for me, and ten coppers for my second in command. That should satisfy you."

Depending on size and quality, a silver coin could be exchanged for between fifteen and twenty copper ones. Eskkar didn't like the fact that Bracca would be earning almost double. Nevertheless, the pay was better than Eskkar expected.

"Ten a day will do for now. But we'll talk more about that later, friend Bracca."

"Of course, friend Eskkar. What could I do without you? Now, let's get these men off their lazy asses and start them working up a sweat. We don't want Icarnar to think you're not earning your pay."

Once again Eskkar's anger rose at the casual way Bracca had taken command. No doubt women and children would soon be ordering Eskkar around and telling him what to do.

Bracca sauntered toward the horse pens, and Eskkar trailed along behind. No matter how annoyed he might be with Bracca, Eskkar preferred to have a real task at hand than to stand around doing nothing. At least he now understood what needed to be done, and he would be giving the orders for a change, instead of obeying those of some ignorant dirt-eater.

They reached the larger horse corral, an enclosure created by sagging ropes looped around a handful of posts sunk in the ground on three sides, and the rear wall of a tavern forming the fourth. About thirty men, the ones Icarnar claimed could ride a horse, and nine or ten boys waited there.

Most had frowns on their faces, probably wondering how this Sumerian thief and his barbarian companion had managed to arrive only the night before and get themselves placed in charge.

If Bracca noticed the grim looks, his voice showed no sign of it.

"My name is Bracca," he said, raising his voice to boom around the market. "Icarnar has put me in command of you horse fighters. You'll obey my orders from now on, as well as Eskkar's," he jerked his thumb in Eskkar's direction.

"He's my second in command. He'll see to the horses and teach you how to fight. Eskkar likes to kill people, so make sure you don't give him any trouble."

Once again Eskkar's left hand twitched on his knife hilt, as he considered plunging it into Bracca's back. The men standing before him noticed the gesture, their eyes flicking nervously back and forth between their two new leaders. No doubt they assumed Eskkar wanted to kill one or two of them, and not Bracca.

"Get your weapons and your gear," Bracca went on. "We're moving out of the village, and going downriver. Make certain you bring everything you need, because we won't be coming back. Now get moving."

He turned to Eskkar. "Inspect the men, and see what we've got to work with. I'll go and talk to Icarnar about getting food and supplies to the camp. Check the horses first. See if they're all sound, or leave them behind. Then get these dim-witted farmers out of the village as quick as you can."

Before Eskkar had a chance to protest, Bracca turned on his heel and strode off. Biting back an oath at his own bad luck for falling in with the smooth-tongued Sumerian, Eskkar turned his attention to the horses pawing the dung-filled earth disinterestedly behind the ropes.

Most of the men wandered off to secure their weapons and possessions, but three men remained. Two had sacks at their feet, so they clearly had their gear with them. But the third caught Eskkar's attention – a steppes warrior.

"You three, what are your names?"

The taller of the two villagers stepped forward. "I'm Tuvak, and this is my brother Vannar."

Tuvak, short and barrel-chested, had a thick beard and a jagged scar that ran the length of his forehead. His brother, taller and rangy, appeared to be a few years younger. Both had the look of men who'd seen some fighting. Eskkar repeated their names to himself to make sure he wouldn't forget.

He turned toward the other barbarian. Much older, he appeared to have at least thirty seasons. Not as tall as Eskkar, but he carried even more weight in his arms and chest, and the bulging thighs showing beneath his ragged tunic indicated many years on the back of a horse. His long black hair, tied behind his neck, revealed a few strands of gray. Scars from the pox flecked both cheeks.

The manner in which he held himself, arms folded across his chest, proclaimed his steppes origins even before he uttered a word. The warrior had little in the way of possessions, only a long sword and a sack hanging from his belt. "Your name?"

"Sharkal," the man said, biting off the word as if he hated to share his name with anyone, let alone another steppes horseman.

Eskkar ignored the man's attitude. "Have you three everything you need?"

They nodded.

"Good. Who knows the most about these animals?"

The brothers' eyes went to the warrior, who kept his gaze fixed on Eskkar. "Sharkal's been tending them," Tuvak offered.

Naturally these villagers would have assigned the steppes warrior most of the work. Well, it made little difference now.

"How are the beasts, Sharkal?"

The man shrugged. "Good enough, for dirt-eaters."

Eskkar guessed the warrior had only recently left the clans. The strong accent indicated Sharkal still struggled to master the dirt-eaters' confusing language, someone who had to think for a moment to translate his words.

Eskkar felt tempted to ask what clan Sharkal had left behind, but such a personal question would best be saved for a later, more private time.

Instead, Eskkar returned his gaze to the other two. "Tuvak, you and your brother will help me take charge of the horses. Start bringing them to me, one at a time. Sharkal and I will look them over."

The steppes warrior stood there in silence, as the brothers unfastened the ropes blocking the corral and led the first animal over. Eskkar examined the horse with care, checking its coat, the muscles at shoulder and withers, and searching for any defect. He ran his hands over the animal's knees looking for weakness, and examined the hooves for cracks. He straightened up when he finished. "Well, Sharkal?"

"This one's better than most."

By now a few of the men and most of the boys had returned, carrying their possessions in small sacks slung over their shoulders or shoved down the front of their tunics. Eskkar decided it would be easier to move the animals out of the village one at a time.

"Vannar, after Sharkal and I finish inspecting the horses, take them outside the main gate and hold them there. Set up a rope corral if you have to. Make sure they don't get loose, or you'll spend the rest of the day chasing after them. Take the boys with you."

Turning to Tuvak, "you take these men," Eskkar indicated the returning fighters, "and have them line up, one to a horse. Sharkal and I will inspect the rest of the herd." Eskkar pushed the first horse on the rump, moving it in Vannar's direction.

In a moment, Tuvak brought up the second horse and another examination followed. More men trickled back, carrying their burdens, and soon a line of men and mounts formed up. Eskkar scrutinized each animal.

To his surprise, he and Sharkal deemed only two animals unfit for riding, both past their prime. Despite Bracca's suggestion to leave them behind, Eskkar decided they would be fine as pack animals, as long as they didn't have to carry too much weight. Besides, if they went lame, they could always be cut up for meat, and there was no sense leaving them for the villagers to enjoy.

By the time the last horse plodded toward the village gate, the final pangs of Eskkar's hangover began to fade, replaced by a raging thirst.

"I need water," he said to Sharkal, and walked toward the village well, fifty paces away. Sharkal accompanied him, both men ignoring the rude stares from the village idlers, who stood about and gaped at the sight of not one but two barbarians in their midst.

They took turns drinking from the same bucket. When they finished, Eskkar led the way toward the main gate, lengthening his stride in his eagerness to get out of the village and into some clean air. As they left the crowds behind, Eskkar's curiosity got the best of him.

"What clan are you from?" Eskkar asked as they passed beyond the stockade, feeling refreshed for the first time that morning.

"I've nothing to say to you," Sharkal said, not bothering to meet Eskkar's eyes, his accent sounding as harsh as his words.

"No stories about my past, or yours. I want nothing to do with a dishonored renegade who abandoned his clan and now serves thieves and dirt-eaters. I'll follow your orders as long as Icarnar commands it, but choose your companions from the dirt-eaters."

Surprised at the insulting response, Eskkar had to resist the urge to stop and confront the man. For all Eskkar knew, those same words might apply to Sharkal. Instead he kept walking in silence, trying to understand Sharkal's coldness.

Use your wits, Eskkar's father had reminded him often enough. Sharkal must have a story every bit as grim as Eskkar's own, or perhaps the man had done some evil deed that corrupted whatever honor he might have once had. Whatever the reason, the man had chosen to face his fate alone.

"Tend to your duties, Sharkal," he said, keeping his voice even, as if talking about nothing in particular. "You'll help me train these villagers to ride and fight, and we'll make sure they injure the horses as little as possible. And if anyone abuses his animal, let me know. Right now, the horses are worth more than any of them."

"I will." Sharkal's voice held no respect, just acceptance.

By now they'd reached the holding area, about a hundred paces south of the village, where Vannar and Tuvak waited with the men and their mounts.

"Mount up," Eskkar said, taking his horse's halter from one of the boys. "We're going to walk the animals to our new camp. Sharkal, bring up the rear, and make sure no one decides to leave with one of our horses."

They rode without any order, the men chattering among themselves like women washing clothing at the river. Eskkar hoped no mounted riders from Tuttul happened along, or all these fools would be slaughtered.

The cavalcade slowly passed through the farms and fields, as the river bubbled along at their right. The areas under cultivation grew fewer in number and disappeared completely in a few miles.

Eskkar had no trouble locating the wide meadow bursting with wildflowers and tall grass that Bracca had suggested. The flat grassland stretched along the tree-lined river bank, and looked like an ideal place to train both horses and fighters. The river would provide plenty of water, and there would be firewood as well.

"Halt," Eskkar shouted. "We'll camp here." Sliding off his mount, he tossed the halter to one of the camp boys. They'd walked and run along behind the horsemen, eager looks on their faces. "You boys, if you want to eat tonight, watch the horses. If any get loose, none of you breaks bread."

"Yes, Master," one of them shouted. They took the halter ropes from the men and began tying them together.

At least none of the boys found Eskkar's leadership offensive. No doubt they were glad enough for any opportunity to work with the horses.

"Line up the men, Tuvak," Eskkar ordered, ignoring the boys for the moment.

When the men formed a single line, Eskkar strode slowly down its length, counting each man and trying to decide which ones had wits and which ones did not. And, just as important, which ones would obey orders and which would likely make trouble.

The second group often, but not always, related to the first. A man with keen wits could still be a troublemaker. Eskkar remembered his father once saying that, to command fighting men, the leader had to keep the troublemakers in line, and the ones who thought too much under control.

Now Eskkar faced the same situation with this untrained bunch of farmers and villagers. Like any collection of men, their abilities would range from the lowest, those scarcely able to obey simple instructions, to those who would think too much for their own good. His task demanded that all of them accept his authority.

He reached the end of the line and returned back to the center where he faced his new fighters, all thirty-one of them. Not much to look at, but he doubted Tuttul had any better.

"Starting today, you are going to learn to fight from horseback. We'll be riding across the countryside soon enough, so I need to know who can ride and who can't. You'll do what you're told, as soon as I tell you. And don't even think about taking a horse and riding off with it. If you do, I'll personally track you down and kill you. Everyone understand?"

Feet shifted about, but no one said anything. Good. Only a complete fool would admit they didn't understand something that plain.

"Tuvak, Vannar, and Sharkal each will be leaders of ten. If they don't obey my orders and perform their duties well, they'll be replaced by someone who can. Right now, Sharkal and I will match everyone with a horse. After you're assigned a mount, you're responsible for it. Not the camp boys, not anyone else. You."

Eskkar glanced at the sun. Noon would be upon them soon enough.

"We'll get some training in today. Tomorrow, we'll ride first thing in the morning, and late in the afternoon. The rest of the day we'll first care for the horses, then practice with our weapons. Remember one thing. As far as I'm concerned, your horse is more valuable to me than any of you. I can always find more men. So make sure you take good care of your animal, or you'll regret the day you were born. Understand?"

Heads nodded, and a few mumbled something in reply.

"UNDERSTAND?" Eskkar's bellow rolled across the meadow, startling some birds into raucous flight.

A chorus of "Yes, Master," answered him, shocked out of the men by the force of Eskkar's authority.

"That's better. When I give an order, I want to know that you heard it. And don't make me raise my voice again. Tuvak, get everyone moving."

Not much of a speech, but it would do for a start. With only thirty-one men, he'd have more than enough time to get to know each one.

Meanwhile, he gave Sharkal instructions to make sure that the biggest and strongest horses went to the heaviest men, and that a poorly trained horse wouldn't be assigned to someone who could barely ride. It was a difficult task, but the warrior had been in the village for at least ten days, and should know something about some of the men and most of the horses.

Tuvak, Vannar, and Sharkal took over, divided the men into three groups, and started the task of assigning the horses. Eskkar brought out his own mount from the herd and swung up onto the animal's back. He could see better from the horse. And probably think better, too.

He watched as Sharkal rode up and down the meadow, taking one or two riders with him each time, to get a feel for both the mounts and the men's horsemanship.

Satisfied Sharkal and Tuvak had the men under control, Eskkar dismounted and walked his horse over to the camp boys standing nearby. "You boys, get over here," he ordered.

In a moment, nine boys ranging in age from ten to as old as fourteen seasons faced him. Eskkar studied them with as much care as he'd given the horses or men.

For a moment, he remembered the days when he'd tended warriors' horses and rode with them across the land. Boys, even the sons of dirt-eaters, were ever-fascinated by horses. Probably every youth facing him had run away from some grubby farm, and the chance to be around horses and fighting men would seem like a dream come true.

Camp boys could make a big difference in how the horses were treated and how well the men functioned. A camp boy could be abandoned or sent packing at any time, for any infraction. They received no pay and drew the dirtiest tasks, all in hope of someday becoming a warrior. Or in this case, a mounted fighter. Whatever reason brought them here, Eskkar didn't intend to waste any resource at his disposal.

"Why are you here?"

"To learn how to ride a horse, Master," one said.

"To fight," answered another.

Eskkar waited until the talking stopped. "Before you learn to fight, you need to learn to ride. And before you can ride, you'll learn how to care for the horses and guard them. Until then, you'll do as you're told. You'll get no coins and you'll work hard, but you will eat."

Eskkar gestured toward the thirty-one fighters scattered over the meadow, some still arguing over who should get which horse. "The men will mistreat you and take advantage of you. You'll have to put up with that as well. If you're not careful, you'll end up as bed partners for them, so watch your step."

They laughed, some nervously, others with a trace of worry at the remark. More than a few of them nodded knowingly. Not that Eskkar intended to allow anything like that, at least not until the men had proven themselves in battle. Afterward, the men could work out whatever arrangements they wanted.

"If you work hard and follow orders, you'll have a chance to ride, and eventually you'll learn how to fight. For now, I'll give three of you to each subcommander," Eskkar went on. "You do what they tell you. If any of you want to go back to the village, now's the time to get out. Otherwise, report to Tuvak and get to work."

The boys dashed away, eager to start their duties. Eskkar knew the feeling. The life of a camp boy was a hard one. Even so, they'd just been given the chance, maybe not a good chance, but a real one, to learn how to fight and ride. Not many boys would pass that up to return to their farms or shops as common laborers facing a lifetime of dreary toil.

Eskkar heard hoof beats and turned to see Bracca riding toward him, a new linen sack slung over his shoulder. Somehow he managed to find another good horse.

"Are you sure this place will work?" Bracca dismounted and glanced around. "It's farther from the village than I thought."

"Do you want our men drinking the foul water flowing out of the village? Any closer, and half the men will be sick by tomorrow morning. Anyway, it's time to talk of other matters."

Eskkar grabbed Bracca by the arm and led him aside, moving far enough away from the men so that the two of them couldn't be overheard.

Suddenly Eskkar's mask of friendliness slipped away. "What do you think you're doing?"

He tightened his grip on Bracca's arm. "By every demon's name, I should split your carcass in two. I studied this rabble on the way here. Half of them look like they've never seen a horse, let alone swung a sword from one. They're a hopeless lot."

"Hold your temper, Eskkar. I've just finished talking with both Icarnar and his master, the Noble Jorak. They plan to start the attack on Tuttul as soon as possible."

Bracca pulled his arm free and raised his hand to stop Eskkar's protest. "All we need is one little raid. You and I can do it ourselves, if we have to. We take a couple of men, ride close to Tuttul, burn a few huts, scare a few farmers, then run back here and boast of our success. No one will be the wiser."

Eskkar grunted in disgust at the idea of killing helpless farmers and then lying about it, but knew Bracca spoke the truth. As far as the two of them were concerned, it didn't matter who won the war, as long as they could enrich themselves in the process.

"And suppose Tuttul's fighters are better trained than this rabble. We could end up dead on our first raid."

"Look, we're getting well paid. If things look too bad, we can always take a few horses and slip away in the night. These fools will be too busy killing each other to waste time chasing after us."

Eskkar hadn't considered just riding off. "We've got the coins from the tavern, and I see you've already gotten yourself a fine horse." Bracca's new mount, a sturdy mare, looked almost as good as Eskkar's. "Maybe we *should* think about moving on."

Bracca shook his head. "Why the rush? No one's swinging a sword at our heads yet. Besides, this war could earn us plenty of loot. First there's what we'll earn riding around the countryside, picking the farmers clean. And if we can take Tuttul, the fat merchants and traders will flee. We'll be the ones sent to track them down."

He grinned. "Think of the gold and gems they'll be carrying. A few days work and some luck could set us up for life."

"Or we could end up dead. I don't like the idea of dying for some greedy merchant."

"We're going to end up dead one of these days, so why not here? At least there's a chance for some real gold. Not to mention that we're the ones giving orders for a change." Bracca clasped Eskkar's arm. "Stop thinking about what can go wrong, and start thinking about how we can take advantage of the situation. And if you can whip this rabble into shape, we just might end up rich instead of dead."

The opportunity for a good supply of gold had never entered Eskkar's thoughts. Despite Eskkar's usual caution, Bracca's persuasive words sounded reasonable. It might be worth sticking around, at least for a few more days, to see what would happen.

"All right, I'll do it, damn you. But you have to help, not go back to Dilmun and sit on your ass in some tavern."

"I knew I could depend on you, friend Eskkar. Just tell me what you need."

Eskkar turned away and faced the empty landscape. What would it take to get these men ready to fight? Though he'd never trained men before, Eskkar understood what needed to be done. Now would be as good a time as any to learn if he could do it. His father had spoken to Eskkar almost every day, as far back as he could recall, describing each and every aspect of warfare and tactics, the how and why men fought, and the best ways to lead them.

Eskkar remembered his own training with the warriors, what he experienced, and what he witnessed. To prepare men for any serious fighting took a lot more effort than these dirt-eaters imagined. Still, to get started might not take that much.

He took a deep breath and faced Bracca. "Here's what I want. You deliver all of it, and I'll get these ignorant farmers into shape. But it's going to take more than three days, so do what you can to extend our training time." Using his fingers, Eskkar listed the items he wanted, and the quantities. "And I want the first supplies delivered by this afternoon. In fact, if you can't deliver them, don't come back."

Without waiting for a reply, Eskkar strode back to where the men waited, most of them squatting on the ground.

"Sharkal," Eskkar shouted, as he approached. "Take half the men. Mount up and move your men to those rocks over there," he paused to scan the meadow. "That should be about three hundred paces from here. Line them up eight paces apart. We'll begin by teaching the horses how to move toward an enemy. Take Tuvak with you."

With a nod, Sharkal started separating the men into two groups.

"Vannar, you'll stay with me," Eskkar said. "We'll take the other half. I want the men mounted and in a line, eight paces apart, starting from this spot. Get moving."

Eskkar headed toward his own horse, but one of the stable boys had already slipped the halter on the mount and met Eskkar halfway. The lad stood taller than the others, and Eskkar guessed the youth had decided to take charge of his leader's horse.

Eskkar paused to check the halter. "No, that's not right. This isn't some old nag pulling a wagon that you're leading to market. Watch me."

He slipped the halter loose, then retied it, steadying the horse with one hand. "Like that. The first loop goes behind the ears. The two ends extend along the head, you make another loop, and tie it right behind the jaw."

The boy followed Eskkar's movements, his eyes wide with excitement. "Yes, Master."

By the time Eskkar finished, Sharkal and his fifteen men had ridden out, the fools shouting to each other, excited to begin their training. Eskkar formed his own rank, making sure the line stood even, with each man properly spaced. He took station at one end of the line while Vannar anchored the other.

When Eskkar felt satisfied with the even line of horses, he guided his stallion in front of his fifteen men, so he could watch their faces. Some were excited, others looked worried. A few babbled away, like village washer women.

"Shut up. I don't want to hear another sound out of any of you. If you're chattering away like women at the well when we go into battle, you won't be able to hear my orders and you'll all end up dead. Is that clear?

He glowered at them. "IS THAT CLEAR?"

A chorus of confused replies answered. "From now on, the only words I want to hear come out of your ugly holes are 'yes, Commander,' or 'no, Commander.' Nothing else. The first man that utters anything but those words will be shoveling horse shit all day tomorrow. Is that clear?"

"Yes, Commander."

"Louder, you scum. When I give you an order, I want to know that every one of you useless turds heard and understood it. IS THAT CLEAR?"

This time the response echoed over the field, unnerving the horses for a moment, and making a few skittish animals step back and forth.

"Good. Now keep that line even. That's the first lesson you need to remember. Always keep the line even."

He waited until the horses again stood in a straight line. "To start, we're going to walk our horses toward the other riders. Remember, walk . . . get back here, you fool!" One chagrined rider had started to move forward.

"Wait until I give the order." The man had to ride around the line to get back in place. Eskkar waited, his face grim.

"WHEN I give the order, not before, we'll all start our horses walking together. And we stay together. I want the whole line to move as one, and I want us to go straight toward Sharkal's men. Do you dolts think you can handle that?"

"Yes, Commander!" This time the response came in unison.

Eskkar looked across the field. Sharkal already had his men lined up. Eskkar drew his sword, lifted it into the air, then lowered it to signal his readiness. Sharkal matched the signal; his men stood ready as well.

"WALK."

Eskkar's line started moving, as did Sharkal's a moment later, both bands of horsemen pacing slowly toward each other. Right away, Eskkar's line became jagged. Some horses walked faster than others, and the men had trouble controlling their mounts.

"Keep the line even, damn you," Eskkar shouted. "You, in the lead, slow your horse. The line must move as one."

Despite his shouts, the line remained jagged. The horses were part of the problem, unused to the strange pace or even the presence of another horse beside them. They became uneasy as the other line approached, and Eskkar heard Sharkal's shouts as he, too, struggled to control a ragged line.

Vannar's voice rose from the other end of the line, and Eskkar nodded in satisfaction. At least he had one subcommander who understood orders. He'd kept Vannar with him to see how quick the man grasped Eskkar's training concepts.

The lines drew closer. "Make sure you walk your horse through the gap. Maintain the line. Keep your horse centered in the gap. Close up, you idiot, you're falling behind!" This to one rider whose horse slowed down at the sight of the oncoming horses.

At last the lines finally met, Eskkar guiding his own horse through the center of the gap before him. "Keep going, don't stop. Maintain the line."

The two groups passed through each other. Eskkar maintained the slow pace until his men reached the starting place of Sharkal's men.

"Halt," Eskkar shouted. "Turn your horse around and get ready . . ."

He swore again, but this time at himself. He'd forgotten to tell them how to turn.

"When I say turn, everyone turns to the left. Remember that. Always to the left, unless I order different. If two riders turn in opposite directions, the horses will be face to face for a moment, and that might upset a skittish animal."

They nodded in understanding. "Good. Even up the line again, damn you. Don't make me tell you every time."

Eskkar took a deep breath. If he kept yelling like this, he'd have no voice by nightfall. "We're going to go back. Damn you, wait until I give the order!"

Another over-eager oaf had started his horse walking, and now he, too, had to circle the line to regain his position. When the sheepish rider again readied himself, Eskkar raised his sword, waited for Sharkal's acknowledgement, then lowered it and yelled the order.

Once again the two lines plodded toward each other. Eskkar kept shouting orders, correcting those who walked too fast or two slow, or couldn't keep their mounts moving in a straight line. The lines closed in on each other a second time.

This time the horses reacted better, already less nervous about the sight of approaching animals. The two lines crossed each other in nearly perfect formation, sixteen horses passing through sixteen horses with scarcely an ear twitching or eye rolling.

When Eskkar's men neared their starting place, he had his commands ready.

"Wait for my order to turn, and remember, turn to the left. Wait for it. TURN."

Two men turned the wrong way, and Eskkar damned them both. He'd have to make sure they knew their left from their right. Some simpletons never understood the concept. He might have to tie a bit of rope around each dullard's left hand.

When the horses finished their turn, Eskkar halted them, exchanged signals with Sharkal, and started the process again.

The sun moved across the sky, and the lines paced past each other ten, fifteen, and finally twenty times. But the last three times, the lines crossed perfectly, and the commands to turn, halt, and walk had been ingrained in every brain, man and beast.

It helped that the horses had tired somewhat, even as they adjusted to the stupidity of their riders and their apparently senseless desire to move back and forth over the same ground.

"This time, men," Eskkar said as they waited for orders, "we're going to move the horses at a trot. A trot, you hear me. Nothing faster, and the first man who lets his horse break into a gallop will stand guard all night."

Eskkar raised his sword, so Sharkal could see it and this time pumped it twice, the usual steppes signal for a trot. He waited until he was sure Sharkal had explained the change and stood ready.

"TROT." Within ten paces Eskkar's line broke down, jagged and uneven, as the riders struggled to control the pace. The faster animals had to be restrained, and the slower speeded up. Still the process went faster, since even the dullest of his men now understood the basic idea.

By the time the two lines crossed ten times at a trot, each line of men and horses held steady. He signaled to Sharkal, and waited until the horseman brought his group over to rejoin Eskkar's.

As everyone reached the starting point, Eskkar gave the order to halt, then dismount. He called to the horse boys, and they rushed over from where they'd been watching the training spectacle. A glance toward the west told him not much daylight remained before the sun set.

"Boys, take the horses to the river, let them drink, then hold them at the corral."

Facing all his men, Eskkar ordered them to sit on the ground, a half-circle forming around him.

"We're finished with the horses for today. Tomorrow, we start again with a walk, until we can do it perfectly. The same with the trot. If you master that, we'll try a canter. Any questions?"

No one said anything, but some of the men exchanged glances. "Speak up, damn you," Eskkar said. "Ask your questions."

"What's all this about?" The words came from a brawny young man with a thin beard. "We won't be walking our horses toward the enemy. We'll be riding at them." Other voices murmured agreement.

Eskkar crossed his arms and shook his head at them, as if embarrassed by their lack of wits. He'd been expecting this question.

"The reason for all this is simple enough, though most of you seem too stupid to understand. In a horse battle, I want our line of riders to smash the enemy at the same time. Every horse should arrive and strike together. If some of you over-eager donkeys rush ahead, you'll be the first ones targeted by Tuttul's fighters. Try to remember that, if you remember nothing else. If you're out front, all their arrows will be aimed at you."

He paused to let that sink in. "And if you lag behind, the enemy will see the gaps in the line, and send his men into those empty places. That means the laggards will be overwhelmed and killed, too. So if you want to stay alive long enough to collect your pay or pick up some loot, you need to hit the enemy's line together, give him the full shock of your charge."

Eskkar looked around at a sea of blank faces and open mouths. Apparently the idea that there might be some tactics involved in fighting from horseback hadn't occurred to most of them.

"We've only a few days to work together before the fighting starts," Eskkar went on, "and I don't have time to explain the reason for every order. Do what I tell you, and you might just survive your first battle. For the rest of the day, we're going to work on our sword-play. I want to see if any of you know which end of a sword to hold."

With Sharkal's help, he formed the men into two lines six paces apart, facing each other.

"All right men, draw your swords."

Blades slid from their scabbards.

"Hold the sword straight out from your body. Like this," Eskkar demonstrated using his own blade. "Extend your arm and keep it rigid."

Holding his own weapon extended, Eskkar strode up and down the lines. Almost at once some arms began to tremble from holding the weight of the blade.

"I said to keep your arm rigid," Eskkar bellowed, using the flat of his sword to push up any blade he saw dropping. Sharkal did the same, the two of them moving back and forth, looking closely at each man.

Soon arms began to shake, and the men's faces turned red from the strain and their breath came raggedly from their chests. Feet shuffled, but another order stopped that.

"Stand still, damn you. You think you can move around like a bunch of old women?"

With a gasp, one man dropped his arm. Two more followed quickly. Eskkar gripped the first man by the tunic and pulled him into the center of the lines. "All right, everyone lower your arms."

He ignored the loud sigh of relief that greeted the order. "What's your name, you weakling," Eskkar asked the one he'd pulled from the line.

"Cignar." The man's lips tightened at the insult.

Still holding his own weapon, Eskkar took a half step toward the man. With a quick thrust, Eskkar struck the man right in the chest with the heel of his left hand, the blow sending Cignar to the ground, the breath knocked from his lungs.

"You'll address me as 'Commander.' If you forget again, I'll use something else on you beside my open palm."

Eskkar raised his voice to address the men. "This man, Cignar, wants to fight beside you. Which of you wants to ride next to him, if he can't even hold his blade up for a few moments?"

No one answered, and no one met his gaze. "Get back in line," Eskkar ordered, ignoring Cignar as he rose from the grass and moved sullenly back to his position.

"In a fight, each of you must depend on the man next to him, to protect his exposed left side. Your sword arm needs to be strong enough to take a few strokes in a battle. Right now, all your puny arms are weak as a rich merchant's daughter. Sharkal, show them."

Sharkal stepped forward and drew his sword. Like Eskkar's, this was a long horse sword, at least a hand and a half longer than the shorter blades the men carried. Eskkar faced him, and raised his own blade, standing close enough that the tips almost touched. They stood there in silence, each blade fully extended, both arms rigid.

Eskkar stared straight into Sharkal's eyes, and the barbarian outcast met his gaze with a stony look of his own. Both men stood there, immobile, as the moments passed, each trying to will the other to lower his blade first. Despite their longer and heavier weapons, they soon exceeded the time the men had held their shorter blades.

Eskkar had no intention of lowering his arm first. But he'd seen the smoldering anger in Sharkal's eyes, and knew that the warrior had no intention of yielding either.

Within moments, it became more than a mere demonstration; it had turned into a test of strength between the two men. Eskkar felt the first tremor in his arm, though it hadn't visibly moved. He concentrated all his effort into keeping his arm rigid, his eyes fixed on Sharkal, trying to unnerve the man as he attempted to do the same to Eskkar.

The rest of the men watched, fascinated by this battle of wills. Time passed. Both men's arms now trembled, and even Eskkar's powerful shoulder began to weaken. But he refused to quit first. His men, and that included Sharkal, had to see him as invincible.

He wanted them to be more afraid of him than any enemy in their path. Defeating Sharkal in this contest would strengthen their faith in their leader. Nonetheless, Eskkar felt his face growing redder with each heartbeat, and he saw the same effect on Sharkal's.

Pain slowly worked its way up the length of Eskkar's arm. His shoulder started to hurt, taking more and more of the strain from his arm. The blades were in constant motion, neither man fully able to control his muscles. Already they'd held their weapons rigidly extended for at least three times the duration the men had maintained.

"By the gods," Tuvak exclaimed, breaking the silence, "put them down, before you kill yourselves."

Eskkar ignored the outcry. "Are you growing tired, Sharkal?"

"No, Commander. Do you wish to stop and rest?"

Eskkar would have smiled if he dared unclench his jaw. "Your arm grows weaker. Perhaps you should lower your blade."

"It's your arm that is shaking, Commander," Sharkal said, his face turning ever redder. "Perhaps we should lower our blades together."

Not a moment too soon, Eskkar thought; he knew he couldn't last much longer. Pain lanced up his arm and shoulder, and reached into his neck. He kept his voice even as he replied. "Give the count, then."

"One." A long pause, in the hope that Eskkar would fail before the count ended. But Eskkar expected that trick, too, and his arm remained extended. "Two."

This time the pause dragged on and on, Sharkal still no doubt hoping Eskkar would fail at the last moment. But Eskkar, his brow covered in sweat, kept his arm extended.

"Three."

Both men let their sword's point fall to the ground. They stood there, breathing heavily. With a nod of approval to his opponent, Eskkar turned back to face his men, and took a mighty breath.

"Now you see what a real warrior like Sharkal can do. So let's try that again. Raise your blades. Extend your arms. Show me how strong you are."

He kept them at it until their arms ached with weariness. Only then, when their strength had gone, did he start the next part of the exercise. "Swing your sword over your head, like this," he demonstrated. "Lunge and thrust like this, then recover."

Their tired muscles made the men's movements erratic. "Pitiful," Eskkar said, shaking his head in disgust. "Show them, Sharkal. And keep them at it."

Their arms would be stiff tomorrow, but they'd work through that soon enough. Eskkar left the men practicing and he strode over to the where the boys had corralled the animals.

"You boys, it's time you began earning your food. You do want to eat, don't you?" He didn't wait for the reply. If they had anything else in their lives to look forward to, they wouldn't be here.

"I want two of you to act as lookouts at all times." He pointed to the two youngest lads. "We'll start with you two. One to the north, and one to the south. Keep your eyes open, and call out if you see anyone approaching. Can you do that?"

They nodded, too excited for a moment to speak. "Good, get started now. For all we know, men from Tuttul could be riding toward us at this moment."

Their eyes went wide at the thought, before they dashed off. He smiled at the sight. Now that he thought about it, Tuttul's horsemen could be around, though he doubted they'd waste time this far south.

Eskkar turned to the oldest looking boy, the one that had brought out Eskkar's horse earlier. "You, what's your name?" Tall and thin, the boy had dirty brown hair that reached to his shoulders and clumped down over one eye.

"Sargat, Master," the boy replied.

"You call me 'Commander,' like the rest of the men, not master," Eskkar corrected.

"For now, Sargat, you're in charge of all these boys, at least until you fail to obey my orders or do something stupid. I want you to divide the boys into shifts. Two on watch at all times, and two guarding the horses at all times. Send some out to gather firewood, and the rest of you start digging a fire pit. When that's finished . . ."

"Commander, men are coming," Sargat said, pointing back along the trail to Dilmun.

Eskkar turned and saw Bracca riding his horse slowly toward them, followed by three men, each one leading a pack animal straining under the weight of its burden.

"Get busy." Eskkar dismissed the boys, and paced toward Bracca. "I didn't expect you to return so soon."

"The village is bursting at the seams," Bracca said, swinging his leg over the horse's neck and dropping to the ground with a contented sigh. "I kept complaining about all the supplies we needed, and Icarnar gave them to me just to shut me up. So I decided to get out of there before he came up with something else for me to do."

For a brief moment, Eskkar almost felt sorry for Icarnar, having to listen to Bracca's steady stream of words. "Did you get everything?"

"Even I'm not that good a talker, Eskkar. This lot will have to satisfy you for today. It should be enough. I'll bring out the rest tomorrow morning. I'm going right back to Dilmun."

"And a nice warm bed at the inn with a nice warm girl or two, while I'm out here sleeping on the ground, doing without."

Bracca shrugged. "Well, why not come back with me? We'll try some new girls. You don't have to stay here with these clods. I know another inn that has even better . . ."

Eskkar had no intention of returning to that stink hole of a village, no matter how many girls Bracca lined up. "You go. I'll stay here. Just get back here by mid-morning with the rest of the supplies."

"Suit yourself, you thick-headed barbarian. How are the men doing, in case Icarnar asks?"

"Tell him they'll soon be ferocious fighters, if he gives me a year or two to train them."

"That soon, eh? Well, then, since you're in such a foul mood, I'll leave you to your work and return to the comfort of my tavern."

"Make sure you get back here by early tomorrow. I could use more help."

The livery men had finished unloading the pack animals and stood waiting. Bracca swung onto his horse. "Don't let any of these farmers slit your throat while you're sleeping."

Eskkar smiled. "And who's going to watch your back tonight?"

Bracca's jaw dropped for a moment, then he laughed. "Perhaps I'll need three girls, then. Don't worry, I'll tell them all about you. They'll be so grateful for not having to service you, they'll probably pay me."

He wheeled the horse around and the little troop started their return journey to Dilmun.

Eskkar stood there, shaking his head at Bracca's departure. The damn braggart probably would summon three whores, if only to boast about it in the morning. "Curse all these dirt-eaters," he muttered to himself, as he faced the men still practicing their sword play. "Sharkal, that's enough of that. Bring the men here. We've got work to do."

By sunset, Eskkar allowed himself a brief moment of satisfaction. Bracca's provisions provided the basic necessities for a training camp, and with a plentiful supply of men, Eskkar put everything to good use. A long fire pit had been dug, banked by a line of stones, and the camp boys stacked enough firewood to last another day or two.

One of Bracca's pack animals carried seventy loaves of bread, eight dead chickens, a basket of green beans to add to the stew, and a large copper pot for cooking. Not enough food for so many, but enough to get through the night and tomorrow morning.

Sargat disgorged another pack's contents: a small bronze axe, two shovels, sharpening stones for the men's swords, and forty empty water skins. The third animal carried blankets. Eskkar had asked for forty, but counted only twenty. Some of the men would be cold tonight. He also asked for a hundred paces of heavy rope, and the same length of lighter rope. Eskkar guessed he'd received about half of each kind.

With the supplies settled, Eskkar led the weary men into the camp, where they no doubt expected to get some rest. Instead, Eskkar ordered everyone to work. First he made sure they constructed a decent rope corral, one that would actually keep the animals from bolting should they pick up a strange or frightening scent. Then he ordered them to finish digging the fire pit, and after that, a latrine.

Every man received a water skin, and Eskkar ordered each man to rinse it thoroughly in the river before filling it. "Unless you want to get sick and spend tomorrow puking your guts out. And don't expect a replacement if you lose it," he warned.

Meanwhile, Sharkal cut up the lighter rope into halters, making sure that every rider would have a strong new headstall of adequate length. Tomorrow Eskkar planned to instruct each man in the proper way to tie and use one.

Two of the boys had grown up on a farm, and knew not only how to gut and clean chickens, but how to cook them. Soon the smell of roasting chicken and stew floated on the air, putting everyone in a good mood. By then the men had a keen appetite. They'd worked hard all day, with nothing to eat since breakfast.

After they finished eating, Eskkar ordered the men to sharpen their swords, with Sharkal inspecting each one, and permitting no one to sleep until he approved. Eskkar made sure his own blade held its usual sharp edge. He hadn't had time to hone it since the fight the previous night.

The men sprawled on the ground, all of them trying to get as close to the fire as possible. Those too slow in their sharpening found themselves farther away. The camp boys had no blankets, and they had to huddle together to try and stay warm throughout the night.

Eskkar told Tuvak to assign eight men as guards, starting with those who had performed poorly on one or another of today's tasks. They'd relieve each other every quarter of the night, and the threat of losing more sleep in the future might make the others pay closer attention to their training lessons, which would begin anew at first light.

At last Eskkar settled in for the night. Since he owned a good blanket, he didn't bother trying to get close to the fire. It would soon die out anyway.

To his surprise, he found himself thinking about the day's events, wondering what else he should and shouldn't have done, or what he could do better tomorrow. Training the men felt oddly satisfying, almost as if he were back with his family and the Alur Meriki, listening to his father's words and watching the warriors practicing their skills.

As a boy, he had followed his father everywhere he could, studying the older boys and warriors, and imitating their lessons. Now he found he could recall many such days where the older and more skillful warriors' knowledge was imparted to the younger. Sharkal, of course, knew all the same drills, and probably even better.

Eskkar guessed the warrior would never be comfortable with the dirt-eaters. He'd lived too long with his clan to ever adapt to the ways of farm and village. For Sharkal, even more so than Eskkar, each day would be bitter, a sharp contrast to the memories of his clan life.

Despite his problems, the man's skills made everything go much smoother. Even with Sharkal's disdainful attitude, Eskkar would sleep easier tonight, knowing Sharkal would be there in the morning. Finally Eskkar drifted off to sleep, his mind still sorting out ideas and tasks for the morrow.

Before the first rays of the sun cleared the horizon, Eskkar woke. He strode around the camp and checked on the two guards. The first appeared tired but awake. The other sat on the ground, his head nodding; he didn't look up as his commander approached. Eskkar kicked him in the shoulder and sent him sprawling.

"Get up," Eskkar said, as loud as he dared without upsetting the nearby horses.

Jolted out of his daze, the man cried out and fumbled for his sword.

"Too late for that, you lazy dog. You'll pull another guard shift tonight, and if I catch you sleeping again, I'll wake you up by slitting your throat. You," he said to the other man, his eyes wide in the morning's first rays of sunlight, "wake the others."

Eskkar heard the hoarseness in his tone. All that shouting yesterday had strained his voice. Unlike Bracca, Eskkar wasn't used to uttering more than a few words a day.

In moments everyone was stumbling around, most of the men groaning with stiffness and tired muscles. Even Sharkal yawned as he walked around the camp, making sure everyone was up.

The camp boys, most rubbing sleep from their eyes and still shivering from the night's chill, brought out the sack containing bread, and made sure each man received exactly half a loaf – today's breakfast. It wasn't much, but Eskkar knew there would likely be days when no food would be available for his men.

His men. The words sounded good in Eskkar's mind. His men would be hungry soon enough, and Bracca had better arrive before noon, or the training would have to be postponed.

Eskkar went down to the river and drank his fill. Then he went downstream and relieved himself. When he returned, Sharkal and Tuvak had the men waiting for him.

"Today, men," Eskkar began, "we're going to repeat some of what we did yesterday." He knew it was always best to let the men know what to expect each day.

"We'll walk the horses at each other, then trot, then canter. If you do well, we may even try a gallop. Once I'm satisfied you can handle that, we'll close up the ranks. The horses have to learn to go forward, even if they can't see a clear path in front of them. Otherwise, they won't charge ahead when we attack. So we'll gradually close the gap between horses, until there's just enough room for the horses to slip through."

He searched their faces for the glazed eyes that would denote incomprehension, but everyone seemed to follow his words.

"As soon as we master that, we'll begin the runs waving our swords over the horses' heads, and shouting our war cries. They've got to get used to the noise and seeing the flash of bronze behind and in front of them. Any questions?"

He sent his eyes over their faces once again, but no one spoke or looked confused.

"Good. Sharkal, Tuvak, Vannar, get the men mounted and lined up as they were yesterday. This time I'll ride behind the lines. I want to study the horses and the way each man rides. Get moving. We've got a lot of work to do today."

19

The sun crept higher in the sky before they resumed training, as Eskkar gritted his teeth and shook his head in disgust. It took far longer than it should to get halters on the horses and lead them out of the corral, despite plenty of help from Sharkal and the more experienced men. At least today, the men's wits weren't slowed by too much drinking, gambling, and whoring the night before.

Despite sleeping on the ground, they'd had a good night's rest and enough bread to satisfy them until midday. Stiff muscles soon loosened as the training began, though Eskkar could see that many of them, those who hadn't ridden lately, had sore bottoms. Well, he could do nothing about that; a few more days work should toughen them up.

Training resumed, picking up from yesterday. The lines of mounted men crossed again and again, moving through walk, trot, and canter. Eskkar, sometimes riding with the men, other times riding behind them, suspected that the horses had grasped the required tactics faster than some of his men.

As he expected, the beasts had grown accustomed to moving in a line, and the men took confidence from their mounts.

The first gallop of the morning went smoothly enough, to Eskkar's surprise. But he repeated the exercise three more times before he grunted in satisfaction.

"Good work, men," Eskkar shouted. "Everyone stay mounted and gather at the center of the field."

Facing a half-circle of thirty-one riders, Eskkar explained the next phase of the training.

"What we're going to do now is gradually close the gap between riders. You've done well so far, but for this we'll keep the horses at a canter. The horses have to believe that there will always be a gap for them to pass through when they charge. If they don't, they'll hesitate at the last moment, or maybe even dig in and toss you off their backs. While I don't much care if you break your necks, I don't want any of the horses injured. Any questions?"

"What happens in a real charge? There won't be any gaps in the enemy's line."

Eskkar had planned to explain that next. "A good question." He studied the man's face and guessed that he had his wits about him. "What's your name?"

"Parcala, Commander."

"Well, Parcala, in any charge, there will always be gaps in the enemy's line. Some horses will be faster or slower, or a beast might even trip and fall. A few may take fright and turn tail, or veer off to the side. Your horse will see those gaps and head for them. It's your task to make sure the horse goes where you want it to, and that's straight ahead at the enemy before you. You want to pass as close to that enemy as possible, no more than an arm's length away, so you have plenty of room to strike with your sword."

"But what if there is no gap?" Parcala asked again.

Eskkar shook his head at their worried faces. "Then it's up to you to make one. Let's say a solid line of men is riding toward you, no gaps in their line. What are you going to do?"

The men glanced back and forth at each other, but no one spoke.

"You're going to create a gap, Parcala," Eskkar said, "by intimidating your enemy. If they see you coming at them in a solid front, as fast as you can ride, screaming your war cry and showing no intention of slowing down or turning aside, then it's their horses that will turn away, or your enemy will lose his nerve and pull up."

He looked them over carefully, and saw doubt remaining on many of their faces.

"Do you know why barbarians are such ferocious fighters? Why you dirt-eaters can't stand before them? It's because they're better horsemen, and because their mounts are better trained. A barbarian's horse goes where it's pointed. It's so used to being properly handled that it will attempt any slope or charge any enemy. The horse *knows* its rider knows what's best. Isn't that right, Sharkal?"

"Yes, Commander."

"Lucky for you men, we won't be facing any barbarian horsemen. None of you would last more than a heartbeat against them. The enemy we'll be facing will be as ill-prepared as you were before we started. It's my job to give you an advantage, to make sure you and your horses are better trained than our enemy. That way, when we do face Tuttul's horsemen, it will be *they* who turn away and flinch at our charge."

The men's faces betrayed their concern. "So, as I keep telling you, follow orders exactly, if you want to live through your first battle."

"Commander, suppose we charge as you say, and there still is no gap," Parcala said doggedly.

"In that case, you drive your horse straight at your opponent's animal. The horses will collide, both animals will probably have broken legs, and you'll be knocked off your horse and onto the ground. But so will your opponent. You'll be dazed and in pain, but so will your enemy. Make sure you get to your feet first, kill your dismounted enemy, and start looking for another horse."

Eskkar lowered his voice, this time to emphasize his words. "Because there's nothing more terrifying than being on foot, an easy kill, while mounted men are battling all around you. You find a horse, or kill someone and take his, do whatever you have to do, just get another mount under you. Remember that, Parcala."

"Yes, Commander."

"Enough questions for now," Eskkar said. "Let's get back to work."

He kept the men at the canter exercise until nearly noon. Gradually they closed the gap between the riders until there was just enough room for each horse to pass. Most of the horses behaved well; the few that didn't required extra control from their riders. When Eskkar gave the orders to cease and dismount, every man swung wearily down from his equally tired horse.

"Sharkal," Eskkar ordered, "get the horses cleaned up and rubbed down. Take them over to the river. The men, too. They stink worse than the horses."

Better to scrub the horses at midday, when they'd have a chance to dry while the sun remained high. Eskkar set the example, one of the first to reach the river. He scooped water over his horse, then rubbed him down with a blanket. A quick dunk in the water removed some of the horse smell off his own body, and he washed the blanket as well. He turned his stallion over to one of the boys as Bracca arrived, once again leading three pack animals.

"You're late," Eskkar said.

"And you smell like horse sweat," Bracca answered, sliding down from his mare and patting her on the neck.

Eskkar shrugged. Even after his dip in the river, it was probably true. A few days of steady riding, and he hardly noticed the powerful smell that could make a dirt-eater gasp and step away. "Did you bring the grain?"

"Yes, ten sacks of it. The villagers complained more about giving up the damn grain than they did about the blankets, the ropes, or the food. I think they're afraid the fields will be burned and they'll be starving this winter."

As long as he got what he wanted, Eskkar didn't care how many villagers starved. "The horses need the grain. If we're going to push them hard, they need to be well fed."

"I know, I know," Bracca said, "the horses are worth more than the men. Icarnar keeps saying the same thing." He lowered his voice and drew Eskkar apart from those unloading the pack animals. "Speaking of the men, how are our illustrious fighters coming along?"

"Better than I expected. Sharkal is a big help. He's worth five of any of them." Eskkar realized the question wasn't an idle one. "Why? What's happening?"

"A rumor reached Dilmun today. Horsemen from Tuttul are burning farms and fields a day's ride from here."

"Damn the bad luck. I need more time."

"You don't have it," Bracca said. "You know what happens when crops burn. The farmers panic. You'll have to ride out tomorrow. Find these horsemen and stop them. At least slow them down, make them back off."

Eskkar mulled the problem over for a moment. When he met Bracca's gaze, Eskkar realized the man had more to say.

"What else?"

"The rumor," Bracca said, "and it's just a rumor, remember that ... claims there are at least a hundred horsemen."

"And you expect me to lead thirty untrained men against a hundred? What kind . . ."

Eskkar stopped and considered Bracca's words. "They can't have that many men. Horses, I mean. There aren't that many horses in this whole countryside. Besides, if a farmer sees ten or fifteen raiders, he's frightened to death. Right away swears he saw a hundred of them."

"Well, how many do you think Tuttul might have?"

Eskkar had already started figuring. "They wouldn't send a small band on any raid this close to Dilmun. We've barely enough men to raid them, for that matter. No, I'll guess they've forty or fifty men, probably less than that. Any more and they'd already be here."

"Can you drive that many off? You'll be outnumbered."

"Don't you mean, can *we* drive them off? You'll be at my side, won't you, friend Bracca?"

"I suppose I'll have to, to make sure you don't get yourself killed."

"I didn't know you were so concerned about keeping me alive."

"I'm not, friend Eskkar. I just want my horse back, if you do get killed."

"It is a good horse," Eskkar admitted. "I'm getting used to his gait."

"It's the best horse in Dilmun, damn you. I'm still not sure how I let you talk me out of him."

Bracca shook his head at his own stupidity. "Can you stop Tuttul's horsemen?" He didn't wait for an answer. "I told Icarnar we'd be leaving at dawn tomorrow."

"Well, then *you* have that long to figure out a way to stop them," Eskkar said.

"Don't look at me, barbarian. You're the horse fighter. You'll come up with something." He walked back to his horse and swung up.

"Where are you going?"

"Back to the village, to try and get you more supplies, more men, more horses, anything I can think of. I'll be back by nightfall." He wheeled the horse around and cantered off, leaving the pack horses and their handlers scrambling after him.

Eskkar stood there, running his fingers over his chin, trying to think. Stopping another band of horsemen wouldn't be easy, especially if they outnumbered him. Given another eight or ten days, he would have the men ready. But tomorrow?

He saw Sharkal and the others returning from the river. "Tuvak, Vannar, Sharkal, come over here."

Leading them away from the holding corral, he sat down on the ground and motioned to his subcommanders to join him.

"Bracca says there's a band of Tuttul's horsemen raiding the land to the west," Eskkar said, giving them the bad news in a calm voice. "A large band, but no one knows for sure how many there are." He knew if he mentioned a hundred riders, half his force would desert before dawn.

"Tuvak, Sharkal, take three good riders and find these raiders. I need to know where they are, and how many. We don't want any horsemen catching us by surprise. Make sure you're back here by nightfall."

Eskkar knew a successful patrol would give everyone more confidence in their leaders. "Tuvak, listen carefully to Sharkal. He knows how to ride a patrol."

Eskkar faced Sharkal. "Tell him what you're doing, and why, at every step of the way. He needs to know what to do. Will you do that?"

"Yes, Commander."

"Good. There's more grain from Dilmun in the sacks. Give the horses a good feed, then get going."

"Can I go with them?" Vannar asked, looking anxiously at his brother.

"No, I need you here, to help with the training," Eskkar said. "You'll go on the next patrol. Don't worry, you'll get your turn."

"Yes, Commander," Vannar said, though he didn't look happy about being separated from his brother.

"And we'll need another senior man," Eskkar said. "What about that Parcala? He's looks like a good rider. Anyone think he can't handle it?"

No one had any objections.

"Good. Have him help you with the men, Vannar. More sword practice, first on foot, then later we'll mount them up."

While the horses rested and grazed, Eskkar put the men through a long session of sword practice. He walked them through the simplest routine he knew, an overhand swing, advance, thrust, overhand swing, retreat. They repeated the steps over and over.

If he had more time, Eskkar would have ordered Bracca to provide practice swords. While even a wooden sword might poke out an eye or knock a man senseless, it wasn't likely to kill anyone.

By the time Eskkar let his men mount up, their arms were stiff and their muscles strained, exactly how he wanted them. Tired arms would move slower, and they were less likely to hurt themselves or one another. Although all the men knew which end of a sword to hold, few had ever fought from horseback. And using a sword from the back of a horse required not only a different way of thinking, but different types of strokes.

He positioned the mounted men in a half circle facing him, and waited until he had every rider's attention.

"I'm going to show you how to use a sword from horseback. First I want you to forget what you think you know about fighting and listen to me. When villagers fight on horseback, they ride toward each other, come to a stop, and start swinging their weapons. They want to fight one on one, and most of the time, the horse is just another obstacle. Isn't that so?"

The men glanced at each other. "Yes, Commander."

"If you've ever faced barbarians," Eskkar went on, "you know they don't fight that way. They let the horse do most of the work, and they keep their mounts moving. To a barbarian, a wounded enemy is almost as good as a dead one. So they don't slow down when they meet their enemies. They try to ride through, taking a quick cut at their opponent's head or shoulder, or even at the horse's head. Then they move to the next man, and the next, always pushing forward, until they've cut through the line.

He had their attention. They understood that his words might mean the difference between life and death.

"As soon as barbarians reach their opponent's rear, they wheel about and charge again, shouting their war cries. The constant movement collapses the enemy's lines and creates confusion and panic. The dirt-eaters see barbarians everywhere, in front and behind. They panic and start looking over their shoulders, afraid some bloodthirsty warrior might be coming behind them."

Eskkar paused to take stock of his men. Aside from the occasional horse twitching and moving, every man's eyes stayed fixed on their commander. At least none of these fools claimed they knew how to fight from horseback.

"In a horse fight, don't worry about your back. As long as you keep moving, your back is safe. So keep the horse pushing forward, and hack at anything that moves within reach. And don't forget to shout your war cry. Your horse will be used to the sound, while your enemies won't."

"What's our war cry?" Parcala obviously felt comfortable raising the question.

Eskkar took a deep breath. Even the most basic concepts needed explaining the first time. "We'll have two war cries. 'Dilmun,' and 'Kill.' You'll shout them as you ride toward your enemy, and yell even louder when you attack. Remember, you want to confuse and frighten not only the men you're facing, but their horses as well. Understand?"

"Yes, Commander."

"Damn you all to the pits, am I talking to men or old women? DO YOU UNDERSTAND?"

"YES, COMMANDER!"

"That's better. And that's how loud you shout your war cry. Now let's get to work."

He and Vannar split the men into two lines, each man only three paces from the horse and rider beside him. The first time they rode toward each other at a trot, swords out and held high in the air.

As the two lines passed, the riders clashed their weapons against those of the approaching riders. Keeping the swords high made sure no one got hurt, and the clank of bronze on bronze was yet another sound the horses needed to recognize.

Again and again they reformed the lines, responding to Eskkar's basic commands: Walk, Trot, Canter, Gallop, Draw Swords, Wheel Right, Wheel Left, Regroup, and, of course, Form A Line.

Eskkar didn't dare give them anything else, lest they get confused. The last thing he needed was some oaf forgetting a command during the heat of battle.

The sun slid down toward the horizon, but he kept them at it until the horses tired. Only then did he tell Vannar to lead both men and mounts to the river, water and wash down the horses and make sure the camp boys fed the animals a double helping of grain.

"Then bring the men back here. They need to practice sword strokes on their feet as well as from horseback."

By the time it grew too dark to practice, the men were staggering, exhausted, their muscles sore as they eased themselves to the ground and gathered round the campfire. Eskkar felt grateful to have them so far away from Dilmun. No one would get drunk and start trouble.

Any wine they'd brought with them yesterday had long since been pissed away. And since most of them didn't have any coins, they wouldn't be gambling away their hard earned pay and turning surly. Instead, they ate their fill, too tired to do anything else.

They'd scarcely finished eating before one of the boys on watch called out that Sharkal had returned. A few moments later, the warrior and the rest of the patrol walked back into camp, leading their mounts through the deepening darkness.

The boys took the horses from them, and the men made room around the fire for the returned scouts. Tuvak wanted to talk, but Eskkar waved him silent. From Sharkal's approach, Eskkar knew there was no immediate danger. "Eat first, then we'll talk."

The patrol wolfed down their food, all except Sharkal, who took his time finishing his meal. He wiped his mouth on his arm and looked inquiringly at Eskkar. By then everyone had crowded around, weary muscles forgotten, waiting to hear the news.

"Tell us what you found, Sharkal," Eskkar said. He understood the look the warrior had given him, but Eskkar wanted the men to hear what they faced. Better to give them the worst now, than have them find out when they faced their enemy.

"We covered about sixteen miles to the west and began sweeping northward. Tuvak spotted smoke and we headed toward it. They'd burned a farm, the house, corrals, everything. Killed the dirt-eaters, nine or ten of them. I counted fifteen or twenty horses from the tracks. Their trail came from and headed back toward the west. We followed their tracks, keeping off the ridgelines, until we found their camp."

"Did they see you?" Eskkar needed to know that fact above all else.

"No. Only Tuvak and I went ahead on foot. We climbed a hill overlooking their campsite. I counted at least fifty-six men. There might have been a few more out on patrol."

Eskkar heard the intake of breath at the mention of the enemy's numbers. Every man's eyes turned toward him, and he made sure his face showed no concern.

"They had some women in the camp," Sharkal continued. He, too, gave no importance to the number. "Some of the men were lined up to rape them. Others had wine. There was much loud talking and laughing. We watched for a while longer, then slipped away. We headed back, keeping to the hard ground to try and hide our trail. These dirt-eaters may not even notice our passing."

Eskkar didn't think that likely, but he kept his face impassive. "How did they look? Like fighters or rabble?"

"Not horsemen, not warriors. Like these men," he gestured to those surrounding the fire. "The camp had no discipline. I didn't see any pickets or patrols."

"Mmm," Eskkar said, taking his time, choosing his words with care. "We should be able to finish off fifty or so of their untrained rabble."

Around the fire, he saw men looking at each other. The first fear had already taken root. The serious looks of Tuvak and the other patrol members had made the men nervous, and now, hearing the size of the enemy force, half his men would be thinking about slipping away in the darkness.

"Commander!" One of the camp boy's high pitched voice carried through the camp. "Master Bracca is riding in."

"Ah, just in time," Eskkar said. "Our leader arrives."

As long as he didn't bring more bad news, Eskkar thought. He turned to Sharkal. "How far to their camp from here?"

For the first time, Sharkal's eyes showed a trace of surprise. "Maybe twenty-two, twenty-three miles. Mostly flat land all the way."

Both men glanced up at the night sky. The moon had just risen. It would be at its brightest soon, and nearly full tonight.

Bracca strode into the firelight, but took one look at the hushed gathering and kept silent.

"Men," Eskkar began, letting his eyes go around the circle, "our enemy has no discipline, no guards. They're used to killing unarmed farmers and their wives in their sleep. Their numbers mean nothing. We'll crush them."

He directed his next words to Bracca. "The day after tomorrow. But first, we'll soften them up a little, and tip the odds even more in our favor."

Eskkar stood. "Vannar, I want you, Parcala, and two others, the best riders we've got. And Sharkal. Get your horses and weapons. Pack enough bread and one water skin for each man. Nothing else. We're leaving as soon as you're ready. Get moving."

Everyone was on their feet, and the talking began. Eskkar ignored the clamor, and led Bracca away until they were out of earshot. "Well, anything new?"

"Icarnar and his master want to know if you're ready to drive Tuttul's raiders off. I'm supposed to ride back and tell them you'll be on your way."

"I need you here tonight with the men, to stiffen their backbones. If you have to, send a camp boy back to the village to tell them we're sending out a raiding party tonight, and we'll be on the move tomorrow. That should satisfy them."

"You're going to ride to their camp at night? Are you crazy?"

"No one likes riding at night less than I do," Eskkar conceded, "but there's enough moonlight, and it can be done, if you know how. Sharkal and I know how. With a little luck, we'll reach their camp by dawn."

"And what am I supposed to do while you gone?"

"You make sure none of the men desert. Double the guards for tonight. Tell them it's in case Tuttul's raiders show up. But keep a close watch. Promise the men more copper if you have to. Just don't let any slip away, and by the gods don't lose any horses!"

"And if you don't come back, then what do I do?"

"What I'm sure you do best, friend Bracca. Slip away yourself before it's too late."

"What can you possibly accomplish with six men against sixty?"

"I'm not sure. But I'll think of something by the time we get there."

Not long after, Eskkar left camp with Sharkal, Vannar, Parcala, and two of the most skilled horsemen in the group. Eskkar led the way on foot, guiding his horse by the halter, while the rest of his men remained mounted. He strode as quick as he could, stretching his legs and making the horse move at a fast walk.

Each man's orders were to follow the exact trail of their leader. Despite the relatively slow pace, the men had to stay alert, eyes watching the ground.

The moon had just risen, and in the dim light, either man or beast could stumble. A sprained ankle for the men, or a broken leg for the horse, and the mission would be over for the unlucky victim.

When his legs grew weary, Eskkar mounted his horse. He let Sharkal take the lead position, again guiding the way on foot, while everyone else rode behind, keeping the horses to a slow and steady pace. When Sharkal wearied, he turned to Vannar to take his place. The moon had climbed high overhead, the extra light helping both man and beast pick their path.

They kept exchanging the lead position as the moon raced across the sky. By the time the silver orb began its descent, they had covered more than fifteen miles, and Eskkar knew they were drawing closer to their enemy's camp.

Sharkal took the lead again, maintaining the steady pace and showing not a hint of fatigue, though the warrior had already covered the same ground earlier that day. To Eskkar, the landscape remained unchanged, a monotonous gray earth dotted with an occasional bush, clumps of grass, or tree catching the moonlight.

Mile by mile, they continued on. No creatures of the night disturbed their passage. He felt the tiredness in his legs, and even the horses began to slow down.

If Sharkal missed the trail, or followed the wrong landmarks, they'd have a long and hard ride back to Dilmun's camp on spent horses. Eskkar's patience wore thin, but before he could ask Sharkal if he had lost the way, the warrior stopped so suddenly that Eskkar's mount bumped into Sharkal's.

"Not far now," Sharkal said. "Stay here with the horses while I take a look."

"No, I'll go with you," Eskkar said. For this he needed to see with his own eyes. "Vannar, keep a close watch until we return." He slid to the ground and handed his halter to the man, and followed Sharkal's shadowy form into the darkness.

As they walked over the hilly ground, Eskkar checked on the moon's progress. It was sliding toward the horizon and dawn would be upon them before the moon completely disappeared. The night journey had taken longer than Eskkar expected, and now they didn't have much time.

Ahead of him, Sharkal dropped to his knees and clambered up the side of another low hill. Eskkar followed his example, and in a moment, both men were flat on the ground, peering over the crest of the hillock.

"This is where you spied on them today?"

"Yes, this is the place."

Eskkar's opinion of his fellow warrior moved up. To ride so many miles at night, and reach a specific location on the first try was more than Eskkar could have accomplished. Not only was Sharkal older, but the warrior had spent his whole life on the trail.

Eskkar put those thoughts aside as he stared down at the camp beneath him. "Count the men," he ordered.

The campfires had gone out, but a few embers still glowed. Eskkar spotted the small stream gurgling between a scattering of trees. The horses were penned in amongst the trees, though he couldn't make out the ropes that held them.

He searched the camp, but saw no men walking the perimeter. If Eskkar led a large band like that into enemy territory, he would insist on at least four men patrolling the camp, with two horses at hand and ready to ride.

There were guards of course. Eskkar made out two, and there might be others. But they looked lax, and at this late portion of the night, clearly didn't expect anything except the dawn.

"I see sixty-six men, Commander," Sharkal whispered. "There may be more on the far side of the stream."

It didn't matter how many men they had. Eskkar hadn't come this far to turn around and head back without attempting something. Only the ones on guard mattered, and they looked more asleep than awake.

"We can follow that gully right to the camp, I think. We should be able to get close enough."

"We could slit the guards' throats easy enough," Sharkal suggested. "We could round up ten or twenty horses without too much trouble."

"No time. Besides, we're not here to steal horses or slit a few throats. If we can stampede the herd, it will take them a day or two to round them all up, especially if they think we're lurking around looking to pick them off. That will give our men another day of training, and enough time to get here and drive off this rabble. We'll scatter their horses and be on our way. Let's get back."

"As you say, Commander." His tone left no doubt of his disapproval.

Eskkar understood Sharkal's reluctance. A warrior expected to accomplish something with a raid, not simply ride back to camp with an empty hand.

"Look, Sharkal, if you can catch a few horses without slowing down, do it. But only after we stampede the herd. Just remember, tonight we're not raiding for horseflesh. And I don't want you getting yourself killed or captured over these sorry excuses for horses."

They slipped below the crest and descended the hill. It didn't take long to reach Vannar and the others, nervously waiting Eskkar's return. They clustered around their leader, waiting to hear what Eskkar and Sharkal had seen.

"There's about fifty or sixty men asleep on the other side of the hill," Eskkar explained, speaking rapidly. Dawn wasn't far off, and they had to move fast.

"Vannar, you and two men follow Sharkal. He'll lead you right to the horses. You four are going to stampede the herd. Use your swords on them, and scream like demons. The noise and pain and smell of blood will get the horses moving. Slash the ropes and scatter the herd, drive them across the stream if you can, but panic them so much that they run and keep running. Just make sure you don't run into the ropes. Once the horses have stampeded, loop around to the south and get back here."

He gripped Parcala's shoulder. "You and I will ride through the camp, shouting at the top of our lungs. That should help keep everyone distracted and away from the corral. We'll have to make ourselves sound like twenty, so don't stop screaming."

Eskkar kept his voice confident. He needed Parcala to trust him. "Just follow my lead. We can do this. Don't stop to fight anybody, but slash at anyone that gets in your way and keep going. After we ride through the camp, we'll swing around to the east, away from the horses. As soon as we all meet up here, we'll ride like the wind back to our camp."

"Only the two of us? What if . . ."

"No time to talk. Dawn's almost here. Just follow me, Parcala, and you'll be fine. Believe me, they'll be too confused and too slow to react. We'll be through them before they can find their swords."

Without waiting for an answer, Eskkar grabbed his horse's halter from Vannar's hand, and started away, Sharkal right behind him. Eskkar resisted the urge to look back, to see if Parcala and the others were following.

Eskkar knew this was one of those moments when the men had to trust in their leader. But then he heard the faint sounds of the horses moving behind and breathed a small sigh of relief. Only a coward would have turned back now, and these dirt-eaters wanted to prove themselves as hardy as a pair of barbarians.

As they drew closer to the camp, Eskkar halted and waited until Sharkal reached his side.

"Let's walk the horses in, as close as we can, until someone gives the alarm. If the guards see us walking horses toward them, they might think we're scouts returning. You might get all the way to the corral."

"I'll get as close to the horses as possible," Sharkal said. "Then mount and attack."

"Good hunting, Sharkal," Eskkar said. "Give me a few moments head start. Parcala, keep a tight grip on your halter and follow me."

The horse corral lay closer to their approach than the sleeping men, so Eskkar and Parcala had the farther distance to travel. They walked normally, not bothering to try and conceal their footsteps, their horses plodding along behind, but neither of them making any unnecessary noise. Closer and closer they drew. Someone should have given the alarm by now, or at least called out a challenge.

Instead, they drew within fifty paces of the sleeping men and still no one had raised a shout.

"Mount up," Eskkar whispered, and swung himself onto his horse. No sooner had he settled himself on his horse than Sharkal's war cry boomed out over the camp, the piercing shout shattering the night.

Eskkar voiced his own cry and kicked his horse forward, sending the animal straight toward the center of the camp. He drew his sword and he held it up high, where the first rays of the false dawn glinted off the bronze blade.

Still bellowing his war cry, Eskkar drove his horse to a full gallop. A shadow moved in front of him and he swung the long sword down, striking something that elicited a howl of pain.

His path took him near a tent and he slashed at the tent rope as he shot past. More shadows moved and he saw the flash of swords, but already the camp was in chaos.

To his left, horses screamed in fear from the corral, their hooves pounding the earth as they burst through the flimsy ropes attempting to get away from Sharkal's frightening presence.

Jolted from their sleep, Tuttul's raiders didn't know what was happening, only that they were under attack. Their shouts added to the confusion, as men stumbled awake, running into each other, and fumbling for weapons while cursing whatever unknown evil had befallen them.

Eskkar broke through the edge of the camp without striking another blow. A rumble of hoof beats came from the corral area. He pulled his horse up, and glanced behind at the camp. No one shouted orders, and no men formed a battle line.

He wheeled the excited stallion and pointed its head toward the camp. A second pass through their confused ranks would really panic them. Eskkar saw Parcala's teeth gleaming in the light. He, too, had turned his horse around, ready for another charge.

"Again," Eskkar shouted, and drove his horse forward, charging back into the disconcerted crowd of milling men, both riders screaming their war cries.

They parted as Eskkar and Parcala thundered through, and Eskkar swung his sword three times, twice making some contact that added new cries of pain to the demoralized and undisciplined enemy.

This time Eskkar and Parcala kept going, galloping back toward the meeting place where Sharkal would be waiting. Vannar and the two other riders were there, but Sharkal hadn't arrived. Eskkar pulled his horse to stop. Twisting his head, he looked at what remained of the corral area. All of the horses had broken free, except for two animals that had fallen to the earth. Tuttul's men pointed swords at their attackers, but without horses, there was little they could do.

Then Sharkal trotted into sight, leading three horses. Somehow the wily horseman had gathered halter ropes and captured the extra mounts.

Eskkar shook his head, but couldn't keep the smile from his face. Sharkal never halted, just passed through them before increasing his pace to a canter.

"Let's get moving," Eskkar said, as he fell in behind, "unless you want to stay and fight all of them."

Not that Eskkar worried about that. He guessed half a day would pass before Tuttul's men recovered their horses.

Eskkar and his men rode off, laughing at their enemies. Eskkar gradually caught up with Sharkal. "Only three horses? I thought you'd get at least six."

For a moment, an angry frown passed over Sharkal's features. Then he saw the smile on Eskkar's face.

"I could go back and round up a few more," Sharkal said.

Eskkar chuckled, and after a moment, Sharkal joined in. But they kept riding.

Noon had passed before they returned to their own camp near Dilmun. Eskkar had stopped several times to rest the horses. None of Tuttul's men had given pursuit, and he didn't see any need to push the weary animals.

When they crossed over the stream, one of Bracca's scouts spotted them and gave a shout. Parcala and the others rode on ahead, whooping and laughing as they announced the success of their raid.

"Stay with me, Sharkal," Eskkar said, though he knew Sharkal wouldn't demean himself by joining the celebration.

They dismounted and handed the horses over to the camp boys. Bracca waited for them, hands on his hips, standing apart from the others.

"So it went well?"

"Well enough," Eskkar said. "Sharkal even had time to steal a few extra horses, which we can use."

"What about Tuttul's men?"

"We rode right through their camp," Eskkar said, "caught them by surprise just before daybreak. Scattered their horses. They'll spend the rest of the day chasing after their mounts, and maybe part of tomorrow, too. They'll be lucky if they get back all of them."

"Good. That may keep Icarnar and the Village Elder off our backs for awhile." He took a deep breath. "What's next?"

Eskkar had discussed that with Sharkal and the others during the ride back. "First, we get some rest, then we ride out. We should have just enough time to cover more than half the distance between us and them by nightfall. Then in the morning, we find their camp, and drive them off."

"Just like that?"

"Just like that," Eskkar said. "With last night's successful raid under our belts, the men will follow where we lead. I doubt Tuttul's men will be expecting us to return so soon. Once they see us, they'll either run for home, or we'll smash them."

"Well, that's settled then," Bracca said, the sarcasm plain in his voice. "The fact they've still got more men isn't a concern to either of you, I suppose."

"They're dirt-eaters riding horses," Sharkal said. "Even these men of yours can break them."

Bracca shook his head. "You barbarians always want to attack, attack, attack." He shrugged. "In that case, I'd better send word to Icarnar, so he can start the victory feast."

"If you want to lead the men yourself, friend Bracca, you can give the orders."

Bracca swore. Even if he wanted to take command, he knew the men wouldn't follow him into battle. "No, you're in charge of the fighting, friend Eskkar. I'll follow your orders for now."

"A wise choice." Eskkar turned to Sharkal. "Let's get something to eat while Commander Bracca deals with our fearless leaders in Dilmun."

Eskkar ate enough for two men, washing everything down with plenty of fresh water. Meanwhile, Tuvak, Vannar, and Parcala took charge. The horses were given all the grain they could eat, and the men ate a huge meal. Sharkal inspected every halter in the troop.

The three captured horses enabled them to pack some extra food, and Eskkar brought the two oldest camp boys along to tend to the horses. Soon Eskkar led the entire force, including Bracca, out of the camp and heading west at an easy pace.

They made good time, and Eskkar changed his mind and decided to cover about two thirds the distance to the raiders' camp before halting for the night. That should keep his men far enough away from any raiders still chasing after missing horses, but leave Eskkar's force close enough to reach Tuttul's camp the next day, and without tiring the horses.

All the same, when they stopped at sundown, Eskkar made sure they posted six guards around the camp. He didn't intend to have his own horses raided, or any of his men's throats slit while he slept.

Exhausted, he slept through the night, leaving Bracca to check on the guards and make sure they remained alert and watchful.

The morning arrived without incident, and Eskkar felt refreshed, as much from the success of yesterday's raid as from a good night's sleep. The men finished off most of the food, and drained their water skins. There would be several streams along the way, and he wanted the men to travel light.

Today his men stayed quiet, knowing they were likely to be fighting before sundown. They behaved like any group of untested troops, alternating between overconfidence and nervousness at the coming encounter, but not one man had deserted, and none of them looked afraid of facing Tuttul's raiders.

Eskkar's bold raid had given them faith not only in themselves, but more important, they now had complete trust in their leaders.

That, Eskkar knew, would be crucial to winning the battle. If his fighters believed they would win, all he had to do was get them into the right position. That meant he had to first find his enemy, then pick the ground for the battle.

"Sharkal, we're breaking camp," he said. "Take two men and scout ahead. See if you can locate our enemy."

The rest of the troop gathered their gear and mounted up. Eskkar saw the excitement on their faces, and he felt pride in these men, who trusted both him and the training they'd received.

The men formed a double column, the same formation they used yesterday. He told Bracca to bring up the rear of the column, as much to stop the endless questions as to have an alert and experienced fighter back there.

Eskkar led the men in the same direction that Sharkal had chosen. As Eskkar rode, he studied the landscape around him with care, looking at the low hills with their scattered trees.

The land they traversed was mostly flat, but there were occasional slopes and even a few deep ravines that obstructed their passage. Twice they encountered small streams, and each time Eskkar halted his men. Water was too precious to waste, and he made sure every man and horse drank their fill.

The sun had reached its zenith, when Sharkal galloped back to rejoin them.

"They're still at the camp," he said, without wasting a moment. "Couldn't get close enough to count the men, but it looks like they've recovered most of the horses."

"Doesn't matter. We're not going to attack them there anyway," Eskkar said. "I thought they'd be on the move by now. They must not be expecting any more trouble. Did they spot you?"

"No."

Eskkar knew Sharkal would have said if he'd been spotted. His question was meant to reassure the men that they still had surprise on their side.

"Then let's take the fight to them," Eskkar said.

They retraced Sharkal's tracks, keeping an easy pace so as not to tire the horses. They didn't have far to go. Topping a low rise, Eskkar saw Tuttul's camp up ahead.

"Halt," he called out, as the rest of the men reached the crest of the hill.

Someone in the enemy camp gave the alarm, and Eskkar saw every man there turn his face toward the hilltop. For a brief moment, the men from Tuttul just stood there. Then panic set in, and Eskkar watched them dash about in confusion, shouting orders and feverishly collecting their weapons.

Bracca guided his horse beside Eskkar's. "Why are you stopping? We should have charged them before they could get ready."

"If we did that, they'd fight," Eskkar replied. "They'd have no other choice, and they wouldn't have time to lose their nerve. Besides, you don't attack an enemy that can duck behind those trees."

"So when are you going to attack?"

"I'm not," Eskkar said. "They are. Now keep quiet and let me and Sharkal plan the battle."

"I don't see much of a plan," Bracca grumbled.

"You want to take charge, friend Bracca?"

Bracca swore under his breath, but shook his head. "I hope you are not going to get all of us killed."

Eskkar didn't bother to answer. He focused on the landscape in front of him. The enemy fighters milled around, struggling with their horses and mounting up. A few fools already had swords in their hands as they pranced their horses back and forth.

Still, he knew the decision not to attack was sound. By the time Eskkar's men crossed the mile and a half that separated the two forces, Tuttul's men would have overcome their surprise and moved into the trees.

"I count around sixty horses, Commander," Sharkal called out.

"Let's flank them, and see what they do," Eskkar said. He raised his voice to carry over the nervous chatter of the men. "We're going to ride around their camp, until we find a suitable place to fight. Stay in the column of twos, and follow me."

At the head of his men, Eskkar rode to the southwest, angling away from Tuttul's camp. He kept the horses to a trot, a gait he knew the animals could maintain for some time without tiring.

As they rode, Eskkar kept his eye on the enemy. They'd stopped milling about, and every man had mounted and formed a rough line. Even so, he saw plenty of confusion in their ranks, with men dashing back and forth.

They probably expected either an immediate attack, or thought Dilmun's horsemen would retreat from Tuttul's superior numbers. Eskkar's unexpected flanking movement must have surprised them, and no doubt they were considering what to do. He hoped he could keep them confused a little longer.

"Where are we going?" Bracca pushed his horse alongside Eskkar's once again.

"Somewhere, anywhere where we can find good ground. I want them to attack, but at a place that I choose. So we'll ride around until we find that place, then we'll wait for them."

"Suppose they attack us before you find a place that suits you?"

"Then that's where we'll fight. Or maybe we'll just ride away. I won't know until it happens. Now keep quiet, and let me think."

They covered nearly half a mile before Tuttul's horsemen began moving toward them, a large mass of horses in no particular order. They, too, kept their horses to a trot, and the gap between the two forces began to diminish with every step.

"Commander, that hill there," Sharkal said.

Eskkar heard a hint of excitement in Sharkal's normally dour voice.

"I see it," Eskkar answered. He, too, had noticed the hill.

It didn't look like much, a long, sloping incline that rose gradually to a flat-topped crest. Eskkar would have preferred something with a little more height, but this would have to serve.

He changed direction, moving away from Tuttul's forces, and his column of men followed. They reached the slope and trotted to the top of the hill.

"Form a line facing them," he shouted.

The men might have only trained together for a few days, but if there was one thing they'd learned, it was how to form a line.

In moments, thirty-three men sat astride their horses and watched their enemy approach. The camp boys, holding the halters of the extra horses, took position behind the line.

"Tuvak, Vannar, you take the right. Sharkal, Parcala, take the left. Bracca and I will take the center. Remember to wait for my commands."

The subcommanders moved away from the center of the line and took their positions. Eskkar urged his horse in front of the line and faced his men.

"The enemy will be here soon," he said, keeping his voice as calm as if they were all back at the training ground.

"We'll let them come to us. If they try to flank us, we'll charge straight down the slope, smash them, and regroup a quarter mile ahead. Remember, we want to strike them as a single line, so wait for my command. Everyone understand what we're going to do?"

"Yes, Commander," the answer came raggedly, some voices high pitched in their excitement.

"I can't hear you!" Eskkar's bellow echoed out over the hilltop.

"YES, COMMANDER!"

That resounding shout would have reached Tuttul's men, and who now knew they had a fight on their hands. A few of his men laughed at Eskkar's training camp words, which helped steady everyone's nerves.

Eskkar grinned at his men. "That's better. When we charge, that's how loud I want to hear you, remember that. But until I give the order, not a word. If we keep silent, it will make them fear us even more."

He ran his eyes up and down the line. Hands shook, lips trembled, men's chests rose and fell deeply, and they kept wiping their hands on their tunics, all the usual signs of impending action. Regardless, no one looked ready to bolt and run.

"Just follow orders, and you'll all live to brag to your children about today. ARE WE READY?"

"YES, COMMANDER!"

He smiled at the deafening response. "Good. Now wait for the order to attack. Nobody moves or talks until then. Show them what real horse fighters look like."

Eskkar guided his horse back into position at the center of the line. Tuttul's horsemen had slowed their approach, and now they halted at the foot of the incline, just over a quarter mile away.

A knot of men formed at their head, while their leaders pondered what to do next. Clearly they didn't like the idea of charging uphill. Trying to flank Eskkar's position would only weaken their center.

By now Tuttul's horsemen understood that they faced a disciplined force of trained fighters, and the longer they hesitated, the more their fear would grow.

Eskkar looked up and down his line of riders. Some gripped their halters too tight while others swallowed again and again, their neck apples rising and falling. Yet no man wanted to show weakness to his companions. They had their fear under control, and he expected no more from them.

Tuttul's men betrayed their excitement, wheeling their horses back and forth, waving their swords in the air, and shouting curses at their opponents. None of Eskkar's men had drawn their swords, and he knew they wouldn't until he gave the order. Though by now their sweating palms would be itching for the feel of a weapon.

"How long do we wait?" Bracca asked.

"We wait until they decide what they're going to do. If they try and flank us, we'll attack their center before they can get into position. What I really want is for them to start up the hill. And that's what they will do, as soon as they figure out it's their best chance."

"I'm starting to regret letting you join up with me, barbarian," Bracca muttered. "Damn you, you ARE going to get me killed."

"You just follow my lead. Keep your horse right beside mine, not a step ahead or behind. And remember to yell your head off."

Shouts floated up the slope as Tuttul's leaders made their decision. Those in command rode back and forth in front of their men,
until the riders formed a rough line facing the crest.

"Good. They're going to keep their men together and come
straight at us," Eskkar said. "It's the best they can do."

The enemy would meet Eskkar's force head on, and try to
destroy them with their superior numbers. The right tactic, he knew,
but did Tuttul's men have the stones to face his? He'd know soon
enough.

Now Eskkar's own impatience set in, as his enemy prepared
to attack. It seemed to take forever, but at last they readied themselves. Their leader shouted an order, and Tuttul's horsemen surged
forward.

"Men, when I give the order, we'll go right to a canter, then to
the gallop," Eskkar called out, loud enough to be heard across the
hilltop, but not by the enemy. "Don't draw your swords until you're
at the gallop, then yell your heads off."

With a ragged shout of their own, Tuttul's forces began moving
up the hill, still about six hundred paces away. Their battle line soon
sagged, with knots of riders ranging ahead of their companions, as
Eskkar had expected.

He waited until his enemy had advanced about two hundred
paces. Now they were less than four hundred paces away. "At a
canter, NOW!"

His men surged forward, the line a bit uneven at first, but to his
satisfaction as he glanced right and left, it soon straightened.

The two opposing lines seemed to be rushing toward each other
over the shaking earth, but Eskkar knew that was the battle fever,
sharpening his senses and speeding up the passage of time. Another
look showed his men cantering together, the horses forming a solid
front as they moved down the hill.

"At the gallop, NOW!"

Heels kicked at the horses' flanks, and the line surged forward,
his riders reaching full speed down the slope in only a few strides.
Hooves pounded the earth, and Eskkar felt a thrill of excitement
rush through him.

He drew his sword. "SWORDS." He had time for one last glance to either side. Every man had his sword out as they tore down the slope.

"KILL!" Eskkar screamed the word over the din of the hooves and the shouts of his men. "KILL KILL KILL!"

The approaching line of the enemy had already broken apart in several places and turned into an uneven mass of horsemen, and Eskkar saw men pulling back on their horses. To the riders coming up the hill, the sight would be frightening.

Despite their advantage in numbers, half of Tuttul's men were slowing down, afraid to face the thundering wall of horsemen rushing toward them. Eskkar's men screamed their war cries, leaning forward against their horse's neck, swords extended and glinting in the sunlight, exactly as they trained.

With a sound like rolling thunder, the two forces smashed together.

Eskkar saw a face before him, and he aimed his sword at the whitish blur, the blade biting on something soft for a moment as he tore past, his mount glancing off the shoulder of another rider's horse just to the rear of the first man. This one jerked at his halter, trying to turn the animal around and run. Eskkar swung down with his sword, using all his strength as he struck the helpless rider across the back.

The center of Tuttul's fighters collapsed under the attack. Horses and men went down, both screaming in pain, while suddenly rider-less beasts galloped in every direction. Guiding his mount, Eskkar struck at everyone within reach, killing one man outright, and making another fall from his mount.

By then Dilmun's forces reached the base of the slope, the place where their enemies had mustered their force only moments ago. Eskkar jerked hard on the halter, trying to slow his excited horse that wanted to keep running. "Pull up!"

Behind him Eskkar heard the first cries of wounded men and horses. The sound would strike even more fear into his enemies.

"Pull up! Pull up!" Sharkal's deep voice carried even over the horse and battle noise, echoing Eskkar's command.

Eskkar swung his horse around. "Follow me! Wheel left! Follow me! Wheel left and attack!"

Sharkal and the others took up the shout. It took only moments to complete the turn, and now Eskkar's men galloped at those fighters who'd been ignored as Dilmun's force drove through the enemy's center.

Bloody swords rose up again. This time Sharkal led the way, screaming a war cry that sent terror through anyone in his path.

Those enemy horsemen who'd avoided the downhill charge now faced the nearly intact line heading toward them. What remained of Tuttul's right flank, now outnumbered, had no stomach to face up to Eskkar's fighters. They'd seen their center go down under Dilmun's charge.

Many of those in Eskkar's path scattered, seeking only to get out of the way. With Tuttul's battle line in ruins, the fighting turned into a melee, with friend and foe mixed together. But it didn't matter. Tuttul's men had already lost the will to fight when Eskkar's men smashed through their midst for a second time.

Eskkar searched for their leader, but even if he had survived, he'd lost all control of his men. They fled in every direction, running for their lives, and intent only on getting away from Eskkar's band.

In twos and threes, Dilmun's fighters pursued their enemy. Eskkar saw Sharkal and Vannar chasing a handful of men.

Eskkar found himself closing in on three horsemen. The hindmost turned his head, and Eskkar saw the man's white face. He didn't even have his sword any more. The fleeing man tried to turn his horse aside, but before he could, Eskkar closed the gap and thrust his sword into his back.

The other two men pulled up, determined to fight rather than be killed from behind.

Eskkar engaged the closest man, trying to smash through his defense before the second could turn his horse. Their horses, biting and kicking, moved apart, and Eskkar saw the second rider closing in on him.

Eskkar's horse, still not properly trained to respond to his commands, fought the halter, almost tossing Eskkar from its back as the remaining enemy fighter struggled to guide his half-wild horse against Eskkar's.

Then Bracca arrived with a shout, as he drove his horse into that of Eskkar's second enemy, catching him from behind, and Bracca's sword swung down with enough force to knock the rider from his mount.

The Tuttul fighter Eskkar had engaged ignored his companion's death. He broke off contact and kicked his horse to a gallop. Dirt clods flew high into the air as the man raced for his life.

Bracca's victory shout lasted only a moment, as three more enemy horsemen rode at him, swords outstretched. Eskkar turned toward them, but with a sudden movement, his mount dug its fore-legs into the earth. Unable to hang on, Eskkar flipped forward over the animal's neck, his hand slipping from the horse's mane.

He tumbled once, then rolled to his feet, as Tuttul's fighters pressed Bracca's horse backward.

Bracca swung his sword at enemies on both sides, until his horse rose up, lashing out with its hooves. He blocked another thrust, but his frightened mount kicked out with its rear legs, and Bracca couldn't maintain his seat. He slid backward over the horse's rump and tumbled to the earth. Stunned by the impact, Bracca pushed himself to his knees, struggling to regain his wits and his feet.

With a shout, one of the enemy wheeled his horse and raised his sword over the helpless Bracca. But as the man's blade descended, Eskkar leapt toward his friend and struck the horse's hindquarters a savage blow with his sword. The horse screamed in pain and bolted forward, making the rider's stroke miss Bracca's head, though the animal's shoulder struck Bracca and knocked him down for a second time. Eskkar stepped over Bracca's body, and parried a thrust from another of Tuttul's horsemen.

By now the third rider had turned his mount around and gotten behind Eskkar. He drove his horse forward and raised his sword.

Eskkar, still engaged with the fighter before him, tried to duck away. Instead he tripped over Bracca's dazed body, and tumbled hard to the earth.

The horseman leaned down, his blade aiming for Eskkar's head. But before he could deliver the blow, Sharkal joined the fight, putting his horse at the enemy horseman's shoulder. Tuttul's fighter turned to meet this new threat, but Sharkal thrust forward with his longer blade and drove the tip completely through the man's body.

Eskkar untangled himself from Bracca and got to his feet, his sword ready. But the remaining fighter had fled, along with the first man whose horse Eskkar had wounded. Sharkal swung wide, gathered up Eskkar's mount, and trotted back to his commander.

"You need to control your horse better," Sharkal said, as he tossed the halter rope at Eskkar.

Eskkar gritted his teeth and ignored the jibe. He jumped onto the animal's back and steadied the nervous beast until it responded docilely, its sides heaving and head hanging down, as if embarrassed by its performance.

Looking about him, Eskkar tried to make sense of the battle. In the distance, he saw his men trying to run down their enemies. Sometimes they succeeded, other times the riders escaped. It didn't matter. They had won the battle, and driven their enemy from the field.

"By the gods," Bracca shouted, "I didn't believe it would work! I've never seen anything like it."

Eskkar turned to see Bracca climbing to his feet, still clutching his bloody sword in his hand.

"Just hope you never meet the Alur Meriki. They wouldn't have let a single dirt-eater escape alive."

"Doesn't matter how many get away," Bracca said. "They're beaten, and they'll run for home and hide behind their palisade for at least ten or twenty days. And thanks for saving my hide."

Eskkar grunted. "Sharkal saved mine."

Sharkal appeared not to hear Eskkar's words. "I'll go round up the horses."

Before Eskkar could say anything more, the barbarian rode off.

Tuvak and Vannar trotted up, the brothers grinning with excitement. "We did it, Commander! We did it!"

"You and your brother fought well, Tuvak. Now get our men together. We need to capture as many horses as we can. Every horse we catch will be one less for Tuttul. We'll meet at the enemy's camp. Send everyone there."

It took the rest of the afternoon. First Eskkar counted his men. Only three had been killed in the fighting, while they counted twenty-two dead from Tuttul. Probably half that number died in the first clash. Meanwhile, Sharkal and the others managed to gather up nineteen enemy horses.

And the enemy's camp had been captured intact. Three pack animals burdened with all the loot taken from the farms Tuttul's men had raided in the last five days waited there, unattended. Bracca announced that he would take personal charge of searching the tents.

Eskkar smiled at the man's cunning. Well before most of Eskkar's men even arrived, Bracca would have sifted through the captured booty and removed the most valuable items, keeping them for Eskkar and himself. The rest would be returned to Dilmun's Elder, who would of course reward Bracca for recovering so much plunder.

Eskkar kept busy with his men, making sure they didn't start quarrelling among themselves over the loot. His men had already stripped the dead of any valuables, including swords, knives, and even their clothes. This would be his men's share of the booty.

Victors in battle took the spoils from those they defeated, the traditional reward for their valor and victory. It had always been that way, and always would be.

They settled in for the night. Tuttul's men had left plenty of food behind, and even a few skins of wine. Eskkar grunted with satisfaction as soon as he saw there was enough spirits to give everyone a few mouthfuls, but not enough for his men to get drunk.

It took time before his men quieted down. Everyone wanted to talk about the fight, boast about what they had done and how bravely they fought. Eskkar heard every story, some more than once, as almost every man wanted to share his experience with his commander. He let them all talk, knowing how essential it was for the men to relive their first battle.

Even more important, he'd won their trust. They were his men now, not Bracca's, not the Village Elder's, not even Icarnar's. They would follow Eskkar's commands, and no one else's.

The wine disappeared, and eventually the stories ended. The fire burned low, and the men, exhausted from the fighting, sprawled on the ground and slept, drained in both mind and body. Soon, except for the men guarding the horses, only Eskkar, Bracca, and Sharkal remained awake, sitting close around the dying embers.

"You did well today, Eskkar," Bracca said. "I had my doubts, but your training turned this rabble into warriors."

Coming from Bracca, Eskkar knew the words were praise indeed. "We couldn't have done it without Sharkal's help. He did as much to train the men as I."

Eskkar reached across the small gap that separated them, and extended his arm to Sharkal. "I thank you again for saving my life."

Sharkal ignored the outstretched arm. "A warrior does his duty for his commander. I did nothing more, and there is no bond between us."

Letting his hand drop to his side, Eskkar shrugged. Apparently this thick-headed barbarian would acknowledge no friendship, no feeling of kindred warriors.

Bracca, his eyes moving back and forth between the two men, sought to defuse the tension. "Well, duty or not, Sharkal, you're more than welcome to ride with Eskkar and me when this fighting is finished. We could use a good man like you."

"When this fighting is ended, I ride alone," Sharkal said, rising from the ground. "I have business in the northern lands. Meanwhile, I'll check on the guards, Commander."

He walked away without a glance back.

"Not a very friendly fellow, is he? What did he do to get kicked out of the clan, fuck all the chief's wives?"

"Whatever he did," Eskkar said, watching the man disappear into the darkness, "he carries the weight of it inside his heart, and he carries it alone."

"You came to grips with your past."

"I was young when I left the clan, and I'd done no evil deed to haunt me."

"Whatever he did," Bracca said, "a man still needs friends to survive. He's a fool if he thinks he can make it on his own."

"Perhaps he'll change his mind some day," Eskkar said.

"I think all you barbarians have very hard heads. Take yourself for instance. You should be grateful I'm here to look after you. If I wasn't here, you'd have handed over all the spoils to those fools back in Dilmun."

"I am grateful, friend Bracca. We couldn't have won this victory today without your help."

"Well, I'm glad you're finally coming to your senses." He got to his feet. "I think I'll get some sleep."

"Good night, Bracca."

"Good night, Eskkar." He started to walk away, then turned around. He extended his arm toward his friend. "And thank you again for saving my life out there. You took a big chance, one against three."

Eskkar stood, and clasped Bracca's arm. "You would have done the same for me."

Bracca gave Eskkar's arm a mighty squeeze. "You know, I think I would."

⸺⸺⸺

The morning sun on his face woke Eskkar with a start. Blinking, he pushed himself upright, his eyes searching the camp for signs of anything amiss. Muttering an oath under his breath, he climbed to his feet and slung the long sword over his shoulder.

His men were up and about, attending to their duties, duties he should have assigned instead of sleeping late.

"Up at last, I see." Bracca strolled over, chewing on a hunk of stale bread. "Thought you were going to sleep through the whole morning."

"Why didn't you wake . . ."

"They wanted to, but I told them to let you sleep. You've been up for two days. Besides, nothing was happening here."

"A commander should be up before his men," Eskkar grumbled.

"Oh, yes, the mighty horde of Tuttul's remaining ferocious fighters might have returned and attacked us at dawn."

Eskkar opened his mouth and closed it again. Nothing would be gained arguing with Bracca. More than enough sentries had guarded the camp through the night. "So what are your plans? Are you returning to Dilmun?"

Bracca moved closer. "Yes, at once. I need to inform Icarnar of our mighty victory."

He lowered his voice. "And I've prepared two large sacks of the captured loot for our masters. But somewhere along the way, I'll make sure the finest gems and plenty of the gold disappears. That will be for us in case we have to leave this place suddenly. Our masters will get what they deserve."

"And I'm supposed to just stay here, and ride around the countryside? What will you be doing in Dilmun?

"Gathering fresh supplies for you and your men out here. We're practically standing on Tuttul's lands right now. Why go back to Dilmun? Just keep the men riding around, until Icarnar and his soldiers join up with us. With the threat of Tuttul's horse fighters gone, he'll be more than eager to order his rabble to march on Tuttul."

"I suppose I can keep training the men here," Eskkar mused.

"A good idea. And make a few raids on Tuttul's farmers, some payback for their attacks."

"How many men are you taking with you?"

Bracca shook his head sorrowfully. "My good friend Eskkar, you're far too trusting. Which of these men would you trust with so much gold? It's almost a two day ride, and I don't intend to get my throat slit. I'm going back alone. Unless you want to hang onto all the loot until Tuttul is defeated and we get back to Dilmun?"

Eskkar stared at his companion. "And if you decide to keep going with all that gold, friend Bracca?"

Bracca grinned. "Friend Eskkar, you know I wouldn't leave you behind. Besides, when we capture Tuttul we'll earn even more. With your horse skills and my scheming, we'll be rolling in coins before this feud is over."

Once again, Eskkar decided not to argue with Bracca. The man had already made up his mind. Despite his misgivings, Eskkar decided to trust Bracca. "How long will you be gone?"

"Five or six days, I would think. Icarnar hoped to be on the march by then. But you'll get supplies in three or four days." Bracca reached out his hand and clasped Eskkar's shoulder. "Stop worrying. I never steal from someone who saved my life." He laughed. "At least I haven't yet!"

"Damn you, go! But get those supplies to me as soon as you can."

"Yes, friend Eskkar." He laughed again. "I'm on my way."

Well before midmorning, Bracca rode out of the camp, a cheerful smile on his face. Eskkar spat on the ground. He decided there was an even chance no one would ever see Bracca again.

Eskkar spent the rest of the morning securing the campsite, assigning patrols, and building a better corral. He didn't intend to have anyone stampede *his* horses.

Those duties settled, Eskkar started the men training again. They still had plenty to learn. After winning one battle, they thought they were mighty warriors. Tuttul had been defeated only because Eskkar and Sharkal had chosen the battleground and led them to victory.

One fact was certain. Whether Bracca ever showed his face again or not, word of Dilmun's victory would only make their Village Elder and Icarnar even more eager to destroy Tuttul. In a few days, Eskkar's men would be fighting again. So any additional training he could force into their thick heads, the better chance they'd have to survive.

Well before midday, Eskkar called his subcommanders to join him. Sharkal, Vannar, and Tuvak approached, the latter two with grins on their faces.

Eskkar returned the smiles. "The men have had enough rest. Get them ready for training. They've got a lot to learn, and not much time to learn it."

Still, Eskkar let himself bask in a rare moment of satisfaction. He'd overcome his enemies, and taken a group of raw recruits and turned them into passable fighters. Now that training would continue, and Eskkar knew the chance to command and train so many men might never come again.

For better or worse, he intended to make the most of the opportunity.

—⊸⫘⫘⊸—

Neither Bracca nor Eskkar enjoyed the fruits of their victory long. After another month of campaigning, they returned to Dilmun in triumph, and were summoned to the Elder's house to receive their reward. Unfortunately, Eskkar and Bracca found themselves surrounded by armed men.

As for their payment, it consisted of being removed from command of the horsemen, and ordered to leave the village at once, with the warning that if they were seen anywhere within fifty miles of the village, they'd be put to death.

Elder Jorak and his master at arms Icarnar wanted no popular leaders of their fighters, and even as Bracca and Eskkar were arriving in Dilmun, the Elder's son-in-law and twenty of his men were riding out to the camp to take charge of the horsemen.

The two friends, escorted to Dilmun's gate by ten armed guards, rode out together, never to return. They made only a slight detour to recover the extra loot that Bracca had thoughtfully hidden the day after they captured the Tuttul's horse camp.

Eskkar would have liked to say goodbye to Sharkal before they departed, and again offer him a chance to join with them. But they had no opportunity to seek him out, and they traveled south as alone as when they first entered Dilmun, albeit with heftier purses and riding two good, battled-trained horses.

But at least they rode together. For the first time in his life, Eskkar had a companion, someone he could trust, to ride at his side. In the end, Bracca's friendship might prove more valuable than all the gold and gems they'd stolen.

20

Western lands of Sumeria, two years later . . .

Eskkar leaned against the tavern's mud-brick wall, arms crossed against his chest. The small sliver of shade didn't provide much shelter from the sun's relentless heat, but he didn't intend to waste any of it. Eskkar, about to enter his twenty-sixth season, had lived most of his life in the cooler northern clime. Only dire need augmented by Bracca's relentless pleadings had carried him so far to the south.

A drop of sweat trickled down his forehead, and Eskkar brushed it away. His dark brown hair, released from its usual band of leather, swirled around his face from the quick movement, and nearly concealed the penetrating eyes watching the open expanse of dirt and sand that passed for the center of the village.

Not many people walked about, not this early in the afternoon when the heat from the sky shimmered like the fires in a smith's forge. Those men and women whose duties or needs did take them past the village's only tavern plodded along, their heads lowered and eyes downcast.

In his travels, Eskkar had visited many villages, even clusters of mud huts too small for such a lofty title, but seldom had he found any gathering as gloomy and downtrodden as this place. He'd expected something grander, as befitted a village that boasted a gold mine nearby. Apparently whatever gold men pulled from the earth went somewhere else, probably back into another hole in the ground hidden underneath the Village Elder's house.

Wiping more sweat from his brow with the back of his hand, Eskkar glanced up at the sky. The sun had moved past the height of its daily climb across the heavens, but the warmest part of the day still approached. Today promised to be as hot as yesterday and the day before, and it would likely be even hotter tomorrow.

Bracca swore that summer's midpoint still remained ten days away, but with Bracca you never could be sure what he said was the truth. Some dirt-eaters – they called themselves farmers – claimed to know the secrets of the seasons, such as when summer began or ended. No true warrior concerned himself with such foolish things.

Each day brought its own burden, too hot, too cold, too dry, too wet, and a man had to face whatever the gods sent. People of the steppes rode, hunted, or fought everyday. Winter or summer mattered little, and knowing about these things in advance mattered nothing at all.

Eskkar cursed at the bad luck that dogged his path and had taken him so far to the south that the Great Sea washed the shores less than a day's ride away. Most of all, he cursed Bracca and his silver tongue that had beaten down Eskkar's objections with the lure of the Great Sea, which Eskkar had never seen.

The fascination lasted only a few moments. Eskkar had waded into the surf, but the moment he felt the water's tug strengthening around his legs, he struggled back to shore, with no further interest in either the hot sands or cool water.

Bracca had also promised villages full of willing women eagerly waiting their arrival. That had turned out to be an even greater lie than the magic of the sea. Women were to be had, of course, but only after coins were handed over to their stern-eyed fathers or masters. And as usual of late, for Bracca and Eskkar, coins were in short supply.

The last of the wealth they'd taken in the fighting at Dilmun had vanished six months ago, the aftermath of a night of drunken celebration. Eskkar had slept through the robbery, which had probably saved his life. Bracca, not as fortunate, had stirred during the theft, and received a blow on the head, one that likely would have killed anyone sober.

In the morning, the two companions found themselves with nothing but their clothes and their weapons. The two fine horses they'd ridden from Dilmun were gone as well. On foot, the pair had continued their journey south, toward what Bracca claimed would be a land full of easy coins and balmy weather.

Now they had traveled all the way to the Great Sea, with nothing to show for it. At last Eskkar had demanded they head north, and the first steps on that journey brought them to the pitiful village of Marcala.

Voices sounded in the distance, and Eskkar turned his attention to the worn track that led to the edge of the village. Two dirt-eaters drawing water from the well did the same, so he guessed something out of the ordinary approached. The voices grew louder, more boisterous, a curious mix of rough laughter and a woman's wails.

Eskkar saw a group of men approaching, not from the farmlands to the west and south, where laborers might be expected, or from the river to the north. Instead they came from the east, the one direction Eskkar and Bracca had not yet traveled.

Last night the innkeeper mentioned that the Village Elder lived in that direction, in his great house and tents along with his family, herds, and guards, all surrounded by lush farmland. He lived as befitted the ruler of the village of . . . Eskkar couldn't remember the name of this place. Not that it mattered. Even the smallest collection of dirt-eater huts and tents always boasted some pretentious name.

The men had drawn closer now, close enough for him to see that this was not some collection of farmers, but a group of armed men, four or five of them leading the way, with a straggling line of ten or twelve farmers plodding behind like sheep being led to the slaughter.

The group would pass this hovel that claimed to be a tavern, since it stood near the center of this collection of mud huts, less than twenty crumbling structures by Eskkar's count. The tavern also held the distinction of being the largest establishment in the village, as well as the only ale house.

He frowned at the approaching group. Any crowd, let alone one with armed men, meant the possibility of trouble. Esskar took a long stride and ducked his head inside the tavern's door. "Bracca!"

Esskar didn't need to say anything more. He heard his companion's annoying voice, even more annoying when Bracca was attempting to wheedle favors out of a stubborn innkeeper, cease abruptly.

In their months together, Bracca had learned Esskar's moods and voices well enough to recognize the sound of trouble. Bracca, as the dirt-eaters declared, didn't need to fall down a well to get a drink of water.

A moment later, Bracca glided through the doorway. "What is it?"

Esskar jerked his head to the east. While his friend studied the crowd now only moments away, Esskar glanced around the rest of the village, searching for anything out of the ordinary, any sign of other danger drawing near to them. Both had learned to look to their backs when men carrying swords were present.

"No bows," Bracca commented, without turning his head.

Esskar grunted. If these villagers were coming for them, they would have brought weapons that could strike from a distance, and not a wailing woman or two. And a village with an elder as prosperous as this one would certainly have a few bows for his guards' use.

So it didn't seem likely that they intended to pick a quarrel with the two strangers. No amount of smiles or soft words could disguise the hard edge that accompanied Bracca's sturdy body, and Esskar's tall frame and frowning visage spoke for itself.

The little procession turned into the open space in front of the tavern, what Esskar knew would be called the marketplace, assuming that this insignificant village imitated the customs of larger and more prosperous settlements.

"Prisoner," Bracca muttered. "Looks like a public lashing."

By now Esskar could see the victim, disheveled, dirty, and with a dazed look in his eyes. His captors pushed him along every few steps, which kept the man stumbling from side to side, and provided more fodder for the guards' jests.

Blood trails showed down the left side of the man's face, and a large bruise covered his forehead. They hadn't bothered to tie his hands. In his exhausted and beaten condition, he offered no threat to anyone.

"Maybe." Eskkar didn't intend to relax just yet. The miserable existence of most dirt-eaters made them poor fighters, but what they lacked in courage and skill, they often made up in cunning. A seeming captive might be just a trick to get armed men within striking distance.

The leader of the band reached the center of the marketplace. A row of tall posts stood there, each one about five paces apart. On market day, farmers and the local craftsmen would fasten their blankets or long strips of cloth to these posts, to provide shade while they offered their wares. But Eskkar had no doubt the thick posts would work equally well for other purposes.

"Tie him up," the leader ordered.

A big man, Eskkar decided, one used to giving orders that were obeyed instantly and without question. Long dark hair grew down to the top of his powerful shoulders, and his neck looked like it might belong on an ox. Scraggly hair sprouted all over his face and bare chest, and a long scar crossed his right arm and shoulder.

Two of the guards bound the captive's hands, laughing as they did so, then shoved him face first against the center post. Another man passed a second rope between the prisoner's wrists, then threaded it through a notch near the top of the stake.

The guard pulled hard once, twice, and a third time, until the groaning man was stretched upright against the stake. What shreds remained of his tunic were ripped down from the neck, exposing the man's back.

"Don't think this involves us," Bracca muttered, as he joined Eskkar in leaning against the wall. At least they had a place out of the sun to watch the proceedings.

The leader noticed the two strangers, and he gave them a long appraising look before he snorted in disgust and turned back to his men. His booming voice carried throughout the marketplace, probably as he intended. "Make sure the rest of the village scum are here to watch the punishment. Get them out of their huts. The Elder said to make sure they learned their lesson."

Leaving the prisoner to his men, the leader headed for the tavern. Bracca had to move aside a half step to avoid the big man's right shoulder.

"I think he likes you," Eskkar said, once the man had passed inside. "Maybe he'll buy us some ale."

"Me, maybe," Bracca said. "Not you. You're too ugly."

"We should get out of here. Whenever villagers get their blood up, strangers are next on their list."

"Especially barbarians. Still, friend Eskkar, you may be right. I was hoping to stay another night here, but there's no work to be had. And without any coins, we'd be sleeping outside anyway, so we might as well be camping away from this dung heap."

The guards' shouts and commands summoned the rest of the villagers. By now anyone within earshot had spilled out of their huts and tents where they'd taken shelter from the heat of the day. They shuffled into the square, most with their heads downcast.

Studying their faces, Eskkar recognized the sullen yet helpless look he had seen many times in his travels. Men beaten down, again and again, until not even the strongest of them dared utter the slightest protest against their masters.

Before Eskkar and Bracca could start on their way, the leader of the guards stepped out of the tavern, a mug of ale in his hand and a thread of brown liquid on his chin. This time he took only a single stride, then turned to face the two men. "What's your business in Marcala?"

Eskkar found himself looking directly into the man's eyes, an unusual occurrence, as few dirt-eaters matched Eskkar's tall figure. The voice grated on his ears, but he kept his tongue in his head and his face impassive.

Bracca had no such problems, however. "We were looking for work, Master . . .?"

"I'm Dargo," he paused to take a sip of ale, "Chief Steward to Elder Tonnar-can."

"Master Dargo," Bracca used his best simpering tone and added a brief bow. "We're looking for work, but it appears there is none to be had in Marcala."

A broad smile crossed Dargo's face. "Plenty of work at the mine for any honest Sumerian, and even your outcast friend. You should go there and speak to the overseer. Tell them I sent you."

Bracca's slightly darker skin and features marked him as a man from this part of the countryside.

Bracca feigned lack of knowledge. "What mine is that, Master Dargo?"

Dargo snorted at their ignorance. "The gold mine, of course. The Marcala mine yields some of the finest gold in the land."

Eskkar had no intention of going anywhere near any mine, let alone one producing gold, the one metal that would drive even timid dirt-eaters to violence. Besides, only slaves worked in the mines, and then only as long as it took for the work to kill them. Most forced to labor under such conditions died in six months or so. Almost none survived more than a year.

Working deep in the pits and shafts, or tending the open furnaces that melted away the metal's impurities, the slaves knew their remaining days were numbered. Only men brutalized and beaten into submission could be forced into such an existence.

"I don't think we'd care to work in the pits, Master Dargo," Bracca said. "We're fighters, not laborers."

Dargo glanced at their weapons and ragged clothing, and snorted. He fixed his gaze on Eskkar. "Your barbarian friend doesn't say much. Is he too proud to work for his bread?"

"My companion is a little slow in the head, Master Dargo, but he knows how to fight."

"Neither of you will do any fighting in Marcala," Dargo said, giving his full attention once again to Bracca. "If you aren't interested in work at the mine, then be on your way. We don't like strangers in Marcala."

Bracca bowed again. "Yes, Master Dargo. We were just getting ready to leave."

A shout made Dargo turn his attention back to the marketplace. The empty space now swelled with villagers, probably fifty or sixty, no doubt close to the entire population of Marcala. They formed a ring around the prisoner, but left plenty of open space for the guards.

Without a word, Dargo walked away, to take charge of the prisoner's punishment.

"At least this time you didn't call me your servant, my good friend Bracca."

"You have no sense of humor." Bracca kept his voice low. "Still, Dargo seems like someone we should avoid."

"There's no fear in the man," Eskkar agreed. The hard eyes that had stared into his own promised plenty of strength, and the worn leather on the man's sword hilt told its own story.

"People of Marcala," Dargo's bellow carried through the square. "This man tried to steal a slave from the mine. The punishment for that crime, as Elder Tonnar-can has decreed, is death by the lash."

A wail of protest rose up. Eskkar saw two guards pushing their way through the crowd. One dragged a woman by the arm, while the other gripped a boy, maybe eight or nine seasons, by the back of the neck.

The woman screamed again, her body shaking as the guard shoved her to the ground. The boy cried out too, in pain from the guard's tight grip.

"Must be the prisoner's woman," Eskkar said. Most dirt-eaters preferred to have the victim's wives and families watch the execution. If the crime were serious enough, the family would be put to death first, while the prisoner watched and anticipated his own demise.

The woman scurried forward on her hands and knees, to fling her arms around the bound man's legs. "Please spare him! He only wanted to help our eldest son! Please don't kill him."

One of the guards grabbed her by the hair and wrenched her backwards, the tightness of his grip adding even more pain to her cries. "You'll have your turn soon enough, bitch, after we've had our fun."

The boy struggled, too, and tried to break free from his captor. But his guard, angered by the boy's struggles, jerked him around and smashed his fist into the tear-streaked face. The boy fell like a stone, blood gushing from his nose and mouth.

"Little bastard tried to bite me," the guard said. His foot lashed out, and the kick lifted the boy off the ground, before rolling him over. "He can follow his father on the post. He won't take long."

The other guards laughed.

"Let's get going." Eskkar pushed himself away from the wall. He'd seen enough executions to know what would follow. The prisoner would be whipped without mercy, his back cut to shreds by the plaited leather whip one of the guards carried, lashed until he sobbed and pleaded to the gods for death to take him.

The executioners would halt the pain just before that moment arrived, to force the dying man to watch the spectacle of his woman raped before his eyes. When they were finished taking her, the lashing would resume until the man's death moans filled his own ears.

The boy might survive his own beating, but even if he did, he would be maimed for life. With the scars of the whip on his back, he would be fit for nothing but a slave's existence.

Bracca didn't answer, an occurrence so infrequent that Eskkar turned to stare at his friend. Bracca's mouth showed a tight line, his eyes fixed on the men in the square. Eskkar recognized the look. He'd seen it often enough, usually right before Bracca shoved a sword into someone's belly.

The first smack of the lash on the helpless man's back wrenched a loud cry of surprise and pain from the prisoner's mouth.

Bracca growled something that Eskkar didn't catch.

"You're not thinking . . . there's nothing you can do," Eskkar said.

Bracca ignored him. He started forward, but Eskkar's hand caught his arm, the powerful grip halting his friend.

"Let me go." Bracca tried to shake his arm free, but Eskkar's grip remained tight.

The lash was in steady motion now, the strokes falling one after another, each accompanied by the man's cries of agony.

"Are you mad? We can't interfere . . ."

"Let go of my arm, barbarian. This is something I need to do. It doesn't concern you, so just get out of here."

More astonished than anything else, Eskkar's hand released, seemingly of its own accord. Bracca moved toward the crowd, loosening his sword in its scabbard as he went. Eskkar watched his companion push his way through the listless gathering of farmers.

For the briefest moment, Eskkar hesitated. This affair was none of Bracca's concern, let alone Eskkar's. Still, he couldn't let his friend go to his death. With a savage oath, Eskkar took a step forward. At the same time he lowered his right shoulder and slid the long sword from its well-oiled scabbard, holding it low at his side.

No one noticed. Every eye remained fixed on the spectacle in the center of the square.

By now Bracca had pushed through the ring of farmers, and moved into the cleared space around the post. He stopped when he reached the boy, lying stunned in the dirt, blood still trickling from his mouth. "I'll take the boy and his mother with me. Now."

The guard wielding the whip paused, his mouth open in shock. No one had ever raised a voice in protest, let alone dared to interfere, at any of the executions.

Dargo, standing on the other side of the clearing, reacted faster than his men. "You'll take nothing. If you're smart, you'll start running now, and hope I don't come after you."

"He's just a child. You don't need to whip him." Bracca reached down and lifted the boy up with his left hand. "Come with me, boy."

The boy's mother, prostrate on the ground, stared upward, her eyes wide with disbelief. She pushed herself to her knees.

The guard who'd kicked the boy was closest. He took a step toward Bracca, his hand reaching for his sword as he moved.

Bracca's sword flashed from its scabbard, a movement so fast that it blurred the eye. The point was thrust into the man's chest before the guard's own weapon cleared its scabbard.

"Stop!" Eskkar's bellow echoed through the marketplace, rising up over the gasp of astonishment from the spectators. The last of the villagers flinched aside as he stepped to the edge of the ring. The tip of his long sword hovered just above the ground, but the sight of the unfamiliar weapon drew every eye.

"There are four of you, and two of us," Eskkar said, putting all the power and strength he could into his voice. "You may take us down, but at least three of you will be dead. And I promise, the next man to draw a sword will be the first to die."

Dargo, his face white with anger and his hand on the hilt of his sword, twisted to face Eskkar. "You dare to interfere with the Elder's punishment? You'll both be sorry you were ever born."

"I doubt the Elder ordered the man's son put to death, or his wife raped," Bracca said. He was moving now with that combination of speed and smoothness that marked him as a dangerous opponent.

Bracca had the boy in one hand, and an instant later lifted up the woman. He backed them away from the post, and moved toward Eskkar's side. The few stunned villagers still lingering in the marketplace shrank aside as he moved through them.

Dargo and his three remaining men stood there. If Dargo gave the order, the men would draw their weapons and fight. But their leader had seen something he didn't like in Eskkar's eyes, and his sword remained in its scabbard.

Bracca moved past Eskkar, guiding the still crying woman, the boy now clutching one of her arms. "We're leaving this place," Bracca called out. "No need for anyone else to die."

Eskkar backed away as well, but moved toward the tavern, until he could grab his pack, still resting beside the tavern's wall. He never took his eyes off Dargo, and he kept the long bronze blade in his hand.

In moments they were moving down the lane and beyond the last of huts, taking the track that led to the west, opposite the direction Dargo and his men had come. Eskkar sheathed his sword. Behind them, the crack of the whip descending on the prisoner's back resumed.

Dargo obviously intended to finish the punishment he'd ordered before coming after them. The woman cried out at the sound and dragged her feet as she looked back toward the huts, but Bracca kept a firm grip on her arm, and by now she had no strength to either protest or resist.

Eskkar knew, as she did, that there was nothing they could do for her husband. If they had tried to free him, Dargo and his men would have fought to the death.

Even if Eskkar and Bracca had somehow managed to kill all of them, and were lucky enough to not have taken any serious wounds, the Elder would soon have a party of mounted men armed with bows tracking them down. That would still likely happen, Eskkar realized.

Taking one last look behind him, he settled his sword over his right shoulder, and shifted the pack to his left. A few quick strides brought him alongside Bracca.

"Where are we going?"

"I don't know." Bracca stared straight ahead.

Eskkar grunted. "Well, then we'll have no trouble getting there." Usually his friend couldn't stop himself from talking. Now Bracca had thrown a fit and gotten them into this mess, and for once he had nothing to say.

"We'll probably all be dead by nightfall," Eskkar muttered under his breath to no one in particular. He thought of himself tied to the post and whipped to death. He grimaced. Not likely, he resolved. They would have to kill him first.

21

Eskkar tried to set a fast pace, but the woman and her son slowed them down. Bracca, too, seemed willing to plod along. By themselves, Eskkar knew he and Bracca would have had a chance to reach the river, where they might have found a boat or possibly some horses to help them get away. Instead they stayed on the trail, the first place Dargo and his men would look for them.

Twice Eskkar tried to speak to Bracca, but the man refused to answer. He just kept moving, his face toward the west. He kept one arm around the woman's waist, helping her along.

Eskkar had never seen his friend like this. Some men, in the aftermath of a brutal fight, acted as if nothing mattered, not even whether they lived or died. No matter how hard or long the fighting, Eskkar had never experienced such emotions, nor had Bracca ever shown any reaction to killing. Besides, his friend hadn't even taken a scratch while cutting down the guard, which made his actions all the more unusual.

The woman, her eyes glazed with grief, hadn't spoken a word since leaving the village. Her boy kept silent, too, but the blow to his face probably accounted for that. Since Eskkar couldn't think of anything to say, the four of them trudged along in silence.

Eskkar, leading the way, kept glancing behind every few steps, though he knew the dirt-eaters couldn't have organized a pursuit this fast. Besides, Dargo and his men had no need to rush. Burdened with the woman and a boy, Dargo knew Eskkar and Bracca wouldn't get very far. Eskkar swore at the situation, but couldn't stop himself from looking to the rear.

Soon enough the woman and boy began to stumble more and more, as they grew tired from the fast pace. By this time the four had traveled almost a mile from Marcala, and the village had disappeared behind a curve in the trail. Eskkar knew they needed a new plan, or they would be dead by sundown.

"Stop! This isn't going to work." Eskkar planted his feet and waited.

Bracca paid no heed, and kept walking. They left Eskkar standing there, but before they had taken twenty paces, the woman's knees buckled, despite Bracca's help. She sank to the ground, wrapping both arms around her son. Bracca took another few steps, then stopped. He kept his face to the west.

"We can't keep going on." Eskkar kept his voice calm, as he walked forward to join them. Bracca's face, usually so expressive, now looked as if it had been carved from wood. He still remained under whatever evil spell had driven him to his rash act. Eskkar decided shouting at him would be a waste of time.

"By now the guards have finished with the whipping, and her man is dead." No one turned to face him, but Eskkar went on, as if he had Bracca's full attention. "They'll head back to the Elder's farm, to gather more men and horses. They won't let the death of one of their men go unavenged. Well before sundown they'll run us down, and when they come they'll have bows with them to finish us off. We're dead if we don't leave these two here and run for it."

Bracca turned to face his companion, but didn't lift his eyes. "I'm not leaving them to that filth."

The words sounded cold, final. Before Eskkar could think of a reply, the woman spoke.

"I can't . . . I won't go any further." Her voice choked, and for a moment, she couldn't speak. "My other son is still a slave at the mine. I must try to help him."

He saw Bracca glance at the woman kneeling in the dust. Weariness showed on his face, or maybe it was some other emotion. Eskkar couldn't be sure. He, too, looked down at the woman. Maybe she could make Bracca's wits return. "What is your name?"

She lifted her head, as if seeing Eskkar for the first time. Blood stained her cheek and her garment, some of it her own, the rest from the boy's face. "My name is Ninamar."

She stroked her son's head. "This is Ubara. Hanish is my oldest son, named after his father. He's still at the mine."

Eskkar dropped his sack. "Well, Ninamar, your man is dead by now. And soon Dargo and his men will be coming for us. They'll kill Bracca and me. You know what they'll do to you and your boy."

She nodded. "Yes, my husband is dead. His body will hang from the post until the morning, covered in flies, and the birds will peck out his eyes. Only then will the people be allowed to cut him down and bury his body."

Her lip trembled, but no more tears flowed. "What can I do to save my sons?"

Eskkar glanced at Bracca, but the man remained rooted where he stood, as if incapable of thought. Eskkar realized that Bracca didn't intend to leave the woman, and unless Eskkar was willing to abandon his friend, they had to find another way. He tried to make his words reasonable.

"Well, we can't just stand here in the middle of the trail. We need a place to hide until after dark. Someplace where they won't find us."

Ninamar shook her head. "They'll find us. They always do. No one's run away from Marcala or the mine in years."

Of course dirt-eaters like Ninamar lived in fear all their lives, terrified of a few men with swords. Still, a pack of wolves could bring down even a lion. And these wolves would be riding horses and carrying bows.

A glimmer of an idea came to him. Eskkar slung his sack back onto his shoulder, then reached down and picked up the boy . . . Ubara.

"Come. First we'll go a few hundred paces north, just to get off the trail, then we'll double back toward the village. If we move now, we might just make it back to Marcala."

"Back there!" Ninamar's eyes widened in fear. "But that's where Dargo will start hunting us."

"I don't think so. He and his men have seen us go down the trail. He'll follow us, then start searching for tracks when he doesn't catch up with us. Hopefully by then it will be dark. We'll find a place to hide for the night, just outside the village, until we figure out what to do next."

Ninamar pushed herself upright. "It matters little which direction we go, I suppose."

Eskkar lifted Ubara onto his shoulder and started moving. As long as he had the boy, he knew Ninamar would follow. He heard the sound of her bare feet shuffling after him. Eskkar extended his hand, and she clasped it.

He left the trail and led the way north, choosing rocky ground that should leave no trace of their passage. Even if their pursuers did notice the place where their quarry had turned away from the trail, Eskkar hoped Dargo and his men would think the fugitives had decided to make a run for the river.

He didn't look back. Either Bracca was following behind, or he wasn't. After about four hundred paces, Eskkar changed direction toward the east, keeping the trail on his right side. He was now moving back toward the village, but on a path parallel to the one they had followed in their flight. He counted on Dargo not expecting his quarry to double back to Marcala.

Hopefully, Eskkar would see Dargo's men on the trail before they saw him. Their pursuers would be mounted, and the horses should kick plenty of dust into the air.

For now the trail from Marcala remained empty. He glanced behind him, and saw Bracca trailing twenty paces behind. Good. At least the man had not lost all of his wits.

Still, Eskkar felt satisfied that he'd stopped his friend's headlong flight. Sooner or later Bracca would return to his senses. Until then, they needed some luck. It might take Dargo a good amount of time to collect what men and weapons he needed for the chase.

If the fugitives could elude their pursuers and reach one of Marcala's outlying farms, they would have the entire night to figure out what to do next. One problem at a time, Eskkar decided. He knew one thing – that if they'd kept walking west, they would have been dead before the sun went down.

Now that he had a goal, Eskkar pushed the pace. He kept the boy on his shoulder, but shrugged the pack off and let it drop, knowing that Bracca would pick it up.

The fast pace soon had the woman stumbling again, but he pulled her along. She did her best to keep up with him. The events of the day had exhausted her, but she refused to let Eskkar get too far ahead with her son.

The pull on his arm went slack. Bracca had closed the gap and again placed his arm around her waist, helping her keep up. Eskkar grunted at the sight. Let his friend struggle with the pack and the woman.

The boy on Eskkar's shoulder wasn't getting any lighter. Besides, Bracca had gotten them into this mess. Perhaps the physical effort would clear his thoughts.

Despite their faster pace, the trip back took longer, as they made every effort to keep out of sight. None of the villagers could be trusted. At least one or two would be glad to take a coin from Dargo for spotting the fugitives. Fortunately, because the guards had swept the nearby farms to make sure everyone witnessed the Elder's punishment, the fields were still deserted. Eskkar saw no one working the crops or irrigation ditches.

He doubted that any of the inhabitants would be eager to return to their labors this late in the day, not with the excitement of both an execution and the killing of a guard to gossip about. Even after Dargo finished off Ninamar's husband and departed, the people of Marcala would likely stand around and jabber among themselves before returning to their huts.

A few would have traded with the tavern owner for a mug or two of ale. Eskkar knew they would speak of little else for the next few moons.

Whatever kept the fields empty, the four of them made it to the outskirts of Marcala before they saw the first group of farmers leaving the village and returning to their homes. Eskkar and his little party, now about five hundred paces north of the village, dropped to the ground and crawled on hands and knees until they made it to the safety of one of the deeper irrigation ditches. They slipped over the top and down into the trench.

Even then, Eskkar didn't stop. He led the way, splashing through the water and staying in the center of the channel. The water reached their knees, and slowed their progress, but they kept moving. The ditch's walls were nearly half as tall as a man.

When they were due north of Marcala, they halted and hugged the ground. No one would see them unless they walked up and glanced into the channel.

On his stomach, Eskkar pushed aside the tall grass and peered over the top of the ditch and watched the last handful of farmers leave the tavern and market. One couple, a man and his wife, crossed within a hundred paces of the hidden group but didn't notice their presence. After that, Eskkar saw no one, except a few people moving in and out of the tavern.

The sun had just passed mid afternoon before he heard the rumble of horses. Lifting his head, Eskkar saw a cloud of dust that turned into a band of nine riders approaching the village from the east, the direction of the Elder's house.

Dargo, recognizable even at a distance, rode at their head. Four of his men carried bows, each with a fat quiver of arrows. They swept through the village at an easy canter and continued down the west trail, as if certain of running down their prey before darkness fell.

Eskkar watched until they disappeared, then slid down into the ditch. Neither Bracca nor the woman had shown the slightest interest in what might be coming toward them.

"Dargo and eight others rode west. They'll be searching for us." He fixed his gaze on Bracca. "If we're going to survive this, we need to find some horses. The only place I know that might have a few left is the Elder's gold mine."

Ninamar gasped at the idea. "We can't go there! He has many guards. They will kill us for sure."

"No, most of the guards have just left. With luck, we can get in and out before they return. They may not even return tonight, if they think we've trying to reach the river. They'll want to pick up our trail at first light."

He turned to Bracca. "If you're not willing to help, you can stay here with the woman and the boy. I'll steal a horse for myself and be gone. They probably won't even come after me, once they have you and Ninamar staked out in the marketplace. After all, you're the one that killed the guard."

Bracca lifted his gaze. He'd said nothing since they reached the ditch. "You didn't have to get involved. I would have finished the guards off . . ."

"You think you could have taken Dargo by yourself, with three of his men at your back?" Eskkar snorted. "You'd have been dead if I hadn't stepped in."

Bracca's jaw clenched, and Eskkar saw rage on the man's face, the first time he'd shown any emotion since they left Marcala.

"Neither of you should have helped me," Ninamar said, speaking quickly to break the tension. "None of us can defy the Elder. Even the gods forbid it. I should have watched my husband die in silence. Now my foolishness will bring death to you both, as well as me and my son."

She clutched the boy to her bosom. "My other boy will die as a slave in the mine."

Villagers and their stupid beliefs. They thought their many gods ruled every aspect of their daily lives, that everything bad that happened to them was foreordained. If a man tripped over a stick in his path, he blamed an offended god extracting punishment for some offense.

Dirt-eaters feared changing the smallest part of their daily routine for the same reason, that it might offend some vengeful and watchful god. As if the gods had nothing more important to do than stare at ignorant farmers slopping the animals. Sheep being led to slaughter saw the world more clearly than they did.

"As soon as it gets dark, I'm going to the mine." Eskkar kept his voice calm. "Ninamar, will you guide me there? If you can ride, I can steal a horse for you and your boy, too."

Eskkar saw her shake her head, as he knew she would. No farmer's wife sweating for enough to eat in the fields would ever have had the chance to ride a horse.

"I can't ride," Ninamar said. "But I will guide you, if you promise to take Ubara with you. I don't care about myself, but now Dargo will kill him, too."

Eskkar didn't really need her to take him to the mine. He knew more or less where it was, and a place that large would be impossible to miss, even after dark. The guards would likely keep some fires burning throughout the night. All the same, by offering to help the boy, his mother would do as Eskkar asked. Hopefully, that would bring Bracca along as well. And if it didn't, and Bracca stayed behind, Eskkar could just abandon mother and son along the way, if they proved a burden. "I'll take him with me."

Bracca moved toward them, until he stood beside the woman. "We'll all go. We'll steal at least two horses, and then run for it. I'm not leaving them behind."

Eskkar concealed his satisfaction. "Good. Then that's settled. We'll move out as soon as the sun sets."

By the time darkness fell, he expected Bracca to return to his senses. Once his friend had a horse between his legs, the woman and her fate would mean little to him. Eskkar let himself slump against the side of the ditch. Already he was covered with mud. "Everyone better get some rest. We'll need all our strength when we get to the mine."

The sun sank slowly toward the horizon. No one spoke, but the same thought remained in each mind. If Dargo and his men were skillful enough to find the place where the fugitives had turned off the trail and picked up their tracks, the horsemen might appear at any moment.

Bracca sat down a few paces away, his feet splashing in the muddy stream of water that filled the center of the irrigation channel. Ninamar clutched her son to her bosom, rocking back and forth. The boy, Ubara, had regained his wits, but said nothing, just kept his eyes fastened on Eskkar.

To break the silence, Eskkar moved beside the woman. He forced himself to smile at the boy and pat him clumsily on the head. "Tell me about the mine, Ninamar."

"What do you want to know?"

He shrugged. It didn't really matter that much. However many guards, however difficult to reach the horses, assuming any remained, whatever the obstacles, they had to find a way in. They would almost certainly have to fight their way out.

Still, maybe Ninamar could provide something useful. And it might help break Bracca out of his silent gloom. "We haven't seen this place. Describe it for us."

She clutched her son tighter. "I hate the mine. For years I went there each morning, bringing fresh bread and whatever vegetables we could spare for the guards. Many of the other farmers did the same. We earned a few extra copper coins every month. Sometimes my husband or our oldest son, Hamish, came with me, to help carry the food."

Her voice faltered for a moment. "Then one day, about two moons ago, just when Hanish, my son, not his father, had finished delivering our goods, Dargo and two of his men walked over to us."

She told the story, slowly at first, but soon the memory came rushing back, and her words came faster. Apparently too many slaves had died in the last few days. Dargo needed more miners so he seized young Hanish, who had fourteen seasons. That made him more than old enough to do a man's work in the mine.

Dargo, however, claimed that Hanish had attempted to steal nuggets from the site, and the penalty for that was to labor there for one year. Dangling his leather whip from his hand, Dargo also suggested that unless Ninamar wished to join their son, she should leave now. Dargo's laughing guards drove Ninamar from the site, sobbing at the loss of her son.

Seeking justice, the next day she and her husband left their farm and walked to the house of the Village Elder. They begged for a chance to see the Elder, but he refused even to speak with them. His servants threatened to beat them if they ever returned.

"Since that day, my husband twice went back to the mine after dark, to sneak in and give food to our son. They don't give the slaves much to eat. That's one reason they die so soon. Last night, when my husband tried to bring food in once more, Dargo's guards caught him."

Eskkar grunted in surprise at her man's courage. He hadn't expected any villager to show such daring. Most farmers treated their sons as hardly more than slaves forced to labor on the land. Girls were valued even less, often sold for little more than a goat or a few chickens.

Regardless, the father had twice succeeded in getting into the mine, which meant it could be done. "Do you know how your man entered the site?"

"Yes. There is a path that leads to the river. A ditch carries water to the mine, so that they can wash away the impurities in the ores. My husband swung around to the far side, and followed the ditch into the camp."

Well, as long as there was a way in, there should be a way out. "Tell me what the mine looks like, where they keep the horses, where the guards sleep – tell me everything. I want to see the place in my mind."

By the time Ninamar finished, the sun had touched the horizon, and Bracca had drawn close, the better to hear the woman's low-pitched words. Eskkar climbed back up to the top of the channel and studied the land.

He let his eyes rove back and forth, from far to near, examining each section until he satisfied himself that Dargo's horsemen had not found the trail. Soon it would be too dark to track fugitives anyway. The moment night fell, Eskkar intended to be on his way toward the mine.

As he finished his sweep, he heard a rasping sound coming from behind him. Eskkar smiled to himself. He didn't need to turn to identify the noise. Bracca's sharpening stone had a sound all its own. His friend might not have shaken loose from what-ever demons possessed him, but Eskkar knew Bracca was ready to kill.

They moved out, traveling in single file, with Bracca bringing up the rear. The moon was nearly full, and gave just enough light to guide their way. The brief respite had given the woman and boy some strength, and both managed to follow Eskkar's tall shadow through the deepening gloom.

Nevertheless, it took some time before they reached the mine, and even longer to swing around to the far side of the site, where the water channel entered the camp.

Eskkar settled down on his stomach and stared at the mine, less than a hundred paces away. As he expected, two small fires burned, providing enough light to get a feel for the place.

He'd also expected to see a fence encircling the gold mine, or at least the slave quarters, but thankfully there was none. Eskkar picked out the corral, and clamped his lip. There were no animals within. If the corral held a few horses, they would have a chance to make their escape. Without the horses . . .

He shifted his position and looked toward the east. A red glow about six hundred paces away and against the side of a hill marked a third fire.

"That's the Elder's house," Ninamar said, following his gaze.

"Do they keep the fire lit all night long?"

"I don't know," she said. "I've only been there the one time, when my husband and I tried to see the Elder about my son."

Eskkar swore under his breath. Another dirt-eater who lived her whole life within a mile or two of the Elder's house, but knew nothing about it. Not that it mattered. That's where they'd find horses, if any were to be had.

There would be guards there, too, but perhaps not as many, and probably not as alert. Slip in, slit a few throats, grab a pair of horses. Nothing would be gained here at the mine trying to rescue Ninamar's son, and wasting their one chance at surprise.

No one spoke while Eskkar pondered the situation. "We should head for the Elder's house," he said, breaking a long silence, "to get horses . . ."

"No." Bracca's voice sounded hard. "We'll get the boy first, then go for the horses. Once you have a horse between your legs, you might not want to come back to rescue the boy."

Eskkar ignored the slur. But something in Bracca's tone told Eskkar that his friend, too, had come to the same conclusion about their chances of success. And yet he refused to give up on the idea of rescuing Ninamar's son.

"If we get the boy," Eskkar said patiently, "but don't have the horses, we'll never get away. Don't forget Dargo and his men might come back here at any moment."

"I'm not forgetting them," Bracca said. "Ninamar and I will get the boy. You get the horses, and meet us halfway between the mine and the Elder's house."

Eskkar opened his mouth, then closed it again. There wasn't enough light to see Bracca's face clearly, but Eskkar knew Bracca was offering Eskkar another chance to escape. One man might be able to slip in, grab a mount and slip out before the Elder's guards gathered their wits.

Bracca must know his rage had brought this trouble on them, and he was prepared to take the consequences. Alone.

"You might kill the mine's guards by yourself," Eskkar said, "you might even get the boy out of the hut, but you'll never get away."

"I'll do it," Bracca answered. "You just get the horses."

Ninamar put her hand on Eskkar's arm. "Listen to your friend," she said, unable to keep the sadness from her voice. "I'll stay with Bracca, and bring out my son. Then we'll meet you halfway. I only ask that you take Ubara with you."

Even she knew if Eskkar got a horse, he wouldn't be coming back. Despite the darkness, neither of them looked at him.

Eskkar thought hard about what they were saying. Both were willing to face death, Ninamar to try and save her oldest son, and Bracca for some still unknown reason. Yet both were trying to give him a way out, one that didn't conflict with his barbarian code of honor.

Nonetheless, he would be leaving his friend to die as surely as if Eskkar put a blade through his heart. Bracca had saved Eskkar's life at least twice, and he had done the same for Bracca. Still, Eskkar knew death would take them all if they went after the boy.

I should go. It was the right choice, Eskkar knew. Unbidden, the words of his father entered his mind. *Never leave a friend behind. Those that do forfeit all honor.* Eskkar hadn't thought of his father in some time, yet now Hogarthak's words rang in his mind as fresh as the day he spoke them.

Eskkar knew he couldn't leave Bracca behind. Since his friend remained determined to help Ninamar rescue her son, that meant they had to free the boy before they escaped.

There had to be another way. They would need time to get the boy and then reach the Elder's house. But there wouldn't be enough time, not with the whole of the camp at their heels. Not unless . . . they needed something to take the guards' minds off the boy. Perhaps there was a way to accomplish both.

He turned his gaze back to the mine. Eskkar counted three mud huts, two of them of a good size, inside the camp. Other structures jutted up from the ground, like bones on a skeleton. Those would be the sluices, troughs, and beams to lift and move the heavy earth.

"What's in the huts, Ninamar?"

"The large one, they call it the pen, that's where the slaves sleep. There are usually about forty or so working at the mine."

The hut didn't look large enough to hold half that number. Eskkar guessed the slaves would be jammed in shoulder to shoulder and head to toe. The stench from so many men would be unbearable, and they would have to relieve themselves wherever they lay.

"Why don't they slip out at night and run?"

"The hut has only two windows, both too small even for a child to slip through," Ninamar said. "And the door is made of thick planks and braced with a beam to keep it closed after the slaves are herded in. Two guards watch the slaves at night."

"Are there any other guards?" Eskkar asked.

"Two more walk through the mine, making sure no one slips in to steal a handful of nuggets. Another ten or twelve guards sleep in the other hut, or when it's hot, on the roof. The third hut is for the workers who supervise the slaves."

Eskkar frowned. Four standing guards would make any effort difficult. Still, these were soft villagers, and might not be alert. "How did your husband get food to . . . Hanish?"

"He crawled around to the back of the hut, put his head in the opening, and whispered Hanish's name as loud as he dared. Then he passed the food through the window. That's how he got caught. That time the slaves inside started fighting over the food, and the guards heard the noise and captured my husband before he could escape."

Eskkar frowned. One shout, that's all it would take, and close to fifteen men would be reaching for weapons, despite allowing for the eight that Dargo had taken with him. The mine, he decided, held nothing but danger.

Even if he and Bracca killed the guards, by the time they pried open the door, fumbled through the slaves to find Ninamar's son, and tried to get away, the whole place would be on their heads. The few moments of confusion resulting from the guards' death wouldn't last.

The silence had stretched out for some while before Eskkar spoke. "No, I've got another way to get your son out. Suppose instead of trying to just free Hamish, we break open the hut and let out all the slaves. Will they run?"

Ninamar squeezed Eskkar's arm at this glimmer of hope. "Yes! They'll take any chance to escape. The worse they can expect is another beating before they're sent back to work. Even if a few are killed, it wouldn't matter."

"Good." Eskkar felt a weight slip from his shoulders at the decision. The odds were still long against them, but he wouldn't, couldn't, leave Bracca behind.

One idea after another raced into Eskkar's thoughts. The plan might not work, but at least they would have a chance. Or so he hoped. "Which way will they run? Back toward the village?"

"I suppose so. Many have kin there."

Eskkar grunted in satisfaction. "We'll need to make sure that they do."

22

They took turns sleeping, or trying to sleep, for the rest of the night. Eskkar's thoughts stayed fixed on the Elder's horses. They remained the key to the plan, and since Eskkar had no intention of galloping a horse through the countryside in the middle of the night, no matter how full the moon, he and Bracca decided to wait until just before dawn to strike.

Eskkar went over how he thought the attack should go. Bracca, thanks be to the gods, decided to forget whatever demons had driven him, and came up with two useful ideas. At least his friend's wits had returned from the madness that possessed him, and none too soon.

As the moon began to dip toward the horizon, the two men and Ninamar worked their way down to the edge of the stream. Although they left the boy behind, he had a role as lookout, to make sure no one from the Elder's house approached them unseen.

By now Eskkar had watched the guards make their rounds of the camp several times, so the three of them knew when to creep down to the edge of the mine. Bracca handed his sword to Eskkar and took the lead, carrying only his knife.

They reached the edge of the mine, and flattened themselves against the ground. Bracca, knife in hand, crawled ahead ten or fifteen paces, crouched down behind a pile of rubble, and waited.

The moon shifted in the sky before the lazy sentry wandered into view, his careless footsteps sounding loud in the quiet night. He strolled along, no doubt thinking that soon his watch would end with the coming sun, and he'd be able to get some sleep. From the deep shadows, Eskkar watched him approach, knowing that the man would be dead in moments.

The guard stepped past the rock pile. Bracca rose up without a sound and struck from behind, one hand clamped over the man's mouth to stop his death scream, while the other plunged the knife into the guard's back.

Eskkar started moving even before Bracca's second thrust went home. He helped Bracca ease the still-twitching body to the ground. Eskkar removed the dead man's sword, leaving it in the scabbard, and handed the weapon to Ninamar, who joined them as soon as she saw the guard go down.

"Take this. You may need it."

He returned Bracca's sword, too. They moved quickly through the darkness, heading for the small fire that still glowed just twenty paces or so from the plank door securing the slaves. There two men sat side by side on a rough bench, close to the fire, which crackled softly.

Again Bracca led the way, his feet making no sound loud enough to be heard over the little noises that came from the flames. He was within four or five paces before one of the guards heard or sensed something and glanced over his shoulder. His mouth opened in surprise, but by then Bracca had covered the distance and thrust his sword deep into the man's throat.

Eskkar, only a step behind, lunged forward with his long sword. The blade slipped underneath the second guard's raised arm. Driven home with all the strength in Eskkar's powerful arm, the sword penetrated the man's chest and passed right through him. With a gasp of surprise, the man sank to the ground, dead before he sprawled out in the dirt.

Eskkar jerked at the blade, but it remained stuck fast, and he had to use his foot and both hands to wrench the weapon free.

Bracca, already moving toward the door, hissed a single word over his shoulder. "Go!"

Ninamar rose from the shadows and ran toward them. She reached the stack of wood standing beside the fire, and started shoving pieces of wood into the flames. The pile of wood, one of several scattered about the site to maintain the smelting fires, was dry as the desert sand from the sun's heat. The fresh fuel caught quickly, and the fire began to grow, its light spreading ever wider.

Eskkar trotted across the mine, taking care to avoid tripping on some obstacle, until he reached the hut where the rest of the guards slept. No door here, just a torn blanket hanging askew.

The doorway didn't face the fire directly, and Eskkar saw that the left side of the entrance remained in the shadows. From within, he heard the various wheezes and gurgles as the guards snored contentedly.

He moved into that darkness and waited. His heart raced, as it always did before a fight. Blood would be spilled, but Eskkar didn't intend for any of it to be his.

Things started happening fast now. The other guard watching the perimeter would be wondering what had delayed his companion's return. Sooner or later he would come to investigate.

From the slave pen behind him, Eskkar heard the sounds of Bracca fumbling with the beam, wedged between the door and the thick mud wall, that kept the slaves imprisoned. While the noise seemed to Eskkar loud enough to wake a hundred guards, it didn't carry far enough to disturb the men sleeping just beyond the hut's blanket.

At last Bracca forced out the beam. With a loud rasp, he dragged the door open. Eskkar took one last look at his friend. Ninamar stood beside the door, and Bracca had shoved his head inside. His voice bellowed into the dim interior. "Slaves! Get up! Get up! You're free. Run! RUN!"

Eskkar slipped his knife from his belt with his left hand. The tip of his sword rested on the ground. Bracca's shouts, loud enough to waken even the most exhausted mine rat, had the slaves up and moving about, jabbering at each other, even if they weren't quite sure what was happening. Still the first one stumbled through the door, looking dazed.

Ninamar grabbed his arm and shouted. "Run for it! Head for the village! Run!" She pushed the man in the direction of the village.

Another man followed the first slave, breaking into a run as soon as he realized he was free. Bracca took up the cry, shouting at every slave who emerged from the slave pen to run for the village. Ninamar's task was to grab her son when he appeared, and take him in the opposite direction.

By then, Eskkar had no more time to worry about Bracca or the woman. The blanket jerked aside, and a man stepped into the doorway, a sword in his hand. With his eyes fixed on the slaves' quarters, he never saw Eskkar standing in the gloom just to the side of the entrance.

Eskkar's sword flashed up and buried itself in the man's stomach. Not a killing stroke, since Eskkar wanted the man alive and screaming. His sharp cries of agony echoed into the night, and had every man inside on his feet. The wounded man dropped his sword and staggered forward before falling to the ground.

A second guard was already in the doorway, and Eskkar used his knife on that one's face, putting all the force of his arm into the thrust. That man went backwards, crashing into those behind him, adding his howls to the shouts and curses that echoed from behind the blanket.

Eskkar moved closer to the side of the door. The men inside tried to peer out, but all they could see was the growing fire, now crackling and snapping, as it sent its flames into the night. The shadows beside the door remained as black as the hut's interior.

Voices rose from within, and men shouted, trying to be heard. No one took command, and the guards, still half asleep, hadn't yet realized that only one man stood outside to bar their passage. They only knew that two men had tried to pass through the door, and both had been attacked.

The man Eskkar had stabbed in the face kept on screaming, his cries if anything louder than the curses of his companions, and adding to the confusion.

Eskkar risked a glance toward the slave pen. The fire's light revealed a stream of men issuing from the hut, urged along by Bracca and the woman, all of them heading in the direction of the village.

A bench, held upright, appeared in the doorway, and Eskkar turned his attention back to the guards. They were using it as a shield. He didn't waste time trying to stab at the man or men holding it.

Instead, he used his foot against the rough wood, unleashing a mighty kick that sent the bench and those holding it back into the hut. A muffled moan came from behind the bench. Eskkar moved closer to the doorway. He thrust his sword twice into the gloom, the second effort eliciting another cry of pain.

Eskkar risked another glance behind him. He didn't know how much longer he could keep the guards inside. They must have at least one bow and a quiver of arrows in there, and sooner or later, one of them was going to remember it, though stringing a bow in the dark was no easy feat.

Bracca's voice carried across the clearing. "Eskkar! Time to go!"

Eskkar bellowed his clan's war cry, a bone-chilling shout that would frighten any dirt-eater. He thrust his sword into the room, jabbing it in every direction. Whether it was the war cry or the sword glimmering in the fire light, his blade met no resistance.

Then he turned and ran, chasing after Bracca, and even farther ahead, the woman and another figure lurching along. Good. Ninamar had found her son.

The four of them ran through the darkness, leaving behind confusion and chaos. With luck, the guards would chase after the fleeing slaves. The camp fire, stoked by the extra wood Ninamar had heaped on it, now boasted flames that rose higher than a man.

They reached the place where they had left Ubara, but never stopped. The boy joined them, and soon they were all breathing hard from running on the sandy ground. Still, they kept going, halting only when Ninamar and her rescued son stumbled and slid to the ground, exhausted.

Eskkar glanced behind at the mine, then ahead toward the Elder's house. In their mad dash from the mine, they'd covered about a third of the way there. Aside from the same small glow that marked the watch fire, he saw no sign of any activity. If their luck held, they'd be able to reach the Elder's house before the guards there had any warning.

"Bracca, let's keep going. The others can catch up and wait for us at . . ."

A drum started beating behind them, each stroke echoing out through the darkness, and loud enough to warn the Elder's guards that something was amiss.

"Damn the gods. They'll be waiting for us."

"Maybe not," Bracca said. "It's probably a signal that something is wrong at the mine."

"Yes, that's the drum they use when a slave escapes," Ninamar said.

Eskkar growled at that bit of information. It would have been nice to know about the drum in advance. They might have been able to toss it onto the fire. Still, it made no difference now. "Let's go. We'll have to keep our eyes open for anyone coming from the Elder's house."

Another glance at the Elder's residence showed the glow from the fire there had increased, sending flames into the night. They started running, moving slower than in their headlong flight from the mine, but still covering the ground at a rapid pace. Before long, they were only a hundred paces from their goal.

Up ahead, a gate screeched open.

"Get down!" Bracca's voice sent all five of them to their knees, hugging a gentle swell in the land.

Eskkar saw a torch bobbing in the air, moving in a wavering line as its bearer ran toward them. "Stay low and keep silent!"

He tugged his sword from its scabbard, then cursed himself for forgetting to wipe the blade before he'd sheathed it. The weapon finally came loose.

Eskkar lifted his head just enough to see three men, one carrying the torch, running toward him. He tightened his grip on the sword's hilt.

Then he realized that the guards were not coming straight at him. They were following a well-worn track that led from the mine to the house. Eskkar and his companions would have crossed it in a few more paces, but they'd come in a direct line from the mine. The path probably meandered between the two sites, following the easiest ground.

With muttered curses at whatever foul luck had ruined their sleep, the three men raced by. The moment they were out of hearing, Bracca, his white teeth gleaming in the moonlight, moved to Eskkar's side.

"That's three less to worry about."

"Should make things easier," Eskkar agreed.

"Regardless, the Elder will keep most of his guards close by, and all of them will be awake now."

Eskkar's grin went unseen in the darkness. His friend sounded more like his usual self, always ready for a fight. "In that case, we'd better swing around and approach from the north. The guards will be looking toward the mine now."

They made their way behind the compound, hugging the shadows and taking advantage of the uneven ground. Soon they were far from the track and at the rear of the cluster of houses. Eskkar took a moment to identify what had to be the Elder's personal dwelling, a large, rambling structure quite visible over the man-high wall surrounding it.

The wall didn't concern Eskkar. He and Bracca could scale it easily enough. All the same, it would help if something distracted the guards long enough for the two of them to climb over it.

"Ninamar, you'll have to help. I want you to move back toward the main entrance, and start screaming. Take your sons with you. Cry for help, say you've been hurt. Just make plenty of noise and keep it up until we're inside. Can you do it?"

"Yes." She clutched the sword she had carried all the way from the mine. "But they'll come out for us."

"Not for a woman crying," Bracca said. "They'll wait until daylight for that. And we won't be long. Go now. We don't have much time. Dawn's almost here."

Eskkar looked toward the east. It remained dark, but the faintest hint of a band of gray marked the coming of the morning sun. "Let's go."

Without waiting for a reply, he started toward the wall. Even if Ninamar didn't help, he and Bracca needed to scale the barrier and get to the horses as quickly as possible. They moved quietly into the shadows at the base of the wall. Eskkar could hear the sounds of men moving about, some shouting orders. Then he heard the whinny of an excited horse.

A moment later a dog started barking, a loud, fierce sound that told Eskkar he would have more than men to deal with.

Off to their right, Ninamar's first scream cut through the darkness. "Help! Help me! I'm hurt."

The dog barked even louder, and another joined in. "Damn the gods. I hate dogs." Eskkar couldn't wait any longer. He slid the sword into his scabbard, straightened up, and jumped for the top of the wall.

For a moment he hung there, pulling himself up by his fingertips just enough to see over the top. A quick glance to the left and right showed no one near, but a crowd of men were moving toward the main entrance about sixty paces away.

"It's clear," he hissed. Eskkar pulled his body up even further, hooked an elbow over the rough edge, and then rolled his leg over the top. Without stopping, he let himself fall to the ground, narrowly missing a cart standing beside the wall.

Bracca, considerably shorter than Eskkar, took a few more moments to drag himself over the top. He, too, almost tumbled into the cart, but managed to twist to the side. He landed awkwardly, one hand steadying himself on its thick wheel.

A vicious growling turned Eskkar's eyes back toward the interior. A dog as large as any wolf was hurtling toward them. He didn't bother to rise, just whipped the sword from over his shoulder. Eskkar held it out, not point first, but with the blade passing across his chest. At the same time, he drew his knife with his left hand and tightened his grip.

The dog, growling even louder, ignored the long edge of the blade glinting in the firelight. He launched himself at Eskkar, who kept the sword level with the beast's mouth, a trick his father had taught him.

Bared teeth snapped on the thick bronze, and he felt the shock of the charge on his arm. At the same instant Eskkar drove his knife upwards into the dog's now exposed throat.

The heavy animal's momentum, its yellow teeth still clenched on the sword blade, knocked Eskkar back against the wall even as it choked to death on its own blood.

By the time Eskkar got to his feet, Bracca was ten long strides away, heading for the corral. A shout rang out, and Eskkar saw a man pointing at Bracca and yelling something incomprehensible. Another dog appeared out of the shadows and sprang toward Eskkar.

He had only an instant to prepare. Even so, for a big man, Eskkar could move fast when he needed to. The moment the dog was in the air, he shifted to the right and swung the sword down.

The long fangs snapped closed on empty air, and an instant later, Eskkar's sharp blade struck the middle of the animal's spine with a loud crunch. The beast howled in pain, and he knew he'd crippled it.

When he turned back to the compound, Bracca had disappeared.

Swearing, Eskkar raced toward the corral, hoping there were no more damned dogs ready to spring at him out of the darkness. A man might show hesitation at Eskkar's size and bulk, but these massive brutes lacked any sense of fear and would tear apart a stranger in their midst.

Clutching his sword and running hard, Eskkar reached the corner of a building, and slammed into another man coming from the opposite direction. Both men rebounded from the jarring collision, but Eskkar's shoulder had caught the shorter man in the face, and he staggered for a moment. The long sword whipped through the air, striking deep into the guard's left arm before he could defend himself.

A shriek of pain accompanied the stroke, but Eskkar was already running, leaving the wounded man in his wake. The faster Eskkar moved, the less likely anyone would catch him from behind.

The corral stood twenty paces away, and Eskkar saw Bracca vault over the top rail. The fire in the courtyard gave just enough light for Eskkar to see a row of halter ropes hanging from the topmost rail.

With his left hand, Eskkar snatched up a handful and shoved them into his belt. The corral's only gate was on the opposite side, so he threw his shoulder against the highest rail. One end tore loose, and he twisted it free.

Before he could pry off the second rail, Eskkar heard footsteps behind him. Without loosing his grip on the rail, he swung himself over and into the corral and jumped back. A figure loomed up out of the darkness, firelight glinting off a blade raised high that slammed into the rail with a heavy thud, where Eskkar's head had been. He still had his sword in his right hand, and Eskkar thrust forward, driving the sharp point into the guard's chest, just below his throat.

With the man's death gasp hanging in the air, Eskkar turned toward the three horses milling about at the other side of the corral. Bracca, his arms spread wide, was herding the nervous animals into a corner of the corral.

Slipping the sword back into its scabbard, Eskkar raced to Bracca's side. Between the two of them, they trapped the three horses against the corral's corner. Before the frightened creatures could decide to escape, Eskkar had the first halter rope in his hand.

"Easy there, easy." He had to calm the brutes down, at least one of them, until he could slip the halter on. While Eskkar could ride just holding onto the mane, the animal wouldn't really be under full control without a halter.

A big stallion, its white markings gleaming in the faint firelight, tossed its head about. The other two animals, probably mares, looked more docile, the sort he would expect dirt-eaters to ride.

The skittish horses, frightened by the blood smell and the noise, shied away. The stallion pawed the ground menacingly, and Eskkar edged away from that beast. Shifting from side to side, always muttering soft words, he and Bracca moved closer.

Just as the horses were about to bolt, Eskkar took two long strides and with a quick flick of the wrist slipped the halter over one of the smaller mares.

For a moment the animal tried to rear, but Eskkar's powerful arm fought the animal's urge to rise up, and he managed to keep the mare's forefeet on the ground. Before the wild-eyed horse could decide what to do, Eskkar moved closer and drew the halter tight.

Meanwhile Bracca, still shifting back and forth with his arms spread, kept the other two horses trapped. Eskkar tossed a halter rope toward him, and soon the second mare was under control.

"Easy, easy," Eskkar kept whispering, trying to calm the first mare they captured. He tossed the end of the halter rope over to Bracca. "Tie them up."

He tried to approach the stallion. The brute, his eyes wide with suspicion, suddenly reared, whinnying in fear or rage, its front hooves lashing out at Eskkar's head.

But Eskkar had grown up around half-wild horses, and he ducked aside with an oath. The horse's cry would turn every head in the compound toward the stable.

The stallion's hooves came down, but before the animal could rear again, Eskkar was at its side. He caught hold of the mane and swung himself onto the horse's back.

Again the stallion lifted its forelegs, neighing loudly, but Eskkar had locked his legs around the animal's middle and gripped the mane with all his strength.

For a long moment, Eskkar was high in the air, clinging to keep his seat. Then the horse's front hooves crashed back onto the earth with a bone-jarring thud.

A moment later, the stallion's back hooves lashed out. One of them struck the corral rail, knocking it into splinters. Before the stallion could buck again, Eskkar lunged forward and slipped the halter over the horse's head. The animal's teeth just missed his fingers, and snapped shut on empty air. Eskkar drew the halter rope tight behind the horse's ears. The partial tie gave him some control over the beast.

A voice called out from the front of the courtyard. "They're in the corral! They're stealing the horses!"

The stallion bolted, but Eskkar had a firm grip on the halter. He guided the animal toward the place where he'd knocked down the top rail. The horse sailed over the two lower rails with ease and broke into a run. Men jumped aside as the horse galloped toward the courtyard gate.

But that gate was closed. Eskkar cursed the efficient dirt-eaters. He and Bracca might have captured the horses, but if they couldn't get the gate open and escape . . .

The horse slowed, as the high wall of the compound loomed up. Dawn was breaking now, and the aroused animal knew better than to crash into the hard mud brick, and the top of the wall stood far too tall to jump.

Eskkar knew what was coming. The stallion planted his feet and slid to a stop, sending a shower of dirt ahead of him. The brute halted a long stride from the gate, just in time to avoid a collision.

Eskkar never hesitated. He swung down even before the horse stopped moving. Holding tight to the loose end of the halter, and with a speed born of a lifetime of practice, he looped the lower end of the rope around its jaw.

Before the animal realized it was under control, Eskkar had snagged the halter down. It took only another moment to secure the other end of the halter to the gate's cross bar.

A laugh sounded behind him. Eskkar whirled, his sword flashing from its scabbard and held extended, the tip level with his eyes, and gripping the hilt with both hands. Four men approached, all with swords in their hands. The stallion snorted and trotted back and forth, pulling at the halter rope that secured it. Its hind legs lashed out in frustration.

"I don't think you're going anywhere."

Eskkar swore as he recognized Dargo's voice. The overseer must have returned from the hunt after sundown, and brought back a few of his men with him.

Eskkar moved away from the horse, keeping the wall at his back. The Elder's men spread out just enough to keep Eskkar pinned against the wall. They would edge in a bit at a time, before they rushed him.

And if he charged at one of them, that man would fall back, and let the other jackals strike from behind. Despite being aroused from their sleep, all of them looked alert and light on their toes. They had done this kind of thing before. Eskkar tightened his grip on the hilt of his sword and took a long breath.

"Leave Dargo to me. You take care of the rest." Bracca's voice cut through the shuffling of feet in the dirt.

Dargo and the other three snapped their heads around as soon as they heard Bracca's words. He had crossed over most of the open space behind the gate, and drawn almost within striking distance. The blade of Bracca's sword rested on his right shoulder.

Eskkar didn't hesitate. The moment the guards' heads turned toward this new danger, he flung himself at the man on his right, the one farthest away from Bracca.

Extending his arm, Eskkar thrust out with the long sword. The man managed to parry the stroke, yet the slight distraction gave Eskkar all the opening he needed.

Both blades were still upraised and in contact, but Eskkar never stopped moving forward, and his shoulder crashed into the man and sent him sprawling to the earth. The next guard recovered fast, and swung at Eskkar's head, but Eskkar had anticipated that.

He shifted his feet into a half turn, just enough to dodge the strike, and now the long bronze sword hissed through the air.

The man, his eyes wide, tried to parry the blow, but Eskkar, gripping the hilt with both hands, whipped the sword down with all his strength. The two blades made contact, and he felt the impact in both arms as his sword knocked aside the guard's shorter blade and kept going, striking the side of the man's head.

A spurt of blood splashed across Eskkar's arm, and the wounded man's scream of agony echoed from the walls as he staggered back, out of the fight. Eskkar ignored that one and kept the sword in motion. He leaped back and with another savage stroke, swung down at the first man he had attacked.

Trying to get to his feet, the guard had no chance to stop the blow, and Eskkar's blade crunched into the man's left arm, shearing through the flesh and cutting into the man's side. A second scream of pain erupted.

Constantly keeping his feet in motion, Eskkar whirled to see Bracca dodging and weaving, trying to engage Dargo and the third guard at the same time.

"Dargo!" Eskkar's word cut through the air.

The courtyard had filled with the sun's first rays. Dargo, sensing death behind him, leapt to the side, away from Eskkar's blade. That gave time for Bracca to fake a cut at the remaining man's head, then lunge forward. He rolled his blade underneath the man's parry and drove it deep into the unprotected belly.

Now it was Dargo's turn to back away. His three men had been cut down in a few strokes, and for the first time fear showed on his face.

Eskkar strode across the open space between them, taking only a moment to wipe his sweating right hand against his tunic. He let his anger flow through his body, as he stared directly into Dargo's eyes, level with his own.

"Let's see how well you fight against me, you coward!"

Either the grimace on Eskkar's face unnerved Dargo, or the thought of facing someone as tall and strong as himself frightened him. "Elder! Bring more men!" Dargo's bellow would have been heard halfway to the mine.

Before Eskkar could close within striking distance, Bracca darted into the space between them.

"Get the horses, Eskkar. I'll take care of Dargo myself."

Eskkar had his doubts about Bracca matching up against Dargo, but something in Bracca's voice told him not to waste his time arguing. Eskkar turned aside and ran back toward the corral. The dull clink of bronze on bronze sounded behind him, and he muttered a prayer to the gods that Bracca knew what he was doing.

The two mares, still tied to the top rail of the corral, remained skittish. The smell of blood lingered in the air, and Eskkar's arrival only added to the scent.

All the same, the two beasts made no real effort to avoid his approach, though both snorted their distrust and tried to shift away. Eskkar's hand had almost reached the nearest halter when the twang of a bowstring made him whirl around.

An arrow hissed right past Eskkar's head, the feather brushing his ear. Two men, one carrying a sword and the other a bow, stood less than fifteen paces away. They must have come from the main house.

Eskkar had no time to wonder how a man could miss at such a short distance. Without the slightest hesitation, he flung himself at this newest threat, giving voice to a frightful barbarian battle cry as he charged the two men, his sword held high.

The man with the bow pulled another arrow from his quiver, but the sight of Eskkar charging toward him made his hand tremble, and he fumbled nocking the shaft. He managed to fit the arrow to the string on the second try, but before he could draw the bow, Eskkar stretched forward with the long sword, driving the blade through the man's chest.

The bowman twisted and fell, his weight wrenching the hilt from Eskkar's hand. The other man cried out when he saw the death blow, as if he felt the pain of it himself, then turned and ran back toward the house, his sword slipping from his grasp.

Eskkar didn't try to withdraw his sword. He kept moving, and in three long strides caught up with the fleeing man, grasped him by the hair, and jerked him completely off his feet. Eskkar pulled his knife from his belt, but before he could strike, the man held up his empty hands, and pleaded for mercy.

"Don't kill me! I'm Tonnar-can, the Village Elder. I'll give you anything you want."

Eskkar had already started the knife down, but he shifted his hand and rammed the hilt of the weapon into the man's forehead. The Elder collapsed like a sack of grain.

A quick look around showed no new enemies. The clash of bronze that had echoed through the courtyard had ceased, so Eskkar ran over to the dead bowman, now lying on his back with the sword's hilt protruding up into the air.

With one foot on the carcass, Eskkar ripped his bloody blade from the body. Two quick strides brought him back to where he could see Bracca and Dargo.

Both men were down, Dargo on his back and Bracca on his knees. Eskkar thought they had killed each other. Then he saw Bracca push himself to his feet, where he swayed from side to side, his sword hanging limp in his hand.

In a moment, Eskkar reached his friend's side. A glance down at Dargo revealed a deep cut across the big man's neck and throat. The body still twitched, but the rapidly expanding pool of blood around the shoulders told Eskkar that Dargo was finished.

He wasted no more thoughts on the dying scum. "Can you get the gate open?"

Bracca, still gulping air into his chest, nodded.

"Good. Hurry." Bracca might be injured or even just exhausted, but Eskkar had no time for that now. They weren't out of danger yet.

Eskkar ran back toward the corral, slowing only when he reached the dead bowman. He snatched up the bow and shoved it over his head and pulled it down across his chest. Scooping up the quiver, he slung that over his shoulder, then lifted the stunned Elder from the dirt and dragged him as far as the corral's entrance.

Leaving the unconscious man there, Eskkar slipped inside and walked slowly toward the two horses, speaking gently to calm down the animals. Untying the mares, he held onto the ropes with a stout grip, and led them from the corral.

As he passed the insensible Elder, Eskkar reached down and grasped the inert body by the wrist, dragging it along the ground.

The skittish beasts didn't care for the dragging body, but Eskkar pulled them along anyway.

By the time he reached the gate, Bracca had swung it open, and was shouting Ninamar's name through the opening. He turned back toward the courtyard as Eskkar joined him.

"Who's that?"

"Says he's the Elder." He handed the halters to Bracca. Eskkar bent down and ran his hands over the man's body. "If he was getting ready to run, he might be carrying some coins."

Underneath the tunic, Eskkar's probing fingers found a small leather pouch. He ripped it free, hefted it for a moment, then shoved it into the quiver with a grunt of satisfaction.

The Elder stirred, but Eskkar ignored him. "Let's get out of here. There may still be men inside the house, and they may have another bow."

He trotted over to where he had tied up the stallion. By the time Eskkar returned with the animal, Ninamar stood just outside the gate, peering inside.

Bracca had his hands full guiding the two mares, and Eskkar struggled with the stallion. Ninamar slipped past both of them, still carrying the sword Eskkar had given her earlier.

Then her voice rose up and echoed against the walls. "Murderer! You killed my husband!"

She swung the sword down, a clumsy enough stroke, but the Elder, just recovering his wits, could do little more than raise his arms. The first blow cut deep into the man's forearm.

Ninamar never stopped swinging, raising the sword up and bringing it down, again and again with all the pent up fury that raged in her breast. "Murderer! You stole my son!"

The stallion reared up at the Elder's cries, and Eskkar had all he could do to keep him from bolting. By the time he regained control of the powerful animal, Ninamar had delivered at least ten wild blows to the Elder, who lay twitching on the ground, blood pouring from his head, shoulders, and arms.

Bracca, the mares now under control, made no move to stop her.

Shaking his head, Eskkar swore under his breath. He hadn't wanted to kill the Elder, who might have some use as a hostage. Now his kin would have half the countryside chasing after the men responsible for his murder.

Eskkar led the stallion away from the bloody courtyard, walking him along until the animal calmed down. When he looked back, Bracca had his arm around Ninamar's shoulder, and she was sobbing against his chest.

The sword she'd carried protruded from the Elder's chest, its bronze blade, now covered with blood, catching the morning sun's rays as they shone through the gate.

After some soothing words to reassure the stallion, Eskkar leapt onto the horse's back.

For a few moments, the powerful animal showed its spirit, but it soon realized it bore an experienced rider. Despite snorting and tossing its head a few times, it quickly settled down and made no more attempts to rid itself of its new master.

By then Ninamar's youngest son, Ubara, caught up with Eskkar. One glance at the boy's pleading face and Eskkar reached down and lifted him onto the horse. Eskkar wrapped his free hand around the boy's stomach.

"Hold onto the mane," he ordered, "but don't pull too tight."

Eskkar touched his heels to the stallion and the animal moved out at an easy canter. With the warm sun at his back, he headed northwest, away from the Elder's house, the mine, and Marcala.

When Bracca, the woman, and her oldest son finally caught up with Eskkar, Bracca had a wide grin on his face. He rode double, with the rescued slave clutching his waist, while he led the other horse.

Ninamar, a look of panic on her face, clung to the second mare, gripping its mane with all her strength. Eskkar shook his head at the sight. He guessed she would fall off at least ten times before midmorning.

In spite of his weariness, Eskkar recognized the look on Bracca's face. His friend had returned to his old self. Whatever evil spirits had possessed him and stolen his wits had departed, washed away in a night of blood. Perhaps Dargo's death had appeased his rage.

Eskkar had to hold back his own smile. Bracca's fury had saved Eskkar from testing Dargo's sword.

Eskkar set a rapid pace. With the Village Elder and Dargo dead, Eskkar guessed anyone hunting him and Bracca would need at least one, maybe two, days before coming after them.

Enough armed men and horses would have to be collected and readied to take up the chase. And now Eskkar possessed a bow, to keep pursuers at a distance.

The way back to the northern lands lay open ahead of them. He possessed a strong mount, and each step of the stallion would bring Eskkar farther and farther from these dry desert lands. He'd had enough of Sumeria.

Despite Bracca's beguiling words, its people were no less brutal or savage than any others Eskkar had encountered. And at least he would get out of this stifling heat.

They splashed across the river and kept going. Just before midday, they crossed another stream and Eskkar decided they were far enough away from Marcala to rest and water the animals and let them graze. He bathed himself in the warm water, washing his body and his clothes, then cleaning and sharpening his sword.

They had nothing to eat, but Eskkar could go a day or two without food if necessary.

The horses attended to, Eskkar sat on a rock, removed the Elder's pouch from the quiver, and inspected its contents – ten gold coins, ten silver, and ten copper. What must be the Elder's emergency purse would give them more than enough to get well away from these lands.

A shadow crossed his eyes, and Bracca slipped to the ground across from him. Eskkar tossed him the pouch.

Bracca hefted it once, but then, instead of examining the contents, he laced it up and handed it back. "Whatever's in there, it's yours. All of it."

Eskkar slipped the pouch back into the quiver. "Why? For once there's plenty for the both of us. We could even give something to the woman."

"You saved my life . . . you saved all our lives."

Eskkar shrugged. His friend's words made him uncomfortable. A warrior did what he needed to do. Gratitude had no part in such deeds.

"Friend Eskkar, there's something I want to say," Bracca went on, "something I've never told anyone. In my tenth season, I watched my father die, cut down at the hands of my Village Elder's men. He fought them, one against ten, until they finally subdued him. Then they tortured him slowly until he died."

Bracca's voice, hoarse with unfamiliar emotion, failed him, and he had to pause a moment before he could go on. "My mother and I tried to run, but they caught us. I never saw what they did to her. I was knocked senseless before they took their pleasure. They thought

I was dead, or they would have cut my throat, too. When I awoke, my father hung from a post, and all that was left of my mother's body was covered in blood. After they finished with her, they hacked her apart and left her to bleed to death."

Bracca needed a moment before he could go on. "Yesterday in the village, the man . . . his woman . . . I might have ignored it all, but when they struck poor little Ubara, everything came back. I had to . . . " Bracca's voice choked, and he couldn't go on.

Eskkar knew the story all too well. His parents, too, had suffered much the same fate. These killings happened all too often, and many children grew up having suffered and endured such things.

"Then you've more than paid your blood debt to your parents," Eskkar said. "Ninamar, Ubara, Hanish, they will live because of you. When they pass beneath the earth, the gods will summon them to stand before your parents, so that they will know who to thank."

Bracca nodded, grateful not to have to speak any further about his past. "So men say."

Eskkar didn't really believe it either, but who could know what lay ahead of any of them. All the same, such words gave comfort. Death came to all. Only that was certain, and in Eskkar and Bracca's case, likely sooner than later. But not today.

This day the warm sun shone down on them, and the stream had cleansed all of them not only of dirt and blood, but guilt and revenge as well. Brutal men who preyed on those weaker than themselves had died. Dargo and the Elder deserved their fate. "It's time to get moving."

"Yes, my barbarian friend." Bracca stood, stretched, and gazed at the horizon.

"You were right after all. It is time to leave Sumeria. It will be many years before we dare return this far south."

More years than Eskkar expected to be alive. He, too, rose, and gathered his things. It was indeed time to get moving.

Two days of riding would bring them to one of the many branches of the mighty Euphrates. They could rid themselves of the woman and her boys there. A few silver coins would see them on a boat heading upriver. The dead Elder's fine stallion would take Eskkar all the way to the northern grasslands.

And if Bracca chose to stay behind with the woman, Eskkar would leave him. Life was precarious enough without foolishly inviting trouble, like they'd provoked in Marcala's marketplace.

Still, something told him that by the time they reached the Euphrates, Bracca would be thinking much the same thoughts, and Eskkar felt glad for that.

Book Two

—⟞⟨Ω⟩⟞—

ORAK

23

The seacoast village of Kuara, just west of the Tigris River, two years later . . .

Eskkar sat at the bare table, ignoring the frowns the innkeeper cast his way every time the man passed nearby. Though Eskkar had chosen the least inviting table in the darkest corner of the inn, he knew he wouldn't be able to sit there much longer, not without ordering something to drink.

The inn, one of the worst in Kuara, consisted of a single chamber not much larger than a one room hut. Still, it started to fill up as the day drifted toward dusk.

Despite its rickety tables and benches, and its filthy dirt floor, crawling with only the gods knew what, the inn's cheap prices for its watery ale insured a large crowd every day, mostly the dregs of Kuara.

Eskkar glanced around the room to see apprentices, laborers, farmers, thieves, and even a few slaves who'd managed to procure a copper coin or two. The rank odor of sweat from so many bodies in close proximity permeated the stale air, making each breath an effort.

Soon a new customer would want the table, and even Eskkar's hostile glare wouldn't deter the innkeeper from demanding that Eskkar either leave or produce copper to buy at least a mug of ale.

And that, Eskkar knew, would never happen. His purse, as empty as his stomach, hadn't felt the weight of even one copper coin for the last two days.

The tattered curtain serving as a door to the outside swayed aside. Two farmers entered, their eyes wandering about as they adjusted to the dim light. Both had brown streaks on their legs, reaching well above their knees, the mud or worse proclaiming to everyone they'd spent the day working like slaves in the irrigation ditches.

For all Eskkar could tell, they might be slaves, their work completed for the day and given some free time by their masters.

The innkeeper waved them in, and Eskkar heard the man's assurances that he had a table for them. Eskkar swore under his breath. Better to get up now, rather than be humiliated when the inn's owner approached.

But the curtain swirled again, and Bracca passed through. His eyes adjusted faster to the gloomy interior than the two laborers, and he maneuvered his way through the crowd to Eskkar's table, reaching it at the same time as the innkeeper.

"I need this table," the innkeeper began, his voice harsh, "for these . . ."

"Bring ale for both of us," Bracca ordered, lowering himself on the wobbly stool across from Eskkar.

"No copper, no ale," the owner snapped.

Bracca had already reached into his pouch. He slammed a tiny silver square down onto the table with enough force to turn every eye their way. "And a loaf of fresh bread as well."

The innkeeper's frown vanished, replaced by a crooked smile at the advent of the coin. Few of his customers could produce silver. "At once," he said, pushing away the two already disappointed newcomers, who would be forced to squat on the dirt floor until someone else left.

"Didn't know the man could smile," Eskkar said, putting his finger on the coin. It felt like real silver, but with Bracca, you couldn't be sure. "And who did you rob to get this?"

"Some rich merchant," Bracca said. "I told him my name was Eskkar, so be sure to run if his guards come looking for you."

The thought that anyone would mistake him for Bracca made Eskkar smile. The two men looked as dissimilar as fire and water. Eskkar, tall and broad across the shoulders, came from the far north. He stood a good head taller than Bracca, too.

For nearly four years, the two men had ridden together, fought together, and suffered hardship and hunger together. They argued often, swore at each other, and even come to blows once or twice. But they had grown closer than brothers as they struggled to stay alive, though always managing to lose or spend everything that they earned or stole.

Bracca had been born not far from this village, and had grown up in this land, or so he claimed. In fact, the only reason the local Sumerians accepted Eskkar in their midst without the usual insults or threats was that Bracca's presence vouched for his northern friend.

To Eskkar's eyes, Bracca looked like a runner, with a slim body held together by ropy muscles much stronger than they appeared. A short sword hung from his belt, pulled tight over a dirty tunic too big for him.

Still, the man could swing a blade with the best of them, Eskkar knew. They'd practiced against each other enough times over the years, and Eskkar's longer reach and greater strength had not always proven successful against Bracca's speed and agility.

The innkeeper returned, faster than expected, no doubt eager to obtain possession of the silver before the two men decided to take their business elsewhere. He set down two mugs of ale with a thump that shook the table.

"The bread is coming, friends," he said, pushing Eskkar's finger aside and scooping up the silver coin. Only then did he dump nine battered and well-worn copper coins, their change for the silver, onto the table.

"Well, that didn't last long," Bracca commented. He lifted one of the copper coins and examined it in the dim light. "I hope these are all good?"

Eskkar shrugged. The innkeeper wouldn't likely try that trick, not on two fighting men. "They'll pass in the dark, I'm sure. And where did you steal the silver, friend Bracca?"

"You had no luck in the market?"

"No, nothing," Eskkar said. "No work to be had anywhere."

"Then count your blessings, barbarian. Tomorrow we leave Kuara, may the gods send pestilence upon this cursed place, in the employ of the merchant Aram-Kitchu. We will help him guard his goods as he travels northward, and perhaps carry a small sack or two. He's agreed to pay us two silver coins apiece when we arrive at our destination. I told him we needed one silver coin in advance, to settle our accounts and buy what we required for the journey."

"And he gave you a silver coin, just like that? He must either be a fool, or desperate for men."

"He is," Bracca confirmed. "But his need is our advantage, and the man hardly flinched when I told him you were a barbarian, though he did mutter a prayer to the gods and made the sign to ward off demons."

"And where are we going?"

Before Bracca could answer, the innkeeper returned, handing each of them a hand-sized loaf of dark brown bread. Eskkar frowned at the pitiful meal. "We need to get some meat."

"We will, after we drink our ale and leave this wretched tavern," Bracca said.

"We'll just take the edge off our hunger with this. Afterwards, we'll get a real meal, maybe a roasted chicken or even a thick slice of beef. I know a place that has both good food and good women. And this time we won't have to share."

Eskkar's mouth watered at the thought of eating a juicy piece of meat. Women, good or bad, could wait. "This merchant who hired us, where is he going?"

"Ah, our employer. His journey's end is some rat hole on the Tigris, a few hundred miles north of here. A village named Opak or Otopeh, or something like that. What difference does it make?"

The name, whatever it actually might be, meant nothing to Eskkar, who couldn't keep track of the thirty or more villages he'd passed through in the last few months, let alone the last two years.

"As long as we're going north, I don't care. I'm still not sure how you talked me into returning to Sumeria."

Two years ago, they'd ridden north from the gold mining village of Marcala, leaving the Village Elder's dead and mutilated body behind. Fortunately, Marcala lay over two hundred miles to the west, otherwise even Bracca's silver tongue couldn't have convinced Eskkar to return to the lands of the Great Sea.

Dead village elders, no matter how greedy or oppressive, were not something dirt-eaters forgot.

"What? You don't like my beautiful land of Sumeria?" Bracca's voice sounded shocked. "Filled with dark-eyed beauties and rich farmers and fat tradesmen begging to be plucked? You want to leave all this," he waved his ale cup at the crowded room, "behind?"

"We've been here fifteen days, and scarcely 'plucked' anything," Eskkar argued, ripping his loaf in two parts and biting into the rock hard crust. He hoped his teeth wouldn't break under the strain.

"Though that tavern whore you hired when we first arrived nearly 'plucked' off your manhood with her knife. Good thing she couldn't find anything that small in the dark."

"An unfortunate misunderstanding," Bracca admitted, squirming a little at the memory. "Perhaps she will be more receptive now that we have something to exchange."

Eskkar had no intention of going anywhere near that one. She'd snatched a knife from under her shift faster than any warrior he'd ever seen. The look on her face convinced him she'd slit both their throats in the dark just for the pleasure of hearing their blood gurgle, let alone for a copper coin.

"Not back there," Eskkar said. "I intend to die with my prick still attached."

"You're probably right. No need to tempt fate again. However, it's been almost ten days since we've had a woman. And we're starting on this long trip. We'll be at least fifteen or twenty days, walking in the hot sun and smelling like pig sweat. There won't be much chance of finding a willing woman on the way."

"Oh, all right," Eskkar said, his resistance fading away, as the ale and bread settled the empty feeling in his stomach. "But this time we get two separate girls. No more sharing."

It had been too long since Eskkar had spread his seed inside a woman, and even then they'd had to take her together. Not that that seemed to bother Bracca. Not much did, and certainly nothing to do with women.

Almost since their first meeting, the man never stopped talking about women, what he liked to do to them, or they to do to him. Dark haired girls, brown haired, golden hair, Bracca could seemingly describe every one of the hundreds of encounters he'd ever had, in great detail. Even assuming most of Bracca's claims were lies, the man's actual accomplishments were still impressive.

"Have no worries on that account, friend Eskkar. Tonight we have coins in our purse. We'll have a good meal first, then spend the rest on women. Perhaps two for each of us."

"One will be enough for me," Eskkar said, "and let me remind you that half of those copper coins are mine."

"Of course, barbarian, how could I fail to divide our wages honestly with you? We share everything, remember?"

Eskkar grunted, this time to hide the smile. They'd saved each other's life too many times to count, but where women and coins were concerned, Bracca couldn't be trusted not to waste the latter on the former.

"Of course, Bracca, my friend. But perhaps I should be the one to hold the coins," Eskkar said, sliding the coppers across the rough tabletop and into his hand, "while you're busy selecting the girls. That way you won't be distracted."

Bracca laughed. "They'll charge more for you, since you're a barbarian, and no self-respecting Sumerian whore would want to have anything to do with your tiny prod, assuming she can get it up for you."

Eskkar shoved the last piece of bread crust in his mouth, stood up and drained the last drop of ale, and dropped the cup on the table.

"We'll see who has to pay extra. I think you'll find that the girls will be begging to pay me for servicing them. Perhaps I'll be able to convince them to do you as a favor to me."

"Follow me, then," Bracca said as he arose, "and I'll guide you to the best women in Kuara." He headed for the door, stepping around a drunk as he went.

Eskkar trailed after him, hoping they wouldn't end up face down in some lane, stripped naked and beaten half to death, before the night ended. It had happened to them less than two months ago, and the last of the bruises had only recently faded away.

⸺⸗⸻

The next morning, his head aching, Eskkar stood beside Bracca on the outskirts of Kuara. The merchant Aram-Kitchu, standing with his back to the sun, looked them both over, disappointment plain on his narrow face marked by prominent eyebrows.

"This is what I'm paying two silver coins for? You promised me a steppes warrior, not some half-besotted clumsy oaf."

Eskkar and Bracca, both squinting into the bright morning glare, began speaking, but Aram-Kitchu held up his hand to silence them. "It doesn't matter."

He turned to his caravan master. "Put them wherever you think best, Tarrata. And make sure they're carrying something besides their thick heads."

Aram-Kitchu stalked away, toward the head of the column, his long brown hair billowing around his head, and shouting orders to his porters as he went.

Caravan Master Tarrata, short and stocky, had long, hairy arms covered with thick muscles, and Eskkar guessed him to have about forty seasons. Tarrata's booming voice grated on Eskkar's ears. His words tended to hiss, perhaps because of a missing front tooth.

Nevertheless, the man looked tough enough to chew leather, missing tooth and all.

"Either of you so-called fighters ever guarded a caravan before?" Tarrata frowned at the two men facing him, both clearly still hung over from a night of revelry.

Both of them shook their heads.

"Thought as much, you low-life scum. Do what you're told, without complaining, or I'll run you off and you'll get no pay. If you give me any trouble, well, I'll kill you myself, just to hear you squeal. Understand me?"

He waited until both men nodded before going on. "You two will bring up the rear. Keep your eyes open for something besides where you're walking. If any bandits attempt to rob us, try to shout a warning before you let them slit your throats. At least that way, you'll be of some use even if you're dead. Meanwhile grab one of the food sacks."

Eskkar eyed the heavy sacks filled with bread and whatever else the guards and porters would eat on the journey. The smallest looked almost as big as Bracca.

In moments the caravan, consisting of eight porters, four other guards, plus Tarrata and Aram-Kitchu, moved out. Following orders, Eskkar and Bracca trailed behind the others. Most of them, Eskkar noticed, appeared almost as bedraggled as he and Bracca.

Aram-Kitchu led the way, his fine tunic outlining his muscular legs in the breeze, with two guards a step behind him. A tall man, nearly as tall as Eskkar, Aram-Kitchu's long strides set a fast pace.

Tarrata and the other two guards marched behind the porters, where they could rush forward to provide protection in case of an attack. Or, more likely, to keep an eye on the porters and make sure they didn't steal anything from their loads and toss it beside the trail, to leave lying on the sand for their friends to find.

Bracca had explained the practice, though how the Sumerian had learned of it Eskkar had no idea.

Eskkar and Bracca stumbled along five or six paces behind everyone, trying to get used to the unwieldy sacks that threatened to unbalance them with every step. Since they carried only food, no one paid them much attention. Dust, kicked up from those ahead, soon covered both men.

"I didn't sign on to be a porter," Eskkar said, wishing his head would stop hurting. "You said we would be guards, not pack animals."

"A misunderstanding, friend Eskkar," Bracca agreed. "But we're moving north, which is want you wanted, so try not to complain too much."

Last night's activities had lasted far too long. After leaving the inn, Bracca led the way to another ale house, where they split a fat roasted chicken accompanied by barleycake, cucumbers, and an onion. They splurged more coins for some real date wine to wash down the feast.

In addition to its food, this establishment also specialized in providing female companionship, at least for those with the ability to pay for such services. Eskkar handed over more of the dwindling number of coins, and fresh wine soon appeared, along with two women.

To Eskkar's deprived eyes, they looked reasonably attractive, but the dimly-lit inn made it hard to tell for sure. Still, the two men had little time to waste, and at least the women seemed willing, exactly what both men needed.

The innkeeper even allowed them to use his private room at the back of the ale house. The women demanded ale as well, and that took another coin.

After consuming more ale, everyone concluded their business and fell asleep, or passed out, Eskkar couldn't really remember exactly what happened. He recalled having two copper coins in his purse when they entered the innkeeper's private chamber.

At least, that's what he recalled. In the morning, even those coins had vanished, probably taken by the girls or the innkeeper while the two men snored off their wine, too besotted to notice anyone robbing their purse.

Bracca stumbled over a stone, muttered a curse, and swung the heavy sack to his other shoulder, staggering for a moment as he made the switch.

"We're fortunate to be carrying the food, barbarian. That means our load will get lighter with every stop. By tonight the sacks will be half empty, and tomorrow we'll just stroll along."

Eskkar groaned at the thought of lugging the heavy sack until they halted for a midday meal. "Maybe we should just throw some bread away."

"I don't think so, my innocent friend. I'm sure Aram-Kitchu knows the exact count of every item in every pack. That's why he's the merchant and we're the ones lugging the sacks."

The trader kept a fairly fast pace, not too difficult since he carried no burden but his sword and a small pouch hanging beneath his left arm.

All the same, Eskkar heard others complaining about the rapid gait. When Tarrata give the order to halt for the midday meal, everyone sank to the ground, legs weary and backs aching.

The Caravan Master unfastened the ropes securing Bracca's food sack, and distributed the bread himself, tearing each loaf in half before handing them out.

"I'm not used to so much hard walking," Eskkar complained, as he unlaced his sandals and rubbed his feet. "I'm a horseman, not a damned beast of burden."

He bit into his bread, eating quickly so as to be ready when the order came to resume the march.

"You seem to have misplaced your horse, warrior. Or have you forgotten how we got into this mess?"

Eskkar hadn't forgotten. Only thirty days ago, they'd possessed plenty of silver and each owned a decent horse. They rode with three others, all good men ready for anything. A band of twenty or so steppes warriors had appeared from nowhere and ambushed the five of them, riding them down so quickly that they had almost no chance for escape.

Eskkar had taken one look at the situation and urged his horse toward a rocky hilltop, Bracca following his lead. The other three, who tried to outrun their pursuers, found themselves cut off and riddled with arrows.

Eskkar and Bracca managed to dodge the shafts directed toward them, and raced their horses until the reached the steep hillock. Abandoning their horses, the two men scurried their way deeper into the rocks, hunched over to avoid the arrows launched at their fleeing backs. Shafts clattered off the stones around them, but none found their targets.

Seeing their quarry scrambling ever higher into the hillside, the steppes warriors decided not to waste time or effort trying to root them out, apparently considering two men on foot not worth hunting down and killing.

In any case, the horsemen had captured all five horses, always their main objective. After looting the dead of anything valuable, they rode off, leaving Eskkar and Bracca huddling high up among the upper ridges until nightfall, when they crept out and slipped away.

Fortunately, the barbarians didn't linger. It had taken Eskkar and Bracca three days to walk to the first village, and another ten to reach Kuara. Once there, Bracca couldn't locate any of his friends or kin. Neither Bracca nor Eskkar could find any work.

For three days they'd begged and pleaded in the marketplace, competing with plenty of others for even the most menial labor. But the two of them looked too much like fighting men, always the last to be hired for any task.

"I suppose this is better than begging or stealing," Eskkar said. "I'm tired of being chased out of every collection of mud huts calling itself a village. At least we're going north, out of this accursed Sumerian heat."

"I'll miss the smell of the sea," Bracca said, "but you're probably right. We'll find more opportunities outside of Sumeria. They're not very tolerant about strangers or those falsely accused of stealing. Even so, I'll miss my dark haired beauties, the finest looking women in the world."

"Back on your feet!" Tarrata's bellow jolted every man. "Get ready to move out."

The porters stood and gathered their burdens. Everyone, including Eskkar and Bracca, complained about the short midday rest.

"I think we'll get to wherever we're going in ten days, if our merchant keeps up this pace," Bracca said.

"If any of us last that long," Eskkar said. His feet hurt, and the muscles in his lower legs felt weak. They'd scarcely completed half of the first day's journey.

He slung the sack over his shoulder, grunting at the weight. "How come you get to carry the lighter sack?"

"Don't worry, it'll all even out with our supper tonight. Just remember to eat a lot of food."

Aram-Kitchu gave the order, and the small caravan resumed its march, heading north, following a parallel course to the Tigris, but about a mile away from the wide ribbon of water. They followed that landmark for about two miles. Then, to Eskkar's surprise, Aram-Kitchu turned away from the usual path, moving more to the east, until they reached the river.

The merchant never halted. He splashed into the Tigris, and started wading across, his caravan dutifully following behind.

Eskkar looked askance at the wide stretch of water. "Is this a ford?" Glancing around, he saw no signs of any boats or rafts, not even a hint that anyone had ever crossed the river here.

"No, my wise barbarian friend, Aram-Kitchu plans to drown himself, and take us with him." Bracca stepped down the bank and into the water. "Do you think he'd risk his neck and precious goods if he couldn't cross here?"

Cursing, Eskkar followed his friend, nearly losing his footing in the mud. Bracca was right. If there were any danger, the merchant would have sent someone else ahead. Probably, Eskkar realized, me or Bracca.

The sluggish water never rose above Eskkar's waist, though some of the shorter men had to struggle when they reached midstream. Then they were climbing on the eastern bank. Aram-Kitchu gave them just enough time to shake the mud from their sandals before continuing.

They kept moving toward the northeast, and within a mile the ground became rougher, with more frequent gentle rolling hills. Eskkar knew that in a few days march northward, the grass would grow greener and thicker, as they moved out of the warmer coastland climate and into the hill country.

The sun nearly touched the horizon before Tarrata gave the order to halt near a small stream for the night. By then Eskkar didn't think he could take another step. Everyone felt the same, exhausted and half-lame. He and Bracca sat with their feet in the water with the others, letting the cool stream soothe their burning feet.

When he felt refreshed enough, Eskkar dove in, cleaning himself and his clothing at the same time. He climbed out, shivering a little, as the two friends walked back to the others.

Tarrata ordered everyone to hunt for firewood, and they soon had a small blaze going. Each man received a strip of dried meat for dinner, along with another half-loaf of bread. Eskkar wrinkled his nose at the sight of the leathery piece of smoked beef, wondering how many months ago the animal had died. He forced a stick through the tough slice, and shoved it into the fire.

"I'll bet we covered twenty-five miles today, despite the weight," Bracca remarked, following his friend's example at the fire.

"Not likely." Eskkar possessed an unusually good eye for distance. "But we might have made more than twenty."

The two found themselves sitting a little apart from the others. The guards, all local men who'd worked for Tarrata before, didn't know Bracca or his companion. The porters, simple laborers from Kuara, resented the fact that Eskkar and Bracca's loads would soon weigh less than their own, and that the two strangers were receiving higher pay as guards.

"What's the rush," Eskkar said. "This Opak will still be there when we arrive. What can another day or two matter?"

"For once you've asked a good question." Bracca kept his voice low. "Either someone's rich uncle is near death, or Aram-Kitchu is carrying something very valuable."

"We're off the regular caravan trail, aren't we?" Eskkar matched his friend's tone.

"Oh, yes, we'll see fewer farmers or anyone else for that matter, if we keep moving northeast. The ground will be rougher, too. But this route to the north is more direct than if we follow the river."

They chewed the rest of their meal in silence, each man thinking about what that might mean.

When Eskkar finished his meat, he tossed the stick aside. "Think we'll run into any bandits?"

"I asked about that yesterday. No caravan's been attacked in two, maybe three months. They say the land is pretty quiet, especially this side of the Tigris."

Eskkar didn't like the whole situation. He hated walking almost as much as he hated laboring for someone else more than a few days. If Aram-Kitchu had traveled in any direction but north, Eskkar wouldn't have joined the caravan.

"Let's hope we don't encounter any bandits, then."

"Thieves and robbers, as even you should know, will be watching the main trail," Bracca reminded him. "No handful of thieves lurking this far east would be strong enough to attack us."

Tarrata interrupted the conversation as he called the caravan guards to the fire. "Two men on guard watch the whole night, starting now. I'll change the guards four times each night. You," he pointed to Bracca, "and you," to one of his regular guards, "take the first shift. The rest of you, shut your mouths and get some sleep. We'll be moving at first light."

Sprawling down on the ground, Eskkar let himself relax, though he unsheathed his sword and kept it beside him. His turn at guard duty, he knew, would come soon enough, and he might as well get as much sleep as he could. Too tired to worry about anything but his aching feet, he fell asleep in moments, adding his snores to those already rising into the night around him.

When morning came, Tarrata roused everyone, using his foot to make sure the laggards got the message. Each man ate his half-loaf of bread, drank as much as he could hold from the stream, and started moving before the sun had lifted a finger's width above the horizon.

The merchant kept to the same rapid pace as the day before, despite the gripes and complaints of those following his footsteps.

Eskkar noticed that even the experienced porters felt the strain. Everyone knew the second day would prove the hardest, until the men's muscles grew accustomed to the pace. Eskkar's legs complained for the first part of the morning, until the muscles stretched out.

His sack, as Bracca foretold, did feel a bit lighter this morning. Nonetheless, the sun seemed to drag its way across the sky. Aram-Kitchu pushed himself as hard as his followers, and they marched at least another twenty miles before they halted for the evening, even more tired than the night before.

Tarrata kept the grueling pace for another four days, ignoring the muttered complaints. Leg muscles hardened even more, and the protests diminished as the men realized they would reach their destination and draw their pay that much sooner.

Orak, by now Eskkar knew the actual name of their destination, drew closer with each stride. The landscape changed as well, with more and more greenery filling in the bare spots.

Wild grasses grew everywhere, and the men stopped occasionally to dig radishes and onions from the ground. They also picked over-ripe apples from the trees to supplement their diminishing supply of increasingly stale bread.

On the seventh day since leaving Kuara, not long after the midday rest period, the caravan snaked its way between hills that overlooked the route they were following. Eskkar, like Tarrata and everyone else, kept his eyes open, always alert to the possibility of an ambush.

Eskkar scanned the trail ahead, saw how it wound between two hills, with the base of a broad and sloping hill on the left, and a much steeper climb on the right. The path looked safe, with no place for men to suddenly fall upon the caravan.

They'd reached halfway around the hillock, when a shout came from above and echoed between the ridges. Eskkar looked up to see a line of men standing on the crest of the hill to their left.

"Stop! Stay where you are if you want to live."

"Demons breath!" Bracca hissed the words in Eskkar's ear.

Eskkar had never seen anything like this before. The brigands, at least fifteen men, held position about sixty paces above the caravan on the highest slope of the hill. Some held bows at the ready. The seemingly safe passageway between the hills had changed into a cunning trap.

If Aram-Kitchu's men moved forward or backward, the bandits had the shorter distance to cover, and would be in position to block any escape. The even steeper hill to their right couldn't be climbed either, at least not while carrying the merchant's goods. The curve of the trail made the perfect trap, and the hill provided the bandits a safe platform to use their bows.

"We're honest traders," Aram-Kitchu shouted up at them. "But we'll kill anyone who tries to rob us."

In reply, an arrow flew through the air, landing a few paces away from where the furious merchant stood, his hand on his sword hilt.

"Tell your men to throw down their goods and their weapons," the bandit leader, a broad shouldered man with a bronze sword in his hand, called down. "You can go back the way you came. Otherwise, we'll kill all of you."

By now Eskkar had the count of the men above him. Sixteen bandits ranged the hilltop, but only two carried bows. An archer anchored each end of their line. The chief, his thick beard visible even from below, stood in the center of his men.

"I'm not giving up my sword," Eskkar said.

"Nor I mine," Bracca agreed.

Both men owned nothing besides their weapons, and without them, assuming they got out of this in one piece, they'd be reduced to working in the fields or digging irrigation ditches to get enough food to stay alive. It might take a year's labor to replace them.

"The fools need to spread out," Eskkar said, jerking his head toward their caravan's leaders.

Tarrata and Aram-Kitchu stood together, and the rest of the men had bunched up around them. Only Eskkar and Bracca, bringing up the rear, stood ten or fifteen paces away.

"They don't know what to do," Bracca said, glancing at the merchant and trail master.

"We're dead if we stay here." Eskkar's gaze fixed on the two bowmen. Each had a full quiver, and shafts already nocked. They could stay up there and kill every man in the caravan beneath them, given enough time. Still, there were only two archers, which lessened that danger.

Bracca came to the same conclusion. "Ahead or back?"

The way past the hillock seemed a bit shorter ahead, and more downhill than the path they'd have to retrace. "I'm going forward," Eskkar said. "Are you ready?"

"Drop your sacks and weapons NOW, or we'll start killing you." The bandit leader's voice echoed ominously over them.

Eskkar thought of tossing away his half-empty sack of bread, then decided against it. "Use your sack as a shield," he muttered to Bracca.

Without another word, Eskkar burst into a run. "Follow me," he shouted to Tarrata, as he streaked past the porters and the merchant in a few strides, racing his way around the base of the slope.

An arrow hissed by, but Eskkar knew a man moving at a dead run across an archer's field of fire wouldn't be easy to hit. All the same, Eskkar shifted the sack to his left side, hoping the bread inside had hardened enough to stop an arrow.

Bracca stayed behind him, keeping a few steps between them. Without waiting for orders, the rest of men broke into a lumbering run, following Eskkar and Bracca.

The bandits burst into movement as well. The archer at the forward end of the line fired another shaft at Eskkar, then ran down the hill, the rest of the bandits following.

If the enemy bowman could get to the base of the hill before Eskkar and the others reached it, he could stand just above base of the trail, and shoot his shafts straight at the oncoming men. And from that vantage point, there would be no way to stop the archer from killing several of them.

Head down, still clutching his sack, Eskkar ran as hard as he could. As he drew closer to the point where the base of the hill met the trail, he saw a narrow ledge only a few paces above the trail, and extending in the same direction. If the archer reached the ledge first and positioned himself, he'd have an easy shot at anyone trying to escape, and still be safe enough from any sword thrust.

Eskkar added another burst of speed, taking only a moment to risk another glance up the hill. The steep slope had the bandits slipping and sliding, most of them using their hands to help control their descent.

With a final effort, Eskkar turned off the path and headed straight toward the ledge. He flung the bread sack up onto the setback and, in nearly full stride, leapt onto a waist-high boulder and pushed off that to throw his body upward.

His hands caught the edge and using all his strength, he swung his legs around and onto the shelf. The archer arrived at almost the same time, sliding on his back the last few paces, clutching his bow in his left hand, and using his right hand to stop from tumbling headfirst onto the ledge.

Despite his awkward landing, the bowman managed to keep his feet under him. He whipped a shaft from his quiver, still somehow fastened to his belt. Ten paces away, Eskkar rose to his knee, but saw that he wouldn't be able to draw his sword and reach the archer before he fitted the arrow to the string and loosed.

Instead Eskkar snatched up the bread sack and hurled it straight at the archer, as the man drew the shaft back and let fly. The heavy cloth snagged the arrow point, and the missile flew into the sack, passing right through the contents but deflected off to the right and down onto the ground.

The archer never got a second chance. Eskkar jerked the sword from the scabbard belted over his shoulder. Taking one step, he threw himself forward, extending into a lunge and burying the sword's point in the man's stomach.

A second bandit arrived with a rattle of loose stones and dirt, clutching a sword. Unable to stop, he tumbled past, a long pace to Eskkar's left, and kept going. The third man, slipping and sliding down the hill, landed off-balance, right on top of the dying archer. By then Eskkar had regained his balance. He thrust the sword once again, driving it into the man's chest.

"Get the bow!" Bracca's voice cut through the shouting and cursing. He'd clung to the ledge and hacked the second bandit in the leg before the man could turn to attack Eskkar.

Ignoring the wounded man's howls, Eskkar bent down, grabbed the bow, and tossed it off the ledge into Bracca's waiting hand. He grabbed the quiver and ripped it from the waist of the dead archer.

Three more bandits came crashing down onto the ledge and Eskkar decided it was time to go.

Quiver in one hand and sword in the other, he turned, took two steps, and jumped down to the path. The force of the landing brought him to his knees, and he felt the last of the porters rush by.

Eskkar rose and started running, every man in the caravan following in Bracca's footsteps. Eskkar, at the rear, prayed that the second bandit archer didn't get a clear shot.

Then Eskkar saw Bracca had slowed, waiting for his friend.

"Give me an arrow," shouted Bracca, reaching back and holding out his hand.

Eskkar extended the quiver. Bracca grabbed a shaft, and fitted it to the bowstring as he ran. They passed some waist-high rocks scattered alongside the trail, and Bracca turned, loosing the shaft in a smooth movement.

The arrow took down the closest of their pursuers, and the others halted, ducking behind any cover they could find. They still outnumbered the caravan's guards, but now they were the ones strung out, without a plan and in disorder.

Bracca took off as swift as a deer, and Eskkar, still clutching the sword and quiver, raced after him. An arrow flew over both their heads. By the time the next shaft arrived, they'd moved almost out of range, and now only a lucky hit would find a target.

Everyone ran as fast as he could, Aram-Kitchu and Tarrata urging them on. The Caravan Master, waving his sword about, threatened to kill the first porter that dropped his burden.

Guards and porters alike kept running, and covered nearly a quarter of a mile before the first porter fell to his knees, exhausted. Tarrata called for everyone to halt. Bracca and Eskkar reached his side, and the three of them, breathing hard, stared back the way they'd come. No one chased after them, and not a bandit could be seen.

"Let's keep moving," Bracca urged. "Before they decide to try again."

"You killed three, four of them." Tarrata still clutched his side, trying to catch his breath. "I doubt they've got the stones to come at us again."

Eskkar didn't like the fact that he couldn't see anyone. The bandits should at least still be watching them, despite the failure of their little trap. Eskkar started walking.

"Where are you going?" Tarrata's voice would have stopped anyone, except Eskkar.

"As far as I can," Eskkar called back, "and as fast as I can."

"Stay where you are, damn you," Tarrata shouted, angry at Eskkar's disobedience.

A moment later, Bracca reached Eskkar's side, and the two men strode along, still trying to get their wind back. Ignoring Tarrata's orders to halt, the two of them pushed past the porters, guards, and Aram-Kitchu, and kept moving.

The merchant stared at them, no doubt unaccustomed to men refusing his orders.

Regardless, Aram-Kitchu recovered fast enough. "Get the men moving," he shouted to Tarrata, before they'd gone ten paces. "Everyone up. Start walking."

Eskkar and Bracca strode along in silence for the next half-mile, neither of them bothering to glance behind them. Tarrata and the others would be looking backwards every other step.

"You think they'll come again?"

Eskkar grunted. He snatched up a handful of grass and used it to clean the blood off his sword.

"They had a good plan, and picked a good place to ambush us. We were lucky. They probably expected us to surrender. If they'd had a few more archers, we'd all be dead."

"Well, bowmen are scarce in these parts, and ones that can shoot straight even scarcer."

Almost no farmers possessed bows, and even if they did, such weapons tended to be small and crude, used merely for hunting rabbits or birds. Even in a village, it took time and effort to maintain a good hunting bow, not to mention the work needed to make arrows, points, and bowstrings. Nor did dirt-eaters have the time to practice with the weapon.

Every bow broke in two sooner or later, and a craftsman needed skill and patience to construct the weapon. Both qualities were in short supply among dirt-eaters, who needed to work most of every day merely to put food in their bowls.

In the steppes clans, men too old to fight spent their days fashioning weapons of all kinds, to earn their food and places riding in the wagons. And the warriors practiced their archery almost every day, not only at stationary targets, but while riding their horses at a full gallop. A group of warriors could launch a steady stream of arrows as they rode to the attack, devastating their victims before they got within reach of sword or lance.

"All the same, why didn't they come after us?"

"Their leader must have held them back," Eskkar said, speaking his thoughts as much to himself as to his friend. "That was a lot of men, this far off the main caravan trail. And all of them looked well-armed. Those were no copper blades they swung at us."

Copper swords, while still common enough throughout the land, had lost favor in the eyes of men who depended on a sword to keep alive. Unreliable in hard fighting, copper swords shattered often enough, sometimes after only a few hard strokes.

Even keeping a sharp edge on them took laborious work and plenty of patience. The stronger bronze weapon kept a keen edge longer, and seldom broke. Every warrior wanted a bronze sword, though the more durable weapon took a great deal longer for a smith to create and temper, and cost much more to buy.

From horseback, the longer blades favored by the steppes warriors could deliver a devastating slashing blow to an opponent.

"So where did all these well-armed bandits come from?"

"I doubt they came from Kuara," Eskkar said, still thinking aloud. "You said Aram-Kitchu had only arrived the day before. And he left in a hurry, without much preparation. No one from there could have overtaken us, not without horses."

"This route would be tough on horses," Bracca mused, "lots of rocks and places to break a leg. Which is probably why the caravans with horses and pack animals use the main route along the river."

"Then these bandits must have come from somewhere else," Eskkar decided. "Either they knew we were coming, or . . ."

"Or what?"

"Or they knew what our noble merchant carried with him when he arrived in Kuara. Maybe they've been following him, knew his plans, knew he intended to go to Orak. They might have learned, or even guessed, he'd take the old trail, and so they got ahead of us. Found the perfect place for an ambush, and waited until we walked into the trap."

"That's a lot of guesses, my barbarian friend. Not to mention a lot of mouths to feed while you're dragging them all over the countryside."

"You like to gamble," Eskkar said. "Any wagers that they've given up?"

Bracca walked in silence for a hundred paces.

"No, I think you're right. They should have followed after us. A few more arrows, and some of the porters would have tossed away their loads, despite Tarrata's threats. Then the bandits would just have to pick up the sacks. Instead, they stopped to regroup."

"That means they're not interested in collecting whatever the porters abandoned. They want something else, maybe something Aram-Kitchu himself is carrying. What goods is he taking to Orak?"

Bracca laughed. "You don't ask a merchant what he's trading, barbarian. Even you should know that."

No one dared ask what might be inside the sack or bundle a porter would be carrying. The less anyone knew about a trader's wares, the safer everyone would be. All the sacks containing trade goods were sealed, and Aram-Kitchu checked each one of them several times a day.

Routine trade merchandise had to be valuable enough to warrant carrying over long distances. If a merchant carried something especially valuable, then the risk and danger would increase. As would the price of the goods when finally delivered.

"None of the porters' sacks look heavy enough to hold gold," Eskkar said. "Perhaps he's trading gemstones."

"Perhaps," Bracca said, without too much enthusiasm. "But plenty of merchants trade in precious stones, and they follow the main caravan route."

He clapped Eskkar on the shoulder. "Well, at least we're not carrying bags of bread any more."

Eskkar smiled. "Yes, and we're not likely to eat anything tonight either. Perhaps Aram-Kitchu will share his private food supplies with us. We did save his goods and probably his life."

"He's a selfish, greedy merchant, like all the others. He wouldn't share his precious dates and honey with his own mother, if he ever had one, not even if she begged on her knees."

"Well, we can ask."

They didn't have to ask after all. Aram-Kitchu ordered the halt himself when darkness began to close in. He untied the bundle that contained his own provisions and dropped it on the ground, and he told Tarrata to make sure everyone got something to eat.

In a near-frenzy of hunger, the men devoured a richer, darker bread than the one they had been eating thus far, with a few dates and an apple. The merchant held back for himself only one item – three tiny pots of honey.

After the meal ended, Tarrata posted guards. For once, neither Eskkar or Bracca drew the first shift.

Tarrata walked to where the two sat. "Aram-Kitchu wants to talk to you two."

Bracca gave Eskkar a knowing dig in the ribs as they followed the Caravan Master to where Aram-Kitchu sat, the sacks containing his goods piled beside him for safekeeping.

"You two fought well today," Aram-Kitchu said. "My thanks to both of you."

"Our lives were at stake, too," Bracca said, sitting down on the ground across from the merchant, though Aram-Kitchu hadn't invited them to sit.

After a moment, Eskkar and Tarrata followed Bracca's example, the four of them forming a little square, all of them so close their feet almost touched.

"I'll see you're rewarded when we reach Orak," Aram-Kitchu said. He turned to Eskkar. "But you should have waited until I gave the order. You shouldn't have . . ."

"The longer we waited," Eskkar said, "the more confident the bandits became. A few more arrows, and your porters would have thrown down their burdens and scattered, running for their lives."

"Keep your tongue respectful," Tarrata ordered, "and don't . . ."

"No, the barbarian's right," Aram-Kitchu said. "But if something like this ever happens again, you follow orders."

"They'll be back," Bracca said, cutting in before Eskkar's blunt talk annoyed the merchant further. "They should have chased after us. My friend and I think they won't give up so easily."

"Tonight? Do you think they'll dare to come tonight?" Aram-Kitchu's voice rose. "Or will they try again tomorrow?"

"Those weren't ordinary hill country bandits," Bracca said, speaking as if he were certain of his words.

"They know you're carrying something of great value, and they must know you're heading to Orak. They may know shortcuts through these hills." Bracca shrugged. "If they get ahead of us . . ."

Eskkar saw Tarrata and Aram-Kitchu exchange glances, and decided they hadn't given much consideration to the thought of further attacks. Eskkar kept silent, preferring to let Bracca with his quicker wits and ready tongue do most of the talking.

"You two seem to know quite a lot about these bandits," Tarrata said, his voice hard. "How do we know you're not . . ."

"Don't be a fool, Tarrata," Bracca said. "If we were part of them, all we had to do was block the way for a few moments, until they descended the hill. Then you'd all be dead."

Aram-Kitchu held up his hand, stopping the argument. "Enough of that. If you think they'll return, what do you suggest?"

"It's too late to turn back to Kuara," Eskkar said. He'd thought about this earlier and the words came easily. "We have to keep moving toward Orak, and hope we can outpace any bandits chasing after us."

"I think we should head northwest," Tarrata said. "We can still cut over to the main caravan route. That'll be safer. We might meet up with another caravan."

"That's what the bandits will think," Eskkar said, "so they'll likely be moving that way. We can gain some time if we leave tomorrow at first light, and if we move as fast as possible, straight toward Orak.

By the time the bandits figure out we're not heading west, we might have covered enough ground to stay ahead of them."

Aram-Kitchu swore in frustration. "What else do you suggest?"

"We'll travel faster the less we're carrying. Leave behind everything that we don't need. Bury your goods if you must. We should take only whatever food is left and the weapons."

"We can still fight them," Tarrata insisted. "We have almost as many men as they do."

"None of the porters has a sword. Besides, they won't fight, they'll run," Eskkar said, keeping his voice low. "They won't die to save your goods. Some of your guards will run too, if things get too tough. The bandits still have one bow and at least twelve men, all carrying swords, against the eight of us. And the next time they attack, they'll have a better plan, one that works to their favor."

"Listen to Eskkar," Bracca said. "He's survived a hundred fights."

"And if we decide instead to go toward the main caravan trail?" Aram-Kitchu asked, his eyes going from one to the other.

"Then you go without us," Eskkar said. "The bandits are probably already moving that way, or we'd have seen them pursuing us. If you go toward the trail, they will get ahead of you. All they're carrying are weapons and food."

"You swore to accompany us," Tarrata said, his voice rising. "You've been paid . . ."

"We've already earned double what you paid us," Bracca cut in, his voice rising in anger. "We're not going to stay and get killed for a few pieces of silver."

"All right, Bracca," Aram-Kitchu said. "You and Eskkar have convinced me. We'll go north. What else do you suggest?"

"Divide the loads equally among the porters and guards," Bracca said. "Do that now, tonight. Leave everything we don't need behind. Then, just before dawn, we wake the men, and start moving north to Orak." He turned to Eskkar. "Anything else?"

"No, but you might want to promise extra silver to everyone. And warn them they'll be running for their lives from dawn to dusk for the next couple of days."

Eskkar watched the merchant and his caravan master exchange glances. Neither man, Eskkar noticed, had denied that something of great value might be contained within the sacks.

—⟨⟩—

Aram-Kitchu and Tarrata took their time rummaging through the packs, shifting goods and selecting what would be left behind. When they finished, the merchant disappeared into the darkness alone, lugging two sacks while Tarrata kept watch until Aram-Kitchu returned, empty-handed.

"He only buried two sacks," Eskkar commented. "He'll still risk all our lives for a few bags of trade goods."

"He's a trader," Bracca said. "What did you expect him to do, leave everything of value behind?"

"Better to lose the goods than our lives," Eskkar said.

"Our lives are worth nothing to him, you big ox. Now get some sleep while you can. Tomorrow's going to be a long day."

Tarrata kept half the men on guard while the others tried to snatch whatever sleep they could. In the grayness before dawn, the march resumed, Aram-Kitchu leading the way.

All the men in the caravan wore grim expressions. Everyone's legs ached, and no one had slept well. When the sun finally cleared the horizon, they saw nothing but the empty hills behind them. If the bandits followed, they remained out of sight.

Eskkar joined the merchant at the head of the cavalcade. Setting the pace as fast as his long legs could force it, Eskkar strode along, making Aram-Kitchu and the others match him stride for stride, even though the merchant carried no burden.

Eskkar decided he wouldn't let the barren landscape either change his plan or slow down his progress. The bandits could be moving on another trail, one running in the same direction. Even though he couldn't glimpse anyone pursuing them, that didn't mean the bandits had given up.

Aram-Kitchu refused to rest until midmorning, when the weary porters begged the merchant to call for a halt. Everyone fell to the ground, exhausted.

"We should rest here, maybe until midday." Tarrata stretched his legs out before him. The four men had gathered together once again.

"I'm as tired as the rest of you," Eskkar said, "but we should stop only long enough to recover our wind." He turned to Bracca, who nodded agreement.

"Damn you, Eskkar," Tarrata said, "you're not in charge here."

"No, we're not," Bracca said, his voice hard with anger. "But if we start walking, half the men will follow us. And I doubt if they'll hold onto their packs. If you stay behind, that's better for Eskkar and me. The bandits aren't going to waste time chasing after a few empty-handed guards, not after they've caught up with the rest of you."

"Stop all this bickering," Aram-Kitchu ordered. He faced Tarrata. "We'd best trust Eskkar and Bracca to get us through this. They seem to know how bandits think."

The merchant tightened his lips for a moment. "I suppose it's better if we push on. The sooner we get out of these damned hills, the better." Aram-Kitchu shifted his gaze to Eskkar. "When you're ready, let Tarrata know."

Eskkar nodded, then stretched out flat on the ground. He closed his eyes and waited until he felt certain the sun had risen higher in the sky. "Let's get going."

Bracca climbed to his feet, but Tarrata turned his eyes toward his master.

"Get the men moving," Aram-Kitchu said, pushing himself upright. "We'll follow Eskkar's suggestions until we're safe."

It took all four of them to get the grumbling men up and on their feet again. Porters and guards, all wanted more rest, but the threat of being left behind got them moving. That and Aram-Kitchu's promise of extra pay when they reached Orak.

Still complaining, the men gathered up their burdens and started trudging along, gradually working the stiffness out of their limbs.

Eskkar sent Bracca, who carried the captured bow and quiver of arrows, a few hundred paces ahead. If the bandits planned another attack, the caravan needed some warning. Bracca had as much hunting and tracking skills as Eskkar, and was a better archer as well. If anyone was likely to spot the signs of an ambush, it would be Bracca.

They stopped when the sun reached its zenith, and again at mid-afternoon. Each time it took more and more effort to get the men back on their feet. Their steps dragged now, their weary legs no longer able to maintain the rapid pace.

The last stretch of the day's journey proved the longest. Tarrata normally stopped the caravan a little before sundown to give every-one time to find firewood and whatever else the land offered.

Instead, Eskkar pushed the men until it grew too dark to walk. When he finally gave the order to halt, men sank to the earth and lay there, too tired even to grumble.

They devoured the remains of their bread and food, wolfing it down dry. The last of their water had gone at midday. As they ate, each man scooped the tiniest crumb that fell, determined not to waste a morsel of the hard bread.

"Tomorrow," Bracca said, his voice hoarse and dry, "we'll need to find water, and soon."

"There's a stream not far ahead," Tarrata said. "We should reach it by midmorning. After that, we'll have another half a day's walk before we get out of these hills."

"How far before we reach some farm, somewhere we can get something to eat?" Bracca asked.

"Not many farms close to the hills," Aram-Kitchu said. "The soil isn't that fertile. And there are too many bandits."

Once again, Eskkar wondered what the merchant carried that made it worth all this risk. Not that it mattered any more, Eskkar decided.

"We covered twenty, maybe even twenty-two miles today," Eskkar said.

"If we can keep up this pace, we can make Orak in three days. We only need to get through tomorrow. If the bandits have gone to the west, they'll never be able to catch up, not without horses. By sundown tomorrow, we should be safe enough."

"What makes you so certain of that, barbarian? You've never been in these parts before. Or have you?" Tarrata couldn't keep his suspicious tongue in check despite his master's order.

"No, he hasn't," Bracca said, more than a little annoyed with the man's hard-headed comments, "but I have, and I've told him where we are. Now keep a civil tongue in your head, or we will leave you behind."

"Be silent, both of you," Aram-Kitchu said. "I know the route well enough, and I think Eskkar's guess is good. Let's not quarrel about nothing. Better to argue all this over a cup of ale in Orak."

"One more day of hard traveling, then?" Bracca asked.

"One more day," Tarrata said, reluctantly. "In that case, we'd better get some sleep."

They arranged the watch into shorter shifts. No one would be able to stay awake and alert for half the night, not after the day's long journey. Everyone slept, occupying any patch of the hard ground and falling asleep the moment their heads rested on the earth. Eskkar kept his naked sword by his side, taking comfort in the hard bronze before he fell into a sound sleep.

24

Dawn found them stiff and sore, and loud groans sounded as the men climbed to their feet. They didn't begin moving until the sun cleared the horizon. Tarrata oriented himself with the sun, and they headed north once again, but this time the caravan master guided the group somewhat to the east.

"The stream shouldn't be too far away," he said, walking beside Bracca and Eskkar. "There were some farmers working the land there, until bandits drove them off."

"Suppose we find bandits at the stream?" Bracca asked.

"Then we kill them," Eskkar said. "We need water. If we don't get it by noon, we'll be finished, too tired and weak to fight or walk."

Just before mid morning, they crossed a ridgeline and saw a farm nestled against the base of a series of low hills. A stream flowed between two hillocks and passed within a hundred paces of three crumbling mud brick huts.

No animals grazed nearby. Two fields, originally seeded with wheat and barley, now grew wild with weeds interspersed among the crops. Neither structures nor land showed any signs of recent human tending.

"Looks abandoned," Tarrata said, as the four of them lay on the crest, peering down at the site.

"We'd better get in and get out," Bracca said. "The bandits must know of this place, too. If they figure out we're not carrying water, they'll guess we might come here."

"At least it's downhill," Eskkar said, getting to his feet and leading the way. His mouth felt dry as the southern desert.

Everyone rushed into the stream, gulping the cold water, until their stomachs could hold no more. His thirst quenched, Eskkar washed the dust and dirt from his hands and face. Splashing across the water, he explored the crumbling buildings, Bracca a step to his rear, bow in hand and a shaft nocked to the string.

Eskkar had to duck his head to get through the entrance of the largest structure, and once inside, his hair brushed against the sagging ridge poles that held up the ceiling. The smell of urine and worse lingered in the room, the sure sign of men too lazy to clean up after themselves.

Despite the litter covering the floor, the room showed evidence of recent occupation. A good supply of firewood stood piled against the wall. Blankets and three clay jars, in useable condition, rested on a bench.

Bones and blackened ashes formed a circle in the center of the floor, beneath the roof opening. An empty water skin hung from a peg on the wall. Eskkar took it down, examined it, and slung it over his shoulder. "We'll be able to take some water with us."

"Not farmers, not living like this," Bracca commented, his foot kicking aside a broken stool. "Living like animals."

"Probably bandits," Eskkar said, stirring the ashes with his foot. "And within the last four or five days."

"Doesn't look like they kept any women here. You'd think there'd be a woman or two with the bandits."

Women would have kept the place cleaner.

"No animals, no vegetable garden, no women, no brats," Eskkar added, finishing the picture. "Not at this place. There must be another refuge nearby."

"That one would have to be closer to the main caravan trail," Bracca said, thinking it through. "Otherwise, by the time word reached this far up into the hills, any traders passing on the main road would have come and gone."

Eskkar remembered his days as a brigand, though his experiences differed. He and his marauders had ridden across the wide and mostly empty northern lands.

These men plied their trade on foot over a smaller area, but one with more activity and richer pickings. And here, in the steep and rocky hills, horses would be more of a handicap than a help, attracting too much attention and requiring more care than they were worth.

"If they kept their raiding small," Eskkar said, "hitting only an occasional caravan, they could do very well in these hills."

"If they thought we went to the west, then . . ."

"Damn Ishtar and Marduk both," Eskkar said. "We've got to get out of here now."

"Why, what's the rush?" Bracca asked.

"I think the bandits use this place as a lookout, to keep watch over the old trail. Men were here, and probably traveled south to join the ambush against us," Eskkar continued, his mind working out the details.

"After we escaped the trap, the bandits probably went toward the main caravan trail, expecting to get ahead of us and set another ambush. But their women and children . . . they've got to have a few of them . . . would be watching the main trail. By now they know we didn't go toward the west, or their women and lookouts would have seen us. And since they know this is the only place we can find water . . ."

"If they've met up with their women soon enough, they could be right behind us," Bracca said, finishing the thought. "If any of these women even exist."

"Do you want to take the chance they don't?" Eskkar didn't wait for the reply.

"I'd better see if anyone's coming up behind us," Bracca said, proving he was no fool. "I'll climb the hill and look. You break the news to the merchant."

Eskkar went back to the stream, where Aram-Kitchu, Tarrata, and the others sat resting, most of them soaking their feet in the water.

"Well, this place looks like a good place to get some rest." Aram-Kitchu had a smile on his face, the first one Eskkar had ever seen. "We can start again at noon and . . ."

"No, we have to keep going," Eskkar said. He explained his thoughts while Bracca went to climb the hill behind the huts to see if anyone pursued them. "They're probably closing on us even now."

"You mean you want to leave right away?"

"Yes, we're guessing they moved to the west to intercept us. But by now they must have discovered from their lookouts that we didn't pass that way. So they'll be heading here. This is the only place for miles to get water."

"The men need to rest," Tarrata said. "At least until noon."

"Aram-Kitchu, Tarrata, we have to leave now. They'll have picked up our trail early this morning. Unless you want to try and fight them off. They could be here at any moment."

"They probably turned back long ago," Tarrata said, shaking his head. "We've kept up a brutal pace. I doubt they could match the ground we've covered."

Eskkar shrugged. "Maybe." He turned to Aram-Kitchu. "Perhaps your goods aren't worth the chase. But Bracca and I are leaving."

The mention of his goods brought a frown to the merchant's face. He turned to his caravan master. "We'd better keep going."

"The men need rest," Tarrata insisted. "We can't go on much longer."

"We've had our fill of water," Eskkar said. "There's nothing to eat here. We'll only be hungrier the longer we stay. We can still make a day's march before dark."

He turned and walked to the stream to rinse the water skin thoroughly before filling it. By then Bracca had descended from the hilltop.

"I didn't see anything, but we should get out of here. These empty hills don't feel right to me."

Eskkar slung the now-heavy water skin over his shoulder. "Time to go."

The two men started walking, not even bothering to look behind them to see if anyone followed. Before they'd gone a hundred paces, the merchant and Tarrata had the men on their feet, everyone shouldering their burdens, and following after the two fighters. By now even the porters and guards had come to trust Eskkar and Bracca.

Bracca and Eskkar took turns scouting the trail ahead. They pushed the pace as hard as they dared, and the porters stumbled under their burdens.

During the remainder of the morning and into the long afternoon, they saw no signs of any farmers or herders. No smoke rose into the air from cooking fires, and even fertile patches of earth stood uninhabited. With bandits looting and hiding in these hills, any farmers who might have attempted to scratch a living here would be long gone or dead.

When the sun began to set, they crossed another stream, this one hardly more than a trickle of water bubbling from an underground source in the surrounding cliffs. By then even Eskkar had reached his limit and needed to rest.

The last handfuls of food disappeared, wolfed down by ravenous men. There wasn't enough to assuage anyone's hunger, but no one complained. They drank, trying to fill their empty bellies with water, before sinking to the ground, too tired for the moment to post a guard.

The brief meal ended, the four leaders found themselves facing each other once again. By now even Tarrata appeared too tired to argue anymore.

"We saw no signs of anyone following us," Aram-Kitchu said, hope sounding in his voice.

"They can read tracks as well as the next man," Bracca said. "They'll know how far behind us they are."

"If they're not already ahead of us," Eskkar said. "They may follow paths through these hills that even you and Tarrata don't know. They've probably been living here for years, and know every goat track and shortcut."

"Still, we've not much further to go," Aram-Kitchu said. "By early afternoon tomorrow, we'll be back on the main trail, with Orak only two days ahead."

Eskkar nodded his agreement. "If we can match the pace we've set for the last two days, we'll be safe."

"The men will march," Tarrata said, "or I'll kill them myself. Better to be tired and hungry, than rested and dead from starvation, or worse."

Eskkar kept his face impassive at Tarrata's change of heart. No doubt the merchant had convinced his caravan master of the need for haste.

"Then we know what we have to do," Aram-Kitchu said.

Tarrata, Eskkar, and Bracca went to where the guards and porters lay scattered on the ground. The caravan master explained the situation and their plan, telling the men what to expect for the rest of the night and until midday tomorrow.

To Eskkar's surprise, the men hardly protested; either they were too tired to resist, or the thought of reaching Orak alive and with the extra silver made up for the forced marches.

Once again Tarrata assigned guards for the night, this time dividing the men in three groups. Bracca got the first shift, and Eskkar dropped to the ground and slept like the dead until Bracca woke him.

Rubbing his eyes, Eskkar tried to stay alert. The other two men sharing the shift were in worse shape. Twice he had to prod first one, then the other, when they'd started nodding off.

The rest of the shift passed in silence, except for the men snoring away, disturbing any small night sounds that might otherwise have been heard. As soon as he felt his eyes nodding again, Eskkar woke Tarrata and the others.

When his relief were all awake, Eskkar again lay down beside his sword and closed his eyes. This time, at least, he knew he'd sleep until dawn. He heard his own heavy breathing before he fell into a deep sleep, his tired body demanding rest.

Something jarred him from his sleep. For a moment, Eskkar lay there, struggling to figure out what woke him. Then something tugged at his arm, and he realized Bracca knelt beside him, his hand grasping Eskkar's wrist.

"Keep silent. I think I heard something."

Awake in a moment, Eskkar felt his heart beating rapidly as he reached for his sword. Bracca wasn't the kind to imagine things. With sword hilt in hand, Eskkar felt safer.

Bracca stayed beside him, both men kneeling on the ground, their eyes scanning the darkness surrounding them. Eskkar heard nothing, saw nothing. A glance at the dimming stars told him dawn would be on them soon enough.

"Are you sure . . ."

With a shout, the bandits attacked, an arrow whistling through the air to bring down one of the sentries. Like shadows from the demon pits below, the bandits charged at them, shouting as they came. Bracca screamed the alarm, and everyone reached for their weapons as they tried to shake the sleep from their bodies.

The attackers charged from one side, storming toward the caravan. Eskkar remained on one knee, waiting, until a shadow loomed over him. He lunged forward, burying his sword deep in the man's chest.

Leaping to his feet and screaming his war cry, Eskkar wrenched the sword free and swung it at another bandit. This man reacted quickly, and Eskkar's blade clashed against bronze, though he heard his opponent gasp at the shock of the blow.

Before the man could recover, Eskkar moved to his right and struck again, this time feeling the blade bite into flesh. A glinting blade flashed at him in the moonlight, and he jumped aside, then struck back.

A grunt of pain and a curse answered the stroke, but Eskkar heard movement behind him. Ducking low, he flung himself to the side, as a sword hissed past his head, a clumsy but powerful stroke that would have cut him in two if it landed.

Every man in Aram-Kitchu's caravan fought with the desperation born of knowing what would happen if they yielded. The attack wavered, as bandits, porters, and guards mixed together, and the darkness made it difficult to tell friend from foe.

Eskkar swung his sword in a wide arc, clearing a space around him. A man moved to Eskkar's left, and he struck at the man's back, a cutting blow. The wounded man stumbled forward, howling in pain.

Bracca's voice boomed over the clash of weapons. "Caravan," he shouted, trying to rally the men around him, "to me! Form a line on me."

Eskkar realized he'd managed to place himself on the wrong side of the fight. A shadowy mass of men moved toward Bracca, most of them bandits, more than enough to overwhelm Bracca and whatever defenders remained.

Screaming his war cry, Eskkar launched himself at the attackers, charging into them from behind, hacking right and left, moving constantly, cutting at every looming shadow or any spot of paleness that might be a face.

The attackers hesitated for a moment, surprised to find someone behind them. By then Bracca had rallied the survivors into a knot of men, all facing their onrushing opponents. The clash of bronze mixed with the shouts of men cursing at each other as they fought, and drowned out the cries of the wounded.

Notwithstanding, two bandits turned to face Eskkar, and he struck at first one, then the other, but neither stroke landed. They moved apart and came toward him, bared teeth gleaming in the faint light, their swords raised.

Eskkar took a step backwards, trying to keep both men in front of him. Their swords flashed at his head. Dodging and weaving as he retreated, Eskkar somehow parried both strokes, moving away from his attackers as he defended himself.

They continued the attack, working together, looking for a chance to break through Eskkar's guard. He jumped away and tried to move around them to reach Bracca's position.

Instead, he tripped over a body and fell hard on his back. With a shout of victory, one of his attackers loomed up, his sword already swinging down. Eskkar twisted to one side and threw himself at his attacker's legs.

Eskkar's shoulder smashed into the man's knee, bringing the bandit down on top of him and knocking the breath from Eskkar's lungs. His sword useless at such close range, Eskkar dropped the blade and snatched his dagger, thrusting it into the man's stomach a moment before his enemy could bring his short sword to bear.

The other bandit loomed over them both, his sword held low, trying to determine friend from foe on the ground. Using all his strength, Eskkar shoved his wounded attacker aside, and scrambled backwards along the ground, attempting to get to his feet.

The bandit's sword came down in a wild swing, and Eskkar felt a burning pain erupt in his leg. Cursing, he rolled back the way he'd come, getting close to his attacker and thrusting up with the knife.

The man's sword knocked Eskkar's knife stroke aside. His assailant took a step back, to gain his footing for a killing blow, but now it was Eskkar's enemy who stumbled over some obstacle in the dark and landed on the ground.

Ignoring the pain in his leg, Eskkar tried to regain his feet, but another shadow crept up behind him. This new assailant carried no sword. Instead, the bandit wielded a club, which he swung blindly through the darkness as Eskkar sought to move aside.

Something smashed against Eskkar's head. Stunned, his arms turning to water, the knife slipped from his hand and Eskkar pitched headfirst to the ground, tasted the earth in his mouth, felt the ground swirling around him for an instant, until everything turned to blackness.

When he regained consciousness, Eskkar found himself on his back, the sun shining into his eyes. Blinking against the brightness, Eskkar's head felt as if it would split in two, and more pain throbbed in his leg.

He reached down and touched a rough bandage wrapped around his left thigh. Bracca, his tunic and face spattered with blood but smiling all the same, walked toward Eskkar, using his shadow to block the sun from his friend's eyes.

"Glad to see you're still alive." He waved his hand at the bodies surrounding them. "Thought you were finished when I first saw you. Most of the others are dead. You missed the best part of the fight."

Still dizzy, Eskkar pushed himself into a sitting position, trying not to think about the pain in his leg and the pounding in his head.

"What happened?" His tongue felt thick and dry, and his eyes wouldn't focus.

Bracca shrugged. "We finally killed enough of them. Eleven dead bodies . . . drove another five or six off after Tarrata killed their leader. Even so, they managed to grab a few of Aram-Kitchu's sacks before running off. And Tarrata's dead. Took a wound and bled out after the fight. Too bad. The old man fought well."

For Eskkar, for any warrior, those words meant the highest praise, to fight well and die in battle, killing your enemies.

"Who's left?"

"Let me see," Bracca said, looking around to make sure. "Aram-Kitchu, one porter, one guard, and you and me. That's it. You should have seen the merchant fight. Killed a bandit himself. Didn't think he had it in him."

Gazing about him, all Eskkar could see were bodies, blood, and flies. Aram-Kitchu limped over, still holding his sword. A bloody bandage was wrapped around his head, and another encompassing his left arm.

"Can he make it?" Aram-Kitchu asked, pointing his sword at Eskkar. "Or should we finish him off?"

It took a moment for Eskkar to grasp the merchant's words, but before he could even mouth a protest, Bracca's laugh echoed out. "The big ox will make it. This is just a scratch for my barbarian friend."

"We're not slowing down for him," Aram-Kitchu said, his tone sending a chill through Eskkar. "If he can't keep up, he gets left behind, or we finish him." He gestured with the sword again.

"I'll kill him myself if he can't keep up," Bracca said, laughing again. "Are you ready to go?"

"Nearly," Aram-Kitchu said. "I need to bury my goods and mark the site. It won't take long."

It didn't. Apparently the surviving bandits had snatched more than half of the trader's goods as they ran off. Eskkar's head had started to clear by the time Aram-Kitchu returned. He carried one small sack over his shoulder, and the porter and guard each carried another, larger one. "I don't suppose you two are going to carry anything?"

Eskkar glanced about for his sword, but only saw his knife. He picked it up, wiped the blade on the tunic of the nearest dead man, and managed to get to his feet, flinching against the pain in his leg.

"Where's my sword?" he growled. "I want to kill that damned merchant myself."

"Plenty of time for that," Bracca said, slipping his arm around Eskkar's shoulder. "I'm sure your sword's lying around here someplace. No self-respecting fighter would want the damn thing anyway. Might as well use a club to kill people."

"I'll use it on you if you don't help me find it."

Bracca laughed again. "You don't appreciate the humor of it all. Now that you're wounded, Aram-Kitchu knows he can kill you anytime he wants, so you'd better start acting nice to both of us."

"Not likely," Eskkar said, gritting his teeth. His leg really hurt, and he knew the long walk ahead might still kill him. Well, he wasn't dead yet. With luck from the war gods, he might survive this ordeal, too.

⁕

Luck turned against them when the weary survivors reached the main caravan trail. They encountered no others on the road, no helpful travelers going their way to give them aid.

The day after the fight, Eskkar's wound became infected. He washed it with water and bandaged it tight, as the healers had taught him, but still the wound swelled and bloody pus continued to ooze from beneath the bandage.

Without a healer, without any curing herbs, they could only press on, hoping to reach Orak before any of them died. None of the others, concerned about their own injuries, gave a thought to helping Eskkar. Without Bracca's insistence, Eskkar knew they would have left him behind.

The gods favored them in one respect. At least they didn't encounter any more bandits seeking their goods or their lives.

"Not much further now, Eskkar," Bracca said. "We're almost there. That's Orak up ahead." He stopped for a moment, to give his companion a chance to rest his leg. The others did the same, sinking gratefully to the ground.

Eskkar heard the strain in his friend's voice. Bracca had supported him for the last two days, and was nearing exhaustion himself. He talked constantly, trying to keep up Eskkar's spirits.

Meanwhile, Eskkar's wound kept shooting pain through his leg and up into his belly, making it hard to think. He lifted his eyes and forced them to focus on the road ahead. They'd just climbed a gentle slope that wound between two steeper hills.

Bracca helped Eskkar sit on a rock, so he could take a moment's rest. He straightened out his injured leg, wincing again at the pain. Glancing around, Eskkar saw the Tigris, its waters looking brownish in the fading light.

About two miles away, a good-sized village nestled in a curve of the river, surrounded by green and brown planted fields crossed with irrigation ditches. Smoke from twenty or so fires in the village trailed up into the still air.

"Get moving." Aram-Kitchu, despite his wounds, had recovered most of his strength, and all of his purpose.

"We can stay here a little longer," Bracca suggested, as the others wearily climbed to their feet.

"No. I'll make it," Eskkar said, trying to keep the weakness out of his voice. He would die like a warrior. No dirt-eaters would see him twitching in pain.

Once again supported by Bracca's arm around his waist, they pushed on.

When they descended the low rolling hills, the road wove its way between lush fields of wheat, barley, millet, flax, as well as smaller vegetable gardens growing onions, cucumbers, and other even more exotic crops. Irrigation canals flowed like snakes through the tall growth, bringing precious streams of water to the thriving plants.

Now, close to the end of their journey, they passed by others on the road, people who stared at them wide-eyed. All five were in rags, blood spattered all over what little clothing still clung to their bodies.

Eskkar and Bracca looked particularly frightening, despite their injuries. Even wounded, Eskkar retained the barbaric look of the steppes about him, while Bracca's darker skin marked him as a sinister stranger from the south.

"About time," Eskkar said through gritted teeth, trying not to show the pain. Growing up as a boy, he'd learned that warriors didn't show pain.

That, he now decided, was another lie told around the campfires at night to impress young boys. He'd never felt pain like this before, not from any of the wounds whose scars crisscrossed his body.

"If I didn't have to carry your sorry ass," Bracca said, "we'd have been here long ago."

Despite the burning in his leg, Eskkar laughed. He'd known Bracca for almost four years, and the man still made him laugh at the strangest times.

"Keep moving, you two," Aram-Kitchu called out over his shoulder. "I don't want to die here on the road, a mile from the village."

Eskkar, still leaning heavily on Bracca, gritted his teeth in anger. "Damn fool can't even see. It's almost two miles to the village."

This time Bracca laughed. "At least Aram-Kitchu's walking on his own."

Eskkar wondered about the merchant's concern. "Why doesn't he go on ahead?"

"Because I'm the only one still fit to fight, and he doesn't want to enter the village without a guard."

Somehow they made it to the gate. Two guards stood at the stout wooden barrier, casting dubious looks at the five ragged and blood-spattered men hobbling toward them.

No doubt Eskkar and Bracca, despite their wounds, would have been turned away as unsavory characters, forbidden to enter. But Aram-Kitchu acted as if he'd lived there all his life. He mentioned the names of some merchants, and that, plus a copper coin tossed to one of the guards, cleared the way.

Aram-Kitchu obviously had visited Orak before. He led them to a decent enough inn, and Bracca eased his companion to the dirt floor inside the common room. This early in the day, there were no customers, so Aram-Kitchu and the remains of his caravan had the place to themselves.

Eskkar must have blacked out for a few moments, because when he came to, an old woman was pouring water into his mouth. Ale followed the water, and by then a healer had arrived.

Eskkar lay there, still in a daze, while Aram-Kitchu and the healer bargained over the fee. The amount would be hefty, as all needed treating. Naturally the healer began with the merchant, the man paying for his services. Bracca would have been next, but he waved the healer over to Eskkar, already working on his second cup of ale.

The strong brew eased the pain as it quenched his raging thirst, and Eskkar scarcely noticed when the healer, an old man with a bald pate, knelt beside him and untied the bandage.

"Mmm, your leg is infected," he said, pulling the cloth away as gently as he could, "badly infected."

"I could have told you that." Eskkar had almost passed out when the healer's knife cut through the bandage. He gulped down the rest of the ale.

"Someone get me more ale, so I've something to hold back the pain while this old fool prays to his gods."

"I've already offered my prayers to the gods today," the healer said, ignoring the anger and pain in Eskkar's voice. "I usually find that once is enough. My name is Ventor."

The man's words distracted Eskkar enough so that he hardly flinched when the healer unwound the last of the bloody bandage.

The old man inspected the wound for a few moments. "Get him up off the floor," Ventor said. "That table will do."

He left his patient, returning in a few moments with a bucket of water. He washed Eskkar's wound, dribbling the water in small amounts, but kept the stream pouring until the bucket was empty, and Eskkar's leg completely soaked.

"I need my wound healed, not a bath," Eskkar complained. He'd gritted his teeth to hold back the pain.

"I think you need the bath more than a bandage," Bracca said, dragging up a stool and sitting beside his friend with a sigh of relief.

"You smell like you've been sleeping with pigs. Give him another bucket, healer, this one over his head."

Ventor ignored both men, extracting a cloth pouch from his box of implements. He unwrapped the cloth with care and took out a handful of pungent herbs.

Eskkar looked at them, but didn't recognize the leaves and cuttings. "What are those?"

But Ventor had no intention of giving away his secrets. Instead he carefully placed the herbs over the wound, making sure no part of the cut remained uncovered. While the healer worked, Bracca called for more ale, and soon Eskkar found another cup in his hand.

Ventor began re-bandaging the leg, winding a long strip of cloth loosely around Eskkar's thigh. When he finished, he took the cup from Eskkar's hand.

"Listen to me, barbarian. You must not move your leg. You must stay here for a few days, and I'll have to return in the morning to change the dressing. Otherwise, you'll die for certain. You'll probably die anyway, but if you move about, nothing, not even the gods, will save you. Do you understand me?"

"My name is Eskkar, healer, not barbarian." His head felt as if he were underwater, his eyes unable to focus. Something in the herbs stung the open wound and started it throbbing again.

"I did not mean to offend . . . Eskkar," Ventor said. "I only wanted to be sure I had your attention. You can have one more cup of ale for the pain, but no more."

He turned to Bracca. "Will he stay still? The herbs are scarce this season, and I don't intend to waste any more if he's going to kill himself like some ignorant fool."

"He'll stay put, I promise you," Bracca said. "I'll put my knife through his other leg if he tries to move, just to make sure."

"Curse you both," Eskkar said. The leg hurt worse than before, and the pain coursed through his body in waves. He didn't think he could move his limb, let alone stand. "Get me more ale, and I'll stay here until I die."

"Or live," Ventor said. He turned to Bracca. "Now, what's your name? Let me take a look at that arm."

Eskkar drifted into an unsettled sleep, and when he awoke, he found Aram-Kitchu had returned to the inn. Eskkar and Bracca looked up in surprise at the merchant's transformation.

Bathed, a clean bandage on his arm, his hair carefully arranged, and wearing a new tunic and sandals, the man appeared almost completely recovered from his journey. Even the large bruise on his forehead had nearly faded away. Under his arm, he still carried the sack containing his treasure.

"I've brought you your wages, Bracca . . . Eskkar," he said. "And I'll pay the innkeeper in advance for a room, so you can recover without disturbing his other patrons."

Aram-Kitchu reached inside his tunic and drew out a small pouch. He counted out ten silver coins and dropped them in Bracca's hand. "You two saved my life, and I always pay my debts. So I offer you both my thanks. If you ever need work again, come to me."

Bracca hefted the coins, holding them up so Eskkar could see them, too. "You are more than generous, Aram-Kitchu, especially for a greedy merchant. Now I don't regret saving your life and your goods."

"What was in the sack?" Eskkar asked. He felt light-headed, but his curiosity remained. "I want to know what was so valuable it nearly got me killed."

For a moment, the merchant stared at them, his eyes moving from one to another. Then he smiled. "It was never in the sack, barbarian. That was only a handful of gemstones to keep everyone's attention."

The smile turned into a laugh at the looks on their faces. Aram-Kitchu glanced around the inn. This early in the afternoon, they were alone in the common room. Even the innkeeper had gone off on some business or other.

Aram-Kitchu reached inside his tunic and pulled out a bulky square of material. Unfolding it, he carefully removed its contents and held it up before their eyes.

Dumfounded, Eskkar gazed wide-eyed at the necklace dangling from the merchant's hand. The thick links and spacers were made of gold, and no doubt of great value, but the real worth of the necklace lay in its primary jewels – twelve glistening pearls, each as big as a robin's egg.

"By the gods," Bracca said, his eyes wide in wonder, "are they real?"

Eskkar had seen pearls before, but always small ones, tiny droplets of pale white used to accent a golden pin, a woman's hair comb, or even a ring. Tears of the gods, men called them. But these pearls commanded the eye, each one a match to the others, all a brilliant, shimmering white with the tiniest hint of pink.

"They're real enough," Aram-Kitchu said, "taken from the waters of the Great Sea."

He folded the cloth over the necklace, and returned it to his tunic, looking around once again to make sure no one noticed. "A fisherman discovered a cache of them. No one has ever seen their like before, nor likely will again."

"What are they worth?" Bracca's voice echoed his wonderment.

"Their worth is nearly beyond measure, but for ignorant louts like yourselves, I suppose you could say they're worth more than a caravan filled with gold. Now keep your mouths shut about this and don't make me regret showing it to you."

A moment later, the merchant and his treasure had vanished.

Bracca's eyes went to the ten silver coins still in his hand.

"Doesn't look like much now, does it? I could have slit his throat anytime in the last three days. Both of us could have been rich. We'd never have to work again. Women, wine, anything we wanted."

"You'd manage to spend it all in a few months," Eskkar said. He felt dizzy, and his voice sounded strange in his ears. "You're not meant to be rich, Bracca, my friend."

"It might not be too late to steal it," Bracca mused out loud. "Perhaps I could manage something, hire some men." He hefted the silver in his hand. "You picked a bad time to get yourself injured, my friend."

Eskkar laughed, a real laugh that filled the common room. "Too late for that. If I know anything about merchants, he's on his way to sell the necklace as we speak. Before the sun moves a hand's breadth, someone else will own it, and no one, except the owner and his plump wife, will ever see it again."

Bracca sighed. "Well, for a moment there, I thought we could be rich. At least I have his silver."

"Half his silver, Bracca. And give me my five coins right now, before you get drunk and gamble them away or lose them in the dirt."

"You're so suspicious," Bracca said, as he reluctantly counted the coins into his partner's hand. "You should learn to be more trusting of others."

"Oh, I am," Eskkar said, his head falling back against the hard table. Another wave of dizziness swept over him, and he managed just a few more words, and only half in jest, before he passed out. "It's you that I don't trust, my good friend Bracca."

25

When Eskkar awoke, the morning sun beat down on his face through a vent hole in the ceiling. He pushed himself into a sitting position and discovered he lay on a bed, a ragged blanket covering his body. The room itself was tiny, barely more than an alcove, with a torn and fraying blanket serving as a door.

Eskkar had no idea where he was or how he got there, until he heard the innkeeper shouting at someone. Another glance at the slanting sun told him that a night and most of a morning had passed. He'd never slept through an entire day before in his life, wounded or not. Damn that healer, the man must have given him a potion to render him unconscious, probably mixed in with the ale.

His body ached, his muscles stiff and sore. When Eskkar touched his leg, a stab of pain went through his limb and he felt heat from the wound even through the bandage. A hand to his burning forehead confirmed that he still had the fever.

Suddenly aware of his thirst, Eskkar looked around for water, but the chamber held nothing but his sword lying on the floor beside him. At least someone had cleaned the blade and washed the dried blood from the hilt.

"Water."

Eskkar could scarcely get the word out, so dry was his throat. A woman pushed the curtain aside and glanced in at him. She appeared familiar, but he couldn't recall if he'd seen her yesterday or last year.

"Water," he croaked again, louder this time.

"In a moment." She let the curtain drop.

He sagged back onto the bed and closed his eyes, too exhausted to move. He must have fallen asleep, because when he opened them, the woman knelt beside the bed, a pitcher of water and a cup in her hands.

She held the cup to his lips and Eskkar drank it down, the lukewarm water as satisfying as the coolest mountain stream. He emptied two more cups before his head fell back onto the blanket, as helpless as a new-born kitten.

"I'll be right back," she said, setting the pitcher and cup on the floor beside the bed.

No sooner had she left the room than Eskkar felt the urge to piss, an insistent demand he could barely contain. "Damn that healer," Eskkar repeated, certain now that he'd drunk some evil potion.

But before he pissed himself and the bed, the woman returned, this time carrying a cracked chamber pot. Wordlessly, she helped him struggle upright, so that he could sit on the side of the bed. He managed to hold himself back until she got the pot positioned before him, and then relieved himself with a sigh of satisfaction.

After he finished, the woman helped him lie back on the bed. Drained by the effort, Eskkar closed his eyes for what he thought was only a brief moment, but when he opened them again, the woman had gone, and the sun had moved a good distance across the sky.

His forehead still felt flushed and his thirst had returned. The water pitcher remained on the floor, right next to the now empty chamber pot. He managed to lift the pitcher and quench his thirst, and fell back on the bed. Once again he lapsed into a fitful sleep. When he awoke, the chamber had darkened, and he knew dusk approached. Too tired to even think, he just lay there, his mind empty.

The blanket covering the doorway shifted and Bracca entered the room.

Eskkar forced his eyes to focus. To his surprise, Bracca wore a new tunic, the clean linen encircled around his waist by a thick new leather belt. The sword hanging from it, however, remained the same one Eskkar had sold to him long ago.

"By Marduk's shovel, it stinks in here." The loud words grated on Eskkar's ears, almost painful.

"No need to shout, damn you," Eskkar said, grateful to get the words out without his voice cracking. He struggled to sit up, and didn't have the strength to protest when Bracca helped him so that his back rested against the wall. "How bad is my leg?" He dreaded asking the question, but he needed to know.

"Your leg? The leg's healing as well as can be expected, or so says Ventor. He's your healer, in case you don't remember. The man's probably a fool. No proper healer would waste his time on a barbarian, even for ready coin."

"Good. I'll be back on my feet tomorrow," Eskkar said.

Bracca laughed. "Your wits have left you, my friend. Ventor says there's still an even chance the fever will kill you. Either way, you'll be in this bed for the next four or five days, maybe longer. In fact, you're as likely to die in it as get out of it." He laughed again at his own joke.

"I'll get up and when I do . . ."

Bracca sat on the edge of the bed, the extra weight making the frame creak ominously.

"Listen to me, barbarian," he said, his voice barely above a whisper. "I'm leaving Orak at dawn. Aram-Kitchu has asked me to be his caravan master. We're taking a boat downriver to Sumeria, to pick up another cargo of trade goods, then we're going east toward the Indus. We'll probably be gone eight or nine months, maybe longer. If we survive."

Eskkar stared, his mouth open. Somehow, he'd expected Bracca to stay with him, at least until his wound healed. Instead, his friend was planning to travel across the world as a merchant's lackey.

And to the Indus. Eskkar knew that half the caravans that ventured into those distant lands never returned.

Bracca waited until he saw Eskkar understood his words.

"I've paid the innkeeper for your room and food for the next ten days and his wife has promised to care for you during that time.

Ventor will be back at least once a day, if he has any honesty in him, to chant more prayers over your wound, or whatever it is he does. Though I've never yet met a healer I'd trust when there's a copper to be lifted from a sick man. So don't promise him or anyone else any coins, no matter what they say."

The mention of copper made Eskkar think of his pouch, and he fumbled at his waist.

"I took it, Eskkar," Bracca said, "after I carried you in here. Someone would have slit your throat for those five silver coins."

He leaned even closer. "Do you remember the road south, the place where we first saw Orak? It was about two miles . . ."

"I remember," Eskkar said, still trying to adjust to Bracca's departure.

"We sat you down on some rocks," he said, and this time Bracca did whisper, his lips almost at Eskkar's ear. "You left bloodstains all over one. I'll bury your pouch under that rock. You can pick it up when you're able. I couldn't leave it with you, out of your wits and helpless, and there's nobody to trust in this mud heap village, not with five silver coins."

Bracca straightened up. "I'll look for it on my next trip here. If it's still there, I'll know you're dead, and I'll treat myself to a night of drinking and whoring in your memory. If not . . . leave word for me with the innkeeper where you have gone, and I'll do the same the next time I visit Orak. Who knows, maybe we'll fight together once more, barbarian."

Gazing at his friend, Eskkar knew it was more likely they'd never see each other again. Time and distance would separate them almost as much as the dangers Bracca would face.

"If you can wait five or ten days, I'll come down to Sumeria. I can . . ."

Bracca shook his head. "You don't know Aram-Kitchu. It seems when he gets the trading fever, he waits for no one. That's why he's so successful. He moves quick, faster than the other traders. Always gets the best prices. I doubt we'll be in Sumeria for more than a day or two, and then we'll be gone."

He sighed at life's little injustices. "Stay here and get well, Eskkar. As villages go, this one isn't too bad, and at least they don't run away in fear at the sight of an ugly barbarian from the steppes."

Eskkar realized his friend was actually leaving. "I owe you for all this," Eskkar said. "Maybe someday I'll get to return the favor."

Bracca filled the water cup and handed it to him. "Drink up. Ventor says you should drink plenty of water."

"Curse all healers." Eskkar took the cup and drained it, embarrassed that his fingers trembled with weakness.

"Maybe not this one. I watched him work on your leg. It had swollen up like a dead sheep's stomach, and he had to slit it open to let out the pus. I don't think you'd be alive without him."

"I still don't trust any of them," Eskkar said. "Mumbling chants and incantations over your body while they cut your purse."

"Glad to see your sense of humor has returned," Bracca said. "Try not to kill anyone for the next few days."

He stood and stretched. "I have to go. Aram-Kitchu suddenly can't seem to do anything without me at his side, protecting his miserable carcass. I've become the merchant's bodyguard as well as caravan master. Soon I'll be wiping his ass for him, too. A wretched existence, and no doubt I'll come to an evil end from all this honest work."

"When you get a chance, steal him blind," Eskkar said, surprised to hear himself laugh.

"Now that's a good suggestion. I'll keep my eyes open for the first good opportunity." He gripped Eskkar's hand hard for a moment, then stood. "Heal yourself, old friend. We fought well together, and I'll remember you."

"Take care of yourself, friend Bracca. May your feeble Sumerian gods look after you."

"I'd better go," Bracca said with a laugh, "before we start crying like two old women."

Bracca vanished through the doorway, the blanket swinging vigorously from his passage. His voice sounded from the main room, speaking to the innkeeper. While Eskkar couldn't hear the words, he knew what Bracca would be saying.

He'd be telling the man and his wife to keep their guest well cared for, or there would be one less innkeeper in Orak when Bracca returned.

Eskkar had received help from many people over the years, but never as much as from Bracca. The man had saved his life at least twice in the last few days, and Eskkar knew he wouldn't have made it to Orak without his friend's assistance.

Eskkar slumped back on the bed and closed his eyes. Even the effort of talking with Bracca had sapped his strength, and he knew he'd soon be falling in and out of sleep. There was a heaviness in his heart over Bracca's leaving that bothered him almost as much as the pain in his leg.

The man had become the closest thing to a real friend Eskkar had since he left his family, the Hawk Clan, and the Alur Meriki. He and Bracca had traveled together, fought together, argued over every trifle, and cursed each other ten times each day.

Now Eskkar would be alone again, friendless, with no one to guard his back or care if he lived or died.

To his surprise, he realized that wasn't going to be what he would miss most. The tough little Sumerian had made him laugh, and a friend and companion who could manage that feat wasn't likely to ever come along again.

His eyes closed, and he drifted off to a fitful sleep, filled with dreams of sadness and gloom, knowing Bracca would be gone when he awoke.

———

Days passed, endless mornings and evenings filled with pain, delirium, and unconsciousness mixed with uneasy sleep. Eskkar had vague memories of shouting and calling for his sword, of hearing the healer's voice, of being held down on the bed while he cursed those around him.

When the fever finally broke, he awoke to see the sun shining brightly through the roof hole. It must be midmorning, he decided. His mind felt clear, though his body seemed to have no strength.

Glancing around, he recognized the inn and the tiny room Bracca had arranged for him. Eskkar even remembered the innkeeper and his wife.

With a swish of the curtain, Ventor the healer entered the room. "Well, Eskkar, you're awake. I'm glad to see the fever has broken. For a time, I thought you were on your way to meet the gods, despite my extravagant application of the healing herbs."

He carried a small stool with him, and sat beside the bed, lifting the filthy blanket and examining his patient's leg. "Your wound has closed. You'll have another scar to add to those you already have, what you barbarians call marks of bravery."

Eskkar tried to sit up, but felt as weak and helpless as a babe. "How long ... have I been here?"

"Seven days, no, this is the eighth day since your friend left you in my charge. I must say the innkeeper has complained often to me about your ranting. He claimed the demons were speaking with your voice and in some strange tongue, and demanded that I take you away. I'm afraid I had to promise him more coppers to let you remain, though I think he'd prefer if you left sooner rather than later. At least his wife feels kindly toward you."

"I don't remember."

"No reason you should. The gods and I were fighting over your spirit. This time I overcame them, though I must admit a lesser man than yourself might have succumbed. Your vitality and will saved your life, with my help, of course."

Eskkar had no idea what his vitality might be, and cared even less. "Then I'll live?"

"Yes, it seems likely. The evil spirits have departed. Now you need to regain your strength. You've done little but lay here and whimper in your sleep since you arrived."

"Help me up," Eskkar said.

With Ventor's assistance, Eskkar sat up, then struggled to his feet. At first he could barely stand, the room turning about him, but the dizziness passed. The healer helped him to the chamber pot, and Eskkar managed to relieve himself without help.

"I'm sure the mistress of the house will be glad of that," Ventor said, after Eskkar finished. "She's been cleaning up after you twice a day, at my order."

"I'll piss on my own from now on," Eskkar said, angry at the thought of wetting himself like a newborn.

"Good. I'll return before dusk to see how you're doing. Try to eat as much as you can. And walk up and down the lane whenever you can, until you regain your strength."

Ventor departed, but a few moments later, the innkeeper's wife returned, carrying a bowl of stew and some bread. She gave him a quick smile and clucked at his progress before returning to her duties.

The smell of the stew drove all other thoughts out of his head. Eskkar sat on the bed and wolfed down the food, wiping the bowl clean with the last of the bread. He would have eaten another bowl, if they'd offered him one. Afterwards, he fell back asleep, exhausted. He woke after a long rest, and this time managed to get upright on his own.

His weakness infuriated him. Eskkar wanted to fall back on the bed, but determination kept him upright. He managed to walk through the common room, and out into the lane. The sun felt good on his face, and he took a deep breath. Moving with care, he managed to take a few painful steps down the lane.

Even that effort made his muscles tremble, and he had to lean on the inn's wall. Eskkar turned around and returned to the entrance, where he rested a few moments, before repeating the journey.

The innkeeper's wife sent her son out to help Eskkar, a strapping lad of thirteen or fourteen seasons, who walked beside Eskkar to make sure he didn't fall. He kept it up until he couldn't take another step, then returned to his bed and collapsed.

Three more days passed before Eskkar felt strong enough to move about Orak on his own. By now he no longer attracted attention. The curious villagers had grown accustomed to the tall barbarian stumbling about the lanes. A few made unflattering remarks about his heritage, but Eskkar's scowl as much as his rapidly returning health soon put an end to that.

The innkeeper had returned Eskkar's knife, but announced he would keep the long sword until his customer's account was paid up. Two more days passed before Eskkar felt capable of leaving the village by himself. He hobbled to the hilltop to the south. The silver coins waited for him exactly where Bracca had said they would be.

Eskkar felt grateful for his friend's foresight. But Eskkar's leg had taken longer to mend than either Bracca or the healer anticipated, and the cost of staying at the inn mounted.

Even Ventor, despite what Bracca had paid him in advance, soon demanded a copper coin for each day, claiming the scarce herbs his patient required in large quantities were expensive.

When Eskkar returned to the inn and settled all his debts, only three silver coins remained. They wouldn't last very long, not if he had to pay for his food and his keep along with Ventor's services.

He wasn't strong enough to chance sleeping in the lanes, so he struck a new bargain with the innkeeper. Eskkar would sleep in the common room, and eat one meal a day there, along with a single cup of ale. That meant he had a place to stay for at least the next twenty days, before the last of his coins ran out.

Before that happened, Eskkar needed to regain his health and strength. He walked greater distances each day, pacing around the village, and up and down the river. It took another eight days before he felt strong enough to seek work.

That brought him to Orak's large and burgeoning marketplace, a crowded and noisy bazaar full of people buying and selling everything imaginable. Unfortunately, there were many others seeking work, and most found as little success as Eskkar.

Orak, as he soon discovered, was a rapidly growing and prosperous village. But such growth and expansion came in uneven spurts, and the need for unskilled labor varied from day to day, and season to season.

All the same, he took whatever work he could get. If there was nothing in the market, he tried his hand at unloading the boats that arrived nearly every day.

Some days work might be plentiful, with every laborer finding some toil that would at least put food in his belly. Other times, a man might spend the whole day in the market with nothing to show for it.

Eskkar faced an additional problem. As a barbarian, he would always be the last to be hired. No merchant or craftsman wanted to take a chance on a tall barbarian with a sword over his shoulder, not as long as the supply of local labor remained eager and available.

By now his silver had already disappeared, and he had only a few copper coins remaining.

Eskkar stopped sleeping at the inn. That luxury, while needed during his recovery, could no longer be afforded. Each night he slept in the fields surrounding the city, hoping no one would murder him. He returned each day to seek work in the marketplace.

If the supply of laborers appeared too plentiful there, he would visit the houses of those wealthy enough to afford horses, seeking any employment even if it meant mucking out the stables and corrals.

Orak, he soon learned, was ruled not by one village elder, but by five families who called themselves "Nobles." Together they established the rules for trading, administered justice, and provided for the village's defense. They employed a small garrison to protect themselves, of course, but also the rest of the inhabitants.

These guards had their own barracks and stable. They maintained a small number of horses, wretched beasts from what Eskkar had noted, used to chase down thieves, murderers, or escaped slaves who fled the village.

At least once a day, Eskkar visited that stable as well, generally to the frowns of those attending the animals, but he had no luck in selling his skills with horses.

All in all, Eskkar had been in Orak for over forty days, and the last of his copper coins were about to vanish.

Dusk fell as he sat on the floor of the inn, finishing his stew and trying to stretch out his single cup of ale. Tables, of course, were reserved for those paying for food and ale in quantity.

A loud voice made him look up, and he saw three men enter. They carried the short swords the dirt-eaters were so fond of, and that identified them as members of Orak's guard.

He recognized their leader, Ariamus, who called himself the Captain of the Guard. A burly man carrying plenty of muscle on his frame, he stood almost as tall as Eskkar.

Ariamus took a table, and in a loud voice ordered a pitcher of ale for himself and his companions. The innkeeper scurried to fetch the brew, and Eskkar returned to staring into his own nearly empty cup, wishing he could afford to have it refilled.

"That cup looks empty."

Eskkar looked up to find Ariamus standing over him. "It is."

"Join me, then, and I'll fill it for you." Without waiting for a reply, Ariamus turned and walked back to his table.

Reluctantly, Eskkar got to his feet, and followed the Captain of the Guard.

"Sit, barbarian," Ariamus said, waving his hand at his companions to make room. "Fill his cup."

Eskkar cautiously took a seat, careful to keep his feet beneath him in case he had to move quickly. In his experience, little good ever came from dealing with village guards.

"Yes, Captain," one of the men said with a wide grin on his face as he sloshed more ale into Eskkar's cup. "Barbarians like ale, don't they?"

"That's Marrata, my second in command," Ariamus said. "The other friendly face belongs to Gatus, one of my guards."

"My name is Eskkar." He nodded politely to each man. "And my thanks for the ale."

He took a drink from the full cup, then set it before him. Eskkar waited, keeping his curiosity from showing. No one in Orak had ever bought him ale before, so this Ariamus clearly wanted something from him.

"I hear you've been looking for work with horses," Ariamus said, sipping from his cup.

"Yes."

"Well, barbarian, I might have some work for you," Ariamus said, getting down to business. "I need someone who can follow a trail, chase after runaway slaves, and bring them back to Orak. Ever do any tracking like that?"

"I've hunted runaways before," Eskkar answered.

"And I need someone to care for the horses. I'm sure you know all about that."

"I thought you had a horse master."

Ariamus laughed, a loud noise that filled the inn and turned every eye toward him. "I did, until this morning. Then I caught the miserable thief trying to steal from my own purse."

"Well, he won't do that again," Marrata added, smacking his lips after draining his ale. "We broke both his arms and crushed his fingers, then drove him out of Orak. If he lives through the night, he'll be lucky."

Eskkar guessed that Marrata had done the breaking and crushing, and probably enjoyed every moment. Something about Ariamus, however, made him appear even more loathsome than most dirt-eaters. Still, Eskkar needed the work.

"Then there's the occasional thief or murderer," Ariamus said. "They're harder to catch and tend to fight when you corner them. I don't suppose you have any problem killing anyone that didn't want to come back to face punishment for his crimes."

"Alive or dead, I can bring them back," Eskkar said. He glanced at the third man, Gatus, an older man who kept his eyes on the table and his mouth shut.

"Good . . . that's good," Ariamus said. "For helping with the horses, I'll pay you one copper every three days. For every slave you bring back, you get two coppers. One copper for thieves, and three for murderers."

Eskkar frowned. Horses represented a valuable asset to any fighting force. "Not much payment for caring for your horses."

Ariamus waved his ale cup. "There aren't that many horses, and not much else to do, barbarian. And there are stable boys to do the mucking. You get one free meal a day, same as the other guards, assuming they put up with your company. Most of them have no use for barbarians. But if you work out, who knows, you could become one of the village's guards. Then your pay goes up to a copper every other day."

"Captain, someone his size will probably eat as much as any three of the men." Marrata rapped his cup on the table and laughed heartily at his own joke.

"My second in command is right," Ariamus said, joining in the laughter. "You'll probably cost me more than you're worth."

Hesitating, Eskkar took another sip of ale as he considered the offer. The pay wasn't enough to live on, and the food served to the guards would probably turn his stomach.

And Ariamus appeared to be the worst kind of commander – petty, arrogant, brutal. It would take months, maybe even a year, to earn enough to buy a decent horse, and that only if he got lucky recapturing runaway slaves.

Eskkar felt the walls of the inn closing in on him. With no horse and with an empty purse, he'd be trapped in this village like a rabbit in a snare, able to move about, but unable to escape.

The silence dragged on, and Ariamus decided to sweeten the offer. "You can sleep in the barracks. Not much, just a slab of wood and a blanket, but it's better than sleeping on the floor here or in the streets."

He picked up the pitcher of ale and topped off Eskkar's cup. "At least you're not likely to get your throat cut while you sleep."

"I'll do it," Eskkar said. He had no other choice, but already he hated himself as much as he knew he would end up hating this Ariamus. To assuage his helplessness, he drained off most of his ale.

"Well, that's settled," Ariamus said contentedly. "I'll be on my way, then. Gatus, stay and finish your ale, then take our new stable hand to the barracks and show him what to do."

Ariamus pushed himself to his feet and headed for the door. Marrata gulped down the last of his ale and followed his commander.

Gatus shook the pitcher of ale and grunted in satisfaction at the sound. He refilled both their cups. "Drink up," he said, his voice gruff. "That's the last time you'll ever get any free ale from our Captain of the Guard."

"How bad is Ariamus . . . Gatus?" Eskkar thought he had the name right.

The man met Eskkar's eyes for the first time. "As bad as you think, barbarian." He took another sip. "What's your name again?"

"Eskkar."

"Well, Eskkar, you'll soon learn more than you want to know about Ariamus."

Gatus drained his cup. "Welcome to Orak."

26

Two years later . . .

The skittish stallion tossed its head and snorted, its ears moving back and forth, and Sharkal eased the animal to a stop, keeping a tight grip on the halter. Obviously the horse had seen or caught the scent of something that disturbed it. He glanced around the horizon, searching for any danger, but saw nothing, no farms, no villages in sight. Only empty grassland fit for little except herding.

Then Sharkal noticed the trampled ground forty or fifty paces ahead. With a touch of his heel, Sharkal rode slowly toward the disturbance, loosening his sword in its scabbard. His mount snorted again, and this time Sharkal understood. The animal had caught the scent of blood, and now Sharkal spotted the red streaks on the grass, where something had crawled along, leaving the blood trail in its wake.

A few more paces forward, and Sharkal halted again. He patted the horse on the side of the neck, to calm its fears. Closer to the blood smell, the horse might bolt and toss its rider, and he didn't intend to spend the rest of the day chasing after it.

He stared down at the man lying face up in the grass. Blood covered the man's hands and the front of his tunic. He'd pulled himself along the ground until he could go no farther, then must have rolled onto his back with the last of his strength.

Staring down, Sharkal saw the wound in the man's chest, and knew he was dying.

The death of one more dirt-eater meant little to him. Sharkal had watched uncounted numbers of them die in his lifetime, many by his own hand. This one appeared no different from the others, an insignificant grubber of the earth crawling on his belly across the ground, a blood trail marking his passage.

The dying farmer lifted his eyes. "Help me, stranger."

The voice sounded weak and full of pain. Sharkal said nothing. Fresh blood still oozed onto the man's dirty tunic.

"Please, help me," the man pleaded, his eyes wide as he fought against the pain. "I don't want to die alone."

Sharkal swung down from his horse and stepped within a pace of the man. "There's nothing I can do for you. You've lost a lot of blood. You'll be dead soon."

"I know. My farm . . . it's just over the hill." The effort to speak made him cough, and bloody foam appeared on the man's mouth.

"My family . . . please . . . please take me to them." Another cough, this one accompanied by a gasp of pain. He tried to pull himself closer to Sharkal's horse, but the effort exhausted him. The dirt-eater again raised his eyes imploringly.

"Please . . ."

Nothing would be gained by helping the man. Sharkal knew he should ride on. Here in the middle of nowhere, east of the Euphrates River, the victim's kin might think Sharkal had done this, might blame him. Best to leave and avoid trouble.

Instead, he knelt beside the man. Lifting him by the shoulder, Sharkal moved the blood stained tunic aside. The movement wrenched another bloody cough, and the dirt-eater shook spasmodically for a few heartbeats.

Sharkal saw that the wound to his chest was too small for a sword. Probably a knife that had slipped in under the man's ribs and penetrated deep enough to pierce the lung. Men wounded like that always died, and usually after a lingering agony.

"It's a bad wound. Death will take you soon."

"I know. My farm . . . it's not far . . . take me there. Please, I beg you." He lifted a shaky hand and pointed in the direction he'd been crawling. "Please don't leave me."

With a grunt at his own foolishness, Sharkal slid one arm beneath the man's legs and picked him up, lifting him like a child. But even Sharkal's powerful muscles strained as he set the man on the horse, and he almost lost his footing when the animal shifted uneasily.

"Hold onto the mane," Sharkal ordered.

The injured man weighed too much for the horse to carry Sharkal as well, so he would have to walk beside his mount. Holding the halter with one hand, he supported the dirt-eater with the other. A touch on the horse's neck started the animal moving. The man groaned with pain, but held on, swaying with each step the horse took.

"Thank you . . . stranger."

Sharkal swore under his breath. He should have left the man to die. Nothing Sharkal could do or say would change the man's fate.

They didn't have far to go. As soon as they reached the crest of the hill, Sharkal saw the tiny plot of green that marked the farmer's land. The horse plodded along, tossing its head every few steps at the too-tight grip on its mane. Sharkal wanted to speed up the pace, but anything faster would kill the dirt-eater before they reached his farmhouse.

As they drew close to the farm, a dog began to bark, joined almost at once by another. Two women working in the field looked up, surprised to see a stranger leading a horse and rider toward them.

Sharkal heard one of them call out. A man and a boy appeared from behind the hut, all four of them standing and staring. Then one of the women recognized the rider.

"Tarrae! It's Tarrae." She dropped the stick she'd been using to dig in the ground, and rushed toward Sharkal and his burden.

He eased the horse to a halt ten paces from the hut and lifted the man down. The frantic woman had to help unclench the dying man's fingers from the horse's mane, but they got Tarrae into the shade at the side of the hut.

"What happened to my brother? Who did this? Who are you?"

The questions came from the oldest of the dirt-eaters, his hands clenched tight around a digging stick. Fear and suspicion showed in his eyes. Sharkal observed the resemblance between him and the injured man.

"I found him on the other side of the hill. He asked me to bring him here."

The women ripped apart Tarrae's tunic, one of them crying out when she saw the wound. The boy ran to fetch a bucket of water, as they tried to help their kinsman.

"He's not the one . . . he helped me," Tarrae gasped. "Two bandits attacked . . . he found me. Brought me home."

Satisfied for a moment that Sharkal didn't intend to murder them all, the brother dropped his digging stick and went to the injured man's side.

"We have to bandage the wound," one woman said, her voice quivering as her body shook.

"Too late for that, Wife," Tarrae said, his voice little more than a whisper.

He managed to take her hand. "I wanted to die at your side, to rest in your arms one last time. I didn't want to die alone."

Tarrae raised his eyes toward Sharkal. "May the gods reward you, stranger." His eyes closed, and he said nothing more.

His wife cried out as she held her husband, her body hunching over as she rocked him back and forth, tears falling onto his bloody chest.

A few more moments, and Sharkal saw the man's hand go limp, and knew his spirit had flown from his body to face whatever journey awaited him below the earth.

Not that any dirt-eater could expect much favor from the spirits standing guard at the underworld. Only warriors received the rewards of the gods, and only those warriors who died fighting bravely would enjoy the best of the battle-god's gifts.

All the rest would be servants and slaves for as long as the gods endured. Or so the old ones claimed.

Sharkal turned away and gathered up the horse's halter. He'd wasted enough time already.

"Wait," the brother said, rising from his knees beside the body. "I want to thank you for helping my brother. Is there anything you need, anything we can do?"

"Nothing. All I did was bring him here."

He swung up on the horse, and put his heels to the animal. In a few moments he crested the hill and left the farm behind. Plenty of sun still remained in the afternoon sky, and Sharkal continued on his journey to the south, the dead farmer already forgotten.

Not that he had any real destination. One pile of hovels was much the same as any other, and at every farmhouse and in every village he would find the same distrust or even hatred for his barbarian heritage.

Just before sundown, he crossed a stream and decided to make an early camp. After he finished caring for the horse, he built a fire, though he had nothing to cook over it. Last night Sharkal had set out snares, but this morning they remained empty.

Nor had any game animals crossed his path today, even if he had a bow to hunt them. Tonight all he had to eat was half a loaf of stale bread, and that meant he would have to stop at the next village he encountered and beg for work. If the gods felt generous, he might be able to sell his services as a bodyguard.

The fire burned low, and he lay on his back staring at the stars. Thoughts of the dying man returned, and for once Sharkal couldn't dismiss them from his mind, though he knew no warrior should waste a single breath over a miserable farmer too weak to defend himself. The man had probably died without striking a blow at his attackers.

Yet something nagged at him. Tarrae had seen death drawing near, and his only thought was to die in his wife's arms, surrounded by his family. He hadn't cursed his murderers, or implored either his kin or their gods to avenge his death.

He wanted only to be with his woman before he began his gloomy journey to the afterworld.

Sharkal found himself envying the dead man such a comfort. When Sharkal met whatever fate the gods sent, there would be no one to comfort him, no one to say the warrior words over his body. He had no friends, no kin.

At best, only strangers would surround his body, and they would think as little of him as he had of Tarrae. At worst, Sharkal would die in some meaningless fight, accomplishing nothing, with his enemies gloating over his death and mutilating his corpse.

The dirt-eater's life meant something, at least to his family. Many wives shed no tears over their husband's death. But Tarrae's woman had sobbed over her man's passing, his suffering wracking her body with honest grief.

Sharkal recalled his wives, but found no comfort in the thought. Neither of them would have mourned him long, and he cared as little for them. They probably forgot his existence the day he fled his clan.

In his years as an honored warrior among the Alur Meriki, he had his kin and his friends to comfort him. Now all that had vanished, like the smoke from the dying fire before him. He had no one. No man would ever extend the hand of friendship to him. He would die alone.

Eskkar. The memory returned, jumping into Sharkal's mind as though their meeting happened yesterday, not years earlier. Eskkar understood Sharkal's plight, had offered the hand of friendship to him, but Sharkal in his pride refused it. He could have ridden with Eskkar, perhaps formed a close and enduring friendship with another clan outcast like himself.

Instead, he'd felt only contempt for Eskkar, who'd learned to live with the dirt-eaters in a way that Sharkal could not comprehend. Now, alone in the night, Sharkal understood how much like Eskkar he had become.

Eskkar had changed from his own life as a steppes warrior, had somehow adapted and found a way to live among the dirt-eaters. He might never be fully accepted within their society, but at least Eskkar could sit at the outer edge of their campfires at night and take some solace in their company.

Sharkal remembered how Dilmun's fighters cheered Eskkar after their victory. Sharkal had fought just as hard, and the victory was as much his doing as Eskkar's, but the men turned to Eskkar with their exuberant shouts of joy, not to Sharkal.

It didn't matter to them that he, not Eskkar, was the stronger warrior. For those few days, Eskkar had joined their brotherhood, while Sharkal faded into the background, alone.

At the time, Eskkar had praised Sharkal's role, and given him equal credit. But Sharkal had ignored that gesture, even as he turned his back on those who had fought beside him.

The last of the fire's orange embers burned out, unnoticed, but the stars glinted even brighter above. Sharkal gazed at them as he thought about his life. Some of the old men in the clan proclaimed the stars held sway over a warrior's life, but he never believed their stories.

Even so, certain stars moved across the sky, taking their time, a gradual movement almost imperceptible, but over the course of a season, they shifted. Perhaps the gods sent them as a sign that, even for him, it was not too late to change.

Sharkal thought about what he wished for, in his remaining years. A son to carry on his name would be a blessing. Suddenly the thought of taking one of the dirt-eaters as a wife no longer seemed so repugnant.

Most of all, Sharkal wanted a chance to die in battle, with honor, under the eyes of a friend so that he would be remembered, perhaps even recalled in a tale. Nearly ten years had passed since he had dishonored his name and fled the clan, leaving everyone and everything he knew behind. Now, only with another outcast might Sharkal find what he needed.

A few months ago, he'd encountered one of the veterans of the Dilmun campaign. The man mentioned that Eskkar now earned his keep as a soldier in the village of Orak.

Sharkal knew of Orak. Everyone seemed to know about the rapidly growing village on the far side of the Tigris, though he had never visited it. He could reach the village in eight or nine days riding.

With a grunt that startled his horse, Sharkal made up his mind. He would go to this Orak, and search out Eskkar. Perhaps he could fight once again at Eskkar's side. Perhaps the hand of friendship would again be offered. This time, Sharkal knew, he would accept it gladly. If Eskkar turned his face away, so be it.

A breeze shifted the night air, and he felt the melancholy vanish. He thanked the gods for showing him the stars and giving him purpose in his life once again. With the decision made, he rolled over on his side and fell asleep within moments, a sleep deeper and more peaceful than any he'd experienced in many months.

Three days later, a little after midday, Sharkal rode into the village of Nuantek, a dreary collection of fifteen or twenty mud huts located midway between the Euphrates and the Tigris.

He had no coins in his purse, and hadn't eaten anything since yesterday morning, when he finished his last two apples. He would have to find some work here, either that or he'd need to steal food from some miserable dirt-eater.

As he rode between the huts, only a few haggard faces gazed at him. The village looked deserted. There should be more people moving about, staring at the stranger and scurrying around like all the villagers he'd known. A place this size should support at least a hundred inhabitants.

Sharkal found what must be Nuantek's sole inn at the far end of the village, with nothing beyond it but a thick field of wheat that faded into grassland. A thin stream of smoke came from the roof, and a rickety and empty corral was attached to one side of the low structure, only a few paces from the growing crops.

He slid down from his horse and patted the animal's neck.

A bald man with a thick black beard wearing a filthy tunic stepped from the darkened interior, weariness showing on his narrow face which bore recent scabs from the pox. He looked to have about thirty seasons on his thin but sturdy frame.

"You might want to ride on, stranger," he said, wiping his hands on his thighs. "The pox swept through here ten or twelve days ago. I was one of the first to come down with it, but the gods helped me survive. Many of us died, or fled to the farms."

"I had the pox when I was a child," Sharkal answered carelessly, tying his horse's halter to the top of the corral. "I need food and something for the horse. I've nothing to pay with, but I'll take any work, whatever you have, if you need anything done. If not, maybe you have some food you can spare."

Moldy bread and rotting vegetables had filled Sharkal's belly more times than he wanted to admit. He'd begged for such lowly fare before.

The man ran his eyes over Sharkal's powerful frame. "If you're not afraid of getting the pox, I've plenty of work for you right here," the man answered. "My name is Yammar. I'm the innkeeper."

"Greetings, Yammar," Sharkal said, his hunger prompting him to add a slight bow as a sign of respect. "My name is Sharkal, and I'd be grateful for the work. My horse needs at least a handful of grain now."

"Looks a little thin," Yammar said, "but good horseflesh. There's a corral behind the house. I've some feed stored there. Put your horse in the corral while I get the grain."

When Sharkal led the horse to the corral, he stopped in surprise. The rear of the inn lay open to the elements, and almost half of the side wall was missing.

Yammar retrieved a filthy feeding bag from the dirt and stuffed it full of grain. When he straightened up, he saw Sharkal looking into the exposed inn.

"I was extending the walls, adding new rooms, when the pox struck. My two oldest boys are inside, still too weak to move about. I sent my wife and our newborn to one of the farms at the first sign of the disease."

Yammar, like so many of the dirt-eaters, enjoyed talking.

"But I can use help rebuilding the walls ... Sharkal. It's dirty work, but I'll fill your belly, feed your horse, and give you a copper coin for each day's work."

Sharkal considered the proposal. A few days work here, and he'd have enough food and supplies to reach Orak. He hated mucking about in the mud, but he'd done it before, and even worse.

Yammar mistook Sharkal's hesitation, and sweetened the offer. "And I'll give you all the food you can carry with you when you leave." He shrugged. "Not many around to eat it anyway, so I might as well give it away before it rots."

"I'll help you, for at least two days," Sharkal said. "Then I need to ride on."

"Feed your horse, then come inside. You look like you could use a cup of ale with your food."

By the time he finished feeding and watering the horse, Sharkal could scarcely control his hunger. Inside the inn, Yammar poured a tall mug of ale, and handed him a plate of bread and half a cold chicken to go with the strong brew.

Sharkal tore into the meat, washing down every few bites with ale. After he finished sweeping up the last scraps with the bread's crust, Sharkal felt almost content, his belly full for the first time in days.

"Thank you," he said, bowing his head. "Now, show me what you want me to do."

The rest of the day, Sharkal moved mud bricks from the drying area to the rear of Yammar's inn. The heavy bricks, formed out of river mud and straw, had to be carried one at a time, lest the fragile combination crumble or break. Under Yammar's direction, Sharkal lined up almost a hundred bricks.

"I set these out in the sun almost twenty days ago. They're nice and hard now."

Sharkal knew that mud bricks needed plenty of time in the sun to dry out. Otherwise they would fall apart at a touch.

"When everything's in place," Yammar informed him, "the inn will be nearly twice as large."

"The villagers will return?" Sharkal saw no reason why anyone would want to live in this dreary place.

"Oh, they'll come back. Nuantek is a good place to live. We're right at the half-way point between the two rivers, so many will stop here. Once the pox is gone, that is."

Yammar kept him working until dusk, and by then even Sharkal's muscles protested. He stripped at the village well and washed first his body and then his tunic. When he returned to the inn, he felt refreshed and his stomach already anticipated another meal.

More ale and a second chicken awaited him, this one plump with the flesh still steaming. The smell of herbs wafted from the platter.

If the innkeeper could cook this well, Sharkal looked forward to meeting his wife.

Yammar's two sons, both about fourteen or fifteen seasons, joined them at the table. The boys, they might even be twins, looked weak and pale, with scabs from the pox still marking their faces, chests and arms. They asked a few of the usual foolish questions about Sharkal's life and wanderings, and he made the usual polite replies that revealed almost nothing.

The meal completed, everyone went to bed, the boys still exhausted by their illness, and Sharkal tired from the long day's ride and work. He turned down Yammar's offer to sleep in the common room with its permanent odor of stale ale and cooking smoke. Instead Sharkal chose the unfinished chamber, where the familiar stars shone over his head, and he could keep an eye on his horse.

The morning sun woke him, and he heard the innkeeper already up and tending to his sons. Breakfast consisted of a cup of watered ale and a half loaf of bread, consumed in a few hearty mouthfuls. He and Yammar started right in on the bricks. More needed to be formed, then set aside to dry out for a few days. Fresh mud had to be mixed as well, to adhere the bricks.

With Yammar's help, Sharkal dug a deep pit a good fifty paces away from the inn, breaking up clods of earth. They carried sacks of dirt back to the bricks, then buckets of water from the well. The earth and water would be mixed with a little straw, to form a thick ooze that, when dried in the hot sun, would bind the bricks together.

Sharkal carried the bricks, and Yammar set them in place, spreading a thick layer of mud between each brick. The first row went easy enough, the innkeeper using a flat length of wood to make sure the wall stayed straight.

The second row took longer, because each brick had to be set with care directly on top of the row beneath, the center of the brick positioned over the joint of the bricks below.

The weight of each additional row of bricks tended to make the ones beneath shift their position, requiring frequent adjustment to keep the bricks aligned. Sticks hammered into the ground held the bricks steady until the mud dried enough to stop any sliding.

Sharkal hated doing this kind of toil, but he'd learned long ago the warrior way: to set his mind to each task, no matter how unpleasant, and do his utmost to see it completed. He seldom paused, whether moving the bricks or carrying the mud, and at times making Yammar scramble to keep up with his laborer.

They worked straight through until midday, when they stopped to eat and take some rest. The garrulous innkeeper told Sharkal about the village, its inhabitants, the inn, and his family. Yammar related the most recent gossip, including the story about a farmer who fell down his well not long ago.

The clumsy man had too much ale to drink, and apparently had gone to the well to get some water. When he fell in, he somehow kept his grip on the ale skin. Once in the water, the man had no way to climb out, so while he waited for someone to rescue him, he drank the rest of the ale.

In the afternoon, his wife returned from visiting her relatives at a nearby farm. She heard her husband's drunken cries for help, and found him, splashing about helplessly.

Instead of delivering him from his plight, she took the three sheep they owned into the village and sold them at the market. With a few coppers, she'd purchased another skin of ale, and returned to the farm.

She tossed the ale down the well to her husband as a parting gift, no doubt hoping he would get drunk and drown. After that, she disappeared from the village, taking with her the profit from the sheep and whatever valuables the man owned.

Three days passed before the man's cousin visited the place, and dragged the farmer out. By then his skin had softened so much from being in the water that he couldn't walk for almost five days. The cousin had carried the hapless farmer to my inn, where he recounted what his wife had done.

"Everyone started laughing, and the farmer grew angry. The angrier he got, the harder we laughed, until we couldn't stop. Men were rolling on the ground clutching their stomachs, and I laughed so hard I pissed myself, and I wasn't the only one. I'd never laughed so much in my entire life. No one could stop. We'd look at each other, or at the fool of a farmer's shriveled face, and burst out all over again."

By the time Yammar finished the tale, Sharkal was laughing with him. Sharkal found himself relating a similar story, about a drunken warrior who abused both his wives. One night he returned to his tent, drunker than usual, and began beating his women for no reason.

When he passed out, the women took his knife, lifted him up, and let him fall on the blade. They let him lie there, face down, until morning, when they claimed they tried to wake him, only to find, to their dismay, that their husband must have fallen on his knife when he passed out, and so bled to death.

Of course, everyone knew what had happened, but no one said anything, and their grinning clan leader pretended not to know what occurred. He gave the wives to another warrior, who was wise enough to treat them better than their former husband.

After that exchange of stories, Sharkal began conversing in more than grunts, and he soon found himself talking about some of his travels and the places he'd seen. Yammar's eyes went wide as Sharkal described the strange lands and even stranger people who inhabited them. The innkeeper, like most dirt-eaters, had never traveled more than a day's journey from his home, and had the usual beliefs of magical creatures that roamed the lands at the far corners of his world.

They worked as they talked, and the conversation made the labor easier. To Sharkal's surprise, he found himself telling Yammar about the customs of the steppes warriors, how they practically lived on horseback, and their constant preparation for battle.

"Barbarians swept through here about eight years ago," Yammar recalled. "Killed a lot of farmers."

"It's their way," Sharkal answered. "They know no other life. To live as a warrior, and die with honor. Only by such deeds can they pass through the portals of the gods."

"And what about you, Sharkal? What do you seek?"

"The same, to fight and die with honor." He sighed. "But I will not have my kinsmen at my side, to witness my courage."

"After the barbarians passed on, we found a grave site," Yammar said. "One of the barbarians must have died, and they took the time to bury him."

"As long as he fell in battle, and was buried with his sword," Sharkal said, "he will be welcomed in the spirit world."

"Enough of such things," Yammar said. "Time to get back to work."

In the afternoon, Yammar's sons joined them, doing what little their strength permitted, mostly mixing the water and dirt. The sun took its time moving across the sky, but when Yammar finally called a halt, new walls almost as tall as Sharkal encircled the additional rooms.

"Another three rows of bricks tomorrow," Yammar said, "and we'll be done, except for the roof. You can stay another day, can't you?"

Sharkal nodded. "Only one more day, then I must continue my journey to Orak.

"Ah, Orak. That place is growing bigger each year. For some unknown reason, everyone seems to want to live there, crowded together with no room to breathe. You have friends in Orak?"

"Just one. His name is Eskkar. It's been years since I've seen him, though."

Sharkal answered without thinking. He hoped Eskkar would remember him and permit such a friendship. "Have you ever traveled to Orak?"

Yammar shook his head. "It's a three or four day walk. Too far to buy or sell goods. My wife and I make do with what we need for the inn from the surrounding farms."

He sighed. "Maybe some day I'll visit Orak. But now it's time to see to dinner. My sons have cooked another chicken, and we've plenty of ale. I know I can use a few cups."

That night Sharkal slept within the walls he had helped raise that day, content with his labors as he examined the bright stars shining overhead. His muscles still protested, but his mind felt at ease.

He thought about Orak and Eskkar, and somehow knew his fellow warrior would extend the arm of friendship, acknowledging

Sharkal as a fellow outcast forced to live their days among strangers. With a friend at his side, perhaps living with the dirt-eaters might be tolerable.

Even this innkeeper had dealt with Sharkal honestly. Yammar hadn't looked at Sharkal in disgust or treated him with contempt as so many dirt-eaters did. Yammar had worked beside him, not afraid to get his own hands dirty, or to labor along side a barbarian. He'd treated Sharkal with the same respect Yammar gave to any villager.

This innkeeper was no warrior, but his sons honored their father almost as if he ruled the village. Yammar might be a mere dirt-eater, but plainly his sons and neighbors held him in high esteem. Sharkal respected the man more than any other dirt-eater he'd ever encountered.

For the third night in a row, Sharkal prepared himself for sleep with a feeling of satisfaction. Yammar, he decided, was like the dirt-eater Sharkal found murdered a few days ago – loved by his family, friends, and neighbors. Sharkal's last thoughts before he slept brought a smile to his lips as he recalled the story about the farmer in the well.

The next day's labor started with the arrival of the village carpenter carrying a handful of long boards on his shoulder. He, too, had been sickened by the pox, but survived, though he looked weak and shaky in his movements.

With Yammar's help, he framed what would become the rear door, and two interior ones, using sawn boards for the lintels and straight logs hammered into the earth to support them.

Meanwhile Sharkal checked the walls. The mud looked dry on the outside, but he knew it would still be soft within. The longer they waited before adding the final two rows of bricks, the stronger the wall would be.

By noon the carpenter had left, and Sharkal returned to carrying bricks. The sound of hoof beats made him look up, and he saw five riders picking their way through the village. He walked back to the inn and watched as they approached.

One glance told him they weren't farmers or traders. All five carried swords, and each horse had a bulging sack tied around its neck, no doubt filled with whatever loot they'd stolen in the last few days.

The advent of the pox in the surrounding countryside would have been a boon to petty thieves. With so many dead, and those still alive weakened by the illness, a healthy man could take whatever he wanted.

Yammar stepped from the inn as the five stopped their horses just outside his door.

"Are you the innkeeper?" Tall and thin, the man's tone announced he led the ragged band.

"Yes, I'm Yammar."

"My name is Velorek. My men and I need food and ale, and maybe a place to spend the night."

"I can feed you," Yammar said, "but the inn is closed." He waved his hand at the mud and muck scattered about. "We're adding rooms, and my sons are still recovering from the pox."

"The pox, is it gone?"

"None have gotten sick in the last ten days," Yammar admitted.

Watching the innkeeper, Sharkal realized that Yammar wanted nothing to do with these men.

"Food, then," Velorek said. He turned his gaze to Sharkal, contempt showing on his face. "You look like a barbarian. Are you?"

"Not any more," Sharkal answered the rude question without rancor. His sword was inside the inn, though he'd kept his knife with him. He met Velorek's gaze.

"Sharkal works for me," Yammar said, before Sharkal could say anything further. "Do you want to eat or stand in the sun all day?"

Velorek laughed. "Well, the sun is still hot, so I think we'll eat. Your barbarian can tend to our horses."

He slid off his mount and let the halter fall to the ground. He stretched to ease his muscles, and headed for the coolness of the inn's interior, his grinning men following in his footsteps.

Before Yammar could say anything, Sharkal said "I'll see to their horses." He knew Yammar didn't want any trouble.

Yammar gave Sharkal a nod of gratitude, and led the way inside.

Sharkal remained uneasy. Velorek had given the briefest of glances to Sharkal's horse, almost too brief. Sharkal's mount was a good one, and while not many dirt-eaters would take a chance stealing a warrior's horse, he wouldn't put it past these strangers.

Five armed and mounted men could cause a great deal of trouble, and to a village like Nuantek already racked with suffering and weakened by the pox, they could do pretty much as they pleased.

Sharkal strode around the back of the corral and entered into the yet unenclosed portion of the inn. His sword rested beside the place where he'd slept last night. He picked it up and carried it outside, setting it down against the end of the unfinished wall. It wouldn't be noticed unless someone entered the corral and walked to the rear.

Satisfied the weapon was at hand, he brought the men's horses into the corral. Since Yammar had plenty of grain, Sharkal watered and fed the horses, knowing that would be what the innkeeper wanted.

He went back to work carrying more bricks to the back of the inn. As he set each brick, he heard the loud laughter and rough voices of Velorek and his men, no doubt enjoying their ale and meat in the cooler interior.

At least Yammar would earn a few more coppers, and the strangers would soon be on their way.

The sun moved across the sky. Yammar came out briefly several times, but stayed close to his customers, no doubt wanting to make sure they didn't get out of control. The boisterous noise from inside the inn grew even louder, as the strangers consumed more and more ale.

Sharkal kept working behind the corral, mixing a fresh batch of mud to bind the bricks together. At first he didn't notice when the noise ceased from within the inn. Then a corral rail creaked. Sharkal looked up, suddenly alert. Velorek and three of his men stood at the entrance to the corral. Sharkal got to his feet as Velorek leaned on the top rail and stared at him, a sneering grin on his face.

"We want our horses, barbarian. Bring them out now."

Velorek didn't try to conceal the contempt in his voice.

"They're your horses," Sharkal said. "Get them yourself."

"We'll be taking yours, too. I like a good mount, and your stallion looks better than mine."

Sharkal didn't answer. He rose to his feet and stepped back toward the new wall. He needed only two steps and a quick glance to see that his sword had disappeared.

The last of Velorek's men emerged from the front of the inn. In his left hand, he held Sharkal's sword.

"As I said, barbarian, we're taking your horse and your sword as well," Velorek said. "Stay out of our way, and you might keep your head on your shoulders."

"If you touch my horse, I'll kill you," Sharkal said. He glanced over his shoulder toward the interior of the inn, wondering where Yammar was.

Velorek saw the look. "The innkeeper can't help you. He wanted too much copper for his miserable food, so we had to knock him around. Not that he'd bother trying to help a foul-smelling barbarian."

Sharkal studied the men facing him across the coral. With the sword in his hand, they might not be so brave. But with only his knife against five swords, they had more than enough ale inside their bellies to give them courage, not only to start a fight but finish it, too.

He could step back, away from the corral and into the inn, and let them have the horse. He'd lost horses before, and one more might not be worth fighting, or dying, over. For a moment, he hesitated, weighing the odds, and knowing the likely outcome if he refused. The stallion, he decided, was worth the risk.

More than that, all his life, Sharkal had fought scum like these. If he let these filthy bandit dirt-eaters take his horse at the same time they insulted him, he'd never be able to live with himself.

Better to face them down. He stepped into the corral, ducking between the rails and moving slowly toward his horse.

The stallion looked up and snorted contentedly at his master's arrival. Sharkal stopped between his own mount and the one that Velorek had ridden.

"Get your horses and go," Sharkal said, putting his hand on the hilt of his knife. "Come near mine, and I'll gut you like a pig."

"You shouldn't make threats against your betters, barbarian." Velorek glanced at his men. "Kill him." He slipped the rope loop off the post and dragged open the gate.

Two of the men drew their swords and entered the corral. The other two moved around the outside of the corral, heading toward the mixing area, to cut off Sharkal's retreat. Velorek followed the first two men through the corral's opening.

Sharkal felt the battle rage sweeping over him, the urge to kill that accompanied every warrior into a fight. But nothing showed on his face as he took a step away from his horse. With a smooth motion almost too fast for the eye to follow, he slid the knife from its sheath and jabbed it into the flank of Velorek's horse.

With a scream of pain, the animal kicked out with its rear hooves, then flung itself straight at the approaching men. The other horses panicked as well, catching the scent of blood and frightened by their startled companion.

In an instant, the corral turned into chaos, the horses bolting around and trying to escape whatever danger threatened them. In their fright, they bumped into each other, until they burst through the open gate.

The two men jerked back as the wounded horse charged past them, trying to avoid being trampled. One of them lost his footing in the mud and muck. Behind them, Velorek also went down, knocked off his feet by an onrushing animal.

Sharkal had worked in and around the corral for two days, and the slippery mess of mud and sand mixed with water had made him slip and fall five or six times. Picking his way through the muck, Sharkal reached one of the first two inside the corral, the man who stumbled and fell.

He saw Sharkal coming and tried to get up, raising his sword at the same time. The unbalanced movement made him slip again, and Sharkal, moving lightly despite his bulk, reached the man's kicking legs and plunged the knife deep into his thigh.

The second man swung his sword, but Sharkal had already shifted his position, moving in closer to his attacker rather than away. The sword flashed past, narrowly missing Sharkal's knife hand, and he rammed the thick-bladed knife all the way to the hilt into his attacker's side.

In almost the same motion, Sharkal used his left hand to grasp the dying man around the chest, and shoved him at Velorek, who'd regained his footing and rushed forward, swinging his sword in a savage cut that would have split Sharkal in half if he hadn't moved aside.

The remaining two bandits ducked through the rails and into the corral. The first one, sword upraised, splashed through the mud and charged at Sharkal's back for the killing blow.

Sharkal shifted again, but had to bring up his knife to parry the sword. The shock of contact hammered up his arm, but the stoutly made blade didn't shatter. Sharkal took one step forward and, with all his strength, drove the heel of his left hand into his attacker's face, sending him reeling back with blood gushing from his nose and mouth.

The fifth man followed close behind his companion, despite slipping once in the mud. He hacked at Sharkal's head with a wild swing. The stroke missed its intended target, but the blade tore into Sharkal's left shoulder, cutting deeply and tearing the flesh from the bone.

With a grunt of pain, Sharkal pivoted around and lunged, extending his body as he thrust his knife at the bandit's chest. The man leapt back, avoiding the stroke, but lost his footing and tumbled to the ground.

By then Velorek regained his feet, stepped over the first man Sharkal had killed, and closed in. He thrust with his sword, the blade burning along Sharkal's side. He barely managed to dodge the worst of the blow. The man with the bloody face stepped beside Velorek, and Sharkal ducked away, keeping the wall of the inn at his back as he faced both attackers.

"Who's next to die," Sharkal shouted. The pain in his arm was like fire, and he felt the hot blood from the wound in his side dripping on his thigh, but he kept the knife moving, waiting for the attack.

"Damn you," Velorek shouted. Despite their swords and the man beside him, Velorek didn't look eager to close in. Instead, he took a half step back, grabbed his companion by his shoulder, and shoved him forward, right at Sharkal. "Kill him!"

Surprised by his leader's move, the man stumbled forward, thrusting with his sword as he did so. The blade's tip struck the barbarian's hip at the same moment Sharkal plunged his knife into his attacker's throat.

The man's weight landed on Sharkal, knocking him against the wall. A gurgling scream erupted from the dying man, but his thrashing body entangled itself with Sharkal's.

Sharkal's foot slipped in the muck, and he struggled to keep upright. He saw Velorek's thrust coming. Sharkal shoved the dead bandit aside. At the same time, he tried to shift away from the coming blow, but Velorek had regained his balance and the sharp blade bit deep into Sharkal's stomach.

The attack brought Velorek within reach, and Sharkal struck back blindly, ignoring the burning pain in his belly that sapped the strength from his muscles. His knife ripped into Velorek's left arm, glanced off the bone, and tore through the muscle as it ripped free.

With a curse, Velorek jerked back, lifted his sword, and swung it down with all his strength, aiming for Sharkal's neck.

"Die, you barbarian scum," he shouted. The blow missed its target, but landed with a sickening thud on Sharkal's shoulder, turning him around and knocking the barbarian face down into the muck at the base of the wall.

For a moment, there was no pain, and Sharkal could taste the wet dirt in his mouth. Death had come for him today, but he felt no fear, only the regret that he had not killed more of his enemies and that he would not be buried as a warrior.

He saw Velorek raise his sword and swing it down, but Sharkal couldn't do anything to stop it. The blow glanced off his skull, peeling back the scalp, but the blade landed almost flat on Sharkal's already wounded shoulder. Then the bright sunlight turned to blackness.

"You pig," Velorek grunted, his left arm on fire. He raised the sword again, but this time he slipped on the mud and landed on his backside. He swore another oath, but a glance at the unmoving barbarian told him the man was finished.

Clutching his sword, Velorek pushed himself to his feet.

"Gods below! I'm bleeding like a goat with its throat cut." He shoved the sword into its scabbard, and clutched at his left arm, wincing at the pain.

He looked around the corral. All six horses had vanished into the open country. Two of his men lay face down in the muck, and Velorek saw they were dead.

The man wounded in the thigh stumbled to his feet, using the corral's rail to hold himself upright. He cursed his own wound and the barbarian too stupid to give up his horse.

The other survivor, at the far side of the corral, also clung to a rail as he wiped the blood from his face, his nose smashed into pulp.

"Get me something to bind this up," Velorek shouted. The burning in his arm grew worse with every moment. He pushed the severed muscles together and clapped his hand over the badly bleeding wound, adding more pain to the jagged cut.

"Get it yourself, you stupid fool," the man with the bloody face replied. "You're the one who wanted to take his horse . . . have some fun with the barbarian, you said. Now my brother's dead, and my nose is broken. I should kill you myself."

"Shut your face," Velorek snarled, "or I'll finish what he started." He stumbled his way out of the corral, cursing with every step, and headed for the inn's entrance. There would be something inside to bandage up his arm and stop the bleeding.

He stepped through the doorway, the inn's interior dim after the bright afternoon sun. A shadow appeared before him, but Velorek never saw the sword in Yammar's hand, not until the innkeeper thrust it so hard into his stomach that the point burst out his back.

Yammar, his head still throbbing from the blow that had knocked him unconscious, had been revived by his sons. As soon as he could stand, he sent the boys to bring the blacksmith and anyone else they could find.

Then Yammar retrieved the old copper sword hidden beneath his bed, and lurched to the door, just as Velorek arrived and attempted to pass through it.

"You bastard," Yammar shouted. The first clumsy thrust had struck low into Velorek's belly, causing much pain, but not something immediately fatal.

It didn't matter, as Yammar jerked the blade free and thrust again and again and again, ignoring Velorek's screams of agony, until the man fell backward out into the sunlight, hands clutching his bloody stomach as his feet kicked at the earth, and he gasped for breath through the pain.

Turning toward the corral, Yammar stopped in shock. He saw no horses within, but three bodies on the ground, covered in mud and fresh blood. Two bandits remained alive.

One supported himself against the corral, clutching his bloody leg with one hand. The other survivor, stood swaying in the center of the corral, blood streaming down his face, but still holding his sword.

"Get out of my corral," Yammar shouted. "Get out . . . get out . . . GET OUT!"

The bandit with the broken nose raised his sword and took one step toward Yammar, then stopped. Yammar's son stood beside his father, clutching a knife in his trembling hand. Shouts from villagers echoed out, and in a moment, the blacksmith arrived, breathing hard, and waving a hammer, with two more men close behind him. One look at the reinforcements, and the bandit turned and ran. He ducked beneath the rails of the corral and headed out for the open country.

The bandit with the leg wound climbed through the corral and staggered after his companion, but his weakened limb failed him, and he collapsed before he'd taken ten steps.

He tried to crawl away, but Yammar caught up with him. The innkeeper thrust down with his sword, a clumsy stroke that drove the blade into the man's buttocks, just above his kicking legs.

A shriek of pain rose up, but Yammar never hesitated. "Die you scum . . . die!" He lifted the sword and hacked clumsily at his victim again and again. The screaming man tried to push himself away, until the effort and loss of blood stopped his struggles and he fell silent.

Exhausted by his efforts and still dizzy from the blow to his head, Yammar slipped to his knees, the sword falling from his shaking hand. He sagged forward, sliding back into unconsciousness from his exertions.

When he came to, he found himself on the ground beside the entrance to the inn, a bandage wrapped around his forehead. He touched it with his fingers and flinched with pain as he felt the size of the lump.

Yammar vaguely remembered that one of Velorek's men had struck him with the hilt of his sword. Yammar twisted his head gingerly and looked into the corral. The bandits' bodies had been dragged out, and lay in the lane, next to the wounded man Yammar had caught and killed. Their leader Velorek lay there, too, his mouth open as he stared sightlessly at the sky. Flies circled and buzzed around them all. When Yammar could focus his eyes, he saw one of his sons and two villagers leading a string of horses back to the corral.

"We got all the horses, Father, including Sharkal's," the youngest said. "Except for one that the bandit managed to catch. He got away."

Yammar shrugged. One man didn't matter. He wouldn't be returning to Nuantek again.

"Father, look at this." His other son, held up a small sack. "I found this inside Velorek's tunic." He held the sack out to his father, who glanced in and saw the glint of silver. "And there's tools and valuables inside the sacks that their horses carried. The bandits must have stolen them."

At that moment, the horses, goods, and silver meant little to Yammar. "Sharkal, is he dead?"

The boy lost his smile. "No, but he's dying. We put him in the shade."

The blacksmith strode over. He and a few other villagers had chased after the fleeing bandit.

"Are you alright, Yammar? We need to get rid of the bodies. We should bury them. Otherwise they'll stink up the village in this heat."

Yammar shook his head, but a flash of pain made him regret the action. "No graves for these thieves. Use the horses to drag them away from the village. Let them rot in the fields. They deserve no better."

He saw Sharkal's big frame, lying only a few paces away. "Help me up. I want to see him."

With the blacksmith's help, Yammar pushed himself to his feet, leaning against the wall of the inn for a moment, until the dizziness passed. His head still pounded, but he moved into the shade and dropped down on his knees beside Sharkal, and held his hand.

Sharkal's eyes opened at the touch, but it took a moment before he could speak. "Glad you're alive." The whispered words came slowly, through the pain.

"Four of them are dead, including Velorek," Yammar said. "You were brave, to fight so many. My sons and I, we owe you our lives."

A coughing spasm racked Sharkal's chest, and another trickle of blood ran down his chin. "I'm sorry that we couldn't . . . finish your wall."

Sharkal had to force himself to breathe, so he could get the words out. "Will you . . . send word to Eskkar in Orak. Tell him I'm sorry I couldn't . . . join him."

"I will. I swear it."

"Bury me . . ." Sharkal's eyes closed, then opened. He tried to speak, but no words came.

Yammar leaned closer. "With your sword. I remember. With your sword. I swear it."

Whether Sharkal heard the words or not, Yammar couldn't say. The hand he held went limp, and Sharkal's breathing ceased. Tenderly, Yammar closed Sharkal's eyes.

Yammar felt the moisture in his own eyes. He tried to brush them away, then he reached out to his sons. They helped him up, and once again a wave of dizziness swept over him. When he turned away, he saw the blacksmith waiting.

"I'll drag the bodies out to the fields."

"Yes. Except for Sharkal. My sons and I will clean and wrap his body, then bury him as best we can. If not for him, these scum would have killed all of us. I will never forget him."

He gazed down at the body, remembering how they had worked and laughed together.

"Damn them all to the demons," Yammar muttered. A rush of tears streamed down his cheeks. "I was going to ask him to come back here when he finished his business in Orak. I believe we could have been friends."

27

The village of Carnax, in Sumeria, near the great southern sea, 3156 BC . . .

Children squirmed and squeezed their way through the marketplace throng, their high-pitched voices lending a festive air to the proceedings as they attempted to get closer to the condemned, the better to witness the spectacle. Two guards tied the struggling man to the stake, ignoring the curses and threats he spewed at them. They threaded a strand of rope under his arms and fastened it high to the thick post, to keep the victim stretched upright.

A coil of rope across his chest pinned the man to the stake, while another loop secured his feet. Most of the crowd cheered in anticipation, though a handful of sullen faces made no attempt to hide their anger.

The sun had reached its highest point in the sky, the time set for the execution. The hot, humid air intensified the strong smells of many unwashed bodies in close proximity. Already it overpowered the grilling meat and animal odors that normally dominated the marketplace.

Trella had twice before watched men put to death, but both times as a child peering from behind an older playmate, and always from a distance. Now in her fourteenth season, she stood close to her father, Sargat, who occupied the place of honor usually reserved for the Village Elder.

Sargat and Ranaddi had been friends since childhood. When Ranaddi took power as leader of Carnax eighteen years earlier, he proclaimed that his long-time friend and supporter Sargat would be his most trusted advisor and dispenser of justice.

Together, the Elder and his advisor ruled Carnax and the surrounding countryside. They'd guided the village's growth and managed its affairs efficiently and fairly. The inhabitants accepted Ranaddi's authority because they knew no other way, and expected nothing different tomorrow.

Since Sargat administered Elder Ranaddi's justice evenly, few complained of inequity or mistreatment. Over the years, Ranaddi grew even more powerful and extended his rule to the adjacent farms.

Secure in his wealth and power, he would rule as village elder as long as he lived, and when Ranaddi died, one of his sons would succeed him, and for the inhabitants of Carnax, everyday life would continue.

None of this mattered to the prisoner. Abbas fought the ropes that bound him to the post set deep into the earth. He spat at one of his captors. The offended guard responded by punching the condemned man in the stomach, a powerful blow that knocked the breath from his captive's lungs.

The crowd shouted approval at the deed. Almost no one felt sympathy for Abbas, the unpopular son of a wealthy trader. His arrogant superiority had offended many in the last few years. Finally, in his wildness, he killed Ranaddi's oldest son, a callous murder that angered everyone in Carnax. And now the people took delight in Abbas's punishment.

By now nearly everyone in the village and nearby farms had pushed their way into the marketplace. Trella knew that people were drawn to the taking of human life, fascinated by the spectacle, and even the execution of a common thief or murderer would generate a sizeable crowd.

This day's event held more drama. The death of Abbas would prove to all that even the powerful could face the ultimate punishment for their crime. For that reason alone, craftsmen set down their tools and farmers left their fields unattended, as they congregated in the marketplace to witness the killing.

Others, of course, just wanted to see blood spilled, and to them it mattered little who died or for what reason. Trella guessed it was much the same in the other villages scattered throughout the land of Sumeria.

Though she knew other villages existed, some larger or more impressive places than Carnax, especially those on the coast of the Great Sea, Trella also knew she would never visit any of them.

Women seldom traveled far from their homes, except perhaps when they were given in marriage. But her father had shown her Ranaddi's trading maps, precious and secret documents, that located villages scattered throughout the land.

The nearly three hundred men and women who inhabited Trella's birthplace were more than enough for her. She knew every one of their faces and names, where they lived, what they owned, even how much they owed the Village Elder. Her ability to recall such details kept her at her father's side, as he, in turn, stood beside Ranaddi.

Today, however, her father assigned her a different task. Sargat wanted to identify those who showed anger at the execution, anyone who might harbor ill will against Elder Ranaddi or his justice. Her father, entrusted with ensuring the killing proceeded smoothly, worried he might miss those hints of emotion that revealed men's inner thoughts.

Troublemakers needed to be identified, and those who complained too loudly over Abbas's death would be watched closely in the future. They might even find themselves banished from Carnax, the usual punishment for those few who chaffed under Ranaddi's rule.

Trella moved off to the side, still at the front of the crowd, where she could best observe not the proceedings but the villagers. As Sargat's daughter, no one tried to push her aside, not that the guard standing only a stride away would have permitted it.

A long and plain linen scarf covered her head and shoulders, ostensibly to ward off the hot sun. But it also concealed her thick black tresses and masked the still-growing breasts that marked her as a woman.

She kept the scarf pulled low over her forehead, making it difficult for others to see her eyes as she searched the crowd. Trella conducted her surveillance so well, so skillfully, that no one noticed her, not even those whose names she added to the list she kept in her head.

There weren't many names to record. Only seven showed their displeasure, either by the way they stood, their clenched fists, or the tension in their shoulders and neck. Those less subtle, or perhaps more angry, gave away their secret thoughts by the frowns on their faces.

Another shout drew Trella's attention back to the condemned man – Abbas, the son of Fradmon, one of Carnax's most powerful merchants. Tears now streamed down Abbas's face, as at last he saw the strands of his life coming to an end. His tunic couldn't conceal the urine dripping down his legs, as fear weakened his belly muscles.

The leader of Ranaddi's guards entered the open space between the prisoner tied to the post and the villagers of Carnax. An undercurrent of anticipation swept through the people at the sight of the executioner, the one who would deliver Ranaddi's justice. Other guards held their spears with both hands to push back the surging crowd that threatened to overwhelm them in the press to get closer to the condemned.

"Abbas should be tortured before he dies! A curse on his family," a woman shrilled, her voice rising over the village square.

Two companions pulled her away from the unruly crowd, trying to comfort her.

Trella recognized the voice of Ranaddi's daughter-in-law, the wife of Ramen, the man Abbas killed. Two days earlier, the men had quarreled over some trifle, both of them drunk after a long night of drinking.

Whatever provoked the incident, no one disputed the facts. Ranaddi's son had thrown his cup of ale in Abbas's face, then turned to leave the tavern. Abbas, infuriated by the insult, plunged his knife into Ramen's back.

Once again Trella lifted her eyes to scan the villagers. No one paid her the slightest attention, all too eager to see the killing, to watch a man die for his crime.

Even without the excitement, few people ever noticed Trella. She almost always attended her father, an insignificant girl who acted more like his servant than his daughter. Many in Carnax thought her dim-witted, a dull, plain girl of fourteen wearing a drab dress, already past the age for marriage and without any suitors approaching her father.

Her father Sargat knew better, of course. He'd discovered Trella's abilities as a child, a few months before her third season, when she began reading the symbols in her tiny, bird-like voice, sitting on her father's lap.

No one had taught them to her. Few men had the wits to learn them, and those chosen to study were almost always the sons of merchants and traders. But somehow Trella had learned them, as easily as she mastered lessons on weaving and sewing from her mother.

At first her odd abilities amused her family. As she grew older, the other children of the village withdrew from her, aware of a difference between themselves and Sargat's daughter.

Her father, however, perceived something special in his daughter. Her only brother Almaric, older by almost two seasons, took years to understand and master the symbols, and even so, his skill remained far below his sister's.

Sargat indulged himself, allowing Trella to function as his messenger and helper. His decision shocked everyone at first. Women were seldom permitted to join the councils of men, but when Ranaddi ignored the apparent transgression, everyone in the large household soon accepted the young girl's role.

She sat off to the side as Sargat administered the daily functions of life in Carnax, dealing with petty disputes and complaints, setting prices, recording agreements, and performing all the tedious but necessary details that Ranaddi preferred to delegate.

In her seventh season, Trella began telling her father when she thought men lied, always waiting until they were alone, and giving her reasons as calmly as a full grown woman.

Over the years, Trella learned to watch men's faces, their hands, mouths, eyes, and even the way they breathed. She perceived hesitations, tiny movements of the eyes and hands, all indicators, she came to realize, of whether or not a man spoke the truth.

Soon father and daughter began working together, trying to solve the problem posed when a man said one thing but believed another in his heart. Sometimes Sargat would make an excuse to leave the chamber, and Trella would remain.

Alone with the petitioner, she would speak of household tasks while she studied each supplicant with care, observing how they changed their manner and expressions with her father absent.

In attending to her father, being a girl proved helpful. A man, even a young boy, would have been noticed and commented on. Men who would have hesitated to utter their thoughts in front of a young man spoke freely in front of the insignificant girl sitting behind her father, her eyes downcast.

Women were of no consequence and could be ignored. Females might gossip and chatter among themselves, but most men paid little attention to their foolish words or ideas. A woman in a man's house was as much his property as his table or bench, his tools or his weapons, and worthy of as little notice.

Elder Ranaddi, aware of these "tricks" as he called them, started using Trella as well, allowing his advisor's "attendant" to also wait on him, and remain in his most private chamber while he dealt with important affairs, arranged trades, and managed the lives of his people.

Almost no one else knew of the role she played. Her mother, Damkina, distraught at her daughter's "unwomanly" abilities, predicted no good would come of all this learning, and argued with her husband that Sargat spoiled their daughter.

Almaric, her brother, understood that his sister was unlike other girls, but soon learned to keep the secret and to tell his friends little about his seemingly dullard sister.

In this way, Trella grew into a young woman, sitting on the floor beside her father, filling his water cup, peeling apples, fetching him whatever he commanded, a silent servant as unnoticed and unimportant as the room's furniture. She wore plain and drab dresses that concealed her growing figure.

Trella even avoided jewelry, the better to make sure she attracted as little notice as possible. Only with her immediate family and trusted servants did she put aside the scarf, comb out her long tresses, and let her smile reveal the even features of a comely young woman.

As she reached the age for marriage, neither Sargat nor Ranaddi felt any need to marry her off. Her usefulness to them far outweighed any bride price she might fetch.

Six months ago her first bleeding came, and the family's women initiated Trella into the mysteries of sex and birth, and all the other secrets women held close to their bosoms. Afterwards, she continued to help her father as before, and he promised to arrange a marriage for her in the coming year, as soon as he could find a worthy, and wealthy enough, suitor.

Trella knew her father would miss her and her skills, but Sargat understood a grown woman needed a husband. Most girls her age had already given birth to one child and were pregnant with the next.

Still, Trella felt no desire to leave her father's side. She loved him for being her father, but even more for letting her use her talents in his service. Helping him manage Carnax and its problems gave her great satisfaction.

Of course, some day soon she would have a husband and children of her own, but that thought held little interest for her. She felt no attraction to any of the eligible men in the village, and certainly no urge to bear their children.

Her one dread was that she might be married to someone from another village, who would take her away from her father. Trella much preferred learning more about the administration of Carnax, a process she studied each day.

Postponing the day of her betrothal into the vague future, Sargat brought his daughter deeper into the mysteries of life. Trella learned all about the ways of the farmer, the artisan, the craftsman, the weaver and the tanner. When to schedule markets, when to plant the crops, how to draw water from the river.

These and a hundred other details of daily life in the Village Elder's house passed before her eyes. She even learned the mysteries of bronze, gold, and copper that few understood. At her father's side, Trella grasped all the secrets of village and farm, along with the application of authority necessary to rule both.

By her twelfth season, there was little in Carnax that she didn't know. And what she saw, what she learned, she remembered. Other people often forgot the simplest of things, or made foolish mistakes, but not Trella. She seldom needed to hear or see anything more than once. After that, she could recall it from her memory at any time, even years later. Trella's worth to both her father and to Ranaddi grew. As her contributions increased, so too did their efforts to make sure others remained unaware of her talents.

Most of all, Trella learned about the ways of power, the ways to command men. To rule, a man had to be both ruthless and cunning. It helped to rule fairly and wisely, but Trella learned that, in the short term, such qualities as mercy or justice held little sway.

Threats or even force were often required to maintain order over unruly, ignorant, or dishonest men. Another potential threat came from the handful of other traders or prosperous craftsmen who yearned to take Ranaddi's place. Some, like Fradmon, grew ever more envious of the authority the Village Elder held over them. The ways of power remained both complex and uncertain.

All the same, Trella studied each situation Sargat and Ranaddi encountered, and she often spent a good part of the evening discussing such matters with her father. By the time she grew into a young woman, she understood almost as well as Sargat not only how to rule, but what it took to rule successfully.

Trella pushed all these thoughts from her mind, as her father stepped into the open space of the market and raised his hands to quiet the crowd. In a few moments, everyone fell silent, eager to hear Sargat's words. The time for the execution had arrived.

"Villagers of Carnax," he began, "Abbas, son of Fradmon, has been condemned to death for murdering Ramen, the son of our

Village Elder. Let everyone see the justice of Ranaddi, our leader. Those who commit murder will be put to death. A life for a life. Let the justice of Elder Ranaddi be carried out!"

Shouts of glee rose, and the crowd pushed forward, and again the handful of Ranaddi's guards struggled to contain the press of bodies.

No dignity remained for the victim. Indeed, Abbas sagged against his ropes, tears streaming down his face while his lips moved soundlessly. He had bitten his lower lip and drool mixed with blood flecked his chin. Trella moved her eyes from the soon to be dead man and scanned the faces of the spectators.

Another man pushed his way through the gathering, shouldering his way to the front. She saw the anger of his face, anger that he did not try to conceal. Trella recognized him – Sondar, Fradmon's steward – no doubt here to witness the deed and report back to his master.

Fradmon, enraged at the death sentence given his heir, had refused to attend, unwilling to face the crowd's hostility and watch his son's demise.

The guard chosen to administer justice stepped forward and drew his sword. Abbas, his mouth agape, stared in horror as his executioner. Blade at the ready, the guard glanced at Sargat, await-ing the command to strike.

"Kill him," her father said, his voice firm.

"No! By the gods, don't kill me . . . I beg you . . . spare my life . . . spare . . ."

The soldier thrust the sword home, a deep stroke that tore into the helpless victim's stomach. Not a killing thrust, Trella saw, but a low stabbing that would ensure Abbas died slowly and screaming in pain.

Ranaddi had demanded that much for his son's death, and Trella had listened while Sargat privately instructed the one who would carry out the sentence.

A shriek of agony rose over the market, and the crowd cheered their delight. Blood gushed from the murderer's belly, some spurting onto the dirt at the executioner's feet. Abbas's head fell forward, and he stared at the great wound.

As the guard withdrew his blade, more blood flowed from his stomach and dripped down his legs. His eyes glazed and his mouth hung open, as his life's blood drained from his body.

At least the time for pain and fear had passed, Trella knew. She ran her eyes over the villagers again. As the victim died, every face revealed its true sentiment, the mystery of death removing for a few brief moments the mask that men wore to conceal their emotions.

She saw Sondar, Fradmon's steward, shake his head in disgust and spit on the ground. Then, for a brief moment, a cold smile crossed his face, before he turned away from the spectacle. He forced his way through the crowd, disappearing amidst those still cruelly taunting the dying man. The steward would report the death and the manner of dying to his master.

Before long, Abbas stopped twitching, then the bleeding ceased as well. The executioner stepped close, and this time drove his sword deep into the dead man's chest, so there would be no doubt that the criminal had died. When the guard withdrew his sword, he turned to Sargat and nodded.

"The execution is ended," Sargat said, his solemn voice carrying over the chattering of the excited and restless spectators. "Return to your homes and your labors." He stepped away, to report to Ranaddi the afternoon's events.

The corpse sagged against the post, a public reminder of the penalty in Carnax for murder. The curious moved closer, to get a better look, some reaching out to touch the still-warm body that would remain there until sundown. Only then could Abbas's family claim their son.

Trella wrapped her scarf closer over her face and, eyes downcast, followed two paces behind her father. When they reached home, she would have much to tell him.

———————

Ranaddi lived in a spacious farmhouse on the edge of the village. Behind the house, extensive fields of wheat and barley waved in the light afternoon breeze, the clean scent flowing over the house and

into the courtyard, where the fresh smell of growing things struggled against the odors of goats, sheep, and oxen.

Chickens wandered about, pecking at anything that moved
beneath them, clucking contentedly whenever they found something
edible. The house formed three sides of a rectangle, with the open
courtyard facing the village lanes. For protection, the outer wall, the
one facing the fields, contained no windows, only scattered, small
openings for ventilation.

The structure had been enhanced many times over the years,
with new rooms added, older ones enlarged, and doorways carved
out or filled in. Ranaddi kept the village masons busy working on his
dwellings, and Trella could scarcely remember a time when laborers
were not hard at work setting one mud brick upon another.

The Village Elder resided in the long central arm of the structure,
his sons and their families occupied one side, while Sargat and his
family lived in the remaining section. Except for a few key atten-
dants and guards who had rooms in the big house, most of the servants, slaves, guards, and the farm workers who tended Ranaddi's
crops lived across the courtyard, within the village proper.

Sargat and his family occupied five rooms, a luxury only sec-
ondary to that of Ranaddi. Trella shared a room with Ninani, one of
the household servants, a young woman occasionally summoned by
her father to pleasure him.

Her brother Almaric, befitting Sargat's heir, enjoyed a room all
to himself, although the tiny alcove had little space for more than a
narrow bed and a chest that doubled as a bench.

Her father and mother had their own room, of course, and Sargat
had another chamber, the largest in his house, which he used as both
a work and storage room. Shelves lined the walls, sagging under the
weight of clay tablets that held the records of all the Elder's dealings
with the villagers.

Each tablet noted a single transaction – who owned which house
or plot of land, or how much each tenant owed the Village Elder or to
any one else. Trella spent most of her days in her father's workroom,
helping the scribes and making sure the records were protected and
safeguarded.

Returning from the execution, Trella followed her father through the courtyard and into Ranaddi's quarters, passing through the common room and entering what Ranaddi called his audience room, a substantial and high-ceilinged chamber where he oversaw his trading ventures, and conducted important village business.

The Village Elder waited for them, sitting by himself at his table, a cup of date wine close at hand. Trella noted that Ranaddi had already comforted himself with several cups.

Ranaddi waited until the servant closed the door behind them, leaving the three alone. "How did he die?"

"Badly, as you expected, but slowly, as you ordered," Sargat answered, occupying the bench across from Ranaddi and motioning to Trella to sit beside him.

"Abbas begged and pleaded for mercy, called out for his father to save him. He even entreated help from the gods, vowing to amend his ways. Almost to the very end, he never believed such a thing could happen to him. Your guard stabbed him well, and he suffered greatly before he died."

"Not long enough, I'm sure. I wanted to put him to the torture, damn him. And damn Fradmon for fathering the murdering coward."

"Torturing Abbas would not bring back your son," Sargat said.

"Better to give him the same justice as any common murderer. This way you remain aloof from those who favor their own. Torturing him would almost certainly start a blood feud. A life for a life, and now it can end. Even those friendly to Fradmon accepted your decision."

"It was your decision," Ranaddi said, his fist striking the table and nearly upsetting the wine cup. "I wanted to see him suffer, to feed him to the flames piece by piece for what he did. Stabbing my son in the back . . ."

Trella's father said nothing. She had heard this argument several times since the murder, until Ranaddi finally yielded and accepted his advisor's counsel. She kept her eyes down, her hands folded in her lap, pretending not to notice the Elder's emotion or his grief.

The silence stretched on, until Ranaddi regained control of his anger. "And what of the crowd? How did they react? How many of Fradmon's followers attended?"

Trella saw her father's gesture, the tiny movement of his little finger that meant she should speak. "I watched the crowd, Elder. Almost three hundred people filled the market, and nearly all shouted for Abbas's blood."

She kept her voice low out of habit. Even in Ranaddi's house, servants enjoyed eavesdropping into their master's private affairs. "Only seven showed displeasure at the execution."

Trella recited the names. "Sondar, Fradmon's steward arrived at the last moment. His face was full of hatred and he spat on the ground. He left before Abbas died, as soon as he saw the thrust would be fatal."

"No one else from Fradmon's house attended?"

"No, Elder. I saw only Sondar. Not even any of the servants."

Ranaddi clenched his fist again. "A messenger from Fradmon arrived while you were gone. He's leaving Carnax tomorrow, taking his family and a few servants with him."

"A wise decision on his part," Sargat said. "To remain in Carnax would likely bring more confrontation and trouble. Fradmon knows he's not strong enough to challenge you."

"He and his family should be put to death."

"Fradmon will have to start over in another village," Sargat said, still trying to mollify his friend. "His trading ventures will suffer greatly. He will have to pay much to reestablish himself, build a new home, find more servants. Fradmon will endure hardship for many years as a result of his son's crime."

"It is not enough." Ranaddi's anguish changed his voice. "My wife cries each night, my daughter-in-law demands vengeance, and my hand itches to drive a sword into Fradmon's heart."

"I agree it is not enough," Sargat said. "But anything else will only bring more bloodshed. It was the son, not the father, that struck down Abbas."

Ranaddi sighed. "I know you're right, old friend. But you've never lost a son." He took a deep breath, as if to clear his mind of these gloomy thoughts. "What else did you notice, Trella?"

"Only Sondar's face, Elder. His anger clouded his features, but for an instant his face showed a grim smile, as if he'd seen what he wanted to see."

"What do you think it means?"

"I don't know, Elder. I saw hatred on his face, but also satisfaction." She glanced at her father, and caught the almost imperceptible nod, encouraging her to go on. "Perhaps he, too, wanted Abbas dead."

Ranaddi dismissed Trella's comments, and turned his eyes back to Sargat. "Are our men watching Fradmon and his house?"

"Yes. I have two men keeping their eyes on him and his family. And I've told the leader of your guards to station more men here, in case of trouble."

"There's nothing he can do, with his handful of bodyguards."

Her father said nothing, but Trella noticed that he didn't offer to remove the guards. Fradmon employed eight or nine men to protect his family and his goods. Ranaddi's force numbered twice that.

"I must return to my wife," Ranaddi said, his eyes vacant now, staring at the wall. "At least with Abbas dead, my son's spirit will rest. Now the grieving can begin."

"I grieve with you, Ranaddi," her father said. "Come, Trella. The day is still far from over, and we have work to do."

—⁐⁌⁐—

The next day, just past midmorning, Trella stood near the village gates as Fradmon, his family, and his retainers departed Carnax. The cavalcade numbered twenty-two, with half of those women and children.

Of the men, only five bodyguards chose to accompany the merchant and provide protection on the journey. Her father's spies had reported that Sondar left the village at dawn, riding alone.

From the shade of a sycamore tree, Trella studied the departing household concentrating on Fradmon and his wife as they rode by, the only two of the party on horseback. His face bore traces of rage and anger, but Fradmon kept his eyes straight ahead and refused to look at any of the idlers who'd gathered to watch him depart.

A few jeered or called out obscenities as the trader passed. If Fradmon heard their words, he gave no outward sign, but he held the horse's halter in a grip so tight his knuckles blanched white from the strain.

Fradmon's wife had tears streaming down her lowered face. She'd lost a son, and now her home and friends too. Trella could sympathize with that, wondering for a moment what she would do if her family had to leave their home. By then the merchant and his household had passed through the gates.

Trella watched until they reached the crossroads and turned west, the direction her father thought Fradmon would choose. A journey of two or three days would see them reaching the Euphrates, the mighty river that flowed to the Great Sea.

Once across the Euphrates, the villages grew smaller and smaller, but the merchant would have a better chance to reestablish his trading house in the new land. After the little band disappeared into the distance, Trella retraced her steps home, to report to her father and resume her duties.

With the execution over and Fradmon gone, Carnax fell back into its routine. Farmers returned to their fields, craftsmen to their tasks, and workers to their labors. Even in Ranaddi's house, the women's bereavement turned into grudging acceptance.

Death spared no one its sting, and not even Ranaddi's wealth had saved his son. People died all the time, from sickness, accidents, fights, from childbirth or old age, and even a few from starvation.

Justice occasionally added to the toll. Only the month before, a farmer quarreled with and then killed his neighbor. The altercation resulted in another murderer being put to death.

Ramen had been Ranaddi's eldest son. With his death, a good number of tasks, debts, and ownership of goods needed to be shifted to his two remaining brothers. Existing tablets had to be corrected or new ones created, meticulous work that would occupy all the clerks' time for many days.

Trella's part in all this was to make sure the modifications were done accurately. Servants, clerks, apprentices – none could be completely relied upon to perform their duties without supervision. Only blood relatives could be trusted.

Trella knew Ranaddi considered her father and her to be members of his extended family. It was yet one more of the many checks and balances the Elder had established to make sure his servants properly performed their duties.

That day passed, then another, and the excitement of the last few days slipped away, replaced by the usual struggle to survive. On the third day after the execution, a little after the sun passed midday, a farmer staggered into Carnax, near exhaustion and barely able to speak.

The guards at the gate escorted him to Ranaddi's house, where the trembling man gasped out a tale of bandits attacking farmhouses along the eastern stream that marked the border of the land Carnax defended, about a half a day's ride from the village.

Ranaddi ordered the leader of his guards to take some men and drive the raiders away. Trella paused in her work to watch six guards gather their horses and weapons from the Elder's courtyard. They rode off, eager to pursue their quarry, all of them glad for the opportunity to leave the village behind for a few days.

The Elder's men would search for these marauders and either kill them or chase them far from Carnax's land.

When the dust from their departure settled, Trella returned to her father's workroom. Bandits were a common enough occurrence, and the guards knew how to deal with them. The rest of the day and evening proved uneventful. She ate a quiet dinner with her parents, and went to her bed chamber early.

The murderers came just before dawn, slipping through the fields behind Ranaddi's house. They numbered only fifteen, but they carried ladders to help them scale the fence, and the two guards on duty had already been struck down by assassins within the enclave.

The attackers swarmed over the fence and burst into the Elder's courtyard before anyone gave the alarm. With a third of Ranaddi's force away chasing bandits, the intruders outnumbered the sleepy and surprised guards, killing many of them before they could seize their weapons to defend themselves.

The crash of splintering wood woke Trella, as men smashed down the door to Sargat's house. Loud voices shouted in anger, and heavy footsteps moved through the house. A woman screamed, the sound cut short.

Trella heard the clash of swords coming from the courtyard. She jumped out of bed and fumbled her dress over her head, while strange voices echoed in the house.

Torchlight flickered through the thin curtain that gave Trella's alcove its privacy. The servant, Ninani, who shared Trella's room awakened also, crying out in fright and clutching the blanket to her chest.

Before Trella could reach the curtain, it was swept aside. Light from the crackling torch illuminated the chamber, sending shadows crawling over the walls.

Trella glimpsed a bearded man with a naked sword in his hand. Blood glinted on the blade. She recoiled at the sight, her heart thumping in her breast.

The intruder, seeing only two harmless women, grunted in satisfaction and stepped back into the common room. By now screams of pain and shouts of rage filled the entire house.

Trella heard her father calling for help, and she crept to the doorway, twitching the curtain aside in time to see a second man with another torch enter the house's common room, this one also carrying a blood-stained sword. She let the curtain fall back, but not before she saw two men dragging her father and mother from their chamber.

The man with the beard saw the curtain's movement and whirled around, sword at the ready and raising his torch, until he realized Trella was no threat. "Get them out here," he ordered.

Another man, his clothing smeared with gore, crossed the common room in two strides and tore the curtain down. He seized Trella and Ninani by their hair, yanked them into the main room, and forced them to the floor.

Trella's eyes darted around. She saw her parents on their knees, her mother clutching her father. A man with a sword stood behind them, and Trella heard him order them not to move.

Sargat's bodyguard lay on his back near the house's entrance, blood dripping from a gaping wound in his stomach. Another body rested beside that of the guard, this one the older woman who cooked their food and tended her mother's spice garden. Trella trembled at the thought of someone striking down such a helpless servant.

Now so frightened she could hardly breathe, Trella remained on her hands and knees, hardly aware that a man's hand still clasped her thick hair. To her surprise, no one moved. The intruders just stood there, waiting. Only a few heartbeats passed before two more men entered the room, each carrying a bloody sword.

To her horror, Trella recognized them both – Fradmon and Sondar. The steward had not abandoned his master after all. With a chill, she now understood the expression on his face at the execution. Even then, Sondar must have known of Fradmon's plan to take revenge.

"Ah, Sargat, the loyal servant who carried out my son's death," Fradmon said, his clipped words expressing such hatred that Trella gasped. "I've come to repay you for murdering my son."

"This is madness, Fradmon," her father said. "The villagers will not stand for such violence."

Even in her terror, Trella heard neither fear nor anger in her father's voice.

"The sheep that live in Carnax will be on their knees before me at dawn, or they'll be as dead as you are."

Trella's mind began to function, taking in the situation even faster than her father. Such a deed as this was beyond the pale. Fradmon intended to murder them all, to take his revenge for his son's death.

The grinning trader saw his words take effect on Sargat. "I'll give you no worse than you treated my son. Stand him up."

The man behind her father jerked him from his knees, then held him upright.

Fradmon stepped closer. "I'd put you to the torture for a few days, but I want to spend more time with Ranaddi." Fradmon laughed, a horrible rasping sound that would have terrified anyone.

"But I'll start with your wife. You can watch her die first."

With a sudden movement, Fradmon swung the sword up and down, the blade cleaving into Trella's mother's neck. Blood spurted from the wound, drops scattering over both Fradmon and her father. Her mother cried out, a horrible sound, and her hands waved about wildly; she slipped to the floor, her hand reaching out toward her husband.

"Your son and witch daughter will amuse my men before they die," Fradmon said, "but not for long, I promise you."

"The gods will curse you for this deed," Sargat said, his voice resigned. He forced himself to stand erect. "They will strike you down . . ."

Fradmon shoved the bloody sword into Sargat's stomach, then twisted the blade, opening the wound even wider. Her father groaned, a long cry of pain wrenched from his throat.

"Just as you killed my son. Now you can lie here and feel the same pain he did. Die slowly, old man." Fradmon jerked the sword from Sargat's stomach with a grunt of satisfaction.

His hands clutching at his stomach, Sargat fell heavily to the floor on his back, his wide eyes fixed on his killer. With the last of his strength, his left hand sought that of his wife, but Trella knew her mother was already dead, the life gone from her body.

Trella stared at her parents. In the flickering torchlight, she saw the awful pain on their faces, and waited for the horror that would soon be hers.

"Tie up the rest of them," Fradmon said, as he strode across the room, ignoring the bodies in his way, and disappearing from sight, with a grinning Sondar following behind him.

Unable to move, Trella didn't even struggle as they bound her hands, then did the same to Ninani. Another of Fradmon's men dragged Trella's brother into the room, pulling Almaric's unconscious body by both arms.

At first she thought the assassins had killed him, too, but when they bound his hands, Trella knew her brother still lived. A large bruise covered half his face, and she guessed he'd been knocked unconscious trying to defend himself.

For a moment, hope stirred in her breast, knowing that he was alive. Then thoughts of the terrible fate that awaited them filled her mind, and Trella wondered if he might be better off dead. Her tears started and she felt her body shaking, as she thought about what they would do to her first.

She tried to move closer to Almaric, but her captor caught her by the arm and flung her hard against the wall.

"Move again, you little slut, and I'll really hurt you." He grabbed her by the hair, shoved her head hard against the wall, then pushed her down.

Dazed, Trella sank to her knees. The room spun around her, and her eyes closed from the pain. She felt her cheek striking the hard packed earth floor, then nothing.

28

When Trella opened her eyes, the sun shone through the shattered doorway. It took only a moment before memory returned, along with the wretchedness of her situation. She pushed herself upright, struggling against the coarse rope that bound her hands.

Looking around the room, she saw the bodies of her parents only a few steps away, the buzzing flies already feasting on their blood. Her face felt bruised, her hair tangled over her swollen eyes.

"Are you all right, Trella?"

Ninani, her father's concubine, sat an arm's length away, her back against the wall. Almaric lay beside her, his head on her lap, bound as well and still senseless.

"What happened to me?" Realization came slowly, and Trella had difficulty getting the words out.

"One of the men threw you against the wall," Ninani said, "and you struck your head. I think you fainted after that."

Trella had never fainted in her life, but the force of the blow combined with the shock of watching her parents murdered must have rendered her unconscious.

She looked around the shambles of the communal room. Debris littered the floor, everything from the remains of a broken chair to pottery shards, and even food normally stored in the cupboard.

Blood from her parents' bodies pooled nearly to Trella's feet. But there were no guards, and the house seemed curiously silent.

"Where is everyone?"

"They all went to Ranaddi's rooms," Ninani said. "The screaming over there was very bad, but it's mostly quiet now. It's just as well you didn't hear it. I think they must all be dead. Fradmon's men will probably come back soon to kill us, too."

Even confused and in pain, Trella knew they wouldn't likely be killed, at least not yet. "They won't kill you," she said. "They'll give you to Fradmon's men. If you survive that, they'll probably let you live."

"And you, Trella?"

"I think Fradmon and his men will take me, too. After that, I'll probably be killed." She said the words calmly enough, but the horror she envisioned made her lips tremble.

A shadow darkened the doorway, and one of Fradmon's assassins entered. Trella recognized the same man who'd bound her hands. His tunic and legs were splattered with blood, and more blood had crusted around his sword hilt, where he'd sheathed his weapon without cleaning it.

He said nothing, just dragged the two women to their feet and shoved them roughly against the wall. Then he tried to wake Almaric. After much pushing and shaking, Almaric moaned.

The bandit swore in anger. "Be easier to just kill him now." Instead, he draped Almaric's arm over his shoulder and half-carried him toward the door. "Get moving, you two," he ordered. "Fradmon wants to see you."

Ninani started to cry, and Trella felt her own fear rising, but the man had her brother upright and on his feet, and she didn't want to be separated from him.

Outside, the chaos in the courtyard appeared even worse than in the house. More bodies, at least ten, sprawled about the courtyard – guards, servants, men, and women, even a goat. A child's body lay beside its mother. Two dogs, bloody flesh hanging from their jaws, interrupted their feeding on the goat long enough to growl at Trella's passage.

She wanted to shut her eyes from the sight, but fear of tripping and falling into the blood-soaked earth kept her stumbling forward, eyes fixed straight ahead.

Ranaddi's house looked even worse than Sargat's, with debris and blood gore almost covering the floor. Seven or eight bodies, those of the household servants and guards, littered the Elder's common room, all of them dead. Helpless servants had died, killed for no reason other than that they lived here.

Someone had dragged the dead aside to clear the way to the audience room, where their captor pushed Trella and her companions. The coppery reek of blood, the acrid stink of urine and worse, permeated the air. Even the breeze wafting in from the wheat field through the open door couldn't overcome the stench. If Trella had anything in her stomach, she would have vomited.

An unconscious Ranaddi, his swollen and battered face barely recognizable behind crusted blood, sat bound to his chair, sagging against the ropes that held him. The naked and bloody body of his dead and mutilated wife was shoved against the wall. Trella couldn't count the stab wounds that had pierced her legs and stomach.

The other members of Ranaddi's family had died here as well, their corpses shoved into one corner of the chamber. Ranaddi must have been forced to watch their torture and death before his own ordeal began.

Fradmon sat on a bench, his back against the table, with his legs stretched out. Trella's gaze fixed on him, and she felt her heart racing. The man she saw only two days ago riding out of the village had vanished, replaced by the demon resting only a few paces away.

His tunic was splashed with blood and bits of flesh. His sandaled feet could scarcely be seen, as if his feet and ankles had been painted in varying shades of red. Blood covered his hands, and some of it, she realized, was his own. A crude bandage wrapped around his right hand, and she guessed his grip had slipped as he stabbed one of his victims.

Fradmon's face showed the most change. His lank gray hair hung limply around his eyes, strands clotted with blood as if trying to conceal his features. His eyes bulged almost like a frog's, but he stared into nothingness.

The man responsible for the carnage hadn't noticed the new arrivals' presence. His cheeks looked sallow, almost white where no blood spatter showed, and his chest heaved, long, rasping breaths, one after another, as he labored to draw air into his lungs.

He's close to death himself, Trella thought. The effort to destroy and torture his enemies had exacted a price even Fradmon had not expected to pay.

The guard escorting Trella broke the long silence. "What should we do with these three?"

Fradmon ignored the question, his eyes fastened on the ceiling above Trella's head.

"Master, what should . . ."

"I heard you, fool," Fradmon said, lowering his eyes and peering at the new arrivals.

Trella scarcely recognized the hoarse voice.

With an effort, Fradmon sat upright on the bench. His hand reached down, and Trella saw a long bladed, blood-stained knife resting on the floor at his feet where he'd dropped the weapon.

"Who are they?" His fingers fumbled with the knife, but he grasped it, then rested the weapon on his knee.

The guard shrugged. "I don't know, Master. We found them in the other house."

Fradmon regarded the newcomers once again. "Oh, yes, the children of Sargat, the loyal servant, the one who put my son to death."

He laughed, a deep rumbling sound that sent a shiver through Trella, and ended with Fradmon gasping for breath. "Ranaddi can watch them die, the last of his household, though I don't think he'll recognize them."

Ninani uttered a small cry at the sentence of death. "Master, I'm just a household servant," she said, the words rushing from her as she dropped to her knees. "I've done nothing to offend you. Please, Master, let me serve you."

Fradmon ignored the plea as he pushed himself to his feet, his eyes focused on Trella.

"And this one, the witch daughter who watches and watches, like a spider waiting for its prey. You stood there while my son died, watching . . . watching. Now it will be my turn to watch, and for you to beg me to end your suffering."

Almaric, his comprehension returning, struggled feebly against the guard who still supported him. "No, you mustn't hurt my sister. Let her go."

The guard grabbed him by the arm and swung his fist into her brother's stomach. Trella started to plead for him, but Fradmon had taken two steps forward, and now he rammed his bandaged fist into Almaric's face.

Fradmon had the knife in his hand, and Trella thought he'd stabbed her brother. Then she realized he'd used the weapon's hilt. The punch, delivered with all of Fradmon's strength, knocked the boy from the guard's grasp.

Trella saw blood spurt from Almaric's mouth and nose as he staggered backward, his head striking the doorframe.

The blow delivered, Fradmon ignored his latest prey. Instead, he turned his head slowly toward Trella, the only one still standing. She caught the rank odors of blood and death that emanated from the merchant, and felt herself gagging at the smell.

A crooked smile appeared on his face, and her horror grew when she saw his teeth were stained with blood. Fradmon took a step toward her, and raised the knife. There would be no rape or torture, she realized. He meant to kill her, slowly and painfully.

A shadow crossed the doorway. "Well, Fradmon, have you finished paying your blood debt?"

Fradmon, a pace away from Trella, paused and turned his head toward the voice.

Sondar stood there, framed in the doorway. With a glance downward, he stepped over the body of Trella's brother. "I came to say farewell, Master."

Even in her fear and confusion, Trella caught the hint of disdain in Sondar's words, heard the contempt no longer concealed.

Fradmon's brow wrinkled, almost as if he had to recall the name of his chief steward and head of his guards. "Did you unearth Ranaddi's hidden treasure? Did you search all the secret places?"

"Yes, we did. We found everything right where he said it would be. Plenty of gold and silver, even a good supply of gemstones. Enough to restore your wealth twice over."

"Good. Bring it here," Fradmon ordered, his blood lust temporarily forgotten. "You'll have your reward soon enough."

"I've already taken payment for my services, Fradmon," Sondar said. The insolence in his voice penetrated even Fradmon's clouded mind.

"What are you talking about? I said bring it here. At once."

"I think not, *Master*. Or should I say, *former master*. My men and I are leaving, and we're taking all the horses, and all of Ranaddi's riches with us."

"How dare you speak to me like that," Fradmon bellowed, his forehead flushing red with rage. "I am your master. You've sworn to obey me!" The vein in his forehead bulged.

Sondar laughed, throwing back his head at his master's words.

"Not any more. I've helped you take your revenge for your fool of a son. He was a pig, and I enjoyed watching him die. Now the fool of a father can take the blame for what's happened here. The villagers will be blaming you for this night's work."

Furious, Fradmon took a step and raised his knife, but Sondar lifted the hand at his side, and Trella saw the gleaming bronze blade he held at the ready.

The sight stopped Fradmon in mid-step, the point of the blade only a hand's length from his heart.

"Guards! Guards!" Fradmon's voice echoed throughout the house. He stumbled back, away from Sondar, the knife slipping from his hand. "Your master needs you! Guards!"

"Your men now serve me, Fradmon. I had to kill two fools who remained loyal, but the rest were glad enough to be rid of you."

Fradmon's fury erupted and his reason vanished. He launched himself at his tormentor, bloody hands outstretched like claws seeking his rebellious servant's eyes. But Sondar stepped into the charge and struck his former master in the chest with the hilt of his sword, knocking the merchant backward to the floor.

Fradmon, drool and blood oozing from his mouth, stared up at his steward.

"You're even more stupid than I thought, Fradmon, to try something like that. I'd prefer to kill you myself, but better to have the villagers take their revenge on you. They'll hunt you down for what's happened."

Sondar laughed at the prospect. "Meanwhile, my men and I will disappear with all of Ranaddi's gold. If I were you, I'd run for it, before Ranaddi's guards return. They'll be here soon enough. By now they must know they'd been lured away on a fool's errand."

He turned to the grinning guard still standing beside Trella. "Put these three with the others. We don't want any witnesses left alive."

Trella stood there while the guard again lifted her brother to his feet, slapping him until he regained consciousness, then leaning him against the wall. He turned his attention to the girls. "You two, take his arms and keep him moving. If he falls, I'll kill him and you, too."

With a shove, he pushed Trella toward her brother. Her hands were numb from the ropes, but she slipped his arm between hers. Ninani got to her feet, and took Almaric's other arm, and together they shuffled slowly to the door.

As Trella turned sideways to ease through the chamber's entrance, for a moment, she faced the bloody room and its contents. Her last sight was of Fradmon on the floor, his eyes closed, hugging his knees to his chest. A low whimpering sound came from his open mouth as he rocked back and forth.

Then she was through the entrance, and a moment later in the courtyard. Horses waited there, with armed men laughing and making jests. The guard shoved Trella and Ninani toward a group of captives cowering against the side of the house.

Sondar, mounted on his horse, awaited them. "Is that the last of them?"

"Yes, Master."

"And the rest of the villagers? Did you search the houses?"

"Yes, Master. Everyone else has fled to the fields. Carnax is empty."

"Then these will have to do. Get them moving."

Trella saw that she and her brother were not the only captives. More than fifteen or twenty other servants, most of them women or young men, stood there, many with their hands tied before them. Sondar's men moved among the prisoners, shouting and pushing everyone into motion.

Trella shuffled forward with the others. As they passed through the deserted lanes of Carnax, she saw more bodies strewn about. Many of the village's inhabitants had died, while Sondar's bandits searched the whole village for loot and plunder.

She had no more time to think about the dead, as she struggled to keep up. Sondar and his men rode horses, and two other mounts served as pack animals, no doubt carrying the wealth stolen from Ranaddi and her father. Trella counted twenty-six prisoners, sixteen women and ten men.

Sondar had nine riders obeying his commands, and two of them carried bows. All had swords. More than enough men and weaponry to make resistance impossible and prevent any foolhardy attempts to rescue the prisoners.

They passed through the open gate and onto the eastern road, Sondar's harsh voice shouting at them to move faster. Trella had no idea where they were going, but any place seemed better than the blood-filled village behind her. Whatever fate awaited her, she knew that Sondar's arrival had saved her life. The insane Fradmon would certainly have killed her and her brother.

Two of Sondar's men guarded the prisoners. Both carried rope whips that they used freely to keep everyone moving. Trying to keep up with the horses meant a brutal pace.

Soon Trella had to stretch her legs to the utmost, and she felt herself breathing hard. But if one of the captives slowed down, the rope lashed out, a stinging goad that continued until the victim stumbled into a run and caught up.

One stroke across her back proved enough for Trella. She kept up with the others, staying at her brother's side. She had no sandals, and wished for the new pair she'd received only a few days before, probably still tucked beneath her bed. Tonight her feet would be blistered and sore.

Almaric remained dazed; he still suffered from the blow on the head. He said little, and had trouble keeping up the pace, despite his stronger frame and longer legs.

Again and again Trella had to support him when he stumbled. She wanted to talk to him, to encourage him, but the guard raised his rope at every prisoner's attempt to speak or plead for mercy, and so the helpless captives trudged in silence over the empty landscape.

They covered the ground at a rapid pace. At first Ninani walked alongside Trella and Almaric, but she soon fell back to the rear of the prisoners, and Trella had to watch over her brother alone.

By midmorning, she found herself farther away from Carnax than she'd ever been. As she walked along, she wondered where they were going. Sondar said that he planned to ride hard and fast, to put as much distance between himself and the village. But Trella knew that he wouldn't get far escorting so many prisoners.

The sun moved higher in the sky, and by now everyone was staggering and gasping for breath. Thirst burned Trella's throat. The horsemen carried bulging water skins, but made no offer to share any with their captives.

One by one, the prisoners began to stumble and fall, and finally no amount of lashing with the rope could keep them moving. At last Sondar ordered a halt, to let them rest for a few moments.

Trella and Almaric collapsed on the ground. Sweat caked with dust kicked up by the horses covered her brother's face and chest, and she knew she must look much the same. Sondar dismounted, and he and his men took their ease sitting on the ground and laughing as they passed around a wine skin.

They boasted of their bravery back in the village and bragged about all the gold they'd taken. The prisoners pleaded for water, but none of the bandits paid them the slightest attention. Some of the women sobbed, while others trembled in fear.

Almaric lay on the ground, seemingly unaware of what was happening. Trella worried that he might not be right in the head. He needed rest and water, and she knew he would get neither from these murderers.

"Enough rest," Sondar shouted, glancing up at the sun's progress. "Get them on their feet."

The grinning men flexed their rope whips as they ordered everyone to start walking. Trella helped Almaric stand, using her bound hands to get him upright before any of their captors decided to use their whips. She walked beside him, alert in case he should start to stumble. Soon they plodded along once again, still heading east.

Midday came and passed. They moved off the barely visible trail that led to a nearby village, cutting across country, heading for some unknown destination. She heard Sondar shouting up ahead, though in her exhaustion she couldn't understand the words.

The men with the ropes started using them, urging their captives faster and faster. Trella saw a line of trees crossing their path, and soon she heard a cascade of water rushing over the rocks, the bubbling sound growing louder as they approached.

Driven by thirst, they stumbled along, the sound drawing them. In a daze, Trella saw a group of men standing beside a stand of willow trees that bordered the stream. Not that she cared. All that mattered now was the water.

Like all the others, she staggered the last few steps until they reached the stream, pulling her brother along with the last of her strength.

Trella dropped to her knees, then was knocked over by someone pushing her from behind. She didn't care. She lay face down in the slow moving water, gulping down the cool liquid that tasted better than any drink that ever came from the well in her family's compound.

As soon as she could lift her head, she looked toward her brother. Almaric drank as well, thought not as much as she wished. Hopefully the fresh water would revive his spirit.

Trella drank again, until she could hold no more, then let her swollen hands soak in the cool water. That reminded her about her feet, and she shifted her position until she sat on the stream's edge, her legs in the water. Somewhat refreshed, she looked around at the men behind her, their voices finally reaching her ears.

"Get them out of the water," a strange voice cut through the air. "They'll drink themselves sick."

"They're your problem now, Drusas," Sondar said.

"Not until I examine them, and I won't pay for anyone too sick to travel."

Trella flinched at the name. The stranger had stood with his back to her, but now she recognized him. Drusas the slave dealer. He spent his days traveling across the countryside, buying and selling slaves.

Rumors said he forced many of his captives into slavery. Strangers on the road, men drunk after a night of drinking, young boys and girls snatched up at night from the lanes or fields, anyone he could get his hands on. Drusas bought and sold slaves as easily as a farmer traded fruit at the market.

A flesh merchant, one so revolting that Ranaddi and her father showed repugnance in their occasional dealings with him. For the first time, Trella understood exactly what her fate would be. She would be a slave for the rest of her life.

After all that had happened to her family, Trella thought she would never feel shock or surprise again. But the sight of the slave master stunned her. The life she had known since childhood had ended. Now Drusas would own her body.

And when he was ready, when he got a good enough price, Drusas would sell her to someone who would be her master, her owner, with the power of life and death over her.

No doubt Drusas obtained many of his slaves by such evil dealings, this time abetted by Sondar. The former steward, not content with Ranaddi's loot, must have struck a deal with Drusas, to sell the slaver whatever household servants and villagers Sondar could lay his hands on.

By completing the transaction far from the village, it was unlikely any of the surviving villagers from Carnax would ever learn of the slave dealer's foul practice or what happened to their kin and neighbors.

"Get them out of the water," Sondar shouted. "Hurry!"

His men waded into the river, pushing the slaves out of the water, and using their ropes to herd the exhausted men and women back on the river bank.

"Line them up," Drusas said. "Men here, women there."

Rough hands shoved Trella away her brother, and the helpless slaves formed a long line, their backs to the stream.

Drusas walked down the line accompanied by two of his men, their calculating faces revealing no trace of sympathy for their latest lot of slaves.

Unlike Sondar's bandits, Drusas's slave masters carried real whips, long strips of plaited leather with a loop on one end to fit snugly over their wrists. The other end, supple from much use, gleamed with a reddish tint, and Trella wondered how much blood it took to darken each scourge.

One by one, Drusas examined the slaves, estimating their worth. He asked each their trade, what skills they possessed, how many seasons each had. No one refused to answer. The dread Drusas exuded would frighten any man or woman.

Then he stood before Trella. She lowered her head, her tangled hair half-hiding her face, afraid to meet his eyes.

"Ah, I remember this one. Sargat's daughter, the one who knows the symbols. Look at me, girl."

The last words snapped out, and Trella lifted her head. She stared directly into his eyes, and realized he stood only a finger width or two taller than she did. He had a thin nose and a small mouth.

She saw not a single blemish on his face, only smoothness with a trace of beard. Drusas didn't carry a whip as his men did. Instead he held a beautifully carved stick in his hand, and he used it to lift her chin even higher.

"Your name?"

"Trella."

He struck her across her upper arm, where the short sleeve of her dress protected her flesh. The blow stung, but she flinched more from surprise than pain.

"I'm your master now, Trella, and you'll address me properly."
He spoke quietly, only loud enough to be heard, but his tone indicated that he expected to be obeyed. "Do you understand?"

"Yes . . . Master." Her lips trembled, as much from saying the
hated word of submission for the first time as from the fear the man
inspired.

"You don't look like you'd fetch a good price right now, but we'll
see what we can do." With a deft movement, he slipped the end of
his stick under the left shoulder of her dress, and jerked it down,
exposing her breast. "Good sized, and still unblemished. Are you a
virgin?"

The odd question surprised her, as much as the broad smiles on
the faces of the men standing on either side of their master. Trella
felt her face flushing with the shame of standing exposed to her new
master.

Drusas struck her again, a bit harder this time, on the other
shoulder.

"Answer at once when you're spoken to, slave."

"Yes, Master."

He frowned at her. She realized her mistake and made the proper
answer. "Yes, Master, I'm still a virgin."

Slaves were always instructed to answer each question fully and
politely, to make sure they understood each command, just as they
were expected to show the proper docility and obedience.

She wanted to pull her dress up, but knew better. Her body
belonged to her master now, not her. If he wanted her to stand there
naked, she would have to obey.

"Treat this one with care, Zug," Drusas said, turning to his chief
steward, a tall, lean man with dirty black hair, standing beside him.
"She'll need to be trained, but we might be able to get something
extra for her."

Without another glance, he moved down the line to the next girl.
Trella pushed her dress back in place, fumbling with her still-bound
hands. She looked over to where her brother stood, his own misery
apparent in his slumped shoulders. He'd watched her answer the

questions, unable to do or even say anything. Now he couldn't meet her eyes, shamed by his own helplessness.

Trella used the time to count Drusas's men. The slave dealer had waited at the stream with eight guards and ten male slaves. With the addition of those seized from Carnax, Drusas would have thirty-six slaves to sell. She'd never heard of so many slaves in one group, and wondered where and how the slave master planned to dispose of so many.

Drusas didn't take long to complete the careful appraisal of his latest acquisitions. After a bit of haggling with Sondar, the former steward collected his payment and mounted up. Within moments, he and his men galloped off in high spirits, trailing a cloud of dust behind them, glad to be rid of the human merchandise they'd delivered.

To Trella's horror, her brother and three other men were separated from the rest of the male slaves. After a few words with Drusas and Zug, two of the slave dealer's men started herding the four prisoners to the north.

"Almaric," Trella shouted, forgetting the command to keep silent.

Zug took a long stride toward her, raising his whip as he moved. "Open your mouth again, and I'll strip the skin off your back."

She shrank away, her eyes fastened on the plaited leather, waiting for the blow to fall. But Zug lowered the whip, and she remembered Drusas's words to treat her with care. However, she knew there were many ways to give pain without marking or breaking the flesh.

Zug leered at her. "That's better. Don't make me come back."

She watched in silence as her brother marched off. Drusas must have an unfilled order for male slaves. To her dismay, she remembered that, only a few day's march away, one of the villages operated several silver mines. She prayed to the gods that would not be her brother's fate.

Slaves never lasted long in the mines. Digging the ore from the hard earth deep underground and burning away the impurities in foul-smelling, smoky fires took a heavy toll on the mine's workers. They sickened and died, often in a matter of months.

Trella felt the tears welling in her eyes as she tried to keep her brother in sight. Once he turned to look back, but one of his guards used the whip. In a few moments, Almaric vanished behind a low rise. With a sinking feeling in her heart, she wondered if she would ever see him again.

The rest of Drusas's men bustled about, showing efficiency in their actions as they packed up their camp and readied their new merchandise for the next journey. Before long, the slave caravan headed south.

On the march, they kept the slaves separated into two groups, with men in the first and women in the second. Drusas kept up a rapid pace, but not as brutal as the one Sondar demanded. No doubt the trader wanted to make sure his new property arrived in good condition.

As they trudged along, Zug wheeled his horse up and down the line, his whip swinging easily in his hand.

"When we stop for the night," he called out, "you'll be fed. Provided you keep up and do as your told. If you don't, then you get a taste of the whip for supper instead of food. So if you want to eat, keep moving and keep quiet."

Trella heard some women crying, and saw their shoulders shaking as the realization of their fates settled in. Two of the women servants who walked with Trella had husbands among the men, and they would likely be separated from them as well.

Trella blinked back her own tears. Crying wouldn't help. In fact, it would make the slavers' control of her even easier. Before long, she and the other women were too exhausted for any more tears.

Their captors rode, and Zug pushed the slaves hard. All the guards used their whips freely, especially on the men, and kept everyone at a quick pace that forced the women almost to a run. Whenever anyone slowed down, Zug or one of the others came by, always eager to use their whips to maintain the pace.

The sun crept slowly across the sky, and Trella wondered how much longer she could keep up. She'd always been physically strong, and while her well muscled legs might be capable of maintaining the pace, the lack of sandals meant that each step grew more and more painful. She concentrated on where she placed her feet, trying to avoid rough stones or hard patches of earth. Only three of the women had sandals; the rest were barefoot.

As the male slaves wearied, Drusas's guards used their whips, lashing the men for the slightest provocation, or no for reason at all. The slavers cursed and shouted at their prisoners to walk faster. The sun began to sink in the west, and they reached a tiny stream bordered by a sparse line of shrubs and low trees.

The horsemen slowed as they approached the bubbling water. Even though the sun hadn't yet touched the horizon, Trella heard Drusas give the order to halt.

All the slaves fell to their knees, exhausted by the long journey, too tired even to seek the stream's water. When a few of the braver ones tried to approach the running water, the guards drove them away.

"You slaves drink when I say so," Zug shouted.

Taking their time, Drusas and his men drank their fill and washed the dust from their faces. Then the horses were watered, fed, and herded into a rope corral. All this activity occurred at a leisurely pace, while the parched slaves, their mouths open, gazed at the unapproachable water only a few steps away.

Finally Zug let the male slaves enter the stream. All too soon, and well before they could satisfy their thirst, Zug raised his whip and drove them out again. Only after the male slaves had cleared the water did he call out for the women to come forward.

Trella wasted no time. She rushed to the water, threw herself down, and gulped the cool liquid as fast as she could. The order came to move away from the stream quickly enough, but at least Trella had quenched her thirst.

The women, their shifts muddy and clinging from the water, huddled together as they sat on the ground. Miserable, they stared in silence while the slavers erected a small tent for Drusas. Meanwhile, the male slaves built a fire and gathered wood, all under the watchful eyes of the guards.

Once again Trella noticed how efficiently Drusas ran his camp. The male slaves outnumbered their eight captors, but tired and exhausted from the long day's march with nothing to eat, the slaves had no strength to resist the armed and rested men watching them.

These men must have handled hundreds of slaves over the years, and they knew how to perform their trade efficiently.

Drusas and half the guards ate first, taking their time over their bread and fruit. But three guards kept their eyes on the slaves at all times, and one of them carried a bow and wore an arrow quiver on his hip. The message was clear. Anyone trying to escape would be killed.

Food, when it finally became time for the slaves to be fed, consisted of stale bread and scraps of fruit tossed on the earth before them. Trella struggled with an older woman from the village over the loaf of bread they had to share. The long day's activity had left the slaves ravenous, and every scrap was consumed, wolfed down as quickly as possible. Even after the last of the food disappeared, the new slaves remained hungry.

Trella observed the careful way the food was dispensed, and realized the guards gave out only enough food to keep the slaves strong enough to walk, and not a crust more. Exhaustion took control after eating, and the slaves stretched out on the ground. There would be no blankets to shelter them from the cool night.

A guard returned, and this time he untied the ropes from the women's hands. Trella let out a gasp of pain when the cords were removed, and her swollen hands burned and tingled after the long day. The short lengths of rope removed from the women were knotted together and used on the men, a loop passing over each man's head, so that one could not move without dragging another.

The men's hands, Trella saw, remained tied, and she guessed at the pain they would suffer through the night. She remembered that many slaves seemed to have impaired hands, and wondered if tight ropes worn day and night might have caused the damage.

The male slaves secured for the night, Zug and two others returned to the women. "That one, and that one," he said, pointing out two of the older and plainer women. The guards grabbed the two women by their hair and led them a few paces away, to the place where the slavers had settled in for the night. The women protested and tried to struggle, but their captors only laughed.

"You'll be smiling soon enough," one man said.

Trella understood what was going to happen even before the other women. Soon it would be her turn. Then she saw Zug returning.

"Trella," he said, walking toward them, "and that one," pointing to Ninani, "you two come with me."

For a moment, Trella couldn't move. Zug, waiting impatiently, lifted the whip always dangling from his wrist.

"Come, Trella," Ninani whispered, her arm lifting Trella to her feet. "There's no sense in being beaten as well."

They followed Zug past the campfire and over to Drusas's tent. The steward lifted the flap, and motioned them inside. Clutching Ninani's arm, Trella crept into the tent.

Inside, a blanket covered the floor, and Drusas sat at the far end, a small traveling table at his side holding the remains of his dinner and a cupful of wine.

"Leave the flap up," he instructed his steward. "There's still enough light to get a good look at our merchandise."

Zug laughed as he pushed the two girls to the center of the tent. There wasn't enough room for them to stand up straight, and, still clinging to each other, they hunched over to avoid the roof of the tent.

"Take off your shifts," Drusas commanded, his voice as flat and emotionless as if he'd asked about their supper.

Ninani slipped to one side, bent over, and pulled her shift over her head. Zug jerked it from her and tossed it near the tent's opening.

Trella, unable to move, stood there. Suddenly she felt the lash of Zug's whip on her buttocks, and the sharp sting brought her back to her plight. She hurriedly pulled her shift off and handed it to Zug, who threw it atop Ninani's.

"On your knees, slaves," Zug ordered. "Your master wants to inspect his property."

Ninani dropped to her knees, and this time Trella followed her example.

"Straighten up," Drusas said, "and put your shoulders back. You need to learn to display yourself properly. Move closer." He rapped his stick on the blanket before him.

Still on their knees, both girls shuffled forward. Now they knelt close enough for Drusas to reach out and touch them.

Zug's whip stung across Trella's back. "Keep your shoulders straight, slave."

Trella straightened up again, the movement keeping her breasts thrust out, and she felt the evening breeze flowing across them.

"Not too hard, Zug," Drusas cautioned. "We don't want to damage our valuable, though very dirty right now, property. Hopefully they'll look better after a bath."

Drusas started with Ninani, examining her skin for blemishes, and running his hand over her arms, breasts and stomach.

"You're right, Zug. She's the prettiest and best of the lot. Not a virgin, but I think she'll fetch a fine price. How old are you, girl?"

"I've sixteen seasons, Master." Ninani spoke the words humbly enough, keeping her voice low and pleasant, as if she enjoyed kneeling naked before a man.

"Not too old yet. I'm sure we can find a good buyer for you." He turned his attention to Trella. "And you, how old are you?"

"I've fourteen seasons, Master," Trella said, answering the same way.

"And you claim to be a virgin? There must not have been any real men living in your father's household. Well, we'll have to make sure. On your back, slave."

Trella hesitated, not sure what he wanted. Zug grasped her by the hair, and yanked her backwards. She fell awkwardly, her legs tangled beneath her. By then Zug was kneeling beside her, no doubt familiar with his master's questions.

"Spread your legs, slut," he said. "Now lift your feet up."

When she didn't move fast enough to satisfy him, he lashed her again, this time across her legs. By then she was in position, on her back, with her legs drawn up and separated.

Trella felt her face flushing again from embarrassment, as her raised loins were held up for Drusas's inspection.

He used his hands to spread her legs even wider, ignoring the gasp of pain his rough touch elicited. He took his time examining her.

"Well, she is a virgin. That will add a few more coins to her price. Now we'll see what else she has to offer."

"What else is there," Zug asked. "They're either virgins or whores."

Drusas ignored his steward's comment. "I've heard you know the symbols, slave, and can add the sums. Is that true?"

"Yes, Master," she answered. Her voice sounded strange in her ears, almost as if someone else were speaking her words. She remained on her back, her feet still up in the air.

"We'll see. Twelve coins and seven coins? How many is that?"

"Nineteen coins."

This time Zug's plaited leather struck the upraised sole of her right foot. "Answer properly, slave."

"Nineteen coins, Master." The words came out with a rush. Her feet, already tender from the day's march, recoiled from the stroke.

"Keep your feet up and hold still," Drusas ordered. He tapped his stick against her vagina. "Unless you want Zug to give you a few strokes here to teach you to obey properly."

He continued with another handful of sums, increasing the complexity of the numbers. The steady tapping on her maidenhead unnerved her, and she had to concentrate to get the sums right.

Looking up, she saw Zug's face grinning down at her, his whip still held ready. Sum after sum, and each time she barely finished speaking the answer before Drusas presented another.

"Twelve and forty-two and thirteen?"

"Sixty-seven, Master."

"It's sixty-five, slave."

"No, it's sixty . . ."

Drusas struck down hard with the stick, and Trella couldn't hold back a scream of pain. "How much is it?" The calm voice showed not the least excitement.

"Sixty . . . sixty-five, Master."

"Very good. Perhaps you are learning after all. One of the most important lessons for new slaves to learn is that they must never contradict their masters. Remember that. Now, back up on your knees."

She started to move, but saw Zug raising his whip.

"Yes, Master," she gasped the words out in a rush.

"You learn quickly," Drusas said. "A slave should always acknowledge her master's commands before rushing to perform them."

Trella saw the small sign of disappointment on Zug's face. He clearly enjoyed his work and wouldn't hesitate to beat her for the slightest infraction.

Trella lowered her feet and pushed herself back up on her knees. She glanced sideways at Ninani, still kneeling there, still upright and holding her shoulders back.

Ninani understood the rules. She'd been given a command, and she was expected to obey it until told otherwise, or until she fainted from weakness.

Trella assumed the correct position, trying to stop her legs from trembling.

Drusas fumbled in a pouch that lay at his side. In a moment he brought out a small bundle, three clay tablets wrapped in a long linen cloth. "Come closer, slave, so you can see the symbols."

Trella shuffled forward, moving close enough to smell her master's wine breath. She looked down at the tablets, each covered with the symbols that marked Drusas's transactions. But she couldn't see them clearly. The light from the sun had started to fade, and the tent's interior had darkened.

"Light the lamp, Zug," Drusas said. "Put your hands on the ground, slave."

Trella leaned forward, placing her hands on the dirty blanket covering the floor of the tent, one hand almost touching Drusas's knee. Her breasts swung forward, filling the space between her arms, as she crouched there, like a dog.

The slave master set one of the tablets on the rug between her hands, and pointed with his stick. "What is this symbol?"

"A man, Master."

"And this?"

"A woman, no, two women, Master."

Drusas moved down the tablet, while Trella concentrated on identifying the symbols. These weren't as easy as those in her father's house. Drusas must have carved these in the wet clay himself, and he lacked the skill to render each symbol crisply, the way a trained clerk would. The blurry, uneven lines made identifying each one more difficult.

By then Zug had the small lamp burning, and he placed it close to the tablet. The smoke from the flame stung her eyes and she could almost taste the burning oil.

Halfway down the second tablet, Drusas's stick touched a symbol Trella didn't recognize.

"I don't know that symbol, Master."

The stick flicked against her breast, just enough to sting without leaving a mark. "A good slave should always speak humbly. You want to be a good slave, don't you?"

"Yes, Master. Yes, I want to be a good slave." She hated the words she uttered, hated the way her voice betrayed her weakness. Trella wanted to burst into tears, to snatch the stick from his hand, but she knew there was no use protesting or resisting.

"Why don't you know that symbol, slave?"

"I've never see it, Master. It has the symbol for a boy but I don't know what the other marks are, Master."

"That symbol represents a boy pleasure slave. Some masters prefer young boys, as I'm sure you know. So this symbol represents a boy trained to give pleasure to his master. Remember that symbol, slave. You may see it again."

"Yes, Master."

"Still, I must admit you know the symbols." Drusas picked up the tablets, wrapped them in their cloth, and replaced them in his pouch. He took his time, making sure the tablets were snugly covered by the linen to prevent any chipping or rubbing that might damage his records.

Trella, still on her hands and knees, risked a quick glance at Zug, and found him seated beside Ninani, who remained kneeling. She saw Zug running his hands over Ninani's buttocks.

"I'm sure I can find one or two buyers who will pay extra for someone like yourself, slave," Drusas said as he closed and fastened his pouch.

"A virgin who knows the symbols and can do sums is a rare commodity. Until then, you are my property, and you will obey, or I will have Zug teach you the penalty for disobedience. And my steward is not as gentle as I am."

"Yes, Master," Trella answered, as humbly as she could. She heard the fear in her voice, but couldn't control it. Her arms and thighs ached from kneeling over in this unnatural position, but she didn't dare move.

Drusas picked up his stick and rapped her lightly across her breast. "Since you are learning so well, you can sit quietly in the corner and watch. For a slave, there is always more to learn."

"Yes, Master," she repeated, the phrase coming more easily with each use. She crawled over to the corner and wedged herself up against the wall of the tent.

Drusas moved to his knees and removed his tunic and undergarment, then stretched out on his blanket, the length of his body facing Trella only an arm's length away.

"You, what is your name?"

"Ninani, Master. My name is Ninani."

"Come here, Ninani, and show me what you've learned about giving your master pleasure."

"Yes, Master." She moved forward on her hands and knees and reached Drusas's side. "What would my master like me to do?"

He touched his flaccid penis with the stick. "You can start by making that hard, and then I'll decide how I want you."

"Yes, Master." Ninani lowered her head, her long hair partially obscuring her face as it cascaded over her master's stomach, and gently lifted Drusas's penis. She took it carefully in her mouth, moving her head up and down.

As Trella watched, Drusas grew hard, and soon Ninani moved her head faster and faster. Keeping her own head lowered, Trella glanced at Zug, and saw his hand reaching beneath his tunic, his eyes settled on Ninani. Trella guessed he would take the girl as soon as his master finished with her.

Trella wanted to turn away, but every few moments, Drusas glanced in her direction, and she saw his eyes examining her body, even as Ninani pleasured him.

From outside the tent, she noticed other sounds that might have been going on the whole time she'd been examined by her master – women crying, men laughing, occasional loud rough voices shouting jests and cheers of encouragement. Trella remembered the two women, and knew they were being raped again and again, that they would have to satisfy all of Drusas's men for as long as they wanted, before their ordeal ended.

By now the slave dealer had grown fully aroused, his member thick and hard, and Trella heard the passion in his heavy breathing. He moaned slightly, and Ninani, her cheeks working hard as she sucked on his penis, increased her efforts.

"Enough," Drusas said. He grabbed her shoulders, and pulled her on top of him.

Ninani swung her leg over him, reached down, and guided her master's penis into her body, before settling down on his hips and giving a long sigh of contentment.

"Our newest slave is quite wet, Zug," Drusas said, relaxing as the girl moved rhythmically up and down. "She enjoys giving pleasure."

He reached up and caressed her breasts bobbing before him, squeezing them hard enough to make Ninani gasp with pain. Then he turned toward Trella, and smiled.

"Soon you will be pleasing your new master like this." He dropped his hands to Ninani's hips. "Faster, slut, as hard as you can."

Trella stared in fascination as Ninani's hips began to move faster and faster. The girl was breathing hard from her exertions, but she knew what to do, and soon Drusas began to thrash frantically against her. Then he gave a shout, and Trella knew he was spurting his seed inside her friend's body.

Ninani didn't stop. She kept moving, murmuring little sounds of encouragement, but watching her master for the first sign that he wanted to her to stop. When he lifted his hand, she ceased moving, waiting for his next command.

"Lick me clean, girl," Drusas said. "You want to make your master happy, don't you?"

Zug, still sitting there fondling himself, laughed.

Ninani lifted herself off the slaver, and took his already shrinking member inside her mouth. Trella, unable to move her eyes away, stared in fascination at Ninani's ministrations.

At last Drusas told her stop. "Enough. Now you can have her, Zug." Taking his time, he dressed himself carefully, ignoring Trella and the others.

His steward moved forward, pulling off his tunic and exposing an erection even fiercer than his master's. In a moment, he had Ninani positioned on her hands and knees, and Zug entered her from behind. He pushed her head down onto the blanket and began driving himself into her body, the slap-slap-slap of their bodies making contact filling the interior of the tent.

Trella saw the pain in Ninani's eyes and heard her whimper, but she said nothing. Trella knew that many women felt pain while they pleasured their men. Zug didn't take long. Perhaps watching his master had aroused him even more than Ninani's body. Soon Zug was crying out as the passion overcame him, and in a moment he threw back his head and grunted loudly.

As soon as he finished, he pushed Ninani away, and replaced his tunic.

"Take them out, Zug," Drusas said. "And make sure no one touches this one." He pointed with his ever present stick at Trella. "At least, for now."

The two girls crawled out of the tent, snatching up their dresses as they left. Naked, they stood and waited until Zug emerged and led them back to where the other women sat stone-faced, watching the guards take their fun with the other women.

He gave instructions to the bored guard keeping an eye on the women, who nodded unconcernedly.

Trella and Ninani pulled on their dresses and fell to the ground, the two of them holding each other. Both started crying, as much from the shock as humiliation.

When the tears finally stopped, Trella turned to her companion. "Are you all right?" She kept her voice to a whisper, not that the guard seemed to care.

"Yes, Trella. I've been taken by two men before, and at least this was over quickly." She shuddered for a moment. "But Drusas frightens me. There's something evil about him. Other men, if you please them, are grateful, even gentle, but him . . . he seemed to feel nothing."

She sighed. "I pray to the gods that he sells me to a good master, like your father was."

With a shock, Trella remembered that Ninani had probably done much the same things for her former master. She had, after all, been selected for her beauty, and her father had purchased her more as a pleasure slave than household servant. "You are braver than I, Ninani."

"No, just older, and more used to the ways of men. But I hope I don't have to pleasure the rest of the guards, like those two." She glanced at the guards, still enjoying their women.

Trella looked over toward the fire. The guards had finished taking the women, but some wanted to take them again. The women lay there, sobbing and crying out in pain, while the guards laughed at their tears.

"Best not to look, Trella," Ninani advised. "At least Drusas wants to sell you as a virgin, so you'll be spared that."

"Yes, for now. But who knows what evil may befall us."

"Only the gods know that, Trella. But I'm sure you'll survive. There's a strength about you that will make men notice you."

"That's what frightens me," Trella answered.

She and Ninani turned away from the spectacle, holding each other's hands. The coarse laughter and loud voices finally stopped, and at last the two wretched women crawled back to the rest of their companions, their bodies shaking and trembling from the ordeal. The other women tried to comfort them, but there wasn't much anyone could do.

Trella stayed close to Ninani. Both girls were exhausted, and Ninani soon fell asleep. As the fire began to die down, Trella gazed up at the stars, and thought about the coming day. This seemingly endless day had seen her parents killed, her life shattered, and she and her brother sold into slavery by the men who murdered her parents.

An monstrous day of evil, she knew, but another day likely just as bad would soon be on her. Trella decided she intended to survive. Even as a slave, she could hope for certain things. Men would rule her life, but as Ninani said, women were all slaves to their husbands and family.

Trella knew that, sooner or later, her father would have presented his daughter to her future husband, and she would be expected to obey him for the rest of her life, to pleasure him as Ninani had pleasured first her father and now Drusas.

As a wife, Trella would also be expected to cook and clean for her husband, and, if she were his only wife, manage his household. Most of all, she would be expected to bear her husband's children, for a woman had no greater duty than that.

Men would be ruling her life no matter what her circumstances. As a slave, she would have even less freedom and opportunities than as a wife, but it might still be possible to have some say over her life.

Trella put the horror of Drusas out of her mind. She considered her possible future, and what she could do to influence the men who were and would be her masters.

Drusas was right. It would be important to impress the man, whoever he might be, who would become her new owner. For the slave trader, a good impression might fetch more silver coins, possibly even a golden one.

For Trella, it might mean the difference between a life of toil and drudgery, or a chance to use her mind. Her old life had vanished, destroyed by a blood feud so brutal that perhaps even Fradmon had fallen prey to his own hatred and burning desire for revenge.

She wanted to mourn her dead parents, her vanished brother, but that could come later. Right now, Trella decided to do whatever she could to influence her fate.

If that meant pleasuring Drusas or even Zug, then she would swallow her distaste and perform any act, no matter how humiliating.

She wanted to live, to salvage something from the life her parents had given her.

Trella knew she was different from other women, even different from Ninani. Her friend had already accepted her new fate as a slave. Ninani would be obedient, and offer herself as a good servant and pleasure girl to any prospective owner, smiling boldly at each potential buyer.

But girls such as Ninani were plentiful enough, and Trella knew she couldn't follow that path. First she didn't have the beauty, and second, she lacked the skills and experience Ninani possessed.

No, Trella would have to present herself as someone different, someone who could help her new owner in any number of endeavors, and in other ways besides the bed chamber. Therefore she needed to be sold to someone who would appreciate not only her body, but also her mind. Assuming, she offered a prayer to the gods, that such a person existed.

By now silence had descended on the camp. Everyone except the men on guard duty had fallen asleep. Trella put all these thoughts from her mind, and allowed her weary body to take control. She needed to rest.

Tomorrow, she would begin her new life, and with each day, she would learn more and more about the role of a slave. For a moment, the vision of her father's body came into her thoughts. She pushed the sight from her mind, and, still holding fast to Ninani, fell into a deep and exhausted sleep.

29

Trella woke with a start. Shouts and curses echoed around the camp, as the guards kicked the slaves awake. She heard the already familiar sound of the leather whip on flesh, almost always accompanied by a gasp or cry of pain. The edge of the sun had just appeared in the east.

She pushed herself to her feet, pulling Ninani up with her. Both girls stood there for a moment, dazed and unsure.

"Get to the river, you fools," a guard shouted at them. "Or you'll have nothing to drink the rest of the day."

Taking Ninani's hand, Trella ran toward the stream, quickly passing the other women still struggling to find their wits. She threw herself down in the mud at the water's edge, and drank deeply, swallowing as much water as she could hold.

"Get out, get out of the water," another guard bellowed. "Line up over here." He pushed the women away from the water, in the direction they would march today.

Trella observed the guards as they ordered the men to drink. She saw Drusas emerge from his tent, and converse with Zug. By then the men slaves were being driven out of the water, the whips rising and falling much more frequently than needed. Trella surmised that the slavers preferred to have the men short on water. That would keep them more tractable and easier to control.

Drusas's men knew the women weren't likely to cause trouble, start fights, or try to run away. Women didn't have the strength or endurance for such resistance. Any women trying to escape would be quickly run down and dragged back to the camp, no doubt to be beaten as an example to the others.

And that, she decided, was why the guards were so savage. They wanted to make sure no one tried to get away. And if someone did try to run, to resist, or even simply disobey a command, they would punish that individual brutally as a lesson to the others.

Depending on the slave's possible value, the offender might even be whipped to death, the ultimate object lesson. After all, as Trella knew well, one slave more or less meant little to Drusas.

Thoughts of escape entered her mind. But like most women, she never learned to ride a horse, and wouldn't get far on foot. Besides, where could a fleeing woman go? She'd be at the mercy of anyone she encountered, and there were worse men roving the land than slavers.

They started the march before the sun cleared the horizon, moving south, and once again traveling at a fast walk. The male slaves led the way, strung out in a long line. They still had ropes around their necks, linking them together, and their hands remained bound. Behind them rode Drusas and his men.

The women, unfettered, followed the guards. The female slaves were allowed to walk together, and Trella stayed close to Ninani's side. Talking, however, was forbidden. A single guard on horseback rode behind the women, his whip dangling in his hand, ready to punish any infraction.

Trella concentrated on her footing. Her bare feet were already tender and sore, and she didn't want to risk injuring them further. A slave who limped would be less attractive at an auction. Still, well before mid-morning, each step brought increasing pain.

Drusas gave the order to halt, and once again Trella sank to the ground. The guard carrying the bread came over, and tossed a few stale loaves toward the women. Trella lunged past another woman to snatch one of the loaves, and had to push her away to keep possession. It took both hands to break the loaf in two, and Trella handed half to Ninani, who'd didn't have the energy even to fight for her food.

They both took bites, ripping through the hard crust for the somewhat softer interior, though even that required plenty of effort to chew.

"This will make us even more thirsty," Trella said, "but it's better than nothing."

"They don't want us to die, I suppose," Ninani said, making a face at the distasteful bread in her mouth.

The slaver trader ordered his men to resume the march, and once again the walking began. The sun grew warmer, and soon Trella felt pangs of thirst, though she'd drunk as much water as she could before their day's trek began.

To take her mind off her parched throat, she considered where they were, and where they might be going. She guessed that they'd traveled close to thirty miles from Carnax, and since they were moving south, that probably meant Drusas was heading for the shores of the Great Sea.

The village of Sumer lay in that direction, probably at least another forty miles. That made sense, she decided. Drusas had gathered a large number of slaves, and he would need a thriving village with a large slave market to sell them.

A shout from the guard riding at the head of the cavalcade made Trella look up, and she saw another caravan coming toward them. This group numbered about fifteen men and ten or so pack animals.

As the other caravan drew closer, the men moved to the side and kept their hands on their weapons, leaving plenty of room between themselves and the approaching slavers. Every honest caravan master viewed slave traders with suspicion. They might attack anyone at any time, looking for more slaves as well as a chance to steal some unwary merchant's goods.

But Drusas waved a cheery greeting as he rode past, clearly uninterested in anything but getting to his destination. Trella saw the men in the other caravan staring, their eyes drawn to the women.

Once the newcomers saw that Drusas and his men intended no evil action, the members of the other caravan began joking and making comments about the women, pointing out Ninani, Trella, and one or two of the others, while they called out obscene suggestions.

Trella had gazed at slaves in the market in much the same way, never really thinking about how the slaves themselves might feel, or even if they felt anything at all. Slaves were a part of life, like sheep or cattle, and powerful men had held other men in slavery since the beginning of time.

The strong ruled the weak, and the weak had to obey. Men of wealth desired, even needed, slaves to serve them, to work in their fields and their homes, to enable their masters to enjoy life. The natural order of life included slaves, and even those enslaved wished for nothing more than the chance or opportunity to take the place of their masters, with slaves of their own.

More than a few men and women became slaves willingly, offering themselves up for sale and hoping to be bought by a kind owner who would provide them with food and shelter. In her father's household, there was little difference between a servant and a slave.

Most masters treated their slaves reasonably well. After all, a slave was a valuable piece of property. Owners didn't starve or mistreat their slaves any more than they would their herd animals.

Slave dealers, interested only in the buying and selling, wanted docile slaves who would make good servants. An intractable or violent slave might mean a lost customer, or, if the buyer were prosperous and important enough, someone who might demand his payment returned.

As she trudged along, Trella thought about the life she had known, the life that had vanished as swiftly as the light from an empty lamp. Most people struggled to attain a simple existence, and often even that was beyond hope. Except for the few wealthy traders, craftsmen, and farm holders, everyone had to labor from dawn to dusk each day, just to stay alive.

And Trella understood better than most the dangers merchants and farmers lived with. A caravan could be lost, wiping out years of work and a large investment. A flood could ruin the land and bring starvation, making a rich farm unproductive for years. Bandits could rob and kill merchants and craftsmen, taking their goods.

Those with wealth needed protection not only from bandits, but from other prosperous traders, who might see violence as a shortcut to additional wealth of their own.

Fradmon fell into that category, she knew. He might want revenge for his son, but his real desire had always been to steal Ranaddi's gold and assume his place as the richest man in the village. Such a man, Trella thought with a shudder, might even sacrifice his own son to achieve his ends.

And, as Trella now understood all too well, the weak could be enslaved against their will. For no matter how someone became a slave, unless set free by their master, they remained a slave for the rest of their lives. Thus they were condemned to do the bidding of others, no matter how hard or distasteful, with the threat of the whip always hanging over their heads.

A slave could be beaten for any reason or offense, or even be put to death. Everything depended on the master. A good one, and a slave might have a satisfactory life. A bad master, however, could turn every moment of his slaves' lives into a torment of pain and suffering. Some slaves ran away, while others killed themselves rather than face such an existence.

Drusas didn't call a halt until midday. He and his men gathered together to eat a handful or two of bread and drink from their water skins, but the slaves got nothing, only the chance to rest. When the order to resume the march came, Trella got to her feet. As soon as she started walking, the pain returned, and she began to limp.

They hadn't gone far before Drusas called another halt.

Trella lifted her eyes, to see the slave master only a few paces away, staring down at her from his horse.

"She's limping," he said, pointing at Trella as Zug rode up beside him. "Get her some sandals."

"Yes, Master," the steward answered. He dismounted and approached the women, his eyes searching the group. "You," he said, pointing at one of the older women who'd been a servant in Ranaddi's house. "Take off your sandals and give them to her. Now." He shook the whip suggestively.

The woman wanted to protest, but Zug took a stride closer and raised the whip. She dropped to the ground and began unlacing her sandals, tears already streaking her face. The moment she had the first one off, Zug tossed it at Trella and ordered her to put it on.

Trella felt the woman's sorrow, but there was nothing either of them could do. She sat and laced the sandals onto her own feet.

A slave's clothes and sandals belonged to her master as much as her body did. Justice . . . injustice . . . the words meant nothing to a slave. The other women stood around in silence, watching dully, grateful for the chance to rest.

"Get them moving again," Drusas said, turning his horse away.

Zug snapped his whip a few times, light strokes that stung more than hurt. Trella noticed he took care to strike the women across the back, where the bruises would be less likely to show, even as he cursed at them for wasting his time.

The slaver column continued south. The unfamiliar footwear felt clumsy. Its previous owner possessed larger feet, and Trella had to step with care to avoid tripping. Even wearing sandals, Trella's already tender feet still hurt, but at least they weren't likely to get any worse.

When she turned her head, she saw the woman eying her, hatred in her eyes. Trella quickened her pace and kept her gaze on the ground.

In the middle of the afternoon, they stopped again. Another caravan approached, a much larger one. Trella saw many porters, pack animals, and even a small flock of sheep herded along by a shepherd and his dog.

She counted at least fifteen guards, so this caravan must belong to some wealthy trader, probably setting out from Sumer. She might even know the trader, or at least know his name.

Drusas rode out to meet the newcomers, while the tired slaves stretched themselves flat on the ground, thankful for another chance to rest. Before long, Drusas rode back, shouting for Zug as he approached.

"Get three slaves ready to go," he said as he swung down from the horse. "This caravan needs porters, so we can get rid of a few here. We'll sell them the weakest ones. Clean them up and give them plenty of water, then bring them over."

Drusas, Trella decided, knew his business. Even out here, a presentable looking slave would fetch a better price than a dirt-encrusted one.

Zug, already off his horse, selected the slaves. One of the guards brought a water skin, and he had them strip and wash the dirt and dust from their faces and bodies.

"Get dressed," he said. "You're being sold to that caravan. So make sure you stand up tall, and look strong and eager for work. If they send any of you back because you look lazy or tired, you'll get twenty lashes. Twenty, do you hear me?"

The men nodded, and he ordered them to move, following behind and flicking his whip suggestively. Trella saw the men straighten their shoulders and stand up straight as they approached their new owners.

"Twenty lashes." Trella shook her head at the horrible thought. "They wouldn't be able to walk after that."

"Perhaps they'll be better off with their new owners," Ninani said, as she sat beside Trella.

"Perhaps." She didn't really believe it. It was more likely that slaves acquired at random on the road would be treated harshly and given the worse duties. By the time the caravan got wherever it was going, its newest additions would be lucky to be alive.

She put the thought out of her head. "We'll be at Sumer in a few days, if that's where we're going."

"Thank the gods for that," Ninani said. "At least we won't be walking any more."

"Yes. We'll be sold at the market to some rich trader."

"Like your father," Ninani said, the words spoken without bitter-ness. "I've stood in the market before. Close your eyes and do what they say. It's not so bad, and I'm sure your new owner will treat you well."

His business concluded, Drusas resumed the march. This time they continued until dusk, when the slaves collapsed tiredly on the hard earth. This was a dry camp, with no well or stream in sight.

Desperate for water, the slaves again had to wait until the camp was established and the guards fed. Two of Drusas men rode off, carrying all the empty water skins, and it was well after dark before they returned, tossing one skin to the women, and two to the men.

Trella managed to get no more than a few mouthfuls before she was pushed away. By the time she shoved her way back, the skin had run dry. Ninani fared even worse. The older, stronger women in the group had lost all fear of their former owner's daughter and his mistress. The struggle for food and water would be ongoing and increasingly brutal, Trella decided.

Zug loomed up out of the darkness. "You, Ninani, get over to your master's tent. And you," he said, pointing to El-lak, a woman four or five seasons older than Trella, the married daughter of Carnax's tanner.

Trella breathed a silent sigh of relief that Zug had chosen El-lak instead of her to return to Drusas's tent.

"Ask for water when they finish with you," Trella whispered as Ninani rose to obey.

A guard came to distribute bread, and Trella snatched a loaf, tore it in half, and began eating, wolfing down the bread as fast as she could.

"Give me the rest," a voice said.

Trella looked up to see the woman who'd lost her sandals. "You've had yours. This is for Ninani."

"Let her get her own food."

Before Trella could answer, the woman reached and seized the bread. In a moment the two of them were struggling over it. A clawed hand reached for her face, but Trella ducked away. The other woman was older and bigger, but Trella had always possessed more strength than people expected.

In a moment, they were rolling across the ground, the rest of the women either shouting at them to stop or encouraging the other woman. Trella's outrage boiled up, and she gripped the woman's hair and practically ripped it from her head.

"Stop!"

The first blow of the whip landed on Trella's attacker. She flinched enough for Trella to push her away and regain her feet before the whip stung across her own shoulders, once, and again, until she moved away. Two more lashes fell on the other woman, powerful strokes that elicited a scream.

"Any more trouble, and you both get ten strokes."

The woman moved away, her shoulders shaking as she sobbed in her misery. No one attempted to befriend or comfort her.

In the growing darkness, Trella had to search the ground with her hand to find the bread, crushed and covered with dirt. She clutched it to her chest and sat there, alone. Her former servants or acquaintances, stayed away. They recognized that Trella and Ninani were receiving special treatment, and that added to their own frustration and anger.

The tears came again, but only for a few moments. *Stop crying, you fool. This is your life now, so make the best of it.*

With silence settling over the women, Trella heard the noise coming from Drusas's tent. A woman's voice cried out in pain. Trella hoped it wasn't Ninani, but couldn't be certain. Surely Drusas wouldn't damage such a valuable slave.

The sound of a whip striking flesh and the cries turned into screams that continued on and on. No one in the camp showed the slightest interest, as the master and Zug inflicted whatever torments they desired on their property.

Finally the master's tent grew silent. Trella saw a flash from the lamp as the flap was pushed aside. Ninani crawled out, naked, and clutching her shift. Her body shook, and she had difficulty getting to her feet.

Zug dragged El-lak by her arms out of the tent, then let her limp body drop to the ground.

"Get the women to clean her up," Zug shouted to the guard.

"You heard him," their guard said. "Bring her back here."

No one moved for a moment, and the guard raised his whip.

"Help them," Trella said, putting as much authority in her voice as she dared. She got to her feet.

"Come, all of you." She ran to Ninani. Putting her arm around her, she helped her back to their place, while the rest of the women reluctantly went to assist the other.

Getting Ninani back to their resting place, Trella shoved the bread in her hands. "Eat this. Hurry, before someone takes it away."

She approached El-lak and found her still crying. Trella examined her as best she could in the darkness, but didn't see any signs of the lash.

"What happened? What did they do to you?"

"My feet," the woman gasped. "Zug whipped my feet."

Trella reached down and ran her hand over the sole of the woman's feet. She didn't feel any blood, but the girl flinched in pain at Trella's light touch.

Recalcitrant women, especially beautiful ones, Trella knew, might be whipped on the soles of their feet, a painful form of punishment that left the rest of the slave's body unblemished.

She'd never heard of anyone in Carnax actually receiving such a beating, but knew it would be very painful. El-lak was no beauty, but obviously Drusas didn't want to damage his merchandise too much.

"Why did they beat you? Did you fail to obey?"

"They just beat me," El-lak sobbed. "I would have done anything, but they just held me down and whipped me. Then they took me."

Trella shook her head in disgust. Drusas must enjoy inflicting pain on his slaves, beating them merely to hear their pleas for mercy, their frantic offers to do anything to please him.

"It's over for now," Trella said, all she could offer in the way of comfort. "In a day or two, he'll put us up for sale, and we'll have new masters. No matter how harsh they may be, they'll be better than Drusas."

She hoped what she said would turn out to be the truth. Trella hugged the older girl for a moment. "Rest now. Tomorrow will be another long march, and you'll need your strength."

Trella moved away from the still-frightened girl, and tried to think. If Drusas took pleasure inflicting pain, that meant her own situation hung by a thread. The moment her value lessened by a few silver coins, that would be the moment she would become his victim.

For now, only his greed outweighed his unnatural lusts. She needed to be sold to another master as soon as possible.

"Thank you for saving me the bread," Ninani said, licking the last of the crumbs from her hand as she crept to Trella's side.

"Did you get anything to drink?"

"No. They just took me again, then made me watch while ..."

"They'll give us water in the morning," Trella said. "Sleep now. Dawn will be here soon enough."

They stretched out on the hard ground. Trella saw the ever-present guard sitting a few paces away, his eyes roving between the men and women, alert and watching. Drusas would be a hard task-master, and his servants knew what awaited them should any of the slaves disappear during the night. A lax guard might even end up taking the escaped slave's place.

Just before dawn broke, Trella awoke and prepared herself. She roused Ninani, to make sure her friend would be ready when they passed around the next water skin. Dawn arrived, and the familiar pattern began again. When the guards tossed a water skin on the ground, Trella made sure she was the one who retrieved it. Ninani got the first drink, greedily gulping down the precious liquid, while Trella kept the others away, then took the skin from Ninani and drank deeply before passing it on.

The day's march began, and Trella gave thanks for the sandals. Her feet still felt tender, but at least the pain of taking each step had lessened. For some reason, Drusas set a somewhat slower pace, though Trella felt certain the slaves' welfare had nothing to do with his decision.

They reached a small stream well before noon, and this time the slaves were allowed to drink their fill. Zug emptied the food bags, and for the first time, the women had enough of the stale bread to assuage the hunger that had dogged their steps for the last three days.

Drusas had another surprise for them as well. First the men, then the women were ordered into the stream, where they were told to wash themselves and their garments. Trella had no idea what prompted this gesture, but she was the first of the women into the stream.

She yanked her dress over her head, and used it to scrub her body of the dirt and filth that covered her from head to toe. Again and again she ducked under the water, always expecting to hear Zug's voice ordering them out.

But Zug and Drusas didn't appear interested, and only the guards remained to amuse themselves by watching the naked women clean themselves.

Ignoring them, Trella cleaned her ragged dress, beating it against the rocks before rinsing it again and again. When she finally pulled the soaking garment back on, she breathed a sigh of relief. At least for the moment, she felt clean. Zug returned, looked the slaves over, and ordered the march resumed.

They plodded along, still holding to an easy pace. Trella had no idea why Drusas had slowed their progress. She thought they were still a day's march, perhaps two, from Sumer. That meant, she realized, another night for someone in Drusas's tent.

She shuddered at the prospect. Even her virginity wouldn't protect her from a painful beating, and she knew there were other ways for a man to take his pleasures from a woman and still leave her maidenhead intact.

The sun had yet to reach mid-afternoon when they crested a low rise, and Trella saw a good sized river not far ahead. One look told her the broad ribbon of water must be a branch of the Tigris.

She remembered the maps she'd studied in her father's workroom. Drusas had guided their journey more to the east than south, and they'd reached the river well north of Sumer, which must be at least a day or two's journey to the south.

As they approached the flowing water, Trella saw ten or twelve mud brick huts set along the bank. A crude corral held goats and sheep, and a wooden jetty projected at least twenty paces into the swirling water. Two boats, one on either side, were fastened to the little dock.

As the slave caravan reached the outskirts of the little village, Drusas rode ahead. Zug guided the slaves to a grassy field near the corral, where the men set up their camp. Smoke rose from two campfires on the other side of the corral, and Trella saw packs and bundles, the kind that traders used to carry their goods.

"What is this place?" Ninani asked, looking about.

"I don't know," Trella answered. "I don't see any fields, and it's too small to be a village."

Then she understood. This must be a way station for travelers, a meeting place for traders, a place where they could exchange goods while avoiding the fees that would be charged in a big village like Sumer.

Even Drusas would have to pay Sumer's elders for the privilege of auctioning his slaves there. If he could sell a portion of his human merchandise here, he wouldn't have to pay so much in Sumer.

Whatever the reason might be, Drusas had timed his arrival so that he and his slaves reached the little settlement well before dusk, and with his goods in presentable condition. That meant the slave master felt he could dispose of part of his human merchandise at this place.

Trella decided this meant nothing good for her. She wanted to be purchased by a powerful merchant, one of the ruling nobles in Sumer or some other large village. Only a rich merchant or craftsman would have the slightest interest in her skills. If she were sold here, only her body would matter.

Of course Trella's hopes meant nothing to Drusas. The guards kept the men and women separate, all the while keeping a close watch over them. The slave master walked down to the river.

He wasn't gone long, however, and when he returned, he spoke to Zug. In moments, the guards rounded up ten of the strongest male slaves and began moving them down toward the center of the village.

By standing on her toes, Trella could observe the gathering place. She saw Drusas disappear into one of the larger huts. A few moments later, at least eight or ten men emerged, fanning out into a half circle, with their backs toward Trella.

The first slave climbed up on something, with Zug standing beside him. The slave removed his tunic, then lifted up his arms and turned around.

She couldn't hear the discussion that took place, but soon enough, the slave stepped down and moved to the side, obviously sold to someone. Another took his place, and the process repeated.

Drusas naturally exhibited the strongest and fittest slaves first, and so the bargaining took longer. The haggling over the weaker, less valuable individuals usually went faster.

The sun still hung well above the horizon when Drusas returned, a contented smile on his face, leading only four slaves that he'd been unable to sell.

"Get the women to the market, Zug," he ordered, before ducking into his tent.

Trella felt her heart beat faster. Without thinking, her hand sought Ninani's.

"Do what they tell you," Ninani whispered. "If you struggle or start crying, it will only be worse."

Zug ordered the women to stand up and form a line. He selected Ninani for the first position, with Trella in the second position and El-lak behind her. Trella realized they would be offered for sale in this order.

Drusas emerged from his tent and, hands on his hips, waited until Zug finished.

"Move," Zug ordered, pushing Ninani toward the market. Trella followed obediently, as Drusas, Zug, and two other guards herded the eleven women along.

When Zug gave the order to halt, Drusas went inside the largest structure, obviously an ale house from the rank odor emanating from the entrance.

"Ale for everyone!" Drusas's loud voice carried throughout the market. "Then we have some pretty slaves for sale that you'll want to inspect."

Trella glanced around. A thick block of wood wide enough to stand on occupied the center of the market. Already a small crowd had gathered, mostly guards or porters waiting for their masters.

One of the women began to cry, but no one paid any attention to her. A few of the onlookers made crude remarks, but Trella ignored them.

The wait dragged on, until at last Drusas emerged from the hut. Three men followed his steps, dressed in fine tunics and carrying swords at their waists, the merchants and traders who would do the bidding. The crowd made way for them, as they moved within a few steps of the auction block.

"Who's first, Drusas?"

Trella risked a glance at the speaker, and saw a burly man with powerful arms who still held an ale cup in his hand.

"Not that you're likely to have any worth buying." The man raised his cup and drank.

"I'm sure you'll change your mind soon enough, Rastara," Drusas said, joining in with the laugh that followed the trader's words.

Zug pushed Trella aside as he took Ninani's arm and practically lifted her onto the block.

"A beautiful young household slave, dutiful to her master, and accomplished in all the tasks of women," Drusas announced.

"Her former master kept her as his favorite pleasure slave, and she warmed each of his nights."

By then Zug had Ninani positioned on the block. "Off with it," he ordered, keeping his voice soft so as not to compete with his master.

Ninani lifted her shift over her head, struggling a moment as her hair got caught before she succeeded. She dropped the shift, shook out her hair, and smiled at the men standing beside Drusas.

The crowd reacted approvingly, admiring the lithe body.

"As you can see, my friends, a true beauty who will harden your member for many years to come."

Zug prodded Ninani, and this time Trella couldn't catch his words. But Ninani moved her legs apart, so that her feet were at the edges of the block, put her hands behind her, and took a deep breath.

This time the onlookers reacted even more favorably, and more than a few edged closer, to get a better look, until Drusas's guards pushed them back.

"Turn around, slave," Drusas ordered, and Ninani obeyed, shifting until she stood in the same stance, only facing the other direction. He stepped beside her, and placed his hand on her buttock.

"Well trained, and obedient, as you can see. Who will bid for this beautiful girl? In Sumer you'll pay double what I can offer here."

"Ten silver."

Trella took a quick look at the bidder, a rough looking man with a large forehead and a hook nose.

"Ah, a jest," Drusas replied, lifting his hands for a moment. "Such a body is worth twice that. Turn around, slave," he ordered, then turned to face the bidder. "Look at that face, and imagine her whispering words of love in your ear."

"Twelve silvers," Rastara said, lifting his cup and sipping at his ale.

"At that price, I'd rather keep her for my own delights," Drusas said, brushing the ever-present stick across Ninani's breast. "In Sumer she'll fetch at least a gold coin, perhaps two."

"We're not in Sumer," the third trader countered.

The haggling went on and on, everyone seeming to enjoy the spectacle and the bargaining. The price crept up a silver at a time, with Drusas extolling her virtues while the bidders invented any number of reasons not to buy.

At last, Rastara offered eighteen silver coins, and the others shook their heads.

"Sold to Master Trader Rastara," Drusas announced. Zug lifted her off the block, and Ninani had to snatch up her shift as he handed her to her new master.

Drusas collected his payment, and Zug turned toward Trella.

"Up on the block," he ordered. "Off with it."

Trella obeyed, pulling her shift over her head with care, not wanting to entangle her thick hair. None of these traders appeared as bad as Drusas. She shook her tresses loose, and assumed the position.

A cool breeze wafted across her chest, and she felt her nipples harden. There was nothing she could do. She put her hands behind her at Zug's prodding, and gazed out over the heads of the crowd. Her lips trembled, and she tried to control them.

"Too skinny," someone shouted.

"And too soft," another voice agreed. "She'll not be good for much work outside the bed chamber."

Everyone laughed, and Trella felt her face flushing with embarrassment.

"Ah, my friends, how little you know," Drusas said, his voice smooth and enticing.

"This beautiful young thing is still a virgin, and not only that, but she knows the symbols and can count the numbers. Those wise enough to purchase her will not want to waste her talents digging in the fields or sweating in some dirty kitchen. I want no less than twenty-five silver coins for this beauty."

"She doesn't look like a virgin."

The crowd laughed, including Drusas. "I assure you she is, honored patrons. But see for yourself, if you doubt my word."

"Everyone knows what Drusas's word is worth," Rastara commented, drawing another laugh from the crowd.

"I am a virgin," Trella said. Better to admit it than have these men spreading her legs apart.

The crowd reacted with an even louder laugh, and a few called out uncouth jests. Zug raised his whip, but Drusas shook his head.

"As you can see, this one has spirit," he said. "And she's eager to offer her gift to her new master, and to help him count his profits by day while she labors over his member by night."

Once again, the same trader opened the bidding, again offering ten silver coins. Trella wanted to close her eyes, but Zug had warned the women about that, so she blocked out the humiliating words and stares. The bidding crept up, silver by silver, until one offered sixteen silver coins.

"Come, Rastara, you're a man of worth who can surely spare a gold coin for such a useful treasure. She'll fetch more than that in Sumer's market."

"I've clerks enough to count my profits," Rastara said, "and virgins enough when I need one. I've no need to pay extra for one who can do both."

Everyone laughed at Rastara's clever words.

No one offered more, and Trella saw Drusas hesitate, a frown on his face. But his greed overcame his desire for a quick sale.

"Then I'll take her to Sumer, where bidders will be fighting over the chance to buy her." He nodded to Zug, who stepped over and practically dragged her off the block.

Trella remembered to reach down and snatch up her dress, before Zug pushed her to the back of the line. "Stay here and don't move."

She jerked the dress over her head and down over her body, breathing a sigh of relief when the garment concealed her. But she hadn't been sold, so that meant there would be another ordeal like this one, and probably more public, in Sumer.

Then Trella realized she would have to spend another night with Drusas. With Ninani gone, the slave master would no doubt turn to Trella to satisfy whatever urges the night might bring. She remembered the angry look on his face when she didn't sell, and knew she would pay for that tonight.

When the auction ended, Drusas had sold half his female slaves, and his smile had returned. He walked over to where Trella stood, jingling his now heavy purse. He stared at her for a moment.

"Zug, where is the merchant from the north? You told him there would be an auction?"

"Yes, Master, I told all of them. His tents are still here, so he hasn't departed."

"I think I'll visit him, and see if he needs any women."

"He won't want any of this lot, Master," Zug said. "All the best ones are gone."

Drusas shrugged. "Perhaps not all. I'll take this one with me." He prodded Trella with his stick. "Take the rest back to camp."

Gripping her by the arm, he led her through the market, toward a group of ten or twelve tents pitched north of the enclave. "You'd better be properly humble, or tonight will be a long one for you. Stay at my side, and do what you're told."

A guard watched Drusas approach, but didn't challenge him. Three tents rested on a slightly higher patch of grass, each about six paces apart. As Trella and the slave trader reached the largest tent, she heard the sound of retching.

Drusas halted, just as a young man rose up from behind the tent. A clump of dirt clung to his knee, but he made no attempt to brush it off. He wiped his mouth with the back of his hand when he saw the visitors. His plain face, half-concealed under long dark hair showed traces of the pain contorting his stomach.

"Honored Drusas," he said, inclining his head. He had to swallow twice before he could continue. "How many I assist you?"

"I want to see Nicar the merchant. You are . . .?"

"Lesu, his oldest son and steward. But my father is too ill to see anyone."

Trella caught a glimpse of a frown that formed on Drusas's face.

"Ah, I'm sorry to hear that. Give him my regrets. I wanted to see if he were interested in purchasing this girl."

"We need no women slaves," Lesu said. "We leave tomorrow to return home and . . ."

Trella saw Lesu clutch at his stomach and swallow hard, before he turned and ran back behind the tent, where he dropped to his knees and vomited once again. She heard the same sound from within the tent, and knew Lesu's father was doing the same.

"Master, perhaps I can tend to the merchant and his son," Trella said. She did not want to return to Drusas's tent with him, not while his anger remained. "I know many of the healing herbs."

"There are no healers or herbs out here," Drusas snapped. "Keep silent or I'll . . ."

The tent flap opened, and an older man ducked through the opening.

"I'm Nicar." He pushed himself upright, one hand pressed against his stomach, and stared at Trella. "You know something about herbs to heal the stomach?"

She started to speak, but Drusas tightened his grip on her arm. "She is not a healer, Honorable Nicar."

"I don't care if she's a dark witch from the bottom of the pits, if she can stop the pain." He leaned forward, peering at her face. "Can you, girl?"

She turned to Drusas, awaiting permission to speak.

He let go of her arm. "Answer him, slave."

"Perhaps, Master. You and your son are both sick?"

"Yes, only the two of us. We ate at the filth-infested hovel they call a tavern last night. We've been sick ever since."

Trella stepped forward, her eyes studying the merchant. Older than her own father, he carried some extra weight around his middle. His once black hair had turned mostly gray, and hung limply over his pale face. She ignored his breath, fouled from the vomiting.

"Your head hurts? And your stomach?"

"My head feels like it's going to burst, and my stomach heaves and heaves, though little remains to come up."

She turned to Lesu, who now stood beside his father. "And you have the same pain?" He nodded.

Food poisoning, she reasoned. Only the trader and his son had eaten at the inn. The rest of the merchant's guards and porters looked healthy. By tomorrow, the worst of the symptoms would be gone, so she had to act fast.

"I can help with your pain," she said. "I'll need barley water and charcoal, to start."

"We've no barley with us," Lesu said.

"I saw sacks of grain in the market," Trella said. "Surely there will be some barley there. And the innkeeper should have some charcoal."

Lesu called out for his caravan master. A broad-shoulder man of about thirty seasons walked over to his master's tent.

"Get down to the market," Lesu said, "and buy a small sack of barley, and a handful of charcoal. Hurry."

The man nodded, and trotted off, taking long strides toward the center of the village.

"We'll need to heat water," Trella said. "I should stay and tend them through the night, Master, if you permit."

Drusas looked dubious at this new turn of events. "I came to offer her for sale, Nicar, not lend ..."

"I'll pay you one, no, two copper coins for the night," Nicar said, "and double that if she can cure the pain. You can have her back again tomorrow."

The slave dealer hesitated for the briefest moment. "Of course she can stay to tend to your needs, Nicar. But she's worth a gold coin, and I need her back untouched. She's still a virgin. You'll be responsible for her."

"I just want to live through the night, Drusas. You can have her back in the morning untouched, I promise it." He turned to his son. "Give Drusas the two coins."

"No need for payment now, not among friends," Drusas said, putting a smile on his face. "Pay me in the morning, when you're feeling better."

He faced Trella, and took her shoulders in his hands, tightening them until she felt ready to cry out.

"You do what you're told, slave," his voice just above a whisper. "Say nothing about yourself, and don't even think about running away. Understand?" Drusas stared into her eyes, to make sure she grasped his meaning.

She nodded, unable to control her fear of the man. If she ran off, he would hunt her down, no matter how long it took, if only for the pleasure of punishing her.

"Then I'll see you in the morning, Nicar," Drusas said, releasing Trella's arms. "May your sickness be gone by then." He strode off, heading back toward his camp.

Watching the slave master depart, Trella felt a wave of relief. Until tomorrow, she would be free from his evil.

Then she put aside all thoughts of Drusas. The day was not over yet, and there might still be much that could be done.

30

Trella was not the only one who watched Drusas depart with an expression of relief. The merchant Nicar, in spite of his illness, appeared pleased to be rid of the man. Trella turned to face the merchant and his son.

"What can I do for you, Master?"

With Drusas gone, Nicar sank to the ground, his legs too weak to keep him upright. "What's your name, girl?" Lesu sat down beside his father.

"Trella, Master." She knelt beside him and put her hand to his forehead. His head felt hot, but not feverish. "Lie here, Master, and rest. I'll see to the fire."

She went to the guard, still pacing about the camp. "Your master needs a fire built right away. Can you gather a good supply of wood and get the fire started?"

Trella found a water skin hanging from Nicar's tent pole. "I need fresh water, Master. May I go to the river to fetch it?"

Nicar nodded without a glance. The river was only a hundred paces away, and she stepped carefully down the river bank, avoiding the rocks and bushes lining the great waterway.

Moving as far out into the stream as she dared without being swept away, Trella emptied the water skin, then rinsed it twice, before filling it to capacity. Only then did she cup a few handfuls of

water into her mouth. She had to use both hands to carry the bulging
skin back to the camp.

One of the porters had started a fire by the time she returned,
and she found a small and dirty copper pot beside it. Frowning, she
took that back to the river and scrubbed it clean. When she returned,
she filled the pot with water, and propped it on some stones so that
the flames licked at the underside.

Nicar's caravan master returned from the inn, a small sack in
each hand. One contained barley, and she emptied three handfuls
of the coarse grain into the pot, stirring the mix rapidly for a few
moments. As the water heated, it would release the healing properties within the barley.

At home, she would have added mint leaves to the mix, to
increase the efficacy. Trella took a few lumps of charcoal from the
other sack, placed them on a rock, and began crushing each one with
a small stone. She worked steadily, mashing every lump again and
again, until she had a good amount of the finely ground black dust.

The helpful guard brought out two cups, as dirty as the copper
pot had been.

"Please," she asked, "would you rinse the cups in the river for
me? They must be as clean as possible."

His eyes widened at her strange request, but he took the cups and
ambled down to the river, while she continued her grinding, adding
more charcoal to the pile before her. Her fingers and hands grew as
black as the dust, but she continued until she felt satisfied she had
enough.

By the time the guard returned, the heated barley water had
warmed enough to give off a pleasant aroma.

Trella remembered her mother's teachings. Their village had no
healer, but she had cared for sick family members and even attended
Ranaddi when he became ill. Trella had stood beside her mother
many times, watching her mix the herbs and potions used to treat
headaches, diarrhea, fevers, cramps, and food poisoning.

She dipped a cup into the barley water and took a small taste.
Hot, but drinkable, she decided. She carried it over to where Nicar

sat, too engrossed in his misery to pay any attention to what she was doing.

"Please drink this, Master. Slowly, a little at a time." When she saw he could hold the cup without spilling any, she filled a second one for Lesu, and gave him the same instructions. As they drank, she added more water and fresh barley to the pot.

Father and son sipped their potions, Lesu emitted a sigh of contentment when the warm and soothing liquid remained in his stomach. Nicar gagged twice, but managed to finish the cup without emptying his belly.

She knelt between them, watching each one closely. When it appeared they would hold down the barley water, she refilled their cups and asked them to consume it as well, and just as slowly.

When they finished, she took Nicar's cup, wiped it dry on her tunic, and filled it with a handful of charcoal. "You will need to swallow this, Master," she said. "A pinch at a time. It will not taste good."

"I know," he muttered. Nicar took a pinch from the cup and put it on his tongue. He had to force himself to swallow the foul tasting embers, but he did it.

"Good, Master. A little at a time. Wash it down with the barley water. I'll heat more for you both."

The charcoal in their bellies would absorb whatever foul food remained, and the barley water would soothe their stomachs. They finished their potions, and both sank onto the ground, both falling asleep in moments. Trella remained between them, watching for any sign of another attack.

She had arrived at just the right time. By nightfall, they might have started to get better on their own. Any earlier, and they might not have been sick enough to need her help. Now Drusas would earn a few extra coppers for her services, which should assuage some of his anger over not selling her.

Wrapping her arms around her knees, she glanced at the river. It was growing dark, and Nicar's guards were watching their master and his goods, not her.

She could walk down to the river and disappear in the darkness. If she ran all night, she might find a place to hide during the day, someplace where Drusas couldn't find her. The idea tempted her, but even if she escaped, where would she go?

If she somehow returned to Carnax, she would find no welcome there. All of her family was dead. Because of her father and Ranaddi, the village had been pillaged.

By now one of the other traders would have proclaimed himself the Village Elder, and would look upon Trella as an unpleasant reminder of the past. Someone would take her in out of pity, so she wouldn't starve, but she would be forced to marry someone right away, or become a concubine in some household.

That assumed she could reach Carnax, a journey that could take her five or six days. She might be raped and murdered along the way, or captured and forced into slavery again. And if Drusas found her . . .

No, safer to stay and pray for a better master. Even if the slave master took her maidenhead tomorrow, within a day or two she could hope for a bigger auction in Sumer, and that she would be sold there. Whatever foul practice Drusas planned for her, he wasn't likely to do anything that would lessen her price.

She thought about Nicar. His guards and porters seemed content enough, and Lesu his son appeared to be honest as well. But Nicar needed no female slaves, so there was little hope with them.

Regardless, she decided to make every effort. Her mother would have let the two men sleep as long as they could, but Trella woke both of them before it grew dark. She made them drink more barley water, and eat a bit more charcoal before letting them return to sleep.

The guards kept the fire going, and she kept heating the barley. Near midnight, she woke them again, insisting that they needed to drink as much of the soothing liquid as they could hold.

Trella slept between father and son, keeping a blanket over all of them, and using her own body heat to keep away the night's chill.

In the morning, she woke to find herself alone and under the blanket. Her hair was a tangle of knots, and her face felt as dirty as the ground she'd slept on. She didn't see Nicar or his son, so she went down to the river to relieve herself and wash her face and hands.

When she returned to the camp, still struggling with her hair, Nicar sat before his tent. Despite facing the sun, his face remained pale and haggard. He lifted his eyes as she approached, and smiled.

"I've forgotten your name, girl."

"It's Trella, Master. Are you feeling better? I can make more barley water."

"My stomach feels as if I've been kicked by a horse. I woke up with a thirst, so I went to the river and drank. Nothing has come up, so perhaps I'm over the worst of it."

"Good, Master. But I would suggest you not travel until the afternoon. Your body will be weak, and you should rest until at least midday."

"Where did you learn so much about healing?"

"From my mother, Master. I watched her as I grew up."

"I'm grateful to her."

"You need to try and eat, Master," Trella said.

He pointed toward the village, and she saw Lesu returning, carrying two loaves of bread, one under each arm.

"I'll heat some water for you both," she said. "That will help keep your stomach calm."

When the water was ready, she carried the cups to father and son.

"Eat with us, girl," Nicar said. "The bread, at least, is fresh. I'll eat nothing else from that filthy inn as long as I live."

Trella dropped to her knees and took the bread Lesu handed her, ripping apart a thick slice that she wolfed down. She'd eaten nothing last night. The bread disappeared, and Lesu handed her another hunk.

"Greetings, Nicar. You seem much better this morning."

Drusas's grating voice made Trella's hand shake, and she saw Nicar catch the movement.

"Greetings, Drusas. Your servant's potions helped us get through the night. I'm in your debt, and I believe I owe you four copper coins."

He glanced at his son, who untied the purse at his waist. "I return your property intact."

Drusas smiled heartily, though it didn't stop him from collecting the coins from Lesu. "Come, Trella, we must get back to camp."

"Can you not leave her here until midday?" Nicar's voice still sounded weak. "We won't be traveling until then, and I might need her services."

"Ah, unfortunately, I must leave for Sumer as soon as possible. The sooner my slaves are sold, the sooner I recoup my investment. Especially this one. She's going to fetch a good price in Sumer, where traders and craftsmen will appreciate her skills. Did I tell you she knows the symbols, and can count?"

He glanced at Trella, and the simpering smile reserved for Nicar disappeared. "Come, we must be going."

"Mmm, no, you didn't. Does she really know the symbols?"

"Nearly as well as I do, Nicar. Test her yourself."

Shifting a hunk of bread to his left hand, Nicar picked up a twig and scratched a symbol in the dirt. "What's this, Trella?"

She moved beside Nicar, so she could see the symbol as he drew it. "A bullock, Master."

Nicar cocked his eye at her in surprise. He brushed the symbol away with his hand, thought for a moment, and drew another. "And this one?"

"I see the symbols for logs, two logs, but the symbol is much bigger than I've ever seen it drawn, Master. Would the symbol represent one of the great trees grown in the northern lands?"

Nicar nodded his head in approval. "The great oak trees from the northern forests. Not many make their way this far south. You did well to recognize it." He smiled at her. "And you can count your numbers as well?"

"Yes, Master."

"And without using her fingers or counting stones," Drusas interjected, as if pointing out a particularly strong muscle of a beast of burden. "Set her a problem."

Once again, Trella demonstrated her skill at counting. Like Drusas, Nicar's problems quickly grew more and more complicated.

In her father's workroom, she would have used counting stones to help with the calculations. The last few she had to struggle to complete correctly.

"So you can see that she knows how to count." Drusas's voice sounded as proud as if he had taught her himself.

"And what price are you asking for this slave?"

"One gold coin, and ten silver ones," Drusas answered.

Trella bit down on her lip. A good gold coin might be exchanged for twenty silver ones, again depending on their quality.

A fully trained pleasure girl might fetch that price. A man could buy a fine horse for less than that. She knew Drusas would have sold her yesterday for eighteen silver coins, if anyone had offered the price.

"I doubt you'll get any takers at that price, even in Sumer," Nicar said, shaking his head.

"Not many merchants would want a woman knowing too much about their business. They talk too much." He picked up his bread and began chewing.

"In Sumer, the buyers appreciate quality slaves. Did I mention that she's a virgin as well? So she'll be able to please both day and night for many years to come."

"What good is her virginity after the first night? Besides, she's rather plain for a bed companion. Much too thin for my taste."

"I agree she needs a little fattening up. A woman should have a little meat on her bones, to cushion her rider. But she'll plump out very nicely once she's in a prosperous household. Her hips are good enough, and she'll have no trouble dropping her babes."

"I already have two pleasure slaves at home," Nicar mused, rubbing his chin.

"And another one promised to you, Father," Lesu reminded him. "Don't forget your brother's gift."

Drusas frowned at the interruption. "Show Nicar your hips, slave. Take off your shift."

Trella had been following the conversation, watching as Nicar skillfully initiated the bargaining process. She caught the signal he'd given his son, though Drusas hadn't noticed. Now she decided to take a chance. She shifted her weight to her knees, and lifted her dress up past her waist, but her hands fumbled with the cloth, letting it drop down again.

"I said take it off, slave," Drusas snapped, his voice cutting through the morning. Every eye in Nicar's camp turned toward the little group.

"I'm sorry, Master," Trella said. She pulled the dress up over her head, struggled with it to untangle her hair, but at last got the garment off. She stood up, moved her legs apart, and clasped her hands behind her back.

"A clumsy girl," Nicar commented, running his eyes over Trella's body. "Nothing worse than a clumsy virgin, eh, Lesu?"

"Nothing, Father. She is very thin and plain."

"Small breasted, too. And I prefer girls with brown hair. No, I think not, not at that price. But I'm sure you'll get at least fifteen silver coins for her at Sumer's market."

Trella recognized the bargaining technique. The potential buyer disparaged every virtue, while the seller extolled every flaw. She knew her breasts were not small. She exhaled a breath and eased her shoulders forward a trifle, attempting to make her bosom appear smaller.

"I turned down sixteen for her yesterday, right here," Drusas said, his temper rising.

"Well, I don't know much about buying slaves, but I think you should have taken that price, for this one, at least."

"You could give her to your cousin, father," Lesu said. "He likes thin girls with small breasts. Though I'm not sure he'd want one who knows the symbols."

Nicar's son, Trella saw, continued to do his part by distracting the seller and finding more flaws in the merchandise.

"Not ones with their bones practically poking through their skin," Nicar said. "Still, my cousin is a fool, so he might enjoy her. I'll give you fifteen silver coins."

Drusas, his lips tight, shook his head. "I'll take her to Sumer. I'll fatten her up myself, if I have to. She's worth at least one gold coin and five silvers."

Trella's heart jumped when Drusas mentioned the lower price, a serious drop from his initial price.

She realized Drusas wasn't used to negotiating this way. He auctioned off his slaves, letting his buyers determine the final value of his goods. Drusas didn't need to bargain. A low price on one slave would usually be compensated by a higher price on another.

She glanced at Lesu, still munching at his bread, and realized how skillfully he supported his father negotiations.

"I might give you sixteen," Nicar said. "After all, I'd have to lug the girl all the way up north. No doubt you've been starving her, and she'll probably eat half my provisions."

"One gold and two silvers, Nicar. That's the lowest I'll go."

Nicar shook his head. "She's no pleasure girl, anyone can see that. I can buy as good or better at home. Sixteen is my final offer."

"I won't sell her at that price."

"Then you'll have to hope for better in Sumer," Nicar said. "Are there many buyers there for clumsy girls who know the symbols?"

"I'm sure many will look on her with favor," Drusas declared.

"Perhaps," Nicar said, brushing his mouth with the back of his hand.

"A young girl who knows the symbols will draw much attention. After you display her, I'm sure everyone in Sumer will be gossiping about her."

"I was wondering about that," Lesu said. "Where did you find her? What foolish village would teach its girls how to count?"

Trella saw Drusas's eyes narrow at the idea of such impertinent questions. People would talk, and once she were sold, her new owner might not care if his slave talked about her past. If anyone in Sumer knew her father or about the attack in Carnax, someone might ask other unpleasant questions.

Drusas no doubt had encountered such problems before and knew how to discredit them. Still, it would be an inconvenience to the slave master, perhaps requiring Drusas to extend a bribe to those asking questions. And if Drusas didn't mention Trella's skill with the symbols, her price would be much lower.

"Father, it might be nice to have a woman to pleasure us on the way home."

"My son's prick is thinking for him again, I see." Nicar frowned at Lesu, sighed, then nodded knowingly to Drusas. "Our young are not as strong as we were when we grew up. They're lazy, drink too much ale, and fill their days thinking of women. They want only to spend their father's silver, not earn their own. Married less than three months, and already he's grown tired of his wife and wants to spray his seed in every woman he can."

Drusas had never bothered to take a wife, and with so many women available, wondered why fools like Nicar and his son ever did.

"Still, your son is right. The slave could service you both on your journey," Drusas said, smelling the hint of a sale.

"I can pay nine silvers, Father. If you match that, we can both enjoy her charms on the way home."

"And I'd have to share her with you?" Nicar laughed. "I know how much profit I'd get out of that arrangement."

"Father! Of course you could have her first, and whenever you chose."

"Oh, I suppose so," Nicar said, a hint of annoyance in his voice. "Eighteen silver coins, then, and for a clumsy virgin. I hope my friends back home never learn of my stupidity."

He sighed. "Consider it a gift from my son's prick."

"No, I have to have at least one gold coin for her." Drusas shook his head. "Put your dress on, slave. We're going back to my camp. Hurry."

"Well, then, good day to you, Drusas," Nicar said affably. "May your business prosper in Sumer. We just came from there, and we saw many slaves in the marketplace. Some trader brought twenty girls in by boat from the western lands."

Drusas frowned at the news, no doubt wondering if it were true.

Trella snatched up her dress and tugged it over her head while her heart sank. Nicar wasn't going to buy her, and the slave master would take his anger out on her.

Drusas grabbed her arm and jerked her to his side. "Good day to you, Nicar." The words held the barest hint of politeness.

Trella stumbled and nearly fell, so hard had Drusas gripped her.

"Are you sure you can't leave her with us until midday?" Nicar's voice stopped the slave dealer's departure.

"You're not going to be able to sell any of your slaves in Sumer for at least ten or twelve days."

"Father, I'm still feeling ill. Can you not offer Drusas a few coppers more for the slave?"

"Mmm, perhaps." Nicar rubbed his own stomach. "Think on this, Drusas. You've already earned four coppers for her services. I'll add six more to the offer. Eighteen silver and ten copper coins."

"No, nothing less than a gold coin."

"Listen to yourself," Nicar said. "You'll have to take her to Sumer, fatten her up, and hope to sell her in a month or so. And you'll pay the Elder's fee for the privilege. All for a few extra coppers. You'll likely end up getting less than what I and my foolish son are offering you."

The slave dealer, a moment ago ready to depart, hesitated, considering the merchant's words. He frowned at Trella, as if she had caused him all this difficulty.

"Perhaps you're right. I'll take nineteen silver coins for her."

Nicar shook his head. "Not from me. I'm not that big a fool. Good fortune to you in Sumer."

He bent over and entered the tent, while Lesu got to his feet and headed to the river.

Drusas stood there, his lips trembling in anger. "Wait! I'll take your offer. Eighteen and six."

After a long moment, Nicar's head reappeared from within the tent. "Oh, I suppose so."

This time his voice sounded weary. "I'm still too weak to bargain with someone as skillful as you, Drusas." He sighed. "Lesu! Come back here. Pay Drusas his coins."

Drusas's hand slipped from Trella's arm, the first acknowledgement that she was no longer his property. She'd been sold! She stood there, almost in a daze, as Lesu returned, opened his pouch, and carefully counted out the coins into Drusas's outstretched hand.

The slaver examined each coin with care, making sure of its worth. Then without a word or a backward glance, the slave dealer stalked off toward his camp, no doubt intending to take his rage out on one of his remaining slaves.

For the first time in many days, Trella felt safe, away from Drusas's horrible presence. She sank to her knees, overcome for a moment. She wanted to cry, but fought against the tears, until the weakness passed.

"Drusas is not much of a man," Nicar said, settling to the ground and smiling as he watched the slaver depart. "But I wanted to thank you for your help last night, and buying you away from him seemed like the best way."

She wanted to tell him what had befallen her, the story of her father, and Carnax and Fradmon and Sondar, but she bit back the words.

Her past meant nothing anymore, and she couldn't burden Nicar with it. There was nothing he could do to change what had happened. He'd bought a slave girl for a more than fair price, and he would expect her to be a dutiful one.

"May the gods reward you for buying me from Drusas, Master. I will serve you well," she said. "Whatever you wish."

No doubt tonight Nicar, or possibly even Lesu, would summon her to their tent. She would be expected to pleasure them. But somehow that no longer seemed something to dread. Nicar possessed many of the same qualities as her father, and she guessed he would treat her well.

"I'll not need you as a bed partner until we arrive home. Nor will Lesu, I'm sure, since he spends all his days and nights thinking about his wife. I heard her threaten to cut his balls off if he takes another woman."

Lesu laughed. "Don't believe everything my father says, Trella. My wife is a very dutiful woman."

Nicar patted Trella on the shoulder. "For now, all I want is some more barley water before we start out. It's a long journey home, and the sooner I leave this land behind, the better I'll feel."

"Where is your home, Master?" Wherever it was, it would soon be her home, too.

"It's far to the north. A village on the Tigris called Orak."

The End

Acknowledgement

My special thanks to Linda Roberts. Her help with editing, proof-reading, cover design, and marketing made this book come together. She took charge of all the many details and polished the final result to ensure a high quality product.

Also thanks to photographer Gordon Vanus, who helped with the map and design challenges. Please visit Gordon's website to view his fine art photography at www.gordonvanusphotography.com.

Honorable mention goes to Norton the Cat, the latest arrival in our happy family, whose constant presence on my lap, keyboard, and desk kept the work moving, although not always in the right direction.

This book overcame many obstacles to see the light of day. Many advised that a collection of long and short stories would not be well received. Thankfully, my early readers encouraged me to publish this collection.

These are the stories that I (and Eskkar) wanted to see in print. As always, I welcome any and all comments, either by email or my website guestbook, at www.sambarone.com.

If you'd like a personalized copy of any of my books, including *Eskkar & Trella – The Beginning*, please contact me through my website for details.

About the Author

Born and raised in Queens, New York, Sam Barone graduated from Manhattan College with a BS degree. After a hitch in the Marine Corps, he entered the world of technology.

In 1999, after thirty years developing software in management, he retired from Western Union International, as VP of International Systems. He moved to Scottsdale, Arizona, to take up his second career as a writer.

Seven years later, the author's first Eskkar story, *Dawn of Empire* was published in the USA and UK. It has since been released worldwide.

History and reading have always been two of Sam's favorite interests, and he considers himself more of a storyteller than a writer. "I write stories that I would enjoy reading, and it's a true blessing that others have found these tales interesting, informative, and entertaining."

Sam and his wife, Linda, along with their two cats (Minga and Norton) have recently moved and enjoy a quieter life in Prescott, Arizona.

His books have been published in nine languages, and he receives correspondence from all over the world. Sam enjoys hearing from his readers, and invites them to visit www.sambarone.com.

Battle For Empire

Eskkar & Trella's saga continues in *Battle for Empire*, the fifth story in the Eskkar Saga. Once again, Eskkar takes up his sword in a desperate struggle to save not only his city, but the Land Between the Rivers. And this time he had to deal with his rebellious son, Sargon, who threatens to destroy everything his parents have worked so hard to create.

Here's a preview of the story.

3113 BC, the Palace in the city of Akkad, in the Land Between the Rivers . . .

"Tell me a story, Grandmother."

The childish words caught Trella by surprise. She rose from her seat at the window to find Escander standing a few steps behind her. The words and intonation might be those of a little boy, but the youth facing her had already entered his manhood.

"And who let you into my rooms unannounced?" She frowned at him and shook her head, annoyed only at herself for not hearing his approach.

"You did, Grandmother, else your guards would have stopped me." His voice now held all the confidence of a young man. "So you must still want to see your favorite grandson."

"I'll speak to the guards about their carelessness later. No doubt they've been sleeping at their post again."

Escander smiled at her jest.

The hard-eyed and well-trained bodyguards from the Hawk Clan remained ever alert outside Lady Trella's quarters. They had a very short list of those allowed entry to her chambers unannounced. King Sargon, her eldest son, as well as her two other children, Zakita and Melkorak.

Escander's name came next. After that, except for a handful of trusted servants and close companions who had served Trella through the years, everyone else, including her other grandchildren, had to seek an audience or wait for approval to enter Trella's wing of the Palace. Even now, the King's Mother had many enemies, and not all of them dwelt outside the Palace.

Her frown faded. Trella held out her arms and let Escander embrace her, her forehead resting easily on his shoulder. His body felt warm and reassuring, strong and full of life against her.

Trella remembered how often she'd held the boy as a child. He needed her touch then, more even than her own children. *Tell me a story, Grandmother.* Escander was always pleading and cajoling her while growing up, using the same words and plaintive voice she'd found difficult to refuse.

Escander occupied a special place in her affections. Sargon had carried his son Escander to Trella when he was little more than two years old, the boy sobbing, his face buried in his father's shoulder. The poor child had just learned of his mother's death, and Sargon, his own grief scarcely under control, handed the frightened and bewildered boy to Trella.

"Please care for him, Mother." Sargon touched the boy's cheek and brushed away a tear. "He means so much . . . there's no one else I trust with him." Sargon, too, had tears in his eyes. He'd loved only two women in his life, and both had died in childbirth.

From that day, Trella raised Escander as her own child, though she never let the boy forget the memory of his real mother, a good woman who cared deeply for both Sargon and their son.

Trella brought her thoughts back to the present. She separated herself from her grandson's embrace. "And what brings you to me now? It's after midday. I know you returned to the Palace last night. Were you too busy to visit your grandmother?"

Almost a month ago, Escander had ridden north, traveling with his uncle Melkorak to inspect the border villages and their garrisons. They had returned to Akkad yesterday.

"The night was late when we arrived, Grandmother, and I didn't want to disturb you. I planned to come this morning, but Father summoned me. We spoke for some time. He said . . ."

Escander met her eyes. "He's sending me to the steppes, to visit our allies and learn from them. But before I leave, he wanted me to speak with you . . . to ask for your help."

Trella studied her grandson carefully. Just entering into his six-teenth season, Escander appeared taller than she remembered, more man than the boy who'd ridden out with his uncle almost a month ago. Escander's shoulders had grown broader, his arms thick with muscle, much like his grandfather, Eskkar.

The young man's light brown hair would have swirled around his gray eyes but an unadorned strip of black leather kept his long hair away from his face and off his neck. A broad forehead gave his face a rugged look. His keen wits and quick tongue nearly matched her own.

It was his mouth that intrigued Trella the most. Escander had the same mouth and jutting chin as his grandfather, Eskkar. And when Escander smiled, Trella saw the stamp of her husband's face on the boy, Eskkar's blood flowing through their grandson's veins.

The youth had indeed grown into a man, Trella reminded herself. Already he knew the ways of power, and the many secrets of Akkad's rulers. Now the time had come for Escander to prove not only his manhood, but his readiness to take the crown of Akkad someday.

And for that, he needed to travel to the steppes, to learn the grim ways of warfare, where lessons came only through battle and at the risk of his life. Sargon's firstborn son had died there. Now Escander would follow the same path, and possibly meet the same tragic end.

"Do you approve of what you see, Grandmother?" He smiled.

Again Trella saw Eskkar's features reflected through her grandson's face. This time a pang of loneliness swept through her. "Don't question your elders."

She'd been gazing at him for some time. "You come to see me with no warning, asking silly questions."

"My father said there were many things I should know before I leave." Escander met her eyes, his expression serious.

"And what could an old woman tell you that the King could not?"

"You're not so old, Grandmother." Escander reached out and touched her cheek. "You've scarcely changed since I was a child."

"Which, as I recall," Trella said, unable to conceal a smile, "wasn't that many years ago."

She pushed his hand away. In one more year, she would reach her sixtieth season, and her hair had long since turned to gray. Nevertheless, she thanked the gods that her wits remained sharp, even if her body had thickened somewhat with age and the burden of birthing three children.

At least she still stood upright, and retained some of the grace that had marked her girlhood. And men yet looked at her with favor, and while she might smile back, she had never taken a lover.

"I don't think your father sent you here to talk about your childhood."

Trella linked her arm within Escander's and guided him to the wide table that butted against the window overlooking the garden below, one of two within her private chamber. Four chairs, each with a thick russet cushion, added a touch of luxury to the otherwise sparse furnishings. "Now, tell me exactly what he said."

"That you should tell me about my grandfather, that it would help me in the north." Escander settled into the chair beside her. "And about Father's own journey there. All about it. The good and the bad."

"Oh, Sargon said that, did he?" Trella leaned back in her chair. "Is my son now afraid to speak to his son? Perhaps I should talk with him, not you."

Escander reached across the table and took her hand. "Be serious, Grandmother. Everyone knows there are secrets only you know and understand, about the dangers in the steppes, and what happened to my half-brother there. Father knows, but he can't . . . won't talk about it."

"It's too painful for him." Trella squeezed Escander's hand for a moment.

Her thoughts went back to those days of danger, of pain, and of sorrow. And of happiness. Those feelings, too, had faded away, replaced with a sense of serenity as she drew closer to her end of days.

She lifted her gaze, looking over the boy's shoulder and beyond the window, at the green and brown hilltop little more than a quarter mile away. Lately Trella spent more and more of her time staring at the sight. Her husband Eskkar was buried there, near the crest of the hill. The unmarked grave dove deep into the earth.

Obeying Eskkar's final wishes, Trella had washed and dressed the King's body in his warrior's garb by herself. Then she placed the great sword on his breast and folded his hands around it. No gold or jewelry adorned the body, only his favorite cloak with the Hawk Clan emblem draped over the burial shroud.

For many years, two elderly women lived nearby, watching the site for Trella, lest any foolish grave robbers seek to loot the grave. But by now no one showed any interest in the spot, its location almost forgotten.

"Tell me a story, Grandmother." Escander still held her hand.

He'd followed her gaze, and knew where her thoughts had taken her. Once again she heard the child speaking, but the earnest eyes that met her own looked anything but childlike.

"You've heard all the stories, Escander. There's nothing more to tell."

"I've heard all the tales of the mighty Eskkar and his brave son Sargon, who fought together to save the city. Now it's time for me to learn the truth, so that I will know what dangers to expect. The secrets only you and Father know."

"The truth," Trella mused, "after all these years, the truth is hard to remember . . . even harder to tell."

"No one speaks of the time when my father went to the north. Is the truth so difficult to reveal? Is that why he asks you to do it?"

"The good and the bad, that's what he asked?"

"The good and the bad," the young man repeated, his voice serious. "Tell me the truth, not a story, Grandmother."

"It would take hours, even days, to tell you everything." Trella leaned back in her chair. "When are you leaving?"

"My father the King agrees that it might take some time for you to instruct me. He said the Hawk Clan could enjoy a few more days guzzling wine and chasing women before my journey begins."

"My son becomes even more presumptuous as he grows older."

"Everyone knows, Grandmother, that you're the only one he listens to. At least, since my mother died."

"If only that were true." Trella's eyes softened the words. Sargon did still come to her for advice and counsel, and when he didn't seek her out, she had other ways of getting her ideas and thoughts into his mind.

Power, she reminded herself, comes in many ways, and Trella still retained much of the authority that had once been hers alone. "Everything? He said to tell you everything?"

"Yes, everything." The boy settled back in his chair and made himself comfortable, now that he saw her acquiesce.

She gazed into his grey eyes, and realized that the boy she'd raised from a child had truly gone, replaced by the calm young man with the aura of strength before her. Eskkar, she remembered, had much the same aura, a powerful presence that men deferred to almost without thinking. "You know what your journey to the steppes means, Escander? What it really means?"

"It means that I will be king someday, if I pass the test, and if one of my brothers or sisters doesn't have me killed first. Or I'm being sent to my death, like my brother before me."

Trella nodded in understanding. After Sargon's first wife died, he'd taken to his bed chamber a long string of willing women, who produced a multitude of sons and daughters. Trella had tried to restrain Sargon's passion, warning him about what might happen in the future, but in this, her son had refused her advice.

Now every one of those sons and daughters, encouraged and guided by their scheming mothers, could make some claim to the throne. The danger that Trella had foreseen had come to fruit. The heir to the kingdom of Akkad stood in the way of his kindred eager to rule. The thrust of a knife or a drop of poison hung over his head. Escander did indeed have many enemies.

"You must always be aware of your siblings," she said. "But I will keep watch over the most troublesome."

Escander shrugged, in just that certain way Eskkar used to do. For a moment, Trella almost lost control of her emotions. She'd loved Escander's grandfather since their first night, and now as her life drew to a close, her heart went out to this boy.

"Whatever happens here will happen." Escander dismissed any concerns with a shrug. "I know the ways of the palace and its intrigues. But what I will face in the northern lands is still hidden. That's why I need to hear the truth now, and not from the steppes barbarians. Besides, if I ever do come to rule, I'll need to look every man in the eye and read their thoughts, the way only you can, Grandmother."

They both knew what this journey to the steppes meant. Trella had often wanted to warn him, to tell him what he needed to know and what dangers lurked in his path, but it remained her son's place to tell him these secrets.

Escander would be on his way before anyone learned of his departure, but tongues would whisper about his destination, and the plotting would begin. Even so, she felt satisfied that at last King Sargon had grasped what needed to be done, even if he couldn't do it himself.

She stood up and went to the door and called out to a servant. "Ask En-hedu to join me."

Trella waited by the door until En-hedu arrived from her rooms down the corridor, then the two women whispered together for a few moments. Trella returned to the table and sat. "En-hedu will watch the door, to make sure no one hears our talk."

"And what if En-hedu listens?"

"En-hedu doesn't need to listen, she knows the truth. She was there for much of it."

Trella poured water for herself, and a half cup for her grandson. She gestured to the pitcher of wine, but the boy shook his head. Trella had spoken to him often about the dangers of too much wine, and he had learned at least that lesson well.

"Where should I begin?"

"Start with when you first met King Eskkar."

"No, you've heard those stories before. And even if they seem like tales to impress children, what you've heard is mostly true. Your grandfather truly was a great man." She took a sip from her cup. "Your story, what concerns you, began long after the building of Akkad's great wall, the wall that saved us from the barbarians." Trella closed her eyes for a moment, to count the years. "Twenty-seven seasons ago, when Sargon was much the same age as you, that's when your story begins."

"So long ago," Escander said in surprise. "How can . . ."

"The very young and the very foolish," Trella said firmly, "think that everything starts with them, and that only their days are important. But to rule wisely, a king has to think many years into the future, and must always remember the failures of the past.

She sighed. "Eskkar learned that lesson well. A wise leader plans for six months ahead; a great leader plans six years into the future. The events from long ago can affect you today, Escander, but if you're not interested, you can go and let an old woman return to her rest."

"No, no, I'll keep silent, I swear it. Not another word."

"When you have questions, good questions, ask them," Trella said. "Otherwise, how can you learn anything? Do you want to plod along like your half-brothers?"

"You know the answer to that, Grandmother. That's why you've favored me all these years, though you tried hard not to show it."

"Let me see, then." Trella drummed her fingers on the table.

"In that time, the lands under Akkad's control stretched ever further south, ever closer to those of Sumeria. As the Sumerian cities expanded their influence northward, the border disputes began. The age of mighty cities had arrived, and it was inevitable that Akkad would clash with the growing power of Sumeria. In those days, the southern cities grew even faster than Akkad, since they had the trade on the great ocean as well as the Two Rivers."

"Then came the war with Sumer," Escander said. "That's when my grandfather proved once and for all his greatness as a leader. His tactics in that war are still talked about among the soldiers."

Trella shook her head. "The only thing good about that war was that the actual fighting ended quickly. Eskkar gambled his life and the existence of Akkad in one battle, and only his luck saved them both."

"The cities of Sumeria still defer to our leadership." Escander's tone implied that it would always be so. "We can take care of the Sumerians if need be."

"Ah, the arrogance of youth, who thinks that what is, will always be. I hoped you would know better. Yes, they still respect our power. Just as they wait for Akkad to make the slightest mistake, so they can attempt to overthrow our rule once again."

Trella had spent most of her life in that struggle, determined to ensure that the city of Akkad never lost its power. Still, it remained a natural conflict of interests that would likely never end.

He nodded, accepting her rebuke. "I take nothing for granted, Grandmother. I lay down each night to sleep wondering if I will awake in the morning."

"A wise thought to keep in your head." Trella let her thoughts return to the past.

"Where was I? Oh, yes. After the Sumerian War, we overcame other minor battles and skirmishes, raids and marauders, good crop years and bad. Despite all these difficulties, the city grew greater and stronger each day. Akkad spread to both sides of the Tigris, and Eskkar built this palace for us on the west bank."

She paused for a moment, remembering those happy days.

"So, after many years of peace, we were caught by surprise when the new threat of war came from the east. Eskkar looked to his son to assist him. But Sargon, your father, had grown into a rebellious and lazy young man. A great disappointment to us both. He sorely tried your grandfather's temper, which he could never quite control."

"I've heard that King Eskkar could bellow and roar like a lion, though never at you, Grandmother." Escander squeezed her hand again. "But my father, a disappointment? I've never heard anything about that."

"Few remember those days," Trella said, "and even fewer want to speak about them. So while Akkad basked in prosperity, a new war loomed."

"Meanwhile, your father, the heir to the kingdom, wasted his time drinking, gambling, and whoring with friends as shiftless as himself, despite our strictest commands. That's when a stranger arrived from Sumeria, and brought with him the first stirrings of the Great War to come."

"Ah, the mysterious stranger, whose name no one knows."

Trella smiled. "In truth, at that time no one in Akkad knew his name or face, save Eskkar."

"But now . . . after so many years? Why is his name still hidden?"

"Because as long as he still lives, he might yet be of help to Akkad in the future. The bond between him and Eskkar proved stronger than time or distance. And even if he has passed beyond the veil, he might have whispered his secrets to his heirs, and his sons may still carry the obligation."

"So to this day, only Sargon and I know his name. Now I will share that secret with you. The man's name was Bracca, and he was a companion of Eskkar's during much of his youthful wanderings. They shared so many dangers that each owed the other his life."

"I've never heard that name. And after this Bracca came, King Eskkar went north once again, to the barbarian lands, to seek allies."

"Now you want to jump ahead in the story, just as you always did as a child. No, at that time, Eskkar's focus remained on Akkad's old enemy, the barbarian clan from the steppes, the Alur Meriki."

She shifted in her chair. "You must learn patience. Even in the steppes you will find enemies."

"Enemies? But I've offended no one outside the palace, let alone in the north."

"Eskkar had many enemies throughout the land, even among the clans of the steppes, and some of them may still be alive. Those who've died may have passed their hatred of your grandfather to their children. Blood feuds can span generations. Your name will bring danger from many sides, and you will have few friends to stand by you. That is why the test worries your father so much."

"But if I survive . . . if I return . . ."

"You will survive. I see Eskkar's spirit in you, and that gives me hope. He always managed to outwit his foes."

"He had you to help him, Grandmother. And the luck of the gods. I've heard those stories, how he often gambled his life in some desperate battle, trusting to chance to see him through. But my luck remains to be tested."

"Don't believe all those tales about your grandfather's luck, child. Eskkar succeeded because he always managed to outwit his enemies. Now, try and keep silent for a few moments."

"Yes, Grandmother."

"Where was I? Oh, yes, the stranger came to the palace to talk to Eskkar. The second Great War had already begun, though, Eskkar and I didn't realize we were at war. By the time we found out what had happened, it was nearly too late."

"But everyone said how strong and . . ."

"You said you wanted to hear the truth, all the secrets. Now keep silent, and listen to the truth about your father, Sargon. What you hear might just save your life."

She sighed again. "I remember the night it all started, the night the stranger arrived to see your grandfather and brought with him the news, both good and bad, of what was to come."

Battle For Empire will be available in Summer 2012.

2996144R00382

Made in the USA
San Bernardino, CA
24 June 2013